IT IS A WORLD OF ICE.
IT IS A WORLD OF BLOOD.
IT IS A GODLESS WORLD.

He felt no pain, just a solid blow in the square of his back as if someone had thrown a stone. No pain, yet his legs were no longer his own and he sprawled face-down into the damp leaf litter. He clawed at the earth, struggling to rise. His legs would not obey him. He reached behind to finger the arrow buried in his back. He felt something rising in his throat.

Then there was a powerful grip upon his arm and he was turned over. The arrow snapped and sent a lance of pain clean through him, transfixing sternum and spine. He cried out and crushed his eyes tight shut against it. When he opened them again, blinking through the mist of tears, there was one last surprise. It was not into the pale face of a Kyrinin that he looked, as he had expected. Instead, he met the gaze of one of his own kind: a black-haired woman, clad in dark leather, with a sword sheathed crossways on her back. . . .

"You should know why you die," she said, "so know this: the Children of the Hundred have come for you, for all of you. The Bloods of the Black Road will take back that which is ours, and where you go now, all of Lannis-Haig will follow."

Lekan's mouth moved. There was no sound. The blow fell, and he plunged toward the Sleeping Dark.

PRAISE FOR
Brian Ruckley

"A gripping story that builds to a grim cli enjoys heroic fantasy should miss this."

"An epic tale of revenge, betrayal, and greed . . . an intriguing and imaginative story." — **DREAMWATCH**

WINTERBIRTH

THE GODLESS WORLD

Book One

BRIAN RUCKLEY

www.orbitbooks.net

New York   London

Orbit
Hachette Book Group USA
237 Park Avenue, New York, NY 10017
Visit our Web site at www.HachetteBookGroupUSA.com

First published in Great Britain by Orbit, 2006
First American edition, September 2007

Orbit is a trademark of Little, Brown Book Group Ltd.

Library of Congress Cataloging-in-Publication Data
Ruckley, Brian.
    Winterbirth / Brian Ruckely. — 1st ed.
        p.   cm. — (Godless world ; bk. 1)
    ISBN-13: 978-0-316-06769-0
    ISBN-10: 0-316-06769-5
    I. Title
    PR6118.U55W56 2007
    823' .92 — dc22   2007009451

        10 9 8 7 6 5 4 3 2 1

                    Q-MB

Printed in the United States of America

For my parents, who, in all senses,
have made everything possible

CAST OF CHARACTERS

THE TRUE BLOODS

Haig
Lannis-Haig
Kilkry-Haig
Dargannan-Haig
Ayth-Haig
Taral-Haig

Haig Blood

Gryvan oc Haig	The High Thane, Thane of Thanes, on campaign in Dargannan-Haig lands
Kale	Gryvan's bodyguard and Captain of his Shield, on campaign in Dargannan-Haig lands
Aewult nan Haig	Gryvan's first son, the Bloodheir
Mordyn Jerain, the Shadowhand	Chancellor of the Haig Blood, a Tal Dyreen
Tara Jerain	The Chancellor's wife
Torquentine	A man in Vaymouth
Magrayn	A woman in Vaymouth, Torquentine's doorkeeper
Behomun Tole	Gryvan's Steward in Anduran
Lagair Haldyn	Gryvan's Steward in Kolkyre

Lannis-Haig Blood

Croesan oc Lannis-Haig	The Thane, lord of Castle Anduran
Naradin nan Lannis-Haig	Croesan's son, the Bloodheir
Eilan nan Lannis-Haig	Naradin's wife
Taim Narran	Captain of Castle Anduran, on campaign with Gryvan oc Haig in Dargannan-Haig lands
Kennet nan Lannis-Haig	Croesan's brother, lord of Castle Kolglas
Inurian	Counsellor to Kennet, a *na'kyrim*
Anyara nan Lannis-Haig	Kennet's daughter
Orisian nan Lannis-Haig	Kennet's son
Rothe	Orisian's shieldman
Kylane	Orisian's shieldman
Lairis	Kennet's wife (deceased)
Fariel	Kennet's elder son (deceased)

Kilkry-Haig Blood

Lheanor oc Kilkry-Haig	The Thane
Ilessa oc Kilkry-Haig	Lheanor's wife
Gerain nan Kilkry-Haig	Lheanor's first son, the Bloodheir
Roaric nan Kilkry-Haig	Lheanor's second son, on campaign with Gryvan oc Haig in Dargannan-Haig lands

Dargannan-Haig Blood

Igryn oc Dargannan-Haig	The Thane, in revolt against the authority of Gryvan oc Haig

THE BLOODS OF THE BLACK ROAD

Gyre
Horin-Gyre
Gaven-Gyre
Wyn-Gyre
Fane-Gyre
and The Inkallim

Gyre Blood

Ragnor oc Gyre — The High Thane, Thane of Thanes

Horin-Gyre Blood

Angain oc Horin-Gyre	The Thane, lord of Castle Hakkan
Vana oc Horin-Gyre	Angain's wife
Kanin nan Horin-Gyre	Angain's son, the Bloodheir, campaigning south of the Vale of Stones
Wain nan Horin-Gyre	Angain's daughter, campaigning south of the Vale of Stones
Igris	Kanin's shieldman, campaigning south of the Vale of Stones
Aeglyss	A *na'kyrim* in the service of the Horin-Gyre Blood, campaigning south of the Vale of Stones

Inkallim

Theor	First of the Lore Inkall
Nyve	First of the Battle Inkall
Avenn	First of the Hunt Inkall
Cannek	A Hunt Inkallim, campaigning south of the Vale of Stones
Shraeve	A captain of the Battle Inkall, campaigning south of the Vale of Stones

OTHERS

Huanin
Kyrinin
Na'kyrim

Huanin

Edryn Delyne	Captain of a Tal Dyreen trading ship
Tomas	First Watchman of Koldihrve

Kyrinin

Ess'yr	A woman in the *vo'an* of In'hynyr
Varryn	Ess'yr's brother, a warrior

Na'kyrim

Yvane	A *na'kyrim* living in the Car Criagar
Hammarn	A *na'kyrim* living in Koldihrve
Cerys	A *na'kyrim*, the Elect of Highfast
Tyn	A *na'kyrim*, the Dreamer in Highfast
Eshenna	A *na'kyrim* in Highfast, originally from Dyrkyrnon

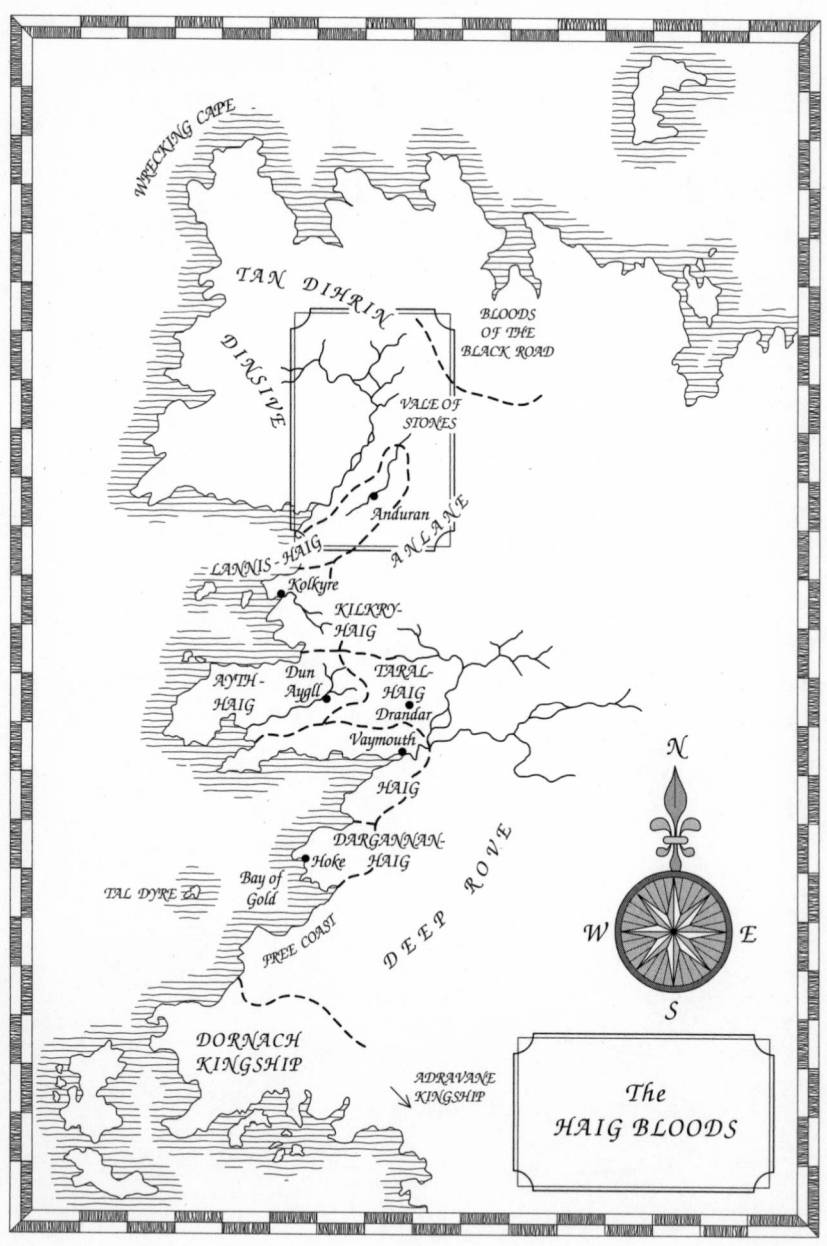

The
HAIG BLOODS

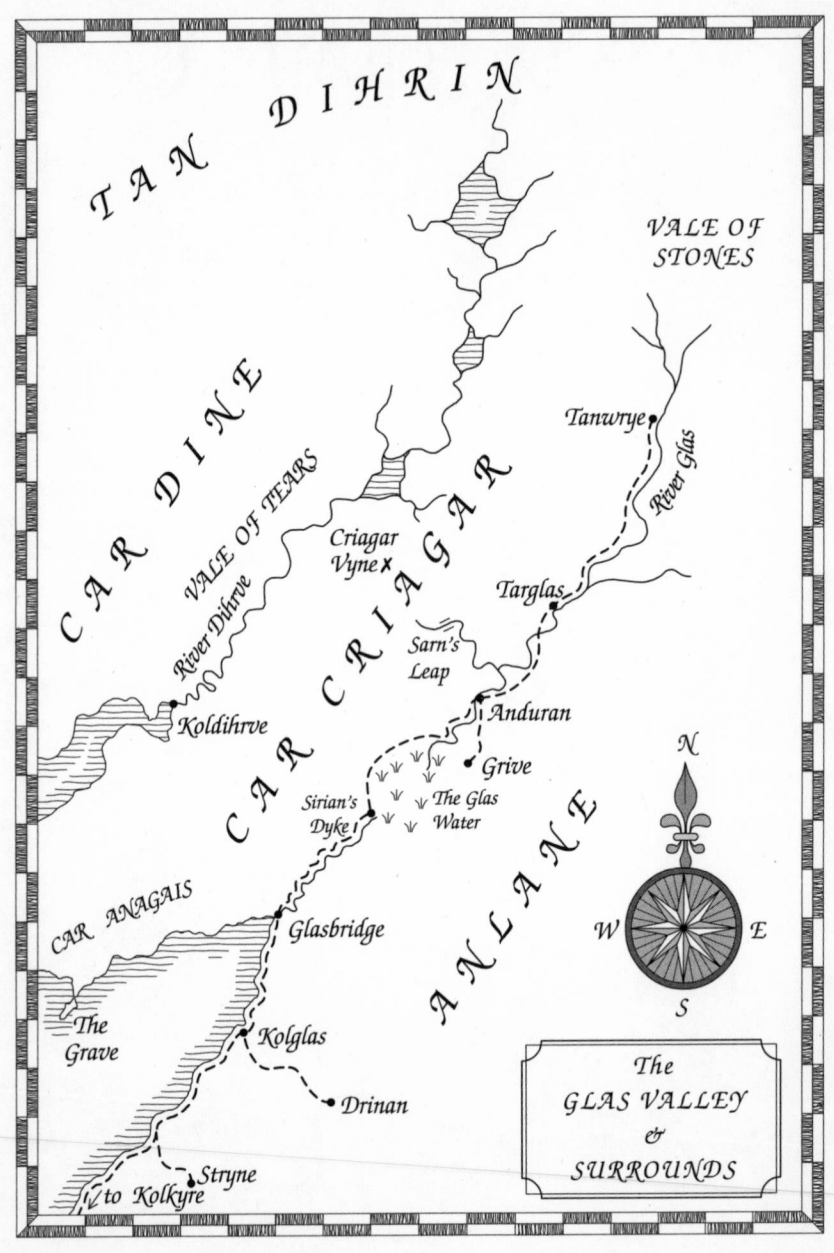

The
GLAS VALLEY
&
SURROUNDS

WINTERBIRTH

PREFACE

They say the world has fallen far from its former state.

In the beginning there was but one race. It failed the Gods who made it and, though it wounded their hearts to do so, they destroyed it. In its place they fashioned five which they put in the world to inhabit it, and these were the races of the Second Age: Whreinin and Saolin, Huanin and Kyrinin, and Anain.

The sky turned a thousand thousand times and beneath the gaze of the Gods their children prospered. Cities, empires, rose and fell. But at last the Huanin and Kyrinin wearied of the cruelties of the wolfenkind, the Whreinin. Despite the will of the Gods they made war upon that race, and they destroyed it utterly and it passed out of time and history. For this deed are the Huanin and Kyrinin named the Tainted Races. And upon that deed were the hopes of the Gods broken, for they saw that what they had made was flawed beyond mending, marred by an unyielding vein of discord and hubris. The Gods took council upon the highest peaks of the Tan Dihrin, where the rotating firmament grinds sparks from the mountain tops, and they chose to look no longer upon the failure of their dreams and to suffer no longer the rebellions of their children. They left the world, departing to places beyond the thoughts or imaginings of any save their own kind, and with them went much that was best in the peoples they abandoned.

This is how the Second Age ended and the Third began. It is how this came to be a Godless World. That is what they say.

PROLOGUE

I The Third Age: Year 942

The solitude of the wild goats that made their home on the rock faces above the Vale of Stones was seldom interrupted. The Vale might be the only pass through the high Tan Dihrin, but it was a route that led nowhere: the bleak and icy shores of the north were home only to savage tribes. There was nothing there to draw traders or conquerors up from the lands of the Kilkry Bloods to the south.

When a sudden river of humanity began to flow up and over the Vale of Stones, it therefore sent unease darting through the herds of goats on their precipitous territories overhead. Bucks stamped their feet; does called for their kids. Soon, the cliffs were deserted and only the mute rock was left to witness the extraordinary scenes below, as ten thousand people marched into a cold exile.

The great column was led by a hundred or more mounted warriors. Many bore wounds, still fresh from the lost battle on the fields by Kan Avor; all bore, in their red-rimmed eyes and wan skin, the marks of exhaustion. Behind them came the multitude: women, children and men, though fewest of the last. Thousands of widows had been made that year.

It was a punishing exodus. Their way was paved with hard rock and sharp stones that cut feet and turned ankles. There could be no pause. Any who fell were seized by those who came behind, hauled upright with shouts of encouragement, as if noise alone could put strength back into their legs. If they could not rise, they were left. There were already dozens of buzzards and ravens drifting lazily above the column. Some had followed it all the way up the Glas valley from the south; others were residents of the mountains, drawn from their lofty perches by the promise of carrion.

A few of those fleeing through the Stone Vale had been wealthy — merchants and landowners from Kan Avor or Glasbridge. What little of their wealth they had managed to salvage in the panic of flight was now slipping through their fingers. Mules were stumbling and falling beneath overladen panniers, defeated by the desperate whips of their handlers or the weight of their loads; the wheels and axles of carts were splintering amidst the rocks, cargoes spilling to the ground. Servants cajoled or threatened into carrying their masters' goods were casting them aside, exhaustion overcoming their fear. Fortunes that had taken lifetimes to accumulate lay scattered and ignored along the length of the Vale, like flakes of skin scoured off the crowd's body by the rock walls of the pass.

Avann oc Gyre, Thane of the Gyre Blood and self-proclaimed protector of the creed of the Black Road, rode amongst the common folk. His Shield, the men sworn to guard him day and night, had long since abandoned their efforts to keep the people from straying too close to their lord. The Thane himself ignored the masses jostling all about him. His head hung low and he made no effort to guide his horse. It followed where the flow carried it.

There was a crust of blood upon the Thane's cheek. He had been in the thick of the fighting outside Kan Avor, his beloved city, and survived only because his own Shield had disregarded his commands and dragged him from the field. The wound on his cheek was little more than a scratch, though. Hidden beneath his robes, and beneath blood-heavy bandaging, other injuries were eating away at his strength. The lance of a Kilkry horseman had pierced the Thane through from front to back, breaking as it did so and leaving splinters of wood along the tunnel it drove through his flesh. He had a fine company of healers, and if there had been time to set his tent, to rest and tend to his wounds, they might even have been able to save his life. Avann had forbidden such a delay, and refused to leave his horse for a litter.

What was left of the Thane's armies came behind. Two years

ago the warriors of Gyre had been one of the finest bodies of fighting men in all the lands of the Kilkry Bloods, but the unremitting carnage since then had consumed their strength as surely as a fire loosed upon a drought-struck forest. In the end virtually every able-bodied man — and many of the women — of the Black Road had taken to the field at Kan Avor, drawn not just from Gyre but from every Blood: still they had been outnumbered by more than three to one. Now barely fifteen hundred men remained, a battered rearguard for the flight of the Black Road into the north.

The man who rode up to join his Thane was as bruised and weary as all the rest. His helm was dented, the ring mail on his chest stained with blood, his round shield notched and half split where an axe had found a lucky angle. Still, this man bore himself well and his eyes retained a glint of vigor. He nudged his horse through the crowds and leaned close to Avann.

"Lord," he said softly, "it is Tegric."

Avann stirred, but did not raise his head or open his eyes.

"My scouts have come up, lord," the warrior continued. "The enemy draw near. Kilkry horsemen are no more than an hour or two adrift of us. Behind them, spearmen of Haig-Kilkry. They will bring us to bay before we are clear of the Vale."

The Thane of Gyre spat bloodily.

"Whatever awaits us was decided long ago," he murmured. His voice was thin and weak. "We cannot fear what is written in the Last God's book."

One of the Thane's shieldmen joined them, and fixed Tegric with a disapproving glare.

"Leave the Thane be," he said. "He must conserve his strength."

That at last raised Avann's head. He winced as he opened his eyes.

"My death will come when it must. Until then, I am Thane, not some sick old woman to be wrapped warm and fed broth. Tegric treats me as a Thane still; how much more should my own Shield?"

The shieldman nodded in acceptance of the reprimand, but stayed in close attendance.

"Let me wait here, lord," said Tegric softly. "Give me just a hundred men. We will hold the Vale until our people are clear."

The Thane regarded Tegric. "We may need every man in the north. The tribes will not welcome our arrival."

"There will be no arrival if our enemies come upon us here in the Vale. Let me stand here and I will promise you half a day, perhaps more. The cliffs narrow up ahead, and there is an old rockfall. I can hold the way against riders; spill enough of their blood that they will wait for their main force to come up before attempting the passage twice."

"And then you will be a hundred against what, five thousand? Six?" Avann grunted.

"At least," smiled Tegric.

An old man fell in the crowds that surrounded them. He cried out as a stone opened his knee. A grey-haired woman — perhaps his wife — hurried to help him to his feet, murmuring "Get up, get up." A score of people, including the Thane and Tegric, flowed past before she managed to raise him. She wept silently as the man hobbled onward.

"Many people have already died in defense of our creed," Avann oc Gyre said, lowering his head once more and closing his eyes. He seemed to shrink as he hunched forward in his saddle. "If you give us half a day — if it has been so written in the Last God's book — you and your hundred will be remembered. When the lands that have been taken from us are ours again, you will be named first and noblest amongst the dead. And when this bitter world is unmade and we have returned into the love of the Gods I will look for you, to give you the honor that will be your due."

Tegric nodded. "I will see you once again in the reborn world, my Thane."

He turned his horse and nudged it back against the current of humanity.

*

Tegric rested against a great boulder. He had removed his tunic, and was methodically stitching up a split seam. His mail shirt was neatly spread upon a rock, his shield and scabbarded sword lying beside it, his helm resting at his feet. These were all that remained to him, everything he had need of. He had given his horse to a lame woman who had been struggling along in the wake of the main column. His small pouch of coins had gone to a child, a boy mute from shock or injury.

Above, buzzards were calling as they circled lower, descending toward the corpses that Tegric knew lay just out of sight. His presence, and that of his hundred men, might deter the scavengers for a while longer, but he did not begrudge them a meal. Those who once dwelled in those bodies had no further need of them: when the Gods returned — as they would once all peoples of the world had learned the humility of the Black Road — they would have new bodies, in a new world.

From where he sat, Tegric could see down a long, sloping sweep of the Stone Vale. Every so often he glanced up from his stitching to cast his eyes back the way they had come. Far off in that direction lay Grive, where he had lived most of his life: a place of soft green fields, well-fed cattle, as different from this punishing Vale of Stones as any place could be. The memory of it summoned up no particular emotion in him. The rest of his family had not seen the truth of the creed as he had. When Avann oc Gyre, their Thane, had declared for the Black Road they had fled from Grive, disappearing out of Tegric's life. In every Blood, even Kilkry itself, the blossoming of the Black Road had sundered countless families, broken ties and bonds that had held firm for generations. To Tegric's mind it was a cause for neither regret nor surprise. A truth as profound as that of the Black Road could not help but have consequences.

An old man, dressed in a ragged brown robe and leaning on a staff, came limping up the Vale. He was, perhaps, the very last of the fleeing thousands. Though they were close to the highest point of the pass, the sun, burning out of a cloudless sky, still had strength. The man's forehead was beaded with sweat. He paused before Tegric, resting all his weight upon his staff and breathing heavily. The warrior looked up at the man, squinting slightly against the sunlight.

"Am I far behind the rest?" the man asked between labored breaths.

Tegric noted the bandaged feet, the trembling hands.

"Some way," he said softly.

The man nodded, unsurprised and seemingly unperturbed. He wiped his brow with the hem of his robe; the material came away sweaty and dirty.

"You are waiting here?" he asked Tegric, who nodded in reply.

The man cast around, scanning the warriors scattered amongst the great boulders all around him.

"How many of you are there?"

"A hundred," Tegric told him.

The old man chuckled, though it was a cold and humorless kind of laugh.

"You have come to the end of your Roads then, you hundred. I had best press on, and discover where my own fate runs out."

"Do so," said Tegric levelly. He watched the man make his unsteady way along the path already trodden by so many thousands. There had been, in the gentle edges of his accent, no hint of the Gyre Blood or the Glas valley where Avann had ruled.

"Where are you from, old father?" Tegric called after him.

"Kilvale, in Kilkry lands," the man replied.

"Did you know the Fisherwoman, then?" Tegric asked, unable to keep the edge of wonder from his voice.

The old man paused and carefully turned to look back at the warrior.

"I heard her speak. I knew her a little, before they killed her."

"There will be a day, you know, when the Black Road marches

through this pass again," Tegric said. "But then we will be marching out of the north, not into it. And we will march all the way to Kilvale and beyond."

Again the man laughed his rough laugh. "You are right. They've driven us from our homes, cast even your Thane out from his castle, but the creed survives. You and I are not fated to see it, friend, but the Black Road will rule in the hearts of all men one day, and all things will come to their end. This is a war that will not be done until the world itself is unmade."

Tegric gazed after the receding figure for a time. Then he returned to his sewing.

A while later, his hand paused in its rhythmic motion, the needle poised in mid-descent. There was something moving amongst the rocks, back down the pass to the south. He carefully set aside his tunic and half-rose, leaning forward on one knee.

"Kilkry," he heard one of his warriors muttering off to his left.

And the shape coalescing out of the rock and the bright light did indeed look to be a rider. Nor was it alone. At least a score of horsemen were picking their way up the Vale of Stones.

Tegric laid a hand instinctively on the cool metal of his chain vest. He could feel the dried blood, the legacy of a week's almost constant battle, beneath his fingertips. He was not afraid to die. That was one fear the Black Road lifted from a man's back. If he feared anything, it was that he should fail in his determination to face, both willingly and humbly, whatever was to come.

"Ready yourselves," he said, loud enough for only the few nearest men to hear. They passed the word along. Tegric snapped the needle from the end of its thread and slipped his tunic back on. He lifted his mail shirt above his head and dropped its familiar weight onto his shoulders. Like smoke rising from a newly caught fire, the line of riders below was lengthening, curling and curving its way up the pass.

The horsemen of Kilkry were the best mounted warriors to be

found in all the Bloods, but their prowess would count for little where Tegric had chosen to make his stand. A titanic fall of rocks from the cliffs above had almost choked the Stone Vale with rubble. The riders would be greatly hampered, perhaps even forced to dismount. Tegric's swordsmen and archers would have the advantage here. Later, when the main body of the pursuing army came up, they would be overwhelmed, but that did not matter.

He glanced at the sun, a searingly bright orb in the perfectly blue sky. He could hear the buzzards and the ravens, could glimpse their dark forms gliding in effortless spirals. It did not seem a bad place, a bad day, to die. If, when he woke in the new world the Black Road promised him, this was his last memory of his first life, of this failed world, it would not displease him.

Tegric Wyn dar Gyre rose and buckled on his sword belt.

II The Third Age: Year 1087

Mist had draped itself across the village, so that water, land and air had all run together. The domed huts were indistinct shapes, bulging out of the morning vapors here and there like burial mounds. Dew lay heavy on the cut slabs of turf that covered them. A lone fisherman was easing his flatboat out into one of the channels that meandered through the reedbeds around the village. There was no other sign of life save the wispy threads rising from the smokeholes of one or two of the huts. Not a breath of wind disturbed their ascent as the trails of smoke climbed high into the air before losing themselves in the greyness.

One larger hut stood apart from the others on raised ground. A figure emerged out of the mist, walking toward it: a youth, no more than fifteen or sixteen. His tread left deep prints in the mossy grass. Outside the hut he stopped and gathered himself. He stood straight and looked around for a moment. He breathed the damp air in and out, as if cleansing himself.

As the deerskin that hung across the opening fell back into place behind him, the interior was cast into a deep gloom. Only the faintest light oozed in through the small hole in the center of the roof; the peat fire had been dampened down to embers. The youth could make out the indistinct forms of a dozen or more people sitting motionless in a semi-circle. Some of their faces were touched by the glow of the embers, lighting their cheeks a little. He knew them, but it was an irrelevance here and now. On this morning they were one; they were the will of the place, of Dyrkyrnon. In the background, all but beneath the reach of even his acute hearing, a dolorous rhythm was being chanted. He had never heard the sound before, yet knew what it was: a truth chant, a habit borrowed from the Heron Kyrinin. They were seeking wisdom.

"Sit," someone said.

He lowered himself to the ground and crossed his legs. He fixed his eyes on the firepit.

"We have sat through the night," said someone else, "to give thought to this matter."

The youth nodded and pressed his thin lips tight together.

"It is a heavy duty," continued the second speaker, "and a sad burden that we should be called upon to make such judgments. Dyrkyrnon is a place of sanctuary, open to all those of our kind who can find no peace or safety in the outer world. Yet we came together to determine whether you should be turned out, Aeglyss, and sent away from here."

Aeglyss said nothing. His face remained impassive, his gaze unwavering.

"You were taken in, and given comfort. You would have died at your mother's side if you had not been found and brought here. Yet you have sown discord. The friendship and trust you were offered have been repaid with cruelty. Dyrkyrnon suffers now by your presence. Aeglyss, you shall leave this place, and have no discourse with any who make their homes here. We cast you out."

There was a flicker of response in the youth's face then: a trembling in the tight-clenched jaw, a shiver at the corner of his mouth. He closed his eyes. The peaty smoke was thickening the air. It touched the back of his throat and nose.

"You are young, Aeglyss," the voice from beyond the smoldering fire said, a little softer now. "It may be that age will teach you where we have failed. If that should be the case, you will be welcome here once more."

He stared at the half-lit faces opposite him, a cold anger in his look.

"You came to us out of a storm," said a woman, "and you carry the storm within you. It is beyond us to tame it. It is too deep-rooted. When it is gone, or mastered, return to us. The judgment can be rescinded. You belong here."

He laughed at that, the sound harsh and sudden in the still atmosphere. There were tears welling up in his eyes. They ran down his cheeks but did not reach his voice.

"I belong nowhere," he said, and rose to his feet. "Not here, and therefore nowhere. You are afraid of me, you who more than any should understand. You talk of comfort and trust, yet all I see in the faces around me is doubt and fear. The stench of your fear sickens me." He spat into the embers. A puff of ashes hissed into the air.

Aeglyss cast about, trying to find someone in the enveloping darkness of the hut. "K'rina. You are here. I can feel you. Will you deny me too?"

"Be still, K'rina," said someone.

"Yes, be still," Aeglyss snarled. "Do as they tell you. That is the way of it here: tread softly, always softly. Disturb nothing. You promised to love me, K'rina, in my dead mother's place. Is this your love?"

Nobody answered him.

"I loved you, K'rina. Loved!" He spat the word as if it was poison on his tongue. He could not see through his tears.

"I only wanted . . ." The words died in his throat. He sucked a breath in. "This is not fair. What have I done? Nothing that another might not do. Nothing."

The shadowed figures made no reply. Their obdurate will lay between him and them like a wall. With a curse that almost choked him, Aeglyss turned and strode out.

After he had gone, there was a long stretch of quiet. Almost imperceptibly at first, then louder, there came the sound of stifled sobs from somewhere in the shadows.

"Save your sorrow, K'rina. He is unworthy of it."

"He is m-my ward," stammered the woman.

"No longer. It is for the best. He has too much in him that is wild and cruel. We cannot free him of it, for all that we have tried."

K'rina subsided into silence, muffling her grief.

"He's right in one thing," someone else said. "We are afraid of him."

"There is no shame in that. He is stronger in the Shared than anyone we have seen in years, even if he lacks the knowledge to use that strength as he might. When he was only playing cruel games, whispering in ears and working a child's tricks, we might overlook it. But now . . . the girl still cries in the night. If he remained amongst us there would be greater sorrow in the end."

"Wherever he goes in the world, there will be greater sorrow," said a man with wild, dark spirals etched upon his face. "It would have been better to put an end to him. Blood will fill that one's footprints. Wherever he goes."

CHAPTER
1

Winterbirth

The Third Age: Year 1102

There are rites and rituals sunk so deeply into the fabric of a race that their roots are long forgotten. In the northern lands, where the fierce cycle of the seasons rules life with a snow-bound fist, the Huanin have marked the arrival of winter since before there was a written medium to record the means of that marking. Across count-less centuries the ceremonies have changed, remaking themselves according to the temper of the peoples who performed them, and the thread linking each to its predecessors has been forgotten. But the ancient theme lives on.

Before there were kingships, the cruel tribes of the Tan Dihrin practiced bloody rites to win the protection of the Gods against ice and storm. When the Kings rose in Dun Aygll, their subjects in the north kept to the old ways though they forgot what they meant, and though there were no Gods left to witness their rituals. The kingdom fell, as the works of mortals do, but through all the chaos that came after, through the turbulent birthing of the Bloods, the seasons turned as they always had and the people of the north remembered that the turning must be marked.

Thus, to the Kilkry and Lannis Bloods, and to the Bloods of the Black Road in the farther north, there is a night late in the year that stands, more than any other, for the passage of time. On that

night the world passes into cold and darkness to await its reawaken-
ing in the following spring. It is a night of mourning, but it is a cel-
ebration also, for in the slumbering of the world that is winter lies
the promise of light and life's return.

from Hallantyr's Sojourn

I

A horn sounded clear and sharp across the blue autumnal sky. The
baying of hounds wound itself around the note like ivy on a tree.
Orisian nan Lannis-Haig turned his head this way and that, trying to fix the source of the summons. His cousin Naradin was
ahead of him.

"That way," Naradin said, twisting in his saddle and pointing
east. "They have something."

"Some distance away," Orisian said.

Naradin's horse was stirring beneath him, stepping sideways
and stretching its neck. It knew what the sound meant. It was
bred to the hunt, and the horn pulled at it. Naradin jabbed the
butt of his boar spear at the ground in frustration.

"Where are the cursed dogs we were following?" he demanded.
"Those useless beasts have led us nowhere."

"They must have had some scent to bring us this way," said
Rothe placidly. The elder of Orisian's two shieldmen was the only
one to have kept pace with him and his cousin over the last mile or
so. The forest of Anlane was open in these parts — good hunting
country — but still it was forest enough to scatter a party once
the chase was on.

If the hounds had stayed on a single course it would have been
different, Orisian reflected. Instead, the pack had divided. It was
only bad luck that he and Naradin had followed the wrong dogs.
Orisian could not summon up much regret. He knew his cousin

would feel otherwise, though. As of four days ago Naradin was a father, and tradition said he must put meat killed with his own hand on the table on the occasion of the baby's first Winterbirth. For a farmer or herder that might mean killing one of his stock. For Naradin, heir to the Thane of the Lannis-Haig Blood, something more was called for.

"Well, let's answer the call," Naradin said, tightening his horse's reins. "They might keep the quarry for me, if we can get there quickly."

Orisian started to turn his mount, struggling to couch the huge spear he had been given for the hunt. The Lannis boar spear was a weapon for a grown man, and though he was sixteen he did not yet quite have the strength to handle it as deftly as did Rothe or his cousin.

"A moment," said Rothe.

Naradin glanced at the aging warrior with something approaching irritation. "We must be off," he insisted.

"I thought I heard something, sire," the shieldman said.

The Bloodheir did not look inclined to pay any heed, but before he could reply there came the distinct cry of a hound from the south. It was a cry of sighting, not scenting.

"It's closer than the others," Orisian observed.

Naradin looked at him for a moment or two, wrestling to control his horse. Then he gave a quick nod and dug his heels into the beast's flank. Orisian and Rothe went after him.

The turf flowed beneath them. The fallen leaves clothing the ground shivered and shook. Birds burst from the treetops: crows, a raucous clamber into the sky. Orisian trusted his horse to find its own way through the maze of trees. It was a hunter, trained in the stables of his uncle, the Thane, and it knew more than he did of this kind of business. Over the crashing of their progress he could hear the hounds up ahead, not just one now but several.

They found the dogs at a thicket of hazel and holly. The animals were gathered where the undergrowth was thickest, jostling and snapping in feverish excitement. They bounded this way and that, lunging sometimes toward the bushes without ever venturing too close. Naradin gave a cry of delight.

"They have something, for certain," he shouted.

"Sound your horn," Rothe called to him. "We need more spears."

"They'll have answered the other call. We can't wait or we might lose it."

Rothe scratched at his dark beard and shot a glare at Orisian, who in his turn felt a twist of unease. Naradin's enthusiasm could get the better of his judgment at times. Boars did not come small or meek in Anlane.

"You hold here," Naradin said. "Give me a couple of minutes to work around and then set the dogs in. And if something comes out this side, don't kill it. It's mine today!"

He urged his horse onward without waiting for an answer.

The boar came through the dogs like a hawk flashing through a flock of pigeons. It scattered them, some leaping high and twisting from its path, others darting aside. The beast was huge, its forequarters great grinding slabs of muscle, its tusks yellow-white blades the length of a man's hand. It plowed after one of the hounds as the others snatched at its haunches.

Naradin spun his horse. "Mine!" he cried.

The point of his spear swung toward the boar as it shook itself free of dogs and came toward him. It was an old, forest-wise creature and turned at the last minute, going for the horse's belly. The spear blade skidded off its shoulder, slicing through hide to bone. Naradin's mount sprang over the boar's head. It almost made the leap. A tusk brushed its leg and it reeled on the soft ground. It kept its feet, but Naradin was snapped forward. He lost his left stirrup and was thrown around the horse's neck. He hauled on the reins, the strength of his arms the only thing keeping him from falling. His weight twisted the horse's head around and it began to stagger sideways. It would go to ground in a moment. The boar closed again. The dogs were coming, furious and bloodthirsty, but too late.

Orisian and Rothe were side by side as they charged in. It was impossible to say which of their spears struck home first, Orisian's on the beast's hip, Rothe's parting its ribs. The impact jarred the spear out of Orisian's inexpert grasp. Rothe was better prepared. His lance knocked the boar onto its side and he put his own and his horse's weight behind it. For a few breaths he held it there, grimacing with exertion as the haft of the spear bucked in his hands.

Naradin had slipped out of his saddle. He drew a long knife from his belt.

"Quickly," Rothe said through gritted teeth.

The Bloodheir did not hesitate. The boar reached for him. Its great, desperate jaws almost had his arm as he drove the knife into its barrel chest. He sought, and found, its heart.

Afterward, as they sat on the ground beside the huge corpse with the hounds dancing around them, Naradin laughed. Orisian could see the joy in his cousin's eyes, and it made him laugh as well.

"That's one to remember," Naradin said. "See its tusks. That's an old master, that one. A lord of the forest."

"I thought we were in trouble for a moment," said Orisian.

"I would have been, if you two had not been here." Naradin drank from his waterskin, then spilled a little on his hands to wash the boar's blood from them. He offered the skin to Orisian. The water was cold and sharp, drawn from a forest stream only an hour or two ago. It had all the chilled clarity of the autumn day in it.

"Luck rode with us all today," said Rothe. Orisian knew his shieldman well enough — they had been together for six years — to hear the words Rothe did not speak. The warrior would not presume to tell the Bloodheir what he thought of taking on an old boar with too few dogs and only three spears.

"We should call the others," Orisian said. "They'll want to see this."

"In a moment, in a moment," Naradin said as he got to his feet.

The dogs milled about him. He went over to the boar and knelt. He laid a hand, in near-reverence, upon its flank. Something took his eye then.

"Look here. There's another wound. None of us put this mark on it, did we?"

Rothe and Orisian knelt beside him. There was a puncture wound in the boar's side, behind its shoulder. Blood was caked on the rigid hairs around it. Rothe crumbled some away between his fingers.

"That's a day or two old, I'd say."

"I thought it strange it should stand and fight like that," Naradin mused.

Orisian leaned closer. He could see something nestled there in the flesh. He slipped a knife into the wound and twisted, feeling the resistance of something harder than muscle. Another turn of the knife brought it close to the surface, where he could draw it out and drop it into his palm: an arrowhead, flat and sleek.

"It was in deep," he said.

"Can I see that?" Rothe asked, and when Orisian nodded he took the little piece of metal and held it up, frowning as he turned it. The lines crossing the backs of the shieldman's fingers were a first premonition of old age, but he held the arrowhead precisely, delicately.

Naradin looked a touch disappointed. "It's not quite the same, to know he was carrying that in him already," he said.

Rothe returned it to Orisian.

"That," he said, "is Kyrinin-made. It's a woodwight's arrow."

"Woodwights?" exclaimed Naradin. "Hunting here?"

Rothe only nodded. He looked around, surveying the silent trees, the still undergrowth. His mood had changed. He stood up.

"The White Owls have been causing trouble this last year, haven't they?" Orisian said to his cousin.

"Yes, but we're not a day's ride from Anduran. They would not dare to come so close." He examined the arrowhead himself. "He's right, though. That's White Owl."

Orisian had not doubted it. Rothe had fought the Kyrinin of Anlane often enough to know their weapons. He looked up at his shieldman. There was a rare tension in the big man's stance.

"Time for the horn, I think," Rothe said without breaking the roving passage of his eyes across the forest. "We should not stay here any longer than we must."

Naradin did not demur. He put the horn to his lips and sent out a long, low call, summoning the hunters to the kill.

* * *

The next morning Orisian gazed out from the battlements of Castle Anduran, watching the grey clouds gather around the Car Criagar to the northwest. The great mountain ridge loomed over the valley of the Glas River, though it was but foothills to the vast uplands that lay invisibly beyond. There were the remnants of ancient towns up there, long abandoned by their forgotten inhabitants. Now no one lived amongst the rocks and the clouds.

He had been here in his uncle's castle for a fortnight, and the weather had changed even in that short time. The sky had grown heavier. The land, the fields and forests, had darkened beneath it. The earth and the sky knew what was coming and eased themselves into it, shedding the gentle sentiments of autumn. There would be snow, even here on the valley floor, in a few weeks. Winterbirth was close.

It was not the most auspicious time for a birth, but that had not dimmed the celebrations attendant upon the arrival of the Thane's first grandson. They had lasted for days, capped by the hunt to find Naradin his boar. Now that all was done, an air of contented exhaustion had settled over the castle and the town that lay beside it. It was a lull between storms, for the imminent revels of Winterbirth would match those just gone in intensity, if not in duration.

With the approach of that festival the time had come for Orisian to go home to Kolglas, to the castle in the waves. A flight of geese passed over, honking to one another as they tracked the valley seaward, preceding Orisian on his way. His gaze followed them for a while. He had come to this high place for a last look at the broad vista, with the valley his uncle ruled stretching out beyond his eye's reach. Kolglas had more limited horizons, in more ways than one.

The sound of footsteps drew his attention back. Rothe emerged from the narrow stairwell beside him.

"The horses are ready," said the shieldman in his ever-gruff voice. It always made Orisian imagine that stones were grinding together somewhere in his throat. "Your uncle is in the courtyard to bid you farewell."

"Time to go, then," said Orisian. "It will be a cold ride back to Kolglas."

Rothe smiled. "Just as well that fire and food await us on the way."

They descended the spiraling stairway and emerged onto a wide, cobbled courtyard. By the gatehouse on the far side, grooms held three horses that blew out clouds of steaming breath into the morning air. Kylane, Orisian's second shieldman, was meticulously checking the horses' hoofs, oblivious of any offense the implied lack of faith might cause to the grooms. Orisian's uncle, the Thane Croesan oc Lannis-Haig, stood close by.

Croesan took Orisian's hand in his. He was more than a head taller than the youth and grinned down at him.

"Two weeks is too short a visit, Orisian."

"I'd gladly stay, but I must be back at Kolglas for Winterbirth. My father should be out of his sickbed soon."

Croesan's smile faltered for a moment and he nodded.

"Doom and gloom are deep-rooted in my brother's guts. Still, Winterbirth may lift his mood. In any case, do not let Kennet's ills cloud the festival for you, Orisian."

"I won't," Orisian said, knowing that it was a promise he might not be able to keep.

Croesan clapped him on the back. "Good. And tell him to visit us soon. It might light a fire under him to see how things are changing here."

"I will tell him. Where's Naradin?"

The question brought a broad grin back to Croesan's face in an instant, and the grand and grave Thane of the Blood was nothing but a proud father and grandfather.

"He will be here in a moment. He told me to keep you here until they come, to make sure my grandson has the chance to say farewell."

"Well, I am glad we found him his boar," Orisian smiled. "I hope the baby appreciates it."

"Indeed. Naradin will bore the boy with tales of its killing when he's old enough to understand, I'm sure. He'll grow up thinking you and Naradin great heroes, and the finest hunters the Glas valley has ever seen."

The thought made Orisian laugh. "He'll be disappointed, then, if he ever sees me at the hunt."

Croesan shrugged. "Don't be so sure. By the time he's old enough to know the difference, you'll be a match for most of my huntsmen. Anyway, you'll return for the child's Naming, since you were here for the birth?"

"If I can," said Orisian, and meant it sincerely. The Naming of an infant destined one day to be Thane was an event that would embody all the history, all the bonds that made the Lannis Blood what it was. Nothing could more strongly signify a long history and a hopeful future, and after the depredations of the Heart Fever and the sufferings of his father, Orisian was learning to value both of those.

Naradin and his wife Eilan emerged from the keep. The Blood-heir was carrying his baby son in his arms, and walked with almost comical care and precision. He had not yet learned how to relax around a life that seemed so fragile.

Croesan leaned close to Orisian and murmured conspiratorially,

"Can you believe they have made me a grandfather, Orisian? A grandfather!"

"I can hardly believe Naradin is a father, let alone you a grandfather," smiled Orisian. That, he reflected, was a half-truth, though an innocent one. Naradin had, for as long as he could remember, seemed ready and hungry for fatherhood. Nothing less was expected of one who bore the future of the Blood upon his shoulders.

Eilan embraced Orisian. She was a beautiful woman, but it was for her gentle and generous spirit that he loved her; and for the way those attributes reminded him of his own mother.

"Journey well, Orisian," she murmured in his ear. "Take my love to your sister."

Naradin inclined the baby toward Orisian.

"Now, little one," the Bloodheir said, "say goodbye to Orisian."

The tiny face gazed blankly out from the nest of thick blankets, lips working moistly and soundlessly. A pink tongue gestured vaguely in Orisian's direction.

"There," said Naradin with satisfaction. "I could not have said it better myself."

"Probably not," agreed Orisian. "Look after him well, and salt some of his boar for me. I will see you at the Naming."

Orisian swung up into his saddle, patting the horse's muscular neck in greeting. Rothe and Kylane flanked him as he rode out through the massive gatehouse. When Orisian glanced back over his shoulder, Croesan, Naradin and Eilan still stood together, each one raising a hand in farewell. With a last wave, Orisian and his shieldmen turned south through Anduran's crowded streets toward the road that would carry them down the valley and on to Kolglas and home.

By the time the three riders were beyond the city's edge, almost vanished into the distance, Croesan oc Lannis-Haig was watching them go from one of the highest windows of Castle Anduran's keep. As he often did, he felt a twinge of sorrow for Orisian, and that brought forth the familiar mixture of feelings for the boy's father, Kennet: the bond of love that brotherhood instilled, colored by frustration and pain. The sadness in Kennet's heart seemed only to have deepened and grown blacker in the five years since the fevered deaths of Lairis and Fariel, his wife and elder son. It kept Kolglas and all who lived there under a burden of loss. Croesan had lost his own wife many years ago, and thus knew something of what afflicted Kennet, but he had given up any hope of salving the grief that sometimes made itself his brother's master, and it pained him that the past weighed so upon those he loved. Orisian and his sister Anyara had, after all, lost as much as Kennet, and still found the strength to bear that loss upon shoulders much younger and less sturdy than those of the lord of Castle Kolglas. The Thane sighed and set those thoughts aside as he turned away from the window.

A manservant was waiting by the door. Croesan glanced at him.

"Find the Steward," he said, unable to keep a hint of weariness out of his voice. "Ask him to come."

The servant nodded and left the chamber. Croesan ran a hand through his thick hair. He gazed around the room. A huge table, made in one of Anduran's finest woodshops fifty years ago by order of his great-uncle Gahan, ran most of its length. The walls bore three broad tapestries. Time and sunlight had faded them somewhat, but they still showed the delicacy of touch that marked them as the work of Kolkyre craftsmen. They had been commissioned by Sirian the Great himself, the first Lannis Thane, and showed scenes from the battle that forged the Blood. Croesan regarded the images for a little while. They were, perhaps, not inappropriate as a backdrop for the conversation he was about to have.

Hard upon the heels of the servant trying to announce his arrival, the Steward swept in: Behomun Tole dar Haig, emissary of the Thane of Thanes within Croesan's lands. He gave a casual bow and Croesan gestured him toward a chair, simultaneously dismissing the servant with a curt nod. Behomun's sharp, clever features and ill-concealed arrogance never failed to aggravate Croesan. The man had the satisfied air of one who knew things others did not. A sneer lived surreptitiously at the corner of his mouth, eagerly awaiting any opportunity to creep out of hiding and cavort upon his lips. He was, however, the eyes and ears of Gryvan oc Haig, the High Thane, to whom Croesan had pledged allegiance, and as such he had to be treated with a degree of care. He was like an itch Croesan could reach but was not permitted to scratch.

"I gather young Orisian has left," said Behomun, his tone solicitous. "It was remiss of me . . . I meant to inquire after his father's health. Have you heard how your brother fares?"

"I had word from the south yesterday," Croesan said levelly. "I am told the battles have not gone well for Igryn; that the Dargannan Blood will soon be subdued."

"I have had the same word," agreed Behomun, unperturbed by Croesan's disregard for his question. "It seems the rebels will be brought to heel before winter is far advanced, and the Haig Bloods will be united once more."

"I am also told," continued Croesan, "that the men of Lannis have acquitted themselves with honor in those battles. So much honor, I believe, that barely a handful will return to their homes."

"Your Blood has always produced warriors of the greatest courage, sire."

Croesan arched an eyebrow and stared at Gryvan oc Haig's envoy. "Honor and courage will not feed the orphans of Anduran or Glasbridge through the coming winter. They will not guard my lands from the woodwights or from the Gyre Bloods. I have near one in six of all my people dead from the Heart Fever just five years ago, and the best quarter of the fighting strength I had left taken south, on the High Thane's command, to die so bravely.

"The last time we sent so many men south we had the armies of

Horin-Gyre marching on our frontier within weeks. We won then. Who is to say what will happen if the Black Road comes across the Vale of Stones again? You know as well as I, Behomun, that there has been more skirmishing in the Vale these last few weeks than for many a year. And my own son killed a boar with a woodwight arrow in it not a day's ride from this castle. When have the White Owls strayed so far into my lands before?"

"The woodwights can hardly threaten a Blood as versed in the arts of war as yours. Kyrinin bows and spears are no match for the swords of Lannis-Haig. And as for the Bloods of the Black Road, I am certain that if they were to come against you, your strength would turn them back as it has always done, Thane."

"Oh, spare me your flattery, Steward," said Croesan in exasperation. "This is not Vaymouth. You can save your velvet tongue for Gryvan's court. I'd hate for you to wear it out for my benefit."

Behomun's manner changed. That sneer was close, testing its leash. "As you wish. Perhaps a different response will find more favor: that your troubles are not to be laid at the door of Gryvan oc Haig. The White Owl Kyrinin hunt your woodcutters and herders because you set your people to clear the forests of Anlane. You must have known that would stir up trouble as surely as a stick poked into a wasp nest.

"And if your northern borders are less well guarded against the Black Road than you would wish, you should have agreed to the High Thane's requests for land to settle his veterans upon. An army of proven warriors would now fill the very farms that the Fever emptied, if you had found a place for them. In any case, if you believed there was a serious threat, you would surely not have allowed Taim Narran and the others to go south at all. It would not be the first time you defied a command of your High Thane."

"The warriors Gryvan wanted to settle here would take no oath of loyalty to me. To my Blood," Croesan snapped.

The Steward snorted and waved a hand. "Every one of them loyal to the Haig Bloods, already bound to Gryvan oc Haig himself. As are you and your Blood, lest you have forgotten. Why put them through your old rituals?"

Croesan paused, his gaze lifting for a moment from the Steward's face to the tapestry on the wall behind him. Sirian was there, riding down the fleeing forces of the Gyre Bloods. Croesan felt old, almost too tired to engage in futile arguments with this man who cared nothing for the past. When the tapestry was made, little more than a century ago, none would have questioned the worth of oaths. None would have thought them to be empty rituals. But Kilkry had been the highest amongst the True Bloods in those days, and many things had been different. Now Lheanor, the Kilkry Thane, bent the knee to Gryvan oc Haig as the rest of them did.

"Had I known," Croesan said at length, "that Gryvan would punish my refusal by taking the lives of my men, I might have thought longer." Behomun started to protest, spreading his hands in denial of what Croesan said. The Thane spoke over him. "But my answer would not have changed. Any man who would be a warrior for the Lannis Blood must swear fealty. It is not so long since the same law was kept in Haig lands, Behomun, though your master seems to have forgotten it."

"Times change."

Croesan sighed. "They do, though there are few truly new things in the world. We had Kings once before. Rats and dogs have inherited their palaces in Dun Aygll. I am told the new mansions in Vaymouth rival that lost glory."

"The High Thane has no wish to make himself a king."

"As you say. But it is of no matter now. I am sending word south to Taim Narran that he is to return with those of my men who still live as soon as Igryn oc Dargannan-Haig is taken. I wished only to tell you that. I would not want a hurried departure to be taken amiss."

The Steward nodded. "Narran is yours to command, of course. I am sure the High Thane will not wish to delay his return."

"I hope he will neither wish it nor do it," replied Croesan. Behomun smiled.

* * *

The road south from Anduran was a well-traveled one. Orisian, Rothe and Kylane passed cattle herders and farmers, as well as carts carrying fleeces, furs and carved furniture from Anduran's workshops down to the harbor at Glasbridge. Late in the morning they overtook a line of half a dozen timber-laden wagons, the gigantic workhorses raised by Lannis woodsmen laboring in their harnesses.

They had crossed the Glas River not long after leaving Anduran, and the road now followed close by its northern bank, protected by a low dyke. Though the river was high, fed by rains in the uplands beyond Lannis-Haig's borders, it was still a long way from over-topping the bund and threatening the road. The open fields to its south had no such protection and they were patterned with pools, the harbingers of winter floods.

After a time the track began to skirt round to the north of the Glas Water. The great wetland swallowed the river, hiding its course amidst a maze of pools, channels and marshes. In a month or two, there would be an unbroken sheet of pale water covering a great sweep of the valley floor. Riding along the fringes of this wild place, Orisian could see, faint in its misty heart, the ruined towers of old Kan Avor. The broken turrets and spires of the drowned city rose above the waters like a ghostly ship on the sea's horizon. The sight, as it always did, stirred a faint unease in him. He had gone there once, as a child, with his brother Fariel. It had been high summer, exceptionally dry, and the waters were low enough for them to ride through some of the city's desolate streets. The muck- and weed-crusted ruins loomed over them, obscuring the sun. Orisian had thought it a haunted, ugly place and he had not been back, for all Fariel's good-natured taunts at his fearfulness. Fariel had never been one to pay much heed to fear.

"They should tear it down," said Kylane, seeing the line of Orisian's gaze. "Does no good to have that foul place rotting there. And fine farmland sunk along with it, too."

"People need reminding," muttered Rothe. "The Black Road is still there, in the north. Without those ruins to remind them, how soon would people forget? There's too many have done that already."

Kylane shrugged. "You can't fault people for enjoying peace. It's better than thirty years since the last battle."

"You can fault them if they start to believe peace is forever. Every day, those beyond the Vale of Stones wake up thinking the Gods will return if only they could subject us all to their precious creed. You don't imagine they've stopped wanting to get these lands back just because they haven't tried in the last thirty years, do you?"

Here, close upon the edge of the Glas Water, the road was in poorer repair and stretches of deeply rutted mud often blocked their way. As they worked around one such obstruction Kylane gave a cry of surprise and reached precariously down from his saddle. When he hauled himself upright again, he was brandishing a trophy: a human jawbone.

"One of the Glas Water's treasures," he grinned at Orisian. "You know some of the farmers say it's good fortune to unearth one of these?"

Orisian grimaced. "I've heard it," he acknowledged. "I don't think we need good fortune that badly at the moment, though."

The ancient bone was pitted and stained the color of soil. Kylane examined it with mock curiosity.

"Hero or villain, do you think?" he asked.

Beneath the mists and sullen pools of the Glas Water lay the graves of thousands who had died on Kan Avor Field, the final battle in the war that drove the followers of the Black Road — led by the Gyre Blood, whose stronghold Kan Avor had been in those days — north beyond the Stone Vale. The fires had burned day and night across this land afterward, yet still had not been enough to consume all the corpses.

After the exile of Gyre, Kan Avor had slowly declined under uncaring masters but its final ruin came later, when the Lannis Blood was created and granted rule over the Glas Valley. One of the first commands of Sirian, the new Thane, had been for the burning and flooding of the city. Kan Avor's slow, waterlogged decay was a permanent reminder of his determination to stamp his authority upon his new domain.

"Villain, I say," decided Kylane in answer to his own question. "Black Road through and through, this one." He sent the bone spinning away with a flick of his wrist. "No fit traveling companion for the nephew to the Lannis Thane."

Daylight was fading as they came toward the Glas Water's southern end. A clutch of low houses came in sight through the thin drizzle that was beginning to fall.

"We'll pass the night at Sirian's Dyke?" Kylane asked.

"Why not?" agreed Orisian. "It'll be a short day to Glasbridge tomorrow. Try not to lose too much sleep in the name of drink and dice, though."

Kylane laid a hand upon his chest. "Why, Orisian, you know I'm not one to surrender to such temptations."

Rothe, riding a little ahead of them, snorted in derision but said nothing.

Sirian's Dyke, Orisian had always thought, was a gloomy village. Thirty or forty small cottages clustered together, surrounded by dank stands of spindly trees. The only structure of any size was the resthouse. The lights at its windows provided at least some promise of warmth and cheer. Its outbuildings — stable, smithy and wheelwright's shop — clung to its walls like children seeking protection at the skirt of a nursemaid. All was dominated by the great, harsh line of Sirian's Dyke itself. The massive dam of timber, stone and earth, standing higher than a man, stretched out from the edge of the village and vanished into the twilight. Here was the means by which Sirian had drowned Kan Avor. In all the years since its construction, most of the village's inhabitants had worked in the pay of successive Lannis Thanes to maintain this bulwark against the will of the river and keep Kan Avor bound in its watery chains.

With their horses stabled for the night, Orisian, Rothe and Kylane entered the inn. The landlord appeared at their side before they had even found a table. He bowed to Orisian.

"Welcome, welcome. It is an honor to have you as a guest, my lord."

The inn was half-full with a mixture of villagers and travelers. A hush fell across the room as Orisian and his shieldmen settled at a table, but it did not last: the Thane's kinsfolk were not such a rare sight in this place.

Orisian slumped in his seat, savoring the warm air upon his skin and the rich smell of food. He pulled his boots off and flexed his feet. He was trying unsuccessfully to remember what he had eaten the last time he stayed in this inn — it had been good, and he was hungry — when a serving girl came over and bobbed in front of him. She gave him a smile as warm as a thick bed. He smiled back and waited for her to ask him what he wanted. She said nothing, and for a couple of seconds the two of them regarded one another thus. Her smile grew only more expansive, her eyes more liquid as she stood there. Kylane laughed.

"Ale and food," said Rothe firmly, "whatever you have that is good."

The girl looked at him as if puzzled by his words, and her smile slipped a fraction without quite losing its hold upon her mouth.

"Yes, sire," she said, and departed with another nod of her head to Orisian.

"And wine and water, please," he called after her, and was granted another glimpse of her radiant face over her shoulder.

Kylane was still chuckling. "Terrible effect you have on women," the shieldman observed.

Rothe glowered at his younger comrade in arms. His disapproval was wasted, since Kylane was already casting around the inn, seeking a game or perhaps a companionable-looking woman of his own.

Orisian kicked amiably at Kylane's shin. "It's not me," he said, "it's whose nephew I am."

"You give yourself too little of your due," said Kylane distractedly. "No tavern girl would think you ugly, even if you'd a goatherd for an uncle."

Orisian smiled, as much at the furrowing of Rothe's brow as anything. The older man often gave the impression that he despaired of Kylane's levity, but Orisian knew the two of them shared a deep-rooted mutual respect. Rothe had been his shieldman since his tenth birthday. Kylane had only taken up the task this last summer — an ominous sign, Orisian suspected, that the aging Rothe was grooming a successor — but even so it earned him the right to a familiarity few others would dare. Being shieldman to a nephew of the Thane did not bring with it the responsibilities of guarding Croesan himself, but still it was no mere ceremonial role. Kylane had made a promise, just like Rothe before him, that set Orisian's life at a higher value than his own.

They drank and ate well, the landlord accepting payment from Rothe only after a show of reluctance. They were given the best rooms in the house. Former residents, Orisian guiltily suspected, had been evicted at short notice. As his thoughts flirted with slumber Orisian found them, to his vague surprise, drifting toward Kolglas. In his mind's eye he gazed upon the castle in the sea and realized that he would be happier to be back home than he had expected. Sleep came quickly and he could not linger upon the realization.

* * *

Lekan Tirane dar Lannis-Haig was running faster than he had ever run before. Terror drove his pounding legs. He flew through the forest as if a pack of wolfenkind were on his trail. He bounded over the uneven ground, staggering but never quite losing his footing. He thrashed through bushes, bramble stems tearing at his clothes. Some large animal, startled by his careering approach, crashed away. He barely noticed. The fear of what was behind him beat down upon his back like a hammer.

The light was failing. Soon darkness would swallow the forest and then he would be finished, for those who came after him needed the light less than he. Still there was a sliver of hope. He was not certain where he was, or how far he had come, but the track from Kolglas to Drinan could not be much further. If he could reach that road there might be travelers to give him aid. Failing that perhaps he could still make the safety of Kolglas, flying down a clear and known path. The town must be no more than a few miles to the north. And that, in its way, was a part of his terror: that his pursuers should be so keen for human blood that they would come this close to the garrison of Kolglas. The woodwights had not been this brave, or foolhardy, in many years.

It had never crossed Lekan's mind, as he set out the day before in search of forest meat for his family's Winterbirth celebration, that anything more dangerous than boar or bear could be awaiting him. There had been no Kyrinin in the lands around Kolglas since before his father's days, and though it was common knowledge that the White Owls were raiding in strength through the woods of Anlane further to the east, there had been no strife here save a few horses stolen from hamlets near Drinan.

He had been standing beneath a great ash tree, unbreathing and still as he searched for sign of the deer he had tracked through half a mile of thickets and groves. A mark in the earth, perhaps the faintest imprint of a hind's foot, caught his eye and he bent to look more closely. The sound was so sudden and unexpected that at first he could not put a cause to it, and when he saw the arrow shivering in the tree trunk his incredulous mind instinctively denied its meaning. Yet it was, beyond doubting, a Kyrinin shaft. And then he was off, casting bow and quiver aside, flinging his backpack away to lend speed to his flight. There had been no sign save the arrow itself, no sound but its hissing flight and sharp crack into the wood. Still he knew they were behind him, and close, and that he had no hope save the strength of his legs.

He swept past a tree, a great gnarled oak that seemed familiar. He had not been this way for a long time but it was, he was sure, a tree he had climbed in as a child. If he was right, the track, the longed-for path that might carry him to safety, was only two or three hundred paces further on. The thought lent new life to his tiring muscles and he leapt forward with still greater urgency. The hope burned stronger.

He felt no pain, just a solid blow in the square of his back as if someone had thrown a stone. No pain, yet his legs were no longer his own and he sprawled face-down into the damp leaf litter. He clawed at the earth, struggling to rise. His legs would not obey him. He reached behind to finger the arrow buried in his back. He felt something rising in his throat.

Then there was a powerful grip upon his arm and he was turned over. The arrow snapped and sent a lance of pain clean through him, transfixing sternum and spine. He cried out and crushed his eyes tight shut against it. When he opened them again, blinking through the mist of tears, there was one last surprise. It was not into the pale face of a Kyrinin that he looked, as he had expected. Instead, he met the gaze of one of his own kind: a black-haired woman, clad in dark leather, with a sword sheathed crossways on her back.

"The woodwights have brought you down, but it is fitting that the killing blow should come from a truer enemy," she said in a harsh, rough-edged accent Lekan did not recognize.

There were other figures gathering behind her. Lekan could not see them clearly. The warrior languidly drew her sword over her shoulder. She saw the confusion in Lekan's eyes.

"You should know why you die," she said, "so know this: the Children of the Hundred have come for you, for all of you. The Bloods of the Black Road will take back that which is ours, and where you go now, all of Lannis-Haig will follow."

Lekan's mouth moved. There was no sound. The blow fell, and he plunged toward the Sleeping Dark.

II

The second day's ride was easy going and Orisian and his shield-men made good time. From the Dyke down to Glasbridge the road was well maintained. The flat ground close by the river was good cropland, and there were countless small farms. A chilling rain that fell for most of the day kept all save a few people off the road, though. Two or three riverboats drifted by. Orisian and the others could easily have found a boat to carry them down to Glasbridge, but few horses tolerated such a journey with equanimity and Orisian preferred, in any case, to stay in the saddle.

By midafternoon they were approaching the northern gate of Glasbridge, Lannis-Haig's second town. It was a bustling port, and the scent of the sea and the screeching of gulls filled the air as they rode down toward the harbor. The quayside was swarming with people. Kylane grew animated at the sight of the largest of the dozen boats berthed along its length: a long, fat sailship riding high in the water.

"Look," he said, patting Orisian on the arm. "She's a merchant-man out of Tal Dyre."

The young shieldman had once told Orisian, when somewhat the worse for drink, that he had dreamed as a boy of taking service with the ships of Tal Dyre. Fanciful tales were told of the exploits of that island's sea captains and of the wealth of its merchant lords. Orisian was disinclined to believe such stories now, but three or four years ago they had stirred in him the same yearnings Kylane described. There had been times when he would have given anything to escape the confines of Castle Kolglas and the memories it embodied. Then, as he had looked out over the great expanse of the estuary from his high bedchamber, to ride the waves as the Tal Dyreens did, to leave everything behind, had seemed an enticing prospect.

"The harbormaster is waving to us," Rothe said with a touch of despondency.

Orisian looked toward the harbormaster's rather ostentatious residence a short way down the waterfront. Renairan Tair dar Lannis-Haig was indeed leaning — somewhat recklessly, given his girth — over the edge of a balcony, waving vigorously and hailing them. Passing through Glasbridge on his way to Anduran a fortnight before, Orisian had promised to visit with the harbormaster on his return. He would have preferred to pass the night quietly in the fine house Croesan kept here, but the harbormaster was a difficult man to refuse. Given time, his remorseless jollity could have ground down the most obstinately doleful rock.

"Orisian!" Renairan was shouting. "Here, here!"

"I suppose we cannot pretend we did not hear him," murmured Rothe as scores of heads amongst the crowds turned toward the harbormaster.

"This'll be a long evening," said Kylane under his breath.

Kylane's prediction turned out to be accurate, though not for him and Rothe. Orisian was respectfully paraded before the guests Renairan had invited to dine with them, like a trophy from some polite hunt. The harbormaster hardly needed to prove his importance — his line had long carried great influence in Glasbridge — but the presence of a member of the Thane's family in his house had been too great a temptation to resist. Orisian's two shieldmen, much to their relief, had not been expected to attend.

There was a trace of vanity in Renairan that excluded mere fighting men — even the guardians of his Thane's nephew — from a gathering such as this. Rothe had protested, but even he could not credibly claim that Orisian might be in danger amidst the great and good of Glasbridge.

The dining hall was decked out with holly, juniper and sprigs of pine: traditional decorations for the coming Winterbirth celebrations. In the grate at one end of the hall, pine logs were burning, filling the air with their sharp scent. The smell touched upon raw memories for Orisian, and cast a shadow across his mood. Some of his clearest recollections of his mother Lairis were of her glowing presence at the Winterbirth feasts in Castle Kolglas. Those images were wreathed about in his mind with the poignant scent of pine. She had been the heart of those festivals, her voice their sweetest music.

Orisian did his best to play the honored guest. He gave a report of the festivities surrounding the birth of the Thane's grandson, and Naradin's killing of his boar. Curiosity satisfied, the conversation drifted to the sort of matters that always preoccupied the people of Glasbridge: the fishermen's catches in the last week, the promise of storms on the season's breath, and the prices obtained by the last merchant to sail south to Kolkyre. They were things, in the main, that Orisian knew little about. He had to concentrate to avoid overlooking any of the moments when a smile, a nod or some approving remark was required of him. Before long he was wishing he was with Rothe and Kylane, hidden away in the kitchens or wherever they had found themselves.

As the evening progressed Orisian became convinced that Renairan's wife, Carienna, and his young daughter were talking about him. Now and again, across the landscape of wine jugs and meat and bread, he noticed Carienna watching him with an unguarded, penetrating gaze. For no reason he could name, it made him uncomfortable and he tried to keep his eyes on other things.

The one guest who caught Orisian's interest was the captain

of the Tal Dyre merchant ship, Edryn Delyne. He had met Tal Dyreens before, when they stopped off at Kolglas and paid courtesy visits to his father, but this man was the most impressive of the breed he had ever seen. He was tall and fair-haired and boasted the short, pointed beard that, in the tales at least, was the mark of every Tal Dyre adventurer.

Delyne regaled the party with stories of the fighting far away in the south. Many men of Lannis were there, fighting under Gryvan oc Haig's command against the rebellious Dargannan Blood, and the interest around the table was keen. Delyne assured his audience that the fighting would soon be over and Igryn, the recalcitrant Thane, dead or taken. Renairan and his guests, Orisian included, received this news with only muted enthusiasm. There was no love lost between the Lannis Blood and that of Haig. Orisian had heard it said more than once that the two thousand men Taim Narran had led south in answer to the High Thane's summons would be doing better service if they were marching against Gryvan's palace in Vaymouth, rather than the mountain forts of Igryn oc Dargannan-Haig.

Orisian's eyes grew ever more heavy-lidded as the evening crept on. Though he watered his wine carefully, the heat of the fire and the heavy scent in the air combined with it to lull him toward sleep. Renairan's booming voice caught him unawares. He attempted an alert expression. The harbormaster's laughter told him that his efforts were in vain.

"Too much good food and wine for our young guest, I think!" Renairan said.

Orisian smiled apologetically.

"Forgive me," he said. "Two days' riding takes its toll."

"Of course, of course," cried Renairan. "You must retire, Orisian. You have another day in the saddle tomorrow."

"Thank you for a fine meal," said Orisian as he rose. The other guests stood up as well, acknowledging his departure with small bows or nods. He found Renairan's wife and daughter closing upon him as he headed for the door, and he had to resist a powerful urge to spring forward and make a dash for the sanctuary of his bedchamber. As the meal was noisily resumed behind them, Orisian was held by Carienna's cheerful, yet somehow insistent, gaze.

"Such a shame that we did not have a proper chance to speak," she said, "but you must spare a word for my daughter Lynna before you retire."

She eased the young girl forward.

"Lynna!" prompted Carienna, and the somewhat flustered girl cleared her throat.

"It was a very great pleasure to meet you, Master Orisian," she said, giving him a delicate smile and a practiced curtsey.

"Ah," said Orisian.

"Lynna is almost fifteen," said Carienna in a voice that spilled implications from its edges like honey from an over-full beescomb.

"Really," said Orisian, "I'm . . ." He realized that he had forgotten how old he was.

"Sixteen, I believe," said Carienna happily.

It took Orisian a while to find a kind form of words to take his leave. Rothe was waiting outside his room. The shieldman smiled sympathetically when Orisian told him what had happened.

"Sixteen is a perilous age for the only available man in the Thane's family."

Kylane was quiet the next morning, nursing the after-effects of drink and what had evidently been a costly gaming session with members of the harbormaster's household. Rothe, cheered by the prospect of being back at Kolglas by nightfall, and perhaps by his comrade's misfortune, was livelier. He and Orisian talked happily of hunting, of Croesan and of the growing grandeur of Anduran as they passed along Glasbridge's streets, over the broad river running through its heart and out through the western gate of the town.

They followed the stone-surfaced track along the southern

shore of the Glas estuary. This was a well-populated stretch, with many farmhouses and hamlets lining the way. Little watermills, their wheels creaking round, stood astride the streams flowing down to the sea. Here and there small fishing boats were drawn up on the rocks. At one roadside house they stopped to buy some oatcakes and goat's cheese, and ate them as they rode onward. Kylane's mood lifted a little, his spirits renewed by the food. He recounted tales, harvested over dice the night before, of bawdy goings-on in the harbormaster's house.

In the late afternoon they rounded a small headland and came within sight of Kolglas. The town lay on the far shore of a shallow bay studded with rocky islets, closely hemmed in by the forest. Castle Kolglas stood tall on its isle a hundred yards offshore: a weathered stone bastion so old that it seemed as much a part of the natural landscape as the rocks breaking waves beneath its walls. The tide was out, so the narrow causeway running from the town to the castle was exposed. They could see a small cart moving along it, carrying firewood to feed the castle's hearths. A broad smile came to Orisian's face.

"A race back!" he cried, and kicked his horse into a headlong gallop along the track.

He heard Rothe's exasperated cry, and then the pounding of hoofs as the two shieldmen came rushing after him. The dash around the curving shore did not take long, but the horses were blowing hard as they slowed at the edge of Kolglas.

The main street and most of the little tracks that ran off on either side were busy. Kolglas always sucked people in at Winterbirth, as surely as a full-laden fishing boat drew gulls. The stalls around the edge of the market square were doing a roaring trade in everything from candles to snowboots, and so much money changing hands had created an infectious air of good humor. Some of the stallholders called out and waved as Orisian went by.

The area around the cairn in the heart of the square, by contrast, was almost empty, with only a screaming gang of children chasing one another round and round the small tower of stones. The monument was a memorial to the Battle of Kolglas. Sirian had been only master of Kolglas then, holding it in the name of the Kilkry Thane at a time when the exile of the Gyre Blood and its followers was still young, their hunger to return still raw and urgent. It had fallen to Sirian to turn back the armies of the Black Road when they poured south across the Vale of Stones and down the length of the Glas valley. His reward for the victory: the right to found his own Blood, to rule over the valley he had defended, and to hold it in perpetuity against the exiles in the north.

The cairn had stood here, with children playing around it and travelers resting by it, for well over a century. Despite its long familiarity it retained a powerful symbolic meaning for the whole Lannis Blood. None who journeyed out from Kolglas could say they had truly returned until they had been to it. First Orisian, then Rothe and Kylane, leaned down to lay a hand upon the round, aged stone that surmounted the cairn. It had been smoothed by the brushing of countless fingertips.

"To the castle, then?" Rothe asked, and Orisian nodded.

They went down toward the sea. As they rode out onto the causeway the clouds parted for the first time that day, and the low, late sun cast the faintest of shadows out across the tranquil water. The castle's sheer walls looked almost warm in the light. The gate was open and as they passed into the courtyard beyond, Orisian found himself smiling again. It was, after all, good to be home.

There were few people about: a small group stacking firewood by the stables, and a handful of warriors sharpening swords on a grinding stone outside their sleeping quarters. Half the fighting men of castle and town had gone south to join the war against Dargannan-Haig almost a year ago. The place had been subdued ever since.

Orisian and his shieldmen crossed to the stable block and dismounted. Bair, the youngest of the stablehands, scampered out to take their horses.

"Take good care of them, Bair," said Orisian, "they have been gentle with us."

Some of those taken ill with the Heart Fever had survived its scourges, Orisian's own sister Anyara amongst them. She had been fortunate and was unmarred by the sickness. Other survivors, like Bair, had been damaged. The young boy was mute. Nevertheless, he had one of the most lively and expressive faces Orisian had ever seen, and a nature as unfailingly merry as anyone he knew. With a grin, Bair gathered up the reins and led the horses toward their stables.

"Back to the quiet life, then," said Rothe, feigning disappointment.

"Only for a day or two," Orisian said. "Winterbirth should bring all the excitement you could wish for."

The two shieldmen said their farewells, shouldered their packs and headed for the guards' bunkhouse.

Orisian looked up at the keep. The windows were dark and blank, and the building had a lifeless air. With a slight, belated twinge of foreboding, he hefted his traveling pack and headed for the main stairway.

* * *

From the forest above the road, eyes that were not human had watched the three riders gallop that last stretch to the edge of the town. The light would fail soon. The watcher's sight was sharp, but even he would not be able to make out any movement on the road from this distance once night had fallen. Although the Huanin in the cottages and farmhouses scattered along the coast were as good as blind in the darkness there would still be some small chance of discovery if he went closer, out of the loving embrace of the forest. There was little to be gained from such a risk; it was clear the enemy did not suspect what was about to befall them. They went about their crude, loud lives just as they always did.

The watcher rose. He had been crouched motionless for half the day, yet there was no stiffness in his lithe limbs. He adjusted the position of his bow and quiver on his back and picked up his spear. For a moment he laid his long, tapering fingers upon its point. It would be good to bathe it in Huanin blood. His heart sang at the thought.

He turned away from the feeble necklace of lights springing up in the cottages along the shore and the forest's shadows enfolded him.

* * *

Orisian's bedchamber was cold, but there was comfort in its familiarity. A knock at the door just as he finished changing announced the arrival of Ilain, the keep's oldest chambermaid.

"We were not sure when you would get back, or we could have had some food waiting for you." Warmth and severity rubbed shoulders in her voice. She worked as she talked, gathering up his discarded riding clothes and clutching them to her chest.

"Sorry, Ilain. But I'm not hungry, in any case. We ate as we rode."

"Well," she said, "that will foul up your stomach sure as fish are wet. No matter. You'll want a rest?"

"No. Really, I'm fine."

The chambermaid frowned. "You'll have a fire lit, at least."

"Yes, please," responded Orisian promptly, knowing better than to refuse her again.

She turned, still carrying his clothes, to go and fetch a taper.

"Where is everyone, Ilain?" asked Orisian.

"I think Anyara is with your father. He is still unwell."

"And Inurian?"

Ilain rolled her eyes skyward, and Orisian felt a twinge of instinctive guilt at her displeasure. He had never quite shaken off the childhood memory of Ilain's scoldings. More often than not Anyara or Fariel had been at the root of whatever misadventure incurred the chambermaid's wrath; nevertheless, it had usually been Orisian who was left to face the consequences, never quite as adept as the other two at identifying the ideal moment to disappear. He was too old now for her to scold, but when Ilain disapproved of something it was not well concealed. Inurian was counselor to Orisian's father, and the closest thing to a friend Kennet nan Lannis-Haig had. That was not enough to make everyone in the castle comfortable with his presence.

"He is in his rooms, no doubt," Ilain said, and swept out.

Orisian hesitated. He knew he should visit his father, but he had a strong urge to put that off a while longer. It was a much easier thought to go to Inurian. That at least would be a meeting that had only uncomplicated feelings attached to it.

The door to Inurian's chambers, which lay on the top floor of the keep, was closed as always. Orisian listened for a moment. There was no sound from within. He knocked.

"Come in, Orisian."

As he entered he at once caught the unique scent that always greeted him here: a tantalizing, rich mixture of parchment, leather and herbs. The room was small and crowded. Book-lined shelves filled one wall; racks of jars and pots packed with herbs, powders, spices, even soils, another. An ancient, scored table held a scattering of papers, maps and a neatly arranged collection of dried and wizened mushrooms. To one side, a curtain concealed the tiny bedchamber in which Inurian slept. In the narrow window Idrin the crow was bobbing up and down on his perch.

A handful of carved wooden figurines and a small pile of manuscripts cluttered the desk. Inurian himself was sitting behind it, leaning back with his arms folded across his chest. He was a small man of middle years, with a mop of pale brown hair interspersed here and there with grey strands like threads of silver. The one thing that anyone meeting him for the first time would notice, however, was that he was a *na'kyrim*: a child of two races. In him,

Huanin and Kyrinin were blended. His Kyrinin father had given him penetrating eyes of a pure flinty grey and the fine features and thin, almost colorless, lips of his inhuman kind. When he came from behind the desk and reached out to greet Orisian, his lean, long fingers and clouded nails also betrayed his mixed parentage.

There were other, invisible, marks too. Inurian would never have children; no *na'kyrim* could. And there was the Shared, that mysterious, intangible realm lying beneath the surface of existence. It was beyond the reach, and the understanding, of purebred Huanin and Kyrinin, yet the intermixing of their blood sometimes gave a *na'kyrim* child access to its secrets and powers. Those in whom that contact with the Shared flowered were named the waking. Inurian was one such.

Orisian could not remember a time when Inurian had not been here, in his little rooms at the summit of the castle. He had come to Kolglas before Orisian was born, finding in Kennet nan Lannis-Haig a rare thing in these days: a human who would offer friendship to a *na'kyrim*. It was not a sentiment all in the castle could share. The War of the Tainted had ended forever the days when Huanin and Kyrinin walked side by side; there was little goodwill for the offspring of any union that defied the weight of that history, and even less for those woken into the Shared. Still, Inurian had stood loyally at the side of the lord of Kolglas for years. And since the deaths of Lairis and Fariel, and Kennet's decline into misery, he had become steadily more important to Orisian as well.

"How was your journey?" Inurian asked, his voice smooth and warm.

"Cold. A little damp."

Idrin croaked in the window, and Inurian chuckled.

"Well, we are both pleased to see you in any case. Is Croesan well? And Naradin's child safely born?"

Orisian bent over the table, peering at the mushrooms arrayed there and prodding one. "Yes, to both. Croesan has a very healthy grandson. What are these for, Inurian?"

The *na'kyrim* waved a dismissive hand. "Curiosity. One eases the birthing of calves, another soothes aching joints and so on. Nothing of great consequence."

"You've been into the forests again, then."

"Indeed. The slopes of the Car Anagais hold many secrets for those who know where to look."

"When can I come with you?" asked Orisian.

Inurian shrugged. "We'll see," he said. "Soon, perhaps." It was what he always said.

Orisian went to stroke Idrin's glossy breast. The crow blinked and ducked his head in the hope that Orisian would pet the nape of his neck.

"I cling to the slender hope that if I search long and hard enough I may yet find a cure for disobedience in crows," muttered Inurian.

"But an obedient Idrin would not be Idrin," said Orisian.

"True."

Orisian sat on the corner of the desk.

"My father?" he asked quietly.

Inurian returned to his seat with a sigh. "For him I have no cures, I'm afraid. Not that I could administer them even if I did, as he will see no one save your sister. She has tended him ever since you left for Anduran. His grief must run its course, Orisian. He will remember himself soon."

"He'll come to the feast?"

"I'm sure. You know these moods pass."

"I do. It seems they take longer each time, though. I am afraid that some day one will come that does not leave him."

Inurian regarded the youth for a moment, sadness tweaking at the corners of his mouth.

"Shall we go hunting on the first day of winter?" he asked.

Orisian brightened a little at the suggestion.

"We could. I've missed the hawks while I was at Anduran. Uncle Croesan prefers crashing through the forest with packs of hounds. I had to go along with him, but it's not really my idea of hunting."

"A fact of life: Thanes must make more noise about their business than ordinary folk, whatever that business is."

"What is planned for Winterbirth, then?" asked Orisian.

"Oh, I would be the wrong person to ask," said Inurian. "You know half of what goes on here is a mystery to me."

"Hardly."

"Well, in any case, I have not been paying much attention. There will be all the usual gluttony, of course. I heard something about entertainers as well. There's a troupe of acrobats or something similar coming to town. Masterless men."

Orisian raised his eyebrows in surprise. Masterless men, those who owed no allegiance to any Blood, were not an unknown sight in these parts, but most of them were solitary traders or hunters from the hills and mountains to the north. They entered Lannis-Haig lands only to ply their wares in Glasbridge or Anduran. He could not remember ever having heard of more than two or three traveling together.

"I imagine I will be called upon as well," continued Inurian, "since there will probably be the usual granting of boons."

"No doubt," said Orisian. He understood little of the strange, unpredictable gifts some *na'kyrim* possessed — the Shared was something Inurian did not talk about — but he did know that Inurian disliked ostentatious displays of his talents. They would be to the fore in any granting of boons.

"Your father likes it," Inurian said. "At least he has in the past. It may . . . cheer him a little."

Orisian nodded. "I suppose I should go to see him."

"You should," agreed Inurian. "He will be glad of it. Never forget that he loves you, Orisian. Sometimes he may forget himself, but the real Kennet loves you dearly. You know that I, of all people, could not be wrong about that."

That much, Orisian recognized as the truth. There were no

secrets from a *na'kyrim* with the gift of seeing what was within. Inurian always knew what lay in the heart.

"I know you're right," said Orisian. "But it is hard to remember, sometimes."

"Come to me when you need reminding," smiled Inurian gently.

"I always do, don't I?"

"Do you want me to come with you?" Inurian asked him.

Orisian was tempted only for a moment. He shook his head resolutely. Whatever burdens there were, they were for him and his father to bear. He could not expect others to shoulder them on his behalf; not even Inurian, who he knew would willingly try.

He paused outside his father's room. This door, unlike that guarding Inurian's secrets, was old and grand, with patterns of flowing ivy carved into its panels. The torches that lined the spiral stairway had stained its timbers over the years so that to Orisian it had always seemed to project a glowering presence. He laid his hand flat upon the door, feeling its grain under his fingertips. The wood was cold.

A gust of chill air greeted him as he entered. A window was wide open. The room was gloomy, and the only sound was the shifting of the sea outside. His father lay in the great bed against the far wall. Kennet's grey-haired head rested on pillows; his arms lay limp across the bed cover. His eyes were closed. There were deep lines in his face as if his skin had folded in upon itself beneath the weight of sorrow, and heavy shadows lurked beneath his eyes. His visage had gathered at least another decade to itself in the last few years.

Anyara, Orisian's elder sister, was sitting by the bed and looked up as he came in. She was tired, he could see, and her long auburn locks were lifeless. She put a finger to her lips and mouthed, "He's sleeping."

Orisian hesitated, midway between door and bed. He could have left, absolved of some responsibility by his father's slumber.

He went instead to close the window. Kennet stirred at the sound of his footsteps.

"Leave it."

"I thought it was cold," said Orisian. His father's eyes were red and empty.

"I prefer it."

Orisian came to stand at Anyara's side.

"You've come back," said Kennet.

"Barely an hour ago."

Kennet grunted. Speaking seemed an effort for him. His eyelids fluttered, and closed. Anyara laid a soft hand on Orisian's arm and looked up at him. She squeezed gently.

"Croesan wished you well," said Orisian. "He wants you to visit him. I think he would like to show you how Anduran is growing."

"Ah," said Kennet without opening his eyes.

"Will you be well for the Winterbirth feast?" asked Orisian, the question sounding hasty and harsh even to his own ears. He did not know what he could say that would reach the father he remembered, and loved.

His father turned his head on the pillow to look at him. "When is it?" he asked.

"Father, we were talking about it only this afternoon," said Anyara. "It's the day after tomorrow. Remember? There will be acrobats and songs and stories. You remember?"

Kennet's gaze became unfocused, as if he was looking no longer upon the here and now but on memories more real to him than the present.

"Inurian told me that the acrobats are masterless men," said Orisian, knowing from his own heart that remembrance of Winterbirths past could bring as much pain as warmth. It was often this way between the three of them: conversations skirted around dangerous territory. As much was unsaid as was said. Knowing the pattern made it no easier to break.

Kennet sighed, which prompted a shallow, dry cough that shook him.

"The day after tomorrow," he said after the coughing had subsided. "Well, I must be there, I suppose."

"Of course," said Anyara. "It will do you good."

Kennet smiled at his daughter, and the sight of that weakened, shallow-rooted expression was almost enough to make Orisian turn away. "Go with Orisian," he said to her. "You should not be always at my bedside. Have someone light some candles here, though. I do not want the darkness. Not yet."

"He is no better," said Orisian as he and Anyara made their way down the stairs. "I had hoped he might be, by now."

"Not much better," agreed Anyara. "But still, he will be there for Winterbirth. That's something. He did miss you, you know. It's good for him that you're back."

Orisian hoped that might be true. His father's affliction touched upon painful places within him. In the months after the Fever had taken them, the absence of his mother and brother had been an aching, unbridgeable emptiness in Orisian's life. It was a wound that had not healed, but had at least become something he could bear. So too it had seemed with his father, for the first year: the sadness deep and immovable, yet accommodated as it had to be if life was to continue. The change had come with the first anniversary of their deaths. After that, these black moods had descended with growing frequency, shutting Kennet off from all around him.

Orisian felt deep sorrow for his father, and a nagging guilt at his own inability to ease his pain. But he had other, less kind, feelings too and they brought with them a different kind of guilt. He sometimes had to battle against bursts of resentment at the strength of his father's attachment to the dead. It was an attachment so intense that it both robbed Kennet of any strength he might have shared with the living and seemed to overshadow — to dismiss — the grief and loss that were lodged in Orisian's own breast. Often, when his father looked at him, Orisian had the sense that he was seeing, or perhaps longing to see, his dead brother Fariel; and Fariel had been so strong, so clever, so fast of hand and eye, that Orisian could never match the man he would now have been.

He and his sister went out into the courtyard. Night was coming on fast, and the temperature had fallen. The clouds of earlier had dissipated, unveiling a sky in which countless faint stars were already glimmering. Soon, that moon would turn, and winter would be born. Brother and sister stood in the center of the yard, gazing upward. Anyara soon lost interest.

"How was Anduran, then?" she asked, rubbing her arms against the cold.

"Thriving," said Orisian. "Uncle Croesan is full of plans."

"As always."

"He's built a great hall on the square and new barns near the castle. All the forests to the south are being cleared for farmsteads and grazing lands. Everyone is busy."

"Well, it's not before time. The Fever's long gone," said Anyara in a matter-of-fact tone, as if she had never been touched by it. Orisian had not forgotten how it felt, when his sister lay at the very brink of death, to think that he was going to lose her as well. Perhaps it had been easier, in a way, to pass those long, terrible days inside delirium than to watch it from without.

Anyara sniffed. "It's cold out here. Are you hungry?"

"A little."

Anyara pulled him along by the arm.

"Let's go to the kitchens, see what's cooking."

"Anyara," protested Orisian, "we'll only get in trouble."

"Old woman!" grinned his sister.

The kitchens filled most of the ground floor of the keep. They were, as always at this time in the evening, a hive of activity. Young boys carried pots and pans from table to stove and back again, while cooks chopped and stirred, pounded and chattered in a frenzy of organized chaos. A row of fat forest grouse were hanging from hooks along one of the roof beams. On one of the tables, a dozen loaves stood cooling, filling the air with their delicious aroma. At first no one seemed to notice that Orisian and Anyara had arrived. A moment later Etha the head cook was hobbling over, wiping her hands on her apron. She was a small, aging woman, whose joints were seizing up and giving her a clumsy stride as time went by. Her spirit, however, was uncowed by such assaults. She clapped Orisian on the arm with a crooked hand.

"Back at last," she said. "Just in time, too. It'll be a fine feast this year. Wouldn't do to miss it."

"I wouldn't want to," he said seriously, and waved at the black-feathered birds above their heads. "Looks like we'll be eating well."

"Yes, yes. And plenty more."

She was interrupted by an angry shout from behind her. Anyara darted past, juggling a still-hot loaf of bread from hand to hand. One of the other cooks was waving a soup ladle after her, flicking thick drops of broth in all directions.

"Why, that girl," muttered Etha. "Still acting the child." She turned on Orisian and poked a stiff finger into his chest. "And you, young man. A year or two younger, but no better excuse than she. You've not been back a day and already the pair of you acting like a brace of thieves!"

Orisian retreated, trying to look abashed. He found Anyara sitting outside, chuckling to herself and tearing off chunks of bread. He joined her, and they devoured half the loaf in silence. It was warm and comforting and tasted wonderful. They chatted for a while, almost shivering in the night air. They could have been children once more, teasing one another and whispering together as their breath formed little plumes of mist between them. Then one of the kitchen boys came out into the yard, banging a big copper pot with a spoon to signal that the night's meal was ready, and they joined the soldiers and stablehands, maids and servants filing into the common hall.

Beyond the walls, the tide had come in. The waves, dusted with moonlight, closed over the causeway, and the castle was alone on its isle of rock.

III

Gryvan oc Haig, High Thane of the Haig Bloods, was roused from a shallow, fitful slumber by his footman's voice. He rolled over and shielded his eyes from the light of the oil lamp the man carried.

"A messenger, my lord," said the footman, "from the fort."

Gryvan pressed finger and thumb into his eyes.

"What's the hour?" he asked.

"Three from dawn, my lord."

The Thane of Thanes grunted and sat up. He moistened his lips, finding his mouth dry and stale from the wine he had drunk the night before.

"Fetch me some water," he said.

His attendant turned and went out of the great tent. The light went with him. For a moment Gryvan sat with his eyes closed, listening to the heavy shifting of the canvas in the night breeze. He felt himself slipping back toward sleep. In the darkness he wrapped his sheet about him and rose, a little unsteadily, to his feet. He was standing thus when the footman returned, seeming more nervous than he had before; knowing, perhaps, that he would have done better to leave the lamp. He held out a tankard of water. Gryvan drained it.

"Give me my cloak," he said.

The footman hurried to gather the thick fur cape from where it lay by the High Thane's mattress. They were high in the mountains here in Dargannan-Haig lands, and the altitude lent the autumn nights a cold edge even this far south. Gryvan settled the cloak on his shoulders. He took its gold-trimmed edges in his hands and crossed his arms. A brief, involuntary shiver ran through him and he puffed out his cheeks. Feeling clumsy, he hauled on his boots. Their leather was cold and stiff.

"So, where is this messenger?"

"He waits outside your council tent."

"Light my way, then."

Hann nodded and Gryvan followed him out onto the hillside.

The High Thane shivered again as if to shake off the weight of sleep. When he had been young, sleep had fallen easily from him. In his sixth decade it seemed to settle ever deeper into his bones. Cold nights far from the comforts of his court taxed him.

The small fires of his army dotted the rocky slopes around him. Faint voices rose here and there from amongst the host of tents. He glanced up at the dark outline of the besieged An Caman fort far above. There were few lights there.

Outside the council tent, flanking the opening, two torches stood in tall metal holders, their flames snapping to and fro in the wind. Guards stood beside them, erect and alert though they were deep into their watches. Kale, Master of the High Thane's Shield, was there too, and a tall, dark-haired man who must be the messenger. Gryvan ignored them as he went inside. He settled himself into a high-backed wooden chair.

"Bring them in, then," he said to his footman.

Kale was first to enter, looking gaunt in the flickering light. His features could have been cut from the granitic hills of Ayth-Haig. Behind him came the messenger: a young man, Gryvan could see now, perhaps no more than twenty-five. The red badge on his breast — a sword and spear crossed — marked him as a mercenary out of the Dornach Kingship.

Gryvan scratched his chin and yawned. The messenger stood before him, some uncertainty betraying itself in the darting movement of his eyes. Kale, as always, was a model of silent, still observation.

"So," said Gryvan, "you've brought me from my bed, when my old limbs crave rest. The urgency must be great, the import of your message truly overwhelming. Let me hear it."

The mercenary ducked his head a fraction. "I am Jain T'erin, captain of one hundred men of Dornach. I speak for them alone, and am here without the knowledge of the Dargannan men in the fort."

"Dargannan-Haig," corrected Gryvan smoothly. "They owe me obeisance still, even if they have forgotten it."

"As you say. They fight for their reasons, my men and I for ours. We have held the fort against you for three weeks, and might do so for another three, but it seems a needless fight. Your armies to the south seek the Dargannan-Haig Thane, and though he is kept from the coast for the time being, he may yet slip away across the water. You would no doubt prefer the men you have encamped here to join the hunt. Our interests may both be served by an understanding?"

Gryvan raised his eyebrows. "So you seek what? Safe passage back to your own lands? Or to exchange Dargannan-Haig gold for mine?"

Jain T'erin smiled slightly, the nervousness all but gone from him now.

"If I have your word on the safety of my men in what would follow, I will deliver the fort to you. After that, we would take service with you if that was your wish. Or return to our homeland."

"Igryn's judgment was ever poor. He cannot even buy loyalty, it seems." Gryvan regarded the messenger for a moment. "You are young to lead a warrior band. Old enough, at least, to see how this battle must fall out, and old enough to try to bring your men safe out of it. There is some courage in venturing out to stand before me, I suppose."

The High Thane closed his eyes for a moment. When he opened them, he fixed T'erin with a cold glare, his face now stern.

"I will tell you my answer," said Gryvan. "You took the coin of my enemy and your men stand alongside his behind walls I have sworn to bring down. Igryn oc Dargannan-Haig mistook himself when he disavowed his oath to me and sought to set aside the obligations his Blood owes mine. He kept for himself taxes that are rightfully mine, for no better reason than greed. He gives sanctuary to pirates and brigands who prey upon the merchants of Vaymouth and Tal Dyre, and the goods they have stolen find their way into his treasury. And when I demand recompense, he imprisons my Steward and denies my authority. The gold Igryn has bought you and your warriors with is mine, little whore-soldier.

"Whatever cave or hovel he is hiding in, my armies will have him soon and he will learn the price of betrayal. As will all who stand against me. Not one stone of the fort above us here will stand. Not one of those within its walls will see another dawn after I have torn them down, and you will be brought before me with your hands struck off and your eyes put out. I will gut you myself and send your head back to your kingling in Dornach."

"B-b-ut . . ." stammered T'erin, "I will give you An Caman. You need spend no more of your people's blood upon it . . ."

Gryvan laughed harshly.

"You think a High Thane is so feeble a thing, so fearful or soft, that the sight of blood would concern him? Has Dornach forgotten so easily the mettle of the True Bloods? If I have to swim through the spilled blood of my own men to do it, I will see every living thing within those walls dead and laid out at my feet. Go back and tell your people they can expect nothing from me but a swift journey to the Sleeping Dark."

The mercenary held out his hands and started to speak. Before he could do so, Kale seized his arms and pushed him from the tent. The High Thane sighed and sank a little deeper into his chair as his bodyguard returned. He sent the footman away with a flick of his wrist.

Gryvan beckoned Kale closer and the warrior stepped forward, inclining his head a touch that he might hear the Thane's soft-spoken words.

"Our friend from Dornach is unfortunate to find himself in a more tightly woven web than he knew. In other times his would have been a welcome offer, but Dargannan is not the only Blood with lessons to learn. I am not done with Kilkry and Lannis. I will see their strength spent and broken on these slopes yet."

"That strength is all but gone, my lord," said Kale. "They sent two thousand men apiece to campaign with you. Less than half that number could now take the field."

"Still, that is more than I will send back to them. They may conceal them better than Igryn, but their instincts are still those of rebels."

The Thane pressed the palms of his hands into his eyes.

"Ah, Kale," he said, "my bones are too old for plotting in the depth of the night. I long to be back in Vaymouth. It's been too long this time."

"Your bones are not so old," said his bodyguard unsmilingly, "and to be always plotting is the fate of the Thane of all the Bloods. Igryn is almost finished. He cannot hide forever. We could be back in Vaymouth in a month, I think."

Gryvan yawned, putting his hand to Kale's shoulder for a moment.

"No doubt," he said. "Well, I'll not sleep again now I've been woken. Slumber's an unreliable companion as the years go by: irresistible when you're in its embrace, then irrecoverable when you're parted from it for a while. Send for our loyal northern captains, and have someone bring me clothes more fitting to receive them in."

Kale gave a shallow bow as he backed away, then turned and passed out into the night.

Taim Narran dar Lannis-Haig, captain of Castle Anduran, was ushered into the council tent by Kale. The two exchanged a loveless glance. Close behind him came Roaric nan Kilkry-Haig, the younger son of Lheanor, Thane of the Kilkry Blood. Gryvan awaited them on his wooden throne, now wearing a fine ceremonial cape and with his sheathed sword across his knees. On either side of him stood Shield guards, resplendent in formal dress as they stared ahead.

"A cold night to be making plans," said Gryvan, "but war makes harsh demands upon us all."

Taim said nothing. Roaric shifted uncomfortably at his side.

"Too cold for pleasantries, I see. So," continued the High Thane, "when light returns, we attempt the walls again. Your companies shall lead the assault."

Taim lowered his eyes, his teeth clenched and his knuckles showing white as he gripped the hilt of his sword. The faintest of winces crossed his face as he heard Roaric draw breath at his side. Taim knew only too well how loosely Lheanor's son held his temper when it stirred within him. The younger man let anger color his voice as he spoke.

"My father gave me two thousand of our finest men to bring in answer to your summons to war," Roaric said, "and hundreds of them have surrendered their lives in your cause. More than half a thousand dead from plagues and fevers or on the battlefield, the same again unable to rise from their sleeping mats. In every battle, and now in every attempt upon the walls of this petty castle, it is Kilkry and Lannis that must be to the fore. Am I to leave every one of my men dead in these hills? When will the other Bloods lead the charge?"

"The hunger for glory of our northern brothers is not what it once was, I see," said the High Thane in a level voice.

Roaric started to reply. Gryvan cut him off. "You should choose your words with more care when addressing your High Thane. It is a long time since yours was first amongst the Bloods. Your father took an oath to me, as did Croesan, the master of our friend Taim here. You stand now under that oath. You are young, and for the sake of your father I will overlook it, but you speak poorly when you call this my cause. It is in the cause of all the Bloods and all the Thanes that one who forgets his duties, as Igryn oc Dargannan-Haig has done, must be brought to heel. There can be no order if such as he go unrestrained. You do not desire chaos, I assume?"

There was a flush of color in Roaric's cheeks and his eyes

showed a wildness for an instant before he mastered himself. "We have not the engines to break An Caman," he said tightly.

Gryvan gave a half-laugh. "This is no Highfast, to shatter armies upon its walls. It is fit only to frighten bandits and robbers. You have scaling ladders, and the courage of your men: take an arm's width of the battlements and the army will be a flood following in your wake." He turned to Taim Narran. "And does our captain of Lannis-Haig share your fears?"

Taim looked up. His face bore deeper lines and darker shades than did Roaric's. His short hair was fading to grey from the black of its forgotten youth. Nothing about his expression betrayed his thoughts save for his eyes. There was a measured, deep-rooted strength about them as he met the High Thane's gaze.

"Neither I nor any of my men fear to die," he said, "though I, and they, would rather have a better reason to greet the Sleeping Dark. They lack the stores within the fort to last another month, and if we waited they would come out of their own accord. Igryn himself is beaten, a fugitive with only the mountains themselves to keep him from capture. You have half a dozen companies out hunting him in the mountains south of here. He will be yours in a day, or a week, and then again this fastness will mean nothing."

Gryvan oc Haig spoke slowly and clearly.

"Perhaps you speak the truth, Taim Narran. I do not care. Understand me well: it is my will that the walls above be broken and that Lannis and Kilkry lead the way. And here and now, my will rules. Your domain is the precincts of Castle Anduran, and they lie very far from here. My domain runs from the Glas to these very hills. I am Thane of Thanes, lord of your lord. Every one of your men who can walk and hold a sword will stand ready at dawn."

"I understand you well, my lord," said Taim, bowing his head. Roaric once again started to speak. Taim touched his arm and turned him away. He liked Roaric despite his youthful failings, and had no wish to see him harm himself still more in the High

Thane's eyes. They walked out of the tent, to wake their men and await the day.

Gryvan grunted and glanced at Kale.

"Roaric is a fool," he said. "It's as well there's another between him and his father's high seat. Our friend Taim Narran is of better stuff, I think."

Kale shrugged. "He knows no loyalty save to Lannis-Haig, lord. Let me set a knifeman on him. It could be done with no finger to point at us afterward, and his loss would wound Croesan to the quick."

"Indeed," laughed Gryvan, "but you allow your dislike of the man to cloud your judgment. My Shadowhand back in Vaymouth would never forgive such impulsiveness. No, we need not take so hasty a step. Taim will lead his men to slaughter tomorrow, though in his heart he would rather strike my head from my shoulders. We should be thankful that the old traditions bind them still in Lannis and Kilkry. Because Croesan has bent the knee to me, Taim will in his turn do my bidding. It would strain his precious honor beyond the breaking point to do otherwise."

The Thane of Thanes rubbed his hands together. "This cold could crack a mountain pine. Have a brazier brought in here. And bread. I must be strong and hearty if I am to savor what the morning will bring."

IV

Orisian woke late, from a dream that slipped away before he could grasp it. In those first bleary instants of wakefulness there was a fleeting memory of his brother's face. He sat up in his bed and looked about the room. He had shared it with Fariel when his brother lived. While the sickness had been stalking the passages and chambers of the castle, this was where Fariel had lain: sweating, muttering, drifting in and out of violent sleep. During those awful weeks Orisian had slept instead in Anyara's room, until she too had fallen sick. Then he had gone with Ilain to the chambermaids' quarters.

For months after his brother was wrapped in a sheet and carried away to The Grave on a black-sailed boat, Orisian had refused to return to this bedchamber. When at last he had found the courage to come back, it had been unexpectedly comforting. He often dreamed of his brother in this bed, and they were almost always fond dreams. His mother Lairis too seemed to have left something of her presence in the room, though Orisian's memories of her had a specificity that those of Fariel never possessed. His image of his mother had turned over the years into a mosaic of details: the smell and feel of her hair upon his face; the warm, strengthening clasp of her hand about his; the sound of her singing. These things infiltrated his dreams, and there were times when he awoke to discover in momentary surprise and confusion that she was not with him. They were lonely times, but soothing in their way, too.

He had just shaken sleep off when Ilain bustled in, bringing water and a cloth. She hardly spoke beyond wishing him a good morning. Her thoughts on the subject of late risers were almost palpable. By the time she left, Orisian was reproaching himself for his laziness.

The day passed quickly. In the morning, he went with Anyara over the causeway into town. They wandered about the market, jostling their way through the amiable crowd. They came across Jienna, the daughter of the merchant who owned fully a quarter of the stall plots. She was the same age as Orisian, and pretty. She and Anyara gossiped gaily, more or less ignoring Orisian. When he did steal into a gap in their conversation to compliment her on her dress, she laughed. Thankfully, it was a friendly, grateful laugh.

Afterward, Anyara poked him in the back and teased him. He reddened and cursed her without conviction. She soon tired of the game and they turned back to idle talk: how many guests would come to the feast in the castle, who would be the Winter King at the celebration, which of the market traders was doing the most business.

They found a stall selling little honey-coated cakes, a delicacy their father had always loved. When they had been children he would often return from visits to Drinan or Glasbridge with packets of them hidden away in his baggage. It had been a regular game for Orisian, Anyara and Fariel to dig through Kennet's belongings in search of the sticky treasures which he, until the very moment of discovery, would deny the existence of. The passage of time had shuffled roles and relationships. Now, Orisian and Anyara bought a small box of the cakes to take back to their father.

Later, Orisian went looking for Inurian. He searched the castle without success. Eventually he was directed out through the tiny postern gate at the rear of the stables. A passageway burrowed through the castle walls and gave out, through a heavy steel-banded door, on to the rocks of the isle's seaward flank. There was a crude jetty, and alongside it a little sailboat: Inurian's, which he must have left there after his most recent crossing to the far shore of the estuary. It was a simple, fast boat, sturdy enough for short trips when the weather was kind. It would not survive in such an exposed berth if caught by high wind or wave, though, and Orisian guessed that it must soon be moved to the town's quayside. He always enjoyed those rare occasions when Inurian took him out on the water, skimming along so close to the surface that an outstretched hand could plow a sparkling furrow through the waves. The short journey from castle to harbor might be a last chance to have a trip in the boat before the winter took hold.

With his back to the great bulk of the castle, not a sign of human life or habitation disturbed Orisian's view north across the Glas estuary to the heights beyond. There was almost no wind and the great bay was as near to stillness as it could come. He stood for a moment watching the distant white shapes of seabirds chasing one another low across the water. The Car Anagais, a rugged ridge of bare mountain tops skirted by dark forests, dominated the northern shore. The summits succeeded one another in a jagged line stretching off in either direction. To the north, he knew, they ran all the way up toward Glasbridge where they merged into the greater ramparts of the Car Criagar, and far to the south they marched down to the blasted headland of Dol Harigaig, where the ridge collapsed into the sea in a welter of broken, jumbled rock. Far beyond Orisian's sight, a bleak island lay there, lashed by the ocean. It skulked off the point of Dol Harigaig, as if the last of the mountains had slid intact into the water and left only its peak above the breakers.

An old story said the isle was the body of a giant, one of the First Race, cast into the sea. It had a more acute meaning for the people of Kolglas now. Dozens of their kinsfolk had found their final, fiery rest there during the Fever, their bodies carried to its huge pyres by boats with black sails. That had been the last journey Orisian's brother and mother had made, bound up in linen winding sheets and crowded in with the other dead upon the deck of a corpse ship. Until that grim year, the island had been called Il Dromnone, an ancient name. Now, everyone knew it as The Grave.

Orisian slipped and slithered along the rocks at the foot of the wall to where he could see Inurian crouching by the water's edge, poking around amongst the stones with a stick. The hem of the *na'kyrim*'s dark robe was trailing in the sea.

Orisian called to him. "What are you doing?"

"Looking for sea urchins."

"Why?"

Inurian sat back on a convenient boulder. "Well, firstly because if you dry them and crush them to a powder they are said to prevent dampness on the chest when taken in broth. I doubt it myself, but who knows? Secondly, because I had a good amount ground up, at which point Idrin chose to knock the bowl over. Most of it disappeared between the floorboards."

"Ah."

Inurian tossed the stick into the water disconsolately. "There are none here, though," he said.

Orisian sat beside him. They gazed out toward the hills. Inurian at last noticed that his robe was sodden and began to wring it out, muttering under his breath.

After a minute, Orisian narrowed his eyes and cocked his head to one side. He thought he could see, so faint that it might be nothing, a hair-thin thread of smoke rising from amongst the trees on the distant shore.

"Can you see smoke?" he asked, knowing that Inurian's half-Kyrinin eyes were a good deal sharper than his own.

"Indeed," said Inurian without looking up. "It has been there for some time. Quite careless."

For a moment Orisian was puzzled, then he understood and glanced at the *na'kyrim*.

"Kyrinin? A Kyrinin camp?"

Inurian nodded.

"Fox, then?" pressed Orisian. "There's only the Fox clan over there, isn't there?"

Inurian's Kyrinin father had been of the Fox clan. Other than that, Orisian knew almost nothing of the inhuman side of his heritage. Though he had never dared to ask, he was almost certain that Inurian went into the hills and forests of the Car Anagais not just in search of mushrooms or herbs but also to visit the camps of the Fox. Much of his longing to accompany the *na'kyrim* on one of those journeys was rooted in the wish to see such a camp. Whatever others of his kind might think of them, Orisian felt more curiosity than anything else about the Kyrinin who lived upon the fringes of his homeland.

"Only the Fox," agreed Inurian. "I suppose they are right to think themselves safe in such an inaccessible spot. Myself, I would still call it careless to give so clear a sign. I would have thought better of her."

"Who?" asked Orisian.

Inurian blinked. "Whoever's camp it is," he said. "Them."

"There's no danger to them there, surely?" Orisian said.

Inurian shrugged. "Your uncle claims that land, even if no one lives there. Now is not the best time for Kyrinin to be so visible within Lannis-Haig borders."

"But if they're Fox . . . it's the White Owls in Anlane who are causing trouble."

Inurian regarded his young companion with an arched eyebrow. "Do you really believe that is a distinction all your countrymen would make, Orisian? You know better than that, or you've not the wit I credit you with. Not everyone thinks of these things the way you do; very few, in fact. Fox and White Owl have been at each other's throats since long before your Blood was even imagined, but to your fellow Huanin they are all woodwights and that is an end to it."

Orisian could not deny it. The War of the Tainted had put a chasm between the two races. The three kingships of the Huanin race — Aygll, Alsire and Adravane — had stood together against the united strength of the Kyrinin clans. For all the savagery of the centuries since, nothing had matched the slaughter done in that vast conflict. The dead had thronged the fields until their stench choked even the carrion-eaters and it was said a man could walk for a day upon the backs of corpses. The Kyrinin city of Tane, the most wondrous city there had ever been, was destroyed. The war had ended only when the Anain, the most potent and secret of all the races, stirred from their unknowable rest to take possession of ruined Tane and raise the vast Deep Rove to engulf it and all its surrounds.

For the victorious kingships there had been no reward. Alsire declined in sad disarray until it was reborn as the lesser Kingship of Dornach, and Adravane began its long retreat into decadence, madness and isolation. Aygll tore itself apart from within and was extinguished in the bloodletting of the Storm Years, its lands inherited by the Bloods that rose from its ashes. All of that marred history was there beneath the surface of the moment in which Orisian gazed out toward the distant campfire of a people he could never know.

"I didn't tell you about Naradin's boar, did I?" Orisian asked. "It had a White Owl arrowhead in it, a fresh wound. And it was no distance from Anduran. No Kyrinin have been seen so close to the city for years, Rothe said."

"Now that is strange," Inurian said. A frown flickered across his gentle features.

"Croesan thought it was just some young hunters, flaunting their bravery by coming so far into our lands."

Inurian shook his head. "The Thane misreads it. This is not a time of year when hunting parties range far. No, that tastes wrong. Whatever the reason is, it's not youths showing off. Croesan would do well to pay more heed to such signs."

The *na'kyrim's* frown deepened. He sank into thought, his eyes locked unseeingly on the rocks at his feet.

Orisian looked back toward the northern shore.

"They should be going to their winter quarters, shouldn't they?" he asked, a trace of wistfulness in his voice.

"Yes," Inurian said, rousing himself. "They're on the move. All the *a'ans* scattered through the forests will be coming together at the *vo'ans,* the winter camps, to wait for spring. A small *a'an,* that one. Ten or twenty people."

Orisian stared at the thin trail of smoke. However impossible it might be, his longing to see for himself what it signified would not go away. Somewhere out there was a world in which the past did not weigh so heavily, where there were no dark, grief-laden walls to loom over him and no reminders of what might have been. If that world did not reside on the pitching deck of a Tal Dyre ship, perhaps it lay in the wandering, forest-bound life of the Kyrinin. Even as he watched, the firesign faded away, until there was no hint that it had ever been. He looked at Inurian.

"Inurian, do you ever wish . . ."

Inurian interrupted him. "It's unwise to dance with wishes unless you've the mettle for it. Wishing for what is not is a fast way to poison your heart." The *na'kyrim* tousled Orisian's hair with rough affection. "Your heart's a lot less poisoned than most I've known, Orisian. I like it that way."

Orisian held his tongue. A vague sense of longing stayed with him.

"Once Winterbirth is out of the way, I must move my boat to a safer berth," said Inurian. "Would you perhaps help me with that?"

Orisian smiled.

* * *

The sun rose upon the last day of autumn. Its pale touch brushed the snowfields and peaks of the high Tan Dihrin, and then swept down toward the valley of the Glas. It fell first of all upon the fortified town of Tanwrye, nestled at the foot of the Vale of Stones, marking the northernmost border of Lannis-Haig. Behind the walls, weary men were leaving their watches and bowls of gruel and bread were being passed out from steaming pots.

The grey light flowed on, south and west, over the reeds and rushes of rough grazing land toward Targlas. Cattle roused themselves from sleep, and snipe and plovers stirred amongst the tussocks. Reaching Targlas, the sun picked out columns of smoke rising from a hundred hearths as the drovers, herders and trappers warmed their cold and drowsy bones. A flock of sheep was being driven out, their shepherd shouting at his dogs. The great River Glas wove its way past the town, and the sun followed until it found Anduran.

The city was already half-woken. Traders were setting up their stalls in the square and dogs chased one another down side streets. The great castle by the Glas opened its gates even as the first hint of dawn fell upon it. Torches upon its battlements were doused and a flock of crows clattered up into the lightening sky. Beyond Anduran, the dawn reached the flat pools and misty islands of the Glas Water, lifting the marshes from their slumber. The ruins of old Kan Avor came sluggishly and reluctantly out of the night. Herons fell away from those broken walls on outstretched wings, heading out over the water to hunt. The day's first light found men already at work on Sirian's Dyke, repairing sections of the great dam that might not hold through the coming season.

At last the sun came to Glasbridge, and to the sea. The docks were alive and bustling as fishing boats opened their holds and crowds gathered to haggle over the best of the catch. The Glas poured its waters into the sea, and the light rushed on over the widening bay, picking out the foamy wave crests. To the north it played across the rocky ridge of the Car Anagais and rippled over the treetops of the dark forests along the shore. To the south, it chased the darkness from the hamlets and farmsteads along the coast, until finally it fell upon Kolglas. Like a great granite hillock, the castle on its island was lit by the day, and the lamps burning in its windows were one by one extinguished.

When this new day had run its course and passed into night, winter would be born.

In that bright morning the Thane of the Lannis-Haig Blood rode out from his castle and into the heart of Anduran. Half his household came with him. Croesan's Shield marched at the head of the procession, bearing pennants. The Thane himself rode just behind them, flanked by a dozen crossbowmen. His mount was a magnificent grey charger bedecked with silver armor and trailing ribbons from its halter and saddle. Behind Croesan came Naradin the Bloodheir and his wife Eilan, riding side by side and waving to those who lined the streets. In their wake followed a succession of retainers, officials and distinguished visitors from Glasbridge and Targlas. All were extravagantly dressed, as if they were some luxuriant pageant fresh come to town, and with the flags and banners snapping in a fresh wind it was a spectacle as fine as any Anduran had seen since the Bloodheir's wedding two summers gone.

The street running down from the castle through the Crafts' Quarter to the wide square in the middle of the town was packed with people, all cheering their Thane to the echo. The new Feast Hall was an imposing presence on the western side of the square: a great timber edifice that dwarfed the houses clustered on either side of it. Its heavy doors sat in a carved frame, surmounted by the Lannis crest. Before the building a wooden stage had been set up. Croesan drew to a halt and dismounted. As his Shield hurried to form ranks on the platform, he went alone with Naradin and Eilan into the great hall.

Despite the excitement outside there was a quiet grandeur about the deserted chamber. Its vaulting oaken beams, its walls and the very air they enclosed seemed imbued with expectancy.

Croesan turned to the young couple and smiled.

"It will be the happiest Winterbirth Anduran has seen in many years," he said. He put his arms around their shoulders, holding them tight against him. "To be a grandfather must be the finest thing in the world," he chuckled.

"Even for a Thane?" asked Eilan.

"Especially for a Thane. At this moment my grandson means more to me than all our lands and castles put together."

"Have a care," said Naradin, "someone might hear you."

Croesan laughed and released his son, who eased himself down into the nearest chair. Eilan kissed the Thane on his cheek.

"You'll be the finest grandfather any boy could wish for," she said.

"Thank you," said Croesan. "I hope you are right."

"Of course she is," said Naradin.

Croesan walked toward the high table. He stood beside the immense chair that would be his seat during the night's revels and laid his hand upon it.

"It is a strange thing, to feel you have arrived somewhere that you have been traveling toward without knowing it. Anduran thrives, my grandson sleeps in the castle. I can see the future through his eyes. He will sit in this chair years from now, surrounded by his people, and by his own children. For tonight at least, I can imagine that there is nothing more for me to do."

"Until tomorrow," said Eilan wryly.

"Until tomorrow," agreed Croesan. He sighed, a momentary distraction from his pleasure. "Your mother would have been so proud of you," he said to Naradin.

The Bloodheir had never known his mother — she had died in his birthing — but still a grave expression came across his face. "And of you," he said.

Croesan shrugged that off. "I have only done what was required of me," he said. The smile came bursting back upon his face. "None of it has given me half the joy of becoming a grandfather. I have the liberty of imagining I have nothing more to do, but the same cannot be said of the pair of you."

Eilan raised her eyebrows at him.

"I will want a granddaughter next," Croesan continued. "And more after that. I wish to be plagued by boisterous children in my dotage. I require a throng of them to pull at my beard and play tricks upon my failing eyesight and disturb my rest with laughter. Now that truly would be a happiness beyond measure."

Eilan laughed. Naradin put on a face of mock horror.

"You will allow us some time to recover from the first, I hope," he muttered.

He received a hefty jab in the ribs from his wife for that.

"Us? What have you to recover from?" she demanded. "The effort was mostly mine, as I recall."

"Enough, enough," said the Thane. "No arguments."

He looked around him once more, and made a deep, satisfied sound somewhere at the back of his throat.

"I am not done with building yet," he said. "I would give you, and your son, a gift. A house, fit for future Thanes, where you can spend the summers. No, humor an old man. We will build you a grand house in Grive, close enough that I can come and stay when the years weigh so heavily that I need a few days' rest away from Anduran. We will make gardens where your children can play, and stables and kennels for your horses and hunting hounds."

"That is a happy thought," said Naradin. "Thank you."

Eilan embraced the Thane and kissed him once again. Croesan smiled contentedly and ran a hand through her fine hair.

"Will you give me a little time with my son, Eilan? Perhaps you could keep our guests outside amused for a few minutes more. I am sure they would rather have your company than mine, in any case."

As the Bloodheir's wife left the hall, there was a resurgence of excited cries from the crowds.

"They love her almost as well as you or I," observed Croesan.

"Not as well as I," said Naradin. "Anyway, they would cheer a well-dressed donkey today. It has been a good year; they're ready to celebrate."

Croesan nodded. "The best year in a long time. There's one shadow I can't quite escape, though, even now. I wish with all my heart that Taim Narran was here to share all of this with us. Winterbirth will not feel right without that man here. I should not have let him go south."

"What else could you do?" his son asked. "You could hardly refuse the High Thane's direct command in such a matter: we might argue over tithes and levies and the settlement of his warriors on our lands, but a call to arms is different. And Taim would never have allowed you to send so many of his men without him. You know what he's like."

"Better than he knows himself. He hasn't the heart for the life of the sword anymore. It's only his loyalty that's kept him from seeing it. This bloodletting in Dargannan-Haig will have been hard for him."

"One more mark in the ledger against Gryvan oc Haig," said Naradin.

Croesan ran his hand over the arm of the great chair and glanced across at his son. "As you say. One more amongst many. Do not forget them. I hate to speak of such things on what should be a joyful day, but you should know that I fear Gryvan is not done with us yet. From the Steward's hints, I think our High Thane is about to demand extra tribute, to meet the costs of subduing Igryn."

"The blood of our warriors is not enough for him, then," muttered Naradin.

"Apparently not. A part of me would long to refuse him if he does make the demand, but I would have your counsel on it. These decisions are no longer mine to make alone. The safety of our Blood will fall to you before very many more years have passed."

"Do you know where Lheanor stands?" asked Naradin. "If Gryvan means to grind us down still further, he will have the same in mind for Kilkry."

"He will," agreed Croesan. "He sees no difference between Lannis and Kilkry, and I would have it no other way. I have sent word to Lheanor. It is time he and I met again, in any case."

Naradin shook his head. "Has Gryvan really become so blind that he sees no danger in driving such wedges between the True Bloods? Does he no longer care that we are the ones guarding his borders against the Black Road?"

"Ah well, there is the nub of it, isn't it? The Gyre Bloods have not bestirred themselves for thirty years. It seems they're more interested in arguing amongst themselves than in renewing their feuds with us. Only Horin-Gyre out of all of them even bothers to send scouts and raiders over the Vale of Stones anymore. I keep reminding Behomun that there are still skirmishes being fought up there, but I fear his master Gryvan knows as well as we do that — for the time being at least — the threat from the north is not what it once was. Thus he feels free to play his games. After all, with Kilkry at our side we could still turn back the entire Horin-Gyre Blood; Haig is a different matter. If it came to open war, Gryvan could count on Ayth and Taral to join him against us. We would last a few months at best."

"So," said Naradin, "however we might long to defy Gryvan oc Haig, we will bite our tongues and do enough at least to avoid an open breach."

"Yes," Croesan sighed. "I pledged loyalty to Haig when I became Thane, as you will no doubt have to do when my time is done and yours arrives. Gryvan may not put much store by that promise, but I hope we can hold to it even in the face of his provocations."

The Thane clasped his hands together and shook himself, as if to shed such unwelcome thoughts.

"Let's not dwell on such things any more than we must," he said. "There are celebrations to get started, and I mean to enjoy them."

Naradin rose from his seat and took his father's hands in his own.

"One day, your grandson will love you just as I do, and as Eilan does. Even the High Thane cannot deprive us of that."

Croesan clapped Naradin on the shoulder.

"That is true, that is true. Now let us go and save your beloved wife from all the excitement."

* * *

Rothe came to find Orisian in his chambers. During their stay at Anduran their routine of regular practice had all but lapsed, and the shieldman was insistent that it should now be resumed. Thus Orisian found himself out in the castle's courtyard, parrying the big man's weighty blows as they circled each other. They used wooden practice swords, but still the impacts sent stinging shivers through Orisian's hand.

When he had been younger he had found such exercises embarrassing. They all too often attracted a small audience of onlookers. He had little instinct for swordplay, and it had been a long and sometimes painful learning process. He was at least good enough now that his work did not provoke outright mirth amongst any observers. Today, in any case, everyone was busy with preparations for Winterbirth and hardly a glance was spared for the two mismatched sparring partners. The one exception was Kylane, who paused to watch as he wandered past. His presence distracted Orisian, who at once received a cracking blow on the back of his knuckles. Kylane strolled off, chuckling under his breath and shaking his head; perhaps, thought Orisian, lamenting the ineptitude of his future charge.

At the end, as Orisian sat breathless on the cobblestones, flexing and massaging his sword hand, Rothe grunted in muted approval.

"You'll be a swordsman yet."

"If my arm doesn't fall off first," replied Orisian.

Rothe offered him a broad hand. As Orisian took it and hauled himself upright, he could feel the hard ridges that scarred the warrior's skin. Rothe had spent most of his life with a sword in his hand, fighting Kyrinin in Anlane or Black Road raiders in the Vale of Stones, and had been marked by the weapon. He had never married; Kylane said — always out of Rothe's hearing — that his sword was too jealous of his company to allow anyone to come between them. Though it was not a life Orisian would choose he had never seen any sign of regret in Rothe.

"What would you be if not a shieldman, Rothe?" he asked on impulse.

A crude smile formed in Rothe's beard and the great man shrugged in a small, almost vulnerable way.

"There are other things of worth," he said, "but none I know anything of. How could I say what else I might be than what I am?"

Late in the afternoon of that day, Orisian looked down from a window in the keep upon a strange scene. The acrobats who were to perform at the feast were filing through the castle gates and into the courtyard. They were big men, their bulk accentuated by rough fur jackets and capes. They wore leather boots and trousers, and each carried a small pack over his shoulder. The last few to enter were laden with small chests, barrels and cloths and a pair of long, thick poles that looked freshly cut.

There were perhaps a dozen in the company. Orisian had never seen so many masterless folk together. All were long-haired, their locks tied back and dyed in exotic hues of rust and gold. They walked lightly despite their size. When Orisian looked more closely he realized that there were a few women amongst them, a trifle smaller than the men but dressed just the same and looking no less powerful.

He found Anyara loitering in the doorway at the foot of the keep, watching the new arrivals with frank fascination.

"They're very . . . big, aren't they?" she said.

"I suppose. They all look the same."

"Well, perhaps they're all related," smirked Anyara. "You know what they say about the breeding habits of masterless folk. Still, they look well enough put together to me."

A few of the castle's guardsmen were gathered outside their quarters. Muffled laughter every now and again suggested some coarse discussion of the female newcomers, yet not one of the acrobats so much as glanced across. They worked with practiced efficiency, in silence, as they arranged their equipment on the cobblestones and checked over it.

"It must be a good show, with so many of them," mused Orisian. "Where are they going to perform?"

"Ilain said they were going to give a show inside the hall, then do some tricks out here in the yard later."

"Where do you suppose they're from? It must be Koldihrve, or somewhere near there, for there to be so many. Don't you think?"

Anyara shrugged. "Or somewhere on the Kilkry coast. There are still masterless villages there, aren't there?"

As they watched, Bair the stablehand wandered across to peer at the collection of wares arrayed in the courtyard. He reached out to touch a coil of thick rope, but one of the acrobats flashed out a hand to seize his wrist. Surprise flung Bair's eyes and mouth wide, and had he not been mute he would surely have cried out. The man shook his head a little before gesturing Bair away. The boy edged backward, continuing to watch with wondering eyes from one of the stalls in the stable block.

Orisian glanced up at the sky. It had darkened in the last half hour as the sun sank away. The castle yard was falling into shadow. Torches would be brought out soon, for Winterbirth was a night when darkness must be held at bay.

"We should be getting ready," he said to Anyara. "The feast will be starting before long."

She nodded, turning to follow him into the keep with an almost wistful glance back over her shoulder toward the party of acrobats.

Inside, early arrivals for the night's feasting had begun to assemble, gathering in small knots in the great hall. There were bundles here and there of the gifts they had brought for the Thane. Already the mood was jovial. Animated conversations filled the hall with sound. Etha was moving along the tables, checking the trays of bread and flasks of ale and wine that had been set out. She was oblivious of the crowds around her as she muttered under her breath, no doubt compiling a list of reprimands for those who had laid the tables.

"It'll be a long night," said Orisian, remembering Kylane's words at Glasbridge with a slight smile.

"Of course it will," said Anyara. "It always is."

Inurian intercepted them as they made their way up to their rooms to change.

"There you are, there you are," said the *na'kyrim*.

"Here we are indeed," Anyara agreed with great gravity.

"Your father asked to see you both," Inurian said. "He sent me to find you."

"He's up, then?" Orisian asked, feeling a little surge of hope. Perhaps the clouds had lifted at last.

"Come and see," Inurian told him, beckoning them to follow as he set off up the stairs.

They found Kennet standing in the middle of his bedchamber, frowning in concentration as he examined the fur of the heavy cloak he wore. He looked up as the three of them entered, and even in that first glimpse Orisian could see that his father had come back at least some way to himself. His eyes had a focus and life that had not been there for a long time.

"This cloak is not what it once was," the lord of Castle Kolglas said glumly.

Anyara ducked under his arms and hugged him around the chest. Kennet swayed fractionally and for a moment seemed unsure what to do; then he returned the embrace.

"There are plenty of furs in the market," Anyara said as she stepped back. "We'll buy you a new one."

Kennet smiled at his daughter and cupped her face for a moment in his broad hand. "Very well, then. That's what we'll do."

As Orisian watched him, he could not help but think how old Kennet looked. He might have hauled himself out from under the shadows once again, but there was a price to be paid. However much brighter his eyes were, the skin beneath them was dark, the lids above them limp and heavy. When Kennet smiled, as he did now, turning to Orisian, the expression had to work its way up from some deep place where it had been left, forgotten and unused, for many weeks.

"Orisian," Kennet said, "come here and let me see you."

He regarded his son with gently appraising eyes.

"You look well," he said.

"And you look better," Orisian replied. He felt a familiar relief settling into him, tension easing. It was what he always felt when his father recovered from one of his dark moods: the lifting of the fear that one day the paralyzing grief would not retreat, but would settle forever into Kennet's heart and bones.

"I am," Kennet said. "Perhaps it was those honey cakes you bought for me that did it, eh?"

"Or the promise of eating and drinking to wild excess tonight, perhaps?" suggested Inurian.

"Be still," Kennet chided the *na'kyrim.* "Just because you do not share our human failings is no reason to spoil our enjoyment of them, old friend."

He cast an arm around Orisian's shoulder, and reached out to draw Anyara close on the other side.

"Will you forgive me my weakness this last little while?" he asked them softly.

"There's nothing to forgive," murmured Orisian.

"And it is not a weakness to be sad," Anyara added emphatically.

Their father squeezed them tighter for a moment and then released them.

"Whether it's a weakness or not, you should know I am sorry for it. I would spare you it if I could. I love you both dearly, and you deserve better . . ." His voice faltered, and for the briefest of moments a kind of anguish was in his face. He shook his head sharply, almost angrily. "I must rest a little before the feast. Just a little. But listen, first let us make a plan. Once Winterbirth is done, we will make a journey. It's been too long since we were outside these walls together, the three of us."

"Where to?" asked Anyara. "Anduran?"

"No," said Kennet a fraction too quickly. "There will be time enough to see my brother later. Just the three of us."

"Let's go to Kolkyre," Orisian said quietly. "To the markets, and the harbor." He had visited the seat of the Kilkry Thanes only a couple of times himself — he liked it for its vigor — but he knew his father loved it. Kennet had always said the winds there came clean from beyond the western horizon: the air you breathed there was new, without a past.

"Yes," smiled Kennet. "Kolkyre. That's a fine city."

* * *

Far away in the north, beyond the Vale of Stones, a sprawling, gargantuan castle — a labyrinth of angular walls, towers and rough stone — lay across the bare rocky slopes of a mountain. Points of fiery light stood out where torches burned against the impending night, their flames tossed to and fro by the wind. Flecks of snow spun around the fortress. Here on the northern flanks of the vast Tan Dihrin, winter's cold breath had begun to blow many days ago. But still, by ancient lore this was the night of Winterbirth, and only with the new moon could the season of ice truly be said to have arrived.

Deep in the castle's guts, in a chamber draped with wolfskins and tapestries, stood a great bed. Posts as thick as a warrior's thigh supported a pendulous canopy and beneath it lay a shrunken, frail old man who while he dreamed had gathered his sheets and blankets about him like a cocoon. At the foot of the bed, stretched out upon a bearskin rug, lay a dog: an aging hunting hound with a dense coat of wiry, grizzled hair.

The door to the chamber eased open and a boy stepped in, bearing a lamp that he shaded with his hand. The dog raised its head but made no sound. The boy went soft-footed to the bed. The man lying there gave a groan and rolled. The boy took a startled step backward and the light flickered at the shaking of his hand. There was a rattle in the sleeping man's throat. He coughed and his rheumy eyes opened. His jaw worked as he moistened cracked lips.

"Forgive me, my lord," murmured the boy. "You told me to wake you."

The man brought a thin hand out from beneath the covers and

laid it upon his face, tracing the sunken hollow of his cheek as if searching for the memory of who he was.

"The healers forbade it, but they did not see me come," the boy said. "Nor did your lady."

"You did well," croaked the man, and let his hand fall away. "The healers are fools. They know as well as I that all their fretting won't stay my death if my Road's run its course." The dog stirred at the sound of its master's voice and came to nuzzle at his dangling fingers.

"It is Winterbirth, my lord. The night will shortly turn."

"Lift me up," the man told him, and the boy raised him into a sitting position and slid a pillow behind his back. The man was light, as if life had already begun to release him from beneath its weight.

"Winterbirth," he breathed. "Tonight and tomorrow will tell all, then. Fate's favor falls upon us or upon our enemies."

Winding its way down the convoluted passages and stairwells, the sound of merriment came from some distant hall.

"Fetch me something to drink, boy," said the old man. "Tonight I must toast the strength of my son and my daughter, who carry our dreams upon the Black Road. There will be no warmth for them this Winterbirth. Only battle and blood."

The boy set his lamp down upon a table and hurried out. The man's eyes closed and his head sank forward a little upon his chest. The dog sat, quite still and patient, and watched him. The Thane Angain oc Horin-Gyre, dying in his vast, wind-scoured fortress of Hakkan, would be asleep once more by the time the boy returned, carrying an overflowing beaker.

V

The great hall of Castle Kolglas was livelier and noisier than it had been in a long time. Many torches burned high on the stone walls, throwing dancing shadows off the garlands of holly and ivy and pine strung between them. A fire blazed in the massive grate and braziers glowed in the corners of the hall. Tables lined with crowded benches ran down its length. Closest to the fire stood the high table where Kennet nan Lannis-Haig sat with Orisian, Anyara and Inurian. There were two chairs — those immediately to the right and the left of Kennet — that stood empty. Plates and cups filled with wine were set out before them as if they waited only for some tardy guests, but those for whom these seats were reserved would never come to claim them. At Winterbirth the dead were uneasy in their eternal sleep, and there was an old custom still kept in some houses of laying places for them at the feast. In Castle Kolglas, though, the table was arranged thus on every night of the year. Kennet sat as he always did, flanked by memory and loss.

The rest of the tables were packed with people from both castle and town. The great and the lowly of Kolglas came together on this night. The feast had begun at sunset, and would continue all through the night until the first dawn of winter. Already, with no more than an hour gone by, the free-flowing ale and wine had raised a hubbub of shouts and laughter. Servants rushed up and down bearing drinks and platters of bread and meats. Those of the guests who had most thoroughly slaked their thirst were thumping tankards on the tables to drive the servers to greater efforts. One of the youngest kitchen maids tumbled over a hunting dog that yelped and darted away. A cheer went up, and cries of dismay as the pitcher of ale she had been carrying shattered. The roar stirred Idrin the crow from his perch on one of the great roof beams and he flapped across to the next, croaking irritably.

Kennet laughed with the rest as the flustered girl struggled to her feet. He was buried in his great fur cloak like some hoary old trapper caught out by the snow. He had been complaining of the cold ever since entering the hall, but he seemed well enough.

"You should speak, Kennet," said Inurian, "before the throng is too rowdy to listen."

Kennet rose to his feet and pounded the table with a clenched fist. The revelers fell quiet, and every face was turned toward the lord of Castle Kolglas. He cleared his throat and took a mouthful of ale.

"I shall keep you from your food only for a few moments," he called out, drawing a muffled chorus of approval, "but there are things that must be said on this night."

His voice moved to a new, slower rhythm, and an absolute hush settled across the hall.

"Tonight is the night of Winterbirth," said Kennet, "and for this one night there shall be no darkness in this place. I bid you keep the fires burning and hold the dark, and the winter, at bay. In the cold months that are to come, let this night of fire and good cheer be a warm memory in your hearts. When the Gods left this world much that was bright and good went with them. But the healing cycle of the seasons remains, and is not the least of the boons left to us. Rest heals many ills, for the earth beneath our feet as for us. Even in deepest winter, summer lies in the roots and in the evergreen and it will return. So let us mourn the slipping of the year into sleep and celebrate the promise of its waking, renewed."

He lowered his head, and when he looked up again his voice had returned to its natural tones.

"There is food and drink enough for twice your number, and there will be songs, and tales, and acrobats and music. But remember while you clear your plates and drain your mugs that many who should be with us here tonight are not. We are not what our forefathers were in the days of the Gods — the world breeds no heroes now — but still we are a hardy folk. Even the hardiest of us may regret our parting from those we hold dear, though. Some who cannot share our tables tonight rest in the Sleeping Dark, taken from us before their time was full; others may yet return. Many of the best of us are far away in the mountains of Dargannan, where they serve the oath that binds our

Blood to that of Haig. I know many of you would wish it otherwise, and your misgivings are mine.

"Nevertheless, our honor — the honor of the Lannis Blood — is upheld by their service. Without the Gods to guide and watch over us, we must find other things in the world to hold fast to. Honor is not the worst to choose. Therefore I bid you keep in your thoughts those honorable men who fight in the south as we celebrate the year's turning. Let us hope that they, like the spring, shall soon return."

There was a great cheer at that. The noise roused Idrin once more and as Kennet sank back into his chair, the black bird swept down and alighted upon Inurian's shoulder. Kennet glanced across.

"Can you not keep that bird under control, Inurian?" he asked above the din. "Put it out of the hall or tie it down. Must we have it flapping about?"

"I am sure Idrin would no more wish to miss the evening's entertainments than the rest of us, my lord," Inurian said, passing a tidbit from his plate to the crow, "and his sulking would be a sore trial to me if he was denied."

Kennet looked doubtful. "Well, keep it away from me, then, if its delicate feelings will allow that much at least."

A faint smile at the corner of Kennet's mouth belied the harshness of his words. Inurian shrugged to dislodge Idrin and the crow flapped back into the roof. Orisian turned his gaze to the hall's door. Almost in that instant, the figure he awaited bounded in to a howled reception that mixed welcome and mock horror, raising the din to new and deafening heights. The Winter King had arrived at the feast.

A tiny, dancing figure trailing a cloak of pine needles and crowned with holly and mistletoe capered about in the middle of the hall. It was Bair. His face twitched in imitation of lunacy as he essayed a wild dance. He had been well coached by Etha and the other staff to whom the selection of the Winter King fell each year.

Bair darted along one of the tables, snatching scraps of food from the guests' plates, upsetting beakers and tankards as he went. Whatever morsels he managed to purloin he stuffed into his mouth so that his cheeks bulged. The victims of his thievery made a pretense of trying to seize him. He worked his way thus around the hall until he eventually leapt up onto one of the tables with an extravagant sweep of his pine cloak that sent dishes spinning. The guests spattered with food and drink cried out in good-natured protest as Bair vaulted to the floor in front of the high table where Kennet, Orisian and the others sat. Orisian could not help but laugh to see the excitement shining in the stablehand's eyes. Anyara threw a chunk of bread at the Winter King, and was on the point of following it with the contents of her goblet when Kennet rose and leaned across the broad table. Bair, his eyes still dancing with merriment, stepped forward and bowed his head that the lord of Kolglas might more easily take hold of him. Kennet laid one hand on the boy's shoulder and with the other lifted the green crown from his head, taking care to ease it free from his lank hair. Then Bair turned about and Kennet took the cloak of pine needles from him. He folded it and laid it upon the table, resting the wreath of holly and mistletoe atop it. Bair scuttled away. The Winter King was no more.

Kennet raised his arms. "Burn the Winter King's robes," he called out. One of the shieldmen sitting closest to the high table sprang from his place. Taking up the cloak and crown, he carried them with due ceremony to the broad, roaring fire in the hearth. There he paused and looked back to Kennet.

"Burn them," came the repeated command, and it was taken up by all those in the hall. Orisian shouted out with the rest and cheered as the shieldman cast his burden onto the fire. The pine cloak hissed as gouts of smoke billowed out. The fire was so fierce that it was cowed only for a few moments, and it spat and crackled with vigor as it consumed the Winter King's vestments.

The annual game, played out in one form or another in halls

across the Glas valley and beyond since before there had been such a thing as Bloods, was done and gradually the guests settled into the comfortable chatter of any great feast.

Trays of food — more than Orisian could remember seeing at any Winterbirth before — came and went until he lost all track of what he had been offered. The servants, ever more red-faced and wild-eyed, rushed from kitchen to hall and back again. Their own celebrations would come afterward, when none in the great hall could force down another scrap. For the time being they were at the beck and call of an ever more demanding and drunken horde. Orisian's eyes were growing wine-weary and a pleasant warmth was running through his face, when he heard Kennet say to Inurian, "It is time for the boons, my friend. If we wait any longer it will be impossible to hear ourselves think."

Orisian stirred himself and sat up straight in his chair. Inurian went to stand a little behind Kennet. Shieldmen were marshaling a small group of guests at the far end of the hall. These were the petitioners whose names had been drawn by lot, winning them the right to seek one favor from their lord on this tradition-steeped night.

The first to approach the high table was a small, slight man. Orisian knew him: Lomas, who lived on the fringe between town and forest and grazed a small herd of cattle on the wood pastures. Lomas bowed to Kennet and, with exaggerated care, laid a hide parchment case bound with a red cord on the table. The case was empty: it was no more than a symbol of the petition he wished to present.

"You seek a boon of me?" Kennet asked, and Lomas stammeringly confirmed it was so.

"And if I hear your case, will you undertake, on the strength of the oath you swore to the Blood, to accept any response I make whether it be in your favor or not?"

"I will," the cattle herder said and Kennet, satisfied, took up the parchment case. "Speak, then," he told Lomas.

The petition was a simple one, much to the disappointment of the audience. There was always the hope that some scandalous dispute would enliven proceedings and give the gossips something to warm their tongues with in the long, dark evenings to come. All Lomas wished was to be excused from the Bloodtithe for a year, since several of his cattle had died with the hoof rot. When the herder had finished, Kennet nodded and beckoned Inurian forward. He consulted with his *na'kyrim* counselor in whispers too soft to reach those thronging the other tables. Orisian caught most of it, however.

"He speaks truly," Inurian was murmuring. "He is afraid, but only of the occasion and of the chance that you might deny him. There is no deceit in him, I think."

There must have been many times down the ages when a benevolent lord had been tricked into granting an undeserved boon. None who came before Kennet nan Lannis-Haig would even make the attempt, not since Inurian had come to Kolglas. At every granting he stood at Kennet's side, and every petitioner knew that their true intent could not be concealed from the *na'kyrim*.

"Very well," Kennet said to Lomas. "Your tithe is remitted for one year. I suggest you spend the time reminding yourself of the rules of proper husbandry, since the hoof rot is easily avoided if you give the beasts the care and attention they might expect."

Lomas, abashed and relieved in equal measure, retreated back down the hall, offering profuse thanks as he went. Good-natured catcalls accompanied him all the way. Someone shouted advice on the prevention of the hoof rot in cattle.

One by one the rest of the petitioners advanced, presented their red-bound cases to Kennet and made their requests. Each time, Inurian leaned forward to whisper into his lord's ear. Orisian watched Inurian with avid attention, seeking without success for any outward sign of the powers the *na'kyrim* was employing. The mysterious gifts of those who carried both Huanin and Kyrinin blood in their veins might be a source of wonder, fear, curiosity or envy, depending upon the observer's temperament. For Orisian, it was fascination that stirred. Even so there was, at the back of his mind, the knowledge that this divining of truth sprang from the same source — the Shared — as had the awful powers wielded in the years before and during the War of the Tainted. *Na'kyrim* of now unimaginable capacities had fought alongside both human and Kyrinin during that long bloodletting. In its final months, doomed Tarcene, the Aygll King, had been possessed and enslaved by one such: Orlane Kingbinder, the greatest of all the fell *na'kyrim* lords of those times. Tarcene's own daughter, in despair, had cut his throat with a hunting knife.

The days when *na'kyrim* made and unmade kings were long gone now. There were few *na'kyrim* left in the world and none with the strength of the olden days. Yet mere centuries could not quench the memories of what had been, and there were, amongst the attentive faces in the hall of Castle Kolglas, more than a few that betrayed unease. For those inclined to see it, a touch of the dark past lingered in Inurian's benign divinations.

The mood was too merry, however, and the wine too abundant, for many to dwell on such concerns for long. One of the petitioners — Amella Tirane, who tearfully begged that the forests be scoured for her missing husband, who had failed to return from a hunting trip — drew a subdued chorus of sympathy; the others gave more cause for amusement than sorrow. In the fifth and final case Marien, a widow of notoriously short temper and sharp tongue, asked Kennet to intercede in a dispute with her neighbors. Ignoring the mounting hilarity in the hall, Kennet listened as she described the sleepless nights she had spent as a result of the noises coming from the adjoining cottage; noises, she declared with all the gravity of her years, that a man and wife were entitled to make, but not every night and not with such abandon that they kept others from rest.

Orisian did not hear whatever advice Inurian offered to Kennet.

His father explained to Marien that however much he sympathized with her distress, he could not bring himself to interfere in the matter of a marriage bed. The widow returned to her seat exuding disgruntlement.

Only after the mirth had died down did Orisian, alone of all those in the hall, note the sad, weary expression that was on Inurian's face, and wonder what the *na'kyrim* had seen in Marien's heart to put it there.

The business of feasting resumed in earnest. Orisian drank deeply from his cup and it was refilled by one of the serving girls as soon as he set it down. He felt warm and happy. His father seemed at peace in a way he had not been for weeks, and for tonight at least the good humor of the moment was enough to keep memories of the past at arm's length. Orisian slouched in his chair, allowing a sense of contentment to settle over him.

Kennet leaned toward him.

"When we go to Kolkyre, we shall have a sword made for you, Orisian. They have the best weaponsmiths north of Vaymouth there, you know. My father had one made for me, in the year he became Thane."

"I'd be proud to have it," Orisian said, aware in a distant sort of way that the wine had rubbed the precision off his voice. "Mind you, you might want to ask Rothe if I deserve it. I don't think I'm the best pupil he's ever had."

Kennet dismissed the suggestion with a wry smile. "If you think that man'd ever say a word against you, you've not got the measure of him yet. Anyway, he told me months ago that you'd be a fine swordsman one day. Once you stopped worrying about not being good enough."

"I . . ." Orisian started to say. He was cut short by a flurry of activity at the far end of the hall. The acrobats had entered, and the cheers that greeted them made conversation impossible for the moment.

Like an exploding flock of great birds, they spread around the hall and immediately set balls and clubs flying in spectacular cascades. The guests whooped and clapped as the patterns the jugglers conjured into being grew ever more complex and intricate. The tempo rose inexorably. Two of them leapt up onto opposite tables and spun a flurry of clubs between them, across almost the whole breadth of the hall. Others lit brands from the fire. The flames whipped through the air.

Orisian was impressed. This was not what came to mind when he thought of masterless folk. The lone hunters and traders who drifted into Lannis lands tended to be ragged and wild-looking, fitting the common image of the masterless as lost, bereft of the bonds a Blood bestowed. Whenever he had seen such folk, they had struck him as fragments of the wilderness itself come loose, ill at ease with the order of town or village. These acrobats were altogether different: strong, focused upon their art, exuding confidence.

One came to the fore. He carried small glass orbs in his hands; when he began to juggle them they glinted and flashed and became a shimmering arc of reflected firelight. At first faintly and then louder, there was a rapid clinking as he adjusted the flight of the globes so that they clipped one another on their way through the air. There were appreciative gasps from the watchers. Orisian almost laughed in pleasure, and glanced around at those beside him. Anyara and Kennet were as entranced as he, their eyes fixed upon the dancing, flickering spheres. Only Inurian wore a different expression. He too was watching intently, but puzzlement had scored thin furrows across his brow.

Orisian turned back to the show in time to watch as one of the orbs plunged toward the flagstones, only to be delicately caught upon the top of the juggler's soft hide boot even as the groans of disappointment started. He bowed amidst the acclamation that followed, then raised his arms for quiet. As the noise subsided he spoke in a soft, oddly accented voice that sounded somehow as if it did not fit in his mouth.

"We need more space than this hall can offer. Please join us outside, for it is not so cold, the night is still young and the best tricks are yet to come."

With this he spun about, and led the rest of the company trotting out through the hall's main door. At once, people leapt to their feet to follow, upsetting more than a few tankards and platters in their haste. Inurian rose more slowly. He was frowning, almost wincing, as if afflicted by a sharp headache.

"What's the matter?" asked Orisian.

The *na'kyrim* blinked and smiled, plucked out of distraction by the question.

"I feel a little . . . odd," he said. "I am not sure: something . . . out of place. Perhaps the granting of boons taxed me."

"Come on," said Orisian, taking his friend's arm and feeling sharply in that moment the strength of his affection for the *na'kyrim*. "Let's not miss the rest of the show."

"No," said Inurian, "let's not." But there was still more concern than enthusiasm in his voice.

The crowd spilled out into the courtyard, their misting breath and excited voices filling the confined space.

Atop the southern corner of the castle's walls, two warriors stood watch. The circular tower they looked out from was open to the elements, but they could shelter from the night breeze by ducking down behind the battlements and warming their hands at a small brazier. The flames did not help their night sight, but at Winterbirth it was more important to have light and heat than to worry overmuch about such things.

A while ago, a serving girl had brought them bread and thick, fatty slices of beef from the kitchen. The emptied tray lay on the stone floor. The men were content enough. They were well fed and it was not as cold as it might have been. From down below in the courtyard they heard the shouts and cheers of the crowd as the celebration moved out from the great hall. They did not pay much attention to it. Their watch was over the shores of the bay south of Kolglas, though there was little to see save the dark, looming outline of forested slopes.

The sound of the trapdoor creaking open snapped their eyes away from the coastline. A figure emerged from the darkened stairwell beneath. It was one of the performers: a woman dressed in leather boots and breeches and a dark hide jacket.

"What are you doing here?" demanded one of the watchmen, his hand going by reflex toward his polearm where it leaned against the battlements.

The newcomer smiled thinly.

"I have brought the show to you," she said in a deep voice.

There were already glass spheres in her hands, appearing as if formed from the substance of the night air. In a second she was weaving the orbs in a sinuous pattern. They caught the yellow flamelight of the brazier and worked it into glinting arcs. The guards' objections faded as their eyes followed the extraordinary dance of light.

The juggler took a step closer to them. "Watch with care," she said softly.

"Very clever," one of the men said, "but still . . ."

She darted forward, her arms flashing out. The tiny blades she had slipped from her jacket cuffs sliced across the throats of the two men. Her glass juggling balls fell to the ground and shattered. The watchmen slumped to the ground, their eyes wide, reaching to stanch the blood that erupted from their necks. She followed them down, kneeling and punching both knives home beneath the angle of their jawbones. The men died all but silently.

The juggler rose cautiously. She checked around the castle walls for any sign of alarm. There was no hint of movement: Kolglas kept only a skeleton guard on this night, and those unlucky enough to have drawn the duty had their eyes turned outward and their ears filled with the cheers and applause from the courtyard. The woman moved to the brazier, stepping over the spreading slick of blood. She produced leather gloves from inside her jacket and pulled them on. Without hesitation, she reached into the heart of the brazier and lifted out a double handful of red-hot charcoal. She cast a final quick glance around. Satisfied that she remained unobserved, she leaned over the battlements and opened her hands. A scatter of yellow and orange motes fell away from the tower, tumbling and fading and vanishing into the water and rocks below.

The woman crossed to the trapdoor, slipped into the body of the turret and set off down the spiraling stairway that would bring her out once more into the courtyard.

South of Kolglas, the road followed the rocky shoreline. A few hundred yards beyond the town's edge, scrub and trees pressed close, squeezing the track between them and the sea. The darkness was intense. The town itself was out of sight, hidden by a low knoll, its presence betrayed only by the glow of its bonfires tingeing the sky. The castle offshore was marked by the light spilling from its windows. There was no sound save the slapping of gentle waves upon the shore, the slight shifting of autumn's last few leaves in the breeze and the low murmur of celebration that drifted across the water from the castle.

A great stag came out into the open and walked a short way down the track. It paused and lifted its heavy-antlered head, testing the night air for scents. Tension came at once into its frame, and it looked uneasily at the forest. It bounded down the track a distance before plunging back amongst the trees and disappearing.

There was no movement for long minutes. Then, out across the water, a shower of tiny lights fell from the near corner of the castle's battlements like failing fireflies. They were there for no more than two heartbeats, faint, and then they were gone, leaving only a rapidly fading afterimage in the eyes of those who had been watching for them. The undergrowth shivered and they emerged onto the roadway. Darker shapes amidst the shadows of the night, they moved across the track in silence: warriors, men and women, with swords strapped across their backs. One by one they came to the shore, waded into the chill water for a few strides and then struck out with powerful, measured strokes. In a few moments thirty of them had crossed from forest to sea and were swimming out toward the castle's looming form. They were virtually invisible in the darkness, but in any case the only guards upon the walls who might have seen their approach lay dead beside a brazier atop the corner tower.

They came out of the water crouching, moving across the jumble of rocks to sink into the deepest dark at the foot of the castle's walls. In single file they began to make their way along the wall, pressing themselves against its cold stone, sure-footed on the wet, uneven surface. At the next corner they paused. A single man eased his way out on his belly over the shell-crusted rocks to look toward the castle's closed gate. The tide was falling fast now, and here and there the rough surface of the causeway broke the water between castle and shore. The town was awash with torches and the light of bonfires. There was no one at the water's edge. The scout slipped back to join his companions, free his sword from its bindings and wait in the shadow of the ancient castle.

In the courtyard of Castle Kolglas, all was fire and movement. The audience was crowded along the front of the keep and around to the stables, shouting and cheering to encourage the acrobats to ever greater feats. Kennet himself stood at the top of the short stairway leading up to the keep's main entrance. Orisian stood before him, and felt his father's hands resting upon his shoulders. There was pleasure in that sensation.

The throng of people was boisterous as they jostled good-heartedly for position. From the steps Orisian could see clear over their heads to the broad flame-lit space where the acrobats tumbled. They spun across the cobblestones, flinging burning brands from one to another. The two long poles he had seen them carrying into the castle were brought to the center of the yard, and men held them upright while a woman scampered barefoot up each one. At the top of the poles, the women tensed themselves for a moment, then in the same instant sprang free, twisting as they passed each other in mid-leap. The poles swayed violently as they landed but they clung on with ease, and acknowledged the roar of approval that rose up from the crowd.

Orisian heard his father give a short cry of wonder.

"A fine show, is it not?" Kennet shouted in his ear, squeezing his shoulders.

Orisian nodded vigorously. Anyara, who was at his side, glanced at him and smiled, and he felt a lightening of his heart. This, at last, was a Winterbirth to savor.

Torches were tossed up to the women atop the poles, who threw them back and forth at reckless speed. When they were done they let the brands fall, to be caught by men below. As some of those on the ground launched themselves into another spate of dazzling tumbling, the men supporting the poles hoisted them off the ground, taking their full weight upon their clasped hands. Their faces taut with effort and concentration, they moved, step by cautious step, toward the gatehouse.

"What are they doing?" asked Inurian, coming up to Orisian's side. Idrin sat on the *na'kyrim*'s shoulder, his head cocked to one side as he blinked at Orisian.

"I don't know," Orisian said, keeping his eyes on the spectacle.

"Something is wrong," muttered Inurian.

One of the acrobats was hoisting a great barrel above his head now, his face rigid with effort. Orisian dragged his gaze away to look at Inurian.

"What?" he asked.

"I don't know. I can't focus. There's something about these people . . . but I can't reach it."

The crow launched itself from Inurian's shoulder and flapped up, a fragment of darkness ascending into the black canopy of the night.

"Oh, don't worry so," laughed Anyara. "Enjoy the show!"

Inurian grunted and shook his head slightly. Orisian's mood dimmed. Inurian could feel the texture of the thoughts in a man's head. There was no one Orisian trusted more, and if the *na'kyrim* was troubled there must be some reason for it.

A chorus of gasps snapped his eyes momentarily back to the acrobats. He was just in time to see the two women spring from the poles and vault over the battlements onto the top of the gatehouse. A guard had come to the edge there, to see what was happening. One of the women seemed to crash into him and they both fell back out of sight. It was clumsy, out of place. Orisian half-turned to say something to his father.

The men who had been holding the poles aloft suddenly released them and they toppled, at first slowly and then very fast, toward the spectators, who cried out in alarm and began struggling to get out of the way. The man raising the barrel in the center of the courtyard gave a great cry and flung it down. It smashed onto the cobblestones, splintering apart. Short swords spilled out between the broken staves. Two of the acrobats were throwing burning torches, arcing them into the crowd. Everyone was shouting, and there were screams of shock.

"What is this?" Orisian heard his father say in a puzzled, uncomprehending voice.

The poles crashed down to the ground. A dark shape came tumbling from the top of the gatehouse, thumping onto the cobblestones. It was the guard. In a flash of torchlight, Orisian glimpsed the unnatural angle of his neck and his open, lifeless eyes. The men who had dropped the poles were at the gate now, lifting its great bar and pulling it open. The swords that had been concealed in the barrel were being snatched up by male and female acrobats alike. They turned upon those who moments ago had been acclaiming them. In an instant, the courtyard was filled with chaos and battle.

*

The warriors outside the walls rose from their hiding place at the sound of the gate creaking open. They bounded forward. In the same moment a rider came splashing out on the causeway from the town: a young man, thrashing at his horse's hindquarters.

"Awake the castle!" he was crying, "awake the castle! Wights attacking the town! A White Owl raid!"

As his fellows poured through the open gate to join the melee inside, one man turned and crouched to meet the rider. He reached up over his shoulder and smoothly brought his sword out of its sheath. The messenger came on without slowing, still crying the alarm. In the second before he would have been trampled, the warrior stepped aside and slashed across the horse's front legs. The impact sent the sword spinning out of his hands, but the animal screamed and crashed down, throwing its rider. The young man tried to get up. His arm had been broken in the fall and it would not take his weight. The warrior slipped a knife out of his boot and cut the man's throat. Ignoring the writhing horse's screams, he retrieved his sword and walked through the castle's gateway, blades held loosely on either side.

Within, all was tumult. The folk who had gathered to celebrate Winterbirth were scattering, struggling over one another in a vain attempt to find safety. Those who had been acrobats joined with the warriors now spilling in through the gate and moved purposefully through the panicking throng. They paid little heed to the townsfolk and castle staff, hacking at them as they might undergrowth that obstructed a forest path. Their quarry was the fighting men of Castle Kolglas.

Here and there amongst the crowd, blades clashed. It was an unequal fight. The warriors of Lannis-Haig were more numerous, but they were unprepared and half of them were at least part-drunk. Even when they came to blows with their enemy, it was like fighting shadows. The invaders were as fast as thought, each swordstroke flung against them finding nothing but air or being met by a deflecting sweep that flowed seamlessly into a killing thrust.

Orisian's disbelieving eyes followed a warrior as he hacked one of Kennet's shieldmen down. The man's heavy shirt had been torn asunder in the fighting, and hung in tatters. Beneath the beads of seawater still clinging to that taut back, Orisian saw a dark, menacing shape stretched across his shoulder blades and spine. A tattoo: the image of a raven, its wings widespread. Orisian's mind went numb at that sight, and what it meant.

In the same moment the cry went up from somewhere in the crowd, giving voice to Orisian's thought: "Inkallim! Inkallim!"

Orisian's father brushed past him, descending the stairway. A sword was in his hand, and a terrible black rage in his eyes.

"Inkallim," Orisian heard him say as he plunged into the fray and was swept out of sight.

Inkallim: the ravens of the Gyre Bloods. They were the elite warriors of the Black Road, serving the creed itself rather than any Thane, and they bore a fearsome reputation. Orisian shook himself out of his shock. Anyara was close by him, clutching his arm with fingers of iron and staring in horror at the carnage before them. A group of men and women — Orisian recognized merchants from the Kolglas market — broke up the steps, desperate to reach the sanctuary of the keep. They surged forward, oblivious of Orisian and Anyara.

"Wait!" cried Orisian uselessly. He and his sister were brushed aside and fell together from the stairs. They landed in a heap, Anyara's weight slamming Orisian against the stone of the courtyard. His vision spun and his chest seized so that he could not draw breath.

Somewhere far away he heard a voice, perhaps Rothe's, raised above the noise of battle and terror. "Lannis! Lannis! Guard your lord!"

Then there were strong hands lifting Orisian up. He blinked, and looked into Kylane's face.

"Are you hurt?" his young shieldman demanded.

Orisian shook his head. He still could not breathe.

"Anyara," shouted Kylane, "are you hurt?"

"I'm fine," she said, staggering to her feet. "Just bruised."

Air filled Orisian's lungs in a great rush and he reeled at the relief of it.

"Where's my father?" he gasped.

"In the thick of it somewhere. We must get you to safety," said Kylane. "Are you armed?"

Orisian showed his empty hands, and Kylane pushed a knife into one. As he felt the weapon's hilt in his palm, another question occurred to him.

"Inurian, where's Inurian?" he asked.

"I don't know," Kylane said. "Forget that now. The two of you are what matters."

Anyara started to cry a warning but somehow Kylane was already moving, responding to a threat felt rather than heard or seen. He ducked low and spun, catching the Inkallim warrior darting toward them across the right knee with his sword and shattering the joint. The man half-fell and Kylane hacked at his neck. He pulled the blade free and glanced back at Orisian and Anyara.

"Stay close to me, behind me. We'll hide you in the keep."

They nodded.

Kylane led them around to the front of the steps, and the horror that had befallen the castle flooded their senses. The courtyard was littered with bodies. Unarmed townsfolk lay dead alongside warriors. The cobbles ran with dark rivulets of blood. Close by the front of the bunkhouse a knot of Lannis men was ringed by Inkallim. In the gateway, five Inkallim were standing, some watching the slaughter impassively, others staring out toward the causeway. To the left, at the far end of the courtyard, a more open battle was ebbing and flowing. His heart lurching, Orisian saw his father, Rothe and half a dozen others fighting with quiet desperation to keep an equal number of Inkallim at bay. He stumbled to a halt, impaled by the sight. One of the Lannis warriors went down, clubbed to his knees. Kennet took a stunning blow to the side of his head and staggered as if drunk. Instinctively, Orisian rushed across the courtyard, tightening his grip upon the dagger.

"Orisian," cried Kylane in desperation from halfway up the steps. "Stay with me!"

But it was too late. Orisian's mind was roaring and his feet carried him toward the melee. Two of the Inkallim who had been guarding the gate — one man, one woman — broke away from their fellows and sprinted toward him. Orisian jerked to a halt and half-turned. In a detached way, he recognized that he could reach neither his father nor the sanctuary of the keep. The warriors closed on him. The cries of the battle faded and he heard, deep within his ears, the drumbeat of his heart.

Kylane flew past Orisian to come between him and the onrushing Inkallim. The shieldman managed to get his sword up to block the first blow. The impact knocked his own blade down, too far out of position to fend off the strike the female warrior delivered to his exposed flank. He thrust his left arm into the path of the sword and took its full strength between wrist and elbow. The blade almost severed Kylane's arm, leaving a ragged protrusion of bone as his hand snapped back. He lurched to one side. He slashed out, putting a shallow red furrow across his assailant's thigh. Her face did not register the blow. She calmly followed Kylane as he reeled sideways, and cut the shieldman's head from his shoulders with a single, two-handed swing.

Bile burned in Orisian's throat, and he cried out as he lunged forward. He heard Anyara shouting something at him from the door of the keep. He flung himself at the Inkallim who had killed Kylane. The woman swept him aside with an elbow. Orisian sprawled to the ground. He felt a thudding smack in his midriff and he was spinning through the air, lifted bodily by the force of the kick. His vision was blurring.

"Is it the boy?" he thought he heard the woman ask.

Orisian struggled to rise. The pain that lanced through his ribcage pinned him down. His eyesight cleared and he saw a sword being raised.

Rothe came then. The great shieldman rushed down upon them. The two Inkallim spun away from Orisian, stepping apart. Groaning at the agony it cost him, Orisian stretched and planted his dagger firmly in a heel. The blade was snatched from his hand as the warrior kicked out in surprise. It was enough to unbalance the Inkallim, and Rothe's sudden lunge knocked him flat. Orisian scrambled for the fallen man's sword arm, clinging to it with all the despairing strength of someone clutching a branch in a flood. Rothe parried a blow from the woman, turning the point of her sword down. He carried a long-bladed knife in his left hand, and in the blink of an eye he had driven it twice, to the hilt, into her stomach. She fell. Even as Rothe turned, the second Inkallim broke Orisian's weakening hold and rose to one knee. Rothe's sword almost took the man's jawbone from his face.

Rothe pulled Orisian to his feet. The female warrior was still alive, curled up and making strange coughing sounds as she clasped her hands over her stomach.

"Kylane . . ." murmured Orisian. That sent waves of fire across his chest and he could say no more. Rothe ignored him.

Leaning against his shieldman's side, Orisian saw that the door of the keep was closed. There was no sign of Anyara. He looked around. The battle was almost over. A handful of Lannis men were left by the sleeping quarters, stumbling over the dead as they fought with quiet, vain desperation. To the left, a solid rank of Inkallim had hemmed Kennet and his few remaining defenders, including Inurian, tight against the castle wall. Rothe had left his father's side to come to him, Orisian realized, not knowing what to make of the thought.

He glanced toward the castle gate, half-expecting the garrison from the town to pour in and save them. If this were anything other than a nightmare, they would surely do so. Figures were indeed moving beneath the gatehouse, coming in from the causeway, but they were not Lannis men. More Inkallim, a few on horses, and at the head of them a man whose appearance added yet another layer of unreality to the scene: a *na'kyrim*. Much younger than Inurian, taller and more lithe, but unmistakably a child of two races.

Then Rothe was dragging him across the courtyard toward the stables.

"Keep's closed," Rothe snapped. "We've got to get you out."

"Father . . ." Orisian gasped.

Inkallim were coming for them. Rothe threw Orisian into the stables. He sprawled amongst the straw, knocking a bucket of water flying. His nostrils were filled with the smell of the place, and with the scent of smoke. Somewhere out of sight a fire had started. The horses were stamping and snorting. A small body was lying in the straw, its blank eyes staring into Orisian's: Bair. The side of the boy's face had been cut open, exposing bone. Orisian struggled to his feet, leaning on the flank of a horse that heaved against him as it slipped toward panic.

Looking out into the courtyard, he saw Inurian struck down, caught on the side of the head by the hilt of a sword. The newly arrived *na'kyrim* was riding forward, crying, "Keep him alive. That one is mine."

The last shieldman at Kennet's side stepped in front of his lord to intercept a swordstroke, and died. Kennet, shouting wordlessly, his face contorted by rage, cut down one more of the Inkallim before he was overwhelmed and pinned up against the wall. He was held, his arms pressed upon the stone, and the sword was pulled from his hand. He kicked out at his attackers. They were beyond his reach.

Orisian started forward, aware that he had no weapon but not caring. His path was blocked as a horse lurched across in front of him. Rothe was belaboring it with the flat of his sword, driving it and the others out from the stables toward their pursuers. Without pause, the shieldman swept around, gathering Orisian with his free arm and bearing him backward into the shadows.

"No!" Orisian could hear himself crying.

Over his shieldman's shoulder, he saw Kennet spitting curses at his captors. Then one of the Inkallim stepped forward and sank a knife deep into Kennet's chest. Orisian howled. His view was cut off as Rothe brought him to the postern gate at the back of the stables. He struggled to break free of his shieldman's grip. Rothe tore the bar from the door and dragged Orisian through the short tunnel to the outer portal.

They emerged on the brink of the sea, where there was no smoke and no light and the night air was shocking. Orisian stumbled over the rocks, slipped and fell. He staggered to his feet. Then Rothe was at his shoulder again, steering him toward the jetty and the dark shape of Inurian's boat.

"No!" shouted Orisian. "We have to go back!"

Rothe threw him bodily into the boat and tossed his sword after him. He tore at the mooring rope and, gasping at the exertion, pushed the boat from the jetty.

Orisian stood unsteadily.

"Rothe, no!" he shouted.

He felt a solid thump in his side. Strength fled from his legs and he slumped down. He clutched at the hilt of the throwing knife that was embedded in him. He stared at it. There was no pain.

There were figures rushing over the rocks. The Inkallim moved fast, as if in full daylight.

The boat surged out onto the water. Rothe vaulted in. He knelt by Orisian and paddled with a single oar. They eased out from beneath the towering walls of the castle and into the open expanse of the bay.

Orisian lay back, feeling the world slipping away from him. He looked up at a sky scattered with a thousand tiny cold stars. Water lying in the bottom of the boat soaked the back of his head. He could feel blood flowing over his hand where it lay on the knife in his side. He heard waves slapping at the boat's prow. He heard Rothe's labored breathing. And he saw his father's face.

He closed his eyes.

CHAPTER
2

Kyrinin

Huanin scribes will tell you that the Kyrinin are all one; that their likeness one to another binds them together and sets them in opposition to all humankind. These scribes are blind to that which they do not understand. When the Walking God, the God Who Laughed, made the Kyrinin, when he strode across the world calling them into being, he made not one clan but many. Huanin and Kyrinin fell to slaughtering one another only long after the Gods had left the world; the Kyrinin clans have been shedding one another's blood since the first dawn of their existence. And few have bathed their spears more often than White Owl and Fox.

The White Owl babe learns hatred of the Fox with the taste of its mother's milk. The child of the Fox knows that the White Owl are its enemy before it has the words to express the knowledge. When the Kyrinin clans were in their greatest glory, before the War of the Tainted and before Tane, that wondrous city of every heart's desire, fell and was submerged beneath the Anain's Deep Rove, Fox and White Owl knew no peace. Much changed in the re-ordering of things that followed the defeat of their kind by the Huanin, but each preserved their hatred of the other, guarding it as jealously as they guard the ever-burning fires of their winter camps. To be of the Fox is to be the White Owl's foe, and to be of the White Owl is to be, from first breath to last, the foe of the Fox. Stone is less enduring than their enmity.

I

The army had made camp in a high valley. A sea of a thousand tents covered the grass, rock outcrops rising above it here and there. Hundreds of war-horses were tethered on the shallow lower slopes of the surrounding peaks. The sun stood above the head of the valley. Eagles and ravens drifted across its glare as they surveyed this vast intrusion upon their mountainous domain.

Gryvan oc Haig stood before the greatest of all the tents. He was resplendent in his finest garb: the crimson cloak of the Thane of Thanes, a cuirass of shining metal beneath it; a scabbard studded with gemstones at his side and his great-grandfather's golden chain about his neck. His hands rested on the hilt of his sword. The point of the blade was pressed into the earth at his feet, as if to signify that the land itself had submitted to him. Kale and others of the High Thane's Shield stood to either side. Hundreds of warriors were gathered before them in a gigantic semi-circle. At its focus, kneeling before Gryvan, was Igryn oc Dargannan-Haig. The defeated Thane was yoked to a heavy log, rough ropes fixing his arms to it at the wrist. The skin there was rubbed away. Another rope held his neck more loosely.

Gryvan was regarding his prisoner with undisguised satisfaction. "Where is your pride now, Igryn?" he asked.

Igryn made no reply. His head hung low.

"Trussed like a common thief," mocked Gryvan. "A fate fit for a traitor, do you agree? For a faithless dog? For one who knows less of duty than the least of the masterless?"

There were cries of agreement and jeering from the ranks of the assembled army. Gryvan stilled the voices with a raised hand, and looked around the close-pressed warriors before him. He swept his gaze over them, and let them see in his eyes that he was one with them.

"See what your enemy has come to," he cried out. "See the fruits of his arrogance. He is laid low by the strength of your arms."

That brought forth enthusiastic cheering.

"Lift up his head," Gryvan said to Kale.

Kale stepped forward and seized Igryn's thick red hair in a tight knot, wrenching his head back so that his battered face angled up toward the Thane of Thanes. His beard was matted and discolored by dried blood. A recent wound stretched from temple to jawbone on one side of his face, the skin at its edges ragged and raw.

"Your family came to my grandfather to beg his aid against the armies of Dornach, when you were nothing more than pirates and cut-throats," said Gryvan. "The price of that aid — of raising you up to be Thanes in your own right, of turning your little fiefdom of bandits into a Blood — was your pledge of loyalty to Haig and to Vaymouth. Better men than you, of Bloods that had a long history before yours was even a dream, see fit to honor that pledge. Yet you broke it, and thought to cast it off as if it were nothing more than a shawl. You have withheld the tithes that are owed to me, and given sanctuary to pirates, and imprisoned my Steward. Worse, we now find that you have so far forgotten your proper state as to buy Dornach men to serve in your armies against me. Have you nothing to say for yourself, Igryn? Are you impervious to shame?"

The captive Thane parted his lips in a crude smile. There was blood in his mouth.

"Nothing," he said.

If Gryvan was disappointed he did not show it. "Very well. It is a long journey back to Vaymouth. Perhaps you will rediscover your tongue by the time we get there. Then we can discuss who might make a fitting replacement for you as Thane of these misbegotten lands."

The High Thane lifted his sword and slid it back into its ornate scabbard, turning his back upon the kneeling figure. Kale released his grip on the man's hair, and Igryn's head fell forward as he swayed upon his knees.

Gryvan beckoned Kale to him. He spoke softly, his words meant only for the master of his Shield.

"I do not wish him dead. It will be useful to have a living reminder for those others who chafe at my bit in their mouth. The thought of Igryn rotting in a jail may give them pause, at least for a time. But even a prisoner can be troublesome if he has some claim to a throne, so he must live yet be unfit to rule. The Kings knew the way of these things. Their Mercy served well in the past. It is time to renew that tradition. See to it tonight."

As Igryn oc Dargannan-Haig was dragged away, the mood amongst the dispersing crowds was buoyant. Taim Narran kept his eyes down as he wove through the throng. He did not want to meet the gaze of some jubilant Haig warrior and be forced to pretend to feelings he could not share. He had come to see the humiliation of the captured Thane only out of a sense that he ought to witness the moment that so many of his men had died to bring about. Now all he wanted was the solitude of his own tent; failing that, if he must have company, let it be that of his surviving comrades. The men of Lannis had camped out on the fringes of the assembled army, keeping a wary distance from the far more numerous bands of Haig, Ayth and Taral warriors that made up the bulk of Gryvan's force.

Passing by a row of great wagons, Taim was dragged out of his reverie by a familiar, irate voice. He looked up to see Roaric nan Kilkry-Haig berating the master of the wagon train. The Kilkry Thane's son was shouting furiously, his face blushing with anger. The target of his fury maintained an impassive calm, and showed no obvious sign of being intimidated by Roaric's status.

Taim sighed. The standing of the Kilkry and Lannis Bloods seemed to sink lower with each passing day. Poor Roaric understood that as well as anyone, yet his only response to the anger and pain that knowledge engendered was to grow ever more bitter and confrontational. It did not bode well for the future.

"Roaric," Taim said quietly, laying a hand on the younger man's arm.

Roaric whirled about and almost unleashed a further torrent of abuse. As soon as he recognized Taim he mastered himself and let out a long, deep breath.

"I'm sorry," he muttered. "I thought you were another one of Gryvan's lackeys."

"Walk with me," said Taim. "I have wine and good salted beef waiting for me. You're welcome to share it."

With a last vitriolic stare over his shoulder, Roaric allowed himself to be steered gently away. The heat in his cheeks slowly subsided.

"I know it does no good," he said, as if anticipating a reprimand from Taim. "But they treat us with such contempt. That man has cut the food supplies I need for my wounded. He says everyone is treated the same, but I've seen no sign of Haig men going hungry."

"I can spare some supplies," said Taim quietly. "We've been hoarding them against the journey home."

"I was not asking for that," replied Roaric.

"I know, but the offer is an honest one. Lannis and Kilkry stand together, remember?"

"Thank you."

They walked on a way in silence. A small audience had gathered around two men who were rolling on the grass, throwing ineffective punches at one another. As the combatants slithered sideways Roaric and Taim had to step around them. The crowd of onlookers cheered and called for greater effort, perhaps a little blood.

"At least it's all done," Taim muttered. "There'll be no more battles, now Igryn is taken."

"No," agreed Roaric. He glanced almost nervously at Taim. "I have lost more than a thousand of my father's men."

"You did not lose them so much as they were taken from you."

"Still, I am ashamed. I should have done more. My father will be horrified to see how few of us return. Perhaps if he had sent Gerain in my place . . ."

"Lheanor chose you to lead, not your brother," Taim interrupted him. "He will not blame you for what has happened, and you should not blame yourself. If the Bloodheir had been here instead of you the outcome would have been just the same. Gryvan would have made sure of it."

"Oh, I know. In my heart, I know that. But what a pitiful state to find ourselves in! My family were High Thanes, and now here we are beholden to the whim of Gryvan oc Haig. We bow and scrape and run back and forth at his command. For a hundred and fifty years we led the True Bloods. It was Kilkry Thanes who stood against the Black Road when it appeared; it was us who had to keep the Bloods together when Gyre threatened to break everything apart. It's Lannis that's held our borders against them for a century or more, Taim. And what does Gryvan care for all of that? Nothing. Haig rules now, and that's all that matters to him."

"Roaric . . ." Taim began to say soothingly.

"You know it's true. Ayth and Taral are so tightly bound up with Haig they hardly deserve to be called Bloods anymore. Now Dargannan's broken and Gryvan's got his eye on us. He'll call himself king one day, or if not him his son. You'll see."

"I don't know what will happen in the future. What I care about today, what you should care about, is getting the men I have left back to their homes. Let Croesan and Lheanor decide what happens beyond that. Winter is here, Roaric. Get your men back to their warm fires and warm beds and loving wives. Time enough to be angry then."

Roaric did not look wholly convinced but he lapsed into an acquiescent silence. Taim was half-tempted to put an arm around his shoulder. He might be a Thane's son, but there was something of the child in Roaric's raw anger and injured pride.

*

With the fall of night, the valley began to freeze. The air was crystal sharp. Despite the bitter chill, there was celebration through much of the camp. Gathered around glaring fires, small bands of men forgot the weariness in their limbs and sang, shouted and drank their fill. Here and there amongst the warriors danced women who had followed in the army's wake all the way from Vaymouth. Dogs bounded from fire to fire and group to group, barking and chasing one another through forests of legs. Already, though it was yet early, there were slumped forms on the ground, where men had staggered away from the circle around a fire and succumbed to wine-induced slumber. The frosted night might yet claim a few lives spared by the battles of the last weeks.

Taim Narran made his way through this chaotic scene. He shrugged off efforts to draw him into each noisy crowd, and waved away the wineskins that he was offered. Such revels were familiar to him. As a young man, shaken and thrilled by his first taste of battle, he had been in Tanwrye for the days of excess that had followed the victory over the Horin-Gyre Blood in the Vale of Stones. It had not been the greatest of battles: a few thousand invaders, lacking the support of the other Gyre Bloods. Still, it had been intoxicating. The Lannis Blood had stood against their old enemies, traded blows with them and emerged triumphant.

Tonight, however, there was no joy or excitement in him. There was little of anything save a vague relief at still having his life and the distorted reflection of that relief: guilt at living on when so many of the men he had brought here did not. He was tired, in his heart as much as his bones.

He came to the tent of Gryvan oc Haig, and waited while one of the guards sought permission to admit him. As he stood there, stepping from one foot to another in an effort to distract himself from the deepening cold, he sensed eyes upon him. Kale was standing a short distance away, half in and half out of the shadows at the side of the tent, watching him impassively. For a moment their gazes met. It was Taim who looked away.

"Come to beg scraps from the high table?" asked Kale softly.

Taim tensed. The man's words, and their cargo of contempt, ignited anger in his breast. He had thought himself the master of his feelings, but now found them suddenly leaking through the bars of their cage.

"Have a care, Narran," he heard Kale say, as if the man could read his mind. "They say you are the best sword in the Glas valley, but you play in a larger game now."

Another surge of hatred ran through Taim, and he found himself irrationally laying his fingers upon the pommel of his sword. But when he looked up, uncertain of what would happen next or of what he wanted to happen, Kale had gone.

By the time he was brought at last before the High Thane, Taim was surprised to find a great emptiness inside him. He had expected to have to struggle to master his anger, to bite back the words he longed to say to this man. Yet he was only weary, as if the brief confrontation with Kale had drained away his last meager reserves of passion. In a way, he was thankful for it. He had advised Roaric nan Kilkry-Haig to hide his fury, and knew he had to live up to that advice himself.

Gryvan oc Haig was slouched across a spill of great cushions that had been laid out before his throne. He was gnawing idly at a leg of mutton, a golden goblet clutched in his other hand, as he watched a semi-clad dancing girl who bobbed and writhed in the center of the tent. Behind the Thane of Thanes, flanking the empty throne, musicians were playing a sinuous tune upon lyre and pipes. They wore airy shirts of white damask in the style of the entertainers who attended the merchant princes of Tal Dyre. There were ten or fifteen people scattered around the edge of the carpet upon which the girl danced: captains of the Haig Blood's armies, officials of Gryvan's court, and warriors of Taral-Haig and Ayth-Haig. Each had before him a silver platter of meat, bread and fruit. There was no sign of Roaric. Neither the Kilkry nor the Lannis Blood had been invited to this gathering.

Gryvan detached his gaze from the dancing girl for a moment, and waved the tattered joint of meat he held in Taim's direction.

"Our Captain of Lannis-Haig," he called above the sound of the music. "Join us."

Taim shook his head. "No, thank you, sire," he said, shifting to one side as the dancer came between him and the Thane of Thanes.

Gryvan gestured at the girl. "Stop that," he snapped. "Enough."

The musicians fell instantly silent. The dancing girl stepped to one side and squatted down. Taim moved forward without thinking, as if sucked in by the void she had left. The carpet beneath his feet was richly patterned with flowing loops of flowers and foliage. It was a strange, incongruous sight here in the wild mountains of Dargannan-Haig.

"Will you take a drink with us?" asked the High Thane.

"Forgive me, sire, but I only came to speak with you. I did not know you had guests."

"Ha!" laughed Gryvan, setting down his food and wiping his fingers on one of the cushions. "Of course I have guests! What else should I be doing on such a night as this?"

"Of course," said Taim. He was uncomfortable beneath so many attentive gazes. He knew he had no friends here. It had been a mistake to come, but he had been thinking less than clearly since the slaughter at An Caman Fort. The companies of Lannis and Kilkry had battered their way into that fastness eventually, at the cost of two hundred or more lives. What had followed — the methodical massacre of every prisoner taken — had seemed just as wasteful. All the more so since only days later word had come of Igryn's capture. The once mighty Thane of the Dargannan Blood had been cornered in an abandoned shepherd's hovel, with nothing left of his Shield save a handful of famished, exhausted warriors.

"Well," said Gryvan, "if you will not join us, you had best tell me what you came to say."

"Sire . . ." began Taim. A sharp groan interrupted him. Behind the circle of feasting captains and courtiers, curled upon a straw mat like a child in frightened sleep, was Igryn oc Dargannan-Haig. His back was to Taim and his knees were clasped up against his chest. Even so, Taim could see that there was a dirty bandage about his head. As he looked, the defeated Thane's shoulders shook, and a shiver ran through his great body.

Gryvan glanced at his prisoner.

"Ah yes," he said lightly. "You see, even our disobedient friend Igryn has joined us this evening."

"He seems unwell," murmured Taim. He knew what he was looking at. They had called it the Mercy of Kings long ago: the fate of lords who reached for the throne and fell short.

"Sadly, yes," said Gryvan. "He has been parted from his eyes, the better that he might reflect upon his folly. Tell me what you want, Narran."

The edge in the High Thane's voice drew Taim's attention smartly back. He cleared his throat.

"I would like to take my men away, sire. In the morning."

Gryvan raised his eyebrows. "We march in two days' time. You know that. Just today I have sent riders to Vaymouth, to prepare a triumphal reception for us all."

An utter silence had come over the room. The High Thane's guests watched in rapt attention. Taim felt a heat rising in his face.

"My men long for their homes, sire. They have wives to return to. So do I. Winterbirth has come, and it is a month's journey back; longer with the wounded and sick we must carry with us. The weather in Kilkry and Lannis will be worse each day we delay."

"But what of the celebrations here?" asked Gryvan with apparent concern. "Do your men not deserve the chance to rest, and to mark the victory they have shared in?"

The words pricked Taim, and he felt, at last, a faint stirring of that anger that Kale had woken.

"Neither they nor I have the heart for it," he said.

The High Thane regarded him for a few seconds. He seemed on the point of saying something. Instead, abruptly, he relaxed back into his voluminous cushion.

"Ah, what matters it now? Go, if you must. Take your men off. I will not prevent it."

Taim found himself exhaling with a relief that he struggled to conceal. He bowed to the Thane of Thanes and stepped backward.

"Thank you, my lord. We will be gone before dawn."

He turned to lift the flap of the tent.

"Narran," said the High Thane quietly behind him.

Taim paused, partway out into the night and the cleansing grip of its cold air, and looked back. Gryvan was staring at him with narrowed eyes.

"How many men will return with you to Anduran?"

"Eight hundred, if you count those who may yet die," said Taim in a flat voice.

Gryvan nodded thoughtfully without releasing Taim from his glare.

"Tell Croesan I asked, will you?" was all he said.

II

By the time the boat ground its keel up against rocks and lurched to a halt, Orisian could not rise. His shirt was plastered to his skin by blood. His head was pounding, as if his heartbeat was seated there rather than in his chest, and he could not draw breath without sending shards of pain darting through his body. He coughed agonizingly and felt thick liquid bubbling inside him. He heard Rothe springing from the boat, boots crunching on a stony beach.

"We must get away from the shore," Rothe said.

Orisian tried to say that he could not move. Only a vague mumbling came from his lips. They felt dry and ready to split. He ran his tongue over them but found that too was desiccated. Then

Rothe had him around the waist and was lifting him out of the boat. Orisian cried out in pain.

"Forgive me," he heard Rothe whisper.

Orisian could see nothing now save blurred patches that ebbed and flowed at the edge of his vision in time with his heartbeat.

"I can't see," he croaked into the darkness.

Rothe did not reply. They were moving, but Orisian could not tell anything beyond that. His flank was hot and wet, yet there was a cold numbness stealing into his hands.

"Stay with me," he heard someone say desperately, very far away. "Stay with me, Orisian."

Then he was lying upon some soft, yielding surface. For a moment his vision cleared. Trees were arching over him, bending down out of the night as if to lay their outstretched twigs on his face. He would have turned away had there been any strength left in him. There was a strange, harsh sound, which after a moment or two he remembered as the bark of a fox.

"A fox," he murmured, wanting to laugh.

A shape loomed up. It was Rothe, leaning close.

"What?" said the man.

Then Rothe sprang away. Orisian heard a gasp, a sighing sound as if a wind had run through long grass, and felt the jarring impact of something heavy hitting the ground. Figures leapt over him where he lay: pale shapes that seemed detached from the earth. Ghosts, he thought.

The last thing he felt before he fainted was many hands upon him, lifting him up.

* * *

The Fever had left dark corners in Anyara's mind. Now, five years on, the memory of the hallucinatory dreams of her sickbed was not quite so strong as it had been in the first weeks of her recovery. Still she was sometimes seized in the late evening by a sudden fear of falling asleep: a fear that she might not wake, might be lost forever in that fierce borderland of death where all dreams were nightmares. It had never occurred to her that the stuff of fevered delirium might pursue her out from that territory into the waking world. On the night of Winterbirth the air was thick with it.

She fell when Kylane thrust her through the open door of the keep. She regained her feet in time to see him set himself between Orisian and the Inkallim, and in time to see him beheaded. A strangled cry died in her throat as she was hauled back from the door by a burly merchant. He slammed the door shut and barred it. Cries and the clash of weapons bled in through the wood.

"Hide! We must hide!" shouted the merchant.

A small group of terrified townsfolk — those lucky enough to have been standing within reach of the doorway — were huddled at the foot of the stairs. The merchant turned upon them, waving his arms as if he was herding sheep.

"Upstairs," he cried.

They scrambled up the stone stairway. The merchant grabbed at Anyara, seeking to drag her with him. She saw something in his eyes that lay between terror and fury, and was afraid of it. Instinctively, she slipped from his grasp and darted into the feasting hall.

It was deserted. When the fighting started the servants had scattered to the kitchens or whatever other place they thought might offer some sanctuary. The fire still burned. Food littered the tables: half-eaten joints of meat, scattered hunks of bread, here and there a tankard turned over in the rush to get outside and see the show.

She stumbled to a halt, held by the incongruity of this scene of interrupted celebration and the violent tumult she could hear outside. A pounding at the door of the keep startled her. For a moment she thought it was someone else seeking refuge, and she started back. Then she heard a harsh voice shouting in an accent she barely understood, and a shiver of fear ran tingling through her back.

The barred door was strong, she told herself. It would hold for a time. She should find a dark corner to hide in until it was safe to come out. She snuffed out the faint inner voice that asked what would happen if it was never safe to come out. And yet she could not hide like a child. The need to see, to know what was happening, gnawed at her. Her father was out there, and Orisian. Out amongst the shouts and the ringing clatter of sword against sword.

She looked at the tall windows of the hall. They were raised up high, but if she put a bench beneath them, if she stood upon it and stretched up, she might be able to see out onto the courtyard. Frowning with concentration, she seized the end of the nearest bench and made to drag it across.

The window exploded inward as if struck by a great stone. Shards of glass spun across the room, forming a glittering cloud that wreathed the dark figure flying through the air. Anyara jumped backward. The bench fell from her hands. The Inkallim landed on one of the great dining tables, sending platters and cups skittering away to the floor. He crouched like an animal, balanced on the balls of his feet as he looked around. There was blood across his naked forearms. Splinters of glass glinted in his flesh. He fixed his eyes upon Anyara. She tensed to flee.

A second massive shape was silhouetted in the window, appearing in an instant and leaping into the hall. The first warrior sprang the moment Anyara's attention was distracted. She spun on her heel and made for the doorway. Before she had gone more than a couple of strides a great blow on her back flung her forward. Her feet left the ground and she flew toward a brazier that stood by the door. The impact ran through her, jarring her shoulders. Dazed, she felt a fierce heat enveloping her as the brazier crashed to the ground. She rolled away, scattering hot embers from her back. Her vision was spinning, but she sensed the looming shape of the Inkallim rising above her. There was a shaft of yellow light that must be the flames reflected in the blade of his sword. She kicked out at his legs. He danced back, avoiding the blow with ease. Before she could move again she felt a swordpoint pressing upon her chest and a strong hand grasped her hair, straining it against its roots. Her head was lifted and then smacked once, sharply, down into the stone floor. She felt a wet burst of blood on the back of her scalp.

"Be still," hissed the Inkallim.

"Let me go," she shouted.

Then she was being lifted, her arms locked behind her. Her nostrils were filled with the scents of burning, of blood, of sweat. The second Inkallim came up in front of her and grasped her face between thumb and fingers. He turned her head from side to side, examining her. He grunted and said something that Anyara did not catch. Her captor might have been made of stone for all the impression her struggles made. The two men exchanged a few more, almost whispered, words then wrestled her toward the door of the keep. They checked the stairway. The shadows were still. The second warrior lifted the bar on the door, and Inkallim poured into the building. They darted up the stairs, bearing slaughter with them in their grim eyes and already bloodied blades.

Anyara was thrown out into the courtyard. She tumbled down the steps and lay upon the cobbles, fearing to move lest her body should fail to support her. Someone seized her and raised her roughly to her feet. She narrowed her eyes against the glare of the flames that were consuming the stables. There were bodies scattered all around the castle's courtyard. Pools of blood shone blackly, each alive with reflections of the fires. Smoke writhed around between the castle's confining walls. The few horses had been brought out from their stalls, and Inkallim were wrestling to control them. The animals stamped and reared, shying away from the conflagration and throwing wild flame-cast shadows. At the foot of the far wall, a small cluster of corpses was gathered. Hunched at their heart, not quite fallen but slumped and bowed on his knees, was her father. Even as she watched, he seemed to be sinking, slipping down to the ground.

"Father," she cried out. The hands that held her arm tightened painfully.

A group of Inkallim were coming toward her, blocking her view. They were dragging Inurian by the arms. With them came a lean *na'kyrim* Anyara had never seen before.

She kicked and struggled. Inurian looked up. Blood was pouring from a wound on his head and he could not stand.

"Anyara," he said.

"Quiet," the other *na'kyrim* snapped.

They hauled Inurian and Anyara to the horses. Inkallim were emerging once again from the keep, moving purposefully but without urgency. Anyara glanced up at the windows. They were all dark. She and Inurian were bound and thrown across the necks of two horses, warriors settling into the saddles behind them. A gust of wind spun sparks and smoke around the courtyard, searing her eyes. The horse skittered to one side and she almost slid off. A firm hand held her in place.

In moments the Inkallim had gathered. They were fewer than they had been at the start of the battle, but not by many. One of the women was shouting curt commands Anyara could not catch. Half a dozen of the Inkallim mounted the other horses, and they led the way out through the gate. The rest jogged in tight formation alongside the animals bearing Inurian and Anyara.

As they emerged onto the causeway, Anyara felt the sea breeze on her face. She strove to raise her head, but she was bouncing up and down with the horse's trot and the strain on her neck was too great. She glimpsed the town ahead, though. It was brightly lit, not just by the torches and bonfires of Winterbirth but also by still greater blazes. Houses were burning. Above the splashing clatter of the horse's hoofs upon the part-exposed causeway, the sound of screaming and shouting reached her ears. There was fighting in the town.

The dash up from the seafront was a chaos of cries, of plunging figures, of clashing blades. The Inkallim never broke stride, pounding up the narrow street toward the square, battering aside any townsfolk who blocked their path. Some of the town's garrison, drawn by the sound of fighting in the castle and the faint sight of smoke rising from its battlements, had begun to make their way down toward the causeway. They were too few and taken too unawares to stand against the Inkallim. Even so, Anyara thought, the raiding party would emerge at any moment into the square, there to be surrounded and cut down. But they turned down a side street. Some of the Inkallim peeled off to hinder pursuit, and she heard screams and the ring of blades.

It grew darker as they moved away from the center of Kolglas, then they passed by the beacon of a burning cottage and Anyara felt waves of heat washing over her and smoke rasping down into her lungs. She turned her face away. When she looked up again they had come to the very edge of the town, emerging onto the main road that ran south along the coast. Without any signal she could detect, the band of warriors broke away from the track and plunged into the black forest.

The fringes of the forest were open, kept clear of undergrowth by the town's stock. As they went on the wildwood closed in about them. Twigs and tendrils clawed at Anyara's cheeks. She pressed her face into the horse's neck, feeling the massive muscles working rhythmically beneath its skin. In the last instant before she sealed her eyes, shutting out the horrors of the night if not those within her own mind, she caught sight of half-hidden figures running alongside them; no Inkallim these — lither, paler — but they moved too fast and the night-bound forest was too dark for her to tell quite what new piece of nightmare had risen up to join their flight.

That first night in the Forest of Anlane seemed to last an eternity. After an age, they paused and Anyara was set upright on the horse.

Her bonds had torn tracks of stinging pain around her wrists. It was too dark for her to see clearly. The wind was rising, shivering through the leafless canopy of the forest above her. She looked around for Inurian, and saw a hunched figure seated in front of a rider a few yards away. Then the massive arms of her Inkallim captor embraced her as he took up the reins once more and nudged the horse on. She felt his chest pressing against her shoulders and tried to ease herself forward. As the horse got into its stride she slid back and could not help but rest her weight against the warrior.

They kept a steady pace, weaving through the ever-thickening forest. To Anyara, peering out over the horse's bobbing head, it seemed that they were traveling blind. Trees loomed up out of the darkness, boughs leapt at her. Now and again at the very edge of her vision she saw people running ahead. Some were Inkallim, judging by their bulk. Others, more distant, were those same less substantial figures she had noticed before, lean and rangy shapes that ghosted silently through the woods. The realization came that these were Kyrinin: woodwights of the White Owl clan were guiding the Inkallim through Anlane. Perhaps they too had set the fires in Kolglas that kept help from coming to the castle. The thought put an icy needle into her heart. She was in the hands not only of the enemies of her Blood, but of her very race.

As dawn's first light began to bleed through the roof of the forest, the trees solidified out of darkness. They sloughed the night and gradually took on form and substance. Anyara's thoughts had run off on pathways all their own, and she came to herself with a start as if roused from a waking sleep. She swayed on the horse. Her eyes, her back, her throat all ached and she feared she might fall at any moment. She looked about her. They were following a narrow, almost overgrown trail. Ahead of her, Inkallim were running in single file, keeping a steady, careful pace. She could see no sign of the Kyrinin. She craned her neck to try to see behind, and glimpsed other horses and riders before her captor slapped at her face.

After an hour or so, when the grey shades of dawn had become the clear light of day, the relentless pace slowed a little. The path widened. Anyara felt exhaustion and cold settled deep inside her. Although it was warmer now, the night's chill had taken root in her body and would not relinquish its hold.

Another horse came up beside her and she turned to see Inurian seated in front of a smoke-blackened warrior. He looked pale and drawn. Blood had crusted his forehead and laid dark stains down his left cheek. Anyara started to say something, then bit her lip at the sound of a third horse coming up behind them. It drew level and she recognized the *na'kyrim* who had appeared after the fighting in the castle was over. He was a good deal younger than Inurian and to Anyara's eyes his skin had a hungry pallor about it. His pale hair hung lifelessly to his shoulders.

There was excitement in the newcomer's face as he leaned toward Inurian, as if the dawn, the flight and the warriors all around brought forth in him a feral joy.

"My name is Aeglyss," he said.

Inurian fixed his eyes upon the path ahead.

"You did not sense me, did you?" Aeglyss said. "Nor did you get inside the minds of those Inkallim. I wasn't certain I could hide their intent from you, you know. You, the great *na'kyrim* who can see a man's thoughts. I promised the ravens I would do it, let them play out their little charade, but in my heart I didn't know. But, see! I was the stronger, was I not? My gifts proved the greater."

Still Inurian ignored him. Aeglyss seemed to relax a little, sinking back into his saddle and adjusting his hands upon the reins.

"How old are you?" he asked after a moment or two, his voice calmer now, more measured.

"Old enough to have seen your kind before," Inurian responded. There was ice in his voice.

"And what kind is that?"

"Dogs that think they are wolves."

Aeglyss laughed at that. There was a ragged edge to the sound, as of a man laughing at word of some disaster.

"They would have killed you but for me, little man. The Children of the Hundred have no great liking for *na'kyrim*. They tolerate me only because they know I can help them. I saved you from their tender mercies, and you should not forget it. We will have much to discuss later."

He glanced dismissively at Anyara, then kicked at his horse. It lurched forward, trotting up the trail to the head of the column.

"What a . . ." Anyara started to say, but a sudden tensing of her guard's arm warned her to hold her tongue. She looked across to Inurian and he had time to nod before the horses parted once more and he was carried ahead and out of sight.

They followed paths that Anyara often could not make out. The tracks wove through what seemed to be impenetrable undergrowth. They went fast, the Inkallim jogging along, the horses grouped in the middle of the column. The Kyrinin reappeared in the midmorning. They drifted in and out of sight, running figures passing amongst the trees on either side without a rustle or a footfall. Haunting birdcalls, which Anyara did not think were made by any bird, ran through the forest every so often.

They stopped without warning, in early afternoon as far as Anyara could tell from the sun's angled rays, beside a forest stream close-fringed by willows and alder. She and Inurian sat against rocks while their Inkallim guards drank from the stream. The warriors who had been acrobats bowed their heads into the water and rinsed the dye from their hair. It made Anyara think, absurdly, of villagers washing clothes by a millstream. Eddying clouds of amber and red swirled away down the current. Then began the meticulous task of re-dyeing. The warriors produced packets of powder from their belts and pouches. Mixed with water, it made a thick paste that they worked through their hair. It took some time. When they straightened, every man and woman had sleek black locks. Anyara looked away. The Inkallim, she remembered being told, wore their hair black in token of the birds that once accompanied the God called The Raven: Death.

A few Kyrinin came in and squatted with Aeglyss and some of the Inkallim, talking in hushed tones. Anyara could not help but catch her breath at their closeness. She had only seen Kyrinin once before, and they had been dead, brought out of the forest by the warriors her father had sent to hunt them down. The skin of these strange, fearful figures was so colorless it seemed almost translucent to her. The characteristics that Inurian had inherited from his Kyrinin ancestors were here before her in their purest form: fingers long and precise, tipped by uniform white nails; eyes of a flat, unnerving grey; fine, sharp-featured faces; pale hair that had an almost luminous sheen. Two of them bore markings she had heard described in stories. Thin blue lines ran in great, whorling spirals and curves across their faces like ferocious masks. If the tales were true, these were the tattoos worn as badges of honor by the most savage warriors of the Kyrinin. Only now, seeing them in soft conversation just a few yards away, did Anyara understand how truly unhuman these people were. As much as anything, the difference resided in their air of detachment and self-assured grace; the way in which they held themselves and the unspoken language of their movements and gestures.

After a minute or two the Kyrinin rose and headed back the way they had come, vanishing from sight.

"Gone to check for pursuit," muttered Inurian. He seemed less haggard and drained than he had in the early morning.

"They'll not find any," he continued, talking as much to himself as to Anyara. "We've come too far and fast. None but other Kyrinin could keep to this trail and match our pace." He chewed at his bottom lip. "Where are we going, though?"

An Inkallim swordsman loomed up before them. He gestured toward Anyara with a deerskin pouch of water. She resisted the urge to shake her head. She was thirsty, and would gain nothing by denying it. The warrior held the pouch as she took a few sips. He offered it to Inurian as well, but the *na'kyrim* ignored it.

"Not to a White Owl *vo'an*, surely?" Inurian mused as the Inkallim strode away. "And not all the way to Kan Dredar?"

"We'll find out sooner than I'd like," said Anyara glumly.

Inurian glanced at her, as if only reminded by her voice that she was there.

"That is true," he said. "That is true."

"Do you know where we are?" Anyara asked him.

Inurian frowned. "Not with any certainty. We have been heading deeper into Anlane all the while, north and east. We crossed the track from Kolglas to Drinan in the night. It makes little sense, unless they mean to spend the winter here and I think even the Inkallim, with Kyrinin aid, would not choose to do that."

Anyara sighed. She caught the eye of one their guards, who was glowering at her, and lowered her gaze.

"They must be mad to even attempt this," she muttered. "Whatever it is they're attempting."

"Not mad," said Inurian. "It makes sense, if you believe what they do. They have nothing to lose, after all. Failure only means death, and they cannot reach the world they crave without dying first. This world is hateful to them."

"Why are the White Owls helping them?"

"That, I would be interested to know," muttered Inurian, "but I think our unpleasant friend Aeglyss will be a part of the answer."

They were quiet for a little time.

"Inurian . . ." Anyara said after a while, "my father . . ."

His arms tugged the bonds that held them, and she thought he wanted to reach out to her. The cords would not yield.

"I am sorry, Anyara. We tried to guard him, but there were too many."

"Orisian?"

"I don't know. I would have given anything to prevent this, but I was too slow, too mistrusting of my own instincts. What gifts I have were not enough. I knew something was amiss, but . . . somehow Aeglyss blunted the edge of my perceptions. I've never before wished for a greater, or different, strength in the Shared, Anyara. Now I wish for nothing else."

He hung his head. Anyara almost wanted to turn away, so clear an echo did his pain find in her.

"And it is only days ago that I warned your brother against wishing for what is not," Inurian said quietly.

They sat together in silence, each of them longing in their own way for the world to be other than it was.

They slept that night in a narrow clearing, stopping long after dusk had fallen. Anyara and Inurian were kept apart. She huddled down, resting her head against a grassy tussock. Grief and despair were writhing in her and she felt close to tears. That she would lock in. They would not hear her cry. A coarse blanket was thrown over her, but it did little to obstruct the mounting cold. She thought that the numbing pain in her wrists and hands, the hard ground and damp grass, the creaking of the trees all around, would keep her from sleep. Instead, her exhaustion flooded up from within and carried her off in minutes.

Time and again she came partway awake, shifting to ease some building pain in her back or arms. Strange sounds, filtered through the veil of drowsiness, reached her: the plaintive call of an owl; the flap of wings above the trees, and once the lilt of soft, unintelligible voices whispering close by. When someone kicked her awake, before dawn had even begun to erode the darkness, the blanket had slid away from her and she could hardly move, so stiff and sore was her body. She felt as if she had closed her eyes mere moments ago.

They made Anyara and Inurian walk for a while that morning. A rider — one of the female Inkallim — went before them, leading them by ropes. Whenever they tried to talk to one another she would tug at their bonds. Anyara felt as weak as she had in the first days after the Fever had broken. They had been given nothing save water since being seized from the castle, and her head was light. She stumbled along, and fell now and again. Each time she was dragged along the trail a short distance and Inurian shouted at the rider ahead until she reined in her horse and allowed Anyara to struggle back to her feet.

Aeglyss came and rode behind them for a stretch.

"Did you sleep well?" he asked.

Inurian straightened his back and walked on. Anyara looked over her shoulder.

"I'm hungry," she said.

"No doubt," said Aeglyss, but his eyes were fixed upon Inurian. "Did you sleep well, I asked."

Still Inurian paid him no heed.

"I need some food," insisted Anyara.

"Your hunger is not so bad," said the *na'kyrim* at length, in a voice now gentle, slow and deep. The sound of his words soothed Anyara in some strange way. "It is not as great as it was. A strong girl like you could go on without eating for hours yet, days even. Think instead of the fall of your feet. Let that rhythm be your only thought. Your legs are strong. Pay no heed to your hunger."

Anyara felt her sense of herself shift a little. Aeglyss was right: there was an easing tempo in the rise and fall of her steps. They were steadier now. She did not stumble anymore. She lost herself in the feeling of walking, and heard the rest of what was said distantly and without real understanding.

"She should be quiet for a time," said Aeglyss. "My voice has always been one of my better features. I can be very . . . persuasive, but she is particularly easy."

"She is exhausted," snapped Inurian, "and weak from hunger, and shock. It is a childish trick, and one I doubt you could play upon someone wakeful and healthy."

"Ah, but I can, I can. I am stronger than you think. But at least now you have something to say. I thought I would have to continue talking to myself."

"I am sure you would not find that too great a burden."

"Come now, Inurian. We should not bicker, you and I. We are *na'kyrim* together. Our kind has enough enemies without fighting amongst ourselves."

"This is not a fight I started, and I would rather not be reminded that we are of the same kind."

"But we are," said Aeglyss urgently, "we are. I saved you, did I not? Kept the ravens from killing you? The girl they were content to take alive, but you they would have killed in a moment if not for me. *Na'kyrim* must stand by one another, for no one else will."

"Forgive me if I do not thank you for saving me from murderers you brought with you."

Aeglyss gave an exasperated sigh. "I wish only your friendship, Inurian," he said. "You have seen what I can do. The Shared wakes strongly in me, you can see that. But I am still young; I have more to learn. I have heard there is no one with greater knowledge of the Shared than you. Some people speak highly of you. That is why I came to Kolglas, you know. The Inkallim came for the Thane's family. I came for you."

When Inurian did not reply, Aeglyss went on, now quietly insistent.

"You could teach me. And I could lend you my strength. How many have you known who could oppose your own insights as I did? I could raise us both up. And I have powerful friends. Without me, the White Owls would never have agreed to help the Gyre Bloods. None of this would have been possible without that help. Horin-Gyre is in my debt. When all of this is done, I will be one of the powerful myself. You could be a part of that."

"Leave me be," said Inurian.

Aeglyss said nothing for a few moments, then, "Very well. You will think differently in time. Girl. Anyara!"

The sudden sharpness of his voice jolted Anyara. She lifted her head, which had grown heavy. Her eyes were clear, as clouds she had not been aware of until that moment parted.

"Are you hungry, girl?" Aeglyss asked.

And in that instant, the hunger was back, gnawing more than ever at the pit of her stomach and sucking the strength out of her limbs. She almost lost her footing and fell. Inurian was looking at her, concern and some kind of pain in his face. She tried to smile, but could not be sure whether she managed it. She risked a brief glance behind. Aeglyss was gone, fallen back out of sight.

"I was almost asleep," she said.

"Not exactly," replied Inurian gloomily before a harsh tug on the ropes reminded them of the wisdom of silence.

They marched on over ever rougher terrain. Long, low ridges ran through the forest, and the company followed trails up and over them. They crossed tiny streams and wove around the great boulders that dotted the slopes. The forest was open, a mixture of birch, pine and lichen-armored oak. Anyara was sure they must still be within the lands of her Blood, but she saw no sign of either stock or men. Herders would only come so far into the wild lands in the summer, and then only if they could find no grazing closer to home.

Some time after noon they did come across some men of Lannis-Haig. It brought no cheer. They were angling down a slope toward a brook that Anyara could hear gurgling over rocks ahead. When they came to the stream, she saw that there had been a hunters' camp here. It was ruined now, the tents cast down, the cooking fire doused. The three men who had made it lay there, all dead. Anyara stared at them as they walked past. One of them lay on his back, his blank face upturned, his tongue poking out from between his lips. He was young, perhaps sixteen. Orisian's age. She felt a tightening in her throat and looked away.

Not long afterward they were hauled up onto horses once again, and the company increased its pace. Anyara's stomach was by now growling with such insistence that it was almost painful. She found herself struggling to keep at bay tendrils of sleep. The enclosing arms of the Inkallim rider kept her from slumping to the ground. She was drowsily aware that they were climbing, rising up some steady slope.

Later, only half-conscious, she felt a breeze on her face and strong hands pulling her from the horse. She was thrown to the ground, unable to move. Her leaden eyes opened and she saw clouds scudding across a dimming sky. For the first time in what seemed an age, no branches hemmed in her view. Far, far above, an unbridgeable distance from the patch of rough ground upon which she lay, an eagle glided serenely over the forest. She fixed her eyes on it for a time, and could almost imagine her thoughts riding its great wings away into the stillness.

Around her, the Inkallim were making camp for the night. They had halted in a high clearing near the crest of a ridge. The land rose, for this short space, above its mantle of trees like the back of a whale breaching the surface of the sea.

Then Aeglyss was kneeling beside her. He leaned over, his face filling her vision. She stared into his grey eyes and saw nothing there. He rolled her and cut her bonds with a knife. Sudden pain and waves of heat pulsed through her hands. The skin had gone from her wrists.

"Stand up," said Aeglyss, hauling her erect.

She staggered. A supporting arm appeared around her waist, and she found Inurian at her side.

"Look," said Aeglyss.

She did not understand what he meant and in her utter exhaustion she stood there, letting her weight fall against Inurian. His arm tightened about her and held her up. Then Aeglyss laid a hand upon her shoulder and squeezed.

"Look," he hissed, pointing.

She followed the line of his outstretched arm. The forest fell away beneath them, sweeping off down a long slope and out over the flatter ground beyond. She was looking across the roof of Anlane, and felt dizzy at the sight. The trees stretched almost to the limit of what she could see, but there was, far off to the north, the grey suggestion of open ground and still further out, so faint it was more a shading in the light than anything else, there was a line of mountains towering above the earth: the Car Criagar, looming over the Glas valley.

"What?" she asked, hearing the word as if it had been uttered by someone else.

Inurian's arm tightened again, and she wondered why.

"See the smoke," said Aeglyss.

Again, she looked. And she could just make out, rising from somewhere in the space between the forest and the mountains, a black smudge of smoke climbing up. It occurred to her that there must be a very great fire somewhere by the river.

"I don't understand," she muttered.

"You will," Aeglyss laughed, and walked away.

She looked up at Inurian's face. He was staring northward, then he sighed and bowed his head.

"I think I know where we are going, now. It is Anduran, Anyara. Anduran is burning."

III

The air was filled with the stench of acrid smoke. The wind gathered it up from the town and danced it around the castle. The sun was a pale disc behind a veil of grey. Croesan oc Lannis-Haig gazed up toward it, watching the ashes of Anduran spiraling into the sky.

He was standing atop the castle's main keep. Somewhere beneath, in the hall, his advisers and officials held council. All of them had climbed to this vantage point when they first smelled the smoke. He had sent the others back after a few minutes. He alone stayed, held fast by the sight of his city burning. There were flames here and there, spouting up from amongst the buildings. Mostly, there was just the smoke. It seethed like an immense exhalation of the earth itself. Strangely, there was hardly a sound save the distant crackle of fires and the occasional groaning roar as some building surrendered. No screams, no cries, no pounding of feet along the alleyways. That eerie absence put an extra morbid twist into Croesan's sadness. It was as if the city had already been dead, and this was just the cremation of its corpse.

They had been in the grand new hall upon the square when the messenger arrived. Croesan had been as happy as he could remember for a long time, filled with a lightness of spirit, an anticipatory excitement, that belonged more properly to children. The hall was filling with hundreds of people, all laughing, all chattering as they awaited the start of the great feast of Winterbirth. Then the messenger had come and turned it all to dust.

The man had ridden without pause from Tanwrye, bringing word of an army coming down through the Stone Vale, of the renewal of the bloody dance between the Black Road and the True Bloods. It had been more than thirty years since the armies had last marched. Then, aged seventeen, Croesan's own first taste of battle had been beneath the walls of Tanwrye, riding with his father and brother to drive back the forces of Horin-Gyre. As he heard the words of the haggard messenger, surrounded by the luxurious accoutrements of a feast that would never now happen, Croesan was returned for an instant into the skin of that youth he had been. Nothing had changed, in all the years that had passed. The Thane must once more ride out from Anduran and face his Blood's old foe.

Within an hour of the messenger's arrival, two hundred men — half of those garrisoned in the city — had marched out from Anduran's northern gate and Croesan's riders were spreading through the farmland around the city, raising his people to arms. In a couple of days, he could have another half a thousand men ready to make for Tanwrye. But it was not to be.

In the depth of the night, one of his shieldmen had come to find the Thane. He was shut in a high room of the keep, talking with Naradin and with his captains. They were making plans that would never be enacted.

"There is a farmer outside, my lord," the shieldman said gravely. "We sent him away at first but he came back, and has others with him now, telling the same story. Otherwise we would not have . . ."

"What are you talking about?" Croesan demanded. His earlier good humor was long gone, swept away.

A disheveled man with matted hair and a scrawny beard pushed partway through the door, restrained by shieldmen.

"The Black Road, sire!" he shouted. "It's marching out of Anlane! Thousands, burning farms, burning homes."

There were mutters of disbelief around the table. The Thane's shieldmen were bodily lifting the farmer from his feet and bearing him backward, out of the chamber.

"My own farm, there on the forest's edge, is gone, lord!" the man cried.

"You say there are others who tell the same story?" Croesan asked.

And soon enough all believed it. Farmworkers and herders, woodsmen and hunters were arriving in Anduran, all of them flying from the destruction of their homes and lands. In the first few hours of darkness, an army had come out from beneath the forest's silent canopy onto the open fields. Somehow, by some unimaginable means, the enemy had crossed all the wild and trackless immensity of Anlane, through the domain of the savage White Owl Kyrinin, and brought an army to within reach of Anduran itself: an impossibility had come to pass.

Whole families poured into the city through the night, loaded onto carts or riding on scrawny horses, fleeing their homes and seeking safety. In the darkness, fear worked its way into hearts. Rich and poor, mighty and humble alike came to the conclusion that their best hope lay in flight. By winter's first dawn the road south to Glasbridge was in its turn filled with a steady stream of townsfolk. And by that same dawn there was an army in sight from the walls of the castle.

Croesan had known then that the town at least was lost. Tanwrye was his Blood's great bulwark against the Black Road: its strength had always been relied upon to block the route through the Vale of Stones. Anduran's own walls were in poor repair, half of its garrison — already reduced by the demands of Gryvan oc Haig — was on the road for Tanwrye. Croesan's castle might be held against assault; Anduran itself could not.

That too was when he understood that he, and his Blood, had after all unlearned things they once knew. Peace had worked a malign flaw into their memories. They had forgotten that to stand against the implacable Black Road required a fire in the heart and in the blood to match that which burned in the northerners; that their guard could never be dropped. Croesan had thought himself mindful of the dangers. Now, breathing in the ashes of Anduran, knowing that half the inhabitants of the city had fled in terror before the enemy was even sighted, he tasted the cost of misjudgment.

The Thane was roused from his black reverie by the sound of someone coming up behind him.

"You should not stand so exposed within sight of your enemy," said Behomun Tole dar Haig. "I saw crossbows down there earlier."

Croesan grunted. "They're too busy setting fires," he said.

Behomun stood beside him for a moment, gazing out across the rooftops, through the haze. "They will regret their actions when the rain and cold come."

"They are not foolish," muttered Croesan. "They have spared the barns, and many of the houses. They know what they are doing."

"I came to see if you would return to the council. It is becoming a trifle overwrought below. Your people would benefit from a firm hand to guide them."

"My people once more, I see. They belong to Gryvan when he needs them to fight for him in the south, but they are mine again now."

Behomun shrugged. Since the siege began, something of his insouciant arrogance had left him. "That was no part of my meaning," he said softly.

"Perhaps. But this should never have happened. The High Thane thinks of the south, always the south. He drools over the riches of the Free Coast and Tal Dyre like a fox in a lambing field. When Kilkry ruled, the other Bloods sent men here, to our lands, to guard against the Black Road. Now it's our warriors who are summoned to the south. There's the result: a sky filled with the smoke of our homes."

"There's no point in you and I debating the rights and wrongs of it, and in all honesty I would have little heart for it. My own family is trapped here just like yours. What's done is done."

"It is done," echoed Croesan distantly.

"The town could not be defended," Behomun said, guessing the Thane's thoughts. "We would likely all be dead if you had made your stand upon the walls instead of here in the castle."

"I know that well enough. Too many are dead in any case, though."

"You could not have taken more in. Every corridor is choked with families. There are more people than horses sleeping in the stables."

Croesan nodded. It was a strange thing, to find Gryvan's Steward so devoid of argument and conflict.

"You could have left," he said, looking Behomun in the eye.

"True, but I am Steward of the Thane of Thanes here. I had some notion of duty." Behomun glanced wistfully toward the west. "It was probably a foolish choice. Now I must trust to your walls to keep my wife and children safe."

"I hope they do so," said Croesan.

"It cannot be long before relief comes. Lheanor will come from Kolkyre, or your own people from Glasbridge and Kolglas. The Black Roaders have over-reached themselves, however much they preach humility. There are no more than a few thousand of them in the city. So long as Tanwrye holds, and we do the same here, they will go no further south."

"Oh, yes. They will lose this war. But my Blood has already

paid too high a price for the victory." Croesan shook himself as a shiver ran through his back. "Come, we had best go down. I have indulged myself by remaining here. I have duties too."

* * *

As they made their way northward, down from the high ground through the ever-thickening forest, Anyara found herself watching the back of the female Inkallim walking in front of the horse. She had never dreamed that she would set eyes upon one of them. The Inkallim — warriors and acolytes, executioners and assassins — were the stuff of whispered childhood tales. Lack of sure knowledge about them had allowed such an accumulation of rumor and myth that they had become, in the minds of those living south of the Stone Vale, colossal, gore-drenched incarnations of death itself.

Anyara wondered how many this lean, wiry woman who marched before her had killed. Women did not take up arms amongst the Haig Bloods. Her father had once told her that necessity had made it commonplace throughout the Bloods of the Black Road, not just amongst the Inkallim: they needed every warrior they could find in the early years of their exile beyond the Vale of Stones, when there had been wild Tarbain tribesmen to subdue and pursuing armies of the Kilkry High Thane to repel. Whatever the reason, it was proof of the cruel demands the Black Road made of its followers.

They halted for a while and Anyara sat with her back against a tree. She and Inurian were kept apart. One of the Inkallim brought her some dry biscuits. He freed her hands so that she could eat. When he was gone she turned them this way and that, examining the raw weals about her wrists. They hurt, but it was nothing she could not bear.

She rested her head back against the tree trunk. Looking up through the naked branches, she watched the passage of heavy grey clouds across the sky. Rain was coming. The days after Winterbirth were often rain-soaked in the Glas valley. She was distracted from her thoughts by a dark flash of movement high in the tree beneath which she sat. She angled her head to try to catch its source. Almost hidden in the very crown of the tree, she saw a black bird hopping from one branch to another: a crow. She looked away, only for something to make her turn back. The crow sat there, patiently riding a branch's movements back and forth. It came to her, with absolute certainty, that this was Idrin, Inurian's crow. She opened her mouth, and closed it again, not knowing what to do. She looked for Inurian. He was sitting thirty or more paces away. He was watching her. She raised her eyebrows at him, wondering how to convey her news. She could not be sure, but she thought there was the faintest hint of a smile on his lips then and, so fast it could easily have been missed, a flicked wink of one eye as he turned away from her.

The hours flowed into one another. She lost her sense of direction. The stars were obscured at night and the sun hidden during the day by banks of cloud. She shivered, and ached, and slept poorly. Occasionally, Aeglyss would ride alongside her and watch her in provoking silence. She struggled to ignore him, and would not meet his strange, half-human eyes.

In those long, lonely hours on horseback, she found herself prey to bleak thoughts and imaginings that she could not fend off. Her father had laughed that night in the feasting hall, when the jugglers had played their part. He had been happy. She could see his face when she closed her eyes. She could see his slumped figure as well, propped limply against the castle wall. She had not seen Orisian's body in the courtyard; it could have been there, nevertheless.

Inurian was somewhere behind her on the trail, and a longing to be near him filled her. Orisian had always been closer to the *na'kyrim* than she had. Somehow the knowledge that Inurian, perhaps alone in all the world, could see into her heart and lay bare the pain and fears she held caged there had made her keep some distance between them. For all that, he had never been anything other than kind and now he was all she had left. He alone remained of all the people who had filled spaces in her life.

In the afternoon they unbound Anyara and Inurian and at last let them sit together while the horses were watered at a stream. She pressed her face into his shoulder. Still she would not cry, but the contact met a raw need in her. Inurian was massaging and probing at his right knee. He left off to put his arm around her shoulders.

"Be strong a while longer," he said.

"Yes. I know, I know."

"You noticed Idrin, then."

Anyara smiled at him. It was better not to talk about all the other things that teemed in her thoughts.

"Has he been following us all the way?" she asked.

"Oh, yes. He has always been stubborn. It is a trait of crows in general which he has refined to its purest form."

"When we were young, we used to tell each other that the Inkallim could turn themselves into crows," Anyara murmured.

"Perhaps you had heard people calling them ravens. An easy confusion for children. But no; the Whreinin and the Saolin were the only races made with the talent of shapechanging. The Anain have no true shape at all, and so cannot be counted."

"I half-thought the Inkallim were just a story anyway," Anyara said wearily.

"A pity they are not."

They were quiet for a little while after that. Anyara found other recollections of childhood fears drifting into her thoughts: the debris of long evenings she, Orisian and Fariel had spent trying to scare each other with whispered tales.

"Is Aeglyss like one of the *na'kyrim* in olden days?" she asked. "The ones that were so terrible?"

Inurian shook his head slowly.

"No, I don't think so. That was all a very long time ago, Anyara. There's no need to fear something so long gone. Aeglyss is strong, certainly: the Shared seethes around him. But I don't think he really knows how to use it. There are so few of us now, we've forgotten most of what the *na'kyrim* knew all those years ago. There've been no great masters of the Shared for a good three centuries, not since the years after the War of the Tainted. Anyway, the tales of them have probably been bloated by fear and by the passage of time."

"Well, I hope no more stories will be coming to life," Anyara said.

"I hope so too," replied Inurian. There was a distance and seriousness in his tone that made her want to shiver. He sensed it, and gave her a broad smile.

"Do not worry," he said. "No more stories."

Soon after, their captors came and dragged them once more to their feet.

A steady rain had been falling for the two hours since the Inkallim made camp. They were spread along the edge of a field of rough grass, with a scrawny copse of alder trees behind them. The few Kyrinin — ten or twelve — who had stayed with the party after they left the sheltering forests of Anlane had taken cover beneath the trees. A scattering of crows was huddled in the branches above, waiting for the rain to pass.

The Inkallim had set up makeshift awnings as soon as they came to a halt, hacking down thin saplings from the copse and spreading capes and canvas sheets between them. They were clustered beneath them now, talking softly, cleaning their weapons and chewing on biscuits and dried meat. They held little pots out to collect the rainwater, and drank from them. Their horses were tethered at the edge of the copse. Inurian and Anyara had been left, their hands and feet bound, to sit without protection upon the dank grass. Their hair and clothes soaked through, they watched the few cattle that were listlessly grazing out in the center of the field. Anduran was less than an hour's walk away. The rain-blurred shapes of the city's buildings were dimly visible to the north. There was no smoke there now; the fires must have been dampened down.

Aeglyss wandered across to them and squatted down, ignoring the rain. Inurian lowered his eyes and stared at the patch of ground between his feet.

"What's happening?" demanded Anyara. "Why have we stopped?"

"We are to be met by Kanin nan Horin-Gyre. It is an honor," smiled Aeglyss.

"The Horin-Gyre Bloodheir? They're the ones doing this? Well, he could just as easily have met us in Anduran, beneath a roof."

Aeglyss shrugged. "Who knows why the powerful do the things they do? I am told he wanted to meet us outside the town."

"He'll only kill us anyway," muttered Anyara. "Probably wants to do it out of sight."

"Oh, not you, my lady," Aeglyss assured her. "He was content to have some of your family taken alive. He can find a use for you, I am sure, or his sister will. If you want to fear someone, I would choose her."

He glanced at Inurian, who was pointedly ignoring the exchange.

"Your friend here may be another story, naturally. The Bloodheir may well prefer to see him dead. Unless I can dissuade him, of course."

With a show of boredom, Inurian looked up. "None of the Gyre Bloods are renowned for their clemency. I doubt such as you can sway him."

"Such as I? I brought the White Owl clan to his Blood's side. If the White Owl had taken up their spears against him instead of being his guides and feeding him, how could he have brought his army through Anlane? Without me, he would not now be camped at the gates of Castle Anduran. I think you will find that the Horin-Gyre Bloodheir remembers his friends."

"The White Owl will not thank you for what you have done," Inurian said.

"What do you care, Fox?" snapped Aeglyss. "They'll thank me well enough when the Lannis Blood is gone."

Inurian looked over toward the dour group of warriors gathered beneath the awnings.

"Better Lannis than the Inkallim and the Bloods of the Black Road. The White Owl will learn that soon enough." He turned back to Aeglyss. "Was your mother or your father of the White Owl?"

The younger man hesitated, taken unawares by the question. For a moment it seemed that he might not answer.

"My mother," he said. "And my father was of the Horin-Gyre Blood, so have a care what you say, old man."

Inurian regarded him for a moment. "You must have been born not long after the battle at Tanwrye thirty years ago," he said. "Your father escaped into Anlane after the Horin-Gyre army was defeated? He was taken by the White Owl?"

The blow came too quickly for Inurian to avoid it. Aeglyss struck him hard across the side of the face, knocking him to the ground. Anyara lunged at Aeglyss, but he pushed her away. Inurian lay there for a few seconds, then righted himself. Blood oozed from the corner of his mouth. It was washed away by the rain.

Aeglyss laid a single finger upon Inurian's chest. His eyes were brimming with cold anger. Anyara could see a muscle clenched so tight in his jaw it might have been a rod of iron laid over his bones. She had a terrible, momentary sense that the *na'kyrim* was about to burst and spill some awful, burning spirit of anger and hatred over them.

"Better not to speak of things you know nothing about," Aeglyss hissed, and rose to his feet. "Let's wait and see what Kanin wants to do with you," he called over his shoulder as he stalked back to join the Inkallim.

Anyara turned to Inurian, a look of concern on her face. Inurian spat inelegantly.

"I'm fine," he said. "His parentage would appear to be a sensitive subject." He leaned a little closer to Anyara. "Have a care of that one. Whatever happens to me, keep away from him. He may be more dangerous than I thought."

"He seems dangerous enough already," Anyara muttered.

Inurian shook his head. "It's mostly bluster. Beneath the surface, he's all bound up in a knot of anger and pain. He is poisoned by it. Nevertheless, there is more power in him than he knows. When he's angry like that, I can feel the Shared in him like a thundercloud. If he knew how to draw upon it, he would be capable of a great deal."

"In any case," said Anyara with forced lightness, "nothing's going to happen to you."

Inurian smiled at her. "Just remember. Stay away from him."

There was a sudden flurry of activity amongst the Inkallim. They were getting to their feet. Peering out through the grey rain, Inurian and Anyara could just make out a group of riders coming toward them across the farmland.

"It's Kanin," said Inurian. "The Bloodheir is coming."

The heir to the Thaneship of the Horin-Gyre Blood was a tall, strong man in his late twenties. His heavy black hair was matted down by the rain. It gave him a roguish, rather bedraggled look. Had Anyara not known who he was, she might have thought him handsome. Instead, she felt the stirring of hatred. Of all the Bloods of the Black Road, it was Horin-Gyre, with its strongholds at the northern end of the Vale of Stones, that had always posed the greatest threat.

A dozen warriors of his Shield had come with the Bloodheir.

Their mail hauberks rang softly as they dismounted. They tied their horses at the edge of the copse, ignoring the Kyrinin amongst the trees, and came back to stand in a loose group behind Kanin nan Horin-Gyre.

Aeglyss went to greet the Bloodheir. Kanin brushed past him without even meeting his gaze. He looked around, his sharp eyes running over the Inkallim who were coming one by one from beneath their shelters, the Kyrinin warriors now getting to their feet amongst the trees, and finally Inurian and Anyara, bound upon the wet grass. He smoothed his hair back from his face with a leather-gauntleted hand, watching the prisoners intently.

"Who is the halfbreed?" Kanin asked. His voice was strong, imbued with the instinctive authority that was his birthright.

"Kennet's counselor," said Aeglyss eagerly. "We thought he might be of some value."

Kanin walked toward Inurian and Anyara. His warriors followed. He knelt on one knee and took Inurian's chin in his hand, forcing his head around so that their eyes met.

"I have heard of you, I think. Inurian, is it?"

Inurian remained silent. Kanin released him and turned to Anyara.

"The Thane's niece, I presume," he said. There was a hint of suppressed mirth in his eyes and the set of his mouth. "A pretty prize."

Anyara scowled at him.

"But not in a pretty mood, it would appear," said Kanin as he rose to his feet. "You had better accustom yourself to new arrangements. This valley is returning to its rightful owners."

"You have tried that before, and failed," said Anyara tartly.

The Bloodheir laughed. It was a rich sound. "Not this time. This time the past will be buried."

He turned toward the Inkallim. "Kolglas?" he asked.

One of the warriors stepped forward, all languid precision and restrained power.

"Burned," he said.

"And Kennet and his son?"

"The Thane's brother is dead. The boy escaped across the water, but was wounded. He is probably dead by now."

A tiny moan escaped Anyara's lips. Kanin ignored her.

"Probably," he said, sarcasm tingeing his tone. "So a child has escaped the famed Battle Inkall. All the Lannis line was to be dead or taken. That was important."

The Inkallim's mouth tightened.

"We answer to Shraeve. She commands the Battle Inkall here, not you."

For a moment, the two men faced one another in the drizzle. Watching them, Anyara understood more clearly than before that the Inkallim were something more than just warriors. This man glaring at the son of the Horin-Gyre Thane did so with the silent will of an equal, drawing upon some strength, some core, that removed any need for deference.

Kanin relaxed and wiped his face. "Very well. You'll find Shraeve somewhere by the market square. You can tell your story to her. At least we have the Thane and his brood shut up in his castle." He shivered, then smiled at Anyara and Inurian. "This weather of yours is inhospitable. We had best get you to shelter in the city. I've picked out fine accommodation for you."

He turned on his heel and made to remount his horse. He stopped abruptly, as if remembering something inconsequential that had slipped his mind until this moment. He looked at Aeglyss.

"I do not want the White Owls to come any further, halfbreed. Tell them if they are seen any closer to the city than this, we will treat them as our enemies."

Aeglyss blinked, starting almost as if he had been struck.

"I thought . . ." he began.

Kanin raised his eyebrows in mock surprise. A flicker of contempt slipped into his voice as he spoke.

"You would not be so rash as to argue with me?" he asked. "The White Owls have what they wanted — the Lannis Blood broken — and we have no further need of them."

"Your father said . . ."

"Do not overplay your hand, halfbreed. My father lies in his sickbed in Hakkan, and I carry his authority here. This is Horin-Gyre land now, and I will not have wights wandering freely across it. You may enter Anduran if you wish, but not them."

"The White Owl will be . . . disappointed," said Aeglyss. "Others — some of their leaders — are not far behind us. They will wish to meet with you, to confirm the pledges made by your father. The settlements in Anlane are to be razed, a gift of cattle and iron made. I promised them these things on your behalf, as your father wished." Anyara noted a strange, soothing kind of resonance slipping into the *na'kyrim*'s voice.

Kanin's expression suddenly darkened and he took a resolute step closer to Aeglyss.

"If I thought, for even a moment, that you would seek to play games against me with your voice, halfbreed, I would split your skull. I know well enough what tricks you are capable of. You may have clouded the minds of the woodwights with your sweet tones, and since they have served my needs because of it, I'll not complain. But do not make the mistake of thinking you can attempt the same with me."

The rain was growing heavier. Kanin wiped the gathering drops from his brow and shook his head a little. He spared a glance for the Kyrinin watching them from amongst the trees.

"When you promised my father you could bring the wood-wights to our side, he made an agreement with you. Now it is over. I want nothing more to do with your savages and I will certainly not be summoned to meet with them. Look at them: forest folk dressed in animal skins. If they want cattle, have them take these." He gestured toward the animals grazing a short distance away. "If they want settlements razed, let them do it themselves, but I warn you, if they burn a single building within a day's march of Anduran, I will kill you and then hunt them down. If they are disappointed tell them to remember that we will be lords of Anduran soon. We make unforgiving enemies."

Aeglyss opened his mouth to speak, but Kanin was already swinging up into the saddle.

"I have more important matters than this to occupy my time. See that the woodwights do not follow us," he said to one of the shieldmen at his side, "and bring the girl and the other to me in Anduran."

With that, the Bloodheir spurred his horse violently, and it bounded forward across the field. Three of his band went after him. The others remained, staring at Aeglyss, who looked around hesitantly. The Inkallim were already bundling up their equipment. A few of the Horin-Gyre warriors rode over to Inurian and Anyara. The bonds around their ankles were cut and they were hauled onto horseback.

"Wait," cried Aeglyss after Kanin's disappearing form. "Give me Inurian, at least. You have no need of him." No one paid him any heed.

Anyara's last glimpse of the *na'kyrim,* as she was carried toward the rain-shrouded city in the distance, was of a lone, shrunken figure gazing after them. She wondered, now that he appeared so forlorn and impotent, how he had ever intimidated her. Behind the *na'kyrim* the White Owls were coming out from beneath the shelter of the trees, closing upon him.

A single black crow rose from amongst its fellows roosting in the copse and flapped lazily through the rain. With a few long sweeps of its wings it turned and followed toward Anduran.

The city was not as Anyara remembered it. Her Blood's proudest creation had been battered by a ferocious storm. Most of the farm buildings on the outskirts were intact, although they had an abandoned air and a feel of incipient decay. There were no people to be seen, no lights in the windows, no smoke rising from chimneys. It was a hollow landscape.

As they entered into Anduran itself the scent of wet, burned wood filled her nostrils. Gutted skeletons were all that remained of many houses. Rubble had collapsed across the roadway in places. The horses stepped over bodies not yet cleared away. A charred, black-crusted arm reached out toward Anyara from across a threshold. A single white sheet, stained by smoke, hung soddenly from an open window. A buzzard sat upon the remnants of roof timber, watching them go by with its head cocked on one side.

They wove their way through the streets, drawing ever closer to the square and to the castle beyond it. There were no more bodies. The dead had been gathered up from these streets. There were still dogs and crows, though, haunting the alleys. There were warriors too, picking their way through the ruins in small groups, gathering what little loot remained. Anyara caught sight of one group, clambering over the wreckage of a house like rats on a body, that differed from the others. They wore furs and hide breeches, and their matted hair was bound into braids with leather thongs. They stopped for a moment to watch the riders pass, then returned to their searching. When they called to each other it was in a harsh tongue that made Anyara think of dogs. They must be Tarbains, she thought: the wild tribesmen of the north who had been there long before the Black Road arrived. If Kanin had brought them south too, little in the Glas valley would escape despoliation.

The buildings that had once lined the southern side of the market square were gone, reduced to piles of blackened debris. One of the fires must have been started there. It had consumed even the bones of the merchants' houses, the shops, the warehouses. Beyond, the square itself was crowded. Ranks of horses were tied along one side, sullen guards watching them from beneath the shelter of overhanging roofs. A train of mules, weighed down with sacks of food and bundles of weapons, was crossing the open expanse. Some thirty caped spearmen escorted it. On the square's western side, a blacksmith's shop was a hive of activity, giving out the roar of fanned flames and the pounding of hammers.

The castle was visible over the rooftops to the north, half-shrouded by the curtains of rain. It was silent and still. Anyara had almost expected there to be a battle raging. Instead it was as if war itself had huddled down to wait for better weather.

Kanin nan Horin-Gyre had occupied the largest house left standing on the edge of the square, the home of a fur merchant who had left in such haste that a bale of fine marten fur still lay on the floor at the end of the dining table. Kanin was seated on it when Anyara and Inurian were brought before him. A handful of hard-faced warriors were lounging around the room, some perched upon the edges of the table, others leaning back in the expensive chairs.

There was a young woman there too, perhaps five years older than Anyara. She wore a light vest of delicately wrought chain metal. There was a golden chain about her neck, and thick, glittering rings upon her fingers. Her hair was long and blackly sleek, like strands of spun obsidian. When Anyara looked at her, she saw only a cold, dead arrogance and contempt.

"Welcome," smiled Kanin. "I have found a throne, as you see." He ran his hands through the dark fur beneath him. "Worth more than the one Croesan sits upon in his castle, I imagine. Had this been my house, I would not have left such booty behind."

"It is your house, now," the woman pointed out.

"Indeed. I suppose it must be." Kanin glanced at Anyara. "Forgive me. You have not been introduced. This is my sister, Wain. And Wain, this is Anyara, the daughter of the late lord of Kolglas."

Wain nan Horin-Gyre inclined her head in mock respect. She was turning one of her rings, round and round on her finger. "A pleasure," she said.

Anyara made no response, striving for an air of disdain despite being soaked to the skin and covered in scratches and dirt.

"Do not mind her rudeness, sister," said the Bloodheir, rising to his feet. "She has had a trying journey. I don't suppose Inkallim and woodwights make for the kind of traveling companions she is used to."

That sent a ripple of wry laughs running around the others in the room. Anyara felt hemmed in, beset by a pack of wolves too well-fed to kill her but too enamored of her suffering to let her go. Fear and anger vied for supremacy within her. Anger won.

"At least I had no choice in keeping their company," she snapped. "You have chosen ravens and woodwights as allies, and Tarbains too. Would none of the other Bloods come with you? Horin-Gyre has even fewer friends than I knew."

Kanin smiled at her. She saw his teeth. "We have those we need, it seems, to break you. And I've seen no men of Haig on the walls of Croesan's castle; no Kilkry horsemen in your valley. Where are your friends, my lady?"

"Coming," said Anyara.

"As are ours," said Wain with the kind of calm certainty Anyara wished she felt herself. "Gyre will be here before Haig. Do you think us fools, playing at children's games? We have watched you for a long time, child, while the Heart Fever ate up your people, while your warriors were called away by Gryvan oc Haig. We have watched and waited for the right time. This is that time."

"I do think you fools," Anyara shouted. "You'll die here. Whether you fear it or not, death . . ."

"Not before you," Wain interrupted her. "Or your father. Did he fear death?"

"Enough pleasantries," Kanin said. Anyara's outburst had not unsettled him in the least, although she thought there was an acid edge to Wain's glare. "I have little stomach for them at the best of times. Our guests had better be shown to their sleeping quarters. The town jail. I hope you will find it to your liking."

Guards moved to march the two prisoners out.

"A word to you before you go, halfbreed," said Kanin, raising an admonitory finger to Inurian, acknowledging his presence for the first time. "I imagine that you possess some of the little tricks of your kind, though I think Aeglyss once told me that yours is a paltry kind of talent. Still, we will keep guards out of your way, I think, and trust to bars and stone to hold you. Be assured that your young companion will be watched, though. She will die the instant there is any suggestion of trickery. If that happens your own death will be unpleasant. You may become a useful gift to someone one day, but do not make the mistake of thinking I value your life any more than that of a dog."

"Such a thought would never cross my mind," murmured Inurian.

"Excellent. Now I am afraid I must send you on your way. Should we meet again, perhaps some time in your uncle's prison cells will have blunted that tongue of yours, Anyara."

He gave an exaggerated bow in her direction. She took a step backward, shying away from the gesture, and cursed herself silently for the reaction. She caught a contemptuous curl at the corner of Wain nan Horin-Gyre's mouth as she was ushered out of the room.

Anduran's jail lay off the long, broad Street of Crafts that passed from the square through the town's northern quarter toward the castle. As she and Inurian were marched toward it, through rain that was now hard and sharp enough to sting her scalp, Anyara stepped over and around the flotsam left in the wake of the town's foundering. As well as the fragments of broken and burned homes, the road was littered with debris dropped by fleeing townsfolk or looting soldiers: here a child's straw dolly, there a single cloth glove, a matron's cap, a baby's shawl. All were sinking, or had been trodden, into rivulets and puddles of dirty water.

The enemy lurked in many of the buildings, sheltering from the rain. Grim, hostile faces regarded Anyara and Inurian from doorways. Once, from the upper floor of one of the houses, someone threw a half-eaten hunk of bread that bounced off Anyara's shoulder. She trudged on.

The jail had the look and feel of a fortress or barracks in miniature. Anyara and Inurian were led through the gate in the long outer wall. Within, two separate blocks of cells lay on either side. Tight, metal-barred windows fixed the newcomers with a gloomy gaze. Guardrooms and sleeping quarters were attached to each of the blocks, but the house of the head jailer stood alone. A group of Horin-Gyre warriors had gathered outside it. They were watching as the bodies of two young men were cut down from the makeshift gibbets that flanked the building.

It was a moment or two before Anyara realized that she and Inurian were being separated. Their captors were steering them apart, Anyara toward the cells on the right and Inurian to the left.

"Inurian," she called.

He was looking at her with something close to anguish upon his face.

"Be strong," he said. "It is not over yet."

Anyara managed a nod, and then someone was pushing her head down and forward as she was forced through a low doorway and swallowed whole by the gloom of her prison.

Later, cast down upon the hard floor of a narrow cell — the door slammed shut and barred, drops of rain splashing in through the tiny window high in the wall — and with no one there to see, she wept at last.

IV

Lheanor oc Kilkry-Haig had been arguing with the High Thane's Steward for some time. Lagair Haldyn dar Haig was not the worst Steward Lheanor had been forced to deal with in his time. Since he became Thane of his Blood, there had been three holders of that office, and by the end of his tenure the second — Pallick — had been almost impossible. Even Gryvan oc Haig had eventually accepted that the man's presence in Kolkyre served nobody and had sent him instead to Igryn oc Dargannan-Haig's court. It was without great surprise that Lheanor later heard that Pallick had been thrown into a jail cell by Igryn. He sometimes wondered if the man's appointment to the post of Steward in Dargannan lands had not been a deliberate ploy to provoke Igryn to rebellion. Gryvan oc Haig, or his Shadowhand, were certainly not above such manipulations, and although few men could singlehandedly cause a revolt through their obstinacy and arrogance, it was probably not beyond Pallick.

By comparison, Lagair's failings were limited to indolence and an all-encompassing indifference to the concerns of others. It made arguing with him a thankless task. Lheanor was an old man, and he found the effort wearying. He was thankful that his son, the Bloodheir Gerain, was here with him, to share the burden.

"I am not disputing your right to act," the Steward was saying. For some reason he was not looking at the Thane, or at Gerain, but staring vacantly at the fire burning in the grate. "I merely insist that you refrain from marching your entire army into the Glas valley until we first have a better idea of what exactly is happening there and second, have word from Vaymouth regarding the High Thane's intent."

"We already have riders on their way to find out what is happening," replied the Bloodheir levelly, "but whatever the details, you cannot deny the need to act. You have seen the same messages we have: more than a hundred people from Kolglas and the villages around there have already crossed our borders. Others are on their way. Kolglas itself has been attacked, the castle and half the town burned, and Kennet nan Lannis-Haig has been killed. White Owl Kyrinin are looting farms, and Inkallim are loose in Anlane. Inkallim, Steward! If the ravens of the Black Road are fighting pitched battles as far south as Kolglas, how can you doubt that disaster threatens?"

Lagair scratched at the side of his nose, frowning with concentration.

"If there is one thing I have learned in all my years," the Steward said — and Lheanor groaned inwardly at this repetition of a phrase Lagair used with self-important frequency — "it is that the obvious conclusions are not always proved correct by subsequent events. I mean, think on it for a moment. Kolglas has been raided, not captured. The entire Battle Inkall numbers no more than a few thousand, to the best of our knowledge, so they can hardly be planning to march all the way to Kolkyre on their own. No, this looks more like a piece of clever hubris, to me. A few Inkallim have somehow managed to sneak to Kolglas, kill the Thane's brother and have now snuck off back to Kan Dredar or wherever they call home. At the same time they've managed to stir up the woodwights, which I freely admit is surprising but hardly a disaster."

Gerain was hiding it well, but Lheanor could see that his son was only a few minutes away from losing his temper. The Blood-heir had a generally equable temperament — certainly in comparison to his brother Roaric — but was quite capable of the occasional ill-judged outburst. There had probably been enough talking in any case.

"Well, we shall know the truth of all this before too long," Lheanor said quietly.

The Steward glanced up and gave the Thane a vacant, pointless smile.

"Our finest scouts are on the road even now, and we'll have their reports within a day or so," Lheanor continued.

"Yes, lord," agreed Lagair. "Quite true. A day or two's patience will cost us little."

"There's a difference between patience and inactivity," Lheanor said. "Whatever the uncertainties, I am entitled to do as I see fit to protect my own borders, and to see to the safety of the Lannis Blood as well. You would not expect me to stand by while another of the True Bloods faces . . . well, whatever they are facing."

Lagair looked doubtful but held his tongue.

"I will look forward to hearing the High Thane's opinions on the matter — no doubt you already have detailed reports on their way to Vaymouth — but in the meantime, I shall take such action as seems to me wise and prudent. I can assure you," Lheanor said with studied clarity, "that I will not go so far as to march my entire army into the Glas valley. You've made it clear you, and therefore Gryvan oc Haig, would disapprove of such a step, and as it would in any case be the act of an idiot, I am happy to promise to refrain from it."

"Yes, very good," said Lagair. His expression suggested he put little value on Lheanor's promise.

"Of course," the Kilkry Thane said, "if, once we know what is actually happening, it no longer seems idiotic, then I will march my entire army wherever I wish. Since it is, after all, mine. That part of it which the High Thane has left me with, at least."

After the Steward had gone, Lheanor took a private meal with his son and his wife, Ilessa. They were all subdued and their mood communicated itself to the servants, who stepped lightly around the table and took care to stay out of sight until they were needed.

There were close ties of friendship and history between the Kilkry and Lannis Bloods. Kennet nan Lannis-Haig had been a frequent, and well-liked, visitor to Kolkyre before the Heart Fever. Lheanor had never known him as well as he knew Croesan, but had believed him to be a good and reliable man. It meant nothing to Lagair Haldyn — and nor would it to the High Thane the Steward served — but for Lheanor and his family, Kennet's death was cause for great sorrow. All the more so if it was truly the work of the hated Bloods of the Black Road.

Gerain was uninterested in his food. He took only a few desultory mouthfuls.

"Will you let me go?" he asked.

Ilessa looked up from her platter to her son, but his gaze was fixed upon Lheanor. For a moment or two, the Thane seemed not to have heard the question. He prodded at the meat in front of him, his brow furrowed.

"How many men do you want to take?" the Thane asked at length.

"Only two or three hundred," Gerain replied at once. He sounded eager, though he was trying hard to maintain a level tone. "My own men: none from the border watches or the castles. Just my own company."

Lheanor sighed and gestured for one of the attendants to remove the unfinished meal before him. He poured himself some wine. A little of it spilled, his hands made slightly unsteady by age.

"Still no word from Roaric," he murmured. "We've heard nothing from him for . . . what? Two weeks?"

"Three," Ilessa said quietly.

"We cannot just sit and wait, no matter how much the Steward may complain," Gerain said. "You told him as much yourself, Father. Out of all the Bloods, Lannis is the only one we can truly call our friends."

"You think I don't know that?" The Thane could not keep irritation out of his voice, but his expression showed that he immediately regretted it. He half-raised a placatory hand. "What times we live in. Both my sons must go into harm's way? You'll allow me to regret that."

"They are their father's sons," said Ilessa. "That is why they do as they do. When you were Gerain's age you would have been the first to ride out."

The Thane returned her gentle smile. They had married young, Lheanor and Ilessa, too young almost to understand what they were doing. Neither had ever suffered even a moment's regret. They had grown old together as willingly as any two people ever had.

"I remember well enough," Lheanor said. His blood had sometimes run hot when he was young. When he was Bloodheir he had been at least as eager, as fired by passion, as Gerain. Looking back from the lofty vantage point of his now advanced years he could not remember when caution — something that could almost be called fear, even — had started to erode that youthful vigor. Perhaps it had been the moment he became Thane.

"I'd not seek strife, but if it comes looking for us we cannot turn away from it," said Gerain. "Let me go. Perhaps Croesan does not need our aid. Perhaps all I can do is tell him we share his sorrow at Kennet's death. But if he does need our aid — our spears — it would shame us to wait for Gryvan oc Haig's permission before giving it."

"You'd find no one in all our lands, except Gryvan's own Steward, to disagree with that. It does not change the fact that he is High Thane. We must tread with care, that is all. I will tread carefully around Gryvan and his Steward; you take your men to Kolglas, and you tread carefully there. I want both of my sons alive to celebrate next Winterbirth here with your family."

V

Orisian struggled up from unconsciousness as if waking from a viscous sleep. He was being carried through the forest on some kind of stretcher. He thought hazily about moving but his body was unresponsive. His gaze jolted in time with the stride of whoever was carrying him. The peeling trunks of birch trees loomed one after another across his vision and passed away. He saw a carpet of rough grass, dark green moss and fallen leaves. Out of the corner of his eye he caught the fleeting image of tall, pale figures walking. There was no sound. It was like a dream. He felt dull, throbbing pain in his side. He could not imagine why it should be there, but it mounted to a stabbing fire that surged and retreated in a remorseless rhythm. He slipped away again into a dark place.

Later he opened his eyes but still could not shed the stupor that clung to him. Voices had roused him. He saw, and heard without understanding. There were sounds, in turn like the chattering of squirrels, the croaking of crows or the movement of leaves in the breeze. He was being carried past strange bulbous tents. He saw a woman crouched in a doorway, her face with its delicate, impassive features trying to tell him something he did not understand. An animal hide was stretched upon a wooden frame. He smelled woodsmoke. Children flurried by. Like something out of nightmare or hallucination, there was a great face woven of boughs and twigs that leered at him. There was a pole thrust into the earth, with deer skulls fastened to it one above the other. They watched him with their dead sockets as he went past and his own eyes faltered and closed beneath their mournful gaze.

When he saw again, there was a face close to his: dusk-grey eyes looking into his own; fragile skin so close he could have laid his lips upon it. He felt the warmth of someone's breath upon his cheeks and brow. He was inside, beneath a curving roof of deerskin. Somewhere very far away he thought he heard a voice he knew shouting his name. It fell silent and as he was laid down upon the ground he lost consciousness once more.

He returned, at first, without knowing who he was. He blinked and turned a little toward the faint light. The movement was enough to trigger pain in his side. He grimaced at it, wondering why he should feel such a thing. The pain eased into an ache and he lay still for a time. His memories came slowly back, but they were unreal and he could not sort truth from dream, or nightmare.

He was looking up at the roof of a strange tent: a broad sweep of animal hide on a framework of poles. Furs were lying over him, filling his nostrils with a musky scent. Once more, he tried to turn his head to look toward the light that was filtering in from somewhere to his left. He was braced for the pain; still when it came it brought a gasp out of him. He lifted his lead-heavy hand and put it to his side. There was some kind of dressing there, warm and moist against his skin. He was taken by a fit of coughing that filled his chest with fire and sent blurring flickers of light across his vision. He watched them dancing inside his eyelids as dizziness swept through him.

Then there was someone inside the tent with him, laying a cool palm upon his forehead and lifting the furs to look at his bandaged flank. He looked into a face from his dreams: a beautiful, pale-skinned face, framed by yellow-white hair, from which clear grey eyes regarded him. The hand upon his brow was withdrawn, and he glimpsed spidery fingers tipped by long, white nails. The thin lips moved.

"Be still," came a voice that was as light and floating in Orisian's ears as a breath of summer wind.

Kyrinin, some small, clear part of his mind murmured to him. The thought drifted away, unable to find any purchase upon him.

"Rest," he heard her say, and he did.

Fariel was there, in a half-waking, half-sleeping place. His dead brother stooped in the doorway of the tent. He was a handsome, almost beautiful, young man now. He held his long hair back from his eyes as he leaned forward.

"Walk with me," he said, and Orisian rose and followed his brother out into the evening.

The forest was bathed in low sunlight, the trees throwing sharp shadows across the grass. Butterflies flitted from light to shade and back to light again. His brother waited for him, holding out a hand.

"Let's go down to the sea," he said, and Orisian nodded. The trees stood far apart, and they made their way down toward the waves. The water was shining. The two of them stood side by side and looked out to the west. The great globe of the sun was just touching its rim to the horizon. A warm breeze was blowing in.

"It's beautiful," said Orisian, and Fariel smiled.

"Very," he said.

"You've been gone a long time," Orisian said.

His brother picked up a stone and threw it far, far out. He wiped his hand on his tunic.

"Not so long, and not so far away."

"No, I never thought you were very far away," Orisian said.

They started to walk along the shore. Birds above them called with voices almost human, mixing alarm and loss.

"I'd like you to come back," said Orisian.

"I can't. I'm sorry," said Fariel without looking at his brother.

"Are you alone? Is . . ." Orisian's voice faded away.

Fariel laughed gently. "Yes, she's with me. And Father."

That brought Orisian to a standstill. He stared at the back of Fariel's head as his older brother walked on a few steps before stopping and turning. Orisian felt a sickness stirring in the pit of his stomach. Gulls were screeching in the air, the sound of screams. The sun was sickening and taking on a red hue.

"Father?" he echoed. Dark shapes were at the corner of his eyes, dancing, taunting.

Fariel pointed out to sea and there, impossibly close, was Castle Kolglas. It was a burned-out shell with smoke still rising from its broken windows, sections of its walls cast down and crumbling, its gates torn asunder and lying like flotsam at the water's edge. As Orisian watched, a great block of stone toppled from the battlements, crashed onto the rocks below and splashed into the sea. He reached out with his arms, as if he could touch the shattered castle. He felt dizzy. Deep inside his head, he saw his father, blood trickling from the side of his mouth, the hilt of a massive knife protruding from his chest. He gagged.

"You'd forgotten," said Fariel.

Orisian bowed his head. "What should I do?"

"I can't say," replied his brother. "No one can tell you that anymore. You'll have to decide for yourself."

Orisian looked up. Fariel shook his head sadly. He seemed to be further away, out over the water. Orisian could not make out his features anymore.

"Wait," cried Orisian, rising to his feet, "don't go."

Fariel said something, but Orisian could barely hear him now.

"Where's Anyara?" shouted Orisian.

His brother faded into the bright demi-circle of the setting sun.

"Don't leave me," Orisian said.

He felt himself falling backward, slumping down toward the earth. He fell into something soft and sank into it.

"Don't leave me," he whispered once, and then all was dark.

When he woke it was with the feel of the faintest touch upon his face. As his eyes focused, he found his gaze returned by the young Kyrinin woman looking down at him. She smelled of the forest, of warmth. Soft fine strands of her hair were brushing his cheek. He moved his lips soundlessly.

"Be at ease," she said in her wondrous voice as she straightened up. "The worst is past."

"The worst," he repeated.

"You saw death and came back."

The dull pain in his flank registered upon his still-cloudy thoughts then, as if to confirm the truth of her words. He stirred, trying to ease aside the furs that lay over him. She laid a restraining hand on his, gentle but firm. Her clear eyes fixed him with a constant stare. There was no imperfection in them, he saw, no flaw in the pure field that surrounded her tiny pupils like a ring of polished flint. Inurian's eyes had not been so perfect. They had had a touch of the human in them. Many things came back to Orisian then, too many to gather and shape. There was a flicker of panic in his breast as if a slumbering bird had woken.

"Where's Rothe?" he asked.

"Rothe?"

"My shieldman. He was with me when . . . he put me in the boat."

"The big man. He is here. He lives."

She was examining the features of his face. He felt uncomfortable, sensing the touch of her gaze.

"Where is he?" he asked.

"Here," she repeated.

"I want to see him."

She rose, towering above him. "Wait. I will ask."

Orisian slid a hand across his stomach. It felt empty, partly from hunger, partly from the bitter, violent memories that were grasping at his thoughts. One took his attention for a moment.

"Fariel," he breathed.

She turned, almost out of the tent. She looked back at him.

"I did not hear," she said.

"I dreamed of Fariel," he murmured.

"Your brother," she said.

Orisian made to ask how she knew his brother's name, but the flap of deerskin was already settling back into place behind her.

Rothe came, and Orisian had to hide the surprise that surged up within him. His shieldman looked different. Some of the bulk had gone from his frame; his face was thinner; his eyes, in the instant before they lit up at the sight of Orisian, were burdened. Orisian caught sight of tall figures outside as Rothe entered. They did not follow him in.

Rothe laid a broad hand upon Orisian's shoulder.

"It is good to see you again," the older man said softly. "I feared . . ."

Orisian struggled to sit up, but Rothe pressed him down.

"Lie still," he said. "Don't tire yourself."

"I'm all right," said Orisian.

"Perhaps, perhaps. Still, it was a bad wound you took, and it would be better not to test it yet. Who knows what harm the wights' meddling might have done?"

Orisian fingered the bandaging around his chest. "They put this poultice on me," he said.

"Best not to wonder what may be in it, then," grimaced Rothe.

"How long has it been?"

"Seven days, Orisian."

"Seven days! I thought two or three, perhaps. I can hardly remember any of it."

"Seven. And moving much of the time. We only arrived here three days ago. They would not tell me what was happening, all the while. Not once have they let me see you. And they took my sword away, my sword I've had for half my life."

Orisian noticed for the first time that there were bruises, almost faded now, upon Rothe's cheek and brow, and a thin red line where some wound across the bridge of his nose had started to heal. He could guess how hard the man had tried to come to his side.

"Well," he said, "at least we are together again now."

"Together as prisoners in a woodwight camp. I tried to get us to Glasbridge, I truly did, but I've no skill with boats and the currents were too strong. They carried us to the Car Anagais. The wights took us almost the moment we landed." A pained expression passed across the shieldman's face. "Forgive me, Orisian, for bringing you away against your will. I had no choice. I could not let you go to your father."

"You're my shieldman, and you saved my life. Should I forgive you that? I was . . . well, let's leave it. Do you know where we are now?"

"Hard to say. There was no break in the forest all the way we walked. I would say somewhere in the Car Anagais still. Perhaps the southern slopes of the Car Criagar, but I don't think we covered that much ground."

Orisian thought on that for a few moments. "What are we going to do?" he wondered.

"Wait until you are a little more healed. Hope these creatures do not take it into their heads to kill us before we have a chance to escape."

"These must be the Fox clan, though," said Orisian. "They would have no real reason to harm us. They're not like the White Owls . . ."

"The thoughts of a woodwight are no more human than his eyes. Never trust them, Orisian. We must guard one another here."

Orisian wanted to say that it would be all right, that this was the clan of Inurian's father, but he knew it would make no difference to Rothe. The shieldman had been a fighter in the service of the Lannis Blood all his life, and throughout that time there had been two constant stars to steer by: the threat of the Gyre Bloods in the north, and that of the Kyrinin who filled the forests around the valley. Even Orisian, knowing that Fox and White Owl were not one and the same, could not keep the tales of massacred woodsmen and of families burned in forest huts wholly from his mind.

The Kyrinin woman came back then. Tension snapped into Rothe's eyes and arms at the sound of her entry, though he did not turn round.

"Enough talk," she said. "Both come out."

"He should rest," said Rothe, still refusing to look at the woman.

To Orisian's surprise, she laughed: a rich, musical laugh like none he had heard before save perhaps, in a way, from Inurian. Rothe was scowling.

"Enough rest," she said. "He is well."

As she came forward to help Orisian rise, Rothe interposed himself. He wrapped a powerful arm around Orisian and eased him up and out of the bed. The woman held out a cape of thick dark fur. Rothe snatched the cape and laid it around Orisian's shoulders.

"Are you strong enough?" he asked.

Orisian thought about it. Although he felt weak and rather frail, there was not so much pain and his body seemed to agree with the Kyrinin woman that he had rested enough. His muscles were stale and ready to stretch themselves.

"Yes," he said.

Still resting much of his weight on Rothe's encircling arm, Orisian followed the woman out into daylight. His eyes had forgotten its feel and he had to squint against the glare, but the instant touch of a breeze upon his face and of the cold air upon his skin was like diving into a cool pool on a hot day. It woke him. He blinked and inhaled deeply, shaking his head a little. The woman was watching him with an amused smile upon her lips.

The sunlight was coming in low and clear from the west. A dog bounded past, yelping as it crossed from light to shade and back again. A small gang of children were in close pursuit, laughing and shouting. When they caught sight of Orisian and Rothe standing outside the tent, they stumbled to a halt and stood in a tight knot, staring at them. Orisian's eyes followed the dog as it ran on and vanished between some huts.

He was in a great camp of the Fox Kyrinin. Domed tents made of hides and skins dotted the forest floor, spreading as far as he could see amidst the trees. Kyrinin were moving amongst them. There were dogs, and a few goats wandered through the camp idly picking at grass or bushes. It was a bright, brisk winter's day, and the scene had a peaceful feel to it.

Then he saw the object standing not far from the hut he had rested in. It was shaped of intertwined twigs and grasses supported on a frame of poles: an intricate weaving which suggested, rather than portrayed, the image of a face. He remembered it from his ill dreams.

"What is that?" he asked.

The woman followed his gaze, but did not respond.

Kyrinin were gathering now. They drifted up as if in answer to some silent summons to stand in a wide semi-circle, watching Orisian and Rothe. Many of them carried spears. Rothe shifted uneasily. The woman said something in her own tongue, and there were a few slight nods amongst the crowd. The children's view of the strange visitors to their camp had been obscured by the arriving adults and they slipped through the forest of legs to the front once more.

"Hungry?" asked the woman.

Orisian nodded. The crowd parted without a sound. As they passed through the ranks of Kyrinin, Orisian felt unease filling him, as if it had leapt the gap from Rothe's body to his own. Intense grey eyes were fixed upon him. These people, so close he could touch one simply by reaching out, were not as he had imagined they would be. He had thought, when he pictured them in his daydreams, that they would be delicate, almost frail. For all the grace in their lean frames, there was a muscular strength and confidence too. Even their silence was more presence than absence. He was glad of Rothe's arm about him, which seemed then as much protection as support.

Beyond the ring of Kyrinin, the woman brought them to a small fire. A girl was turning a hare on a spit. Fat fell into the flames, hissing and snapping. The girl danced away as they approached.

"Eat," said the woman.

Orisian lowered himself to the ground and sat cross-legged. The scent of the meat woke a ravenous hunger in him. Rothe lifted the hare from over the fire and laid it on a stone. They picked scraps of meat from its carcass. Orisian could hardly eat fast enough to meet the need within him. Food had seldom tasted so sweet, and with the warm cloak about him and the air so sharp and fresh he felt, for the first time since he had woken, something like himself. Only when the hare had been reduced to a pile of greasy bones did he pause. He tried to wipe away the juices from around his mouth. They clung to him.

He looked up at the woman standing to one side.

"How do you know my brother was called Fariel?" he asked.

There was no reaction in the Kyrinin's expression. "Inurian spoke of him," she said, then turned away.

"You know Inurian?" he called after her.

She went to the watching crowd and began speaking to some of them. A skinny dog came and made a grab for one of the bones. Rothe waved it away. It growled balefully at him before sitting down just out of reach and fixing the remains of the meal with an obsessive stare. Orisian looked into the center of the fire. He had asked Inurian to let him come on his journeys into these hills many times. And now here he was, amongst the people the *na'kyrim* had known and visited. He had strayed, through a nightmare, into the secret part of Inurian's life he had always been so curious about, and Inurian was not here with him. Nothing was as he had hoped it would be.

"She's coming back," muttered Rothe.

"You must go in again," the woman said.

Rothe and Orisian were parted. The enforced separation brought a thunderous rage to Rothe's face.

"It's all right," Orisian called after his shieldman, though he was not certain of the truth of that. To his surprise, the woman followed him into the tent, and watched as he lowered himself onto the sleeping mat once more. She squatted at his side.

"Do you know Inurian well?" he asked her.

"You must speak with In'hynyr tomorrow," she said.

Orisian looked blank.

"The *vo'an'tyr.* The . . ." She grimaced, apparently frustrated in her search for the right words. "She is the will of the *vo'an.*"

"I see," said Orisian dully.

"Some wish to send you to the willow."

"What does that mean?"

"To take your lives."

"Why?" asked Orisian.

"You are Huanin. Perhaps not friends to the Fox. Some say you should not be here."

"But we were brought here," protested Orisian. "We did not choose to come."

"You would be dead if I did not bring you. The needed medicine was here."

Orisian pressed his hands into his eyes. Perhaps Rothe had been right. There was nothing but danger here. The woodwights were savages after all, their thoughts twisted in strange patterns.

"The *vo'an'tyr* will send for you." She rose and made to leave the tent.

"Wait," he said. "Will you be there tomorrow?"

The woman shook her head.

"Will they speak my tongue?" asked Orisian.

"In'hynyr has often wintered at Koldihrve."

For a moment Orisian was puzzled, then he understood. Koldihrve: the settlement of masterless men at the mouth of the Dihrve River beyond the Car Criagar. It had the reputation of being a wild, dangerous town, all the more so because the Fox Kyrinin had a winter camp on its edge. It was the one place Orisian had heard of where Huanin and Kyrinin still lived side by side.

"That is where you learned it as well?" he asked.

"Enough questions." She made for the doorway.

"What is your name, at least?" Orisian said.

"Ess'yr," she said.

With that she was gone and Orisian was left alone. After a time — a dead space in which thoughts ran unhindered and chaotic around his head — for no one reason that he could name, but for all of them, he found there were tears in his eyes.

They came for him early in the morning. He had been awake a little while. The sound of dogs barking outside had woken him before dawn, and dark thoughts had kept him from sleep once roused. When the Kyrinin entered the tent he was examining his wound, having peeled away the dressing. There was an angry red weal, but it seemed to be healing. He had no time to replace the poultice. Silent Kyrinin warriors led him out of the tent.

A wetting drizzle was falling, as much a heavy mist as rain.

Beneath its veil, the *vo'an* was a silent, muffled place of indistinct shapes. They crossed through a part of the camp he had not seen before, rising up a slope to a grove of trees where one shelter stood apart from the others. There was a patch of bare earth before it, into which tall poles were driven. One had a column of deer skulls attached to it, another the pelts of beavers, a third was twined around with boughs of holly. They sent him inside alone.

The air within had a cloying, herbal intensity that was almost tangible, as if someone had pressed a cloth dripping with scent across his nose and mouth. He wrestled with a sudden wave of nausea. A bright fire burned in the center of the tent, and a crowd of Kyrinin were seated around it. As he stepped in, all turned to look at him. One of the women rose and reached for him. He shrank away from the touch. She grasped his shoulder and pressed him down. He sank to the ground. The oppressiveness of the air seemed a little less, and his head ceased to spin. The woman put a small wooden bowl into his hands.

"Drink," she said.

He lifted the bowl to his lips, and winced as he tasted the hot, bitter liquid it contained. He did not dare to put it aside, since he had no idea what had significance here and what did not. Somewhere inside him, not as far beneath the surface as he would have wished, there was a small boy shivering with fear and loneliness. He knew a time had now come, perhaps the first time, when he could not allow that boy to be a part of his thoughts. He rested the bowl on his knees and looked around with what he hoped would pass for composure.

There were perhaps twenty Kyrinin crammed into the tent, facing and flanking him in tight ranks. Here and there, on the faces of both men and women, he could make out the fine, curling facial tattoos that he thought were supposed to mark out warriors or leaders. In the War of the Tainted, he had heard, the Kings' warriors had cut the skin bearing such brands from the faces of dead Kyrinin, to prove what dangerous enemies they had slain.

Opposite him, across the shimmering flames, was a small woman, older than most of the others. She was wrapped in a cloak of some roughly woven material decorated with black and blue swirls. There were bold streaks of red slashed through the silvery hair that fell across her shoulders. Her features were sharp but there was a furrowing in the skin at the corner of her eyes and mouth that betrayed the passage of years. Her flat grey eyes were fixed upon Orisian.

"I am In'hynyr. I am the *vo'an'tyr*," she said, her voice a light, reedy sound that had a thread of iron within it.

Orisian nodded. The liquid he had swallowed had left a burning track down his throat and into his chest.

"We will talk," said In'hynyr.

"As you wish," replied Orisian faintly. He was at a loss to know what else to say, or whether he should be saying anything at all.

"There are five *vo'ans* of the Fox clan this season," In'hynyr said, "which is a good number. This place we are in now is a good one. The Sun-facing slope with rich forests. There is food to be gathered here. The forest is generous. This season is the first we have had a *vo'an* here since my first child was carried on my back. She has many children of her own now. It has been a long wait for the Fox to return. When there was a *vo'an* in this place before, Huanin from the valley saw our fires and came to seek us out. We led them over rough ground and steep valleys. We traded killings with them and they went away. You are from the valley, thicklegs and heavyfoot?"

"I . . . I am from Kolglas," stammered Orisian, caught unawares by the sudden question. In'hynyr's voice had a rhythmic, lulling quality to it that distracted him from the meaning of the words being spoken.

"Why have you come to this *vo'an*?" asked In'hynyr.

"I was wounded. I was brought here. Ess'yr said . . ." Orisian replied. He tried to continue, but In'hynyr gave a sharp sniff and spoke over him.

"It was known in the Fox clan that there would be war in the valley this season. Our spear *a'ans* in the summer returned from the lands of the enemy with word of a Huanin army. They said the White Owl, who are carrion-eaters, would make war upon the people of the valley alongside this army. The White Owl, who have no memory, make themselves the servants of the Huanin. That is good. They shall suffer for it. It is good, too, that there is war in the valley. If there is war in the valley, we shall be left in peace. So we returned to this *vo'an* after many years."

Orisian was struggling to follow all that was being said. If the White Owls had given aid to the Inkallim, it might explain how they had reached Kolglas. With Kyrinin guides they might have come undetected through Anlane. Yet it seemed an impossible alliance. The White Owls were no friends of humans, and the Bloods of the Black Road certainly none of Kyrinin.

"This is a good *vo'an*," In'hynyr was continuing. "We shall come back here next season if all is well. The *a'an* of Yr'vyrain found you and the big man by the water. Ess'yr of that *a'an* wished to make you well, and brought you here. We gave leave for that, for death had your scent. You are made well now.

"It is a grave matter that you and the big man have come here. When the clans were younger, when the City shone like the sun, one of the Huanin came into a *vo'an* of the Fox, by an ice-free stream in a valley of oaks. He was lost. He was given food and shelter. But he was foolish, and spoke of foolish things like a child who knows not how to be still. After a time the people told him to go. And because the Huanin heart is hot and their thoughts are like fire, he was angry. He took earth in his hand and cast it upon the *torkyr* and cursed the Fox. For this, he was taken and sent to the willow. This did not heal the wound. Many of the people in the *vo'an* sickened and died in the next summer. The flames from the *torkyr* they carried with them were made unclean by his anger."

"You want to kill me because of something that happened hundreds of years ago?" asked Orisian, striving to keep the tension that was knotting his stomach out of his voice.

"This man was sent to the willow a thousand and a half years gone," In'hynyr corrected him. "When the wolfenkind still cast a shadow in the world. When the Fox lived nearer the sun, in kinder lands. But his name is not forgotten. I know the names of the people who died of sickness in the summer that came after. They are not forgotten. We sing for them still. We do not forget. Do you? Do the Huanin forget the past?"

"No, we don't forget, but . . . I am not the same as that man. His mistake . . . his foolishness . . . is not mine." Orisian felt lost. A decision was being forged out of arguments he did not fully understand. He felt powerless. The thought went through his mind that Fariel would have known what to say, what to do. And Inurian would have. He was uncomfortably hot. The walls of the tent pressed in upon him.

"We know that there can be good as well as evil in the Huanin," In'hynyr said. "At the place you call Koldihrve there is peace between Huanin and Kyrinin. There can be good in the people of the valley, too. Two summers gone, a youth from the *a'an* of Taynan was hunting. He was foolish, and a boar wounded him. A man from the valley found him and cared for him. He made him well, and the youth returned to his *a'an.* By this we know that there is good in the people of the valley. Do you have this good in you?"

"I would help someone if they were hurt," said Orisian. "As Ess'yr has tried to help me. Not all Huanin think ill of the Kyrinin, just as not all Kyrinin think ill of us. I wish the Fox no harm."

"You do not wish the Fox any harm," said In'hynyr, as if testing the truth of the words by their taste. She paused, and an intense silence descended. Orisian glanced from face to face. Blank eyes met his. There was no connection to be made with these people; they regarded him with the detachment of a slaughterman picking a sheep for the knife.

"Ess'yr tells us that you are high amongst your people. You are one of the rulers," said In'hynyr.

"No," said Orisian, "not really. My uncle is the Thane. Inurian is my friend . . ."

Again, the curt sniff. He wondered if In'hynyr was displeased. He had thought Inurian's name might buy him some friendship here. It did not appear to work. He cast about for something else that might serve better. It might not be true, he thought, that Fariel would have known what to say. He had not talked to Inurian about the Kyrinin, as Orisian had often done; he had never imagined visiting a Fox camp, would never have even thought such a thing to be possible. He would not have seen any difference between Fox and White Owl.

"My family is no enemy of the Fox," he said. "And we are no friends of the White Owls."

"The man in the castle in the valley fights the White Owl. That is good. Have you also made war on the enemy in Anlane?"

"I have not fought them myself, if that is what you mean. War-riors from my home have, when they raided against our people in the forest. Rothe, the man who is with me, he has fought them. He is an enemy of the White Owl."

Orisian was starting to feel sick again, from the heat, the heady smell inside the tent, the weariness he could feel in his bones.

"All hands are against the Fox," said In'hynyr. "We are a small clan. Eighty *a'ans*. The White Owl, who swarm like bees, are five times as many. Your kind fill the valley like mice in the grass. We are a small clan, but we hold against our enemies. To hold, our sight must be clear like the fox, and our thoughts sharp. Ess'yr felt duty to you, and we allowed her wish to aid you. Our duty is to the *vo'an*. Is the *vo'an* safe?"

"I wish only to return to my own people. I will not tell anyone where the *vo'an* is. Neither will Rothe, if I tell him not to. We just want to go back."

He could speak no more. There was a throbbing behind his eyes. Everything he had ever heard about the Kyrinin, every tale of butchery, was milling about in his head demanding attention:

children killed in their beds in farmhouses; the torture of warriors captured in forest skirmishes. Yet still he clung to the notion that tales were only tales, and they were not about him, here, now. He could not believe that he had escaped the horrors of Winterbirth only to be condemned to death by this small old woman with red in her silver hair.

"Drink," said In'hynyr. For a moment Orisian looked at her, not understanding, then he recalled the small wooden bowl still resting on his knees. Hesitantly, remembering the drink's astringent taste, he raised it to his lips and sipped. The liquid had cooled a fraction and though it still tasted harsh it did not burn so fiercely. His head cleared a little. The oppressive heat seemed to lift itself from his face.

"What is your promise worth?" In'hynyr asked him.

Orisian paused, searching for some form of words that might make the connection he needed with this woman.

"It puts a duty on me," he said. "As you bear a duty to the *vo'an,* as you say Ess'yr felt some duty to me. My promise is a duty I owe to myself, and to you."

"Where will you go?"

"Go? I . . ." He hesitated. Where would he go? His father was gone, perhaps Anyara and Inurian as well. And Kolglas was far away, if Rothe was right about how far they had traveled. "I would go to Anduran first," he said. "To my uncle, the Thane. If what you say is true, my people must make war against the Black Road and the White Owls. I must be a part of that."

Somewhere within the tent, hidden amidst the shadows, someone had begun to sing. It was a soft, chanted song, so low and deep that it was like a distant murmur. Orisian could not even be sure whether there was a single voice or more. He could hear no words within the song. It had a funereal sound.

"I mean the Fox no harm," he said again. "I am not your enemy. If there is war, it will be against other Huanin and against the White Owl. Not the Fox." He could think of nothing more to say.

For a long time, no one said anything. There was only the song, flowing around him. He lowered his eyes and stared at the bowl cupped in his lap, and the liquid within. Its heat was fading quickly. A few fragile wisps of steam rose toward his face.

"Leave us," said In'hynyr at last.

Fighting back a surge of relief, Orisian scrambled to his feet. In his eagerness to take his leave he ignored the pain in his side. Only as he made for the opening in the side of the tent did doubt reassert itself.

"Will we be allowed to leave the *vo'an,* then?" he asked.

"We will think on it," was all In'hynyr said.

VI

He sat cross-legged in the tent's doorway for long hours. They had given him a cloak of marten fur that had a powerful scent as if it was freshly stripped from the animals. He needed it, since each day turned the air a little crisper.

Two weeks, and a lifetime, ago this would have been a dream realized for him, to be in the midst of a camp of the Fox. Even now, despite the gnawing memory of what had brought him here, he was aware of an otherworldly peace and calm in the camp. The Kyrinin moved about with precision and balance, whether adult or child. The oldest of them, shrunken and even a little stooped, retained a natural grace Orisian had never seen in his own kind. The adults were tolerant of the packs of children that darted to and fro amongst the tents. They watched, sometimes joined in with their wrestling and chasing. Orisian never heard any voices raised in anger or excitement.

Showers passed, along with the scudding clouds that bore them, but for much of the time the sky was bright. Sunlight would fling the stark shadows of leafless trees across the camp and set the grass glowing green in memory of summer. Flocks of small birds chattered through the *vo'an.* The Kyrinin came and went. They hunted, gathered firewood, prepared meals just as any villagers might.

But amidst the familiar there were the reminders that he was far from what he knew and understood. The great face woven of boughs, standing like a sentinel watching over the heart of the *vo'an,* unsettled him. Once or twice he saw Kyrinin lay their fingertips upon it and murmur some words. The poles decorated with the skulls of various animals were sometimes, when the light caught them just so, menacing. Perhaps most unnerving of all, he would sometimes notice one of the Fox standing quite still amongst the tents, staring at him. When he returned the gaze there was none of the discomfort a human might show at being so caught out. Always it was Orisian who looked away first.

Once or twice a day he and Rothe were allowed to pass some time together. Rothe's hushed conversation was filled with concern for Orisian, and with plans for escape as soon as the two of them were strong enough. Orisian knew they could not get away if the Fox opposed it; their safety relied on reason and patience, not flight. In his heart of hearts, Rothe must know the same. Perhaps he spoke of escape only because he thought it was what Orisian needed to hear to keep his spirits up. If so, they were equally guilty of imperfect honesty, for Orisian had not told the shieldman about his audience with the *vo'an'tyr.* It would not help for Rothe to know their fate still hung so precariously in the balance. Not yet, at least.

Ess'yr visited him often, sometimes bearing food, sometimes to check his wound, sometimes for no particular reason he could grasp. He came to look forward to the sight of her. Though she seldom smiled, there was an undercurrent of goodwill in her manner. Still, she talked in strange circles, as In'hynyr had done, and he always felt that he missed half the meaning of her words.

Sometimes she would answer his questions. How many people were in the *vo'an?* he asked; two or three hundred, she told him.

Seven *a'ans,* which would disperse once more in the spring. Where was the rest of her family? Her parents had gone to the willow. Her brother was hunting in the Car Criagar.

Then when Orisian posed a question that trespassed beyond whatever unseen boundary hedged their conversation, she ignored him, or walked away. She would not discuss his and Rothe's fate, nor would she talk of Inurian. And when he asked about the great, unearthly face of twigs and branches that gazed across the camp she only shook her head a touch. He learned to tread with care.

At night, he lay longing for sleep amidst the strange smells of the Kyrinin tent, listening to the alien sounds of forest and camp. In those loneliest of hours, in the grip of darkness, he fought a losing battle against the images and memories that jostled within his head. They were of Castle Kolglas on the night of Winterbirth. But the person he longed for most, whose absence hurt more than any other, was someone lost long before: Lairis, his mother. The hole she had left in his life was as cavernous as it had ever been, the wound exposed afresh. He held the furs of his bedding tight about him, as if they were her arms.

On the morning of the fourth day since he had awoken, when Ess'yr brought him a bowl of watery broth, he sensed that something had changed. There was a lightness in her manner that had not been there before. He asked if In'hynyr had made some decision, but Ess'yr ignored the question.

"My brother is back," she said. "He will see you."

The tall, lean hunter Ess'yr later ushered into Orisian's hut was more imposing than any Kyrinin Orisian had yet seen. In the mere act of entering, without a word being spoken, the space became his. His long silvery hair had an almost metallic sheen to it. His taut face was covered by an intricate swirl of dark blue lines tattooed into the skin. The smoke-colored eyes remained impassive, but the corner of his mouth gave the faintest of twitches at the sight of the Huanin youth crouched on the sleeping mat.

"My brother," said Ess'yr. "Varryn."

"I am Orisian," he said, wishing his heart had not picked up its beat.

The tall Kyrinin angled his head and narrowed his eyes. Orisian felt impaled.

"*Ulyin,*" Varryn said, and swept out into the morning.

Ess'yr gazed after him, scratching once at her cheek with a white fingernail. Orisian cleared his throat. "What does *ulyin* mean?" he asked.

"A baby bird; no feathers. They fall from nests." She looked at him. "Bad hunting," she said and went after her brother.

He saw Varryn again that afternoon, when Ess'yr shepherded him out of the tent and over to a fire where a bowl of stew was waiting. As they sat side by side, eating in silence, her brother joined them. Orisian watched him out of the corner of his eye. Caution vied with curiosity for a while, as he took in the dense tattoos that scarred the Kyrinin's skin. Eventually he set his bowl down and turned to Varryn.

"What . . ." Orisian hesitated for a moment. "What do the marks mean? On your face?"

Ess'yr spoke before her brother could reply. "This is *kin'thyn.* Threefold. Very few have the third."

She murmured something to Varryn. Orisian was struck anew at how her voice danced when she spoke in her own language; as if a stream flowed in it. Varryn gave a nod of assent to whatever she had asked him.

"I can tell you how he won the *kin'thyn.* He agrees. Do you wish it?" she said to Orisian.

"Yes, I would like that."

"The first *kin'thyn* when he was thirteen summers." There was something almost reverent in Ess'yr's tone. "He was in a spear *a'an* of Tyn'vyr, crossed into White Owl lands. They hunted the enemy for five days. He put an arrow in an old one from behind a tree.

The second when he was fifteen. A spear *a'an* of the enemy came near. He opened one of them with a knife. Then many summers before the third. Kyrkyn called a spear *a'an,* and they went across the valley, went deep in enemy lands. They found a family by a stream, and sent them all to the willow. Varryn took the fire from their camp. They ran for the river, but the enemy was as wolfenkind behind. Many fell. Kyrkyn, and ten more. Five came out from the trees and back. Varryn carried the fire with him. Only for this is the third *kin'thyn* given. For the enemy's fire."

Throughout the telling, Varryn had regarded Orisian with a fixed, emotionless gaze. It made him want to turn away. Instead he asked, "How do you cross the valley into Anlane so easily? Without us, my Blood, knowing you are there?"

The question was directed at Ess'yr, for Orisian had assumed her brother would not understand, but Varryn rose to his feet, setting aside his bowl though it was still half-full of steaming stew.

"Huanin do not know," he said. He walked off, pausing after a few steps and half-turning. "Eyes and ears are thick and heavy. Like your legs and feet."

Orisian watched the Kyrinin's back as he stalked away.

"Varryn does not like Huanin too well," said Ess'yr.

"No," Orisian agreed. "You don't seem to feel the same way."

"I do not love your race. But Inurian speaks well of you. Of you."

Orisian forgot all about Varryn. Here was a momentary chink in the shield Ess'yr maintained against questions he longed to ask.

"You know him? Inurian, I mean. He has been to visit your camps?"

"I saw you, with the big man, and I knew you. I saw you before, three summers before, with Inurian in a boat. Close to the shore. You did not see me, but he knew I watched. He made a sign."

"We never landed on the Car Anagais," Orisian said, thinking quickly, wondering how to make the most of Ess'yr's willingness to talk. "I always wanted to come with him into the forest. I knew he was coming to your camps, and I wanted to go with him. He always put me off."

Ess'yr looked him in the eye. "Why do you want to come to us? Huanin do not come to a *vo'an*."

"I know many of my people do not like the Kyrinin. They are afraid, I suppose, but it has never been like that for me. I just . . . I just wanted to see what your camps were like. To see how you lived. It's hard to explain, but for the last few years I have often wanted to . . . to be somewhere else than my home. Somewhere different, new. And I wanted to see where Inurian comes from, and where he went on his journeys, I suppose."

"He is important for you."

"Yes. He has been very kind to me in the last few years."

Ess'yr brushed a hair from across her face. The gesture was so casual, so inconsequential, that for a luminous instant Orisian was held by it and freed of all the world beyond that sculpted hand and its languid movement. Ess'yr was quite still for the space of a few breaths. Then she stood up as if arriving at some conclusion.

"Come. I will show you. Perhaps Inurian wishes it."

She led him out of the *vo'an*. As they walked in silence, she ahead and he behind, Orisian reflected that Rothe would have seen this as a chance to escape; to overpower Ess'yr and flee. It was not something Orisian considered for even a moment, though. He doubted he could best the Kyrinin woman even if he tried, and in any case Rothe remained alone in the camp. His shieldman would view it as a grave failing, Orisian knew, but he could not possibly leave Rothe behind. There was, as well, his sense that he owed Ess'yr a debt. He might have died had she not found him and brought him here.

They came to a place where the ground leveled out. The earth was boggy and moss-covered and gave beneath Orisian's feet. Ahead stood a dense grove of willows. From somewhere amongst the trees came the sound of trickling water. Ess'yr drew him to a halt a short distance from the willows. A few small birds, startled by their approach, darted deeper into the thicket. Orisian opened his mouth to speak. Before he could do so he found her thin finger touching on his lips, as light as air.

"Breathe lightly," she said. "Speak soft. This is not your place. You are watched."

Orisian waited for Ess'yr to explain.

"This is a *dyn hane*. A place of the dead. The body goes into the earth. A willow staff is planted in the hands. If it buds, the spirit will go to *Darlankyn*. If it does not bud, they remain. Then they are *kar'hane*: the watchers."

Peering ahead, Orisian could see that amongst the dense-packed, curving trunks and branches of the willow trees were scattered a few thin, leafless poles that must be the unregenerated burial staffs of Kyrinin. The sight of them made him imagine ghostly eyes upon him. The countless branches of the living willows brushed sighingly together. Each tree, he realized, marked the grave of a Kyrinin, its roots entwined about their bones in the soft earth.

"Sent to the willow," Ess'yr said softly.

A cold grave, thought Orisian to himself, in wet ground by a forest stream. He had long known that the Kyrinin buried their dead instead of burning them as his own people did. He could not remember ever hearing about the trees, though. It occurred to him that he might, when riding with his father or with Croesan's household on the hunt, have passed by such places as this. How many hundreds of Kyrinin might have lain in their dead slumber beside his horse's hoofs?

"The *kar'hane* do no harm, if you have goodwill," she said as they walked back toward the *vo'an*.

"And those who are not of goodwill?" asked Orisian.

Instead of answering his question, Ess'yr said, "Inurian likes the *dyn hane*. He names them places of peace. This is why I show you."

"Thank you," Orisian said to Ess'yr.

As they made their way into the center of the *vo'an,* she directed his gaze toward the face sculpted out of branches. As always, it appeared sinister to him, as if a writhing mass of snakes had been suddenly frozen in place.

"You ask what that is. It is . . ." Ess'yr paused, searching for a word or phrase that did not come easily to her lips, ". . . a catcher of the dead. It is *anhyne.* An image of the Anain."

In the moment she uttered the words he could see it, and wondered why he had not guessed it before. The Anain were unlike all the other Races; closer to the Gods, as some would have it. If they had a form at all, which many claimed they did not, it was that of wood, bough and leaf come to life. This, the unknowable thought of the green earth coursing through the forests and wild places of the world, was what the Kyrinin had sought to represent.

Everything Orisian knew of the Anain was half-legend, gleaned from tale and rumor. There were no more than a handful of stories of humans who had encountered one of them and almost all had dark endings. One of those tales every Huanin or Kyrinin alike knew well: at the end of the War of the Tainted, when the Kings had cast down Tane and crushed the strength of the greatest Kyrinin clans, the Anain had roused themselves. They had raised a vast forest — the Deep Rove — where there had been none before, swallowing up Tane and all the lands about it. It set a wild, impenetrable barrier between the human armies and the Kyrinin fleeing away into the east. It, as much as the siege and breaking of Tane, had ended the bloodshed. And here, in the peaceful heart of the *vo'an,* was a representation of that awful power, watching over the playing children and the wandering goats.

"What does it mean?" asked Orisian, finding himself speaking in hushed tones.

Ess'yr frowned slightly. It was a strange sight upon her normally undisturbed features, as though some bird had passed for a moment across the sun and cast a flicker of shadow over her face.

"If the body does not come to the *dyn hane,* the . . . spirit will not rest. The *anhyne* is the guard against this. It brings the Anain close. They guard against the restless dead."

The restless dead, Orisian thought. That was a fit name for them. He did not believe in ghosts — not the kind he understood Ess'yr to mean — but there were other ways for the dead to be restless.

"I didn't know there were any Anain here," he said.

"They come before the eye in few places. What you call Deep Rove. Anlane where the enemy is. Din Sive. But the eye is not all. They fill the green world. You do not see them, but they are here."

She would say no more after that. It was enough to leave Orisian wrestling for hours with a sense, still more acute than what he had felt before, of being watched. No matter that Ess'yr said the Anain were a protection, he had no wish to lie beneath the gaze of such legends. That night he craved the stone walls of Kolglas, their solidity and unchanging presence, in a way he had not for years.

Orisian was woken by hands that stripped the furs from over him, and urgent voices that tore at the slumber clogging his ears. His first instinct, still half-asleep, was to struggle and fight against the bodies that seemed to crowd in upon him. There were too many, and he abandoned any resistance. He was pulled and pushed out into the cold night. Blearily he looked around.

A great crowd of Kyrinin was gathered before his tent: so great that he thought every man, woman and child of the *vo'an* must be assembled there. They stood in silence, their eyes fixed upon him. Those who had roused him melted into the crowd, leaving him standing alone, still a little unsteady. The forest was bathed in radiant moonlight, casting an ethereal glow over the colorless faces that confronted him. He looked up and saw a great white full moon hanging in the sky overhead.

Rothe was pushed roughly forward to join him. The shieldman looked more awake and alert than Orisian felt.

"Stand close by me," he growled as he stood upright and took Orisian's arm in a tight grip. "Show no fear."

Orisian looked around the wall of motionless bodies that faced them. There was no sound save the rasping hoot of an owl somewhere out in the woods. He had the powerful sense that he and Rothe did not belong here, that they had somehow strayed from the waking world and passed into another place. Something was happening, or about to happen.

"Say nothing," he whispered to Rothe, realizing that his shieldman was more likely to make a mistake in this moment than he was himself.

The crowd parted, opening a narrow pathway for an advancing figure. Bare feet showed beneath the hem of a straight hide dress. Strips of fur hung from the shoulders of what must be a Kyrinin woman, but the face that looked upon Orisian and Rothe was that of a great fox. As the head turned this way and that, he could see the bonds that held the mask in place. They lay over long strands of grey hair, marked with streaks of red, that shone in the moonlight. It was In'hynyr, Orisian realized. The recognition did nothing to soften the savage aspect of the mask when she turned back to stare at him. In her left hand she bore a tall staff to which were tied a dozen tiny animal skulls. The bones clicked against one another as she moved. There was an elongated instant of tension as the *vo'an'tyr* faced the two humans, then she swiveled round and spread her arms. She stood thus between them and the host of Kyrinin for a few seconds. Her voice, when she began to speak, was muffled beneath the fox mask but that only made it sound all the more eerie as it spilled out across the clearing. She spoke in the Kyrinin tongue: a tumble of words that sounded almost like an incantation.

"Be ready for anything," murmured Orisian.

In'hynyr spoke on, and every eye was upon her. She shook her staff and the little skulls it bore chattered. Her voice rose and fell. Her breath steamed, rising up as if drawn to the lambent moon.

The fox-face spun about with a cry and In'hynyr thrust an arm toward the two of them. Rothe flinched. Orisian did not stir. He had done what he could to save them when he spoke to the *vo'an'-tyr*; he knew nothing could now change whatever was going to happen. In'hynyr fell silent and a whisper ran through the crowd. Heads were bowed here and there. First one by one and then in small groups, the gathering began to fray and disperse. The Kyrinin disappeared, sinking into the darkness. In'hynyr backed away, keeping her masked face toward Orisian and Rothe, for a few strides and then turned and walked off, alone. In the space of a few breaths, only Ess'yr remained of the throng. She stood regarding Orisian. Rothe's hand was lifted from his arm, and he heard the big man exhale deeply. Ess'yr came toward them.

"What happened?" asked Orisian as she drew close.

"The *vo'an'tyr* spoke," Ess'yr said. "You may leave. Tomorrow. One day more, and you will be sent to the willow. I will come for you in the morning."

At dawn there was a heavy fog laid across the camp. Orisian stretched outside his tent. He had slept little after the gathering had dispersed, tossing and turning for much of what was left of the night, his mind too crowded to allow any rest.

Rothe strode up out of the fog. He grinned at Orisian as he drew near.

"Freedom beckons, then."

Orisian returned the smile. "So it seems."

"I never thought we would get out of this with our hides on our backs," Rothe said, "but here we are. This will be a good tale to tell."

Orisian looked around the *vo'an*. The shifting veils of fog muffled all sound and half-concealed the few figures moving about. The smell of smoke hung in the damp air. It was a muted end to the tale of their sojourn here.

Ess'yr arrived. She held up a pair of scrawny, skinned carcasses. "Break your fast," she said.

He and Rothe watched in silence as Ess'yr spitted the squirrels over a small fire. As they sat there waiting, Varryn appeared. He stood beside them, leaning upon a long spear. Rothe regarded the Kyrinin warrior with unconcealed hostility.

"This is Varryn, Ess'yr's brother," Orisian said. Rothe grunted and turned his eyes back to the fire. Varryn showed no sign of even recognizing their existence. Even when Ess'yr said something soft to him, Orisian detected no flicker of a response. Perhaps Ess'yr saw something he did not, for she seemed unperturbed.

"Where do you go?" she asked Orisian.

He glanced at Rothe, aware that he had not discussed the matter with him. "To Anduran," he said. "The city in the valley." His shieldman nodded.

"It is close, isn't it?" Orisian asked Ess'yr.

"Not far," she said. "We guide you to the forest edge. I and Varryn."

"No need," said Rothe, glaring at Ess'yr.

"It is best," said Varryn. "Our people are in the forest. They may think you the enemy. End with quills in you like a porcupine. We take you fast and safe."

Rothe looked as if he was struggling to restrain himself. "I am sure we can find our way," he said through lips clamped so tight that the words had to battle for their freedom.

"My brother . . . plays," said Ess'yr. "But he is right. We will take you by ways that mean you cannot find this *vo'an* again. We will take you by ways that are safe. We will take you so that we know you have left Fox lands. For these reasons, the *vo'an'tyr* says we take you. That is how it will be." And that was the end of any debate.

A black expression settled over Rothe's face, and Orisian reflected that a journey with the shieldman and a proud Kyrinin warrior in the same party was not going to be an easy one.

"We prepare," Ess'yr said. "When you finish, come to the edge of the *vo'an*. The east."

She and her brother left Orisian and Rothe to pick apart the squirrels. The shieldman muttered in dire tones about the fool-hardiness of trusting Kyrinin.

"We've no choice," murmured Orisian. "I don't think they'd look kindly on refusal. It won't be for long, anyway. They're only trying to protect themselves; making sure we can't find our way back here too easily."

Orisian sucked at a bone. Unnoticed, children had gathered around them. He glanced up to find a dozen or more, come to take a last look at these strange visitors to their home. Rothe tossed the remnants of his meal onto the fire and rose to his feet. The children shuffled to one side to open a path for him.

The two of them made their way to the edge of the camp as they had been instructed. Nobody paid them any heed. They passed a pair of old women cracking nuts on a stone anvil. A younger girl was stretching the still wet and gory hide of a deer across a drying frame. She did not even look round as they walked by.

Ess'yr and her brother were seated together at the fringe of the *vo'an* where the last few tents were spread thinly. Small packs lay beside them, and spears, arrow-filled quivers and bows. Standing in front of them, waiting with a still patience no human child could have achieved, was a young Kyrinin girl. She was watching as Ess'yr and Varryn fed long strips of leather through their hands, knotting them at regular intervals along their length. Afraid to interrupt the air of intense concentration that pervaded the little group, Orisian stood to one side with Rothe. The shieldman's sword and scabbard were on the ground. Without waiting to be invited, he picked it up and began to examine it in the minutest detail.

Each knot was precisely tied and moistened with a touch of saliva before being pulled tight. Like beads upon a necklace, knot after knot was added to the strips. Finally, at almost the same moment, both of them seemed satisfied with their work. Each passed their piece of leather to the child. She took one in each hand and walked off.

Ess'yr turned to Orisian. She brought out a thin knife from

inside her jacket. It was made for throwing, with a smooth wooden hilt that lacked a crosspiece.

"This was in you," she said, holding it out to Orisian. "You have no weapon. Take this."

He took it and slipped it into his belt. It reminded him of his wound, and he felt the flesh there ache for a moment, but it was better to have this knife than none.

"An Inkallim blade," said Rothe almost admiringly. "That's a rare trophy to carry."

Without a word, Ess'yr and Varryn rose, took up their packs and weapons and headed into the forest. Orisian and Rothe glanced at each other. Rothe shrugged. They followed the Kyrinin away from the *vo'an*.

Only after they had been walking for a few minutes could Orisian bring himself to ask Ess'yr what the knotted leather cords had meant.

"One knot is one thought," she told him. "Thought of people, of times, from the life. It is done before a journey. If our bodies do not return, the cord goes to the *dyn hane* and is buried. It will bind our spirits to the willow. We will not be restless."

The two Kyrinin set a demanding pace. The forest was open, with broad stretches of grass between the stands of trees. Every few hundred strides they would pass an ancient oak tree in some sheltered spot. Often their route would change direction beneath the branches of one of the oaks, and Orisian suspected that the Kyrinin were navigating by these gnarled trees, using them as markers on some map they carried in their heads.

"How far is it to Anduran?" he called ahead to them.

"Not far," was all Ess'yr replied, without even turning round.

They came to a more difficult stretch, where a swathe of trees had fallen and a dense thicket of saplings had sprung up around their corpses. Varryn led the way straight into the undergrowth. Orisian and Rothe found it difficult to fight their way through. They emerged, scratched, on the other side to find the Kyrinin warrior awaiting them, leaning on his spear once more, as if he had been standing thus for hours.

"A speared boar is not so loud," he said.

Rothe looked grievously affronted in a way that might have made Orisian smile had he not feared that words between these two might turn into something more physical. The shieldman had, in any case, no opportunity to respond. Having delivered his rebuke, Varryn spun on his heel and was off once more.

"A speared boar . . ." muttered Rothe. "That it should come to this . . . following woodwights through the forest like children. I wore a beard before that . . . that wight was a bulge in his father's breeches."

"It is a sad day," Orisian agreed, "but we had best keep up nevertheless."

They strode after the two Kyrinin, pressing on along the southern flank of the Car Criagar toward Anduran.

CHAPTER

3

The Black Road

In the days when Monach oc Kilkry was High Thane in Kolkyre, when his Blood had ruled over all the others for close to a hundred years, Amanath the fisherwoman fell into a slumber in Kilvale. For three days and three nights she lay thus, and her family thought she had begun her journey to the Sleeping Dark. They sang songs of loss and put oils upon her eyes. But on the fourth day she awoke and began to speak. She spoke of the Hooded God, the Last God, and of how he had remained when his brothers and sisters left the world. She spoke of the Book of Lives he bore and the tales he read from its pages; tales that told the story of every life there has been or ever will be. And those tales she named the Black Road, which is the fated path from birth to foretold death. She spoke of the Kall: the day when humankind would be united by the creed of the Road; when the Gods would answer the call of that unity and return to unmake and remake the world. And she taught that only for those who had been faithful to the creed would there be rebirth in the world that was new.

The fisherwoman's teachings did not please the powerful. The High Thane's men hung her from an ash tree. All the Thanes felt fear, save one. Avann oc Gyre-Kilkry who ruled in Kan Avor heard Amanath's words and took them to his heart. He gathered to him all those who saw the truth, and gave them shelter. And when war came his Blood stood against all the others in the name of that truth.

Avann it was who, when Kan Avor had fallen, led the ten thousand over the Vale of Stones and into the north. The truth that Amanath spoke lives there still amongst the Bloods he fashioned. The flame still burns, and does not falter.

Hear well. This is the truth, for those who have the ears to hear. Put away pride and put away fear. The day of your death has already been read from the pages of the Last God's Book. There is only the fated path. There is only the Black Road.

from an anonymous commentary upon The Book of the Road

I

The vast walls of Vaymouth, shining in the last rays of the sun's light, soared over Taim Narran dar Lannis-Haig and his company. The capital of the Haig Blood had become, in the last hundred years, what might be the greatest city in the world. Its fortifications were on a scale unseen since the Shining City of the Kyrinin was cast down. The southern gate, called the Gold Gate, was open, its great doors of plated iron swung back and chained in place. A handful of guards were clustered to one side, leaning on their spears and watching the approaching band of men impassively. The beggars whose shack-towns seethed around the city's walls lined the road, reaching out to the Lannis-Haig warriors.

As he drew close, Taim felt his familiar distaste for the city, and the ambition its grandeur embodied. He would gladly have passed it by and gone on through the coastal plains toward Ayth-Haig lands and the way north, but several of his men would not survive without rest. Ten had already died on the journey back from the Dargannan-Haig mountains. He was tired of burning bodies on makeshift roadside pyres.

He rode through the gateway and was immersed in the shadow of the walls, as if engulfed by a gigantic beast. A figure stepped into the roadway ahead. With a sense of cold resignation, Taim recognized the man who blocked his path: Mordyn Jerain, Chancellor to the High Thane. Born and bred in Tal Dyre but long ago adopted as a son of Vaymouth, Jerain had been at Gryvan oc Haig's side for nearly twenty years. He was a handsome, brown-haired man whose every movement was precise, poised and considered. He wore his power with ease. He wore, too, a dark reputation. In places where there was little affection for the intricate dealings of the Haig court, the Chancellor was called by the name Shadowhand.

"I was told you were coming," said Mordyn as Taim drew his horse to a halt.

"Of course."

The Chancellor smiled, and it was a smile both glittering and hollow. "I came out to meet you," he said obviously. "There are matters we must discuss."

"I have men with me who need rest and healing. That is my only interest here. I have permission to quarter my company within the walls. We will rest for a little while, and be on our way."

Mordyn's eyes narrowed and he put his graceful hand on the bridle of Taim's horse.

"I am Chancellor of the Haig Blood, Narran. There are many demands upon my time. I do not come to meet travelers at the gate for idle entertainment."

Weariness coursed through Taim, and with it a trace of the anger that lay deep-buried. He looked at the Chancellor's hand, and at the embroidered cuff of his sleeve. A fine tracery of gold thread wound its way through velvet. The coat had most likely been smuggled out of the Adravane Kingship in the far south, into the Dornach Kingship and thence through either the marketplaces of Tal Dyre or the masterless towns of the Free Coast to Vaymouth. The journey placed a dizzying price upon such a garment, and his possession of it spoke as eloquently of Mordyn Jerain's status as any title could. This was not a man to trifle with, but Taim had left much of his discretion on the bloodstained screes beneath An Caman Fort.

"And I do not speak with Chancellors for mine," he said.

He flicked his horse's harness out of Mordyn's grasp and nudged the animal forward. The Chancellor shook his head like a man faced with a petulant child. He raised a hand, and guards spread themselves across the gateway. Beyond them, inside the city, a small crowd was gathering, drawn by the sight of their infamous Chancellor.

"You are tired and the road must have been a long and hard one for you and your men," said Mordyn. "Your impatience is understandable. However, I must insist that you find the time to speak with me. I have news that you will want to hear now rather than later, and I will not give it in the street."

Taim slumped in the saddle as his horse slowed to a halt. Behind him, some of his men were pressing up, and he could feel the tension in them without looking round. All he wanted to do was find a quiet, warm bed and sleep, dreamlessly. His dreams had been unforgiving of late. He wanted to set the world aside, even if just for one night.

Instead, he turned to the Chancellor. "Very well," he said.

He dismounted and passed his reins to the closest of his men. He sent the company on without him, while he followed Mordyn and his honor guard on foot to the Palace of Red Stone.

The palace, one of several magnificent residences constructed for the family and high officials of the Haig Blood, was not far away. It abutted the inner face of the city wall, and was raised up on a terrace from which trailing vines and bushes overflowed. Its walls were inset with blocks of red porphyry. Sentries in immaculately polished breastplates and gorgets stood on the broad steps leading up to the entrance. Their helmets bore plumes the color of corn.

A faint, rich scent in the air distracted Taim as he walked beside the Chancellor through marble halls. The sounds of the city faded behind them, soaked up by the Palace's massive bulk. Pillars as thick as hundred-year-old trees supported a painted ceiling. They passed a fretwork grill set into the wall and Taim glimpsed female faces behind it, watching him go past. He thought he heard whispers and laughter.

The Chancellor led him to an audience chamber. There was a great desk of dark, almost black, wood there, decorated with gold leaf. Mordyn Jerain ignored it and gestured to a pair of cushioned chairs.

"Please have a seat," the Chancellor said. "Can I send for some food or drink?"

A maidservant, hovering between the motionless guards who flanked the doorway, looked hopeful. Taim dismissed the suggestion with a shake of his head and the woman departed.

Taim sank into the chair and was for a moment seduced by its luxurious comfort. He almost had to suppress a sigh of relaxation and relief. The feeling took him a thousand miles, more, away from the memory of the unyielding mountains of Dargannan-Haig. Mordyn's voice dispelled the sensation.

"You will forgive my insistence, and my departure from the usual courtesies, I think, when you hear what I have to say. I was told yesterday that Inkallim have overrun Castle Kolglas."

Taim's mind went blank. He could not unfix his gaze from the knots and whorls in the wooden arm of his chair. He was, he noticed in a detached way, all of a sudden clutching that arm fiercely. The cloying aroma he had smelled in the halls returned. It had a clovey, spicy texture.

"Little is certain," the Chancellor was continuing, "though it does seem clear that the castle was burned, and that the attackers escaped into the forest."

"Kennet?" asked Taim. He longed to believe Mordyn was lying to him. He could imagine no reason for such a deceit, though.

"I cannot say. I expect more messengers at any time. The first knew only what I have told you."

"It is not possible. They could not reach Kolglas. What of Tanwrye, and Anduran?"

For the first time, the faintest hint of doubt seemed to touch the corner of Mordyn's eyes. It was there for a heartbeat before being extinguished.

"There was mention of Kyrinin," he said. "It is . . . well, it seems absurd, but it may be that woodwights had a hand in the assault. You know how confusion thrives at such times, so I would not place much faith in the report. Still, if the White Owls have aided the Black Road it might explain the inexplicable."

Taim could find no words. He shook his head.

"I fear this may be the herald of worse news to come," Mordyn said. "It seems unlikely that the Gyre Bloods would commit the Inkallim so far beyond their borders, in numbers large enough to take the castle, if it was not part of a grander scheme. The whole valley may be beset. Soon, if not already."

Taim glared at the Chancellor. Mordyn was unperturbed. "I speak the truth, Taim. You must know it. The Inkallim do not make empty gestures."

"What . . ." Taim fought to master himself, wrestling with a tide of emotion that threatened to blind him. "What will you do?"

Mordyn arched his eyebrows. "I? Await the High Thane's return. I sent messengers south as soon as I had the news. You no doubt passed them on your way here."

"Wait?" snapped Taim.

"And gather our forces as quickly as we can. Even if there was an army provisioned and ready here now, it would still be three weeks or more before it reached Anduran. That means fighting in winter, and if we are to do that it must be with the strength to be certain of swift victory."

"Lheanor will not wait," said Taim darkly.

"The Thane of Kilkry-Haig will do as his master commands, I imagine."

"He will not wait," Taim repeated. "He is a true friend to my Blood."

"Taim, Taim," the Chancellor said, "your Blood's truest friend now is Gryvan oc Haig. He can bring twenty, thirty thousand men to Croesan's aid. Yes, it will take time, but Gyre will regret its ambition."

"I do not care about Gyre," muttered Taim. "Only Lannis . . . Lannis-Haig . . . and my Thane."

"Of course," said the Chancellor. "I understand that, and I counsel you not to let your fears run too far ahead of our knowledge. This may yet prove to be nothing but a raid. And your Blood has, after all, won great victories over the Black Road before. The High Thane's support, or that of Lheanor, may not even be required."

"Perhaps not. It may well have been so, had I and my two thousand men not been summoned south."

Mordyn Jerain smiled tolerantly.

"We can all share in that regret. You know it was necessary, though. Igryn's open defiance of the High Thane could not stand. The True Bloods are nothing if they cannot hold together in the face of rebellion by one of their own. It was fitting that every Blood should play its part in Igryn's defeat. No, more than fitting: essential. We live in dangerous times. If our enemies saw divisions between us, they would not be slow to act."

"The Black Road is our greatest enemy," murmured Taim. "It always has been. My Blood has not forgotten that. Nor has Kilkry-Haig. The True Bloods might hold together more easily if others shared that view, rather than spending all their time dreaming of the riches that could be theirs if only the Free Coast, or Tal Dyre, or even Dornach, would fall to them."

A decorous cough drew the two men's attention to the doorway. The woman standing there was of a beauty that caught Taim's breath in his throat for an instant. Thick, glossy black hair fell across her shoulders and she wore a silken dress that could not be imagined upon another, so perfectly did it fit and become her. Gold dripped from her ears, her neck and her wrists; a glut of the metal that would have hypnotized a greedier soul than Taim's. It seemed to him that the rich scent pervading the palace clung, as well, to her, so that as she entered she brought it into the room with her.

He recognized her at once: Tara Jerain, the Chancellor's wife. He had seen her riding at Mordyn's side during the ceremonial review of the High Thane's army before they had marched south. Such a presence once experienced was not forgotten.

"Ah," said Mordyn, springing to his feet. "Taim, this is my wife, Tara."

Taim rose and inclined his head as graciously as he could manage. "I am honored to meet you, my lady."

"And I you," replied the woman in a voice as luxuriant as her jewelry. "I am sorry not to make your acquaintance on a happier day."

Taim was a touch surprised that the Chancellor's wife should refer so directly to the source of his distress, then he recalled the rumors that surrounded this woman. There was no shortage of them, and all suggested that she wielded almost as much influence, in her own way, as her husband. She was a worthy wife to the Shadowhand and would, Taim supposed, know all that Mordyn did about events in the north.

"I asked Tara to join us," the Chancellor was saying, "in case there was anything she could do to make your men more comfortable here in the city. She can find them anything they need."

"Indeed," Tara confirmed. "Food, drink, the care of healers. Tell me what your men require, and it is theirs, Captain Narran."

"Their needs will be well seen to," Taim said, unable to keep an edge from his voice. He felt as if he had been waylaid. He was being dismissed; delicately, sympathetically, but quite deliberately.

The Chancellor's wife gave a subtle nod, her eyes fluttering shut for the briefest of instants as if a breeze had touched them. "As you wish," she said.

"You, at least, will rest here for a time," suggested Mordyn. "I will have a room prepared."

Taim turned to the Chancellor. He caught himself before he gave full vent to his feelings.

"Thank you, but my tastes are simple. I will rest with my men, and prepare for the journey on to Kolkyre. And to Anduran."

"You will not wait, then, for the High Thane to return?" asked Tara, her voice all innocent inquiry. "Surely he can only be two or three days behind you on the road?"

Taim smiled at her. It was required of him, even though he felt that what mattered now, all that mattered, was waiting for him somewhere in the north.

"I must go, my lady," he said. "My place is at my own Thane's side. And I have a wife of my own, one I wish more than ever to see again."

Anduran and Glasbridge, the greatest settlements of Taim's Blood, were as villages compared to the enormity of Vaymouth and the masses of its population. People churned up and down the streets as thickly as fish in a drawn net. Taim had refused the Chancellor's offer of an escort and a mount. He knew the way to the barracks well enough, and he craved release from the oppressive solicitude of Mordyn Jerain and his household. Now, struggling through the crowds, he was less certain. Although he had been in the capital of the Bloods twice before, its rough exuberance and scale still wrought a disorientating effect.

Strange smells and sounds assaulted his senses: spices and herbs he did not recognize; music made upon instruments unknown in the north; now and again the cadences of languages foreign to him, the odd native argot of Tal Dyre traders or the coarse-sounding olden form of his own tongue that was still spoken in distant parts of the Ayth-Haig Blood. He was jostled this way and that but knew there was no point in complaining.

Taim wondered at the way life continued in all its chaotic vigor. His own world was shaking, its foundations cracked by Mordyn Jerain's news, yet it was a day like any other in these streets. Far away on the northern border of his homeland, men might be dying; men he knew well from his own time in the garrison at Tanwrye. Here, the traders hawked their wares and the townsfolk went about their business. He felt a kind of loathing for the people all around him.

The barracks themselves lay in the center of the city. It was a long walk. In time the turreted and balconied spires of the Moon Palace, where Gryvan oc Haig's family lived and ruled, came into view above distant rooftops. Around one last corner the press of the crowds thinned as the street gave out onto a wide square. The city's barracks stood austere and massive on its far side. There were performers dotted across the open space, juggling or working sleight-of-hand tricks for appreciative knots of spectators. One was a firewalker whose olive skin and colored tunic and pantaloons said he was a wanderer from the Bone Isles of Dornach. Amongst his audience a small, lean man darted this way and that, the rags he wore shaking as he bounced from foot to foot.

"They are not gone," he cried to the sky. "It is not true. I have seen them, they watch over us still. I met the Gatekeeper on a street in Drandar. The maker! I walked in the Veiled Woods, and saw the Wildling there, feasting on a deer he had killed."

A madman, Taim thought. The executioner's axe would have been over his neck for such words once. Monach oc Kilkry had been merciless when the fisherwoman of Kilvale gave birth to the Black Road. Convinced that such heresies could bring only misery and chaos, he did not flinch even when the strife turned into civil war. Now no one even listens. No one cares about such things, not here where Gryvan rules. Once, stability and order had been the whole purpose of the Bloods. They had, after all, arisen as an answer to the tumult of the Storm Years after the Aygll Kingship fell. Now, it seemed to Taim, they served a different purpose: that of supporting the ambitions of the Haig Blood.

Taim passed in through the barrack gates, ignoring the stern gazes of the guards. He found his men in a hall at the furthest corner of the sprawling maze of buildings, yards and armories. It was then that the burden of his position, and of his news, grew so heavy as to be almost unbearable. He saw exhaustion in the bodies and eyes of his men. They were grimed by the dirt of travel and their clothes were worn. At the far end of the hall the injured and sick lay upon pallets. He could offer none of the rest and comfort they all so deserved, and must raise them up for the long journey to home and, perhaps, a greater battle than the one they had left behind.

It was not so very difficult in the end. Taim took pride in their weary resolution, but for all his tiredness he did not sleep well that night.

II

Anyara's cell in Anduran was cold and comfortless. All they gave her to eat was a thin gruel with a few chunks of dispirited grey bread floating in it. It was brought to her by guards, some of them women, who never spoke. They stood and watched her as she ate. She sensed their contempt for her, and sometimes something stronger: hatred almost. It made her angry. She was the Thane's niece, incarcerated in her own homeland by intruders. It was she who had the right to hatred, not her jailers. Her anger boiled over just once. She flung her bowl at the feet of a guard and spat curses at him. He regarded the gruel sprayed across his boots, and then struck her with the back of his hand. She yelped and clutched her nose in a vain attempt to stem the blood that sprang from it. He hit her again, on the side of her head, and knocked her down. He picked up the empty bowl and carried it away, slamming the bar across the cell door in his wake. After that, Anyara kept her feelings on a tighter leash.

In the nights she craved sleep as a kind of escape. It came only grudgingly. She lay on the battered mattress they had given her, curled like a worm in the stone gut of some great animal that had swallowed her. The Black Road haunted her exhaustion. To her it was a desolate creed. The whole idea that your life, and the death that would end it, was fixed from the moment of your birth was loathsome to her, yet her own impotence now seemed a bitter echo of it. All the strength she had cultivated over the last five years counted for nothing. Others had decided upon a cruel death for her, and there was not a thing she could do.

She could remember, long ago in a world now as tenuous as a dream to her, sitting upon her father's knee in the hall of Kolglas, listening to his tales of old battles. As a young man Kennet had fought alongside his father and his brother against the warriors of the Black Road at Tanwrye. In his soft voice, as he whispered stories of that day in her ear, she heard a bitter respect for his enemy. A company of Inkallim had stood aside and watched as a Horin-Gyre army was surrounded and destroyed before the walls of Tanwrye. Some said it was because the ravens wished to curb the Blood's arrogance, some that the High Thane of Gyre had forbidden the invasion and Horin-Gyre was thus punished for its disobedience. Yet, Kennet murmured, there had been no fear amongst the slaughtered. They had fought on, and died, for hour after hour.

Lairis had scolded Kennet for telling such tales to a little girl in the midst of a meal, but he had reprimanded his beloved wife. "She must know the nature of her enemy," he said.

Though the knowledge did her little good, Anyara thought, she did know her enemy, and how remorseless and resilient their hatred was.

All she could see through the high, narrow window of her cell was a patch of sky. It offered little cheer, wearing its clouds with somber gravity. Sometimes she heard rain on the roof and thought that even those drops would be a comforting touch upon her head if she could just walk for a few moments beneath them. The hours were long. Over many years she had fashioned strong defenses against her fears and pain, against the Fever, death, her father's suffering. Now those defenses were sorely tested.

Most of the guards had heavy footsteps that she could recognize before they reached the door of her cell. When, after three or four days of imprisonment, she heard a lighter step approaching, her spirit lifted at the mere thought of some change in the crushing routine. Her heart fell once more when the visitor stepped through the doorway. It was Wain, sister to the Horin-Gyre Bloodheir. Her long hair was a little less lustrous than the last time Anyara had seen her, her clothes a little more soiled by smoke and dirt, but her gaze was no less hard; no less contemptuous.

She smirked at the sight of Anyara, who managed to stay an impulse to smooth her own hair and clothes. The time had passed when she could pretend to be anything other than cold and hungry and disheveled.

"These walls must never have seen such a distinguished guest," said Wain.

"What do you want?"

"So sharp. Jail does not agree with you, perhaps?" Wain reached out and seized Anyara's wrist, making a show of examining her palms and fingers.

"You are a soft little thing, aren't you?" she mused. "You would not last one winter in the north. Soft women make soft men, it would seem, since your Blood is so easily defeated."

Anyara wrenched her hand away and glared at Wain.

"We are not beaten yet. Croesan will have Kanin's head and yours before he's done."

Wain laughed. She ran her fingers over the gold chain at her neck.

"Your concern for our heads is touching," she said, "but I do not fear what will come to pass. The Hooded God read the tale of my life in his book on the day of my birth; its ending was fixed at that moment. My feet are on the Black Road and no wish of yours will change its course. Anyway, I think it is your death that is written for this time and place, not mine. I came to tell you that we have sent message arrows into the castle. We told your uncle that we have you, and that he must treat with us or see you skinned beneath his walls." She paused as if to observe Anyara's reaction, but seeing none she carried on. "What do you think? How soft have the men of Lannis-Haig become?"

"Not soft at all," said Anyara, hoping that she kept her fear out of her voice. She had known this was how it might go — why else would they have kept her alive except for a game such as this? — but the thought was one she had almost managed to keep at bay so far. There was always hope, she told herself with little conviction. Only the adherents of the Black Road believed that events could follow but a single course.

"Well, you might be right," Wain said. "A pity for you. At least you can rest assured that Croesan will be following you into the darkness. Your precious Thane in his castle will not last long. This land will be ours once again."

"It was never yours. You must mean that it will be Gyre's. The Horin family was nothing but thugs in Glasbridge before you fled into the north, I heard. At least the Gyre line springs from true Thanes, even if they lost the right to the title when they . . ."

Wain took a sudden step forward and Anyara retreated, expecting a blow to come. Wain flexed her right hand, perhaps imagining what damage the heavy rings that adorned it might do. She seemed to think better of it, and laughed instead. She began to turn one of those rings around her finger thoughtfully.

"A little spirit left, then," she said. "It is true that Ragnor oc Gyre will rule here, but it will be my Blood, my brother, that returns his throne to him. But a throne is only the means, not the end. That is what you cannot see. We will rule only to spread the light of the true creed. When that light shines in every heart, then the Gods will return to us."

"You're getting carried away. You can go no further while Anduran stands. And Tanwrye cannot have fallen yet." Anyara saw the truth of it in the other's eyes. She saw danger there as well and did not press the point.

"Such confidence," Wain smiled. "Such arrogance, that you think even the strongest walls can stand if it is written that they should crumble. You think all your hope, all the striving in this fallen world makes any difference to the tide of fate? That is the kind of pride the Gods require us to set aside before they will return. The Black Road exists to teach us humility. If our ancestors had possessed more of it, the Gods would never have departed."

She came forward again, and Anyara fell back until she was pressed against the wall. Wain pinned her arms against the cold stone. Anyara felt an awful strength in the other woman; not just in the iron-hard grip of her hands but in the icy stillness of her eyes. She wondered what Wain was doing here. It could not just be a desire to frighten her or mock her. Perhaps it was just curiosity to see how this soft girl from Kolglas withstood captivity, or the desire to test the strength of her belief against Anyara's denial.

"The Black Road will triumph," the Bloodheir's sister said, "because it is truth, and until it rules the Gods will not return and the world will not be renewed. You and all your kind have nothing to set against that, and therefore you will fall."

Abruptly, she released Anyara and turned her back on her. She left without another word. Anyara massaged her upper arms where Wain had gripped her. There would be bruises there, she knew. That was the least of her worries. No word would come from her uncle to spare her the attentions of the Horin-Gyre executioners. It could not, for her life was nothing weighed against that of the Blood itself.

* * *

There was no sickness in the castle yet. For that at least, the besieged could be thankful. But there was little food, either. The blow had fallen with so little warning that there had not been time to bring many supplies in from the great barns of Anduran. If no more than the castle's normal population needed to be fed, their stores would have lasted for some weeks; twice as many again had poured in as the enemy drew near. In the courtyard, the stables, the great rooms of the keep, people huddled together around whatever few possessions they had managed to salvage. Mothers fed their babies at the breast in the passageways. Rations of food were kept meager to eke out the stores. Hungry children cried, tempers ran a knife edge.

Only at the very end, when the Horin-Gyre vanguard was over the walls and inside the town, had the castle gates been closed. Then, Croesan had thought there could be no more bitter sound in the world than the desperate voices of those left outside.

Hope had stumbled a little in the Thane's breast, this last day. If help was to come from Kolglas or Glasbridge it should have arrived by now, and in truth he was not sure how much they could offer anyway. Taim Narran had taken most of their fighting men south with him. The best, and greater, part of the forces left to Lannis-Haig had been on the northern border and must now be trapped in Tanwrye. The real chance of aid was from Kolkyre, and the old Thane Lheanor oc Kilkry-Haig. He would come if he could, Croesan knew. Kilkry and Lannis had been closely bound since the very day Sirian was made into a Thane. It was all a question of time. The Black Road army that held Anduran in its grip did not have the siege engines to breach the castle gate or walls; such machines could never have been transported down through Anlane. If help came before they could be built, and before the castle's food supplies were exhausted, there would yet be a reckoning with the enemy outside the gate.

The seal of Lannis-Haig was about the Thane's neck. He lifted it in his hand. It bore the image of Castle Kolglas, the wellspring of his Blood. He wondered if his brother was dead, as the message from Kanin nan Horin-Gyre had claimed. It might be so. The fact that Kennet had not yet come to Anduran could only mean that something had prevented him, and it was hard to imagine how the enemy could have taken Anyara — as they also claimed in that arrow-borne message — except over her father's body.

Croesan let the seal fall back against his chest and looked around. The audience chamber had never been more finely decorated. Golden ribbons were strung from the throne up to fans of polished boar spears that glinted on the walls. Wreaths of greenery were hung with the banners of Anduran, Kolglas, Glasbridge, Targlas and Tanwrye, the five towns of the Blood. A red carpet, trimmed with gold, ran the length of the chamber.

It had been in this room that the seal was first placed around Croesan's neck. His father had been dead no more than a few hours, laid low by a fever only months after coming unscathed out of the Battle of Stone Vale. Now three more generations of the Lannis line stood in the magnificent chamber. Croesan looked upon Naradin and Eilan, the latter cradling their baby son in her arms. Husband and wife were dressed in plain white robes that brushed the floor. The baby was wrapped in a cream-colored sheet. Behind them was gathered a solemn group of officials and castle officers. It was a smaller gathering than the occasion warranted. In more normal times, every family of substance throughout the Thane's lands would have been represented here to witness what was about to happen.

To one side, close by the Thane, a silver bowl filled with water rested on an oaken stand. Athol Kintyne, the Master Oathman of the Lannis-Haig Blood, waited before it. His grey hair and beard, his stooped shoulders and his skin like well-worn hide bestowed an aura of aged wisdom upon him. His duties, shared with the dozen Oathmen who served him, lay at the heart of the Blood's life and history. One of those duties was the Naming of infants. That Naming most often took place at the end of the first three months of life. For reasons nobody felt the need to question, the Thane's grandson was to receive his name before he was even one month old.

"We should begin," murmured Croesan.

Naradin and Eilan came forward. They stopped by the silver bowl and bowed their heads to the Master Oathman.

"Who is the child?" asked Athol.

It was Eilan who gave the reply. "He is the son of Eilan, daughter of Clachan and Dimayne, and he is the son of Naradin, son of Croesan and Liann."

Athol nodded. "Wash him," he said.

Naradin and Eilan together removed the sheet from the baby and lowered him into the water in the bowl. They handled him carefully. He made no complaint while Naradin held him and Eilan lifted water in her cupped hands and spilled it over his head. Naradin lifted him out again, and Athol proffered a new, immaculate sheet of purest white satin in which he was wrapped.

"Who is the child?" asked the Oathman again.

There was the slightest of hesitations before Eilan replied, in a clear and strong voice. "He is Croesan nan Lannis-Haig."

Naradin glanced across to his father. There was a sad smile on the older man's face. He had not known of this. He blinked. His eyes had taken on a watery sheen.

Athol stepped forward and tied a fragile strand of cloth about the infant's wrist.

"Croesan nan Lannis-Haig, son of Naradin and Eilan, be welcome amongst us. Bear your name with honor."

There was a ripple of soft approval and congratulation from the onlookers as the Master Oathman straightened and smiled at the mother and father. "A well-chosen name," he said.

"We think so," smiled Eilan.

"There is one other thing," said Naradin. He turned to his father. "Thane, it is my wish to stand in place of my son and to take the Bloodoath on his behalf."

Croesan raised his eyebrows. "It is unusual . . ." He looked to Athol.

"But possible, of course," the Oathman confirmed. "It is permitted for one to stand in another's place in some circumstances." He paused for a moment, a trace of uncertainty crossing his face.

"If . . . if there is the likelihood of death before they are of an age to do it for themselves."

Eilan was stroking the baby's face. She bent over him as if he was all that there was in the world. "Our son has a name," she said, without looking up, "but that is not enough for the grandson of a Thane in such times as these. It would not be fitting should he die with a name, but without a master."

Croesan sighed. His mouth trembled, and for a moment it seemed that he might not be able to speak.

"Very well," he said thickly. "There is no need, since no harm will come to the child, but it is a choice for the parents. Athol, you will accept the Bloodoath from my grandson. Naradin shall stand on his behalf."

"Place the child on the floor, Bloodheir, and kneel at his side," Athol said.

Naradin did as he was told. The white sheet shone against the dark red carpet. The Thane pressed his lips tight together and turned away, fighting in that moment to calm powerful emotions. The baby was making small, inarticulate sounds. His minuscule hands pawed the air as if he strove to grasp some drifting motes that only he could see.

Athol stepped forward, interposing himself between the Thane and Naradin. He spoke in a deep, impersonal voice.

"In the name of Sirian and Powll, Anvar and Gahan and Tavan, the Thanes who have been; of Croesan oc Lannis-Haig, the Thane who is now; and of the Thanes yet to come, I command you all to hear the Bloodoath taken. I am Thane and Blood, past and future, and this life will be bound to mine. I command you all to mark it."

He reached out an open hand to Naradin. "Have you the blade?" he asked. Wordlessly, Naradin withdrew from a sheath at his belt a short, flat-bladed knife with a handle carved of antler. He laid it hilt first in the Oathman's palm. Athol held the knife up and examined it.

"The blade is fresh-forged? Unbloodied? Unmarked?" he asked, and Naradin avowed it was.

"By what right do you speak for the oathtaker?" Athol asked.

"He is my son," replied Naradin.

"It is fitting." Athol went down on one knee beside the baby. He held the knife poised by little Croesan's chubby arm.

"You will give of your blood to seal this oath?" Athol asked.

"I will," said Naradin on behalf of his child.

"By this oath your life is bound to mine," the Oathman intoned. "The word of the Thane of Lannis-Haig is your law and rule, as the word of father is to a child. Your life is the life of the Blood Lannis-Haig."

He laid a tiny cut into the skin of the baby's arm. A bead of blood formed. An expression of offended puzzlement appeared on little Croesan's face. He made a coughing noise that threatened to develop into sobs. Athol caught a fraction of the blood upon the very tip of the oathknife. With his thumb he began to rub the liquid into the blade.

"You pledge your life to the Lannis-Haig Blood?" asked Athol, and Naradin agreed softly.

"You bend your knee to the Thane, who is the Lannis-Haig Blood?"

"Yes," Naradin said.

"None may come between you and this oath," said Athol sternly. "By this oath you set aside all other allegiances. The Blood shall sustain you and bear you up. You shall sustain the Blood. Speak your oath."

Naradin took a deep breath and said, "I speak in the name of Croesan nan Lannis-Haig, son of Naradin and Eilan. By my blood I pledge my life to Lannis-Haig. The word of the Thane is my law and rule; it is the root and staff of my life. The enemy of the Blood is my enemy. My enemy is the enemy of the Blood. Unto death."

Athol leaned forward and laid the stained knife on the baby's naked chest.

"Unto death," he said, and turned away.

Naradin lifted his son in his arms. The baby was crying now. Eilan came and bound his wounded arm. There were tears on her cheeks as she kissed his soft forehead. Croesan the Thane took his grandson. He cupped the baby's head in his great hand and gazed down into a face contorted by mounting unhappiness.

"Hush, hush," whispered the Thane. "The Blood shall sustain you, little Croesan. The Blood shall sustain you."

He put all his belief into the words. He meant them with all his heart, yet knew they were only a part of the bargain. The Blood would not sustain his brother's daughter, imprisoned somewhere in this very city that Sirian had built. Croesan himself had held the crumpled message from his besiegers over the flame of a lamp and watched Anyara's life burn away in his hand. He had no choice, just as there had been no choice but to bar the gates of the castle against his own townsfolk when the enemy drew too near. Yes, the Blood sustained its people. Sometimes too it made demands of them that would break the hardest heart, and Croesan's heart had never been of the very hardest stuff.

* * *

Anyara found marks scratched on the wall of her cell. As far as she could tell, running her fingertips over them, they were nothing more than a counting of days: a dozen short, shallow lines gouged out of the stone by some previous inhabitant of the jail.

Her own days passed with grinding slowness, every minute extending itself as if to savor her impotence. Even so, she found herself wishing it would slow still further, so that the moment when hope died would be delayed. Every morning she woke half-expecting that they would come and take her to be killed.

She leapt up and grabbed at the bars of the tiny window to test their strength, and found they were immovable. She tried to strike up conversation with one of the guards, choosing a man who seemed a fraction less implacable than the others. He did not respond to her approaches and gave no sign of even noticing when she smiled her finest smile and fingered the hem of her ragged skirt for him. For half a day she feigned illness in the hope that they might move her to a less secure place. She writhed upon her mattress, clasping her stomach and copying the sounds she had heard serving women in Kolglas make when they were giving birth. When a guard came in and asked her what was wrong she pretended she could not reply. The woman seized her hair and turned her face upward, holding her like that for a few seconds before snorting and leaving. After a few hours had passed and no one else came she abandoned the pretense.

So much time passed that she almost started to believe they were not going to kill her after all. She resisted that thought. The hope she needed to find was a strong one, not one based on an illusion that the world was going to change its nature and become kind and merciful. She had to look after herself. It was what she had always done.

III

A family — mother, father and two young boys — was being executed in Anduran's main square. Kanin nan Horin-Gyre was there to witness it. They had tried to hide food from one of the Bloodheir's foraging parties. A poorly relaid section of boarding in the floor of their house betrayed a few bags of flour and dried meats, and condemned them all to death. None disputed the order that the children must die as well as their parents. The reasoning was common currency amongst the northern Bloods: if a life must be taken, take those of any who might avenge it at the same time. Still, Kanin had commanded that the family should have quick deaths, their throats cut with sharp knives as they knelt blindfolded upon the cobbles of the square. Cruelty would not have added to the message their deaths were meant to send.

It was not the sullen resistance of these common folk that had brought a black mood down upon the Horin-Gyre Bloodheir. He expected little else; had expected more of it than he had found, in fact. Rather, it was the mere fact that he was standing here in the miserable drizzle watching them die while his true foes were ensconced behind unyielding walls. He had dared to imagine, as he struggled through the seemingly unending wilderness of Anlane with his army, that fate would be kind to them. He had hoped that the head of the Lannis Thane might be on a spike over the castle gatehouse by now. Instead he faced the prospect of a wearing siege, with time as great an enemy as the warriors on Castle Anduran's walls. He strove for the humble acceptance of fate's course his faith demanded, but it was hard.

This war had been a desperate enterprise from the start, conceived in the hope that fate would favor the bold. The border stronghold of Tanwrye was too stern an obstacle to be easily overcome, as the Horin-Gyre Blood had learned to its cost in the past, but when the halfbreed Aeglyss had appeared at the Horin-Gyre fortress of Hakkan, promising that he could deliver the aid of the White Owl Kyrinin, Kanin's father Angain had glimpsed opportunity. Although Kanin felt nothing but contempt for the progeny of such obscene interbreeding — and Aeglyss had struck him from the start as a particularly distasteful and self-serving example of his kind — even he had been exhilarated by the possibility the *na'kyrim* offered up: an entire Horin-Gyre army smuggled through Anlane deep into enemy lands, reducing Tanwrye to an irrelevance. Before Kanin was born, when Angain himself was Bloodheir, the finest of the Horin-Gyre Blood had been slaughtered at Tanwrye by the army of Lannis-Haig. Angain's younger brother had died there while Angain lay in his sickbed, prostrated by a wound taken in a bear hunt. Aeglyss offered the Thane not just vengeance but a kind of healing when he promised that he could open a path to the heart of Lannis-Haig.

Out in the center of the square one of Kanin's shieldmen was reading aloud the sentence. There was not much of an audience. Aside from the Bloodheir and some of his Shield, the only onlookers were a few groups of warriors huddled in their cloaks and a dozen or so residents of the city who had been dragged out to watch. They were poor folk, clad in ragged clothes and keeping their eyes down. They gave every sign of indifference to what was happening in front of them. Kanin knew, though, that they would spread word of Horin-Gyre justice through the small population left in Anduran.

The other Bloods of the Black Road had mocked Angain's proposal at first, not least because the very idea of alliance with a Kyrinin clan was repellent to them. Even when grudging assent was granted, no more than a thousand Gyre swords had been lent, and those only in support of the feint against Tanwrye. More would come, the High Thane pledged, if fortune showed the way; it was obvious what he thought the likelihood of that was. And a hundred or so warriors of the Battle Inkall had come forward, of course, with Shraeve at their head. The thought still twisted a barb in Kanin's guts. The Inkallim had betrayed his family all those years ago at Tanwrye, watching from a knoll while the Horin-Gyre warriors were overwhelmed, and he did not trust them now. Shraeve, though, had been the one who suggested that not just the Thane but all the ruling line of Lannis-Haig should die, and volunteered some of her warriors for an assault on Kolglas. Aeglyss had again delivered White Owl aid for that attack. However much Kanin despised the *na'kyrim,* his value was beyond dispute. Without the food and guides provided by the woodwights, he might have lost half his warriors on the march through Anlane; the other half would probably have been killed in skirmishing if the White Owls had been actively hostile.

Fate had played a cruel trick in the last days before the army was to march. Life began to loosen its grip upon Angain oc Horin-Gyre. His strength slipped away and all his desire was not enough to let him take the field. So when the time had come, Kanin and his sister Wain had knelt at the side of their father's bed, the scent of his sickness filling their nostrils, and promised to put an end to Lannis-Haig for him.

The executioners were tying back their victims' hair. One of the boys — the younger one to judge by his size — was struggling against fear. His lips were shaking, convulsed by the half-strangled sobs that filled his throat. Kanin saw but did not note it. His thoughts had strayed far from what his eyes observed.

They had come so close to success. The attack across the Vale of Stones had trapped most of Lannis-Haig's strength to the north; the castle at Kolglas was fired and the Thane's brother killed; the town of Anduran itself had fallen pitifully easily. Yet it had not been quite enough. The castle held, and the Thane within waited for his allies to come to him. If Tanwrye had been assaulted a few hours earlier, or Kanin himself been a single day later in emerging from Anlane, there might have been hardly a warrior left in Anduran to man the castle. Croesan might have been caught exposed upon the road between his capital and Tanwrye. That had been the intention; the hope. On such fine margins did fate work its will.

Out on the square, blades cut through flesh. Four bodies toppled forward. Legs kicked; heads jerked in time to a slowing beat. Blood poured over the ground, running in intricate patterns along the countless channels between the cobblestones. Kanin wheeled his horse about and nudged it toward the merchant's house he and Wain had made their own.

Wain. His other half; his stronger half, he sometimes thought. He knew very well that the majority of warriors they commanded feared her far more than they did him. The fervor of Wain's belief in the Black Road, and in the Blood, was a beacon for all of them. Those things burned in Kanin's breast too, but in Wain they were informed by a passion so ferocious its light could blind.

Angain had often tried to make his son marry. None of the brides Kanin had been offered — the fawning daughters of great landowners, even the mesmerizingly beautiful niece of Orinn oc Wyn-Gyre — had been a match for his sister. Kanin could not imagine himself marrying until he found a woman who could be measured against Wain and withstand the comparison.

He found her upstairs in what had once been quite a grand bedroom. The merchant whose family had lived here must have been a gifted trader, for the house was as finely fitted out as any Kanin had seen in his homeland save the homes of Thanes and their kin. Wooden panels carved with hunting scenes covered the walls. Ornate iron stands held flickering candles. There were wolf and bear skins laid out on the floor. They had been found in the loft, with dozens of others forgotten or abandoned by the fleeing family.

Wain was seated before a long, narrow table. She had set a burnished shield up on it and was grimacing at her distorted reflection as she ran an antler comb through her hair.

"Done?" she asked, without looking round.

"It is done. I would rather have had them working on the walls."

"Four more pairs of hands will not make the city any more fit to meet an assault," said Wain. "Four cut throats may yield a good deal more food."

"Indeed." Wearily, Kanin unbuckled his leather tunic and cast it to the floor. The light shirt he wore beneath was soaked through.

"I'll have someone light a fire," his sister said.

He crossed the room and took the comb from her hands. "In a while. Let me do that. You'll pull your hair out before you straighten it."

He stood in silence for a few minutes, unteasing her hair with methodical persistence. Concentrating upon the task distracted him from his troubled thoughts. Her locks were beautiful, even dirty and knotted as they were. He could smell smoke and grime and sweat on her.

"You've been laboring?" he asked.

"With the machine-makers. There's enough timber and rope here to make a hundred war engines. It's the hands skilled in the making that we lack; we lost some of our best back in the forest. Still, another few days and we'll be throwing the ruins of their precious city down their throats."

"Another few days. And a week after that to break down the walls or the gate. Or two weeks? Or six? Have we got that long, Wain?"

She shrugged. Looking down at her hands resting in her lap, Kanin could see that she was toying with her rings. It made him smile. The habit had been with her as long as he could remember, and he could summon with perfect clarity the sight of her, an ungovernable, independent child sitting in her night robes and doing the same thing: turning, always turning, the ring on her finger. It happened when her mind was working, as if her thoughts moved with such force that they had to have some external echo. She had long since stopped noticing when she did it, and if ever Kanin pointed it out — which he sometimes did, with a studied air of innocence — she would glare at him with such annoyance that he laughed. That too reminded him of when she was young, of her severe expression whenever she had observed something that offended her child's sense of what was right.

"The guards told me you went to see our prisoners the other day," he said to diffuse the temptation of teasing her.

"I did."

"And?"

"The girl has more strength than I expected. Not as feeble as most of them seem. She is afraid, though, like all of them. They live in fear."

"What about the halfbreed?"

Wain's reflection showed her lack of interest. "I don't think he's said a word since he was locked up. The guards stay out of his way. We should kill him and have done with it."

Patience had never been a part of Wain's armory. When they had been children she had always been the one to court a scolding by loosing her dogs too soon on a hunt or venturing out on the ice too early in the season, before the adults judged it thick enough. Kanin knew it was hard for her, this inactivity. That was why she had gone to bait the Lannis-Haig girl. It was why she drove the workers making the siege engines so hard.

"You never know when even a rat is going to have its use," Kanin said. "Look at Aeglyss. He's served a purpose. Still, we'll see. After they've stewed a little longer in the castle we can let them watch while we finish the girl. Maybe we should kill the halfbreed at the same time."

Wain's hands had become still. As a rule, it meant she had reached some conclusion. Kanin met her reflected eyes. She was excited.

"It's coming soon," Wain said. "I can feel it in my bones. The Road is going to turn, one way or the other. What do you think? Light or darkness for us?"

"One or the other, Wain," he said. "One or the other. Aid will come to us from the north, or to Croesan from the south. This is a horse we can only stay astride. We cannot lead it where we will."

"Yes, yes," and he heard that fierce certainty in her voice that he knew so well, "but still I say something is coming. One way or the other."

A huge man, all muscular bulk, appeared in the doorway: Igris, chief of Kanin's shieldmen. He waited in silence, staring rigidly ahead. Kanin set aside the comb.

"What is it?" he asked.

"The halfbreed asked for an audience. We told him you would not see him." The man's voice was deep and strong.

"Very well," said Kanin. Wain rose and began buckling on her sword belt.

"He's insistent, though," Igris said. "He still waits outside. He asks that he be allowed to speak with the other halfbreed, the one from Kolglas. The guards turned him away when he tried to get in to the jail."

Kanin sighed in irritation. "So he has you running around as his messenger, does he?"

For the first time, the shieldman glanced at his master. His face was impassive, but there might have been the faintest flicker of doubt in his eyes.

"Perhaps he charmed you with that voice of his?" Kanin suggested. "Perhaps you listened a little too closely when he suggested you should pass on his request?"

"No, my lord. I do not think so."

"Well you wouldn't, would you? What do you think, Wain? Perhaps we should rid ourselves of Aeglyss."

His sister was testing her blade's edge with her thumb.

"He's obsessed with Kennet's tame halfbreed. Let them talk to each other. What harm can it do? It might keep Aeglyss quiet for a while, at least."

* * *

There was room in the Shared for Inurian to find peace. By stilling the chatter of his senses and freeing his mind of all contact with the world about him, he could sink back through deep strata of silence and darkness. He could bring about dissolution. It was a feeling none save another *na'kyrim* could hope to understand, and even amongst them precious few could attain it as he did. Time lost its meaning there, in the abyssal places, and the mind could find solace. It was a respite he needed during his incarceration in Anduran.

On the fifth night of his imprisonment he lay down upon the floor. He let his awareness of the cold and of the stone beneath him fall away. He shut out the harsh voices in the yard outside and the whispering rivulets of rainwater trickling down the walls of his prison. His breathing shallowed, taking on a steady trance-rhythm. His thoughts slipped away behind him, like eddies in the wake of a ship. His mind was smoke, attenuating. He was thousands, thousands of thousands. He was Huanin, Kyrinin, even joyful Saolin. He ran within Kyrinin hunters, felt the lovestruck awe of every Huanin mother, the abandoned exultation of the Saolin's shapeshifting.

Even the Whreinin had left their traces in the eternity of the Shared. Although the wolfenkind were long gone, they had once walked the world and the Shared would never forget it. He could sense the wolfenkind's savage cruelty, that had finally driven the Tainted Races to hound them to extinction, but there was no judgment in the sensing of it. The Shared was all things, and there was no good or evil in it, no right and wrong. There was only existence, or the memory of existence.

The Anain alone lay beyond him. They were there, like the rest — theirs was an immeasurable, illimitable presence — but their nature was of a different kind, and not something any *na'kyrim* could comprehend or taste.

Inurian faded, dispersing into the seamless unity that underlay thought and life. He had surrendered himself thus to the Shared many times in his life, but on this occasion the experience was marred. Something tugged at his awareness, refusing to allow its cleansing dissolution. It was as if the last flimsy threads of his mind caught upon some snag and were held. For a moment he strove to dissipate those final elements of his self. The focus grew stronger. The sensation of his thoughts recoalescing was almost physical. It grieved him to be thus denied release. As he ascended toward consciousness, he felt that which had prevented his escape drawing closer: a turbulent shadow casting itself over him and wrapping the sharp stench of corruption around him. Like a drop falling upon the still surface of a pool, something had marred the perfection of the Shared.

He opened his eyes to find Aeglyss standing before him.

"I am not sure what you were doing, but I would like to learn the way of it," Aeglyss said quietly. A faint smile was playing across his pale, thin lips.

Inurian rose and flexed his right knee to ease its protests. The long walk through Anlane, and the damp and cold of his miserable cell, had reminded the joint of a twisting fall long ago on the rough slopes of the Car Anagais. He returned his visitor's gaze unresponsively, burying his surprise and the sudden presentiment of horror that accompanied it. It was clear that Aeglyss was the cause of the turbulence in the Shared; what that implied about the man's potential potency put a sliver of fear into Inurian's heart.

"Can we not even talk to one another?" Aeglyss persisted. "I wish only to learn from you. I need your help — your guidance — to harness the strength I know I possess."

He took a short step closer to Inurian. "Our interests run in the same channel. These people would kill you without a second thought: I have been arguing on your behalf ever since we arrived here."

"That's a lie," Inurian said evenly.

"Ah, so you're interested enough to go scrabbling about inside my head. What do you see there? I could keep you out — I did at Kolglas — but there's no need to. You must know I mean you no harm."

"I don't need the Shared to tell me that you are no friend of mine," replied Inurian. It was true only in part. He was not prepared to give even a hint of how unsettling the things he sensed in Aeglyss were. The younger man carried such a roiling knot of anger and resentment in him that Inurian could almost taste it.

"Use me, then, if you refuse my friendship," snapped Aeglyss. "I hoped for more from another *na'kyrim,* but I should have known better. I've had no better from *na'kyrim* than from anyone else. Why should you be any different?"

It took an effort of will for Inurian not to wince at the sharp, sudden pain that flared in Aeglyss as he spoke. That was what underlay all the more ferocious emotions that burned in Aeglyss.

Beneath the bitterness was pain: a deep-rooted hurt, profound and lonely.

"Help me because I can help you," Aeglyss insisted. "I cannot force you — I know I've not the strength for that, not yet — but if you help me to understand what I am capable of, you will benefit as much as I will. I know I can do things with the Shared no one has been able to do in years. I know it!"

Inurian regarded the other man. He could almost pity him. Almost, but not quite.

"No." He shook his head. "I cannot help you."

For an instant, a terrible fury burned in Aeglyss' grey eyes. Unable to help himself, Inurian glanced away. When he forced himself to meet the other's gaze again, that fury had gone.

"We can talk about it another time, perhaps," said Aeglyss.

He left, closing and barring the door behind him.

* * *

In the first hour or two of daylight, the Children of the Hundred came out onto Anduran's market square. Kanin was there, organizing a party of Horin-Gyre warriors who were about to head south down the valley. Anduran itself might have fallen quickly, but there was troubling, sporadic resistance throughout the countryside. The survivors of a minor battle near Targlas, halfway between Anduran and Tanwrye, had just straggled in: they had been victorious, and probably broken the will of that town's populace, but it had cost thirty lives that Kanin could ill afford.

Already in a foul mood, he watched the Inkallim taking up their sparring positions. Every morning they did this, performing their elaborate and precise ritualistic combats beneath the steely gaze of Shraeve, their leader.

She stood attentive and motionless as the first clash of blades rang out. She was a tall woman, lean and powerful. Her long hair, dyed black like that of all Inkallim, was tied back. Two swords were sheathed crossways upon her back. Never yet had Kanin seen her draw them. She would be lethal, he knew: lethality was the sole purpose of the Battle Inkall. Although only around eighty remained of the hundred or more who had joined the long march through Anlane — a dozen or so Hunt Inkallim had come too, but their business was not on the battlefield — eighty of the Battle were worth at least two hundred ordinary warriors, probably more. They followed Shraeve's command, though. Kanin could no more tell them when and where to employ their skills than he could order the passage of the clouds across the sky. He was not inclined to make the attempt, in any case; he would as soon trust one of the long-dead wolfenkind as the ravens' loyalty to his cause.

Wain put a hand on his shoulder, disturbing his dark musings.

"Come away," she said. "The time of our testing is here."

He looked at her questioningly.

"Our scouts have found an army gathering, between Glasbridge and Kolglas. It's coming up the south side of the valley."

"So soon?" said Kanin. "I'd hoped . . . well, no matter. How many?"

"Three or four thousand, they say. With Kilkry-Haig riders in the van."

That was a bitter blow. Lannis alone, Kanin would have hoped to defeat; an army strengthened by the prideful horsemen of Kilkry was a sterner test. What was coming now would be utterly different from the skirmishing that had been going on up and down the valley for the past few days. He had, at best, equal numbers to stand against the enemy, and hundreds of those would have to remain in position around the castle to keep Croesan from sallying forth. Worse, almost a third of his strength was Tarbain tribesmen who would be grass beneath the scythe of Kilkry cavalry. Shraeve and her Inkallim might be enough to make a difference, but he would not ask for her aid.

"That will be enough to test us, indeed," he murmured.

"We should send for Aeglyss," Wain said. She shook her head

slightly at the doubt on Kanin's face. "He has not given up hope of winning our favor. We can use that. He may be able to persuade the White Owls to give battle once more. It probably won't work, but we lose nothing in the attempt. If he succeeds, we can dispense with him and with his woodwights just as we did before; if he fails, he fails."

Kanin grimaced. "Are we so desperate? We were going to do this together, for our father. For the Blood. I don't want it . . . fouled. In any case, what can a *na'kyrim* and a few woodwights do against an army?"

She shrugged. "I do not know. Is there harm in trying, though? I like him no better than you do, but if fate dictates that Aeglyss is a weapon we are to use against our enemies, that is what he will be. It is not for us to choose."

"I suppose they are good archers if nothing else, the woodwights." Kanin glanced back toward the Inkallim. Their swords were flashing in the low morning sun. Shraeve was watching him, he saw. She ignored her warriors and stared directly at the Bloodheir.

He turned away. "Very well. Let's talk to Aeglyss. If he can turn the White Owls to our cause again, he's got even more talents than I thought. But as you say, we lose nothing in the attempt."

IV

There was no singing or cheering in the ranks of the army that Kanin and Wain led out from Anduran. A grim silence hung over the tight-packed companies of warriors. There was a certain resolution in the quiet of the Horin-Gyre men and women; that of the Tarbain levies who swelled their numbers had more the feel of nervousness about it. Open, massed battle against a strong foe was not the way the tribesmen would choose to make war. They were still raiders and ambushers in their hearts.

Although Kanin and his sister had debated the wisest course

almost to the last hour, the outcome had never seriously been in doubt. They both knew they could not retire northward. If they did, Croesan and Lheanor oc Kilkry-Haig would just gather their forces and come after them. Standing and fighting, victory was still possible if fate allowed it. And if this one victory could be won, Castle Anduran might well fall before their enemies could mount another relief attempt. Wain resolutely confirmed Kanin's instinct: give battle. Test fate, and do it on open ground, too far from the city for Croesan to take a hand. The story of the Road's course was told long ago. It could not be escaped; only faced.

The Inkallim were taking the field, at least, with Shraeve at their head. Kanin had not asked them to come. In this as in all things the Inkallim did as they pleased. They had dyed their hair before marching, though: it was as glisteningly black as fresh pitch. That might mean they would fight.

Beneath heavy skies and a soft rain, they passed by Grive. The little town was still. No smoke rose from the chimneys, its streets were empty and the windows of the houses shut fast. Most of the inhabitants had fled. The remainder hid themselves away. The land here was flat, crossed by narrow ditches, dotted with tiny copses of willow and alder. Abandoned cattle lowed disconsolately as the army went by. Kanin dispatched a handful of warriors to round them up and return them to Anduran. A swirl of crows, kites and buzzards was circling above an unseen carcass. You will be gorging yourselves soon, thought Kanin.

They were not far beyond Grive when Kanin's outriders returned. They reported that the enemy was a few hours away, moving along the southern edge of the Glas Water. Kanin found a place where any attack upon his lines must come across the wet, heavy ground of a wide grass field, and drew up his forces. Ditches to the north and south would hamper any attempt to turn his position; bloody and bruising as it would be, a face-to-face confrontation, stripped of any subtlety or maneuver, seemed to offer his best chance of victory. His two hundred or so mounted men he kept in the rear, with his Shield. The Inkallim arrayed themselves upon his right, behind the main line. They squatted down on the grass. Kanin ignored them. He would not demean himself by asking Shraeve her intentions.

With so few riders, the Bloodheir could not hope to attack. Too many of the horses that had left Hakkan with him had died, or fed the hungry, in Anlane. All he could do was wait, and hope that spears, courage and the muddy ground would suffice against the charge that he knew must come. If Aeglyss could somehow produce some White Owls willing to fight it might help, but Kanin had all but resigned himself to the halfbreed's failure. Aeglyss had been gone for more than a day and time had run out. It was no great surprise: whatever subtle tricks of persuasion and deceit the *na'kyrim* could work with his half-human voice, Kanin had never really believed he was equal to the task of convincing the woodwights to once again serve the purposes of the Black Road. His willingness to make the effort had been embarrassingly effusive, though. The halfbreed's urgent desire to ingratiate himself was pathetic.

Out in the distance to his right, he could see a dark mass looming over the flat expanse of the Glas Water. It could only be Kan Avor, the drowned city that had once been the Gyre Blood's home and now called like an imprisoned lover across all the miles to every northerner's heart. It would be fitting to test the fates here, within sight of those broken-backed towers. And so close to Grive: that had been the home of Tegric, whose hundred men held the Stone Vale against all the Kilkry Bloods for the day the people of the Black Road needed to escape into the north. It was the Inkallim who called themselves the Children of the Hundred, but any warrior might draw inspiration from Tegric's example. Here, today, Kanin would make his own stand.

* * *

Far from Anduran, beyond the vertiginous peaks and heaving glaciers of the Tan Dihrin, light snow was falling on the slopes around Castle Hakkan. In the night not long gone, for the first time in a week, the scouring northern wind had ceased to blow across Horin-Gyre lands and the morning's snow was settling on frost-coated ground.

That frost crackled beneath his feet as Ragnor oc Gyre, High Thane of all the Bloods of the Black Road, strode toward the entrance to the catacombs. His cape of sable fur skimmed across the ground, stirring the thin layer of snow like dust raised into pirouettes by a broom. Behind him marched Angain oc Horin-Gyre's household. The late Thane's Shield came in the midst of the procession, bearing his shrouded body on their shoulders. There was no sound save the trudge of feet and the tolling of the bells that rang from the castle below and all the rocky crags around. The low, flat clouds trapped the sound of the bells in the valley, building echo upon echo until the air shook with it.

The High Thane led the way up to the mouth of the tunnel. It gaped like the bolthole of some huge mountain beast. Torches were burning inside, lighting the passage to the chamber where Angain would join those who had traveled this way before. Ragnor did not enter. He stood to one side of the entrance as the corpse-bearers came forward and went in. Angain's widow, Vana, dressed in the ermine only widows wore, followed them. She went past the High Thane without looking at him. Her dead husband's oldest hunting dog — the grey hound that had kept vigil at the foot of his bed throughout his last days — walked at her side. Its tread was sluggish and weary.

The only other to enter the catacomb, walking behind Vana, was a figure hidden from view by a capacious grey cloak. A great hood covered his face. This was Theor, the First of the Lore Inkall. There was nothing to distinguish his robe from that of the lowliest Inkallim in the earliest years of service; nothing to say that he held a power in these lands as great, in its way, as that of the High Thane.

The rest of the dead man's household waited a short distance from where Ragnor stood. The flecks of snow began to crowd in the air. Nobody spoke. The bells rang and rang, distant celebratory peals now. Ragnor waited.

Angain's Shield, having discharged their final duty, emerged first. A short time later Vana and Theor followed. As they walked up the passage they doused the torches that lined its walls, so that as they moved back toward the light, darkness reclaimed its territory and took possession of the dead Thane. Ragnor inclined his head as Vana drew near to him. He offered her his hand and she fleetingly took hold of it. The dog at her side looked up at Ragnor with torpid eyes.

"He waits in peace, my lady," the High Thane said. "A fortunate man, to leave this bitter world behind."

He was looking at the back of her hand. Many years ago, before she was betrothed, he had tried to bed this woman himself. She had been a magnificent, haughty girl, and she had refused him. That had taken courage, since his temper in those days was extravagant. He looked now at the back of her hand, and wondered at how small and old it was, lying there in his grip.

"Fortunate indeed," she said. "I will see him again. I look forward to that." Her voice was not so frail as her hand. That girl Ragnor remembered was still within. She went to join the others, who crowded around her.

The First of the Lore Inkall stood at Ragnor's side. They watched as the crowd shared out sweetmeats and small beakers of grain spirit. A soft murmur of conversation began to rise, a touch of laughter here and there. They would be telling Vana tales of her husband's first life now, and looking forward to his second. Death was not an occasion for too much mourning in the lands of the Black Road. One by one, the bells around the valley fell silent.

Theor slipped back the hood of his cloak to reveal startlingly silver-grey hair. His lips, nestled within a short beard, were stained black by years of seerstem use. His skin had forgotten its youth and sagged from his cheekbones. Only his eyes retained some semblance of vigor, for they were bright and would have sat well in a face thirty years younger.

The creaking sound of a heavy-laden wagon drew his attention down to the track running along the valley floor. Two horses, whipped on by a group of Tarbains, were straining to haul a flat-bedded cart over the uneven surface. It bore a cage in which a massive bear swayed, giving out a long, low rumble of suppressed fury.

"Destined for Castle Hakkan, no doubt," sighed Theor with a slight shake of his head.

"You disapprove," said Ragnor, eyeing the creature in the cage.

"This baiting of bears upon a lord's death is a relic of Tarbain beliefs from before we came, when the bear was the symbol of their chieftains. Should the Lore Inkall approve of its adoption by a Blood of the Road?"

The wagon rocked, one of its wheels thumping down into a rut. The bear bellowed and its Tarbain captors yelled back and rattled the bars of the cage with their spears.

"It means nothing now," said Ragnor. "Sport for drunkards toasting their master's passing. And good sport, too. Have you seen the dogs they breed in these parts, First? Vicious. They'd give even those monsters your Hunt uses pause for thought. Still, that bear looks as though it will take more than a few of them with it."

The Inkallim's dark lip curled with distaste. "Whatever its merits, it is a corrupt tradition. Angain has gone to await rebirth in a brighter world, not to some mountain guarded by the ghosts of bears. We have enough trouble bringing the Tarbains out of the darkness of their ignorance without our own Thanes endorsing their rites."

Ragnor snorted. "We are all Tarbains now, Theor."

Theor glowered at the High Thane. "There is no Tarbain blood in my lineage. Nor yours."

"If you say so, Lorekeeper. Makes ours the only two pure lines in the north, though. What does it matter? Fane and Wyn, even my own Blood, count many Tarbains amongst their oathbound followers. I've plenty in my Shield who're part Tarbain. And you know as well as I do that man we just laid to rest, may he molder and never wake" — he saw, but ignored, Theor's twinge of distaste at the phrase — "had more than a trace of the wilderness in him. His grandmother's appetites were not very particular, they say. Anyway, if we'd not had the savages' blood to renew our own we'd be breeding nothing but freaks and idiots by now. Looking at some of the offspring my liegemen have produced I wonder if we've had enough of it."

Theor gathered himself for a riposte, but changed his mind and looked back toward the bear.

"Perhaps you are right," he said. "There are few of the Tarbain left who do not bend the knee to you now, in any case. Most are Saved."

"Indeed." Ragnor produced a flask from deep within his heavy cape and unstoppered it. He took a long drink of its contents and wiped his lips with satisfaction. He offered the flask to Theor, who declined.

"Your loss," muttered the High Thane. "A powerful protection against the chill, this stuff. Will you walk with me a way? No matter how keen they are for the revels, the rest will not dare return to the castle until we move, and I'd hate them to get themselves frost-bitten."

They walked side by side, the lord of the Gyre Bloods and the lord of the Inkallim, and the rest fell in behind them like a well-drilled company of soldiers. The High Thane's Shield ensured that a respectful distance was maintained, to give the great ones their privacy. Down at the foot of the slope the bear in its cage followed a parallel course, matching their pace toward the castle where its bloody end awaited.

"You were within the catacomb with Vana for some time," the High Thane mused.

"We spoke a little," Theor said. "She sought my views on whether her husband had been true enough to the Road to earn his rebirth in the new world."

"Can't say I'm sorry to see the back of Angain," Ragnor said. "His was a miserable spirit."

"He was true, in his heart, to the Black Road."

"That he was. Here's to him," and the High Thane took another great swallow of fortifying liquid. Snow was matting down his hair, melting and running onto his forehead. "Bad time to die, with his children off on this mad adventure in the south."

"They do as their fates require," said Theor. "But, yes, it might have been easier for all of us if he had lived a while longer, or if Kanin at least had remained in Hakkan."

"Yet you've got your little war maiden down there with them," chuckled Ragnor. "What a woman that one is! I'd give a lot for a few like her in my Shield."

"Shraeve is . . . her own woman," murmured Theor, "and not easily dissuaded from a course once she is set upon it. She believed Kolglas could be taken. When someone wishes so fervently to test their fate it is their right. Anyway, I do not interfere in the doings of the Battle Inkall. That is Nyve's domain."

"Well, he's trained himself a fierce raven in Shraeve. Still, she might have met her match in Wain. I pity poor Croesan. With Shraeve and Wain for enemies, and Gryvan oc Haig for an ally, he's about as lucky as a man beset by wolves and finding nothing but a donkey to ride away on." He emptied the drinking flask and tossed it away to shatter amongst the rocks. He blew his cheeks out and turned up his collar. "It'll be cold tonight. This cloud won't last once the stars come round."

They walked in silence for a short distance. The cart carrying the bear had become stuck again, and Ragnor glanced down the slope as its Tarbain escort strove to lever the jammed wheel free. They were shouting curses in their harsh language. The cart rocked forward and back again. The haunches of the horses were turning bloody beneath the switches of their handlers. Ragnor gave a snort of disgust.

"Never known how to manage horses, those people."

"There were none here until we came. Tell me, what do you think will happen if Wain and Kanin do not return from south of the Vale?"

"Ah, you want to trade tales of spies? Well, I'm willing. Mine say those Gaven buzzards are eyeing up Horin lands already. Supposedly, Lakkan has ten years' production from his silver mines put aside to offer me for them if Angain's children die. What has the Hunt Inkall been whispering in your ear?"

The Lorekeeper shrugged. "Similar. But Orinn oc Wyn-Gyre covets them too, and would not willingly see them pass to Gaven-Gyre. Angain would have served you better by having a larger family, or keeping the heir he did have safe, at least."

"It's his children who've failed me there," smiled Ragnor. "Kanin's eyes are focused too close to home, and Wain herself is about as welcoming to suitors as that brute in the cage down there. It's a poor example they set, when we spend so much time telling the commonfolk they have a duty to breed. Horin has always been a Blood to make more problems than it solves. I'd not shed many tears over its demise, even if it sets Gaven and Wyn at each other's throats."

"No more than Gryvan oc Haig would shed for the Lannis Blood, I imagine," said Theor pointedly.

"Do you think so?"

"Your father always embraced the Inkallim with his confidence. There were no secrets between him and my predecessor, yet I find myself uncertain of your intent in allowing this war to begin."

"There were ravens there when Angain and I discussed it. Nyve himself on one occasion, I seem to recall. He made a number of helpful observations on Tanwrye's defenses."

The First of the Lore Inkall looked grave. "And I am sure Angain was aware of your full intent, of course. Nevertheless, there were occasions when your father had plans afoot that did not find their way into the ears of the lesser Thanes. At such times, it was to the Inkallim that he turned. He did so when the Horin-Gyre Blood required chastisement in the past, you will recall."

"I do recall," the High Thane said lightly. "They were a still more unruly brood in those days. But come, if you suspect me of keeping secrets from you, say so. The Lore Inkall has always enjoyed the liberty of plain-speaking."

"I make no accusation. I am sure that whatever plots or devices you may have in progress are intended to further the cause of the Black Road. To strengthen the creed, rather than weaken it. Or give succor to its enemies."

Ragnor stopped. After a couple of strides, Theor turned and looked back at the High Thane. Behind them, Ragnor's Shield halted and the entire funeral procession shuffled to a standstill, puzzled at the sudden delay. No voices were raised in query or protest, though. The crowd simply stood in the gently falling snow and waited. When Ragnor spoke his voice was low, ensuring none save Theor could hear, but it was icily precise.

"Not an accusation, but a threat perhaps? I would kill any man who suggested that any action of mine weakened the creed. Save one of the Lore Inkallim, given the privileged position your people enjoy in such matters."

The First of the Lore smiled.

"Such privileges do not extend beyond matters of the creed, of course," continued Ragnor.

"Of course. But do not misunderstand me, High Thane. I make neither accusation nor threat. My only desire is to see an absence of secrets between Gyre and the Inkallim. We are the roots and boughs of the Black Road, the Gyre Blood and the Inkallim. In years past the creed has been saved, or renewed, time and again by the two of us acting in concert. Anything that undermines that unity gives me cause for concern."

"Yes. Well, you are custodian of the creed, and . . ."

The High Thane's words were interrupted by a sudden chaos of cries and creaking wood. He and Theor both turned to see one of the carthorses rearing in panic. Its companion started forward, twisting the cart round. The stuck wheel came free and bounced against a rock as it scraped sideways. The bear was roused by the tumult and half-rose onto its hind legs. The tribesmen yelled furiously. Ragnor saw what was going to happen a moment before they did, and muttered, "What fools."

The bed of the cart tilted, shifting the cage, and the bear reeled sideways. With a slow inevitability, accompanied by a thunderous, splintering crash, cart and cage toppled over. The Tarbains shouted louder still. Both of the carthorses began to buck and struggle. Roaring, the huge bear tore its way out of the wreckage and raised itself up to its full height. The men scattered. One was a fraction slow, and the beast ran him down in a few strides. A single sweep of its paw knocked him flat and its jaws engulfed his head. The bear shook its prey from side to side, and the sharp snapping of the Tarbain's neck was clearly audible to all in the funeral party. As the surviving tribesmen fled down the track, the bear stood over the body for a moment or two then swung around and glared at the throng a hundred yards or so up the slope.

"I suppose we had better do something," said Ragnor. He gave a flick of his head and his Shield separated themselves from the other mourners. Crossbows were released from their bindings. The bear shook itself and came a few paces toward them. It reared up once more and roared.

"Magnificent," the High Thane murmured. Some of his warriors knelt, the rest stood in a rank behind them. They were slotting bolts into place. The bear dropped onto all fours and bounded closer over the rocks. It rose again, bellowing defiance. Angain's hound was barking furiously, as if imagining that his dead master was at his side still.

A dozen crossbows sang and their shafts flowered together in the bear's chest. It swayed, fell forward onto its forepaws, took a few unsteady steps and then slumped down. Its great flank heaved and they could hear its rasping breaths. One of the shieldmen drew his sword and strode down to administer the final blow.

"A magnificent animal, don't you think?" Ragnor said to the Lore Inkallim. "As fearless in the face of death as any true believer could hope to be."

"Fearless or ignorant," Theor said absently. His eyes never left the bear as the warrior sank his sword into its neck. A slight frown settled over his features.

"It's as well you don't hold with the old Tarbain symbols," said Ragnor. "On a day such as today, that might look an ill omen to those inclined to see it that way: presaging the death of a great lord, or changing times or some such nonsense." He turned and marched on toward Castle Hakkan, laughing to himself.

The master of the Lore Inkall did not follow at once. He watched as the shieldman drew his blade across the thick fur of the corpse to clean away the blood. When he did follow in the footsteps of the High Thane, he bore a thoughtful expression. He drew his grey hood up once more to shelter his face from the elements. The snow was getting heavier all the time.

* * *

A black line emerged out of the drizzling mist. More than three thousand, Kanin estimated as the companies fell into position facing his own. Some of them looked to be commonfolk: farmers, fishermen and villagers gathered from the southern Lannis-Haig lands. Many, though, were fighting men. The two lines were not far apart, and despite the leaden air he could hear shouts running to and fro along the enemy ranks, and the stamping of horses and the clatter of their harnesses. He saw a few banners hanging limply. He could identify only a few of them. At the center amidst a mass of horsemen stood one that bore the insignia of Kilkry-Haig. Kanin sniffed and shook raindrops from his hair. He glanced across to Wain. She sat astride her horse close by, the half-dozen warriors of her Shield in attendance.

"It seems we have the chance to make a name for ourselves," Kanin said. "That's the Kilkry Bloodheir, isn't it?"

His sister grinned. "It would be sweet-tasting to win this one."

"As fate falls," murmured Kanin. "We can hope."

The waiting was a torment. The rain eased off, leaving wet clothes plastered to bodies. Kanin could feel his muscles growing stiff in the saddle. The Tarbain men before him were becoming restive, shifting about, muttering and shouting at one another in their barbarous tongue. Kanin rode down the line, quelling them with a fierce glare. The Horin-Gyre warriors amongst the tribesmen were still, quiet. He saw some of them murmuring under their breath as they stared fixedly ahead. He found his lips moving of their own accord, the whispered words coming without thought: "My feet are on the Road. I go without fear. I know not pride." Again and again, over and over. The Hooded God would hear and approve, if the words were spoken with true belief. And if that belief was still in the heart when the moment of death came, he would gather the fallen in to him to rest until the renewal of the world.

Finally, after an hour or more, there was movement. Horsemen began to stream across behind the opposing army, gathering on its left flank. They milled about there as minute by minute their numbers swelled: a hundred, two hundred, and more. At the same time, a line of archers were coming forward, strung out across the field. They advanced to within a long bowshot before kneeling. Kanin felt his pulse speeding, the sense of impending release building within him. Now the answer would come. Whatever happened, it was better than the waiting.

A hissing flight of arrows arced up and over. They pattered down, many falling short, others rattling against uplifted shields or smacking home in thigh or chest. It was a sound unlike any other, the thudding of an arrow into yielding flesh. Kanin's horse skittered sideways as the first cries rose up and it caught the scent of battle. He patted its neck. There was a second volley of arrows, and a third.

"More crossbows to face the horsemen," he called to Wain, and she nodded and cantered off. A few shouted commands sent crossbowmen scurrying from left to right to take up positions opposite the Kilkry horsemen. There was barely time, for a great clamor and blowing of horns rose up amongst the riders, and they wheeled their mounts about and began to advance across the field. Another shower of arrows came in. A stray one passed well over the line and felled a Tarbain warrior standing close by Kanin. He looked up at Kanin with a fixed expression of shock on his face as he died.

The riders came slowly at first, holding their horses on tight reins. Their speed picked up until, in a thundering burst of hoofs and flying clods of earth, they broke into a gallop. And here was another sound that had but one meaning: the visceral, swelling rumble, felt through ground and air, of the charge. It touched upon some leashed part of Kanin, shivering through his breastbone, and he felt it raising him up, bearing him in wild anticipation toward the clash that must follow. A volley of bolts flashed out to meet the charge. Horses crashed down, plowing into the soft ground, flinging their riders beneath the stamping feet of those who came behind. The crossbowmen stepped back, hurrying to reload, and spears sprouted along the front rank. When it came, the impact was like the wordless roar of a thousand voices.

The spear wall was not dense enough to deter all the horses, and the charge swept up and crashed against the footsoldiers. In moments, the right flank of the line was in chaos. Horses lunged through the mud and over bodies as their riders slashed around them. Tarbain tribesmen were already beginning to stream away in terror, flying back past Kanin's position. Knots of Horin-Gyre warriors formed, the cavalry swirling about them. Swordsmen and spearmen hacked and stabbed at the horses, while crossbowmen struggled to pick off the riders. The screams of animals and men flowed together into a single, high cacophony.

Kanin glanced along the rest of his line. Everywhere the Tarbains were wavering, groups of them edging back from their positions, jostling and arguing with the Horin-Gyre troops alongside them. They had been taught to fear cavalry charges by the Gyre Bloods themselves and, unlike the mail-shirted warriors of the Black Road, had only small wicker shields for protection against the arrows that were still cascading down. Kanin swore.

Wain came cantering up. Her face was spattered with dirt, but there was a kind of exultation in her eyes.

"They'll turn our flank soon," she shouted above the din.

"Get down the line," the Bloodheir cried, gesturing to his left. "Keep the savages in their places. I'll hold the right."

Kanin turned his horse about. Behind him, his Shield — a score of his Blood's finest warriors — were waiting in motionless, silent ranks. Igris, their captain and the most stony-faced of them all, was gently stroking his horse's mane. His eyes were fixed upon Kanin. Beyond the Shield, Kanin's few precious cavalry were watching him expectantly. They wanted blood and, in the way it often was with warriors of the Road caught up in the fierce anticipation of battle, it mattered little to them whether it was their enemy's or their own. Fate called for a host of deaths today; those who fell would be answering a call that had been sounded at their birth.

"With me," was all Kanin cried, and then he was off, galloping at their head toward the raging battle on the right flank. A wild freedom filled him as he pounded into the melee. Here, he was just one amongst the many, and this would be a good way for his first life to end. The Horin-Gyre riders plunged in amongst those of Kilkry-Haig, the weight of their charge carrying them on and on. Horse lurched against horse, blade clashed with blade. Crossbow bolts hissed through the air. There was, for long minutes, only blood, and tumult, and death. Then Kanin found there was no enemy before him. The Kilkry horsemen were streaming back toward their own lines. The footsoldiers spilled out from their little clusters, falling upon the wounded and unhorsed. Kanin brought his mount to a protesting, rearing halt. He looked around. The ground was black with bodies. Here and there a crippled horse struggled to rise from the mud. There were despairing cries for help from amongst the corpses. Kanin almost laughed out loud.

He made his way back to where Wain was waiting, his jubilant company of horsemen following behind. Many of them had fallen. The survivors did not care.

"What now?" asked Wain.

"A moment," said Kanin. His heart was hammering and his face was flushed. He mastered himself, setting aside the red lust of combat. He looked across to the enemy, and that helped to calm him. There were still too many. The disciplined Kilkry riders were regrouping, and the archers continued their methodical, relentless work. Companies of spearmen were forming up to advance across the center.

"So close," he murmured.

Wain looked at him questioningly.

"We can only stand and fight," he said.

"These Tarbains are no more use for this kind of work than goats," muttered Wain.

There was a renewed chorus of cries and horns. Across the field, rank after rank of warriors began to move forward. Somewhere, a drum was beating.

"Let us see what is to become of us, then," Wain cried and spun her horse away.

The army of Lannis and Kilkry came on across the grass. The going was difficult in the center of the field and their lines began to break up as men stumbled, the wet earth sucking at their feet. The cavalry came charging up again, tearing the ground to pieces. Kanin led his own riders to meet them. Arrows and bolts whipped between the closing lines. The banner of Glasbridge town fell and was snatched up in a second.

A burgeoning bellow filled the air as the armies sprang together, closing the last few yards in a sudden rush. In that first savage fury of contact it seemed for a moment as if the Horin-Gyre line would break at once, but it held. Just.

Kanin lashed out at any figure that came within reach. He wanted to find Gerain, the Kilkry-Haig Bloodheir whose banner he had seen, but in the chaos of the struggle he had no chance to seek him out. An arrow skimmed off his mail-clad shoulder. He ducked beneath a sweeping sword and hacked at the exposed thigh of its wielder. His blade cut through leather and there was a spray of blood that soaked his glove. His horse stumbled and carried him a few lurching steps sideways before it recovered its footing.

Kanin steadied himself and glanced around. His warriors were outnumbered and though they were taking a heavy toll of the enemy it was only a matter of time before they gave way. Yet even as the thought occurred to him, a great shudder passed through the mass of combatants as if a wave had broken over them. He turned and saw the Inkallim cutting through the fray, a black-clad tempest. Shraeve was in the heart of it, her swords dancing like light. She barged aside a Tarbain, crouched and sprang to bear a Kilkry warrior down from his saddle. The man was dying — his stomach opened — before he hit the ground, and Shraeve was spinning away to slash the legs from beneath a second horse.

None of those on the field, save a handful who had been at Kolglas on the night of Winterbirth, had ever met the Children of the Hundred in combat. They knew of them only by terrible rumor. Now they saw them: leaping, spinning, dancing a bloody path through the battle with all the ease of birds playing on stormy currents of air. In the first few minutes of carnage as the ravens swept out of imagination into reality, and man after man fell beneath their blades, the will of the Kilkry and Lannis warriors who faced them shook, hesitated and broke. First one, then a dozen, then a hundred turned and poured back the way they had come. They trampled their comrades in their urgent desire to escape. Some of the Horin-Gyre riders, wild at the sudden turn in their fortunes, spilled after their foes. Tarbains too rushed forward, eager for slaughter now that they saw their enemies' heels.

The Inkallim halted as soon as their opponents were broken. Their fury was cold, controlled. Kanin shouted, gathering to him all of his warriors that would listen. He knew as well as Shraeve and her ravens that the battle was not won. The flank might be saved but most of the line was a surging maelstrom. Enemy archers, not caring what home their arrows found, were still raining shafts down upon the fight. The center of the Horin-Gyre position was buckling. It was not just Tarbains who were falling back.

All that was left of Kanin's Shield had come to him, and he rallied another forty or fifty warriors. He looked at them, raised his sword in the air and without a word kicked at his horse's flanks and made for the place where the fighting was fiercest. The Inkallim ran alongside him. The world fell into the space between two breaths. Blood and mud were one; the formless howl of battle filled the air, drawing every other sound into itself. Bodies came up against one another and were cut, broken, pierced. The fallen were ground into the earth by the feet of the living.

Kanin found himself for a moment in a patch of clear ground with no opponent to face him. A severed hand lay in a deep hoofprint. There was a broken, abandoned spear. His chest heaved and burned. He knew there was blood on his face because he could taste it. He had no idea whose it was. His horse was shaking. Then Wain was before him, shouting. He frowned. He could see her lips moving, but heard only the cries of the dying and the clash of swords coming out from her mouth.

"See!" he heard at last. "From the forest."

She was pointing with her sword, and he followed its line. He saw a sight that was at first beyond his understanding. Beyond the battle, out across the flat farmlands to the south where there was still grass and sky and quiet, more warriors were coming. It was a company without banners, or horses, and it came in an unordered mass: two or three hundred figures walking in silence.

"What . . . ?" said Kanin in confusion.

"Kyrinin," cried Wain. "White Owls."

She was right, he saw. Even in the dull light of this day, and across the distance that separated them, he could see that this was no human army. It was a sight to astonish any onlooker. The few Kyrinin great clans left in the far east and south were said to still have the will to give battle on open ground, but Kanin would hardly have believed it of the White Owl. That they would do so on behalf of the Black Road — knowingly or not — filled him with a fierce kind of rapture.

The men of Kilkry and Lannis looked with different eyes. They saw a new enemy, hundreds strong, descending upon their flank and rear. A flash of uncertainty sparked through their ranks. Some tried to break free from the melee to face the threat. The archers who had kept themselves back from the main battle suddenly sensed their exposure and vulnerability and began to waver. The Horin-Gyre warriors knew nothing save that the men before them hesitated. They drew in a breath of renewed hope and pushed forward.

The White Owls, still far from the heat of battle, halted. Hundreds of bows were silently drawn. A flock of arrows took to the air, vaulting a huge distance. The second cascade of shafts was loosed before the first had fallen. They lanced down amongst the Lannis rearguard and bowmen.

Shraeve and her Inkallim carved their way through the ranks of the enemy.

"On! On!" cried Kanin. Igris charged at his side.

It became a rout in minutes. Floundering in ever-deepening mud, scores fell: warriors from Kolglas, Glasbridge and Kilkry lands; townsfolk and villagers fighting for their Blood. Their bodies piled up in drifts like heaps of dung waiting to be plowed into the earth. The survivors streamed in panic-stricken disarray southward, pursued by the few mounted Horin-Gyre warriors. Gerain nan Kilkry-Haig died, unrecognized, crushed by his great horse as it fell, hamstrung and gutted by deftly wielded knives.

Groups of Tarbains were capering about the field, looting the fallen and killing the wounded. Kanin watched as his own casualties were carried in from around the field. There were many Tarbain tribesmen amongst those borne past him. They groaned and writhed, fought against their pain. His Blood, like all those of the Black Road, had carved its northern territories out only after a long struggle with these wild tribesfolk. They were, as far as Kanin was concerned, little better than woodwights. Most were now Saved, their eyes opened to the truth of the Black Road, yet he could see, in the way their wounds and suffering afflicted them, how shallowly the creed was rooted in them. His own people, the warriors of Horin-Gyre, were silent as they were carried in. They bore their fates well and it pleased Kanin to see it. There was a strength to be found in acceptance; in knowing the nature of the world. Those whose wounds were too severe would meet the Healer's Blade — the fine knife designed to slip between ribs into the heart that every Black Road healer carried — with dignity, and go gladly toward a new life in the renewed world.

Wain came to fetch him away from them. Several men were with her, bulging sacks slung across their shoulders. They had been collecting heads to be thrown into Castle Anduran.

The Kyrinin had not moved since the end of the battle. Now a small group had separated from the main band of White Owls. They came across the grass, picking their way between and around bodies: a dozen warriors, their faces blurred by sweeping, spiraling tattoos, walking in a loose band with a tall, unarmed figure at its center. It took Kanin a few moments to recognize who it was. Wain was a moment ahead of him.

"Aeglyss," she murmured.

As the party of Kyrinin drew closer, they passed between knots of warriors who fixed them with hostile glares. The White Owls did not seem to notice. Kanin could see an amused expression playing upon Aeglyss' face. It broke into a narrow smile as the *na'kyrim* came up to him.

"You don't seem pleased to see me," said Aeglyss before Kanin could speak. "I hoped for a warmer welcome."

"I am surprised, that is all."

Aeglyss gave a sharp, short laugh at that. "I do not doubt it. But pleasantly surprised, I hope?"

Kanin frowned. It was as if the halfbreed's fawning, obsequious manner of only a day ago had never been. Now, the man reeked of arrogance and self-satisfaction, perhaps even thinking himself some kind of hero. He was as unpredictable and inconsistent as a child.

"You should thank me," said Aeglyss, indicating the battlefield with a sweep of his arm. "If we had not arrived when we did, things might have gone differently."

Kanin followed the gesture with his eyes, taking in the bodies of men and women and horses; the gouged, broken earth, stripped of any hint of green; the Tarbains crossing and recrossing the scene in their search for bounty. It looked ugly to him, now that Aeglyss had come. "I suppose so," he muttered.

"Graciously done," said Aeglyss, his voice weighed down by sarcasm. Kanin made to reply, but the *na'kyrim* was already holding up a conciliatory hand.

"Let us not argue," Aeglyss said. "We are reunited in victory. It would be a shame to sour the moment."

"Indeed," said Kanin.

"I will not trouble you further now," Aeglyss pressed on, "but perhaps we shall have more time to talk once we have returned to Anduran."

There was a silvery, soothing undertone to the *na'kyrim*'s voice with his final words. Kanin felt light-headed, and closed his eyes momentarily. When he opened them again, Aeglyss was already turning and heading back with his Kyrinin escort.

"Wait," shouted Kanin.

"We will follow you to the city, Bloodheir," called Aeglyss without looking back. "I will come to you there."

The Bloodheir stared after the *na'kyrim* and his inhuman companions.

"He seems to think he will now be a favorite of yours," Wain said at his side. She sounded almost amused.

Kanin shook his head. "The man is mad," he muttered.

V

The Craftmasters were bringing gifts to the Thane of Thanes. In the Great Hall of the Moon Palace in Vaymouth, a succession of bearers deposited treasures before Gryvan's throne. It had been the way of things ever since Haig replaced Kilkry as chief amongst the Bloods: a High Thane returning victorious from battle received the tribute of the Crafts, in gratitude for his restoration of peace and prosperity.

The day before, the ordinary folk of Vaymouth had thronged the streets to hail the triumphal progress of Gryvan oc Haig all the way from the Gold Gate to his Palace. The journey had taken two hours, such had been the jubilant press, so urgent the collective need to greet the returning army with their train of yoked prisoners. Now Vaymouth's greater powers made obeisance in their turn.

In the presence of the full assembled court, the Weaponers gave to Gryvan pikes and maces set with gold, the Armorers a helm of solid silver. The Vintners laid before him jars of the best Taral-Haig wines and the Furriers the pelt of a great white bear. One after another, each of the sixteen Crafts paid homage, and Gryvan oc Haig acknowledged each gift with a gracious nod and smile.

Standing a little behind the throne, Mordyn Jerain watched impassively. The Shadowhand had received gifts of his own from some of the Craftmasters — those who took the keenest interest in the fate of the now Thaneless Dargannan-Haig Blood — these last few days. Dargannan was a young Blood, without tradition and history to fall back on at a time of crisis, and Igryn had no son; fighting had broken out amongst his relations as soon as he was taken. With each gift had come a murmured suggestion of how stability might best be restored, which of Igryn's diffuse family might best be suited to replacing him as ruler of Dargannan lands. For all the courtesy and humility the Craftmasters affected, their pride grew year by year. The time might soon come, Mordyn felt, when it would be necessary to remind them that it was still the High Thane who wielded the greater power.

Seated upon the steps that led up to the Throne Dais was a living demonstration of that power. Igryn, the fallen Dargannan Thane, was an eyeless mockery of his former self. His hair and beard had been trimmed and combed, new clothes provided and his empty eye sockets hidden behind a black silken band to make him fit to appear amidst the splendors of the court. Still, he was left to sit upon the cold marble steps like a child or an idiot.

Mordyn did not imagine that the message of humbled power Igryn embodied would discomfit the Craftmasters. They would assume that their ways were too subtle, their ambitions too narrowly defined, to merit such a violent response. Gryvan had meant the blinding for another audience: Igryn's successor, and the troublesome — though now beset by troubles of their own — Thanes of Lannis and Kilkry. The High Thane's instincts had always run toward blunt gestures. Mordyn would have prevented this one if he had been there in the wilds of Dargannan-Haig. The sudden revival of the Mercy of Kings drew too clear a link between Gryvan and those long-dead monarchs of Dun Aygll. It would have been better to kill Igryn outright.

As the Chancellor watched, a servant in the raiment of the

Goldsmiths approached Gryvan oc Haig and, kneeling, unfolded a velvet-wrapped bundle upon the floor. He revealed a necklace woven from hair-thin threads of spun gold. The servant lifted it to display its beauty to the assembled throng before respectfully setting it back upon its velvet bed.

Mordyn suppressed a smile and glanced up. Tara was there, in the crowd lining the hall. The Chancellor savored the familiar feeling of surprise that he should be loved by a woman of such astounding beauty and gifts. So many years of marriage, and still he hardly believed that he deserved such fortune. It was the discreet droplets of gold hanging from her ears that he was looking for now, though. Lammain, Master of the Goldsmiths, had delivered them personally into Tara's hands only two nights gone, expressing the hope that they might be a fitting ornament for such a lady on this day. Later, in one of the more private rooms of Mordyn's Palace of Red Stone, as they lingered over cups of aromatic wine, the Craftmaster had wondered aloud if Gann nan Dargannan-Haig, a cousin of Igryn's, might not be fitted for the Thaneship. Mordyn knew Gann to be a crude blowhard, and knew as well that the Goldsmiths had been secretly enriching the young man for several years. They probably all but owned him by now. The hills of Dargannan-Haig were thickly veined with gold in places, and the idea of a compliant Thane no doubt appealed to the Goldsmiths.

Mordyn had taken care to send the Craftmaster away content that the earrings had bought a worthy audience. Gann would never be Thane — and perhaps Lammain already knew that — but he might have to be found some elevated position that would allow the Goldsmiths to benefit from their investment. At least until the Chancellor could determine exactly how deep their claws were sunk into the Dargannan-Haig Blood.

Gryvan and his wife Abeh were magnificent, seated side by side upon the dais. His crimson cloak outshone anything else in the vast hall and made itself the object of every gaze. Abeh, as ever, had neither the sense nor the inclination to hide the delight all this ceremony and opulence kindled in her. Mordyn was always assailed by the image of a sow rolling ecstatically in mud when he saw the High Thane's wife in such a setting.

Aertan oc Taral-Haig was close to the dais, surrounded by an attentive crowd of his followers. The Thane of Taral spent almost as much time in Vaymouth as he did in his own city of Drandar. He had passed most of the summer ensconced in a wing of the Moon Palace, awaiting Gryvan's return from the campaign. Not for Aertan the discomforts of a hot summer in the dry heart of Taral-Haig, where the petty lordlings who infested his lands could trouble him with their interminable disputes, when the luxuries of Vaymouth beckoned. There's one we needn't worry about at least, thought Mordyn. Aertan's loyalty would never need to be questioned so long as it brought him comfort and wealth. Behind him, skulking at the rear of the crowd as if he longed to be somewhere else, was Roaric nan Kilkry-Haig. Even at this distance Mordyn, experienced as he was at reading a man's emotions, could detect the hatred that lurked in the young man's eyes. It was an impotent hatred, so long as Lheanor his father remained bound by his pledge of allegiance to Gryvan, and Mordyn gave it little thought.

A more problematic figure stood close to the Taral Thane: Alem T'anarch, the ambassador of the Dornach Kingship. With his pale hair tied back from his face, and an ostentatious diamond clasp at the collar of his black cape, the ambassador was an exotic, faintly unsettling presence. Since his return, Gryvan had refused to even meet with T'anarch, despite insistent requests; uncowed, the ambassador had submitted a demand for reparations to be paid to the families of the two hundred or more Dornach hire-swords Gryvan had captured and executed during the campaign. It was an outrageous claim, and the whole dispute smelled to Mordyn like the kind of game-playing that could easily get out of hand. War with the Kingship was inevitable, if the Haig dominion was to continue spreading into the rich lands of the south, but the time was not yet right for that struggle to begin.

The gift from the Goldsmiths was the last. Horns were blown, their notes bounding back and forth in the stone-clad hall like silver in the air. The audience began to flow toward the doors, a slow river of glorious indulgence and self-satisfaction.

When Mordyn went to speak with him in the evening, Gryvan was in a fine mood. Mordyn could smell sweet wine upon his breath. The High Thane had been drinking with his sons while they trained hunting eagles in one of the long, high terrace gardens on the palace's flank. Mordyn had little time for either the Bloodheir Aewult or his younger brother Stravan. Neither matched their father's singleminded hunger for power, and that, as far as the Chancellor was concerned, made them poor inheritors of Gryvan's mantle. Or of his own service. But the Thane of Thanes loved them well, so Mordyn kept his thoughts to himself. There was time yet; one or other of them might some day become what was needed to keep the slow avalanche of Haig supremacy moving.

The brothers had departed to seek livelier entertainments elsewhere by the time Mordyn came walking softly across the grass to join Gryvan. The High Thane was at the edge of the terrace, staring out over his city. A group of huntsmen stood at a respectful distance, the great brown eagles massive upon their arms. Gryvan's shieldman Kale was with them. Both he and the birds watched the newcomer as he took up position at Gryvan's side. Mordyn had been in the service of this man for so long that he could read all but the subtlest of his moods without a word being exchanged, and Gryvan had few moods that would merit the description subtle. Now, the Chancellor could sense that his lord was in an exalted state.

Beneath them, thousands of houses were crammed together, making warrens of narrow streets from which there rose the murmuring of countless lives being lived. Here and there, scattered between the Moon Palace and the distant horizon of the city wall, greater buildings rose above the rooftops like islands in a dark, tumultuous sea. In the distance Mordyn could see his own Palace of Red Stone, its porphyry glowing dimly in the last of the sun, and he thought of Tara waiting somewhere in its deep embrace for him to return to her. There were other grand houses too: the Palace of the Bloodheir, where Aewult hosted revels of a kind Mordyn preferred not to attend; the marble-faced White Palace, where Abeh took her household whenever the High Thane was long out of the city; the Crafthouse of the Gemsmiths, to which a tower taller than anything in Vaymouth save the Moon Palace itself had only this last summer been added. That edifice caught Mordyn's attention for a moment longer than the rest. It was an uncomfortable reminder of his earlier musings on the rise of the Crafts. He did not allow the thought to distract him. He had other concerns to share with his Thane this evening.

"It is a sight, is it not, Mordyn?" Gryvan breathed.

"It is," the Chancellor said softly.

"When I was a child there were fields wide enough to race horses across within Vaymouth's walls. Orchards enough to give every child an apple a day through the season. All gone now; all become houses and workshops and markets."

There was no nostalgia in Gryvan's tone. It was with something close to wonder that he spoke.

"We have sucked the world to us, you and I," he said. "Built a place that draws life to it. Was Dun Aygll ever quite such a sight, do you think?"

"No," said Mordyn, carefully coloring his voice with reflection and thoughtfulness, "not such as this."

"They fell because they grew still, the Aygll Kings. They made nothing new for too long. They forgot to cow their warlords with ever greater glories."

Hardly an accurate assessment of the Aygll dynasty's collapse,

Mordyn thought. They fell because their strength was spent on the battlefields of the War of the Tainted; because the mines in Far Dyne were exhausted, and because the last King of their line who was worthy of the name was turned into a puppet on a string by the *na'kyrim* Orlane. Still, the High Thane could be allowed his drink-fueled fantasies. Even when drunk he usually heeded counsel wiser than that offered by wine.

"The great must never be still if they are to prosper," Gryvan was saying. "They must always be moving onward. The south calls to me. Ah, it's a tempting call. Next year, or the year after, before I am too old for the testing, we must measure ourselves against the Dornach Kingship. If we could humble that nest of thieves and whoresoldiers, what a legacy to leave my son, eh?"

Mordyn could not help but think the High Thane underestimated the toll the passing years were taking upon him. The man was not recovering as quickly from the recent campaign as he once would have done. His face still had a pinched look to it, and there was a tiredness in the skin beneath his eyes that had not been there before he rode out to make war on Igryn oc Dargannan-Haig. A campaign against Dornach would be an altogether more demanding endeavor.

"Indeed," the Shadowhand said, "though Dargannan must first be secured for such an undertaking to succeed."

Gryvan tore his gaze away from the great vista before them. He regarded his Chancellor with a wry smile.

"Ever the practical man," he said.

"I share the vision," Mordyn said and thought, You had not the half of it before you opened your ears to me. "But still, the glories of two years hence are founded upon what we do tomorrow, and next week and next month."

Gryvan clapped him on the shoulder and laughed. "I know, I know. You remind me often enough that I shall not forget it. And we shall pick Igryn's successor soon, though I am tempted to leave his bloodthirsty brood to tear at one another for a while longer.

No great harm can come of it, so long as the thousand men I left there remain."

Mordyn nodded, and judged that the moment was right to share the small concern that had been nagging at him over the last couple of days.

"Appealing though the southern prospect is, I fear we must give some thought to events in the north, my lord."

The High Thane was not so drunk that he did not raise an eyebrow at that, and fix Mordyn with a steely gaze.

"I thought we were on safe ground there, Mordyn. We agreed before I went south that anything that happened in the Glas valley would matter little in the long run."

"Of course," said Mordyn with an ease he was no longer sure he truly felt. "Gyre has as much wish to see the Horin Blood spending its strength as we have to see Lannis being drained of its. Ragnor oc Gyre will not come to Horin-Gyre's aid."

The Chancellor still believed it to be true. He, and therefore the High Thane, had always known there might be an attempt upon the Glas valley once they had summoned Croesan's best warriors away, but Mordyn was certain Ragnor oc Gyre lacked the will to put his full strength behind it. He had a few precious eyes and ears buried amongst the Bloods of the Black Road and knew something of how things stood there. More important, he had the words of the Gyre Thane himself. It would likely trigger instant revolt in the lands ruled by both men if it were known that Gryvan and Ragnor had exchanged messages in the last few years, especially if the content were revealed. No promises had been given, no explicit guarantees, but the outline of an understanding had been sketched: Gryvan would not threaten the strongholds of the Black Road so long as Ragnor extended the same courtesy to the True Bloods. If some of the lesser Bloods — Lannis and Horin the obvious, unstated examples — came to blows, neither High Thane would permit the situation to escalate into full-scale war and neither would permit their peoples to claim any new lands.

Unrestrained conflict was in nobody's best interests. So long as that held true, no great damage could be done by the latest disturbances, save to Lannis pride.

Only in the last few days had a sliver of doubt intruded upon Mordyn's confidence. There had been no word at all from Behomun Tole in Anduran, and the last message from Lagair, the Steward in Kolkyre, reported rumors that the Lannis-Haig capital itself was besieged. The Chancellor was not accustomed to being surprised; that news had startled him. How a Horin-Gyre army could be encamped around Anduran so quickly, given the strength of the defenses upon Lannis-Haig's northern borders, was a mystery. The most worrying possibility — that the Bloods of the Black Road were, after all, united in the assault and had simply overrun Tanwrye with an immense army — was one the Chancellor would not admit to Gryvan, but which demanded some precautionary measures. If it was indeed the case, Ragnor oc Gyre had lost his reason. He must know that sooner or later the Haig Bloods would destroy even the greatest army the Black Road could keep in the field south of the Stone Vale.

"So, if you do not fear Ragnor has played us for fools, what is your concern?" the High Thane asked him.

"I can only admit that it seems the Horin-Gyre forces have moved more swiftly than I — than any of us — thought likely," Mordyn said with as much humility as he could muster. "It is no great worry. We still have time enough to deal with them. No, it is Kilkry-Haig that occupies my thoughts." There was truth enough in this line of argument, Mordyn believed, to convince Gryvan.

"There must be some doubt about how long even the leash of your command will keep Lheanor from the field. We do not want him gaining some glorious victory on his own. Anyway, should he be drawn in before our strength is mustered, this could become a more protracted affair than it need be. The outcome would be the same, of course, but there would be more . . . waste."

"Waste," repeated the High Thane. "And you do hate waste, don't you, Mordyn? Well, you would not raise the matter if you had no answer to it, so let me hear it."

"We remind Lheanor that he is to await the arrival of the armies of the other Bloods before taking the field, my lord. And perhaps hurry along a few men to reassure him that we are making haste. A few hundred should suffice."

Gryvan nodded. "Easily enough done," he said.

"And perhaps," Mordyn went on, "lend a little more urgency to our assembly of the main force? If Anduran is indeed already besieged, there is little to be gained from further delay. The sight of the Black Road hammering at his own door will have given Croesan pause for thought. If he has not realized by now that his best interests lie in maintaining your good favor, he never will."

Gryvan turned and looked out once more over Vaymouth. Night was coming on quickly and the city was falling away into shadow. All across the sprawling capital of the Haig Blood pinpricks of light were sparking as the citizens lit torches, candles and lanterns. The High Thane yawned and rubbed his face.

"Do it, then," he said. "We can use some of the men I brought back from Dargannan-Haig; they've not dispersed yet. The great must keep moving onward, but we might hope for a little more time to rest between our triumphs."

Gryvan laughed at his own words, and Mordyn, satisfied with his evening's work, joined in.

The Chancellor rode back toward his palace flanked by grandly attired guards and preceded by a pair of torchbearers who cleared a path through the thronged streets. Parts of Vaymouth seemed more convincingly alive during the hours of darkness than in the day. There had been a fashion for night markets this last summer, and even though the lazy warmth had gone from the evenings, a few still operated.

The seething crowds parted, in the main without protest, at the approach of the Chancellor's party. Even those who did not recognize him could tell from his escort and dress that he was a man of importance. It was a giddy height for the son of a timber trader to rise to, but then Mordyn Jerain had never been quite like other merchants' sons. As a young boy in Tal Dyre, when Vaymouth was just the name of one more foreign city, he had not been popular with his peers. He imagined he must have been an arrogant child: cleverer than most, more instinctively aware of his own potential even at that tender age. He could not really remember. His childhood often seemed to have been lived by some other person, linked to the man he was now by only the most tenuous of threads. He learned the arts of manipulation as a defense, and they came naturally to him. By the time he left the island at the age of fourteen, he had more allies than enemies amongst the other children, and those who spoke against him would quickly be on the receiving end of a beating.

He liked to think that as soon as he saw Vaymouth he knew he would never return to Tal Dyre. The merchant isle was still a match for Vaymouth, in wealth at least, in those days, but the capital of the Haig Bloods was so vast and crudely vibrant that it was intoxicating to the ambitious young Mordyn. While his father labored to build a business, Mordyn had set about educating himself in the ways of the city. It probably broke his father's heart when Mordyn abandoned his Tal Dyreen roots and took service at the Haig court as a lowly official. Probably, but the Chancellor could not be sure, for he had never seen any of his family again. They had left the city and returned to Tal Dyre many years ago. His Tal Dyreen contacts knew better than to trouble him with any news of them.

The Palace of Red Stone was filled with the scent of honeyed cloves. They had been set on lattices above the braziers. It was an indulgence of his beloved wife that the Chancellor could not refuse. A slight breeze toyed with the silken drapes that hung across the bedchamber's windows. Mordyn could hear the metal-shod tread of one of his guards on the terrace outside. The sound was so familiar he barely registered it, and it did not distract him from his task. With precisely weighted fingers, he worked balm oil into Tara's naked shoulders. The sensation of her slick, pliable skin beneath his touch worked an almost hypnotic effect upon him. He inhaled deeply, savoring the rich mixture of smells: the cloves, the oil, her. There was nothing in his world to match the perfect, complex texture of such a moment.

He laid a soft kiss upon the back of her neck, felt the oil on his lips. She made an appreciative sound. He touched his tongue to her skin.

"I saw you looking at me in the Great Hall this morning," she whispered.

"How could I not?" he asked.

He drizzled more oil over her skin and began to massage her neck. Her head eased forward a little, and she lifted her hair out of his way.

"You must be tired," she said.

"Not yet."

"Did Gryvan give you what you wanted?"

"Oh, yes. It was not so much to ask. Mere sense."

"So there will be war in the north soon? The ladies of the court twitter like a flock of birds. There has not been so much excitement for a long time. War against the Black Road would be so much more . . . traditional than the crushing of a rebellious Thane. There is nothing quite like the toing and froing of armies and reports of distant victories to spice up their lives."

"Distant victories are the best kind," said Mordyn softly. He pressed his ear against her back, listening for her heart. "One or two more of them and we shall have the best-loved Thane the Haig Blood has ever seen." He could hear it. He imagined that his own heart beat in time with hers.

"Yes," she said as she turned to take him in her arms. "Keep the blood and the strife safely distant and we need only concern ourselves with better things."

VI

In Anduran, a great catapult was being hauled across the square by a team of mules. The machine looked like an angular creature from another land, intruding upon the order of the town.

"They're moving the second engine up," Kanin said. Wain peered over his shoulder. They were standing at a high window in their commandeered house.

"Let us hope its workmanship is better than the first," she said. The throwing arm of the first to be put to use had split when it was tensioned. The man who missed the flaw in the wood lost half the skin from his back for the oversight.

"How long before more are ready?" Kanin asked.

"We should have three or four of them by the morning." He knew her well enough to detect the undercurrent of detachment.

"Not enough, you think?" he pressed.

"Who knows? We were granted some time by the victory at Grive, but not much of it. Perhaps they will come out of their own accord once we start throwing heads inside. They might be hungry, or sick, already. Our chances would be better if it was high summer."

"Perhaps," agreed Kanin. Now that the elation of their victory was receding, he knew as well as Wain did that their position was as dangerously fragile as ever. There would be more armies marching up the valley before long. They had sent word commanding part of the army besieging Tanwrye to come south. It may or may not be possible: the Lannis garrison there would sally at the slightest sign of weakness. Other messengers had gone further, making for Kan Dredar. They would plead with Ragnor oc Gyre to unleash his own mighty army, now that Horin-Gyre's daring had brought such a rich harvest within reach. Whether or not the High Thane would respond, Kanin had no idea.

A commotion outside turned him back to the window. Below, a band of Tarbains were driving a bullock along. The animal was recalcitrant, pulling against its halter and lowing in protest. The excited tribesmen jabbed at it with spears and shouted at one another. Points of blood speckled the bullock's haunches.

"Where have they got that from?" snapped Kanin. "Igris!"

His shieldman came in at once and joined him at the window.

"Find out where they've brought that animal from," commanded the Bloodheir. "If it's within an hour's walk have them whipped. They know that all goods near the city are to be handed over and recorded, don't they?"

"They do, but Tarbains are like children. They can't hold a thought in their heads."

"Why should I care?" snapped Kanin. "I don't need you to tell me that they are children. I need you to enforce my orders."

The anger in Kanin's voice straightened his shieldman's back and put an expression of rigid obedience onto his face. Kanin almost said something to dilute the harshness of his words. He chose not to.

Igris went out. Kanin could hear him shouting as he descended the stairs. It was in the nature of anger to be handed on and grow, and it would travel out to the tribesmen on the square.

"The Tarbains will be ungovernable soon," Wain said. "Scores of them have scattered through the valley already. Almost all of the wild ones have gone; even some of the Saved."

"Let them go. We knew it would happen, and they'll give Lannis and Kilkry a little more to worry about. The city and the nearest farms must feed the army, though. If Gyre had given us all the swords we asked for, we wouldn't have to rely on these barbarians."

Below, Igris emerged with a couple of other men and strode toward the Tarbains. He began to berate them loudly and they shouted back, gesticulating with their spears. The bullock, relieved of its captors' harsh attentions, stood quite still and hung its head as if searching for grass among the inhospitable cobblestones.

"I'm going to the castle," Wain said.

Kanin nodded. He did not turn as she left the room. Instead he watched as Igris knocked down one of the tribesmen with a backhanded blow. The bullock wandered off. A brawl developed.

Figures were moving on the battlements of Castle Anduran. From the safe vantage point of one of the houses fronting the castle, Wain could just make them out, although the light was too poor for her to see them clearly. Others were better placed: a few crossbow bolts lanced up from amongst the crude earthworks and wicker shields on the open ground beneath the castle walls. The shapes on the wall disappeared. She was sure none of them had been struck. She had been watching for an hour, awaiting the arrival of the siege engine.

The Bloodheir's sister muttered a soft curse. As she strode back toward the center of Anduran, she was oblivious of the groups of weary, disheveled warriors she brushed past. The slow attrition of the siege filled her with frustration. She knew she must accept whatever fate decreed, and would do so; but the faith permitted — advocated, even — hope. The most unlikely victories could sometimes be won, for nothing mattered but what tales the Last God had told, and fate seldom took account of what seemed likely in the minds of mortals. The arrival of Aeglyss and his White Owls had proved that, if nothing else.

A liquescent cough from some invalid registered upon her thoughts. Signs of disease had begun to appear in the ranks of the Horin-Gyre army. Wounds festered in the wet and the dirt. Hot and cold fevers stalked the streets. The weakest had been culled before they even reached the city; dozens had died on the journey through Anlane. Now a fresh winnowing was under way.

The atmosphere amongst the besiegers was not helped by the presence of a huge Kyrinin warband encamped beyond the semi-derelict city walls. Despite their part in the battle, no one trusted the woodwights, or really understood what had brought them out from their forest lair in such numbers. To her irritation, Wain found Aeglyss in her head once more. Her brother refused to meet with the *na'kyrim,* and had insisted that the White Owls remain out of bowshot of the city.

Wain shared her brother's contempt for all *na'kyrim.* Their very existence was a symptom of that willful disregard for the world's natural order which had led to the Gods' despair. Nevertheless, she could not free herself of the sense that Aeglyss meant something. He had proved his value more than once now. Kanin might refuse to accept it, but fate could use the strangest tools in weaving its pattern.

She found the catapult becalmed on the street outside the jail like a sea monster thrown helpless on a hard shore. One of its axles had broken. Workmen were trying to mend it, and at her approach they bent furiously to the task, each trying to outdo the other in the urgency of his efforts. For a few minutes she watched the repairs. The leader of the group kept glancing at her. Every back was tensed, expecting the lash of her tongue at any moment. It did not come. She no longer truly believed that siege engines were the key to this lock. She left the men to their labors and walked on.

She went to the outer wall of the city. Climbing up onto the rubble of the ramshackle defenses, she stared out over the fields beyond. The tents and fires of the Kyrinin were there, the camp as silent as ever. She stood and watched for some time. She had no idea what it was she was looking for. There was nothing she had not seen before.

She looked down at the stones beneath her feet. They had been great building blocks once, scales of the town's armor. Now they were eroded and chipped, jumbled in a heap and already embarked upon the centuries-long journey to dust. Time and fate paid no heed to the intent of mere mortals.

"Wain."

The soft voice at her shoulder startled her and she almost lost her footing on the loose stonework. His hand was there in an instant, upon her elbow, keeping her steady. She snatched her arm away.

"Do not touch me, halfbreed," she hissed.

"As you wish," Aeglyss said, unconcerned. He glanced out toward the White Owl encampment. "You were watching the camp. What do you see?"

"Savages." His closeness made her skin crawl.

"They would say the same of you. A mistake, to always see only what it is easiest to see."

The urge to turn away from him, from his grey eyes and his corpse-pale skin, was powerful. Yet his voice held her.

"Why is it you and your brother turn me away?" His hand was back upon her arm, and this time she did not withdraw. "I only want to help you achieve what you desire."

"What is it that you think I desire?" she asked tightly.

"The same things as your father, and your brother: vengeance for past defeats, the triumph of the Black Road, honor for your Blood. The end of this world. The Kall. But it burns more fiercely in you than in them, Wain. I can feel it in you as if you carried the sun itself in your breast."

Carefully, she took a step away from him, easing her arm from his grip. She had never feared anyone in her life, yet this *na'kyrim* brought that emotion close. For all that she could break his neck or snap his wrist in a moment, some part of her believed she was the weaker. And his unflinching gaze and his calm, entrancing voice told her that he really might be able to give her what she wanted. He is more than he appears, she reminded herself. He can twist your thoughts, cloud your mind, with that voice.

"You move away from me," he said. "Are you afraid?"

"Not of you," she said. "But I mistrust your voice. What is it that you want?"

"Speak with Kanin. Persuade him to look with favor upon me again. Persuade him to allow me to help you, in whatever way I can."

She hesitated. Hesitation was no more in her nature than was fear.

"I did what I promised before," Aeglyss whispered. "I bent the White Owls to your will. Your father trusted me to aid you. Learn that trust from him, Wain. Teach it to your brother."

A terrible tension was building in Wain, knotting the muscles of her stomach and shoulders, setting her pulse thudding in her head. She could not bear it.

"Very well," she said, without knowing quite why she said it. "I will speak to my brother. Come to us tomorrow morning. We will be holding a council in the hall on the square." She made to climb down from the wall.

"Wait," he said, and she found herself turning back to him. "Why do you despise me so, Wain?" His voice was different now. She thought she heard need. She refused to trust that thought.

"You are what you are," she told him, "and I am as I am. I do not despise you, but you are not of the Road. And you are not of my kind."

"My father was, though. He had the same blood in him that you do. That should mean something. But it's not enough, is it? Not for you. I do not understand what I have done to earn your — and your brother's — contempt. I did nothing but what you wished. I sought only favor in your eyes."

"Fools look for reasons," Wain said softly. "What has been and what will be are one. They are the Road, and happen because they must."

"Will you see me differently if I give you what you want?" He smiled and it was a smile that shook her. "Am I really so terrible in your eyes? You seem so fair in mine. You are not like the others. All I want is for you to trust me, to let me be a part of this with you."

Her breath was light, fluttering in her throat. He reached out toward her. She felt as if she stood upon some towering precipice and the world was rushing away beneath her. Then she saw his fingernails, and they were clouded. She remembered who, and what, he was. She spun away and vaulted down over the great stone blocks to the street below.

"Please . . ." she perhaps heard him say, almost inaudibly.

She forced herself not to run as she strode into the city, and did not look back although she could feel his eyes upon her back like twin embers.

* * *

Inurian did not even hear the other entering this time. He felt his presence, and that was enough to wake him. It was like a breath upon the back of his head; a stone dropped into the Shared. Inurian rolled over. Aeglyss was sitting with his back against the wall, his knees drawn up to his chest and enfolded by his arms. His face was in shadow. There was a silence such as comes in the very heart of the night, when all the world and all its inhabitants are still. Inurian said nothing. He watched his visitor and waited.

Aeglyss spoke. "I never knew my father's name. They killed him before I was born, as soon as they realized I was there in my mother's womb. She would never tell me what they did to him, but they are cruel, the White Owl. For a Huanin, and a captive at that, who had dared to take one of their own as a lover . . . Well. They might easily have taken her life, too. Stilled me before I had drawn my first breath."

Inurian dared not stir. He could almost see the emotion that was coiling and uncoiling itself within the other's frame, like a snake in a fire.

"When I was . . . six? Eight? One of the other children — a girl — ah, what was her name? I can't remember. She was hounding me, tormenting me. Kyrinin are no more gentle with the likes of you and me than Huanin are. That day it was too much. I told her to take out the skinning knife she had on her belt. I told her . . . she put it through her hand. It was the first time I really understood anything about the Shared, understood why they were afraid of me.

"They shut me away. They must have wanted to kill me then, I suppose, but my mother came. She cut through the side of the tent and carried me off. We went into the forest, just me and her together. Do you know what that means, for one of the people to leave the *vo'an,* to go alone out into the winter?"

He gave a sudden, harsh laugh, his bowed head jerking up and cracking against the stone wall. "Of course you know what it means. You know exactly what I'm talking about, don't you? Anyway, it was a bad winter, not a time to be alone in deep Anlane. She kept me alive, though, somehow. She was a strong woman. Ah, and beautiful. As beautiful as any Kyrinin you've ever seen.

"I remember walking through snowdrifts as high as my waist, and some so high she had to carry me on her back. I remember hiding, for days at a time. We left White Owl lands, crossed into Snake and then beyond, and always we were hiding. Can you imagine? I still feel the cold, sometimes, even when there's a fire burning. I can't get warm. It was a long time, always moving, always starving, always alone."

His hands shifted. Inurian saw them twitching.

"There was a storm eventually, worse than anything before," said Aeglyss. "One morning, she just stayed asleep. She would not wake no matter how I shook her. I lay down beside her, and folded her arms around me. I knew . . . I could feel . . . that if I could find the way to use it, the Shared could keep her alive. It was like seeing a light just out of reach, and every time I reached for it, it went away. I could tell that there was warmth in the Shared, but I had no idea how to draw it out. No one had taught me. So she died, and I waited for the end to come.

"They came instead. She had come far enough, you see. She had . . . lasted long enough. They found me beside her and took me into the marshes."

Again, Aeglyss broke off. He looked up at Inurian for the first time. There was not enough moonlight for Inurian to make out his features clearly. Still, there was a pallid, haunted look about the man's face that chilled him.

"That is where I first heard your name, you know," said Aeglyss. "Those fools sitting around in their tents and huts; said you understood more about the Shared than most, even though it was not strong in you. I thought nothing of it, then. And yet all those years later, I found myself in Hakkan talking about Kolglas, and I remembered you. Ha! Almost enough to make you believe in the Black Road, do you think?

"Here we are. You and I, the knowledge and the power. The two halves of something that could be quite new. That is how it ought to be. You must be my guide through the deep places of the Shared. It's there in me: this . . . vastness, that I don't know how to reach, how to use. Do you understand?"

Inurian could sense the other man's need, his longing. Something in Aeglyss was breaking, or perhaps had broken long ago.

"I cannot help you," said Inurian. "I told you that before."

"Cannot?" cried Aeglyss, surging to his feet. His voice lashed out. Inurian felt his skin crawling with the tread of a thousand imagined insects. He might die now, he thought. Now, in this cell with no one to see, he might easily die.

Aeglyss leaned against the wall. One hand hung at his side. The other was pressed to the stone, splayed like a huge, rigid spider. When he spoke again, his voice was quite level. "You can see what is inside men."

"I can sometimes . . . know what is unspoken," said Inurian carefully.

"What do you see in me?" asked Aeglyss.

Inurian closed his eyes for a moment. He lay quite still beneath

Aeglyss' intense gaze. He felt the hard, cold floor of the cell against his side. He focused upon it, shutting out the blackness that strove to force its way into his mind.

Aeglyss laughed bitterly. "You are afraid. Everyone is afraid of me. They always have been. The White Owls wanted to kill me; Dyrkyrnon cast me out. Even these Black Road bitches, after I have brought them to the edge of greatness. Whatever I do for them, they will not let me be one of them. I know that."

Knowing was not the same as believing in the heart, Inurian reflected. Whatever Aeglyss might say, the hope — the need — for acceptance was so powerful in him it leaked out, giving the lie to his words even as he spoke them. He still craved the approval of the Horin-Gyre leaders. His desire to belong somewhere, any-where, was painfully obvious to Inurian.

"The fear is too much for them," Aeglyss continued. "All afraid, but now they do not even know what they fear. I will not be put aside anymore. I will not! You, you of all people, will not turn away from me." He shivered and clasped his arms across his chest. He was swaying. "Who has been the greatest of our kind? Dorthyn who hunted the Whreinin out of the south? Minon the Torturer? Orlane Kingbinder?"

"All were powerful in their ways," Inurian murmured. "Their power added little happiness to the world, but in any case you overestimate your strength if you mean to compare it to theirs."

"You could teach me their ways," said Aeglyss, then, no longer addressing Inurian, "To bind a King . . ." He shook himself. "I think . . . I think I cannot continue like this. I think I will lose my mind. Or die, perhaps. Will you help me, Inurian?"

When Inurian did not reply, Aeglyss turned as if to go. Inurian lifted himself up on one arm.

"I would help you if I could, Aeglyss," he said.

Aeglyss stopped. He stood there, his head bowed, his hands digging into his shoulders.

"Not just for your sake," continued Inurian, "but because of what you might do. It is too late, though. Your heart, your intent — they're too . . . damaged. I have known little love in my life, Aeglyss. All our kind learn what it is to be feared, to be turned away. I am sorry for what you have suffered, but the pain need not lead to whatever place it is you have found yourself in. It need not have brought you to this."

"Help me, then," said Aeglyss urgently. "Do not refuse me. Please, you are the only one who could understand. I will give you whatever you want."

"Is that truly all you have seen in the Shared? Power? A way to bend others to your will?"

"You talk of power as if it is an evil thing. I see a strength that is given to me, but not to others. Only a fool would turn aside from such a boon. What else would you have me see?"

"That all is one. If you use the Shared to harm others, you harm yourself."

"All is one. All is one! No. I don't think so. All is hate, fear, pain. If others seek to harm me — as they will, as they have always done — would you have me lie still and unprotesting beneath their blows?"

"Then I am sorry. I cannot teach you to see what I see; I cannot heal your wounds. You would not use anything I taught you well."

Inurian stretched himself out on the floor and shut his eyes. He could feel Aeglyss standing there for a little while, feel the weight of his presence.

"I will wait for you to change your mind, Inurian," Aeglyss breathed. "But not for long. Not long."

Then he left.

Inurian did not sleep for a long time. He lay awake, staring at the wall of his cell. For some reason, out of all that had been said, it was the names Aeglyss had spoken that haunted him the most: Dorthyn, Minon, and Orlane Kingbinder, most fearful of them all. Great powers they had been in their time; true shapers, who molded the course of the world.

The *na'kyrim* now were but an echo of what they were when the world was younger, and it had always seemed to Inurian a good thing that it was so. The might of the great *na'kyrim* of old bred fear and loathing in those, Huanin and Kyrinin alike, who could never hope to understand it. Worse, it had corrupted the *na'kyrim* themselves, made them drunk with their potency. Many had become the eyes of bloody storms. Such was the company Aeglyss sought to count himself in, and Inurian could almost smell the truth of it. This marred young *na'kyrim,* burning with anger and pain, would cast a long shadow if he ever came by the power he craved. Inurian felt the awful horrors of history crowding in, clamoring to be unleashed once more upon the world.

He knew what it was to be shunned by all, shut out from both of the worlds from which he sprang. All the peoples of the world were outcasts — all craving other certainties to replace those that had departed with the Gods — but none were so bereft as the *na'kyrim,* with no places, no kind, no children to belong to. Yet in Kennet nan Lannis-Haig Inurian had found a man who could look upon a *na'kyrim* and see an equal behind the grey eyes that returned his gaze. He had found a whole family he could love in place of the one he would never have: Kennet and Lairis, whose devotion to one another had warmed all the cold halls of Kolglas; Fariel, wonderful Fariel, who had carried his gifts with a grace that belied his youth; Anyara, who could not hide from Inurian's inner eye the things she concealed so well from others. And Orisian. The boy who grew up in his brother's shadow, only to have his heart broken when it was taken away and he was exposed to the harsh, ferocious light. He had loved every one of them, but Orisian most of all.

And he had failed them, in the end. Lairis and Fariel had been carried off to The Grave, Kennet cut down, going too gladly to his death. Perhaps Orisian still lived — he would surely have known if that one had died — but if he did he was beyond any help Inurian could give for the time being. There was only Anyara now. Somehow, if he was allowed the life to do it, he must find a way to shield her.

Outside the window of his cell there was the sound of flapping wings. He rose and looked up. He could not reach the window and saw nothing but the night sky. There was the soft, rasping call of a crow. Inurian smiled sadly and lay down again.

His rest was fitful. The slabs on which he lay were unyielding and the thin blanket could not keep out the cold. What finally roused him was less immediate, less tangible: a calling in his dreams, as if some distant voice was summoning him. He pressed his hands into his eyes as he lay there in the semi-darkness. The feeble first light of dawn coming in through the high window illuminated the cell. There was no sound save the skittering of a rat's claws somewhere out of sight, and the tapping of half-hearted rain on the roof. He rolled onto one side and sat up. Looking around, his eyes still bleary with sleep, he saw nothing at first. Then the faintest distortion of the air on the far side of the cell caught his attention.

He watched as a shape formed itself out of nothing. It was too tenuous, and the cell too gloomy, for any detail to be visible, but he could tell that it was a female figure that now wavered before him. The rain outside was worsening, its drumming on the roof growing louder.

"I had thought you might be dead," said Inurian.

"I doubt you thought of me at all," came the almost vanishingly soft reply, as if from the walls themselves. Inurian grunted and rubbed at his shoulders.

"And I had not troubled myself to think of you in some time," continued the female voice, "until I stumbled across you now."

"Well, I'm not sorry to see you, Yvane."

There was the thinnest thread of laughter in the cell for a moment, and then a pause. "That's kinder than I would have expected."

Inurian waved a hand irritably, though he knew his visitor could not see him. Not in the way that eyes saw, at least.

"This is not the time to renew old disagreements," he said. "You have come looking here because you felt something in the Shared."

"I know you can't be the source, unless you've changed a good deal since I saw you last." The question had more than a hint of confrontation in its tone.

"Yvane, Yvane, please. I will not argue with you."

There was silence, and then the flat reply: "Very well."

"There is another here. He is what you have felt. His name is Aeglyss. He is young, very raw, but the Shared runs strong in him. Perhaps more strongly than it has in anyone for years."

"Does it indeed," said Yvane. The skepticism in her voice was clear.

"Yes," insisted Inurian. "We were arguing. His anger disturbs the Shared. He's filled with hate, with resentment. It's crowded everything else out of him. You know my gifts, and I tell you truly what he is."

"What's he doing in Kolglas?"

"I'm not in Kolglas," said Inurian wearily. "I'm in Anduran. The Black Road has me."

"The Black Road? Is Anduran taken?"

"It is close."

"Hmph. It never ends, does it? Your precious Huanin live for the chance to wade around in one another's blood. How do you come to be in the middle of it? What about that miserable old chiefling who kept you under his roof?"

"Ah, Yvane," sighed Inurian. "Please."

He bowed his head, shorn of all strength. His visitor's image shimmered as if touched by a breeze, though the air was still.

"Are you a prisoner, then?" she asked.

"Yes. Yvane, if I do not come out of this alive, Highfast should know of Aeglyss. Perhaps even Dyrkyrnon: I think he may have lived there for a time. He said they cast him out. If he continues down the path he's following, it might take Highfast or Dyrkyrnon to rein him in."

There was no reply for a time, then: "They long for these bloodlettings. Gyre, Haig, Lannis, all of them. From the crib they dream of vengeance for some crime or other committed in the distant past. Father kills father, and so child must kill child. It never ends. Leave them to their cruel games. Nobody will thank *na'kyrim* for interfering."

"Aeglyss has already interfered," said Inurian, gazing at the floor. "The Gyre Bloods might think he is their puppet, but I doubt they understand what they're dealing with."

When Yvane did not reply, Inurian looked up, thinking for a moment that she had left him. The outline of her form was still there, a fragment of cloud glowing palely from within.

"I would . . . regret it if you died," she said quietly.

"As would I."

"Perhaps I should see for myself," she said. The pale figure began in that moment to fade.

"No," hissed Inurian, reaching out an arm. "You'll only alarm him. He's dangerous. Yvane!"

But she was gone, and he was alone again.

He sat without moving for a long time. Then he unpicked the lace from one of his boots, and drew it out. Closing his eyes, he began to knot it. One small, tight knot after another along its length, pausing over each to savor its shape beneath his fingertips. Outside, dawn was breaking.

* * *

The Horin-Gyre Blood held its council of war in the feasting hall that Croesan oc Lannis-Haig had prepared for Winterbirth. The high-roofed chamber was in disarray. Tables and chairs had been overturned and all its decorations torn down. A single huge table stood in the center, a dozen or more people gathered around it.

Kanin nan Horin-Gyre was seated in the great carved chair that was to have been Croesan's. His sword lay on the table in front of him. Wain was to his left, his shieldman Igris to his right. Shraeve was there, wearing a cuirass of hardened black leather like the carapace of a martial beetle, and all the captains of the Bloodheir's army. A single Tarbain chieftain, old and haggard in a jacket trimmed with moth-eaten bearskin, occupied one end of the table. He looked as if he might fall asleep at any moment. Aeglyss the *na'kyrim* sat a little apart from the others, his chair pulled back: he was here only by the indulgence of the Bloodheir's sister and Kanin would not grant him a seat at the table.

"We must make the attempt," Wain was saying. Her eyes had a fierce intensity and certitude. "We will not be granted enough time to sit here and wait for the castle to be delivered to us. We must reach out and take it."

Nobody seemed to be inclined to challenge her judgment, though Kanin knew not everyone here agreed with it. He had his own doubts.

"Is there any fresh word from the scouts this morning?" he asked.

One of the warriors shook his head. "There are bands of farmers and villagers roaming around beyond Grive and the Dyke, but no sign of any army yet. They will spend a while longer licking the wounds we gave them at Grive."

"Only until another few thousand Kilkry horsemen turn up," muttered Wain. "Then what? We can't fight them with Tarbains and woodwights."

She cast an angry glance at the Tarbain chieftain at the end of the table. He grinned back at her and said nothing. There were many gaps amidst his teeth.

"We don't know yet how long it will be before help comes to us from the north," Kanin said. "Tanwrye has not fallen, and will not do so for days — perhaps weeks — yet. It can't be taken by storm, unless Ragnor oc Gyre changes his mind and sends his whole army to do the deed. The besiegers may be able to spare us a few hundred spears but it will be no more than that, for the time being at least."

He turned to a small, slender man who sat beside Shraeve.

"Cannek, what do you know of the castle's strength?"

The man looked up. He wore nondescript clothing of hide and soft leather; his face was plain, without distinguishing features. Someone passing him in the street might do so without noticing him, but for the long, sheathed knives that were strapped to each forearm. He was the leader of the dozen Hunt Inkallim who had accompanied the army. The Hunt had its own methods for gathering information, and though Kanin had no wish to know what they were, he was happy to derive whatever benefit he could.

"Well, we cannot be certain, of course," Cannek said with a faint, disarming smile. "We have questioned many of the city's inhabitants, but really they are poor material for us to work with. The common folk, you know, rarely pay enough attention to important matters such as food supplies and garrison strengths."

Kanin nodded with as much patience as he could muster. The Hunt was the least of the three Inkalls that together made up the Children of the Hundred — both Lore and Battle came before it in numbers and seniority — but it had gathered perhaps the darkest tales of all around it. Whatever Cannek might imply, he would not be relying solely on rumors extracted from prisoners. The Hunt had dozens, perhaps hundreds, of ordinary people in their pay throughout the Bloods of the Black Road and, if rumor was to be believed, even amongst the so-called True Bloods. If anyone at this gathering would know what lay behind the obstinate walls of Castle Anduran, it would be Cannek.

The Inkallim flicked a stray hair from the back of his hand.

"They are short of food, though," he said. "Of that we can be fairly sure. As to numbers, it's a matter for guesswork in the main. Few warriors, we think. But how many men were taken in through the gate in those last hours before it closed? Can't say."

Kanin frowned, but quickly forced his face to relax. It would not be wise to show displeasure. Falling out with the Hunt Inkall could only create difficulties. Still, he suspected Cannek could be more forthcoming if he wished.

"Perhaps you should execute that Lannis girl under the walls, as you threatened," mused Cannek.

"That'll achieve nothing," Kanin said. "She's more useful alive, for the time being. Since he was not taken at Kolglas" — he glanced at Shraeve, who ignored him — "we may yet find ourselves dealing with her brother before long. She might have value as a bargaining piece then."

The slight sound of a chair leg scraping on stone from some little way behind him drew Kanin's attention. Aeglyss was leaning forward in his chair, as if straining to close the gap between himself and the rest of them. He should have refused Wain's suggestion that the halfbreed attend, but she had been so calmly persuasive he had given in. She persisted in her belief that he might prove to be of some further use, and Kanin had no stronger argument than his dislike of the man to set against that belief.

"It matters little whether there are fifty or five hundred swords to defend the castle walls," Wain said. "We have been in the hands of fate since the day we marched out from Hakkan. Why turn aside now? Whether we succeed or fail we will have lived out the tales told by the Hooded God willingly and with courage."

She is always so certain, Kanin thought. Always the first to test fate. If all of us could surrender ourselves so willingly to the Road our armies would be an unstoppable flood sweeping away Kilkry, Haig, even the Kingships in the south. If all of us had been as steadfast as Wain, perhaps the Kall would have come years ago.

"There is someone here."

The words were so unexpected, so disconnected, that at first no one was certain where they had come from. Then, one by one, everyone turned their eyes to Aeglyss. The *na'kyrim* was sitting erect in his chair, his eyes narrowing thoughtfully. He cocked his head to one side as if trying to catch the faintest of whispers. He looked up to the roof beams, around to the furthest corners of the hall.

"An uninvited guest," he murmured.

"What are you talking about?" demanded Kanin.

"Hush," said Aeglyss.

The Bloodheir's eyes widened and he surged to his feet.

"Do not presume . . ." he started, but fell silent as the *na'kyrim* suddenly grimaced and staggered upright himself. A ripple of disquiet ran through the hall. Aeglyss took a couple of steps toward the doorway, his right hand clasped to his temple.

"Looking for me . . ." he said to himself. It was clear he was barely aware of the presence of Kanin and the others. He halted and suddenly looked at the dais at the end of the hall. He laughed, though it sounded strained. "How clever, whoever you are. Like smoke . . . a woman, if I see you right."

Following the line of the *na'kyrim*'s gaze, Kanin saw nothing. The dais was empty, occupied by nothing but dust and the fallen decorations of Winterbirth. Igris had risen from his seat and stepped forward. The shieldman looked questioningly at the Bloodheir.

"That is an admirable skill," said Aeglyss as he took a step closer to the dais. "I would dearly love to know the trick of it, my lady, if we meet some time. But not now, I think. No, whoever you are, I'll not have you looking over my shoulder."

His hands twitched at his side as if they wanted to reach for whatever he thought he saw on the dais. His shoulders went taut and his jaw locked in concentration and effort.

"Begone," he spat through gritted teeth. "Begone."

"He has lost his mind," Igris whispered in Kanin's ear. "Let me kill him."

Kanin hesitated, minded to grant his shieldman's request but held by a kind of morbid fascination. Before he could speak, Aeglyss gave a sudden cry and slumped to the ground. He lay motionless. There was blood on his face: he had bitten through his lower lip.

Many miles away, amidst ancient ruins high in the snowbound peaks of the Car Criagar, there was the piercing sound of a woman crying out in pain. It lasted for just a second or two and then died, falling away beneath the wind that surged around the mountains.

In the hall in Anduran, Kanin stared at the unconscious form on the floor.

"Extraordinary," murmured Cannek.

Kanin blinked.

"Take him away," he said to the nearest of his captains. "Give him back to his woodwight friends, or leave him in some hovel. I don't care."

As Aeglyss was dragged out Kanin resumed his seat.

"As my sister was saying . . ." he began.

"I believe the castle can be taken," Shraeve said quietly.

Kanin looked at her in surprise. She had not spoken since they first entered the hall. He had not expected her to take any great interest in proceedings.

"It may cost you most of what strength you have left, but then if you fail you will have no need of strength," the Inkallim said. "And if you succeed . . . well, who knows what may happen after?"

"We are of one mind," said Wain. Kanin glanced at her and saw how chill was the look she fixed upon Shraeve. The two women did not like one another, Kanin knew. Too much alike to rest easily in each other's company, perhaps. But they were alike in determination, in implacability. If both of them were going to argue for the storming of the castle, Kanin already knew the outcome of this council.

VII

To travel through the forest in the company of Kyrinin was a revelation to Orisian. He had been on hunts often enough — riding in his uncle's parties or going more softly with a hawk on his arm — and when he was younger he had played with Fariel and Anyara in the fringes of the great forests around Kolglas, and gone with his father to visit Drinan or Stryne deep in the woodlands, but none of that changed the fact that his heart lay with the open vistas of the coast and the Glas valley.

So it was for most of the people of the Lannis Blood. Even though some grazed their cattle deep into Anlane when the season was right, and woodsmen bred their mighty horses to haul timber to the workshops of Anduran, the forest was not where they belonged. It was a wild place to be cleared, or a source of food, wood and forage that could be harvested only with a wary eye.

Now, following in the wake of Ess'yr and Varryn, Orisian realized what it might be like to see the forest in a different way. It was not just that the Kyrinin went confidently and quickly over land that had no trails; it was, as much as anything, all the things he never even glimpsed. The first time Ess'yr paused for half a stride and lifted her head, just as a deer might, before moving on, he was puzzled. After it had happened twice more, he realized that she was hearing, or smelling, or feeling things that were beyond his reach.

Once he understood that, the forest changed its character for him. Birds that passed croaking overhead seemed to be calling a name he could not catch. Trees looked as though they were human figures frozen in the midst of some contorted movement. On the second day out from the *vo'an,* as the four of them came around the edge of an impenetrable thicket of brambles and saplings, the two Kyrinin froze, snapping into a stillness so deep it was startling. Orisian and Rothe halted as well. Ess'yr and Varryn sank down to their haunches and gestured for the humans to do the same.

They waited thus for what seemed an age. Orisian's muscles tightened in his legs and the wound in his side throbbed. He longed to ask what was happening, and knew that any frustration he felt would be multiplied several times in Rothe. It would infuriate his shieldman to be held thus at the whim of the Kyrinin.

At last, somewhere up ahead, there was rustling and the sharp crack of a fallen branch giving way beneath a heavy tread. A great creature was moving through the forest, climbing up the slope heedless of any undergrowth that might bar its way. The sounds lingered for a few minutes and then faded as the animal passed beyond earshot. Even then, the Kyrinin kept them immobile and silent for a long time. Eventually Varryn rose and without a backward glance set off once more as if nothing had happened.

"Bear. The wind is kind," Ess'yr said.

After that Orisian imagined the creature somewhere above them, a dark, ill-formed presence, watching them from afar.

When they rested they sat a little way apart, Huanin and Kyrinin keeping their distance. Rothe sniffed suspiciously at the food Ess'yr offered. There were little strips of flaking dried meat so desiccated and aged that it was almost black, and a handful of big seeds that Orisian did not recognize. When he split one between his teeth it had a nutty, sharp taste. Rothe gnawed with a wary grimace at the frayed end of the meat. He wrinkled his nose, but teased a strand of the fibrous material loose and chewed on it.

"I would give a lot for a rack of roast boar," muttered Rothe as he probed with a fingernail to loosen scraps of food from the crevices between his teeth.

"Perhaps when we reach Anduran," Orisian said.

"That would be good," Rothe agreed. "And a bench to sit on instead of wet grass, and a bed to go to at the end of the day."

"I didn't know you liked your comforts so much," said Orisian with a smile.

"It's nothing but sense, to wish to be elsewhere than under the stars when winter's come. I've had my full share of rocks for pillows and trees for a roof. The years chip away at a man's patience for such things. Still, I shouldn't be hankering after comforts, meager or otherwise. It's not feasting and sleeping we're headed for."

"No," murmured Orisian. One way or another, it could only be war they were traveling toward; something he felt unready for, something he was not sure he would be able to meet in the way he should. Yet a part of him felt that only war could make sense of the horrors of Winterbirth. Orisian was feeling something he never had before: a desire for blood to wash away blood. The thought felt like a tapeworm lodged in the gut of his mind. He could almost see Inurian shaking his gentle head in disapproval.

Rothe sensed his distracted gloom, and patted him upon the shoulder. It was a soft touch, from those callused, blunt hands.

"We'll come safe through this, Orisian. You'll see. The Blood is strong. And I'll not leave your side, whatever comes."

"I'll be safer than anyone in the valley, then."

"Of course. I've killed an Inkallim. Not even Taim Narran could claim that."

Having Rothe with him was a source of strength to Orisian. In one way alone did the precious shieldman's presence make for a less easy journey, and that was in the tension between him and Varryn. Rothe's frustration — fury, almost — at having to follow where the Kyrinin led was never far from the surface. It showed in the rigidity of his jaw and the way he would sometimes tug distractedly at his beard while he stared ahead.

It was clear that Varryn was not inclined to make the experience any easier. He made no concessions to the humans' lesser agility or surefootedness in the routes he took, and offered no explanations for anything he did. Even to Orisian, whose instinct, however hesitant, was to trust these two Kyrinin, there appeared to be a cold arrogance in Varryn. And his tattoos, the *kin'thyn* that swirled over his face like the dance of blue fireflies, did nothing to soften the impression. Though he felt a pang of disloyalty at the thought, Orisian suspected that even Rothe might not be a match for the Kyrinin, on this ground at least. Perhaps that was part of what lay between the two men; perhaps such warriors instinctively weighed each other's worth, played out some confrontation in their minds to see who would emerge the victor. Varryn's arrogance might be that of the one who had triumphed, in both his own imagination and Rothe's.

Several times, when he lost his footing upon some slick patch of moss or broke a twig with his tread, Orisian heard a muttered "*Ulyin,*" from Varryn. Once, Rothe caught the word as well.

"What do you think *ulyin* means, anyway?" he asked Orisian darkly.

"I don't know," Orisian lied. "Probably 'be careful.'"

As they worked their way along the flank of the mountains it was sometimes hard to believe that they were still within the lands claimed by Croesan's uncle. Once or twice they did come across a path that was too crude and obvious to be the work of Kyrinin. Varryn would not let them follow such routes. Sometimes, too, there were clearings where they saw signs of grazing by cattle, or could make out the scars left by some woodsman's or hunter's camp. None of these marks his people had left upon the forest struck Orisian as anything other than transient. He saw nothing that would not be healed.

He thought of the face of the Anain that watched over In'hynyr's *vo'an.* Ess'yr had said that the Anain were here, even if they did not show themselves. Orisian found himself glancing at flickering shadows, and at the movement of branches stirred by the wind. He started at the clattering eruption of pigeons out of the trees. The sharp barking of foxes in the dusk took on a shivery quality in his ear.

His unease was reinforced by the small rituals Ess'yr and Varryn followed. They never made a fire until darkness had fallen, and then only a small one that they ringed with a makeshift low screen of branches to muffle the light. When the time came, as her brother was decanting the embers of the previous night's fire from the birch bark container he carried and sustained them in, Ess'yr would find a flat stone. She set it at the new fire's side and placed a few scraps of food on it. In an almost inaudible voice, she murmured a few words. After she was done, Varryn would bow his head over the food and whisper the same incantation. In the morning they left the food behind them as they made their way onward.

Orisian hesitated to ask Ess'yr what the act signified. His curiosity must have been poorly concealed, for on the third evening Ess'yr sat beside him at the fire.

"The food is for restless dead. Those who walk. No *anhyne* to guard us here. If one of the restless comes in the night, they will take the food. Leave us."

"The restless dead," echoed Orisian, feeling the stirring of the darkness beyond the reach of the fire's frail light. The unburied dead.

"You fear the dead," he murmured.

"Not fear. Pity. Only those who do not rest."

Orisian was not sure how to behave with Ess'yr. He felt she was less at ease with him now than when they had been in the *vo'an*. It might be because of Varryn's presence, or the fact that she was no longer his healer but his guard, guide and escort. Still, she did not mock him as Varryn did. She would talk to him and tell him things, if not with as much freedom as she had on occasion back in the camp. More often than her brother, she would wait for him and Rothe to catch up when they fell behind.

They came to a stream that bubbled along between moss-covered rocks. There was a pool where the water paused, gathering itself before rushing on down toward the valley that summoned it. While Varryn and Rothe sat in silence, Ess'yr took Orisian to the water's edge and made him kneel down beside her. He did so gingerly, trying to protect his side. The wound had been hurting more for the last day or so.

She pulled up the sleeve of her hide jacket, exposing the pale, sculpted length of her forearm. He watched as she flexed her long fingers. She slipped her hand into the water with seamless delicacy, leaving barely a hint of its passing upon the surface. As she reached beneath the lip of the bank, she looked not at the water or at her arm but at Orisian. He could not look away from those utterly grey eyes.

Her face betrayed nothing: no expectation, no concentration. Its surface was no more ruffled than that of the pool. Her hand emerged, and cupped in it was a small, glistening fish. It was a mountain trout, its flanks speckled with red dots. Orisian laughed, and for a moment there was a smile on Ess'yr's lips as if the sun had touched her.

"You," she said.

He obeyed, sinking his hand into the water. He moved his hand along the bank, feeling the earth, brushing his fingertips over pebbles. He touched something alive and cold and smooth. Closing his hand with all the care he could muster, he raised the fish. As soon as he brought it within a breath of the air it gave a single, contemptuous twist and flicked out of his grasp and away.

His disappointment showed. Ess'yr smiled again.

They caught no more fish, and shared the meager flesh of the one between the four of them. It was enough to make it the best meal they had eaten since leaving the *vo'an*.

Rothe pursed his lips as he peered at the wound in Orisian's flank. Orisian was lying on the ground, his jacket hitched up.

"How does it look?" he asked.

Rothe gave a noncommittal shrug. "It matters more how it feels."

"Not bad. It itches sometimes. Is it healed?"

"Will be soon, if you treat it gentle. Still red." He sniffed at the paste-smeared bandage he had removed from over the wound. "Wish I knew what it was they've used on it, though."

"Whatever it is, it's worked. I'll settle for that."

Rothe grunted and straightened.

Orisian pulled his jacket down and carefully righted himself, still wary of jarring the muscles in his side. "I'm sure they knew what they were doing," he said. "They are Kyrinin cures, all those medicines Inurian has. He never did anyone any harm with them, did he?"

"No, but he didn't cure all the ones he tried, either," said Rothe.

"Well, anyway, this has worked."

Rothe frowned at the poultice in his hand. Orisian glanced over to where Ess'yr sat further up the slope with her back to them. She had said it would be all right to take the dressing off, but shown no further interest. Varryn had disappeared some little while ago: scouting ahead, or hunting. As usual, he had not seen fit to explain what he was doing.

Rothe leaned close, fixing Orisian with a serious gaze.

"We should go," the shieldman whispered. "Leave them. We are not their prisoners now, whatever they may think."

Orisian shook his head, but Rothe was insistent. "This is taking too long. Anduran cannot be far. If we go straight downhill we would surely be in the valley in an hour or two. Orisian, these wights are no friends of ours. We don't need them."

Orisian shot a nervous look toward Ess'yr, afraid that she would hear what Rothe was saying. She had not moved.

"They were told to take us, Rothe. I would get there faster if I could, but their *vo'an'tyr* told them to escort us, to see us out of their lands. They won't let us go off on our own."

"We don't need their permission," hissed Rothe urgently. "And this isn't their land. It's ours; yours. Now is the time to do it. You're almost healed. Her brother isn't here. She can't deal with both of us alone."

Again, Orisian shot a worried glance toward Ess'yr. Her head and shoulders remained as motionless and relaxed as ever. Yet he saw that her right hand rested upon her spear where it lay beside her, and he could not remember if it had been there before. He had a sudden taste of fear and a glimpse of something awful waiting a few paces into the future.

"No, Rothe," he insisted as quietly as he could. "No. Stop now. We stay with them."

The words felt unfamiliar and ungainly on his tongue as he

uttered them. He knew why: he had never, in any sense that mattered, commanded Rothe before. He had never had to. His shieldman blinked, and for just a moment Orisian saw in his eyes the instinct to keep arguing. It was snuffed out. The tension vanished from the warrior's face.

"As you say," Rothe said, and Orisian could not hear in his voice a single trace of frustration or disagreement.

Shortly afterward, Varryn returned and sat silently beside his sister. A squall of rain swept over them. It came down the valley from the north, drenching the forest and rattling the trees for half an hour. In the sodden aftermath, the Kyrinin shook their heads like animals to shed rainwater. Ess'yr leaned forward so that her long hair hung in a curtain and ran tight fingers through it. Orisian watched her squeeze out droplets of water with a few long sweeps of her hand.

The child's body was twisted where it had fallen, one arm bent and pinned beneath the torso. Rothe laid his hand on the dead boy's shoulder and rolled him over. The limbs moved sluggishly. Death's grip had been on him for just a little while, stiffening his joints but not yet locking them. Orisian glimpsed a ruined face — split skin flecked with fragments of tooth or bone, a lot of blood — before Rothe, kneeling down, blocked his view.

The corpse was shod with crude hide slippers. The leggings were of undyed wool. It was the clothing of a poor household: shepherds, perhaps, or woodsmen. The boy lay in a slight hollow. Trees leaned over him. The grass was lushly green and wet from recent rain.

The two Kyrinin were standing back, resting on their spears. They watched as Rothe closed the child's eyes. He had to clean his hand on the grass afterward. He turned the body over again to hide the face.

"Not long dead," said the shieldman. He stood up. He looked tired, Orisian thought.

They could be no more than a day's walk from Anduran, in a fold of the hills that hid the Glas valley from sight. For the last couple of hours they had been walking through parts of the forest that had been well grazed in the summer. Most of the trees were young and spindly; only stumps remained of those that had offered good timber.

"This was in the wound," Rothe said, holding out his hand. In his palm lay a thin piece of horn, worked to a sharp point.

"What is it?" asked Orisian.

"The Tarbains from the north set them into their clubs. That's who killed him: Tarbains." He cast a glance toward Ess'yr and Varryn. "Savages. They're barely human."

"Tarbains," said Orisian quietly. "Then it's bad, isn't it?"

Rothe nodded. He flicked the sliver of horn away. It disappeared into the grass as if it had never been.

"Yes," he said. "If Tarbains are roaming free this far south, it's very bad. They could only have got here with a Black Road army. I'd not have believed it if it was any eyes but my own doing the seeing."

"We should take care of the body," Orisian said.

"The ones who did this cannot be far away. It's not safe to stay."

Orisian looked at the dead boy. Once it had departed, life left no trace. The body had a shapeless quality. It was difficult to imagine it had ever been inhabited. As far as he could tell, all his family had come to this: certainly Fariel and Lairis, perhaps Kennet and Anyara. All of them. He wanted to look away, but could not lift his eyes from a patch on the back of the boy's jacket where some old tear had been carefully repaired.

"How old is he, do you think?"

"I couldn't be sure," Rothe murmured.

"How old, though, do you think?" Orisian repeated, and heard the strange insistence in his voice as if it was someone else speaking.

"Perhaps twelve. Thirteen."

"We should find the ones who did this," Orisian said.

"I don't think . . ." began Rothe.

Orisian pointed to the lip of the hollow. The grass there was trodden flat. "Even I can see the tracks," he said.

"It would be better to pass around, and make for Anduran," said Rothe.

"No. This boy wouldn't be out here on his own. His family, his home, can't be far away. His parents might be searching for him."

"More likely they're dead and the Tarbains are feasting on their hearts, waiting for us."

Orisian glared at his shieldman. Rothe looked back. His face was quite calm, quite firm.

"Then we will kill them," Orisian said. "I am going to follow this boy's trail, whether it's wise or not. These are our people. Should we pass by?"

Rothe stroked his beard.

"I will do it, Rothe. I am nephew to the Thane," said Orisian quietly. Never before had he truly thought that his uncle's position made a difference to who he was, in his heart; perhaps it did, after all.

The shieldman held Orisian's gaze for a moment or two, then knelt and began to examine the ground. Orisian glanced over toward Ess'yr. She and her brother had not stirred. They showed no great interest in what was happening.

"We are going to find this boy's family," he said to them. Ess'yr gave a slight nod. He had no idea what it meant, beyond the fact that she understood his words.

"There were three or four of them," Rothe said. "They ran him down and killed him with clubs and spears. It's easy to say, Orisian, but you understand that if they see us we have to kill them? All of them, if we can. If one escapes, he might come back with more."

"Of course." Orisian heard the coldness in his own voice.

Rothe stood up and faced Ess'yr and Varryn. When he spoke it was still to Orisian, though.

"You've only a knife. The few who did this might not be the only ones around. We may need help."

Orisian looked to the Kyrinin. Both of them were watching him, not Rothe.

"Ess'yr, if there is a fight we may need your help. Please?"

It was Varryn who said, "We have no quarrel here."

"Perhaps not. I will understand if you do not come with us. But if the Tarbains have come this far, they can go further. They will kill Kyrinin as willingly as Huanin."

"We will come," Ess'yr said. "We must take you to the forest edge. We are not there yet."

As they set out along the trail left by the boy and his pursuers, Rothe muttered to Orisian, "I am your shieldman, and you will allow me to keep you safe. Stay back if there is trouble. If you have to fight, show no fear. Whatever happens, do not run. Tarbains are dangerous but they're cowards, too. They're like wolves: quick to turn tail if they decide you have sharper teeth than they do. If you face one, let him see your teeth. And let's hope your friends know how to use those bows."

The boy had not come far. He had crossed a little stream, run beneath the spreading branches of a huge oak that had been spared the axe for some reason, crossed a glade that must be full of flowers in the spring. Not far.

They lay in the damp grass atop a rise, looking down between scattered trees toward the cabin a few score paces away. It was the kind of dwelling hundreds of Lannis folk lived in: square, made of timber and stone, with a little woodshed close by. There were snares hanging on the wall, sheltered beneath the eaves. A pile of unsplit logs lay in front of the woodshed, as if at any moment a man might come out from the cabin with his axe. He might be a charcoal-burner or a fur trapper, or even a honey-maker with hives somewhere out of sight.

The door of the cottage hung open, leaning at a broken angle, and the voices that Orisian could hear were not those of a woods-man and his family. They were crude, abrasive, and shouting in a language he had never heard before. Orisian was tense. It had been so clear, standing over that body in the hollow, that this was the right thing to do; a brief moment of clarity, when things for once had seemed simple. Now, faced with the consequence of his will, he was not so certain. Rothe had been right, of course. It would be wiser to pass by. Yet he was the Thane's nephew, and those who lived here were people of his Blood. Orisian had taken the oath. The enemy of the Blood was his enemy. If it was to mean any-thing, surely it was this?

Then a figure came out of the cabin. It was a man, but one unlike any Orisian had seen before. He was tall, rangy like a lean dog. His hair was filthy and tangled in knots and mats. Dozens of splinters of bone were sewn into the fur jerkin he wore, a speckling of morbid ornament. His arms were naked but for two leather armlets, one at the wrist, one just below his shoulder. The great weapon he rested across his shoulder was vicious-looking: a long cudgel with a thick head from which five or six spikes protruded.

The man loitered in front of the doorway. He spat and scratched at his face. He looked around, and though his eyes drifted over the place where Orisian and the others lay he did not see them. He was relaxed, careless.

The Tarbain went inside again. There was a renewed chorus of loud voices, raised in what sounded like argument. Rothe eased himself back from the crest of the rise. The four of them squatted in a tight group once they were hidden from the cabin.

"Can't say how many are in there," Rothe whispered. "It doesn't sound to be more than four or five, though."

"There's no sign of the boy's family," said Orisian. "They might be inside, do you think?"

Rothe shrugged. "If they are, they're dead, or worse. Tarbains don't take prisoners, Orisian. They'll probably stay here a while, eat and drink as much as they can and then carry off everything else."

"And maybe do the same to the next family they come across?"

"Maybe. Now that we're here, I'd be glad to see them dead. We need them outside, though. If we go rushing in, it's as likely to be us that's buzzard food as it is them."

Varryn whispered to his sister. She nodded, and he was gone, running in a low crouch up the line of the ridge. Ess'yr took an arrow from her quiver and ran its fletching between her lips, smoothing the feathers. It was a delicate, almost sensual, movement. Rothe looked alarmed.

"What's happening?" he demanded in a hiss.

"They must be under the sky, yes? To kill them?" Ess'yr said. She began to crawl up toward the spot from where they had been watching the cabin.

Rothe unsheathed his sword and raised his eyebrows at Orisian before following her.

The voices had quietened. The clearing around the cabin was quite still. A slight wind brushed the highest twigs in the trees. It touched the broken door and creaked it on its one surviving hinge. Orisian realized he was holding his breath.

"What's happening?" asked Rothe again. He was getting close to anger.

Ess'yr pointed. Varryn was there, crouched against the nearest wall of the cottage. Ess'yr rose to one knee and put the arrow to her bowstring. Rothe gave a low growl of irritation, but half-rose himself and hefted his sword. The Inkallim's knife was still in Orisian's belt. He fingered its hilt. As he set himself on his knees his side gave a twinge of protest and he winced.

Varryn stood and walked forward. He carried his spear loosely. His bow was still across his back. He went out twenty paces into the space in front of the cabin.

"This is not how I'd do it," muttered Rothe.

Varryn shot a quick glance up toward them. Ess'yr drew back

the bowstring and held it. Varryn took a few steps sideways, and put himself in the line of sight from the open doorway. He rested the butt of his spear on the ground and stood there.

"Don't forget, stay back," Rothe whispered in Orisian's ear.

There was a chorus of shouts from inside the cabin. Varryn sprinted toward Orisian and the others. The Tarbains spilled out behind him, howling and almost falling over one another in their haste. They saw only a single Kyrinin flying away, and they came after him. There were six of them. Orisian saw teeth bared, cudgels and spears flailing.

The arrow was gone and homed before Orisian even realized Ess'yr had released it. It took the rearmost Tarbain square in the chest. He tumbled over his own feet. Rothe sprang up and ran forward, crying out like a madman, "Lannis! Lannis!"

Another arrow thrummed across the air and found a shoulder. It spun a second man around, but he did not fall. Orisian stood and pulled his knife free. Two of the Tarbains were slowing, realizing that they faced more than a single foe. Two more came on, though, too frenzied to care what was happening. Varryn turned to meet them, halfway up the slope. The first Tarbain to reach him was the one they had seen outside the cabin before. He swung his spiked cudgel. The Kyrinin slipped beneath it and put his spear into the man's belly. It took him off the ground, punching through furs and flesh and stabbing out through his lower back. Varryn let body and weapon fall and met the next Tarbain with a kick to the knee. The two men rolled together, each grappling for an advantage.

The one Ess'yr had shot in the shoulder was fleeing. She put another arrow in his back. Rothe was on top of the last two. He bore one backward with the weight of his charge. The other froze, poised upon the boundary between courage and flight. Then as Ess'yr sighted on him her bowstring snapped. The arrow tumbled to the ground. The Tarbain looked up. He stared straight at her for a fraction of a second, and made his choice. He came bounding up toward her and Orisian, his spear leveled. Ess'yr dropped her bow and stooped to pick up her own spear. The Tarbain came on. Orisian took a step back. The tribesman had no eyes for him; he might have been invisible.

Ess'yr met the Tarbain with a lunge that made him lurch to one side and come to a slithering halt. Fast as a falcon's strike, the butt of her spear came round and cracked into the small of his back. He grunted, but he was strong and the blow barely rocked him. He feinted toward Ess'yr and she backed up. The Tarbain was making a strange noise, half growl, half groan. There were strands of leather and hide twisted into his hair; they shook as he rolled his head this way and that. Orisian rushed at him.

He came from behind and to one side, almost out of sight. The Tarbain's reaction was late. His spear swept round in a flat plane. Orisian ducked it and hit the man around the waist, staggering him. He would not fall and somehow Orisian could not get his knife turned the right way to stab him. Then there was a solid thud and a piercing shriek as Ess'yr's spear sank a foot deep into the tribesman's thigh. Blood flooded out, more than Orisian had ever seen except when a sheep's throat was cut. The Tarbain tried to turn and tripped. Orisian landed on top of him, and drove his knife into the man's chest with every shred of strength he had. The impact made his hand slip off the hilt. There was blood everywhere, all over his fingers, over the knife and on his clothing. The blade stayed where he had put it, though. There was a roar, or perhaps a scream, in Orisian's head, crowding out any thought, bearing him away from himself on a cresting wave of fury and grief. He gripped the knife and pulled it from the man's flesh, stabbed it in again, and then again.

The Tarbain did not move. He was still making strange noises, but they were soft and fading now. The grass all around was a dark, liquid red. Ess'yr was running, sprinting toward the cabin. Orisian did not want to be left alone with the dying man, and went after her.

Rothe had killed his man. Varryn had managed to pin the last and was straddling his chest. As they came near, he whipped an arrow out of his quiver and plunged it into the tribesman's neck. The first man Ess'yr had put an arrow into was crawling on his hands and knees back toward the cabin. He was speaking very quickly in his unintelligible language. For all that the words were senseless, the current of terror that flowed through them was clear. Rothe walked up to him and raised his sword above the back of his neck. Orisian looked away.

They found the boy's father, mother and two sisters in the cabin. They were all dead.

Afterward, Orisian sat on the grass a little way from the cottage. He had his back to it, and was gazing out into the forest. When he looked in that direction, everything appeared normal, as if nothing had happened. The trees were as they had always been. The lichen on their trunks had not changed.

The knife was in his hands. Rothe had retrieved it for him and washed it in a bucket of water they found inside the door of the cabin. Orisian had cleaned himself as best he could. He doubted whether the stains would ever come out of his jacket, though.

His shieldman came and sat beside him.

"You all right?"

"It's not the same as practice, is it?" Orisian said.

"No. You did well, though. Showed no fear, stayed alive; can't ask for much more."

Ess'yr was a short distance away, testing the spare string she had fitted to her bow. Orisian gestured toward her.

"She killed him, really. There was so much blood coming out from where she stabbed him he would have bled to death in no time." Even as he said it he wondered. Whether it was true or not, it did nothing to shift the hollowness in his stomach.

"Probably. Still, you made sure he wasn't getting up again. That's important, Orisian. Leave it only half done and one day you'll be the one doing the dying."

"I thought it might feel better," said Orisian.

"Better?"

"I thought it might even the scales a bit. For Winterbirth. For my father."

"But it didn't."

"No."

"It's a start. Only a start. These men we killed, they were enemies of our Blood."

Orisian was no longer certain that any amount of killing would balance the scales of Winterbirth. What had just happened felt as though it had nothing to do with Kolglas. And if it happened a thousand times it would not give Orisian the chance he wanted to tell his father that he had loved him, despite everything. Ess'yr loosed an arrow into the trunk of a birch tree. It smacked into the wood and shivered there.

"She does know how to use a bow, though, doesn't she?" Orisian said.

"She does. There's no doubting that."

They left the Tarbains for the scavengers. They fetched the boy and put him with the rest of his family into a shallow grave in front of their home. It was a poor kind of end, against the Blood's traditions, but there was no question of making a pyre. There was no knowing who might see the smoke. They ate well, too, and gathered as much food as they could easily carry to take with them. It made Orisian uncomfortable.

"It's food for rats if we leave it," Rothe said. "We've done the best we can for them. They'd not begrudge us it."

They walked in silence through the afternoon. As the first greying of evening had begun they came to the edge of the woods and the Glas valley was before them: a few rolling, sinking slopes shorn of trees, and then the flat lands of the valley floor. It was a huge plain laid out like a blanket of green patchwork. Farmhouses were scattered across it, and a few cattle could be seen here and there, but it was a lifeless view. There were no people in sight, and no smoke rose from any of the buildings. Orisian had a fleeting sense of apprehension. Now, the forest felt safe and concealing compared to that open, exposed ground.

Anduran was out in the center of the valley, couched in a lazy curve of the Glas some way to the east of where they stood. The river still had a faint shine to it even though the sun had almost fallen from the sky. The castle stood tight up against the riverside. The town it guarded lay to its south, a dark discoloration upon the valley. Orisian did not experience the surge of relief he had expected.

Rothe was standing beside him.

"What do you think?" Orisian asked.

Rothe frowned in concentration as his narrowed eyes swept over the landscape.

"A camp," Ess'yr said. "There."

Rothe and Orisian looked. Orisian thought he could see what she was talking about: an indistinct, pale shape sprawled around a darker point at its center, not far from Anduran. It might have been a camp of tents radiating out from a big farmhouse. Certainly, whatever it was, it had not been there when he and Rothe had ridden out from Anduran all those days ago.

"Now what is that?" Rothe was murmuring.

"The enemy," Ess'yr said.

"White Owl," said her brother, and for once there was clear emotion in his voice. He spoke the words as if they tasted vile.

Rothe almost laughed. "White Owls? There'd have to be hundreds for such a camp, and out in the middle of the valley, right next to Anduran? You're mad."

"No," was all Ess'yr said.

"It's impossible," insisted Rothe. "Inkallim at Kolglas and Tarbains here are strange enough, but White Owls at Anduran?"

Orisian was frowning. "It was impossible for Inkallim to reach Kolglas, but they did it. The White Owls helped them do it. In'hynyr said as much, back in the *vo'an*."

Varryn had squatted down. He was no longer paying any attention to the discussion. He stared rigidly out at the camp on the valley floor. Orisian turned to Ess'yr.

"Are you sure?"

"Yes," she said.

Rothe gave an exasperated snort. Orisian ignored him.

"How many?" he asked Ess'yr.

"Many."

"Well, I won't turn back now. We'll just have to go carefully, and see what we find."

"Wait for dark," Ess'yr said. "We go too. We must know what the enemy does. Where you are blind, we can see."

VIII

The catapult's arm snapped forward and an arc of fire vaulted the wall of Castle Anduran. The barrel of oil and pitch roared as it blazed through the air. The thump of its impact somewhere within the fortress was heard by the besiegers. It brought a ragged cheer from the warriors who hid amongst the crude siegeworks facing the castle. They shouted encouragement to the men straining to crank back the throwing arm. There were three catapults in all, and they had been at their work for some time. The smoky stink of their missiles had settled over the whole area. For a time, the castle's defenders had attempted to pick off the men working the machine with arrows, but the range was too long for accuracy and there were shieldbearers standing guard. Now the burning barrels, the rocks, the severed heads went unanswered as the day sank into dusk.

In the streets and houses that faced the castle across the killing ground, there was a subdued bustle of activity. Small bands of warriors, their feet muffled with cloth, moved along alleyways, gathered in abandoned houses and taverns. Their captains silenced any murmur of conversation with murderous gazes. They carried no torches, and in the deepening dark there were trips and falls and strangled curses. Beakers of bracing grain spirit were passed around, one swallow only for each. Some of the warriors slept, some did not. Some murmured in the shadows: "My feet are on the Road. My feet are on the Road." And on and on into the night the catapults kept up their thumping rhythm and threw ribbons of fiery gold into the black sky.

In the last few hours before dawn, the temperature fell. The day's first light brought with it a bitter chill. Clouds piled up around the summits of the Car Criagar to the north. The men atop the battlements shivered and peered out over the town as it emerged from the darkness. The catapults had fallen still, and there was no sign of movement around them. Here and there in Anduran the odd light glimmered. Somewhere a fire-weakened timber gave with a resounding crack.

It was a calm scene, until the eye looked closer. Amongst the barricades and low earthworks that had been thrown up beneath the walls, crowds of Tarbain tribesmen were packed more thickly than ever before. They thronged the ground, pressing themselves down and jostling for any scrap of protection. A few arrows flashed down from the walls, until hurried commands were shouted to save them. Figures were moving amongst the houses that fronted on to the castle; not many, but they moved with haste and purpose. The sentries looked more closely, and they saw spears and polearms. They saw more figures, pressed in beneath over-hanging eaves. The Black Road had gathered its full strength.

Word ran through the castle like wildfire. "They're attempting the walls," some cried; "They'll force the gate," others. Most of the shouts were nothing more than: "To arms, to arms!"

Warriors and farmers, shieldmen and townsfolk took up what-ever weapon they had to hand and went to the walls. They were hungry and cold. They were tired, for the bombardment had denied many sleep. But they went to the walls and they promised one another the Black Road would be bloodied today.

Croesan and Naradin, Thane and Bloodheir, stood together atop the gatehouse. They risked no more than the briefest of glances out over the grim scene.

"They grow impatient," murmured Naradin. "That's a pity."

Croesan grunted. He wore polished mail; a gleaming silver shield hung on his arm.

"They'll not find us easy," said the Thane.

Naradin looked around and back, over the courtyard of the castle. Most of the wooden outbuildings by the keep — stables, blacksmith's forge, hay store — were ruins, burned out during the night's incendiary bombardment. A new fire was being kindled even now: a pyre, onto which the bodies of men and horses had been piled, along with the heads thrown into the castle by the catapults. The keep itself was intact, though it bore the scars of several impacts. A fire had started on one of the upper floors in the night, but it had been quickly extinguished. Naradin cast his gaze along the walls that flanked the gatehouse. More than half of those now gathered to defend them were not warriors at all. They were townsfolk trapped here and left with no choice but to take up arms: apprehensive, exhausted.

"If we had only another couple of hundred trained spearmen they'd find us impregnable," the Bloodheir reflected.

"Well, we don't have those men," said Croesan firmly. "So we trust to the courage of those we do have. If we fail, there'll be others to avenge us: Lheanor, Kennet if he lives. Taim Narran. First, though, let us try to ensure that their vengeance is not required. Our Blood has life in it yet."

Naradin nodded.

"Go to the keep," Croesan said. "Wait there with your Shield, and anyone else you can find in there. Keep Eilan and your child safe. Leave the courtyard and the walls to me. We will meet again once all is done."

Naradin embraced his father. They stood thus for a few moments, clinging to something, then parted and went their separate ways.

The arms of the catapults were cranked slowly back. Baskets of rocks and rubble were manhandled into place. Kanin nan Horin-Gyre stood at the mouth of an alleyway, within sight of Castle Anduran's gate but shielded from arrows by the overhanging roof. A man standing by the nearest of the catapults, twenty paces ahead, watched the Bloodheir intently. Kanin nodded, and in a great crash the three machines sprang once more into life.

Kanin turned to the thin, gap-toothed figure at his side.

"Go, then," he said to the Tarbain chieftain.

The man's eyes were hostile, his lip curled as if preparing an angry response. But he bent his grey head and took a single long stride out into the open. He sucked in a rasping great breath, spread his arms and howled with all the strength his aging lungs could muster. It was a wordless, formless cry.

Hundreds of Tarbain warriors huddled amongst the siegeworks rose up as one, howling in their turn, baying in the sudden release of tension. A seething mass, bearing huge ladders that rocked like twigs on a fast-flowing stream, they poured forward to the castle walls. Many fell, trampled or brushed aside by their comrades. Arrows and rocks showered down from the battlements. Boulders flung by the catapults rebounded from the walls and fell amongst the tribesmen. Still, the ladders reached the castle and were flung up against it.

As the Tarbains scrambled upward, ants on a great boulder, another band of thirty or more men — the strongest of Kanin's own warriors — barged through the throng and up to the gate. They pushed a massive wheeled ram, fashioned from a single straight oak and capped in iron. Before they could bring it to bear on the great timbers of the gate, a cascade of stones and arrows had felled a dozen of them. Others ran up from behind to take their place.

Atop the walls, blows were traded, blood shed. Tarbains fell screaming from the ladders back into the press of their kin below. Some spilled out onto the battlements. Against them, women, old men and boys fought alongside the castle's warriors, hacking and swinging with staffs and clubs, axes and kitchen knives. They killed and were killed.

Croesan the Thane came surging along the wall, his Shield all about him. They pushed to the fore and swung their long-bladed swords. The Tarbains had no protection save their tunics of marten and lynx fur. The dead piled up. The wounded groaned and writhed, and were trodden underfoot. Croesan came to the head of a ladder and shouted out in fury as he slashed at the man ascending it. His shieldmen levered the ladder away from the wall with poles and it toppled. Below, the battering ram was crashing against the gate.

The Thane wiped flecks of blood from his eyelashes. He looked to left and right. There was still fighting, but the castle's defenders had the upper hand. Nowhere had the Tarbains gained a secure foothold. A great boulder smashed against the battlements nearby, and spun on and over down into the courtyard. Croesan glared out at his besiegers, and saw that there was to be no respite. A host of Horin-Gyre warriors was now drawing up in open sight, spears to the fore, swords and axes behind. A desultory volley of arrows came down from the sections of castle walls that were not yet beset. The crack of splintering timber said the castle gate was yielding. The army of the Black Road were swarming around the foot of the walls; more ladders were being thrown up. A flurry of crossbow bolts hissed overhead as Croesan turned away. One of his shieldmen fell at the Thane's side, his helm stove in by a bolt.

When the main gate broke open, Horin-Gyre warriors poured into the breach, pushing back the fractured timbers and spilling through into the passageway beyond. Their way was blocked by the inner gate and there, in the gloom beneath the great mass of the gatehouse, dozens died as missiles darted out from holes and alcoves. The ram rolled in, grinding the dead and wounded beneath its wheels.

The strength of the Tarbains on the walls was spent. They died, or fell back. They had served their purpose, though. The mail-shirted warriors of the Black Road who now swarmed up the walls to take their place found fewer, tired defenders. Croesan was drawing up his Shield, and as many other fighting men as he could muster, in the courtyard, facing the inner gate. When he lifted his eyes to the walls he could already see how this day would end. The Black Road would pay a heavy price for Castle Anduran, but it would be theirs. There were too many of them. However much courage and determination burned in Lannis hearts, it was not enough to outweigh the enemy's numbers. The inner gate shook, shedding splinters and dust as the ram smashed against it once more.

"Lannis!" cried the Thane. He held his sword and shield above his head.

"Lannis!" he shouted, and the men all around him took up the cry.

Then the inner gate surrendered. Croesan charged forward to meet the Black Road.

In the shadow of the gatehouse, around the abandoned ram, back into the passageway, the battle crushed itself into chaos. Spears crashed against shields, were parried, broke, drove through into flesh. It came to the push of body against body. Knives came out and stabbed and slashed furiously amongst the press of legs and bodies. The attackers were driven forward by those coming up behind them, and the fighting began to fragment as the Lannis-Haig defenders were overwhelmed. Entangled groups of combatants spilled back into the courtyard.

Naradin the Bloodheir burst from the keep with a score of men. They cut a swathe through the ranks of the enemy and fought their way to the Thane's side. A spearpoint gouged a bloody track across Croesan's cheek. He slashed it away and hacked down the woman who directed it. Naradin, unbalanced, took a savage axe blow upon his shield, and his arm broke behind it, but he cut through his assailant's wrist, and sent hand and axe tumbling. The Horin-Gyre attack faltered, and was pressed back. The cobblestones were slick with gore; the dead formed banks like windblown leaves. Fighters lost their footing and were pinned down and killed. The Lannis-Haig warriors pushed on.

"To me! To me!" Croesan was crying, at the heart of the fighting. He buried his sword deep in the side of a foe. The blade caught between ribs, and when the man slumped to the ground the Thane for a moment could not free it. He cursed, and hauled at it, and in that moment a sword came down on his shoulder, snapping bone and driving jagged edges of metal into his flesh. Croesan fell to his knees, and took his hand from his sword to steady himself. His shieldmen brushed past him, guarding him as best they could. Naradin tried to lift him with his one good arm. A bolt darted down from the battlements and struck the Thane's son in the throat. He clasped his hand to his neck. He staggered backward and collapsed. Others helped Croesan to his feet. He could not free his sword, and snatched another from the hands of one of his helpers as he let his shield fall from his crippled arm. He looked for his son, but could not see him.

Fresh attackers kept coming. Inkallim were amongst them, and Wain and Kanin and his Shield. The courtyard was once more filled with tumultuous conflict. A ring of shieldmen gathered around Croesan. The sea of invaders washed around it. One by one his guard was cut away, and Croesan the Thane of Lannis-Haig was surrounded by a dozen footsoldiers of the Horin-Gyre Blood. They cut him down with many blows.

The army of the Black Road swept through Castle Anduran like a horde of wild dogs. In stairwells and passageways silent, desperate battles were fought. In the kitchens and the halls, men, women and children were put to the sword. The door to the main keep was smashed open. Up through the keep the conquerors fought, hunting out those hiding in its corners. In the end it was Wain nan Horin-Gyre who led the way as a group of warriors broke down a small door at the head of the keep's spiraling stairway. They found a chamber with bare stone walls and floors. Sitting in a simple wooden chair beside a bed was Eilan nan Lannis-Haig, cradling her son Croesan in her arms and staring at those who had burst in upon them. As they paused, she laid the baby down on the bed. She did it gently, unhurriedly.

"You are the Bloodheir's wife?" Wain demanded.

Eilan said nothing. Wain raised her already bloodstained sword and advanced across the room. Eilan lifted a short sword from where it rested by the chair and stood to meet her.

Afterward, Wain nan Horin-Gyre cleaned her blade on the white bedsheets.

The Bloodheir stood in the center of Castle Anduran's courtyard. He was afraid that his hands might be shaking, so strong were his emotions. The fighting had been done for almost an hour, but his sword remained unsheathed and his shield was on his arm. Sweat still ran down his back. He had to blink to clear his eyes of tears, blood or whatever it was that blurred them. There was a small glass vial tucked into his belt. It held dust: the dust of Castle Anduran, gathered and sealed away to be sent north as a gift to his father.

Wain joined him.

Kanin held out one hand, palm downward, to her. "Look. It's still, isn't it? I can't tell. Does it feel the same to you?"

Wain smiled at him. He almost wanted to sink against her, to take the weight from his legs and lean on her strong shoulders. All the tension, the fierce hope, of the last few weeks had washed out of him like a great ebbing tide. It had taken his strength with it, leaving a kind of elated exhaustion. Corpses littered the ground. They choked the castle's gate. Smoke still rose from charred wood. The castle's defenders had been weaker than they expected but the cost to Kanin's army had still been great. At least a third of all his strength lay dead around him. It had a sort of glory about it.

"It is more than we could have hoped for," Wain said. "Fate has some great purpose in mind, to grant us such victories."

Kanin nodded. His thoughts were less on the Black Road than on his father today. Angain had dreamed of this day for years. Kanin and Wain had made his dreams real. For now, whatever happened next did not matter.

"We can feast in the halls of our enemies tonight," said Wain.

"Yes. And send messengers north. Our father will rejoice. Ragnor oc Gyre will see just what is possible. He must send us aid now; he cannot refuse the chance to hold what we have taken for him."

"Perhaps. We should send the heads of Croesan and his son to Tanwrye. Let the garrison there see that their Thane is cast down. It will rot a little of their hope. And we killed Gryvan's Steward in the keep; he was hiding with his family in the kitchens. His head would make a fine gift as well."

"I will have Igris see to it." Kanin at last sheathed his sword. He set his shield down, resting it against his legs. He flexed the fingers of his sword hand. "Have the girl from Kolglas — Anyara — brought up here tonight, for the feast. It will do her good to see the ruin of her Blood."

He looked up at the keep. "We should take ourselves some rooms up there," he said; then, almost as an afterthought: "Let's bring Kennet's *na'kyrim* here tonight as well. Aeglyss seems infatuated with him. That's reason enough to put an end to him, I think."

* * *

The long cacophony of the castle's fall reached Anyara in her gloomy cell. She did not know its exact meaning but the sound put an edge to her fear. She slumped down and sat with her back pressed hard against the wall of the prison. She covered her ears. The sound of slaughter was blocked out, and worse imaginings filled the void it left. She sighed and lowered her hands. There were cries upon the breeze now, the voices of the hurt and dying.

It lasted for a long time but eventually the noise faded and gave way to a quiet that was in its way more grim. A battle was over, she knew.

Those who came for Anyara hours later were not ordinary warriors. They bore themselves with a haughty arrogance, and their heavy leather tunics were sewn with delicate chain that looked more suited to ceremony than battle. Round shields were strapped across their backs. Some honor guard of the Horin-Gyre Bloodheir's, perhaps, or his Shield, dressed for show.

They bundled her from the cell, along the passage and out into the jailyard. It was near dark. She had only a moment to savor the longed-for sensation of open sky above her before they were pushing her onward. The yard was filled with people rushing this way and that. Amongst them, Anyara thought she glimpsed captives; frightened faces amidst the crowds of Black Road warriors. The cells were filling up. She saw Inurian then, being driven toward her. He grimaced.

"Not the best hosts I have ever known," he said.

Men pushed between them, and Anyara had no chance to reply before they were being hurried out from the jail and into the streets of Anduran. They turned at once toward the castle. Anyara's heart quailed at the sound of celebration that assailed her ears. The last thin sliver of hope she had clung to was melting away. A group of warriors, whooping excitedly, rushed past. One trailed a long skein of material — a fine curtain torn from its place — behind him. An ornamental chain, the emblem of some castle official, hung about the neck of another. The guards escorting Anyara and Inurian moved them aside to let the celebrants go by.

Another burst of shouting came from up ahead and Anyara saw men pulling a wailing serving girl down the street. She looked away. One of her escort pushed her and they resumed their march up the Street of Crafts. The once elegant houses that lined it were now dilapidated and bedraggled like a row of poor mourners. Anyara felt fearful apprehension building in her. Soon they would be out onto the open ground before the castle, and she had no wish to see what awaited them there.

More warriors spilled down the street, clutching torches and capering about in a mad fashion. They were different to those she had seen before: Tarbains who looked like they belonged in some cave or hut of sticks. Some of them were naked to the waist, their torsos streaked with ash and dirt. The tribesmen cried out to the Horin-Gyre warriors as they passed by, but got no response. They were drunk, giddy on the intoxicating combination of liquor, loot and evaded death.

Inadvertently, Anyara met the bleary gaze of one of the Tarbains. She lowered her eyes, but too late. She felt a claw-like grip on her arm as she was dragged to one side. The Horin-Gyre warriors turned on the Tarbains. One of them struck at the man who had taken hold of Anyara with the flat of her sword. Anger sparked between the two groups. They jostled one another as the tribesmen passed from raucous excitement to outrage. A warrior stepped in front of Anyara to shield her from further assault. There were men rolling on the ground, wrestling. Others rushed to pull them apart. Anyara was almost knocked over. Some of the Tarbains had clubs or knives out now; there was a piercing yell as one of them struck home. The Horin-Gyre warriors shed all restraint, and a savage melee began.

Anyara spun about, looking for Inurian. The *na'kyrim* stood a few paces away beside a female warrior whose attention was fixed upon her comrades' struggle. Even as Anyara turned to look, Inurian was sliding a belt knife out of its sheath at the woman's waist. Anyara's attention alerted the warrior and she swung around, grabbing at Inurian. The *na'kyrim* was faster. He stabbed into her throat and she fell, dragging the knife from his hand as she went.

Anyara leapt over the fallen woman. Inurian pulled her through the doorway of a fire-gutted house.

"Run," was all he said as they crashed over blackened timbers in the hallway and stumbled past a ruined flight of stairs. Behind them, there were urgent shouts. Inurian thumped aside a door that hung loose and then they were spilling out into a black, tight alleyway. Inurian had hold of her wrist and she could only follow as he turned right and rushed a few strides along the cobbled alley before diving through another doorway. The voices behind them felt imminent. An open window led them out into another passage. A foul stench said there was an abandoned slaughterhouse somewhere near. Small shadows scattered as rats took flight.

Inurian closed his hand over Anyara's mouth and pulled her down, pressing her into the blackness that had pooled at the angle of walls and ground. She stirred uncomfortably, but he whispered in her ear, "Still."

She could hear his deep, even breathing. The sound of pursuit grew louder. Feet hammered into the alley; muttered curses and urgent exchanges. Some of the hunters ran off. Other, softer treads came closer, and there was the startling crash of doors being thrown open as they peered inside the buildings that lined the passage.

She pressed her eyes tight shut, as if it would in some way mar the sight of those who searched for them. Inurian was as still as a corpse beside her. Someone standing nearby shouted out. Then they were moving away, their voices receding, their footsteps fading into the night. Inurian exhaled and Anyara opened her eyes. Inurian rose to a crouch, glancing up and down the alleyway.

"Quickly," he whispered, "they'll think we are ahead of them for a little while yet. We must get out of the town if we can. I don't know if there are any Hunt Inkallim here, but if there are we'll not be able to hide from them or their dogs. We need to get over the walls."

They scurried along the back streets of Anduran, darting from doorway to doorway and shadow to shadow, seeking always the deepest dark. Where burned-out ruins had replaced buildings they scrambled over and through the rubble, finding shelter in its nooks and crannies. Twice the groups of warriors criss-crossing the city almost had them, and each time they huddled down as small as they could, holding their breath while their pursuers went past.

The minutes stretched as they worked their way closer to the western edge of Anduran. Once there was, from some little distance away, the sound of barking dogs and they glanced at one another. It could mean nothing, but it put the same thought in both of their minds: the Hunt was to be feared at least as much as the Battle Inkall. Assassins and torturers, hunters and trackers, the Inkallim who served in it were said to be an elite amongst the elite. Once marked by the Hunt Inkall, a life had no more value than a Whreinin's promise.

"We must get across the river," said Inurian. "If we can reach the forest, there are Kyrinin tracks I know. We might be able to lose ourselves for a time."

Anyara nodded dumbly. She knew Anduran well, but in the darkness, with the enemy upon them and so much of the town disfigured by fire and battle, she had little idea where they were. Inurian seemed confident of his route, though. She followed without hesitation, trusting in his instincts.

They came to a place where the city wall was crumbling and half-fallen. For a few, tense seconds, they crouched in a doorway, straining their ears and eyes for any sign of watchers. There was only the faint sound of voices far behind them. They clambered up a pile of rubble, grabbing at stems of ivy that had colonized the city's fortifications, and then they were up and through the breach and tumbling into the ditch outside the wall. Anyara could have laughed as she rolled, filled with the heady sense of escape. Inurian was on his feet again in an instant, scanning the night.

"Stay close," he said to her, and he was off before she could reply, racing up and out of the ditch and into the fields beyond.

The moonlight was stronger here, with no buildings to cast their shadows. It made the bushes and trees, barns and distant farmhouses into sinister shapes somehow filled with threat. They waded along a water-filled field drain. When at last they clambered out, Anyara's legs felt numbed to the bone. Her ragged skirt clung to her skin. She was about to ask if they could rest for a moment when Inurian crouched and gestured at her to follow suit.

"See?" he asked, pointing out across the flat fields. At first Anyara did not understand what he meant, but then she picked out the yellow pinpricks of firelight in the darkness.

"Kyrinin fires, I'd say," murmured Inurian. "A White Owl war party, and a huge one." He turned to Anyara and whispered with steely intensity. "The world is turned upside down for them to be out here in such numbers. Aeglyss has a great deal to answer for. He could be as great a threat as the Black Road, Anyara: the more so because he's unstable, unpredictable. Remember that."

"I will," she whispered, taken aback.

"One more thing," Inurian said. He was pressing something into her hand. "It's a foolish thing, but I would be grateful. Take this."

She closed her fingers about the knotted lace.

"If something happens to me," the *na'kyrim* was saying, "and you have the chance, afterward, bury this somewhere where the earth is wet, and plant a willow stake over it. Will you do that?"

Anyara nodded. She might have asked him what it meant, but that did not seem like the right question.

"What do we do now?" she asked him.

"Make for the river. I think . . . ah, I wish I could be sure. I can't be certain. There might be someone, beyond the river, who can help us. I think I can feel her . . . perhaps." There was a wistfulness, almost an ache, in the *na'kyrim's* voice. "I'm not sure. But we must go quickly, anyway. If they put White Owls on our tracks we'll need a big start to have any hope of shaking them off."

"We had best keep moving, then," said Anyara with a resolution she did not feel. Inurian squeezed her shoulder.

"We had," he said. "Stay close and quiet."

The Inurian who led her through the farmland was one Anyara did not know. It was, perhaps, the Kyrinin part of him that had been hidden through all his years at Castle Kolglas. His steps were careful but swift, his movements silent. He found concealing ditches and hedgelines, even low undulations in the apparently flat ground, where Anyara saw nothing. When he paused, becoming so still that he faded into the greys and blacks of the night, she could have believed that she was alone. She fought to calm her thumping heart and the voice in her head that urged wild, abandoned flight. All she could do was focus on Inurian and follow his lead.

There was a sharp barking from somewhere out in the darkness. Anyara knew it was only a fox, but the sound had a chilling edge on this night. Muddy ground clawed at her feet as they skirted a little stand of trees, and she stumbled, her hands sinking deep into the wet earth. As she struggled upright a few pigeons erupted from the branches above. Inurian took her arm in his hand.

"We must run for the river," he hissed, and his urgency clutched at her throat.

"Why?" she gasped. "Because of the birds?" but already he had spun about and was dashing on into the darkness. She flew after him, the thought of losing sight of him filling her with dread.

It was a hard, frightening dash. Every hump and hollow in the ground, every unseen ditch and tangle of bushes or brambles became a trap. Anyara lost all sense of direction and distance. She ran onward, her breath growing ever shorter and her heart straining to burst out from her chest.

They blundered through a bed of nettles. The grass was longer now, and tugged at their ankles. By some unconscious hint of sound or smell, Anyara could tell that they had reached the Glas before it was visible. The riverbank was studded by low bushes and fringed by a narrow strip of tall reeds and rushes. Beyond, the water moved thickly in the moonlight. They came to a halt and looked back, listening for a moment. The night was silent.

"We swim," said Inurian breathlessly. Anyara turned to regard the black, silent river with some trepidation. There was no time for doubt, though. Inurian was already pulling her into the water.

"Swim downstream, across the current," he said, and struck out from the bank. She followed. The cold embrace of the river compressed her chest and made her skin feel hard. The current pushed at her. Inurian seemed to be moving away from her and she had to bite back a rush of panic. She concentrated on her stroke, fighting to keep a rhythm against the weight of her clothes and the river's remorseless tug. At last more reeds loomed up out of the darkness, and a pale hand was reaching for her. Inurian hauled her out and she slipped and slithered through mud and up onto grass. She lay there gasping.

"No time to rest," urged Inurian, dragging her to her feet.

She risked a glance back, but could see nothing.

"We have to hurry," insisted Inurian. "We have to run."

"Are they coming?" asked Anyara as she rushed after him, away from the riverbank.

"I think she's here. I think I can find her."

They made less than fifty paces. Anyara fell. Inurian helped her up. All she heard was a soft thud and a tiny, surprised sound from Inurian, and then the *na'kyrim* was slumping to his knees, his hand slipping from her shoulder and sliding down the length of her arm.

"I'm sorry," he murmured as he went.

She grabbed at him, trying to hold him up, and looked around. Still she saw nothing. As she scrabbled for a grip on his tunic,

Anyara felt the shaft of an arrow sunk deep into Inurian's back. She wanted to cry with frustration. He was too heavy for her to lift.

"Get up!" she shouted at him. "Get up, Inurian! We have to keep going."

She heard something: it might be the splash of somebody entering the river.

He did get up, leaning on her. His head was hanging low. She managed to move him forward and they began a lurching progress through the fields. She had no idea where they were going, but knew that it was movement that mattered. If they did not keep moving they were dead. Nothing else mattered.

"She's close," Inurian said weakly, and he breathed a name that Anyara did not catch.

"Keep moving," she begged him. His weight was increasing. She was not sure how much longer she could bear him up.

She twisted her neck to look back, and she saw them. They were coming: Kyrinin coming out of the night. She took another step. Don't stop, she thought.

She almost screamed when, without a sound, two shapes rose up a few paces in front of her: a man and a woman. Kyrinin, not human. White Owls, she thought, somehow ahead of them and waiting here. A flurry of impressions told her something was wrong, though. The cut and shape of their clothes was different from what she had seen on the White Owls in Anlane; their eyes, as they lifted bows with arrows already nestled against the strings, were not upon Anyara and Inurian but upon the hunters behind them.

"Down," the woman said. Anyara fell, taking Inurian with her, as arrows hissed by in both directions. The two Kyrinin sprang forward, going to meet her pursuers. She could hear someone else moving closer.

"Anyara?" someone was saying. She could not believe the name that went with the voice. She looked up. A big man was rushing past, naked sword in his hand, and in his wake came a smaller figure. She cried out in a potent mix of release and relief, and rose to embrace Orisian.

IX

Kanin nan Horin-Gyre's hands, so recently trembling with wonder at the victory he had won, shook now with anger. He strove to contain it. At this moment he should have been in the hall of Castle Anduran: they should all have been there, rejoicing in the destruction of the creed's foes, marking the day when the Black Road was at last restored to the lands that had once been Avann oc Gyre's. To feast in the halls of Anduran would realize the hopes of Tegric and his hundred when they sacrificed themselves on the march into exile; the hopes of generations of the faithful; most of all, the hopes of Kanin's father. On the foundations of this day, new and greater hopes could be fashioned. It might not be the end of their journey to the Kall, but they had taken a great stride down the path that led to the creed's dominion and the unmaking of the world.

Instead . . . instead, Kanin stood and glared at the nervous warrior who stood before him. She was one of the best of his Shield, and had been charged with bringing Anyara and the *na'kyrim* from the jail to the castle. It was no distance: the work of minutes.

"You hold the Tarbains?" Kanin asked. The words had to force their way out past the rigidity of his jaw.

"We killed two. We have the others." She spoke quietly, with downcast eyes.

"I want their heads on spikes above the jail by dawn," Kanin hissed. "But others can see to that. You . . . you are dismissed, from my Shield, my army. You will walk back to Hakkan and kneel before my mother and tell her that I have commanded you to serve her as chambermaid and washerwoman."

The woman did not need to be told to leave. She backed silently out of the room.

Kanin sat heavily in a chair. This room, a small one in the heart of Castle Anduran's keep, had little left by way of furnishings. Most had been stripped out. Only a chair and table remained. The Bloodheir thumped his fist on the table. It did little to dispel his anger. Restless, he sprang to his feet again. He had promised his father that he would destroy the Lannis Blood, or die in the attempt. Now some girl, and the idiocy of his own people, was making it a lie.

"Where is Cannek?" he demanded of Igris, who stood unobtrusively in the corner. The woman who had failed Kanin so grievously was his responsibility, and Igris knew it as well as Kanin did.

The Hunt Inkallim entered even as his name was uttered. If Igris was relieved at the opportunity to stay silent, he did not show it.

"You wished to see me?" Cannek said. He glanced quickly around the room and, seeing only one chair and the Bloodheir pacing up and down, he stood where he was.

"Every tracker you have, every dog, is to be on the trail. Find them for me."

"Yes. It is being done even as we speak, Bloodheir. They will not get far: a girl and a *na'kyrim* are not likely to escape the Hunt."

"Shraeve told me none would escape the Battle at Kolglas, but one did. They say the boy was mortally wounded but they can't show me the body, can they? See that the Hunt does better, Cannek. I want to see that girl's body."

The Inkallim was unmoved by the bitterness in Kanin's voice. He smiled: a faint, equable gesture.

"If fate favors us," he murmured. "You may be interested to know others are already abroad. The woodwights are busy emptying their camp: dozens of them are making for the river. Quite why they're so agitated, I don't know. They are good trackers, though. It may help us."

Kanin ceased his pacing and stared at the Inkallim.

"Woodwights!" he spat. "I'll not have them interfering. This is nothing to do with them."

Cannek spread his hands in a gesture of impotence. The knives that lay along his forearms pointed out at an angle.

"I am not sure you can prevent them, unless you wish to do so by force. As I say, they are already on the move. And . . . well, I dislike being the bearer of unwelcome news, but that *na'kyrim* of yours, who put on such a performance in the hall: he is with them."

"Aeglyss is not mine," Kanin snapped. "I thought he was in his sickbed."

"So he was," agreed Cannek. "The woodwights were caring for him, I believe. Anyway, he seems to have recovered. Enough to ride with them on the pursuit, at least."

Kanin kicked the chair and sent it spinning across the room. Cannek watched it go with a neutral expression.

"He wants the other *na'kyrim*," Kanin said. "I want the girl. If Aeglyss gets in your way, kill him too."

* * *

Orisian leaned against the bole of a great oak. He fought the urge to vomit. The wound in his flank was throbbing, and he feared he had torn the new flesh there. The pain, and the head-spinning exhaustion he felt, had brought on waves of nausea. Never in his life had he run so far and fast.

Their flight from the river had been punishing. Varryn set a stern pace. His features showed little hint of it, but Orisian knew the Kyrinin was frustrated at their slowness. There was nothing to be done about that. At the best of times, no human could match the night vision of a Kyrinin, or their speed through the darkness. As it was, Orisian was hampered by the imperfectly healed wound in his side, Anyara was already weary and, most of all, there was the fact that Rothe was carrying Inurian in his arms.

The fighting by the river had been over quickly. Ess'yr and Varryn, with Rothe close behind them, had darted into the darkness. Orisian held Anyara. Even as he registered Inurian's slumped form at his feet, the indistinct sounds of struggle reached him. There were fierce impacts, stifled cries and grunts, then a fearful, leaden silence. Rothe reappeared first. He turned this way and that, his unbloodied sword ready.

"I couldn't find them," he muttered. "Too dark for me."

Ess'yr and her brother returned. The two of them whispered to one another, and then Ess'yr gave a sharp nod.

"To the forest," she said. She was distracted in a way Orisian had not seen before, as if her thoughts were elsewhere. "One escaped. Many spears will come soon."

"We must get to Anduran . . ." Rothe started to say.

"You will die," Varryn said.

"There is nothing left in Anduran," said Anyara, and that had been the end of it.

Rothe stepped forward to carry Inurian as soon as it was obvious that he could not stand, let alone run. Ess'yr snapped the shaft of the arrow in the *na'kyrim*'s back. Inurian groaned. Orisian felt an awful emptiness at the sound.

"Shouldn't we get the arrow out of him?" Anyara asked him.

"Not now," said Varryn before Orisian could reply. And with that he was off, plunging into the night.

Orisian kept as close to Anyara as he could. He longed to speak with his sister, to ask her what had happened since that terrible night at Kolglas, but there was not a moment to catch his breath. He could only stay by her, make sure she knew he was there.

Now, panting and aching amidst the first trees of the forest, it was a struggle for him to stay on his feet. Varryn and Ess'yr stood together, gazing back the way they had come. Anyara flung herself down at the base of a tree nearby, her head resting against its bark, rasping breaths rushing in and out of her. Rothe laid Inurian down on the turf, and sat beside the *na'kyrim*. The shieldman's great frame was hunched and shrunken, his arms hanging limp. Orisian stumbled over and knelt next to him.

"Are you all right?" he managed to ask.

Rothe nodded. Even in the gloom, Orisian could see that his shoulders were heaving as the big man struggled to regain his breath.

"Inurian?" Orisian asked.

"Still lives," Rothe said. "But he is badly hurt. I'm sorry."

A sudden flapping sound, and a shape leaping toward him, made Orisian cry out. A scrap of the blackest shadow swept down from amongst the trees and folded itself noisily onto the ground. Rothe too had started away, but then there was a sharp croaking noise, and the shieldman gave a pained laugh.

"It's that cursed crow," he muttered.

Anyara came over. "Idrin. It's Idrin. He followed us all the way."

And then, as the very first smudge of light appeared in the sky, she told them what had happened. Neither Rothe nor Orisian, nor the two Kyrinin when they came and squatted down to listen, said a word as she spoke of Inkallim and White Owls, of Aeglyss the *na'kyrim* and Kanin the Bloodheir. When she had finished Orisian told his own tale.

They were quiet for a little time. Ess'yr crouched at Inurian's side. She laid a hand upon his cheek. They could all see that the *na'kyrim*'s face was tight and washed out of any trace of color. His breath rustled. There was an extraordinary tenderness in Ess'yr's touch upon his face and the still, strange set of her expression. For some reason he could not quite identify, that scene — the Kyrinin woman and the ailing *na'kyrim,* the leafless trees crowded round and the midnight-black crow that stood close by its master, all illuminated by the tenuous, mournful morning light — made Orisian's heart ache acutely. He turned away.

Varryn roused himself. Almost hidden amidst the densely woven tattoos, there was a grave look upon the Kyrinin's face as he regarded his sister.

"We must move," he said. "We lose time."

"Perhaps they are not following," said Orisian, craving even a few more moments' rest.

It was Ess'yr who replied, though she did not raise her eyes from Inurian's pale face. "We killed three," she said. "They will come."

"We go higher," Varryn told them. "Then follow the sun. Back to the *vo'an*."

"Wait," snapped Orisian. He could feel a sudden surge of anger coloring his cheeks. He was tired, and for this moment at least did not want to be ordered about by Varryn. "We have to think. Rothe, we have to head for Glasbridge now, don't we?"

"There's nowhere else, if Anduran's taken."

"We could try for the road, follow it down."

"Perhaps, but not yet. Better to keep to the trees until we're further south. If we can get close enough to Sirian's Dyke, we could make a run for it, join the road there. They can't have taken the Dyke yet?" He looked questioningly at Anyara. She shrugged.

"All right," said Orisian. He was avoiding Varryn's gaze now, afraid that if he met the Kyrinin's eyes he might falter. "We'll do that. We stay together until then. What about Inurian? Can we get the arrow out?"

"Leave it," said Ess'yr, and though her voice was calm it was firm. "He dies if it moves."

It drained Orisian's assertiveness away. He looked at Ess'yr, and saw how her hand lay on Inurian's chest, like a mother's on her sick child.

"Rothe, can you carry him further?" he asked quietly, and the shieldman nodded.

Varryn and Ess'yr led, as always. Sometimes they ran, sometimes they slowed to a long-strided walk. Much of the time, they were traveling uphill. Orisian noted it, and knew it was adding to the distance they had to cover to Sirian's Dyke, but he said nothing. It took all his energy to keep moving forward. In any case, he could see the sense in putting more rough ground between them and any pursuers. It might not make a difference — his father's shieldmen used to say that a White Owl could follow the trail left by a windborne leaf — but any chance was better than none.

Orisian's legs had nothing left to give him and he could see that Anyara had passed into a place where will alone kept her from falling. Rothe's breathing was becoming tortured, as if each step drained the air out of him. On they went, in spite of it all.

Some time after noon they began to track more directly across the face of the slopes. It was less punishing upon the muscles, but their exhaustion was such that each footfall became treacherous. Slick grass, unseen roots and the angle of the ground tricked the weary eye, betrayed heavy legs. Orisian and Anyara almost fell several times, their feet sliding away beneath them. Even Rothe, burdened by Inurian's insensate form, stumbled more than once, lurching like a drunken man but always just keeping his balance.

Finally, when Orisian, Anyara and Rothe had slowed to no more than a clumsy plod, the two Kyrinin came to a halt at the base of a leaning tree. The three humans slumped down and stretched themselves out. Orisian was not sure if he would ever be able to rise again. As he stared up, Idrin flapped in across his field of vision and settled on an overhanging branch. The great black bird cocked his head, looking down at the pitiful figures strewn on the ground beneath him. Orisian closed his eyes.

"An hour. No more," he heard Varryn saying.

It was not sleep that came upon Orisian then, but a kind of daze. His mind fogged over and he thought he was floating upon some river that gently rocked him to and fro. Time slipped by. He heard Idrin cawing, and in his dreamlike state the distant sound was transformed into a man calling out over a great distance. He thought he heard his father, far away.

It was Inurian's moans that roused him at last. He looked around. Anyara was sprawled across the turf, far into slumber.

Even Rothe had succumbed, his barrel chest rising and falling to sleep's unique tempo. Inurian had not moved from where he had been set down. Vague, disjointed sounds were slipping from his lips. It was the sight of Ess'yr that caught and held Orisian's attention. Again she was at Inurian's side. She gazed down into his face, and stroked his brow. She was whispering to him. As Orisian watched, she looked up and met his eyes. The flow of her murmurings never faltered. There was no blame or accusation in her gaze, yet Orisian felt a sudden flush of embarrassment, almost shame. He closed his eyes once more. There was something between Inurian and Ess'yr that demanded privacy.

When Orisian woke, befuddled and cold, he was confused for a moment, wondering why it was a clouded sky that greeted him and not the stone of Kolglas, and why he felt hard ground beneath him and not his bed. Aching, he lifted himself up and remembered.

Anyara, Rothe and Ess'yr were all awake, sitting near Inurian. Above, Idrin was hopping from branch to branch. Almost before Orisian had noticed his absence, Varryn was bounding up out of the forest. He gave the curtest of nods to his sister, who rose lithely to her feet and hefted her bow.

"We turn back," Varryn said to the rest of them. "The enemy are below, and ahead. We are too slow."

"Turn back?" gasped Anyara in disbelief.

Varryn ignored her. "We go higher."

Rothe groaned. "That is madness," he said. "We can't climb forever. There must be a way on to Glasbridge." For the first time in his life, Orisian heard a raggedness in his shieldman's voice. He could only guess what it must have cost the man to carry Inurian so far already.

There was a sharp, still moment in which the Kyrinin and Huanin warriors stared at one another, neither willing to break off the gaze. It was sundered by a sudden croak from Idrin as the crow dropped from his roost and swept down to the grass at his master's side. Inurian stirred, a breathy murmur escaping from his lips. Ess'yr was the first to reach for him, and Orisian looked worriedly over her shoulder as she felt for the *na'kyrim*'s pulse at the hinge of his jaw. His delicate eyes opened. They flicked about as if he did not know where he was. They darted from Ess'yr to Orisian, and a weak smile appeared upon his colorless lips.

"I am cold," Inurian whispered.

"We have no furs," said Ess'yr, letting her hand fall away from his throat.

"Forgiven," murmured Inurian.

Idrin hopped closer and pecked at the sleeve of Inurian's tunic.

"Ah," Inurian said. "Still loitering around." He smoothed the glossy feathers on the crow's back. "Go home, friend. Back to your brothers, Idrin."

The great black bird looked quizzically at the *na'kyrim*, head angling this way and that. Then, without warning, he sprang up into the air and with a few strong sweeps of his wings Idrin was gone, climbing up between the trees and heading out into the wide grey sky to the south. Ess'yr whispered something in her own tongue, and Inurian gave a slight shake of his head in response. He closed his eyes. When he spoke, he caught Orisian by surprise.

"I was sure you still lived, Orisian. It is good to be proved right, for once."

"You are always right," Orisian said, fearing that his voice might crack.

That brought a smile back to the *na'kyrim*'s face, but still he did not open his eyes. "Is Anyara here?" he asked.

"I am," she replied.

"Good."

Orisian saw that Ess'yr had placed her hand over Inurian's. She did not squeeze it, merely resting her skin against his. It was impossible to tell whether he felt the touch.

"Tell me where we are," Inurian said.

Orisian expected one of the Kyrinin to reply, but Ess'yr barely seemed to be breathing and Varryn held himself some distance away. He was facing out toward the silent forest. He gave no sign of having heard Inurian.

"We are on the southern edge of the Car Criagar," Orisian said. "Rothe is here as well. He has been carrying you."

"Thank him for me," whispered Inurian. Orisian glanced at his shieldman, and the big man inclined his head in acknowledgment.

"Where are we heading?" Inurian asked.

Orisian hesitated at that. Still neither Varryn nor Ess'yr showed any inclination to respond to Inurian's questions.

"We were going down toward Glasbridge. There are White Owls pursuing us, but now Varryn says they . . ."

Inurian lifted his head from the ground. His eyes flicked open once more. "Varryn?" he said.

"Yes," said Orisian. "Ess'yr's brother." He could see that Inurian was no longer listening. The *na'kyrim* looked around, and his gaze settled upon the tall Kyrinin warrior standing with his back to them. He clearly knew who Varryn was, but his expression was unreadable. With a wince, Inurian let his head sink back.

"You are in good hands," he breathed, though his voice was toneless and flat.

"He says the White Owls are ahead of us now. He wants us to go up, away from the valley," Orisian continued.

He thought at first that Inurian had not heard him, or had fallen once more into unconsciousness. A moment later those grey eyes met his own. There was a cargo of meaning in the gaze that Orisian could not quite grasp, but it lasted for no more than a second and it was to Ess'yr that Inurian spoke. He said something to her in the Fox language. Ess'yr tensed at his words. Her hand flinched where it lay upon Inurian's. Varryn turned to face them. Orisian realized that some decision had been made; whatever

Inurian's words had been, they had changed the future for the Kyrinin.

"Follow them," Inurian said to Orisian. "They know where to go."

Within a minute, they were moving once more.

They climbed higher and the air grew colder with each hour that passed. They no longer ran; Rothe's strength had at last reached its limit. For once, the Kyrinin did not show any sign of urgency, as if speed was no longer what mattered.

They came to a river, much larger than any of the other streams they had crossed, and turned to follow its course upward. Orisian began to feel a nagging sense of familiarity. For the first time since they had begun their flight, he felt he ought to know where he was.

"It must be the Snow River," said Anyara.

She was right. There was no other watercourse of any size that flowed from the Car Criagar in these parts.

"It must be," he agreed. "I can't see why we're following it, though."

Their exchange roused Rothe from his trance-like exhaustion. He lifted his head and looked around without breaking his stride.

"It is the Snow," he said. "It'll only lead us into a trap if we keep going."

Orisian realized at once what he meant. He had never seen it with his own eyes, but his uncle's hunters had talked of the gorge through which the upper reaches of the Snow passed. At its head it grew sheer-sided and narrow, ending in a high waterfall where the Snow spilled from the crags. The hunters called those falls Sarn's Leap, and called them cursed as well. Few went there. When a man reached the falls there was nowhere to go but back the way he had come. Already the land to either side of them was rising in rocky ridges like the funnel of a wildfowler's nets.

"Ess'yr," Orisian called, "there's no way through here. We can't get past the falls."

She ignored him.

Inurian murmured something. Rothe slowed and looked down at the *na'kyrim* he bore, as if surprised that he was still alive.

"Trust her," Inurian was saying.

Cliffs towered above them when they at last came to a halt. The Snow River was sunk deep in a gigantic furrow of stone. They rested beside it and drank. The sound of Sarn's Leap came from somewhere up ahead, a continuous hiss of cascading water. It was hidden around a curve in the gorge.

"What now, then?" demanded Rothe.

Orisian was staring at the thick stand of willows that lay between them and the waterfall. The trees thronged the floor of the gorge. There was no way round them. He knew what they were.

"We go on," Ess'yr said to Rothe. "They will not follow."

"There's nowhere to go," muttered Rothe. "This is a cursed place. Sarn had no luck here. No one does. Why shouldn't they follow, and trap us at the falls?"

Ess'yr turned her back on him.

"It's a *dyn hane*," explained Orisian. "A burial ground. It must be an old one; abandoned. The Kyrinin dead are in the trees."

His shieldman looked doubtful. "So that'll keep the White Owls off us? Fine, but what do we do once we're at the falls? Fly? They only have to wait. There's no way out of here, Orisian."

"There is," said Varryn.

Orisian felt a sharp premonition of something awful. The Kyrinin's voice had a dead finality about it. The decision had been made some time ago. This was the crux of it.

Inurian was lying on the ground. He raised himself on one elbow and beckoned Orisian.

"Listen to me, Orisian. In the mountains above us there is a ruined city. You know it?"

"Criagar Vyne? I've heard of it."

"Ess'yr can show you the way. There is a woman there: Yvane, a *na'kyrim.* She can give you shelter. I don't think the White Owls will go so far into Fox lands. Perhaps the Black Road won't either." He clasped a hand to his mouth to smother a racking cough. When he lowered it again there were flecks of blood on the palm.

"But we have to get to Glasbridge, or to Kolglas. We must . . ." Orisian fell silent as Inurian seized his arm in a vise-like grip.

"No, Orisian," the *na'kyrim* said raspingly. "Think. It won't take the White Owls more than a few hours to run you down. You're not in the valley now: you're in the forest, and that's Kyrinin territory." Inurian's grey eyes held Orisian fast. They burned with an intensity unlike anything Orisian had seen there before. "Anduran's gone, perhaps Tanwrye as well. Glasbridge will be next. Get Anyara to safety, Orisian. Yvane can get you to Koldihrve, onto a boat there. Both of you."

Orisian found tears in his eyes. He was barely listening to what Inurian said. "You will come with us," he said defiantly, though he could not keep a tremor from his voice.

Inurian closed his eyes. "No," he said. His strength was failing. His hand fell away from Orisian's arm.

"Yes!" Orisian shouted, taking hold of Inurian. The others turned at the sudden outburst. Ess'yr came up on his shoulder. Inurian murmured something to her in the Fox tongue. She reached down and began to prize Orisian's hands away from the *na'kyrim.*

"He cannot come," she said in a level tone.

Orisian pushed her away. "He comes with us!" he cried. He looked from face to face. "He comes with us," he insisted once more.

Anyara was crying without a sound, tears leaving tracks through the dirt upon her cheeks. Ess'yr and Varryn said nothing. Their eyes met his with a steadfast gaze. Only Rothe looked away. The shieldman bowed his head.

"Rothe," Orisian said, "you have carried him this far."

Rothe cleared his throat and gave an uneasy flick of his head, as if shying away from his thoughts.

"He will stay," said Varryn. "We cannot carry him. The climb . . ."

"Climb?" shouted Orisian, driven by some deep instinct to turn his anger upon Ess'yr. "Why did we come this way if you knew we could not take him with us? We should have gone some other way."

The pain he saw in the delicate, normally impassive face of the Kyrinin woman was more than he expected. Its depth took the heat out of him. She said nothing.

"He knows," Varryn was saying. "His idea. There is no other way."

Orisian hung his head. There was a desolate impotence in him he had felt only once before, five years ago, watching a black-sailed boat sail out from Kolglas for The Grave, bearing bodies wrapped in white winding sheets.

"You should have told me," he said in a broken voice. In that moment he felt a fluttering touch upon his hand. Inurian's long fingers were brushing his skin.

"Be still, Orisian," the *na'kyrim* murmured. His eyelids were fluttering. "Be still," he breathed again. "Be strong. I will rest here a while. You must go on."

"I won't leave you here," Orisian groaned.

"You will, because I ask you to. You have always trusted me and you must trust me in this. Aeglyss is coming for me. I can hear him, inside my head. That is why I have come with you this far, to draw him in to this place where he can go no further. His Kyrinin will not willingly go beyond the *dyn hane,* and neither will Aeglyss if he has me. But you must keep going. Others might come: Horin-Gyre or worse. This only delays them. You cannot tarry."

Orisian shook his head.

"Where is Ess'yr?" Inurian asked, and she moved forward and knelt down.

Orisian followed nothing of what passed between them. It was murmured, in the fluid language of the Fox, but his mind was numb in any case and he could not tear his gaze from Inurian's elegant hand that lay still beside his own. He sensed from Inurian's tone that he was asking Ess'yr a question. She did not reply at once. Varryn took a few quick steps closer and snapped something. He was angry. Ess'yr gave an answer, and her brother spun away and strode toward the *dyn hane.* Inurian was smiling. Ess'yr bent and laid a kiss upon his lips.

"Go," whispered Inurian.

It was a moment before Orisian realized the command was meant for him. He shook his head again.

"Take him, Rothe," said Inurian. Ess'yr had risen and was walking away. Her shoulders were rigid, as if only their strength contained something within her.

Rothe took hold of Orisian's arm. "Come away," he said.

Anyara knelt down and embraced the *na'kyrim.* "Goodbye," she whispered, then she stood up and followed after the Kyrinin.

"Orisian . . ." Rothe said, but Orisian shook his hand off and held Inurian as his sister had done. He tried to enclose his body, to gather it to himself. He could feel Inurian's ribcage rising and falling, hear his faltering breath.

"Go," said Inurian in his ear. "He is close. Go, Orisian. I will not forget you."

"I will see you again," said Orisian, and he let Rothe pull him gently to his feet and lead him away.

X

The forest breathed its soft, even breath. Twigs stirred in the faintest of breezes. An owl roosting high against the trunk of an oak blinked and peered down as fleet-footed shapes sped beneath. On a rocky knoll, a black bear nosing for insects in mulch-packed crannies raised its head and turned this way and that, teasing a scent out of the air. Snuffling in irritation, it scrambled down from the rocks and padded away. Bounding forms swept past the knoll, emerging from and disappearing into the forest in the space of a few moments. Mice cowered amidst the springy turf as silent footfalls shook their domain. A single dead leaf, one of the last vestiges of autumn, spiraled down and was tumbled in the wake of a rushing figure before it resumed its descent.

Inurian stood by the river. The *dyn hane* was at his back. The sound of the falls filled his ears. The winter sun had broken through and was lighting the highest parts of the cliffs. The bitter edge was gone from the air. It was very beautiful, he thought. This had always been his favorite time of year.

A face drifted before his inner eye, that of Ess'yr. It bore with it more pain than he could countenance. He set it aside and looked to the still forest downstream. He waited; for how long, he could not say.

How strange it is, he thought, to come to such an ending. I am not done with life. Can it really all be so easily ended? Of course it can, he told himself. It had been a path woven of a thousand small chances, the intersection of countless other lives: one wandering *na'kyrim* happening upon a good man in a castle in the sea; another eaten away by anger and bitterness; a fevered woman long ago sowing the seed of a cult, her garbled words reaching out over all the years to set Thane against Thane; an arrow in the darkness. Just one arrow.

He saw shapes moving amongst the trees. There was no sound to mark their coming. He knew them for what they were. They emerged at first one by one, then a score. A wide arc of Kyrinin stood facing him. And still there was no sound save the rushing water.

Inurian swayed a little. It had been a terrible struggle to rise to his feet. Although the pain had all but gone now, he thought the effort had sundered something deep inside him. He had the sense of his thoughts trying to lift away and drift upward. He had to fight to hold them to him. He glanced up. The sky was a field of pure blue. The light seemed to have such clarity that he could have seen to the end of the world had the rock walls not pressed in so close about this place. For a moment he was rising, floating toward that blue expanse. He caught himself and drew his gaze back to the clearing.

Aeglyss was there now, sitting astride a brown horse. He had passed through the line of Kyrinin and was watching Inurian. The horse was breathing hard and jinking around, breaking up the soft, wet earth.

Aeglyss passed his reins to one of the Kyrinin and swung out of the saddle. He patted the horse's neck as he stepped forward. He came up to Inurian.

"You look weary," he said, tilting his head a little to one side.

"I am tired," agreed Inurian. In his mind the words were clear, yet they sounded heavy and slurred in the wintry air.

Aeglyss was removing his riding gloves now, folding them over his belt and flexing his fingers. The horse behind him was still shifting about, shaking its head.

"Are you dying?" he asked.

Inurian closed his eyes for a moment. "I am," he said.

"Come back with me. The White Owls have good healers. Perhaps we can keep you alive."

Inurian shook his head with care, fearful of dizziness. "No," he said.

"But this is foolish," said Aeglyss. "Why die such a wasteful death? Come back with me. Teach me what you know. Stand with me."

Inurian was silent. Something was rising from the pit of his stomach, drifting up through his chest. His legs, which had felt so heavy not long before, were now weightless. He could hear the feeble beating of his heart.

"Do not leave me. I need you," said Aeglyss softly. "Please." He was imploring, grief-stricken almost. Inurian pitied the other man in that moment.

"I cannot stay," Inurian said. He struggled to focus on the face before him. A fine network of thin red lines was strung across Aeglyss' eyes. He had the skin of a corpse. An angry wound marred his lower lip. There were other, deeper marks that only Inurian could have sensed.

"You've over-reached yourself, haven't you?" he said. "Attempted something that was almost beyond you."

Aeglyss flicked a hand dismissively, though Inurian felt the irritation in the gesture as well.

"Some woman, spying, eavesdropping. I chased her off." He looked over Inurian's shoulder. "Clever, to put the *dyn hane* across the trail. Whose idea was that? The White Owls're hungry for Fox blood, but this will turn them aside. For now. It doesn't matter, of course. You're the one I came for."

"I may be dying," Inurian said, "but your sickness is the greater, Aeglyss. It will destroy you. You must know that." He coughed, and felt salty fluid in the back of his mouth. His throat was burning.

"Please," whispered Aeglyss again, and this time his voice was a caress. Inurian felt the other's will laying its dark fingers upon his thoughts. He hungered to do as Aeglyss asked: to free himself of his suffering, to cling to precious life. This is how it happens, he thought. He shook his head.

"You've not the strength to bind me to your will. Not the skill, certainly."

For long moments Aeglyss stood there, as immobile as his Kyrinin followers, staring. Inurian blinked. There was a cloudiness spreading across his vision, bleeding in from the edges like a fog, and he could see little but Aeglyss' face. He thought he saw many things there: the old anger and hunger, but also something in the eyes and the set of the brow that spoke of puzzlement and pain, like a child who did not understand why he was being punished.

"Last chance," Aeglyss said. "I will forgive you all your insults, if you come back with me. Teach me."

"No."

Aeglyss turned on his heel and walked away. Inurian felt a strange surge of release.

"Aeglyss, wait," he said.

Aeglyss glanced back.

"They will kill you sooner or later," Inurian said. "The White Owls, or the Black Road, or the Haig Bloods. You think you can play their games, be a part of it all. But you can't, Aeglyss. They'll not love you for seeking to be one of them."

Aeglyss seized a spear from the hand of the nearest White Owl. His teeth were bared in a grimace of fury. He strode up to Inurian and drove the spear through his midriff, impaling him upon its shaft.

"No games, little man," hissed Aeglyss.

Inurian slumped. Aeglyss held him up.

"You once called me a dog that thought it was a wolf. Tell me now, Inurian. Which am I now? Dog or wolf?"

"You have a dog's heart."

"Very well. But it beats more strongly than yours."

"I've made my choice," murmured Inurian and felt his last strength passing out between his lips and into the sharp air. It was easier than he had expected to let go.

Aeglyss spat upon his cheek and released the spear. Inurian fell onto his side. Aeglyss stepped back.

"I'm sorry," Inurian murmured.

"Finish him," Aeglyss said in the White Owl tongue. The Shared sang in the words, put a core of command and insistence into them that could not be denied. The Kyrinin poured forward. They crowded around Inurian and he disappeared beneath a frenzy of stabbing spears and stamping feet. Aeglyss stood and watched for a while, then went back to his horse. He gave one sharp cry, of some kind of pain or anger, as he swept up into the saddle.

Riding away, Aeglyss was hunched low. He did not look back. The Kyrinin fell in behind him and were soon swallowed by the woods. The bloodied corpse of the *na'kyrim* from Castle Kolglas lay alone on the damp grass, waiting for the carrion birds. The sound of the falls rolled on.

CHAPTER
4

Car Criagar

From the towering heights of the Tan Dihrin — the World Mountains — spill chains of lesser peaks like arms reaching out across the earth. Of these the longest is the Car Criagar. Less fierce than the Car Dine to its north but still wild and rugged enough, the Car Criagar is a great wall of mountain tops stretched between the valleys of the Dihrve and the Glas. Its lower slopes are clothed in forest, but wind-scoured moors and rockfields drape its peaks. All through summer, snow clings to bowls and slopes that never see the sun. When the season turns and the nights grow longer, the Tan Dihrin sends its breath down from the roof of the world, and the high Car Criagar is lost in shifting snow and storm. Yet in this heart- and soul-breaking place, that has no love for life, there are the carcasses of ancient cities and fortresses. These, it is said, were the dwelling places of a people who lived and ruled long before the Gods departed this world.

They must have been a mighty people, greater in will and capacity than we are today, to have built so grandly in such places. Those who visit the ruins now — Kyrinin, or masterless men, or hunters from the valley of the Glas — come as scavengers, wanderers. They mistrust these abandoned places, and tell tales of ghosts and beasts that haunt them. Perhaps their unease has deeper roots, though. Perhaps they do not wish to be reminded of how far short they fall of those ancestors who lived in the light of the Gods.

from Hallantyr's Sojourn

I

Dun Aygll was a city of stone and marble memories. Lying at the edge of the high grasslands and moors in the north of Ayth-Haig lands, it had been the seat of the Aygll Kings from Abban, the first, to Lerr, the last, the boy king murdered at In'Vay. Palaces still dotted the city — survivors of the fire and ruin that attended the Kingship's fall and of the Storm Years that followed it — but they had fallen into disrepair as the wealth and power of the Ayth Thanes who now ruled there had declined. The remembered splendor of those royal residences, implicit in the crumbling architecture and the mosaics and frescoes that could still be glimpsed behind overgrowing weeds, haunted the city and lent it an air of neglect and decay. Packs of wild dogs roamed the court-yards and gardens in which kings who ruled from the Vale of Tears to the Bay of Gold had spent their days. Beggars and thieves, the destitute and the desperate, were the only people who now found refuge beneath roofs that had echoed long ago to the pomp of ceremony.

Only one palace remained intact: a long, low fortified residence on the town's northern edge where the Thane Ranal oc Ayth-Haig lived in drink-soaked seclusion. Its proper name was the Bann Ilin; many called it the Sot's Palace. The Ayth Blood had fallen far from its early days of influence and grandeur. A succession of dissolute and spendthrift leaders had reduced it to its current state of fawning obedience to the Haig Thanes. Even Ranal's authority over his own lands was tenuous. Whether it was the lords in Asger Tan and Ist Norr on the distant coast, the bandit settlements and goldpanners' camps in the denuded Far Dyne Hills or the companies of Haig soldiers who patrolled the great highways of his territory, there were many within his domain whose loyalty to him was notional at best.

Taim Narran dar Lannis-Haig rode into this fading city at the head of a column of exhausted men. His company was less than it had been. The weakest of his band had been left in Vaymouth, under the watchful eye of one of the few merchants in the city whose roots lay in the Glas valley. No more had died on the road west along the Nar Vay coastline and up through Dramain to Dun Aygll, but the journey had taken its toll. Their food was all but gone and they lived on what they could buy or barter from farmers and traders along the way. Taim had been glad to leave Haig lands behind, and even Dun Aygll, with its grim, dank feel, was a pleasing sight. The Ayth-Haig Blood was little more friendly to his own than Haig itself, but their arrival here meant they were nearing more welcoming regions: a few days further and they would reach Kilvale, on the southern border of Kilkry-Haig. There at last they could be certain of finding true allies.

Rest must come first, though. For three centuries or more a great horse market had been held each year in Dun Aygll. Its stables and sheds lay empty for much of the time, and they provided a temporary home for warriors and animals alike once Taim had agreed on a price with the market warden, a minor official of the Ironworkers' Craft. Only two of the Crafts — the Ironworkers and the Woollers — kept their Senior Houses in Dun Aygll; over the years the rest had migrated first to Kolkyre, when Kilkry was supreme amongst the Bloods, then to Vaymouth when Haig took on the mantle. The Crafts always flocked to power, like buzzards shadowing a retreating army. The two that remained in Dun Aygll were, at least as much as the Thane, the masters of the city. It was to the Crafthouse of the Woollers that Taim went after his men had been settled. His father had been a member, and that, he thought, was enough to mean that the Woollers' House might be a source of the information he craved.

The building was a grand one, set back from the street behind a columned entryway. A beggar, her face mauled by disease — the King's Rot that some held to be a curse bequeathed to his subjects by the last Aygll monarch as he died — held a pleading hand out toward Taim from her station on the steps.

Taim looked up at the building's facade. It must once have been bright with a rainbow of colors, for the minute tiles of a huge mosaic pattern curved and swept across the stonework. Their hues now gave only a muted hint of their former glory. Carved faces gazed down upon him as he passed between the columns and through the open doorway. There was a short passageway, and then a gate of wrought iron blocked his path. Beyond it, he could see a garden laid out around a crumbling fountain.

A skeptical guard gave him admittance and told him to wait while someone was summoned. The official too, when he came, was less than welcoming; only after a show of reluctance did he go to find a more senior officer for Taim to talk to.

Taim sat on a pitted stone bench beside the fountain, gazing at the thin stream of water that flowed from the mouth of a twisting fish. The skill of the mason who had carved the fountain had been overwhelmed by time. The fish was pitted and flaking. Looking around, Taim could see that the gardens were still cared for, but winter had robbed them of beauty. Bare earth, browned stems, piles of fallen leaves and a scattering of scrawny evergreen shrubs were all that could be seen. The gardens filled the center of a great quadrangle, around which a porticoed walkway ran. There was no sign of life. The place had a somnolent feel.

In the end, they sent the Craftmaster's Secretary to talk with him. He was a portly, round-faced man from Drandar, who appeared to have a stock of genuine goodwill for Lannis-Haig. He said he had visited Anduran several times.

"Your Thane, all of your Thanes, have been good friends to our Craft in the Glas valley."

"The wooller's trade is a part of my Blood's life. It has always been so."

"These are sorry times for us all," murmured the Secretary. "No good can come of such disruption."

"Do you know anything of what has happened? There was little word on the road from Vaymouth."

The Secretary grew uneasy. He pursed his lips and brushed dust from the surface of the bench. "It is not usual for word gathered through Craft channels to be shared too widely," he said, but hastily continued when he saw disappointment in Taim's face, "yet your father was, as you say, a member, and you could no doubt get the same information elsewhere. We know nothing that is not known outside these walls, I think."

"I would be grateful for any news," said Taim.

"Of course, of course. That is understandable. Regretfully, I do not think I can tell you anything that will ease your worries. The last word we had was of a battle, somewhere between Anduran and Glasbridge. Gerain nan Kilkry-Haig fell there, and many others. The Black Road was victorious. Anduran is besieged."

Taim's shoulders slumped a fraction. "Gerain's death is ill tidings. He was a good man; his loss will break his father's heart. How can all this have happened, so quickly? Anduran besieged?"

The Secretary gave a nervous shrug. "It is difficult to sieve fact from rumor. There are many wild tales coming out of your lands. Tales of wild men from beyond the Tan Dihrin who eat human flesh, tales of a Kyrinin army pillaging the valley. I am told, though it stretches belief, that woodwights and Inkallim together assaulted Kolglas. A White Owl raiding party attacked the town while the ravens slipped into the castle."

Taim Narran looked bleakly down at his hands. He should be there, at Croesan's side.

"I am sorry," said the Secretary. "You know how such times breed fear and fancy. Perhaps things are not as grave as they appear."

"Even if the tales are only halfway to truth . . ." Taim did not finish the thought. There was, in the end, little to say. The Craftsman cleared his throat. He shifted a fraction closer to Taim.

"Word has been sent out from Vaymouth, summoning new

armies. There will be gatherings here, and in Drandar. The greater strength must triumph in the end, and that belongs to Haig, not Gyre."

"My home will be a wasteland by then. If the High Thane had stood shoulder to shoulder with my Blood, and with Kilkry-Haig, from the start instead of caring only for the southward spread of his shadow, this would not have happened."

He regretted the words as soon as they were out of his mouth. The Crafts were greater powers here than in his own lands, more woven into the fabric of rule and influence. Although the Woollers were not known as great friends of the Haig Blood, it was still rash to speak ill of the Thane of Thanes without knowing when and to whom the words might be repeated.

The Secretary looked at Taim with an indecipherable expression on his face.

"Is it true," he asked softly, "that the High Thane had Igryn blinded?"

"It's true. The Mercy of Kings."

The Secretary nodded slowly. After a few moments' thought he drew a deep breath.

"Gryvan oc Haig stands shoulder to shoulder with none save the Shadowhand. Those two make for poor friends in times such as these. Armies have been summoned, yet there are no great companies on the road. Why is that, do you think? I heard tell of a man — a captain of Haig archers — whose tongue ran free in a tavern near here. He claimed there will be no move north until your Blood is ruined. There will be no more Lannis Thanes in the Glas valley, he said." The Secretary shook himself and glanced around. "Mere rumor, I am sure, but not one you heard in these precincts."

"No," murmured Taim.

"I should return to my business. I have a meeting with the master of our almshouse. The work of the Craft never ceases."

"No," said Taim again. "Thank you. I am grateful."

*

Taim walked back through the streets of Dun Aygll, lost in thought. When he marched south all those months ago, he had promised his wife he would return to her. Now he was doing so, but perhaps too late for her; for all of them. He feared that he was taking his men back to die upon the fields of the Glas valley. It was, at least, a more fitting place to find the Sleeping Dark than the mountains of Dargannan-Haig where they had left so many of their comrades, and the Bloods of the Black Road were a foe worth the sacrifice. But if there was truth in the words of the Craft Secretary — and they were of a piece with Taim's instinct — there must be, somehow, a reckoning with the Haig Blood too. Taim had the clear sense that whatever happened in the weeks and months to come, he would never again know peace or rest. What time was left to him would be bloody.

II

The *dyn hane* swallowed them. As the willows crowded in, daylight was replaced by gloom and shadow. Orisian struggled on, lost in a daze of disbelief. He wanted to cry out, to stop them and turn them back. This was all wrong. It was not supposed to be like this. But Rothe was close on his heels, and they could not stop. And it was, after all, like this.

Thin branches lashed at his face. The trees pressed close. There was no path through this place of the dead. Orisian felt something on his cheek and flicked at what he thought must be an insect, only to find that it was a tear.

They came abruptly out from amongst the trees. A sheer rock face rose before them. Close by, Sarn's Leap plummeted from the heights into a churning pool, throwing out a mist of spray. Orisian looked up, and felt the cold touch of a thousand water droplets on his skin.

"We should go back," he whispered. Only Rothe heard him above the sound of the waterfall.

"It was a grave wound, Orisian. There was nothing we could do. Perhaps they will tend to him."

Orisian stared at the cliff. It was a seamed and cracked wall of stone. Mosses and ferns clustered by the cascade, immersed in its saturated breath. Elsewhere, the cliff was naked of life. Boulders were jumbled at its foot.

Ess'yr had started to climb, following a crevice that angled up beside the falls. Varryn went after, gesturing for the humans to follow.

Orisian and Anyara hesitated, but Rothe said softly, "We must go. We cannot go back now. We've no choice but to trust them in this."

In the moment his foot left the earth, Orisian felt himself to be irretrievably alone. He was as small as a beetle scaling the wall of a tower. His mind was filled by the texture of the rock beneath his fingertips and by the howl of Sarn's Leap. To fall would be nothing; the world had already receded from him. There were surfaces only — the thin skin of rock to which he clung, the transparent roof of the sky above — and nothing at all beyond them, save a void. He could hear its inchoate voice inside his head. Perhaps it was the thunder of the falls, perhaps not.

The crevice petered out. He looked up, and saw Varryn and Ess'yr climbing on above him. He followed, for little more reason than that his body kept moving. The Kyrinin reached a perilously thin ledge that fractured the cliff face. As Orisian hauled himself onto it, they were shuffling themselves sideways, drawing ever closer to the plummeting mass of water. The mist of the falls swirled about them and they disappeared from sight. He stood up to go after them and for the first time looked over his shoulder. He saw the canopy of the *dyn hane* stretching out down the gorge. The waterfall cast clouds of vapor over the treetops, glistening in the autumnal sun. His body swayed as the space sucked at his back. He edged along in the footsteps of the Kyrinin.

Ess'yr and Varryn had entered a narrow, vertical fissure in the rock, half again as high as a man. The Snow River was crashing down through the air within an arm's length.

"Come," a voice beckoned from within, and Orisian squeezed through into the cliff face.

The Kyrinin were waiting inside. In the half-light, Orisian found a tight, oppressive chamber. A flight of steps vanished up into the mountain. A malign breath seemed to descend out of the gullet of the stairway. It laid clammy fingers on his face and sent damp tendrils down into his lungs. The smell of a hundred stagnant years pressed upon him.

Anyara and Rothe came in. Varryn led the way up the stairs. Ess'yr followed, and then Orisian. He discovered what true darkness meant. They went in single file. Orisian fell into a numb rhythm, the distant weariness of his legs growing but not troubling him. He could tell that the stone beneath his feet had been worn smooth. The tread of centuries had bowed the steps. He could hear the others before and behind him. In the lightless tunnel, as black as a distillation of night, patterns began to swirl and writhe inside his eyes. He could not catch them, for they faded when he tried to turn his gaze upon them. And in his strange, lost state of mind, he wondered if it was the Sleeping Dark he would see if he could hold one of these fleeting glimpses. Perhaps that was what lay beyond the wall he was burrowing through. His stride faltered. He almost tripped, and came to a halt.

"Orisian," snapped Rothe from behind them, "keep going, keep going."

He took another step up into the darkness and the shapes were gone.

"Do not stop," Ess'yr was calling back from above.

Do not stop, Orisian thought, and came back to himself with a dizzying sense of immediacy. He felt a fluttering in his chest, the sudden bloom of fear. He reached out and brushed the wall. It steadied him, told him the world was still there even though he was blind. He began to climb again. The minutes dragged by.

Orisian's legs were flimsy twigs, a mass of aches. He thought of his father, brother, mother without being able to recall from one moment to the next what he had thought. For a while he felt Inurian walking at his side. The feeling passed. Inurian was behind him, he knew. They all were, save Anyara and Rothe. He had come loose from everything he had known like a boat slipping its mooring and riding the current out into a limitless sea.

There came a point when the thought was clear and certain in his head that he could go no further. He must stop, let the exhaustion in his legs and lungs abate. Then, without warning, it was over. There were no more steps and he stumbled forward into a flat passageway. Ess'yr and her brother were standing together, waiting for Orisian and the others. He could see them. Ahead, there was a sliver of white daylight that shone in his eyes like a blade of white fire. Robbed of the mechanical rhythm that had sustained him, he slumped against the wall, sliding down to the cold floor. Anyara came and sat down beside him. Rothe stayed on his feet, but grasped his thighs and bent forward, his chest heaving.

Ess'yr gazed down into the black pit they had climbed out of.

"They do not follow," she said.

"I thought that was the whole point," Rothe gasped.

Varryn had moved on. He was silhouetted in the opening for a moment, then stepped outside.

"Come out," he called.

Ess'yr went first. With the last vestiges of his strength Orisian rose and he, Anyara and Rothe followed the Kyrinin out. The daylight was harsh. The wind blew sudden, cold air on to their faces. They gazed up in silence at the landscape before them. They had emerged amongst a great chaos of boulders that hid the entrance to the stairway. A bleak valley ran away from them, rising gradually between stone-crowned ridges into the heart of the range. Not a tree was to be seen as the land mounted in buckled ramparts toward the towering peaks of the Car Criagar. The summits were muffled in clouds. A narrow, fast-flowing river — the Snow — cut its way down the valley between boulders and tussocks of sharp grass, rushing toward the waiting falls somewhere out of sight.

"What a place," muttered Anyara.

The wind was keen, and carried a wintry edge, but it filled Orisian's chest and washed the stale, dead air of the stairway out of him. His head spun, his skin tingled as if his blood was only just starting to flow once more.

Varryn glanced around. "Rest," he said, pointing toward a small dip in the ground close by. "For a little."

They sat on the ground. Orisian pulled at the rough grass. Varryn was murmuring to Ess'yr, his mouth close to her ear. She left him and walked slowly toward the river. She knelt by the water for a long time. Orisian could not take his eyes off her. She undid the thongs that held her clothing and raised her tunic up over her head. Her naked back was white and flawless, revealing every lithe movement of the muscle and bone beneath the skin. She raised handfuls of water in her cupped palms and spilled them over her face and head. It ran down her back and matted down her hair.

He saw Ess'yr lean forward and dip her face, then her whole head into the river. He glimpsed the pale curve of her small breast as it brushed the surface of the water. When she straightened again, she did so violently, flicking her head and loosing a shower of droplets. She held her hands to her face. It all looked like grief.

"She was his lover," he heard Anyara say at his side.

"I see that," he snapped. "I'm not stupid."

He at once put his arm around his sister, ashamed of his vehemence. She leaned her head on his shoulder. When Ess'yr came back from the river the rims of her eyes were red, but she was eerily calm.

"We must move on," she said.

"I cannot," said Anyara.

"Nevertheless," whispered Ess'yr. She stooped to take up her small pack, bow and spear and walked off, heading north into the wilderness.

Orisian stood. Varryn was following his sister. Orisian watched him for a moment or two.

"Anyara, Rothe," he said, "listen to me. Whatever happens from now on, no one is left behind." He looked at each of them in turn. "Do you understand? Enough loss. This is our fight, not theirs." He gestured toward Varryn. "The choices are ours to make. And I will not leave anyone else behind."

First Anyara, then Rothe nodded. Orisian could see the trace of surprise in his sister's eyes. I am not quite the brother she knew, he thought. I am not quite the person I knew myself.

"Let's go, then," he said.

"Fill your waterskins first," said Rothe.

The water of the Snow was icy cold.

They climbed steadily, trudging over tussocks and heather. They followed as close to the river as they could. Sometimes for a short distance they were forced to work their way around boggy patches of ground, but always they came back to the edge of the rushing water. It rained a little. The temperature fell quickly and the raindrops turned to a wet sleet. White smudges appeared on their clothing, but melted away in the blink of an eye. The sides of the valley grew steeper and shed their thin covering of turf and grass, exuding boulders and sheets of rock. The sun was hidden behind a flat grey sky that deadened sound and light. Even what little vegetation there was took on the muted shades of the rock and cloud.

Each of them was lost in their own thoughts. Orisian's legs took each monotonous step unbidden. He felt himself to be huddled in some corner of his mind, longing to forget for a time all that had happened. This was a place he knew, the same place he had found himself when the Heart Fever had picked apart the seams of his life, but it was none the easier for having been there before. He told himself again and again that Inurian might not be dead. He lifted his eyes briefly from the ground. Ess'yr, a little ahead of him, was shivering as she walked. She must be dangerously cold, after her strange, ritualistic bathing in the river, he thought. He knew better than to suggest that they stop.

They came to a broad expanse of moss and rushes — the Snow's source — where they could go no further without climbing on to higher, exposed ground. As they labored upward the wind sharpened its teeth and the sleet drove almost horizontally across the slope. They had to lean to keep their footing. Great rock outcrops reared from the hill like the heads of gigantic creatures frozen in the act of tearing their way out from the earth.

When at last they emerged onto the brow of the ridge, a gale greeted them. Orisian lifted an arm to shield his eyes. What he saw was almost as unsettling as the buffeting wind: the true Car Criagar showed itself. For as far as he could see through the sleet and wisps of low cloud, there were bare slopes and peaks jostling against one another to reach up into the sky. The highest reaches were almost white with accumulated snow and ice. Varryn set off in that direction, into the barren heart of the Car Criagar.

They kept to the lee side of the ridge as much as possible, but as they climbed higher it became more difficult to find a path among the eruptive, cold-shattered rocks, and several times they had to cross onto its exposed face. There, the wind shook them and they slipped and stumbled, scraping hands raw on the sharp stones. The ground plunged precipitously away in vast scree slopes. Clouds were spilling from the peaks ahead, boiling off into the vast spaces of the sky. They had neither the clothing nor the strength needed for such a battle with the elements, yet Varryn led them remorselessly onward and upward.

At last the ridge broadened and opened out into the shoulder of a mountain. The ground rose in a great sweep broken only by occasional gullies and granite boulders. Lines of snow lay across the slope, and the wind strung it out from every hummock. There was a brief pause, then Varryn turned his back to the gale and set off around the mountain's flank.

The light began to fade. Varryn halted beside a massive boulder that lay on the mountainside like the discarded toy of some giant's child. A diagonal fissure divided the stone, running a split through the lower two thirds of its body. The Kyrinin gestured at it wordlessly.

"You don't mean us to spend the night here?" said Rothe. "The cold will kill us."

"Wind kills first," Ess'yr replied for her brother. "This is shelter. We will be close, share warmth."

"No fire?" Anyara asked.

Varryn's only answer was to upend the bark tube he kept embers in. Cold ash was all it held.

"There's nothing to burn anyway, I suppose," Anyara murmured.

They pressed themselves into their unyielding crib. Though the crack was deeper and wider than it appeared from without, it was an oppressive space. There was no room to lie down, and all they could do was slump against the stone. The weight of rock above and around them filled Orisian with a grim anticipation of being crushed in his sleep, but then finding even a moment's sleep in such a resting place seemed an impossibility. The bodies of his companions blocked out most of the light. As Varryn, the last of them, scrambled into place Anyara murmured, "This is some kind of nightmare."

It was the longest night of Orisian's life. The five of them stayed wedged in the hard center of the stone, their bodies shaken by occasional shivers as the night touched, and then retreated from, its coldest hours. Ess'yr had been right, though. The heat they shared kept the fatal chill at bay. Through the long hours he could feel her body against his; her shoulder on his, the length of her thigh stretched alongside his own. Once or twice he thought he felt the warmth of her soundless breath upon his cheek and though he could see nothing, he imagined her face there, so close that a tilt of his head might be enough to touch it.

It seemed an eternity before a diffuse light came seeping through the clouds. Staggering out into the open, Orisian groaned at the pain and rigidity in his joints. The wind had died. Formless banks of flat grey cloud now concealed all the high peaks, but he could feel their insensate mass lurking behind the veil. He gouged and rubbed at his legs with his numb hands, hobbling about like an old man. The others looked just as exhausted and battered as he felt, except for Varryn: he appeared as alert and rested as if he had slept in perfect comfort.

"How much further is it?" Orisian asked.

"Hours," said Varryn.

The weather was a little kinder to them that second day. There was hardly any wind, and instead they had to contend with clammy banks of cloud that drifted across the slopes. At such moments they could see no more than twenty or thirty paces ahead.

Enclosed within a narrow world, with sight and sound stifled, the threat of the hidden landscape felt more imminent than before. Few of Orisian's Blood came here. To climb so high into the Car Criagar at this time of year was something none but the foolhardy would attempt. The great chain of mountains had a grim reputation, for its inhabitants — the Kyrinin who roamed its forests, the great bears that lurked in its wildest corners — as much as in its own right. And there were the ruins: the remnants of cities built when the Gods still watched over the world. There were tales of adventurers who had come seeking relics of those distant days and found only death of one kind or another. Sometimes the mountains killed them, sometimes pits or crumbling walls amongst the ruins, sometimes wild beasts.

Orisian could not say how far they traveled that day. In the afternoon, the weather turned against them. The wind returned and what began as a light snowfall gathered strength until a fully fledged storm was threatening to engulf them. They came over a rise and paused on the crest. The wind clawed at their clothes and snatched the breath from their mouths. Snow flew at them. Orisian bowed his head and winced.

"There," cried Ess'yr above the buffeting wind.

Below them, across a vast flat sweep of land, lay a city. A gigantic crag rose to one side, its highest reaches lost in storm, and spreading out from its foot a sprawling network of broken walls and streets and crumbled houses: Criagar Vyne. In its decay and dereliction, in its utter possession by the mountains and by the turbulent sky, it was as if the rock of the earth had broken chaotically through the surface to express a memory of what had once been in this place. It was a sight so barren that Orisian felt a vague horror of it stirring within him.

"Who could live in such a place?" shouted Rothe.

"Huanin, once," Ess'yr replied, "a *na'kyrim,* now."

Varryn was already striding on, descending toward the ruins. Ess'yr followed him. Anyara glanced uneasily at Orisian.

"We've come this far," Orisian said, shielding his eyes from the stinging snow with his hand. "There'll be some shelter, at least."

* * *

Highfast: squatting atop a massive pinnacle of rock, defended as surely by the precipitous cliffs beneath as by its own thick walls, it was the most impregnable of all the holdings the Kilkry Blood had inherited from the Aygll Kingship. Marain the Stonemason built it, and that feat alone had ensured that his name was better remembered than that of the monarch who commanded him. Its purpose, the need that had driven more than a hundred laborers to their deaths on the crags and narrow paths of the Karkyre Mountains in the decade it had taken to build, was the defense of an ancient road. Since then the current of history had shifted course. The road fell into disuse during the Storm Years that followed the

Kingship's fall. Highfast had become a forgotten fortress, sunk deep into the ferocious solitude of the mountains. There had been bloodshed beneath its walls many times in its long, slow life, but it was a place of peace for those who now inhabited it.

The rocky peak upon which Highfast perched was no mere foundation for its walls and turrets. Marain's armies of workers had burrowed down into the bones of the mountain, threading a warren of chambers and tunnels through the stone. In places, where the cliffs were sheer and invulnerable to assault, those tunnels broke the skin of the mountain. Windows and platforms opened out onto vertiginous views across a plunging gorge. Just as they admitted some small quantity of light, so too these apertures gave access to the unceasing winds that coursed around the mountain tops. Sometimes the network of passageways would reverberate beneath the rushing air, as if they were the lungs of a living giant.

That sound, almost beneath the reach of even her *na'kyrim* ears, was one that usually gave comfort to Cerys the Elect. She had lived within the confines of Highfast for fifty years, and knew all its moods. Its permanence and familiarity anchored her. She felt safe in its body.

She stood now upon a high balcony, looking down on the cavernous Scribing Hall. Beneath the light spilling in through high, narrow windows, a dozen *na'kyrim* pored over manuscripts and books, transcribing, copying, preserving. There was no sound save the rumbling of the wind in the rock, the rustling of quills and the occasional brittle sigh of a page being turned. With its seamless blending of stillness and industry, it was a scene that in years gone by would have taken the edge from any disturbance in Cerys' breast.

Today, her thoughts were not so easily quieted, and she was not alone in that. She had seen it in the faces of a few others, those in whom the Shared flowed most strongly. The pained uncertainty she felt in her own heart was reflected in their eyes. The seed of that uncertainty had been sown yesterday: it had come to her, quite sudden and sure, that one of them — one of the waking — was no longer present in the Shared, but only remembered there. And though she could not be sure, not yet, she thought she knew who it was.

She smoothed the feathers of the great black crow that perched upon the balcony's balustrade.

"Can you tell me it's not true, my sweet one?" she murmured to the bird. It fixed its bead-like eye upon her, and she smiled. "No, you'll be no help to me, old feathers."

The messenger, a thin, gangly *na'kyrim* who rubbed his hands together as if striving to rid them of some clinging stain, found her there, lost in thought above the toiling scribes.

"Elect," he whispered, fearing to disturb the concentration of those laboring below, "the Dreamer speaks."

For thirty years Tyn of Kilvale, the Dreamer, had lain in a chamber high in the Great Keep of Highfast. Young *na'kyrim* tended him, bathing his bedsores, turning him and cleaning him. Often it was the first task given to those newly arrived at Highfast. It taught them patience and passivity. And proper awe for the Shared, for Tyn's slumber was that of one falling away from the world and into the infinite ocean of that incomprehensible space. The Dreamer dreamed, but not as others did.

There were others, too, who attended him. Their duty was more singular. One after another, they would take their turn watching over the sleeping *na'kyrim,* waiting. In his ever-deepening sleep Tyn journeyed down paths unknown to those who still resided in the tangible world, and on occasion something of what he found there would emerge, half-formed, from his splitting, flaking lips. These were the words for which those at his side waited, for they were words trawled up from the deepest, furthest reaches of the Shared; otherworldly treasure cast up on the beach of his bedchamber. As the years passed he spoke less and less often. Seldom now did the Dreamer rise close enough to wakefulness for any fragment to be recorded.

It came as no great surprise to Cerys that this should be one of those infrequent times. Inurian had spent many hours at the Dreamer's bedside in his younger years. She followed the messenger up the winding stairways toward Tyn's chamber, apprehension stirring in her stomach. It would cause her nothing but pain to have her fears confirmed.

To her relief, Cerys found Tyn as deeply asleep as ever. His attendants kept his appearance as healthy as they could. Someone setting eyes upon him for the first time, and not knowing his past or future, might imagine that here was an old man who had fallen asleep mere moments before. For those who knew better there were signs of his long, slow disengagement from the world of the waking. His skin had become a fine veil of ivory. It stretched feebly over the bones of his face. His sparse silver hair lay on the pillow like the collapsed web of a dead spider. The undulations of the bed covering hinted at an emaciated form beneath.

It was not age that had worked such changes upon the Dreamer's body. He had lived for seventy years; not so long for one of the *na'kyrim.* The Shared was drawing him ever further away from the shell of his flesh, and day by day he was sloughing it like the old skin of a snake. Every few months Amonyn would come and lay his hands upon Tyn's chest in an effort to stave off the slow decay of his fleshly form. The sessions always left the healer drained, and they seldom had great effect. Only in Dyrkyrnon or somewhere in the dark heart of Adravane might there be *na'kyrim* who could surpass Amonyn's skills in healing, but that which consumed Tyn was beyond his power to thwart. The most important part of Tyn had ceased to care about the world in which his body slept, and without that interest to call upon there was little even Amonyn could do.

A scribe sat to one side of the bed. The man was leafing through papers. He rose as the Elect entered. He had the look of a man who longed to trade his place with another.

"Elect," he whispered, "I think I have it all, but he spoke only briefly . . . and so fast."

"Spoke of what?" Cerys asked. She leaned over the frail figure in the bed. Beneath almost translucent lids, Tyn's eyes rolled this way and that like beetles struggling under a silken cloth. *What sights he must see*, she thought to herself. *Does he even remember that the rest of us are still out here, in this other place?*

"M-most confused, Elect," the scribe said. "You may comprehend more clearly than I . . ."

He held out the sheets of parchment. Cerys took them without examining them.

"The gist?" she insisted gently.

"Mention of Inurian, I think. Perhaps . . . I think perhaps death, Elect. His death. But something — someone — else, as well. A man, though the Dreamer spoke as if it were a beast: a black-hearted beast, loose in the Shared."

Cerys nodded. It was as she had anticipated. Tyn's words were seldom obvious in their meaning — how could they be, having traveled so far and across such strange territory — but this message was clear enough, and it fitted with what the Shared whispered in her own mind. Inurian was gone, then. She would not be the only one at Highfast to feel that loss keenly. But what of the other part? This other man? Cerys had the deep, instinctive sense that change was in the wind. For a waking *na'kyrim* such instincts were seldom to be ignored, and now they whispered to her that if change was coming it would not be of a gentle kind.

With worry etched upon her brow she went to find Olyn. The keeper of crows was the one to whom the Elect always turned in matters of the deep Shared, since Inurian had left Highfast.

* * *

As Orisian and the others drew closer, more details became visible amongst the mass of ruins. Most of them stood no taller than a man. In places the city was nothing more than a jumble of stone and rock, gathering snow in its crannies, but here and there the rough outline of walls, of doorways and chambers emerged out of the rubble. They came up to the first crumbling wall and passed through a breach into the dead streets beyond. The wind at once fell away a little. Orisian puffed his cheeks out and rubbed at his face. There was no feeling in his skin. Rothe laid his hand upon a massive stone block. Its dark, ancient surface was crusted with overlaid growths of lichen.

"They must have been very great buildings once," he said, glancing round at Orisian.

They picked their way through the bones of the city, as cautious in their steps as if it were the bones of its ages-dead inhabitants they were treading upon. Ess'yr and Varryn were tense, moving like deer that sensed but could not see the hunter. Instinctively, all of them crouched a little to keep their heads below the horizon. The wind howled above them. The daylight would fade soon, and the thought of night casting its cloak over these ruins was unsettling.

A space opened out before them, where snow had piled up in drifts. They paused on its threshold. Looking from face to face, Orisian drew some comfort from the evidence that the unease was not his alone. Even Ess'yr and Varryn were on edge here, far from their protective forests. The two were muttering to one another in clipped sentences.

"We could wander here for hours," said Rothe. "We should find somewhere to pass the night."

"Agreed," said Varryn.

They found a place, in the corner of what had been a small house, where the wind and snow did not reach. A few strips of dried meat were passed around, and they took sips of water from skins that were almost empty. They crowded together, all of them except for Varryn. He sat erect with his back against the wall.

"I will take watch for the first part of the night," Rothe said to him. At first the Kyrinin did not seem to have heard, but then he gave a slight nod.

Orisian, pressed close against his sister, felt her hand reaching for his. Whether it was for his comfort or her own he did not know, but he held tight. Hunger pinched at his stomach. When he closed his eyes sleep seemed a distant hope.

Unprompted, the image of Ess'yr's white, naked back came into his mind. He stirred uneasily. It was followed by the sight of Inurian, alone in the clearing where they had left him. Orisian had watched his mother die. He had seen her lips part and the breath rattle out from her chest for the last time, and her eyes lose in a single instant the undefined luster of life. He imagined the light in Inurian's slate-grey eyes going out. Unconsciously he tightened his grip upon his sister's hand.

"Sleep," whispered Anyara.

He wished he could.

In the darkness of that night the wind moaned without pause over and through the skeletal city. After a time there was no more snow. The temperature fell as the hours went by. Orisian heard Varryn rising and taking Rothe's watchful place. The two said nothing to each other.

Dawn amidst the mists and clouds was a muted thing. The light that came was watery and lifeless. Though the wind had fallen away the sky was an ocean of grey, merging with the snow-dusted peaks and slopes. The cliffs to the west loomed over the city, watching over its corpse just as they must have observed its life. The five of them could have been alone in all the world.

Anyara flexed her arms and legs. "I'll never be warm again," she said.

Ess'yr passed out a small handful of hazelnuts. As the others cracked them open on stones, Varryn scooped up some snow and crushed it against his face, pressing it into his eyes. They sat in a small circle, eating in silence.

"What do we do now?" asked Anyara eventually.

"As Inurian said. Find the *na'kyrim*," said Orisian.

"If she's here at all," said Rothe disconsolately.

"She is here," Varryn said.

"But the word of a dying . . ." Rothe caught himself and glanced at Orisian. "Forgive me," he said.

Orisian smiled weakly. "Inurian was sure we would find her here."

"We will look for sign. There will be tracks," said Ess'yr.

"Why not just shout for her? She'll hear us from miles away up here," suggested Anyara.

"And others will," said Varryn, with an edge of contempt in his voice. The Kyrinin turned his attention to one of the ties on his hide boots, which had come loose.

Ess'yr opened a pouch at her belt and produced some browned scraps of some kind of food. She passed one each to Orisian, Anyara and Rothe and replaced the rest in the pouch.

"Chew, not swallow," she said. "It is *huuryn* root."

Rothe eyed the unappealing chunk of wizened root in the palm of his hand. Anyara had already slipped hers into her mouth and was chewing vigorously, and after only a moment's hesitation Orisian followed suit. The shieldman did the same with a show of reluctance. A bitter taste flooded Orisian's mouth as soon as he bit down. It reminded him of the drink he had been given in In'hynyr's tent, but whether it was quite the same he could not be sure. At first he felt no effects, then a strange, blurred feeling developed behind his eyes. The cold seemed to recede a little from his hands and arms and feet and his weariness was blunted. He poked the root into the side of his mouth and held it there between jaw and lip. Its sharp juices sent tingles running through his gums.

They moved methodically through the ruins. The two Kyrinin kept their eyes on the ground, and occasionally they would stoop and examine some patch of snow, rock or earth. Each time they quickly moved on. In the flat light, with the sun invisible behind banks of cloud, Orisian would have lost all sense of direction but for the towering craggy cliffs that stood above the city. Wisps of snow were trailing from the heights. Once, Orisian caught sight of a pair of great black birds flashing across the face of the cliffs. He lost them against the background of the dark rocks. There was no other sign of life.

As time went by, and the eye grew more accustomed to the patterns in the stone, some of the city that had once been here began to reveal itself. They found what must have been a bakery. Its walls were almost gone, but there was still a cracked and broken oven. They saw a stretch of roadway, a few strides of perfect paving slabs that looked as fresh as if they had never felt a foot. In another area the buildings had been reduced to nothing but a featureless field of jumbled brick and stone, much of it blackened by some ancient fire. Varryn prized a little fragment of pitted bone from the crack between two rocks.

"Skull," he said. "Huanin."

They covered almost half of the city without finding anything to suggest that they were not alone. The invigorating effects of the *huuryn* faded after a few hours and the cold exulted in its reclamation of their bodies. Strength drained away; eyes and spirits alike flagged. Even Ess'yr and Varryn grew progressively more subdued and slow. They found a place to rest. A few mouthfuls of biscuit were all there was to eat, and Ess'yr did not offer any more *huuryn*. Orisian was desperately thirsty, and gulped at a water pouch until Ess'yr gently pulled it away from his lips.

"Slow, and little," she said.

"Sorry," Orisian murmured, though there had been no reprimand in her tone.

Rothe was massaging his left calf, grinding at the flesh with his great fingers.

"How much longer must we keep this up?" he asked of no one in particular. "We could search this place for a lifetime and find nothing. We should be making fires and shouting out at the top of our lungs, as Anyara said, to draw the woman to us."

Varryn, seated a little away from the others, made a soft noise and ran a hand through his hair but said nothing.

"Varryn spoke truth," Ess'yr said. "Enemy might still be on our trail. And if we make noise, perhaps this woman goes away. The Fox say she is mad. She does not want visitors."

"It would make little difference if she did run away and hide," said Rothe. "At this rate we'll all be ice before we find her, anyway."

"The boy and the girl will not die here. I have sworn."

"You have sworn?" snapped Rothe in incredulity. "You have sworn? My life is pledged to Orisian. Neither he nor Anyara have any need of the protection of woodwights to . . ."

"Enough, enough," said Orisian, spreading his arms out. "I am sure Ess'yr does not mean any insult, Rothe. And, Ess'yr, I don't know what it is you think you have . . ."

He saw that neither of the Kyrinin were paying him any heed. As one, their heads had lifted and their faces become fixed masks of concentration.

"What is it?" Anyara asked, but Varryn silenced her with a fierce look. Beneath the fine web of tattoos there was a grim, intense expression. Ess'yr laid a hand upon her brother's arm.

"Sound," she whispered.

Rothe shifted into a crouch, grasping the hilt of his sword. Orisian fumbled for the blade at his belt, hampered by numb and clumsy fingers.

"Where?" hissed Rothe.

"Coming," was Ess'yr's hushed reply.

Anyara shifted onto the balls of her feet. Varryn half-turned and his fingers flashed a terse message to his sister. Ess'yr gave a grunt of assent, and picked up her spear. Varryn began to rise. Even as he came to his feet, he was crouching again, hissing through his teeth.

A figure emerged from behind the crumbled remains of a wall. It was a woman, cloaked in hides, her face all but hidden by a fur hood. She halted and cast her eyes over them.

"You are noisy," she said. Her voice was rough and harsh, as if the mountain frosts had got into it and cracked it just as they had the rocks of this lost city. Still, as soon as he heard her speak Orisian detected the residue of that lilting tone Inurian had. *Na'kyrim,* he thought.

Ess'yr said something cautiously in her own tongue. The woman gave a terse reply.

"Yvane," Ess'yr said, and her usually level voice held a hint of relief.

"Noisy and stupid, to be camped out here in weather like this," Yvane said, switching out of the Kyrinin tongue once more with ease.

"Inurian told us to come here," said Orisian. "He said you would help us."

The old *na'kyrim* fixed him with a glare that made him fear for a moment that they had made a terrible mistake in coming here. Then she turned on her heel and strode away.

"Come then," she snapped as she went. "I can give you food and fire. But do not presume it is anything other than an offer of brief shelter for those in need."

III

Nyve, First of the Battle Inkall, had only one ear. Where the other should have been there was a sprawling scar with a hole at its center. Every Inkallim knew the story. When Nyve was young, freshly admitted to the lowest ranks of the Battle, he had been one of five tasked with guarding a group of Lore Inkallim walking from Kan Dredar to Effen, a remote town in Wyn-Gyre lands. Deep in the broken lands east of Effen they had come across a large band of Tarbain hunters: wild Tarbains, of a tribe then unyoked by the Gyre Bloods, unsaved by the true creed. Ignorant perhaps of what kind of warriors they faced, the Tarbains attacked.

They had many hunting dogs with them, and Nyve lost his ear to one of those before he broke its back. Only Nyve and two of the Lore Inkallim survived, the bodies of more than a score of Tarbains heaped up around them.

They went on to Effen and there Nyve gathered fifty men of the town. He was young, but he was one of the Children of the Hundred and he had a fire burning in his eyes; no one dared to refuse him. He brought them to the scene of the battle, and followed the tracks of the Tarbain hunters back to their source. On the second evening, they found the village. They burned it and Nyve himself decapitated the skull-crowned chieftain and sent his head back to Effen. Then he returned, alone, to Kan Dredar.

Nyve was fifty-five now, and walked with a stoop. His fingers had gnarled with age, the joints swollen and locked. It had been some years since he could hold a sword, yet no one had tried to depose him as First. The mind housed within that faltering body was unblunted. Theor, First of the Lore, liked Nyve. He trusted him. They had risen together through the ranks of their respective Inkalls, and been installed as Firsts within a few months of each other.

They shared a bowl of fermented milk in Nyve's chambers. It was *narqan,* a Tarbain drink adopted long ago by some of the northern Bloods; it had been the traditional liquor of the Battle Inkall for a hundred years. The First of the Battle had to hold his cup between his crippled knuckles. He set it down with practiced precision and licked his lips as he watched Theor draining his own cup.

"That was well done," Nyve said as Theor swallowed the last of it. "You drink it like one of the Battle. Better than you used to, at least."

Theor gave a friendly grimace. He had little liking for *narqan,* but he was the guest here and was prepared to observe the customs of his host.

"It does a man good to overcome his dislikes," chuckled Nyve.

"I am grateful, as ever, for the opportunity to improve myself. How are your joints?"

Nyve regarded his hands as though they belonged to someone else. "They're never at their best at this time of year. I think the wet and cold get into them, though no one seems to believe me; as if I'm not the best judge of it. Who's to say what my own bones are doing better than I am?"

A serving boy came to remove the empty vessels. Nyve watched as he walked away. "That one's second cousin to Lakkan oc Gaven-Gyre, you know. Or third, is it? His name's Calum. I think there's a certain family resemblance, don't you?"

"Poisonous ambition and arrogance are not often visible to the eye. They always think it'll do them good to have one of their own inside," smiled Theor. "They do like to think there are some bonds even we cannot cut."

"Indeed. His parents were horrified when he told them he wanted to enter training, I believe. Lakkan insisted they let him follow his hope — because he wants his eyes and ears here, of course, rather than out of any concern for the boy's desires. He shows some promise. He might even live to join the Battle."

"You keep him close, I am sure."

"Certainly. I wouldn't want Lakkan to worry. And I sleep a little easier myself, knowing what he's about. Just in case, you understand."

The clash of arms rose from outside: candidates training in the yard. Nyve cocked his head to listen, contentment passing across his face like the track of a fond memory moving beneath the surface.

"Has there been any word from the south?" Theor asked.

"Nothing new, since the victory at Grive. I'd thought it would have come to an end by now. The Book's been far kinder to Kanin than I would have guessed."

"His faith gives him strength."

"That and the White Owls. By Shraeve's account, they'd all

likely be dead if that halfbreed hadn't turned up with hundreds of woodwights at his back. Makes you wonder if we shouldn't have taken a closer look at the *na'kyrim* when he was in Hakkan, while all of this was being planned."

Theor nodded. The same notion had occurred to him when he heard the last reports from the Glas valley. "We thought we'd seen all we needed to see. The Hunt watched him closely. He spoke in his sleep, brooded alone; their judgment was that there was little to him but bitterness and the desires of a child. If he can get the White Owls running around at his beck and call they may have underestimated him, though."

"They may. Fate seems to be smiling upon Kanin's adventure in a number of ways. I think Shraeve is starting to believe a great deal might be possible."

"Yes. That was how I understood her last message, too." Theor allowed his tone of voice to convey his meaning.

"You doubt her judgment?" Nyve asked.

"Do you?"

The First of the Battle smiled. His teeth were yellowed and worn. "Perhaps I should send for more *narqan,* old friend, if you want to discuss Battle business."

Theor raised his hands in mock horror. "There is no need for threats," he said.

"Shraeve has served well since she came to us," Nyve said. "It would have taken more strength than I've left in this carcass to hold her back once she got wind of what Horin-Gyre was attempting. She's never been one to take the smoothest path, but she's proved her mettle. Her Road is one bounded by endeavor, and by strife. So be it."

"So be it," Theor echoed with a nod. He knew Nyve could have put an end to Shraeve's ideas of going south, and of taking Kolglas, with a single, soft-spoken word. But there had been good reasons to give her free rein: it was many years since the Battle Inkall had tested itself against the old enemies beyond the Stone

Vale, and Nyve had wanted a loyal pair of eyes to report on events and on the strange alliance Horin-Gyre had forged with the White Owls.

"Still," sighed Nyve, "good fortune may be lapping at Kanin's ankles so far, but he'll need to be carried off his feet by a great flood of it if he's to press his advance much further."

"The High Thane certainly seems to think so. I spoke with him at Angain's interment. He was no more forthcoming than is his wont, but it's plain enough he doesn't mean to exert himself in Horin-Gyre's support."

Nyve rubbed at the scar on the side of his head with a knuckle.

"Still itches," he muttered. "You'd think by now . . ." He let the thought drift away unexpressed, and regarded Theor expectantly. They both knew, in the way of old colleagues, that the time had come for the crux of the conversation.

"It concerns me," said Theor almost casually, "that all our gentle efforts to reaffirm the bonds between the Gyre Blood and the Inkallim have borne such meager fruit, these last few years."

A sound at the door betrayed the return of the serving boy Calum, bearing a tray of food.

"Not now," Nyve said without looking around. Once they were alone again he pursed his lips. "Do I take it that you feel ungentle efforts are required?" he asked softly.

Theor gave a slight shrug. "Perhaps I am growing suspicious, downcast, in the autumn of my years. Or too enamored of times past; when Ragnor's father ruled he barely decided the color of his bedding without consulting us."

"That's true. In truth, it was wearisome, but it served us all well."

"Of course," said Theor, speaking a little more firmly now. "The creed requires a strong hand to sustain it, a strong pillar to uphold the roof beneath which all may shelter. It needs the Gyre Blood. Perhaps Ragnor forgets, as his father never did, that the Gyre Blood needs the creed, too."

"You doubt his fervor," Nyve stated.

"I fear the possibility of his . . . distraction. However much his father loathed Horin-Gyre, he would have been a great deal more interested in Kanin's achievements than Ragnor seems to be. He is more preoccupied with juggling the loyalties of the other Bloods, with securing his power and control. It's not the first time it has happened. It is the nature of rulers to adopt ruling itself as their purpose; look at Gryvan oc Haig. But for us it must be different. The High Thane of Gyre cannot exist merely to be High Thane of Gyre. He must be both warrior and guardian of the Black Road, above all."

"Still rather fiery, even if in the autumn of your years," smiled Nyve.

"I am Master of the Lore. I could hardly be otherwise."

Nyve nodded. "I detect a proposal looming on the horizon," he said.

"Ragnor's inactivity puzzles me. Greatly. He gives every sign of preferring to see the Horin-Gyre Blood extinguished than the return of his own Blood to its rightful place in Kan Avor. Imagine it: for the first time in more than a hundred years we have an army of the Black Road winning battles south of the Stone Vale and the High Thane of Gyre is at best indifferent. No matter how skeptical he was at the beginning, Kanin's successes should at least have attracted Ragnor's interest."

"Strange times, I agree."

"Too strange to be all they appear. I desire to know the mind of our High Thane, and there may be a chink in his armor of reticence. He was not the only one I spoke with when Angain was being consigned to the catacombs. When we were alone, standing over her husband's corpse, Vana told me that she has a prisoner: one of the High Thane's messengers, caught as he tried to cross out of Horin-Gyre lands."

Nyve raised his grizzled eyebrows. However long he had known Theor, it was evident that the Lorekeeper could still surprise him.

"The Horin-Gyre Blood is seizing the High Thane's messengers?"

"Only this one. He made them suspicious. Where, they — and I — wonder, was he going? What need has Ragnor to send word beyond the borders of the Black Road? The man would not say, and the message he bore is in a cipher Vana's people cannot read."

"It goes beyond strange and into perilous for one of the Bloods to be imprisoning Gyre couriers," the First of the Battle said. "And for us to know of it and not — I assume this is what you propose — not make Ragnor aware of the fact."

"We are Inkallim. The creed comes first, always. Before all other considerations. If the creed is threatened, we must know of it. Vana has the same concerns, but cannot get to the truth of it. She offered to pass the messenger and his message to us. To the Hunt."

"Have you talked to Avenn about this?" Nyve asked. He sounded doubtful. Neither of them needed to say that whatever his mission had been, the messenger would not survive the attentions of the Hunt Inkall.

Theor shook his head. "I will never do so, unless I have your agreement to it. You know that."

"I need some more *narqan,*" Nyve said. He rapped on the table at his side. "Where's that boy when I need him?"

He looked thoughtfully at Theor. "You will allow me to think on this," he said.

"For as long as you wish," Theor replied.

Nyve's smile returned. But for his ugly scar, he looked like a jovial old man immersed in a life of ease. "It's a long time since there've been such events as these in flow. It's almost enough to make a man feel young again."

Theor left by a discreet side door, out of sight of the training yards and weaponsmiths. He followed a colonnaded walkway to the rear of the Battle's compound and passed through a gate in the outer wall. His litter-bearers were waiting there for him; until winter tightened its grip, the tracks across the hillside to the Lore sanctum would remain muddy and unfit for the First's feet.

The little snow that had fallen in the night was almost gone, but the air had the heavy taste of more to come. As he rocked along, Theor could see over the trees on the lower slopes to Kan Dredar. Ragnor oc Gyre's city was a brown and black sprawl across the flat ground, an almost formless jumble of wooden shacks milling around the few stone buildings: the city guards' barracks, the market hall, the High Thane's stronghold. The scene was a peaceful one. Cities always looked best from a distance in Theor's experience; closer inspection tended to reveal grime and greed. Buzzards and kites were patrolling over the city as they always did. Theor noted how the birds spaced themselves out, dividing Kan Dredar between them, each circumscribing its patch of back streets with leisurely circles.

A pale shape by the side of the trail caught his eye. It was a small bundle wrapped in a sheet. Theor caught a glimpse of grey, blotched skin; a baby, then. When a weak or crippled child was born, some families would put it out like this, in the woods or on the hillsides, to test its fate. It was a practice the High Thanes of Gyre had outlawed long ago — every potential warrior was too precious to be risked, when only ten thousand had made the journey into the north — but for some of the commonfolk it was a stubborn reflection of their faith. Most likely the mother would return in a day or two, and if the Last God's Book had spared the child it would be taken back into the family and cared for as best they could. This baby's Road had run its course, though.

Theor was carried on in his litter. Care would be needed in pursuing his doubts about Ragnor oc Gyre. Above all, he must carry Nyve and Avenn with him. The Lore was senior and superior to the Battle and the Hunt, but that did not mean they would blindly follow his lead; unity amongst the Inkallim mattered if the Gyre Blood was faltering in the force of its will. At such times — and they had come once or twice before in the century and a half of the Black Road's exile beyond the Tan Dihrin — the Inkallim were the ones who must hold things together.

They had covered two thirds of the way back to the halls of the Lore when his escort slowed. The sound of feet running through the slushy mud came from behind them.

"What is it?" Theor asked with an air of disinterest.

"A boy is coming," said one of his litter-bearers. "A Battle candidate, from the look of him."

Theor waited, folding his hands into his armpits against the cold.

He recognized the message-bearer at once: it was Lakkan oc Gaven-Gyre's cousin, Calum. The message was straight from Nyve's own chambers, then. The boy was out of breath, his cheeks glowing and his clothes spattered with mud. His excitement was obvious.

"First," he said, "First, Master Nyve sent me. He told me to catch you on the path, if I could."

"You have triumphed then, young man."

"He said you should be the one to carry the news back to the Lore."

"Did he?"

"A messenger bird came just as you left. Anduran has fallen, First. Town and castle are in Horin-Gyre hands."

Theor was meticulous in suppressing any sign of the surprise that he felt.

"And Master Nyve said I should say . . ." Calum frowned, recovering the words, "I should say that he will think on matters more quickly now." He seemed pleased to have accurately recalled the phrase. "It is a great day, is it not, First? The Last God's Book smiles upon us."

"It does indeed," Theor replied. "You may tell your master that I share his delight. See if you can't make the return journey even more swiftly than the outward one."

Calum gave a shallow bow and sprang away. Theor watched him go. He saw the boy slip and sprawl to the ground. Mud blossomed languidly into the air. Calum leapt up, undeterred, and bounded on down the path, shaking sodden earth from his hair as he went.

As he resumed his own progress, Theor puzzled over the unexpected news. Events were moving more quickly, and more dramatically, than he had imagined likely. Nyve was right: there would have to be a decision soon. And he would have to remember to compliment Nyve on his still sharp sense of humor. It was a pleasing touch to have one of the Gaven-Gyre elite rushing through the woods to deliver word of Horin-Gyre glory. Lakkan would be spitting bile into his jeweled goblet if he knew.

* * *

Dusk was falling on the Glas valley, turning the land to greys and blues. High in Castle Anduran's keep, Kanin nan Horin-Gyre looked out over the day's end. The city lay beneath him, and beyond it the road south cut its way across the farmland. The White Owls had lit their fires and that nest of orange glimmers out in the fields drew his eyes. The continued presence of the Kyrinin on lands that now belonged to the Gyre Bloods was a bitter disappointment to Kanin, but he could not bring himself to send away so many warriors while they remained willing to fight in the interests of the Black Road.

Since his return from the falls on the Snow River, Aeglyss had kept himself hidden in the White Owl camp. One of Kanin's sentries, who saw the halfbreed's band come back across the bridge over the Glas, had reported that Aeglyss was unsteady as he rode, almost as if he had been wounded, though there was no sign of blood. Strange sounds, as of a man in some delirious death-sleep, had spilled from his lips and his head had hung so far forward that his face was hidden from view.

Kanin had sent messengers to the camp as soon as he heard of Aeglyss' arrival. They returned all but empty-handed, turned away by the White Owls. The only word they brought came from one of the Kyrinin warriors, who barely spoke their tongue. He told them, and they told Kanin, that the *na'kyrim* from Kolglas was dead but others — three Huanin, two Fox — had passed up into the high mountains. The news had cast Kanin into a brief torment of anger and frustration. He cared nothing for the life or death of a halfbreed; that the Lannis girl, probably the last of her line, should escape his grasp was a different matter. The pledge he had made to his father — to return only when all of that hated family had been cast into the darkness — was a vow given to a man Kanin did not expect to see again this side of the Kall. It was an honorable vow, accepting of whatever fate the Black Road might dictate for one who made such a bold promise. And now the girl was gone. Aeglyss had been interested only in the other *na'kyrim,* from the very beginning, and he had let the girl slip through his fingers — and thus through Kanin's.

Some unconscious sense made the Bloodheir turn from the window. Shraeve was standing in the doorway. Igris was behind her, looking for some sign from his master. Kanin dismissed his shieldman with a shake of the head. Wordlessly he gestured toward one of the chairs that stood by a long table, but Shraeve ignored the offer.

"Your sister told me you were here," the Inkallim said.

"Surveying our new domains," Kanin said with a wry snort. He lowered himself into a chair. His father had always told him that to be seated while another stands was to take the stronger position. Kanin had no illusions that one such as Shraeve would be discomfited.

She glanced around the room. Great pale rectangles were visible on the walls where hangings had once protected the stone, and she lingered upon them for an instant.

"The tapestries were unsuitable," Kanin muttered. "I had them burned."

The Inkallim walked by him and stood where he had been moments before, looking out over the ever-darkening scene. The swords crossed on her back made a stark silhouette.

"A veritable army by Kyrinin standards," she murmured. "I had the spears counted . . ."

"Three hundred and a few," Kanin interrupted her. "I had the same thing done. What of it? An army by their lights is little more than a raiding party by ours."

"Or by Kilkry's. Or Haig's," she said, turning to look at him.

Kanin raised an eyebrow. His mood had already been foul before Shraeve intruded upon his reverie.

"You fear the strength of our enemies?" he asked. His unworthy hope that he might cause some offense was disappointed.

"Only children and unbelievers fear. There is no fear in falling asleep . . ."

". . . when you know you shall wake again. I know, Shraeve."

"You counted the White Owl spears," she said. "Have you also looked into the matter of the Lannis girl's companions?"

The question caught Kanin off guard. This was evidently what she had come here to ask him, and it was far from anything he might have expected.

"Five escaped, climbing up into the mountains," Shraeve continued. "The girl and two other humans, and two Kyrinin. A strange combination, do you not think?"

Kanin shrugged, irritated. "These are strange times. I have more pressing puzzles to set my mind to. I would be curious to know how you came by the information, though. I heard it myself only yesterday. You have good ears, or many eyes."

Shraeve swung back to the window and spoke to the evening air. "Fine trackers, the woodwights; almost as good as the Hunt. Cannek asked one of them about the trail."

Kanin grunted. "And did the one he asked survive the experience? If the Hunt is going to turn the woodwights against us, I'd like to know in advance."

Shraeve ignored the question. "Two Kyrinin: a man and a

woman, the man taller and heavier than average for his kind. Three humans. One, of course, the girl you wanted. Another — a man — very heavy, very powerful. A warrior, perhaps. But the third was a much smaller man. Younger, not many years out of childhood, and favoring one side as he ran."

Kanin saw her meaning an instant before she spoke the words: "Kennet's son escaped from Kolglas with one of our knives in his side, and a shieldman bearing him up."

"I see," Kanin said through gritted teeth. He could feel the anger rising up in him again, surging even as he strove to hold it back. He wondered if Shraeve would see the heat it put into his face. "It is time I spoke with the *na'kyrim,* then, whether he wishes to have visitors or not."

"I thought the same," the Inkallim said quietly. "In the morning?"

Kanin rode out from the castle with Igris upon one side, Shraeve on the other, and ten of his Shield behind. Dogs snapped at the heels of the horses. The packs of abandoned, half-wild mongrels that now populated the city had become an irritant to its occupants. They scavenged through the emptied and burned areas, drawing more brazenly close to the watchfires of the warriors with each passing night; they stole precious food, and had mauled a sick man in his sleep. Kanin had issued orders for the animals to be killed on sight, but he forbade his escort to act on that command now. He was not in the mood for distractions this morning.

They passed by the jail. Above its gate half a dozen heads were displayed. The birds had been working on them. These were the Tarbains whose drunken intervention had made the Lannis-Haig girl's escape possible. Most of the tribesmen he had brought south were scattered across the valley now, and he did not care what havoc they wrought so long as they did not interfere with his own foraging and scouting parties. Within Anduran the rules were different, and since Anyara's escape the few Tarbains left in the city had learned that indiscipline would no longer be tolerated.

The little company of riders crossed the great square. The smithy that survived there was the focus of furious industry. Horses were gathered about it in tightly marshaled groups. Every animal fit for war duty had been brought in from the countryside and many of them needed new shoes. Some huge Lannis work-horses were there, too. They were useless for riding or battle — they would not tolerate a man upon their back — but they would be worked harder than any, hauling material to the city walls for the repair works.

They rode on, weaving through a section of the city that had been ravaged by fire. Kanin glimpsed a rat scurrying amongst the blackened timbers. Whatever else might come to pass, he thought with small satisfaction, the Lannis-Haig Blood was humbled. Rats picked over the corpse of its pride. Still, it was not enough. He had promised his father, and himself, more.

At the city's edge a gang of disheveled workers — townsfolk pressed into the service of their conquerors — was laboring on a section of the wall, overseen by Horin-Gyre guards. All around Anduran's perimeter, similar groups were toiling to make good the neglect of many years. It might make a difference, should Kanin find himself beset here by the Haig Bloods; it might even buy enough time for aid to come to him. Within hours of the castle's fall, he had sent word north to Hakkan. He knew that Shraeve had sent both birds and riders bearing the same news to the precincts of the Inkallim in Kan Dredar. By one route or another, Ragnor oc Gyre would know that the Horin-Gyre Blood had achieved the impossible. It must surely be enough to stir the High Thane from his sloth.

As he rode past the workgang, a few grimy faces were lifted toward him. They probably knew who he was. He thought he caught a glimpse of hatred, of unsubdued arrogance, in some of those sullen visages. The perversity of their silent defiance now, after they had shown so little appetite for the defense of their city, annoyed Kanin. Had he not been about other business, he might have paused and ordered the punishment of those who looked at him most directly. As it was, one of the guards barked a command and the workers returned to their labors.

They went out into the fields. As they drew closer to the sprawling expanse of deerhide tents that the White Owls had thrown up, Kanin could see that there were more than the three hundred or so warriors his scouts had last reported. It was an uncomfortable thought, that so many would flock to Aeglyss.

Grey eyes followed them as they made their way toward the center of the camp. They found Aeglyss there in the yard of a great farmhouse. Part-fortified in the style favored by some of Anduran's wealthy farming families, the building was the hub around which the Kyrinin company had arrayed itself. The stock animals had fled, or been rounded up by Kanin's foraging parties. One at least must have remained, though, for they found Aeglyss seated with a group of Kyrinin beneath the gutted, flayed carcass of a cow strung up on a wooden frame. Everywhere that Kanin looked, individual Kyrinin were sitting in silence as others pricked their faces with long, fine thorns bearing dye. Across the skin of scores of faces, dark blue whorls were emerging amongst tiny beads of blood. As they approached, Aeglyss rose to his feet.

"What are they doing?" asked Kanin, looking around distastefully.

Aeglyss followed his gaze. *"Kin'thyn.* There can be no going back now." A mirthless smile tweaked at the corner of Aeglyss' lips. "You would not understand, of course. Well, Bloodheir, this is the harvest of all that we set in motion. There is to be war on the Fox, such as there has not been in generations."

Kanin stared at the *na'kyrim* in incredulity. "War on the Fox?" he cried.

Aeglyss appeared oblivious of the Bloodheir's mood. "You are watching a terrible history being forged here. These warriors are being honored without yet having earned the honor. Not one of those you see being marked can return from Fox lands without drawing the blood of an enemy. So many have not gone to war since before there were Bloods; and every one of them must kill. We are unleashing a storm."

Kanin swung himself rigidly out of the saddle. It took an effort of will to unlock his fingers from the reins, and to restrict himself to a single pace toward Aeglyss. Something in his manner or movement was enough to at least send a flicker of doubt across the *na'kyrim*'s brow.

"Three White Owls were killed by the river, by Fox," Aeglyss said. "There must be payment for that. I have . . . convinced them that we must seize the moment, now when so many spears are gathered together, to strike a blow the Fox will never forget."

"And you think I care about any of this?" hissed Kanin.

"Well . . . the White Owls could not be here in such numbers if you had not broken Anduran. They . . ."

Kanin took another, longer stride forward. Aeglyss fell silent. The Bloodheir was distantly aware that a stillness was spreading out around them; Kyrinin heads were turning, eyes were settling upon them.

"Your wights should be marching south," he said. "They should be in Anlane, lying on the flank of any advance against us, not disappearing into the Car Criagar to settle old scores with the Fox."

"It's hardly fitting for a scion of the Gyre Bloods to belittle the settling of old quarrels," muttered Aeglyss, but the uncertainty in his voice undercut the pointed words.

Without taking his eyes off the *na'kyrim,* Kanin made a sweeping gesture with his arm. He heard horses moving in response. His Shield were spreading themselves in a loose arc around him.

"What happened at the Falls?" he demanded.

Aeglyss looked away at once, a brief dart of his eyes to the ground and back. It was enough to convince Kanin that whatever came next would be a lie, or a half-truth at best.

"Inurian died. The others — we do not know. We found Inurian alone. The others were gone, up into the mountains."

"What others?" pressed Kanin. Another step closer to the half-breed. Some of the nearest of the White Owls were standing up. They appeared relaxed, detached observers, but Kanin could not be sure. Aeglyss shrank a fraction away from the Bloodheir. He was almost backed up against the suspended carcass of the cow.

"Did you leave off the pursuit as soon as you had the halfbreed?" Kanin said. "Was the boy there? Kennet's son, from Kolglas?"

Aeglyss spread his hands. "I don't know that." His voice held Kanin for a moment. It was inside the Bloodheir's head, stilling in just that fraction of a second all the fires burning there; a cooling whisper. "There were others, but I couldn't say if the boy was amongst them. I'd've gone on if I could, but the White Owls would not."

And Kanin could not move. His mind drifted, turning in idle circles. All the anger that had been in him was forgotten, and all he could think was, Yes. Of course.

"I doubt the White Owls would turn back if you had wished otherwise," came Shraeve's voice, sharp, precise and cold.

It cut through to Kanin, piercing the clouds that surrounded him. He struck Aeglyss in the face with the back of his hand, and all of his resurgent fury went into the blow. The *na'kyrim* reeled against the butchered corpse of the cow, and tumbled away to the side. He fell heavily and rolled onto his back. His hands were half-raised to ward off further blows. There was blood on his lips.

Kanin went for his sword.

"Lord," said Igris softly but insistently.

Kanin looked up and saw the thickening of the White Owl crowd around them. Silently, Kyrinin were edging forward. Half of them bore freshly inscribed tattoos upon their faces, blood and dye mixing on their pale skin.

"No need to test the woodwights on this, perhaps," suggested Shraeve. "We do not know how they regard him." The Inkallim remained placidly seated on her horse, her hands resting lightly on the animal's neck. She gave Kanin a slight, wry smile.

The Bloodheir released his sword with a curse. He straightened his back and shouted across the yard.

"I am done with this one. He is nothing to me now, and nor are any promises he made to you. If he made them in my name, he lied."

At his feet, Aeglyss was groaning, garbled words flailing in his bloodied mouth.

"He is a dog," Kanin shouted. "Less than a dog. Do you understand? Who here speaks my tongue? Who speaks for you?"

The Kyrinin did not stir. Their grey eyes were fixed on Kanin, but none responded. There was no flicker of understanding or interest, just those passive, inhuman eyes.

"Dogs!" Kanin cried and swept up into his saddle.

They returned to Anduran in silence. Heavy skies weighed down upon the earth. Kanin could feel the dark mood that had settled over the warriors who accompanied him. He regretted losing his temper as he had, especially over one such as Aeglyss. But the loss of Anyara, and now it seemed of her brother as well, plagued him. And the halfbreed had dared to play with his thoughts . . . that was intolerable.

At length, against his better judgment, he said to Shraeve, "I should have rid myself of him long ago."

"Perhaps," she said.

Her apparent indifference re-ignited the embers of his anger briefly.

"It would not have come to this if your ravens had done their work properly at Kolglas in the first place."

"Nor if your fine warriors had managed to escort a young girl from jail to castle without mishap."

Kanin caught himself just in time as he made to reply. Whatever momentary release it might provide, trading insults with

Shraeve would do little good. He was a Thane's son, but even that did not put him beyond reach of an Inkallim blade. They had killed more than a few of the powerful over the years. Always in the interest of the creed, of course.

Kanin found Cannek in the stables of Castle Anduran. The Hunt Inkallim had seen fit to install their dogs there. Cannek and two of his comrades were squatting amongst the straw, feeding the great beasts scraps of meat. Kanin had to suppress his instinctive wariness of the creatures. The hounds of the Hunt were almost as ruthlessly trained as the Inkallim themselves were, to track and kill humans. Kanin himself had seen a dozen of the Hunt and their dogs raid a Tarbain village in his family's lands, in punishment for cattle-thieving. It had been a spectacle to make even the most hardened of warriors uneasy.

Cannek glanced up as the Bloodheir approached. He scratched the thick neck of the nearest dog, working his fingers underneath its collar. The animal had fixed its soulless eyes on Kanin and there was a low rumble in its throat.

"He means you no harm," the Inkallim said.

"I want to know how the pursuit of the Lannis girl goes," Kanin said.

Cannek rose to his feet. His knees cracked disconcertingly as he did so. He brushed straw from his leather trousers.

"I have not heard anything. But you need not concern yourself. Two of our finest are on the trail. They will not give up so easily as the White Owls did."

Kanin grunted. "I am beginning to mistrust the promises of others regarding the Lannis-Haig Blood," he said stiffly.

"Really. Your discussions in the Kyrinin camp did not go well?"

"I'm sure Shraeve will give you a detailed account if you ask it of her. Where did the trail go, after the Falls on the Snow?"

Cannek shrugged. He made even that simple movement seem

considered and precise. "Up and into the Car Criagar. That is all I know, Bloodheir, and more than I need. As I told you, the best of us are following the scent. They will not return until their quarry is dead."

Two of the dogs suddenly snapped at each other, unleashing a volley of snarls. Their jaws worked with a clattering of teeth. Kanin could not help but take a half-step away.

"Can I be of any more help to you, Bloodheir?" Cannek inquired.

Kanin left with a mute shake of his head. He had made a decision, and there was no point in delaying its consequences. He was tired, after so many days of little sleep and constant tension, but he knew he could expect no rest. If Kennet's offspring made for Koldihrve — and they would surely have to, with Hunt Inkallim on their backs and the White Owls intent on flooding the forests of the Car Criagar with strife — that town was the key. Kanin knew nothing of the place save where it lay — the mouth of the Vale of Tears — and that it was a foul nest of masterless men and woodwights. But it was on the shore, and therefore had boats. It was the only possible way he could see that the Lannis-Haig rats could escape from this trap. Kanin meant to reach it before them.

He knew it was a rash decision, but it felt right in a way few of his decisions had in recent days. Despite all the triumphs since they had marched south, despite the victories at Kolglas, at Grive and Anduran, he felt as if events were spiraling away from him. Aeglyss and his White Owls had certainly spun out of his control, if they had ever been within it; the Inkallim seemed like little more than amused spectators; and all that he and Wain had won still could not be held unless the other Bloods of the Black Road came to their aid.

The one clear and certain thing he could see before him, the only need that he could answer directly, was that there was unfinished business with the family of Croesan oc Lannis-Haig. If he put an end to the Lannis line, nothing that came after could rob him of that. And he would have succeeded where the Inkallim had failed. They, for all their vanity, had let a mere youth slip through their fingers at Kolglas. To be the one who put right that mistake would be a small revenge for their betrayal of the Horin-Gyre Blood at the battle in the Stone Vale all those years ago.

Wain came to him while he was sitting with his captains, making final arrangements for the supplies his company would need. Something in her face made him dismiss the others before she had even spoken. She sat in a chair at his side.

"Messengers have come," she said, looking down at the surface of the table. "Tanwrye still holds, but the land between here and there is subdued. They can spare us some of their strength: a hundred horse will be here in a day, twice as many spears in another two or three. Mostly our own, a few of Gyre."

"These are good tidings . . ."

"The messengers brought other news," she cut him off. "Our father . . . died on the first day of winter."

Kanin bowed his head. He had known this moment must come — had already said his farewells — but still it caught him a fraction unprepared, as was in the nature of such things. It would be a long time now before he saw his father again. The world itself would have to die and be reborn before that could happen.

And would it be wrong to see a sign in this? The lives of men and women were nothing in the vast movement of fate, yet there could be pattern — meaning — in their interplay. Nothing happened by chance. Word of his father's death came on the eve of a journey to finish what was started in his name. There might be significance in that.

Wain was watching him. "You are Thane now," she whispered. "Do not go into the Car Criagar. Your place is here."

"No, Wain. Would you make me a liar to our father? When I meet him again in the renewed world, I don't want the first thing I tell him at the start of that second life to be that I failed our promise to him. Without their deaths, everything that we hold now will be taken away again. Others might forget, but so long as even one of their line remains, they will never stop trying to recover this land. The Thane is the Blood. You know that."

"You should be proclaimed as Thane," she said. "We must . . ."

"When I come back. Not until then." For once, he was the firmer. "I will not be away for long. And you know as well as I that I am not truly needed here. This army is yours to lead as much as it is mine. I and my fifty warriors would make no difference in whatever you may face in my absence: we always knew that all of this would come to nothing if the other Bloods did not march to our aid in the end," he said. "If it is to nothing that we are headed, so be it, but I will not go there without at least trying to finish with Lannis-Haig."

He picked up the fragile vial of Anduran's dust that lay on the table and held it out to her.

"I was going to send this to our father. Send it to Ragnor oc Gyre instead. Tell him that the Horin-Gyre Blood holds the Glas valley for him, and awaits his return to claim what is his."

She smiled faintly, and he planted a soft kiss upon her forehead.

IV

"Inurian is dead, then," Yvane said, after she was told all that had happened.

"We are not certain," said Orisian.

"I think you know it as well as I do," the *na'kyrim* said. "And I do know it." She was staring into the fire, stirring it with a stick. Embers danced upward.

The chamber lay at the end of a short passageway; it was warm and close. Without Yvane to guide them they might not have found it. She had brought them to the base of the cliffs that soared above the ruins, led them clambering over a mass of huge boulders up to a flat platform deep in the shade of the rock face and into the narrow opening of the tunnel that brought them here.

The *na'kyrim* had brewed an infusion of herbs while they told her their stories. They passed it around and each took a few heartening sips. The fire crackled between them and the entranceway. Crude figures had been painted on the walls. The abstracted forms of animals and people processed across the stone, given life by the flickering firelight. The wind moaned across the cave's mouth.

When he thought he could do so without being noticed, Orisian examined their host. Yvane had the same part-Kyrinin features he had come to recognize in Inurian, though her eyes were still more unlike a human's than his had been. Her hands and fingers seemed every bit as lean and long as Ess'yr's. They bore calluses here and there, the legacy of hard years amongst the rocks of the Car Criagar. That time had left its imprint upon her face, too. Her skin was weathered, roughened to a coarser grain than he would have expected in a *na'kyrim*. Her short hair had the sheen of a Kyrinin's but it was a reddish brown: a shade that could only have come from her Huanin parent. Had she been human, Orisian would have guessed that she was well into her fifth decade of life; since she was *na'kyrim*, he knew she must be older.

"Stay rockside of the fire," she said. "The smoke is drawn out through the passageway. And it's best to keep the flames between you and any visitors."

"What kind of visitors?" demanded Rothe.

"Huanin, Kyrinin, animals. Bears." She flashed the shieldman a harsh smile that had barely formed upon her lips before it was gone again. "In winter it's bears scavenging here; in summer, your people from the valley. Treasure hunters and boys who think they're men because they've got some hair on their crotch. They scare off more easily than the beasts do."

"Not all of us," muttered Rothe.

Yvane gave no sign that she had heard, continuing to probe at the fire.

"Inurian said you would help us get safely away from here," Anyara said.

The *na'kyrim* gave a soft laugh. "You Huanin are so hasty," she said. She waved the smoldering stick at Ess'yr and Varryn. "See, your Kyrinin friends are perfect guests. They are still, and quiet, saving talk until host and visitor have taken the measure of one another."

"I did not mean any offense," said Anyara, neatly blending contrition and irritation in her tone.

Yvane shrugged. "None was taken," she said. "Some Kyrinin make poor guests as well. For children of the God Who Laughed, they can be rather dour."

No flicker of a response crossed the faces of Ess'yr and Varryn.

"I imagine your Fox friends are less than comfortable here," Yvane mused. "They tell foolish stories about me in their camps. Talking with the dead and the like."

Orisian could not tell whether or not they were welcome here. All of Yvane's words were spoken in a casual tone, yet there was an edge to them.

"This is where you live? This cave, I mean," he asked. Yvane glanced around as if examining her surroundings for the first time.

"I've not used this place in a while. You were wandering this way anyway, so you might have found it yourselves."

"You were watching us," Orisian said.

"More or less," said Yvane. "When I felt Inurian die I had a suspicion that my peace would not last long. Intuition, if you like; the Shared, if you prefer. I'll admit you're a more unusual little group than I expected. Lannis-Haig and Fox traveling together has never been a common sight. Rarer than a flat calm off the Wrecking Cape, in fact."

She lapsed into silence, and after a few moments the quiet settled so heavily across the group that it would have been a strain to break it. Orisian found the hush less uncomfortable than the talk that had gone before. The fire hissed and popped. The wind rumbled.

Orisian's head nodded. It became too difficult to stay awake. He stirred once, looking around with half-open eyes. Anyara had slumped against Rothe's shoulder and fallen asleep. Ess'yr and Varryn had passed into slumber where they sat, their backs against the stone wall. Only Rothe remained stubbornly alert, his exhausted eyes fixed upon the *na'kyrim* woman who, pointedly ignoring his gaze, was stretching herself out by the fire. Orisian saw no more but wondered, as his mind floated down, how long Rothe would keep his vigil for.

When Orisian woke, the fire was near-dead ashes. A thread of daylight reached in from the outside world. He moistened his lips. They had dried and cracked in the night. There were two dark shapes curled on the floor to his right: Rothe and Anyara. He looked for the Kyrinin, but could see no sign. Yvane too was gone from her place by the fire. In those first few moments of wakefulness, he was nagged by the thought that something was missing. It was only as he rose to his feet that he realized that the monotonous, constant voice of the wind had fallen silent. Walking a little clumsily, since numbness had stolen his legs from under him, he made his way out into the open.

Even without any wind, the cold air brought tears to his sleepcrusted eyes. It was early morning, and he was amazed that he had slept so soundly for so long. The ruined city sprawled out before him, a stark net of rock cast over the even white snow that had fallen in the night.

He started as Ess'yr appeared beneath the edge of the platform, vaulting up from amongst the boulders. He held out his hand and pulled her up. She felt weightless, her hand soft in his.

"You slept well?" she asked, and he nodded.

"Where's Yvane?" he said.

Ess'yr sniffed. "Went at the first light," she said.

"And Varryn?"

"Hunting. There are hare tracks in the snow."

"I suppose we just wait for him and Yvane to come back, then," said Orisian.

And wait they did. Rothe and Anyara woke, cold and grumbling and hungry. There was dry wood beneath some sacking in a corner of the chamber, and Rothe managed to rekindle the fire. They huddled about it.

Ess'yr would not settle. Again and again she rose to go outside for a few moments. When she came back in, rather than sit by the fire she circled about it, examining the crude paintings upon the walls. When Orisian asked her what the matter was, she mumbled something he did not catch. This tiny cavern was as far as it was possible to get from the forests and open skies the Kyrinin loved, he supposed.

After an hour or two Varryn reappeared, clutching a white hare in one hand. He grimaced as he threw his bloody catch to the ground. With a gesture toward his eyes he spun around and went outside again.

"There's not enough wind to pull the smoke out," said Rothe.

Now that his attention was drawn to it, Orisian's own eyes began to burn and weep. After a few moments he headed out onto the broad ledge and sat cross-legged, huddled up to try to keep some warmth in his body. There was no sign of Varryn. Rothe followed him out and sat beside him. The big man clearly wanted to say something, but could not quite bring himself to do so.

"I wonder where Yvane has gone," said Orisian.

"Best not to inquire too deeply into the doings of her kind," said Rothe. "More woodwight than human, that one."

"She's a friend, I think," Orisian said gently. "Inurian thought she would be."

"You will go to Koldihrve, then?" Rothe asked.

"Inurian said it is what we should do."

"I know you loved him, Orisian, and it's fitting you should give weight to his words, but are you sure? It's not that I don't trust him, or doubt his wisdom. I know he understood things people like you and me don't."

The aging warrior looked him in the eye, and Orisian saw quite clearly the love and care that lay just beneath the surface. He saw, as well, that there was grey in the man's beard that had not been there a few weeks ago.

"Orisian . . ." Rothe started, and then had to pause to clear his throat. "Orisian, it may be that you are the Thane now. I think that is most likely the way of it."

It was the thought that Orisian had steadfastly ignored since Anyara told him what had happened in Anduran. He had known he would have to face it, but had hoped for a little more time.

"We can hope not," he murmured, casting his eyes down. Fariel came into his mind. His brother would have made a fine Thane. But no; he set his mind against that thought. It would not help him now. There was no point in imagining a world that would never be.

"Of course, of course," Rothe said hurriedly. "Perhaps Croesan, or Naradin, or even the baby, still live. But perhaps they do not."

"I know it as well as you do, Rothe."

"Yes. I'm sorry," said the shieldman.

Orisian laid a hand upon Rothe's arm. "It's only that I have no wish to be Thane."

"That's only sense. It's a fool who can't see it's easier to give an oath than be given it."

Perhaps, Orisian thought. But who really did the harder thing: Kylane, who made an oath that cost him his life, or me, by being the object of it?

He smiled at his shieldman. "I had an idea you were close to putting aside your sword, before all of this happened. Was I wrong?"

Rothe looked uncomfortable, like nothing so much as a man reminded of some childhood foolishness.

"I had that thought," he said, "or half the thought. Perhaps a farm, like the one I grew up on; just somewhere to rest a while, to let the last years be quieter." His voice hardened, stiffening against the hint of tranquillity: "The thought is gone now, Orisian. Never doubt it. I would not leave your side now even if you pelted me with stones. Not so long as I've the strength to lift a sword."

Orisian smiled. "Oh, I know that well enough, Rothe."

They did not say anything for a time. The smell of cooking meat drifted out and teased at them.

"Tell me what it is you think I should do," Orisian said eventually.

"I will follow wherever you go, but if it were mine to choose I would say we must go to Glasbridge. If you are their Thane, the people must rally to you. You are their strength and you must be amongst them. And if Anyara is right that Horin-Gyre is in the van of our enemies, that is where they will go. Their roots lie there; they must try for it."

Orisian hung his head. He knew that Rothe would indeed follow wherever he led, and would lay down his life in whatever cause Orisian chose. As Kylane had already done. As — a fearful thought — many more would willingly do if he was truly now Thane of the Blood.

"My heart tells me the same thing," he said softly. "But Inurian seemed so certain this was our only chance. I don't think Ess'yr and Varryn would have agreed to come this way if . . ."

A sudden sound distracted him. Yvane had appeared, bearing a great bundle of furs bound up with twine. Orisian and Rothe stood up. There was a scowl upon the *na'kyrim*'s face that cowed even Rothe before she said a word.

"I smell smoke," she snapped.

"We lit a fire," Orisian said. He and Rothe took a step back as she flung the furs to the ground and came stamping toward them.

"Have you no imagination?" she demanded. "Did it not occur

to you that firewood may be a little harder to come by here than in your comfortable castles?"

She encompassed the entire snowy, rocky panorama before them with an extravagant sweep of her arm. "Do you see any trees?" she demanded.

Orisian looked around. Rothe did the same thing. Yvane gave a groan of deep exasperation and stormed into the passageway. Rothe and Orisian glanced at one another with raised eyebrows. They heard the *na'kyrim*'s irate greeting of Ess'yr and Anyara.

"Doesn't do to have one of her kind angry with you," sighed Rothe, puffing out his cheeks. Orisian nodded pensively, but already his attention was elsewhere. He eyed the pile of furs that Yvane had abandoned upon the ledge. He rubbed his upper arms briskly against the cold.

"Do you think those furs are for us?" he wondered.

"I dare to hope," said Rothe, "but let's wait until she tells us so."

Once Yvane had calmed a little she acknowledged, with all the grace and good humor of a bee-stung mule, that the furs were for her visitors. Orisian and the others pulled them on. For the first time in days Orisian began to feel some real warmth coming into his skin as he sat watching the hare char over the flames. Yvane had reluctantly allowed the fire to remain alight, since the animal was already cooking when she returned. They devoured it enthusiastically, heedless of the grease that ran down their chins and the smoke that stung their eyes. Ess'yr cracked a leg bone in two and sucked at the marrow. They melted snow in one of Yvane's clay pots to quench their thirst.

Afterward, Ess'yr went to look for her brother. Orisian could not imagine she was worried about him; he suspected it had more to do with a desire to be under open skies once more. Rothe insisted on keeping watch outside, and left Orisian and Anyara alone with the *na'kyrim*. The shieldman had evidently concluded that however abrasive Yvane might be, she was no grave threat to his charge's safety.

Orisian hesitated at first, fearing the sharp edge of Yvane's tongue if she was still in a foul mood, but he doubted there was time to be too careful of her temper.

"Inurian told us that you would help us. He wanted us to go to Koldihrve, said you could get us there," he said quietly.

Yvane, wiping her lips with the sleeve of her jacket, seemed at first not to have heard. Then as she settled herself back against the wall of the chamber and stretched out her legs she fixed him with an attentive gaze.

"And why is it you want to go to Koldihrve?" she asked. "Not too many friends of your Blood there, you know."

"To find a boat. That was Inurian's idea, anyway . . ." He paused.

"But not yours, apparently," Yvane murmured.

Orisian gave a small, uncertain shrug. He felt he was being almost disloyal to Inurian by even doubting his instructions.

"I am . . . unsure," he said. "At first I thought we could head straight for Glasbridge, or Sirian's Dyke, in the valley. But Inurian and Ess'yr and Varryn seemed certain we would not have reached them."

Yvane prodded the faltering fire with a stick, stirring its embers back into bright life.

"I don't suppose you would, then. If even a Fox with the threefold *kin'thyn* feels it wiser to fly up here, chances are pretty good you'd be dead if you'd not followed. There's not many of them amongst the Fox, you know; bearers of the threefold patterns, I mean. The Fox has never been a big clan anyway, of course . . ."

"Well, we can't stay here," Anyara interrupted.

The *na'kyrim* fixed her with a sharp gaze, arching one of her eyebrows in a pointed gesture of displeasure.

"I mean," Anyara persisted, "that if we cannot get back to Glasbridge overland, it sounds to me as though we have no choice but to press on to Koldihrve and try to find a boat."

"Mind sharp as a needle, that one," Yvane muttered to herself, and returned her attention to the fire.

Anyara glared at their host. Orisian willed her to hold her tongue.

"Inurian tried to get me involved once already," Yvane said unexpectedly. She might have still been talking to herself. "He wanted me to . . . do something about this Aeglyss. Perhaps that's why he sent you up here. It's not as if you really need my help to get to Koldihrve, after all, when you've got those two Fox nursemaiding you."

"Aeglyss?" exclaimed Anyara in surprise. "You've spoken to Inurian about him?"

Yvane nodded. "While he was in Anduran. I took a look at Aeglyss myself. It wasn't the best of ideas; if he had the skill to match his raw strength . . . anyway, I've still got an ache in my head I can't shake off."

"Well, Aeglyss is the one pursuing us. Or one of them, at least," Orisian said. "Even if he didn't kill Inurian with his own hands, it was partly his doing."

Yvane gave a noncommittal grunt. "Inurian didn't say anything about taking care of his waifs and strays. He wanted me to give Highfast a prod, that's all. Get them to take care of Aeglyss."

"I thought Highfast was a fortress," said Anyara.

"It is," Yvane replied. "Never been taken in battle they always say, and I imagine it's true enough. Kyrinin besieged it during the War of the Tainted, and your own kind in the Storm Years, and again in the Black Road wars. Came through it all well enough. There's more to it than that, though; what warriors are left there are more for show than anything. The very first Kilkry Thane gave it to some *na'kyrim* who were looking for a place to hide away and they're hiding there still, or their successors are, at least. It's not much of a secret, but there's probably more don't know it than do."

She sighed heavily. "Some good people there, but not as many answers as they like to think. They've grown as musty as the books they guard, and half of what they chatter about makes no more sense than the croaking of their crows. It takes a certain temperament to shut yourself up with so many words and so much learning. Neither Inurian nor I ever quite had the mettle for it. A shame, in a way. For those who can settle there it is very . . . soothing."

"And Inurian thought they're the ones to deal with Aeglyss?" asked Orisian.

"Inurian always had a tendency to assume the best about people: I suspect he thought the Highfast folk would help sort out whatever mess Aeglyss is creating just because he's a *na'kyrim* like them. He evidently believed this Aeglyss is — or could be — a remarkable young man, gifted with exceptional talents."

Anyara growled some comment on that, but kept it low enough to avoid Yvane's attention.

"If Inurian was right," Yvane continued, "then it may be that only the kind of *na'kyrim* who dwell in Highfast are capable of standing against him." Her eyes glazed over, her voice drifted, following her thoughts down some distracting track. "Or Dyrkyrnon . . . he did say he might have lived there, didn't he?" She hung her head.

"Dyrkynon?" Orisian asked.

Yvane looked up, seeming surprised that she was not alone.

"Dyrkyrnon," she corrected him. "Yes. Another hideaway for my kind. It's not the same kind of place as Highfast, though. There's *na'kyrim* and there's *na'kyrim.* The ones at Dyrkyrnon can be less friendly than a bear with a thorn in its foot when the mood takes them."

There was a moment's quiet. Anyara's face betrayed her impatience.

"Even if you just point us in the right direction . . ." she began, only to be cut off by Yvane's raucous clearing of her throat.

"Excuse me," the *na'kyrim* said. "The wet and cold up here lie heavy upon my chest sometimes. Especially when I'm thinking."

They lapsed into a tense silence. Orisian and Anyara glanced uneasily at one another.

"Did he still have that crow? What happened to it?" asked Yvane.

"Idrin," said Orisian. "He sent him away. Told him to go home, I think."

Yvane nodded as if Orisian had confirmed something she already knew. "Then they will know by now, at Highfast, that he is dead."

She was deep in thought for long moments, and neither Orisian nor Anyara dared to disturb her. Orisian's eyes wandered, drifting over the uneven surface of the walls. He gazed at the figures painted there: animals and people delineated with simple, broad strokes. It was crude work, but suited to this firelit setting. It might have come from an ancient, unformed world.

"Do you know about the Sky Pilgrims?" Yvane asked him.

"I've never heard of them," Orisian said.

"Ah, there's no finer example of the rock-headed foolishness of your race. You know, at least, the story that one of the First Race's crimes against the Gods was supposed to be stealing fire from the roof of the world? Well, in the very early years of the Kingships there were those who thought they could persuade the Gods to return by repeating that journey in penance. They were the Sky Pilgrims. Dozens of them marched through here on their way to the Tan Dihrin. It was not a belief that prospered; hardly a surprise given that most of its followers must have met rather miserable deaths."

"And they made these drawings on their way there," Orisian said.

"I think so. I can't make much sense of them, but then sense was not the most prominent of the Sky Pilgrims' qualities."

"You should not speak so harshly of the dead," muttered Anyara. "I'm sure they were only doing what they thought was right."

To Orisian's surprise, that made Yvane hesitate.

"Perhaps they were," she said. "Inurian's rubbed off on you, I see. He often scolded me for being too impatient of Huanin — and Kyrinin — failings. Told me I should wait until I had rid myself of every flaw before going around picking at everyone else's." She smiled distantly, as if pleased by the memory.

Rothe came bursting into the chamber then. He brought snowflakes with him, and the cold of the outside world that Orisian had almost forgotten existed. The shieldman had a grave expression.

"Come," he said. "I think I saw someone. Younger eyes might be better than mine."

Orisian and Anyara followed him. Yvane did not move from her fireside place, silently stirring the ashes as the fire began to falter. Every step down the short passageway brought the sound of the wind closer. When they emerged onto the dais of rock outside it was to find the sky obscured by flat and featureless grey clouds, the air filled with wind-blown snow. Mists and fogs were seething around the ridges to the south and west. Orisian raised a hand to shield his face.

"Where did you see them?" he said to Rothe.

The shieldman gestured back the way they had come on their flight from Sarn's Leap.

"On the horizon there," he shouted. "I thought I saw someone cresting the ridge, coming just the way we did."

Orisian and Anyara peered that way, into the teeth of the Car Criagar's stinging breath. It was a vain effort: clouds had engulfed the landscape.

"It's no use," Rothe said.

Orisian shook his head in agreement.

As they retreated back into the cliff face, he glanced at Rothe.

"Did you see any sign of Ess'yr and Varryn?" he asked.

Rothe only shook his head.

Waiting was a hardship for Orisian. One way or the other, he probably owed his life to Ess'yr and her brother. But it was not only out of gratitude that he longed for Ess'yr's safe return in particular: he knew, with the acuity of one experienced in the matter of loss, that losing her now would cost him a precious part of what strength he had left. Anyara and Rothe were wrapped in their own silences, each staring deep into the fading embers of the fire. Yvane appeared to have drifted into sleep where she sat.

Ess'yr and Varryn came in almost casually, brushing flecks of snow from their shoulders and hair. A surge of relief carried Orisian to his feet.

"We thought you might be in trouble," he said. "Rothe saw someone on the ridge beyond the ruins."

Varryn glanced at the shieldman as he set down his spear and bow. He squatted in silence and began to work his way through the arrows in his quiver, smoothing their flights and testing the heads.

"Huanin," Ess'yr said as she flicked snowmelt from her forehead.

"You saw them?" demanded Rothe.

Ess'yr gave the slightest of nods. "Saw, at a distance. Perhaps only two. They have dogs."

"Dogs," Orisian echoed. "Hunters, then?"

Anyara shifted uneasily by the hearth. "Perhaps," she murmured, "but perhaps not just hunters but the Hunt. Inurian was worried about it, when we were escaping from Anduran. Perhaps it wasn't just Battle Inkallim that came south with Horin-Gyre."

Rothe groaned. Orisian knew his own face must be revealing the alarm Anyara's words triggered.

"Would the Hunt really come after us? I mean, to pursue us all this way . . ."

"You forget," Rothe interrupted him. "You may be the Thane of our Blood. That alone is reason enough for the Hunt Inkall to pursue us to the end of the world, if they take it into their heads to do so. Even if they do not know it is you they are pursuing, they know Anyara is here. Perhaps they think she is the last of your uncle's family alive. Remember, Orisian, our people might have softened over the years: the Gyre Bloods have not. They'll see this through to the end, whatever that end might be."

"Well, whoever they are, they're going to have an uncomfortable time out there, from the sound of the wind," Yvane said.

Orisian glanced at the *na'kyrim*. She looked perfectly alert and relaxed.

"Whoever they are, we can't stay," Orisian said quietly. "As soon as the weather eases, we will have to move on. Whether you come with us or not."

Yvane returned his gaze for a few moments, then gave a shrug.

"We found a little food," Ess'yr said. She unfolded a pouch of leather to reveal a handful of wizened berries and a clump of unappetizing greenery. She laid them on a stone and the three humans regarded them glumly. Anyara's stomach gave a complaining rumble. Yvane produced some hazelnuts and dry mushrooms from her pocket and added them to the meager array. It was not much; just enough to blunt their hunger. All the while they ate, the sound of the winter storm outside mounted.

Afterward, Varryn rose and gathered his weapons once more.

"Someone must watch," he said flatly as he disappeared out of the circle of firelight.

V

Gryvan oc Haig was in a rage such as none in the Moon Palace had witnessed for many months. As he stormed down the stone corridors, he spat invective at every servant unfortunate enough to cross his path. Kale strode after his High Thane, and behind him came the Chancellor Mordyn Jerain and Gryvan's son Aewult. Mordyn noticed, as the Bloodheir marched along beside him, that there was a kind of satisfaction on Aewult's face. The young man enjoyed such moments, when passions flared and Gryvan showed that he could still make people fear him. If the day comes when Aewult rules in his father's stead, Mordyn reflected, few people will love him as at least some do Gryvan. But many will have cause to fear him.

The High Thane threw open the doors to his private chambers and swept in. The attendants within, startled in the act of setting out Gryvan's robes for his impending audience with the Dornach ambassador, fled with a volley of curses snapping at their heels. Gryvan slammed the doors shut behind them.

"Explain to me, then, what is happening," the Thane of Thanes shouted, red-faced. "Explain to me, Chancellor."

Mordyn steeled himself and locked his features into a calm, open expression. He had known Gryvan for long enough to be certain that this tempest would blow itself out as quickly as it had arisen. Kale, as immune as ever to the emotions raging around him, had drifted to the window to ensure that no one was loitering on the balconies without.

"Which matter would you have me address first, lord?" Mordyn asked. He hoped, and expected, that Gryvan was most exercised over the news that Mordyn himself had just broken to him, rather than that which a messenger from the Steward in Kolkyre had unfortunately delivered at almost the same moment. The first, the Chancellor had an answer to; the second was more problematic.

"The Goldsmiths, the Goldsmiths," snarled Gryvan. He sank heavily into a capacious chair. Aewult made for a small table. Gryvan's servants had laid out some food for him there. The Bloodheir idly surveyed a bowl of apples and grapes.

"Very well," Mordyn murmured. He carefully clasped his hands across his stomach, in as passive a posture as he could manage. "I have been looking into the matter for some time now, and we are therefore well placed to respond to recent events. As I was explaining before Lagair Haldyn's message arrived, Gann nan Dargannan-Haig has killed his half-brother. He took him in an ambush. All of this strife within the Dargannan Blood serves us well in weakening them, but the time has perhaps passed when we can stand aside and watch them hacking away at one another. It appears increasingly possible that if left to their own devices, it will be Gann who rises to the top."

"Yes, yes," Gryvan said. The heat of his anger was already fading somewhat. His brow remained knotted, but his hand was quite steady as he poured himself wine from a jug at his side. "But now you tell me that the Goldsmiths own Gann. Apparently you've known this for some time, but not seen fit to share the information with me."

"Gann's a coward," Aewult said casually, through a mouthful of apple. "Throughout Igryn's rebellion, Gann hid away on one of the islands."

"He is unfit to be Thane," Mordyn agreed, "even if he wasn't a creature of one of the Crafts."

"But he is such a creature," snapped Gryvan. "That is what concerns me. I don't care who rules the Dargannan Blood, so long as they know their place. What I do care about is that the Goldsmiths should think they are entitled to try to make Thanes themselves."

"Indeed," said the Chancellor. "The Crafts have always taken an interest in the doings of Thanes, and have never shied away from spending coin in support of their interests. This goes beyond that. To my certain knowledge the Goldsmiths have not only enriched Gann himself, but paid a dowry for his sister's marriage, made a gift of one of their own houses to his infant son and bribed — I regret to say — our own tax collectors to overlook certain private dealings Gann has had with Tal Dyreen merchants. It is my belief — not certain, but probable — that they also paid for the hire of the Free Coast bandits that Gann brought in to kill his half-brother. They have put Gann so greatly in their debt it's unlikely he will ever be anything more than their lackey."

Gryvan took a noisy swallow of wine, then set the goblet down so roughly upon the table that it spilled. He shook his hand and scattered red droplets.

"I've made them all rich, all of the Crafts. Since Haig took over from Kilkry there has never been such wealth, and they've garnered more than their fair share of it."

"They are ungrateful," agreed the Bloodheir. Mordyn deliberately avoided looking at him. Aewult smelled the prospect of bloodshed and intrigue, and that always excited him. At least

Gryvan was capable of restraint; for Aewult, all too often, the bloody exercise of power appeared to be an end in itself.

"Ungrateful, I could tolerate," muttered the High Thane. "But when they interfere with my own needs, they go too far. We must have a secure, subdued and obedient Dargannan Blood. Nothing of what we seek — not the Free Coast, Tal Dyre, Dornach — none of that can we reach for without Dargannan first safely under our heel. Whoever the new Thane is, he will be my creature, not the Goldsmiths'."

"I have a suggestion," Mordyn said.

The High Thane nodded curtly. He was calm enough to listen now.

"Balance is important in this. There is no need to force a confrontation with the Goldsmiths. It benefits us to remain on good terms with them, and with all of the Crafts, but they do need to learn the limits of their power in this game. I can, therefore, have their piece removed from the board. If we do it in such a way that our hand is not obvious, they will suspect our involvement but be left uncertain. That, I have found, is almost always the best outcome. Uncertainty constrains actions without provoking hostility."

He heard Aewult snort dismissively. He ignored it; now, and hopefully for years to come, it was Gryvan who made the decisions. The High Thane glanced at his son.

"Go and find Alem T'anarch," he said sternly. "Tell him that his audience will be somewhat delayed. And tell him that the delay in no way reflects any lack of respect for the exalted Dornach Kingship."

"He won't believe that," Aewult said.

"He's not supposed to, of course," Gryvan snapped. "Now go."

The Bloodheir went, tossing his half-eaten apple back toward the bowl as he went. It missed, and bounced messily to the floor.

"Very well," Gryvan said. "Use whatever means it is you have for doing these things. Rid us of Gann, and I will trust to your judgment that the Goldsmiths will understand the message."

"I will ensure they do," Mordyn said with a shallow bow.

"And what of Lannis-Haig?" Gryvan asked. This was the second irritation that had driven the High Thane to his brief fury. It was, for Mordyn Jerain, a much greater source of puzzlement and concern than the petty intrigues of the Goldsmiths. He shook his head, a gesture finely calculated to convey both regret and mild uncertainty. It would not be wise to appear over-confident in this area, he knew.

"It is remarkable that Anduran has fallen so quickly, lord. If Lagair Haldyn is correct in his reports, of course. It seems unlikely that he could be wrong about something so . . . substantial."

"Remarkable. You think it remarkable?" There was still a hint of danger in Gryvan's voice. That anger had not entirely dissipated. "I think it rather more than remarkable. I would not have agreed to any correspondence with Ragnor oc Gyre all these months had I known he meant to overrun our lands. However difficult Lannis-Haig might be, the Glas valley is still part of my domain. It will not pass to the Gyre Bloods."

"No," said Mordyn emphatically. However unclear the course of events in the north was, that much he could be certain of. "In all truth, High Thane, I do not know if Ragnor has played us false, or if Horin-Gyre has merely been immensely fortunate. In any case, whatever messages have passed between Ragnor and us in the past, the time has surely come to act firmly. The Black Road must be thrown back beyond the Stone Vale before they can establish a firm grip on the Glas valley."

"Of course. Our armies are gathered. I will send Aewult himself at their head."

Mordyn bit back a flicker of unease. Sending the Bloodheir north at the head of an army would not have been his recommendation; none of the other Bloods were overly enamored of Aewult nan Haig, but Kilkry and Lannis liked him least of all. Now was not the moment to challenge the High Thane's will, though. The Chancellor knew he had stretched Gryvan's patience by waiting so long to inform him of the Goldsmiths' machinations, and by failing to predict the fall of the Lannis-Haig Blood.

He took a step back, fixing his eyes on the tiled floor of the High Thane's chamber. He could remember these tiles being laid, a dozen years ago. Gryvan had brought the finest workmen from Taral-Haig, bought the most expensive tiles the potteries of Vaymouth had to offer. It would take a shepherd three lifetimes to earn the cost of this floor.

"I will see to the matter of Gann nan Dargannan-Haig this evening, if you have no further need of me," Mordyn murmured.

"Go," agreed Gryvan. "He is one fly we can swat with ease, at least."

There were few people in Vaymouth for whom the Shadowhand would venture out on the streets of the city at night. In the normal course of events, there was no need for it: people came to him, in one palace or another. But in the case of Torquentine things were different. For him, the Chancellor of the Haig Bloods would don a scruffy, heavy-hooded cloak and sally forth himself. Nothing he might want to say to Torquentine should be trusted to an intermediary, and Torquentine could not come to him.

The Chancellor made his way down disreputable streets toward the heart of Ash Pit, perhaps the least savory of all Vaymouth's districts. He maintained a wary eye and the shambling gait of one too old and ill to be worth the attention of the city's cutpurses. Almost out of sight, two trusted men — his own hirelings, not the guards that came with the post of Chancellor — followed him. They would intervene if trouble threatened, but even so there was some slight risk in walking these streets after dark. He had made the journey only a handful of times.

He came to a narrow junction and paused. He gave a hand signal and his escort sank into the shadows. The Chancellor crossed the street. The building to which he made his shuffling way was completely anonymous: just one more poorly built house jammed into a long street of its fellows. Yet when he tapped upon the door, Mordyn could feel its strength and solidity beneath his knuckles. No ordinary shack would have a door of heavy oak, banded with iron across its back and barred with a thick beam. Torquentine treasured his privacy.

Mordyn knew, as he waited patiently for a response from within, that he was being observed; that he had been beneath the gaze of hidden sentries from the moment he came within a hundred paces of this place. He doubted they would know him for who he was, but equally they would not believe him to be just another decrepit beggar. It mattered little if they mistrusted his disguise. Many people who came to see Torquentine must prefer to keep their faces hidden.

A haggard-looking woman opened the door. Her pallid, sickly face was disfigured by the tell-tale marks of the King's Rot. Part of her nose was eaten away, and purplish blotches marred her cheek. Mordyn had always thought it an elegant touch for Torquentine to employ such a doorkeeper. Superstition or pure distaste at the sight of her might be enough to repel some uninvited guests.

"Is your master at home, Magrayn?" the Chancellor asked. It was more ritual than genuine inquiry: Magrayn's master never left this place.

The woman stood to one side and gestured for him to enter. He knew the rules, and went no further than a step beyond the threshold as she closed the door behind him. There was another barred door to pass through yet, and only Magrayn could give him permission to progress.

"Show your face," she said. Her voice was slovenly, uneven. The Rot had sunk into her throat.

The Chancellor slipped back his hood and looked her in the eye.

"The visage matches the voice, I trust?" he smiled.

Magrayn grunted and gave a swift triple knock upon the inner door.

"Open up," she called, and Mordyn was given admittance to Torquentine's lair. Hard-faced men searched him and took his knife from him, and he was led down into the cellars.

The man Mordyn had come to see would be thought a monstrosity by some, but to the Shadowhand such a view would be a meaningless distraction. Torquentine was, above and beyond all else, useful. There was more than one network of power in the Haig Bloods, and Torquentine stood at the heart of that which shunned the light of day and the scrutiny of curious eyes. A word whispered in a quayside drinking den in Kolkyre or murmured with lust-loosened tongue into a doxy's ear in Dun Aygll could find its way to Torquentine. A sizeable fraction of the illicit gains of smugglers, thieves, moneylenders and assassins throughout the Haig lands seeped along surreptitious channels to his pocket. He was the spider at the center of a vast, almost invisible web. But if he was a spider, he was one grown fat upon the flesh of his prey.

Alone, the Chancellor entered the chamber in which Torquentine reclined upon a vast heap of cushions. The man was gigantic. His voluminous clothes concealed a body that must weigh as much as three more commonly sized men. The skin of his face sagged and folded itself down. One eye was gone, a ragged scar running across its empty pit from temple to nose. The good eye that stared out at the Chancellor shone with intelligence. Mordyn often reflected that Torquentine's size might serve a purpose in one way at least. It was too easy to judge a man by his girth, to assume that one so bloated could only be dim-witted, or weak, or foolish. Such assumptions would be a grievous error on the part of anyone dealing with Torquentine. To the Chancellor's knowledge there were few people in Vaymouth who were quite as dangerous.

"Chancellor," Torquentine said hoarsely. "An unexpected pleasure. It has been some time since the Shadowhand graced my chambers."

"More than a year," Mordyn agreed as he lowered himself onto an immaculately upholstered bench, the room's only piece of furniture. Small bowls of aromatic herbs and petals rested beside him. Their scent mixed with the smoky aroma given off by the guttering oil lamps. Beneath it all, Mordyn could catch a hint of the malodorous air they were intended to mask. The Chancellor glanced quizzically at the material covering the bench.

"You have new upholstery," he remarked.

"Indeed," rasped his host. "I tired of the previous pattern. And it had been worn by the buttocks of a great many supplicants."

"Supplicants were a thing of the temples we dispensed with long ago," said Mordyn.

"Petitioners, if you prefer," smiled Torquentine. "But men must find something to worship once their Gods abandon them. It is in our natures to make temples of the strangest places, even if it is not Gods that inhabit them."

"Mere mortal that you are, there is nevertheless a great deal of you for men to abase themselves before," Mordyn acknowledged. "I dare to hope I stand more highly in your affections than a mere petitioner at some altar, however."

"Ah, affection. It does not become a man to dispense his precious stocks of that commodity too freely. But what need could you have of my humble affection in any case, honored Chancellor? You have the love of the great and the noble to warm your heart should it grow cold. In any case it was, as likely as not, your gold that paid for the new covering of my bench. You may treat it as roughly as you wish."

"I cannot tarry long," said Mordyn. "There is but a single item I wished to discuss."

Torquentine raised a fat arm in exaggerated distress. "Such brevity, and I have not even had the chance to offer you any refreshments yet."

Mordyn suppressed the urge to smile. Torquentine enjoyed the sound of his own voice, and gave a passable impression of a buffoon.

"I have a small task for you, Torquentine. Nothing too testing, for a man of your capacities."

"I am rigid with curiosity," said Torquentine in a tone of studied disinterest.

"Gann nan Dargannan-Haig. Cousin to Igryn. Do you know him?"

"Of him, of him. An empty vessel, like most of his family. A mouse burdened with the ambition of a rat; overfond of drink and of whores, and pox-ridden to boot. Thinks he has the makings of a Thane. And lacks the sense to recognize himself as a tool of the Goldsmiths, of course. But then you will know all of that already, Chancellor."

"Indeed." Mordyn nodded. "You summarize the man. Well, worthless though his life has been, I am resolved that he should be given the chance to redeem himself, by dying a useful death. I would not suppose to tell you your business, but I thought perhaps a tavern brawl? Or expiry from overindulgence in the pleasures of some whorehouse?"

Torquentine's eye narrowed a fraction. It was a tiny gesture, but Mordyn drew satisfaction from the fact that he had surprised his host. Only once before had he asked Torquentine for a death, and that had been a lowly brothelmaster who tried to blackmail one of Mordyn's clerks. Gann nan Dargannan-Haig was a different kind of victim.

Striking at one who was both a member of a ruling family — albeit a dishonored one — and a possession of one of the most powerful Crafts was a bold move, but the Chancellor was satisfied it was worth the risk. Even if they believed it to be no more than bad luck, his loss would be a setback for the Goldsmiths; a few words in the right places would ensure that they suspected, but could not prove, the hand of the Moon Palace behind the deed. If Lammain the Craftmaster had half the sense Mordyn credited him with, he would recognize it for the warning it was.

"Nothing too testing, you say," mused Torquentine, "yet you ask a good deal, Chancellor."

Mordyn said nothing. Torquentine would not refuse this commission. The benefits of the Chancellor's patronage were great, and Torquentine's reach was long and discreet enough to do the deed without any risk to himself.

"Very well," said Torquentine. "I shall deal with the luckless Gann. The world will hardly suffer from his loss. Imagine: at this very moment he probably lies sated in the arms of some woman, his dreams all of pleasure and ease, and here we sit deciding to put an end to him."

The man's voice faded, and his one eye fluttered and half-closed. After a moment he sighed and returned to himself.

"Such are the vagaries of fortune," he breathed. "A boon in return, though, dare I hope? This is no small request you make of me, so perhaps a little something in addition to the usual payment?"

The Chancellor raised his eyebrows quizzically. The rules he and Torquentine played by were well established. He would prefer to avoid any departure from them.

"Gann is not some street urchin, after all," Torquentine smiled. "Snuffing out his candle will require care, planning. It will be a complicated effort."

"What is it you want, Torquentine?" inquired Mordyn, lacing his voice with a hint of irritation.

The great man on the cushions raised his own eyebrows in turn. It made the scar across his face stretch alarmingly.

"Well, in truth I could not say. Perhaps we could delay the resolution of that question until such time as the answer is more apparent. I imagine a solution will present itself before long. They usually do."

"You seek to put me in your debt, Torquentine," the Chancellor said levelly.

"Oh, come now, let us not speak of debt. We make a bargain, you and I. It is merely that your half of it remains, for the time being, a little . . . ill-defined."

"Done," Mordyn said as he rose to his feet. He heartily disliked the idea of making open-ended promises to the likes of Torquentine, but now hardly seemed the time to argue over trifles. He was the Shadowhand, after all, and promises were easy things to break. "I should return. My wife will be expecting me."

"Ah, the divine Tara. She of such famed perfection. You cannot imagine how it pains me that I should have to rely only upon rumors of her beauty and never set eyes upon it for myself." Torquentine sighed and cast a glum eye over the walls of his chamber as he caressed his oceanic stomach. "To think I have been incarcerated in this cellar for so long, and all for the sake of an ill-disciplined love of nourishment."

To hear his beloved wife spoken of thus by such as Torquentine sent a mild shiver of repugnance down Mordyn's spine as he made to leave. A passing thought held him in the doorway.

"Have you any word out of Lannis-Haig?"

"Lannis-Haig, Lannis-Haig. Barbarians up there, you know. No appreciation for the finer things in life. But what word is it you seek?"

"Whatever may have fallen into those huge ears of yours," muttered Mordyn. He would not usually inquire about such matters in this place, and already half-regretted the question. Torquentine's expertise lay in the rumors of marketplaces and the doings of thieves and brigands. Mordyn had other means of following the course of grander events, though they were not serving him as well as he would wish. He was tired of being surprised by news from the Glas valley.

"Well, I've little to offer that will not already have reached your own capacious ears, I should imagine," said Torquentine, "and half of it's rantings, of course. The Black Road rules in the valley once again; only until our esteemed High Thane deigns to flex his muscles, as all right-thinking folk would tell you. Lheanor's hiding away in his stick of a tower in Kolkyre, mourning his dead son. Croesan's dead too, some say, and captured others."

"And the rest of Croesan's family? Dead?"

Torquentine shrugged. It was an eye-catching gesture, sending ripples through his jowls.

"Or as good as. Yet, what was it I heard? Kennet, the senile one in Kolglas: they found his body after the woodwights and the ravens were done with his castle, but never his children's. I forget their names."

"Orisian and Anyara," Mordyn said absently.

"Indeed. No sign of them, although from what I hear half the bodies were well-roasted, so who could be sure?"

After the Chancellor had gone, Torquentine sat quite still and quiet for a few minutes, furrows denting his sweat-sheened brow. At length, he tugged at a silken cord that hung from the ceiling. A bell rang in the building above. It brought Magrayn down from her post. He beckoned her to approach, and when she was within reach he laid a hand upon her disease-ravaged face.

"Sweet Magrayn," he smiled as he ran a fat finger perilously close to the wound that had eroded much of her nose. She returned the smile.

"Whisper in some ears for me, beloved," said Torquentine. "Cast out some bait. I want to know what has become of every member of the Lannis-Haig line. The Chancellor seems curious on the subject, and where a Chancellor's curiosity leads, there is often some profit to be found."

As the Chancellor made his way back through the shadowy lanes and alleyways, his guardians dogging his footsteps, he was preoccupied. An instinct deep in his guts, born of long years of reading the signs, whispered to him of storms gathering. Events were taking on an unpleasantly chaotic, unpredictable character. Such times could be crucibles of opportunity, and thus welcome, but they were seldom gentle on a man's nerves. Lannis-Haig should not have crumbled so quickly. And those children of Kennet nan Lannis-Haig's: what had become of them, if they were not dead with their father in Kolglas? It might complicate matters if there was some orphaned runt of a boy running around trying to salvage something from the wreckage of the Lannis Blood. That was exactly the kind of situation Aewult would mishandle, preening himself at the head of his precious army.

Mordyn strove to set the thought aside. There was no knowing the truth of any of this for the moment. All would become clear soon enough. But still, he could not shake a sense of foreboding. He had a powerful urge to be in Tara's arms, to take comfort from her familiar, intoxicating charms. He lengthened his stride and hastened back toward his Palace of Red Stone.

VI

The morning in the Car Criagar was bright and crisp and clear, as brazen as if no day there ever started differently. All through the night the winds had raged around the mountain tops, whipping snow and sleet over the rocks. The storm had blown itself out before dawn, calmed by the approaching sun.

Standing on the wide ledge outside the entrance to Yvane's bolt-hole, Orisian gazed across the ruin-veined landscape before him. On days such as this, couched in the grandeur of the mountains, arrayed beneath a broad, blue sky, the city must have been a glorious sight when it lived. Whoever its inhabitants had been, they must have been stirred by the marvelous conspiracy of sky and rock that surrounded them.

Rothe was crouched down at Orisian's side, trying to sharpen his sword with a whetstone Yvane had found for him. His efforts were punctuated by occasional, almost inaudible, curses at the inadequacy of the little stone. Varryn and Ess'yr were down below, cautiously scouting through the closest of the ruins. There had been no sign or sound of intruders in the long hours they had spent in the cave, but neither of the Kyrinin seemed reassured. Despite their reticence and restraint, Orisian suspected they would be as glad as anyone to leave this place. The only question that remained was whether Yvane would accompany them. The *na'kyrim* had gone off some time ago, promising to return with supplies for their journey.

Anyara came to stand beside Orisian.

"A strange place," she said.

"It is," he agreed. "It's amazing. I wish Inurian was here to see it. He could have told us more about it, I expect."

"Yes," said Anyara softly. She looked down at her hands, loosely clasped before her. "I miss him very much. I know I never spent as much time with him as you did, but after Winterbirth . . . he did his best to look after me."

"He always did that," Orisian said. "You, Father, me; he looked after all of us, in different ways. You think you know how important someone is, but it's never real until they're gone." He shook his head disconsolately. "I thought I knew him well, you know. But with Ess'yr, Highfast, Yvane . . . I feel like I know less about him now than I did a month ago."

"You know the most important thing: that he cared for you. That he cared for us all."

Orisian narrowed his eyes, staring into the distance.

"He told me not to wish for things I couldn't have, but how can I not? I'd change everything if I could. Everything, right back to . . . I want to see our father again. See him the way he was when everyone was alive. Is it so bad to wish for something like that?"

Anyara put an arm about his shoulders. Grief was a dangerous territory for the two of them to share. Orisian always feared that if he or Anyara let the other see a fraction too much of the sorrows they had borne, neither would be able to hold back the rest.

"I am afraid, Orisian."

It was not something he could ever remember her saying before. The Fever had taken her to the very edge of the Sleeping Dark; she had once come within moments of drowning in the harbor of Kolglas; still further back, Orisian had a memory of watching her fall from high in a tree outside the town, bouncing and crashing through lower boughs on her way down. Yet she had never spoken of fear. He had learned, so young that he knew it in the same way he knew the trees would lose their leaves in autumn, that fear did not touch Anyara. Now that knowledge seemed, like many other things, an obviously childish thought to be set aside.

"Afraid of what?" he asked.

Anyara almost laughed. "You choose," she said. Then: "Dying. Being alone. You, me, Rothe — we only have each other now."

"And we will not lose each other. But there may still be others, anyway. We have to hold on to that hope."

"Spoken like a true Thane," Anyara said. He looked at her sharply, to find a sad smile upon her face. "Well, you are, aren't you? You must be."

"Oh, Anyara, I hope not."

She squeezed him tightly, all of a sudden the elder sister once more.

"If you are, you will be a good one," she said, releasing him from her grasp.

He looked at her. "Good or bad, I will have to try, won't I? All my wishes are only wishes. I wouldn't have chosen any of this — none of us would — but we are here nevertheless. If there is no one else, I will have to try."

She took his hand in hers and they stood together like that for a little while, brother and sister side by side, looking out over the wasteland where the ruins lay silently beneath the winter sun.

When Yvane returned, she brought little deerskin packets of food, walking staffs and fur strips to bind around their boots.

"Better than nothing," she said as she dropped it all into a pile at her feet.

"Are you coming with us?" Orisian asked her.

"Yes, yes. Some of the way, at least. Perhaps all the way to Koldihrve."

"I'm glad."

The *na'kyrim* gave a little laugh and shot a sharp look at him.

"You shouldn't be," she said. "It's a bad sign, if you'd the sense to read it."

He waited patiently for her to explain.

"I don't know what those Fox have found," Yvane said with a vague wave in the direction of Ess'yr and Varryn, still searching amongst the rubble below, "but I've seen enough to know I'd do well to spend a little time away from here. There's tracks of dogs — big ones, too — and men in the freshest snow. Definitely been someone poking around in the night. And to have kept going through that storm, they must be very serious about their work."

Orisian looked uneasily out over the ruined city. Nothing moved. The broken walls and crumbling stonework lay silent beneath their cloak of snow.

"If I stay behind, whoever it is might go off on your trail but then again they might not. And even if they do, perhaps they'd dig me out of one of my hideaways before leaving. However much I like my solitude, I'm not stupid. I'll take my chances with you."

Orisian nodded.

"Of course," Yvane added sharply, "if you hadn't seen fit to turn up, all uninvited, I'd still have my nice quiet life to enjoy."

"The uninvited guests who came to my home cost me a good deal more than we've cost you," Orisian snapped, and scrambled down from the platform. Fresh snow crunched beneath his feet as he made his way to join Ess'yr. The Kyrinin was crouching down beside a heap of building stones, letting her delicate fingertips drift almost randomly across their pitted, lichen-strewn surfaces. Orisian stood behind her, caught for a moment by the shimmer of the winter sun on her hair.

"Dog," she murmured. She turned her head and looked up at him with those clear grey eyes. She held a fingertip out, and he could just see a short, thick strand of hair on it.

"Yvane says they've been in the ruins during the night. She's coming with us."

"Best if we go now," said Ess'yr. She rose to her feet in a single flowing movement. "We cannot hide from them, so best to be in the open. Then we see them coming."

They followed Yvane north along the base of the cliffs. All of them were tense, wary. Even Yvane seemed uneasy amongst the ruins. Orisian, for the first time in his life, longed for the feel of a sword at his hip, or any weapon better than the little knife he carried on his belt.

They came out of Criagar Vyne with nothing to disturb the silence save the sound of ravens croaking on the rocky heights above them. This time, with the furs Yvane had given them and her staffs to lean on, they were better equipped to brave the bleak lands beyond. It was enough to keep them almost comfortable even when they came out from beneath the shelter of the cliffs and the wind picked up.

On a day such as this — bright and wide — the mountains were a sight to behold. Orisian could imagine that the Car Criagar was asleep, resting in the lull before the next storm swept down from the Tan Dihrin. Great peaks surrounded them, studded by pinnacles and turrets of rock. The stillness was so deep that it was possible to believe they were the only living things to have trodden this path in innumerable years. All the vast age and patient indifference of the mountains was there like a taste in the air as they made their way northward.

Once the ruins were well behind them, the Kyrinin at least relaxed. The open slopes offered little chance of ambush. Even so, Varryn would now and then stand for a time looking back the way they had come. They rested a while in the early afternoon, quietly sharing food and water. The sun was almost hot upon their faces, but it did not last. Thin skeins of cloud appeared across the blue expanse of the sky and by the time they began to search for a suitable sleeping place, the Car Criagar was sinking back into the muffling grey light it seemed almost to crave. There was no rain or snow at least, and as Yvane led them to a notch in the hillside they could hope for a more comfortable night than some of those they had recently known.

Yvane knew what she was doing in choosing that hollow for the night: reaching into a crack beneath a pitted boulder, she withdrew a sack of kindling and firewood.

"Better to have no fire," Varryn said.

Yvane emptied the sack out and began sorting the wood.

"You can have no fire if you like," she said, "but I don't like the cold. If anyone is following us, they'll know where we are well enough with or without a fire."

There was little talking after that. All of them were preoccupied by their own thoughts as the fire held their eyes and the night settled in, closing the world around them down into a small pocket of light.

It was as they settled to sleep that the sound came, as startling as the shattering of glass in the darkness: a brief howl. Moments later a second answered it. They seemed distant, but it was hard to tell.

"Might be glad we have a fire, if it comes to it," was all Yvane said as the sound faded away and an unnerving silence descended.

The last thing Orisian saw before he passed into a shallow sleep was Varryn sitting straight and alert, bathed in firelight, his face turned out toward the night and his hands resting upon bow and spear.

In the morning Varryn was still seated where Orisian had last seen him, as if no more than a moment had passed. The weather had closed in. Yvane exchanged a few words with Varryn in the Fox tongue, but they said nothing to the others. At another time Orisian would have wanted to know what they discussed; now there seemed no point. There was, after all, nothing to do save press on, even if a score of Inkallim were treading in their footprints.

Their path now lay downward and away from the highest peaks, but the Car Criagar would not let them go without one last reminder of its true nature. Low cloud, a hard wind and wet snow accompanied them. The further north they went, and the further from the heart of the range, the more characterless the slopes became. The dramatic rocks and screes of the heights were replaced by great featureless snow fields.

Orisian found himself striding along beside Yvane.

"How long to get to Koldihrve?" he asked her. It was hard work, fighting through the deepening snow, and he was out of breath, but the relentless silence of the mountains had begun to seem oppressive to him.

"Not long," the *na'kyrim* said.

"That's a Kyrinin answer," Orisian observed.

"Where is it you want to go, anyway? Not Koldihrve, I mean, but after that. What are you going to do?"

"Go to Glasbridge, or to Kolglas, if we can find the boat we need at Koldihrve. I have to fight the Black Road; restore my Blood. I have had enough of running, of hiding," Orisian said. And of losing people, he thought.

"Be careful not to dress revenge in finer clothes than it deserves. You can't always get back what's gone. I wouldn't try to, if I was you; disappointment can do strange things to people."

"You don't understand. The Black Road has destroyed my home, my family. They've taken our lands. I'm bound by oath to defend my Blood against its enemies."

"Who is it you think is watching you?" said Yvane irritably. "There're no gods now, if there ever were, so they'll not be your judges. Is it the dead? Better to leave that to the Kyrinin. What will you do when you've killed all of those who killed your dead? Sit back and wait for your own victims' children to arrive, knife in hand, at your bedside one night? Blood for blood, life for life down through all the ages. That's a kind future you're planning for yourself and your kin. Think how much happier the world might be if people sought approval for what they do from their children instead of their ancestors."

"What would you have me do?" demanded Orisian. "Run away? Hide in a cave somewhere?" He allowed anger to color his voice.

"In truth," sighed Yvane, "I don't much care. All your Thanes and warlords always think they are the ones making everything happen, making the decisions. As often as not, they're plain wrong. Life has its own patterns, its chances and fortunes: they trip up great lords just as surely as the commonfolk. Whatever plans you lay, like as not they'll twist and turn in your hands. Just be sure why you do what you do. I long ago wearied of people who spend all their time digging up old hatreds and polishing them up for fresh use. The past's like a maggot in the heart of the present; it fouls it."

Orisian looked down, watched his feet sweeping through the snow for a few strides.

"It's not revenge I want," he said. He had tasted a little of vengeance, when that Tarbain's blood had splashed out over his hands. It had not soothed the ache within him, and it had not brought back any of those who had died. It had not even saved the woodcutter's family. "I want . . . to end it. It's the future I want to see changed, not the past. If you can tell me how to stop what's happening . . . if you can tell me how to stop that without taking up a sword against the Black Road, I'll listen. But I don't think you can. And I know as well as you that nothing will make the dead live again, but that's not the same as wishing they had not died. How could I not wish that of people I loved?"

Yvane smiled sadly. "You couldn't. No one could ask you to." She glanced up at the listless sky. "We have to forgive ourselves for all the ways we failed the dead, you know. And forgive them for all the burdens they leave us; all the ways in which they failed us. Especially for dying."

413

Orisian felt a tightening in his throat, and had to close his eyes for a moment. They strode on without speaking.

They had been walking for what seemed like hours when Rothe stopped. Orisian followed his shieldman's gaze and saw why. Above and behind them, on a low ridge they had crossed less than an hour ago, the wind had whipped the snow up into twisting curtains that danced along the crest. Through those veils, a vague figure could be seen. It flickered in and out of sight as the cloud and snow washed around it. Orisian narrowed his eyes. It might have been an outcrop of rock, but no . . . it shifted slightly, parted. Up there on the ridge, a tall man was standing with a great hound at his side.

"It's the Hunt," Rothe murmured. "It must be."

Yvane began striding with greater urgency through the ankle-deep snow.

"Keep moving," she shouted over her shoulder. "It's not far to the tree line. There's no sense in trying to hide out here."

They fell in behind her, following a course diagonally down the slope. Rothe drew his sword. Low cloud came across the hillside, enclosing them in a dampening mist. They were alone again, struggling across the snow field in the midst of a grey sky. It was worse, in a way, to know what was behind them but not be able to see their hunters. Their pace picked up a little. The backward glances were more frequent, more urgent, but told them nothing.

"Have a care, have a care," muttered Rothe, as much to himself as to anyone else. The mist deadened his voice.

"Faster," Yvane called out, and stretched her stride. The snow hampered them, clinging to their legs as if it did not want them to leave its domain. Orisian wondered how long they could keep this up. He wanted to run, but knew that would only bring exhaustion. Without thinking about it, he pulled his knife from its sheath.

"They are on us!" Ess'yr cried. She and Varryn spun around in the same moment, springing apart and hefting their spears.

"The cloud's thinning," Rothe said, and in that same moment the beast was there.

Orisian had only half a second to take in what he was seeing: a great hound, massive and wild as a boar. It erupted out of the concealing mists in a flurry of snow. Ess'yr was the closest, and it rushed straight down upon her. She sank a little lower at the hips, her thighs tensing. Varryn made no move to help his sister: he was staring fixedly back up the slope in the direction from which the dog had emerged.

The hound sprang. Ess'yr swayed to one side and flung it aside with the butt of her spear. The animal drove a great furrow through the snow as it slithered on down the slope.

"Get back," Orisian shouted to Anyara.

Rothe took a great bound forward, seized Anyara's shoulder and threw her away as the hound rolled to its feet. It was far too agile, too quick, for its size, Orisian thought. Rothe lashed out with his sword. The hound shied away from the blade, gathered itself and leapt for Rothe all in the blink of an eye.

Varryn shouted something in the language of the Fox. Orisian glanced at him, in time to see the Kyrinin duck his head a fraction to avoid a crossbow bolt that flashed out of the misty vapors and as quickly vanished back into them. Varryn dropped his spear and swung his own bow over his shoulder.

Rothe was crying out in rage or pain. He was thrashing on the ground, the hound's jaw locked on the wrist of his arm. His sword was gone, flung away in the frenzy of shaking and pulling. Anyara was shouting too as she flailed at the dog with her walking staff. The crack of wood on bone said she found her mark more than once, but the beast ignored the blows as if they were gnat bites to a bull. Orisian threw himself across the hound's back. He felt the immense strength of its neck as it shook its head back and forth, smelled its musty, thick hair. He stabbed it in its ribcage, again and again, until it went limp.

He looked up in a kind of numb surprise, and saw the Hunt Inkallim coming an instant before even the Kyrinin did. The man seemed to solidify out of the clouds, but did so at full speed, flying light-footed through the snow directly for Ess'yr, brandishing a quarterstaff that was bladed at both ends.

A warning began to form on Orisian's lips but thought and voice could not hope to keep pace with a clash between Kyrinin and Hunt Inkallim. Even taken unawares, Ess'yr found the time to bring her spear up. Without slowing, the Inkallim veered sideways. The point of the spear went across his flank, caught in his deerskin jerkin and snapped him around. He leapt into a spin and his staff came in a huge arc, too quick for the eye to follow. Ess'yr was faster than any human could have been. Still, it was not enough; the blow took her below the sternum, flung her like a child's doll through the air to thump into the snow a few yards away. She lay still.

Rothe surged to his feet, spilling both Orisian and the hound's corpse as he rose. The shieldman clasped a hand about his blood-stained wrist, and took a lurching step toward the Inkallim.

Varryn hissed: an inhuman, piercing sound. The Inkallim flicked his head round. Varryn was motionless. He was perfectly poised in the still moment a hunter would seek: unbreathing, feet firmly planted, bowstring taut, the fletching of the arrow brushing his face. The Inkallim began to move. The arrow was released. In an instant it crossed the space between Kyrinin and human, and cracked into the Inkallim's cheek. The moment the bowstring snapped out of his hand, Varryn was rushing to Ess'yr.

"My sword," Rothe cried.

"I can't see it," Orisian heard Anyara shout.

The Hunt Inkallim turned unsteadily back toward the shieldman. Varryn's arrow stood rigid in his face, rooted in a nest of blood and bone. A mad, desperate grin split the man's face. Blood was spilling out over his lips. Orisian threw his knife: he was unskilled in the art, but it was made for throwing and it found a home high on the Inkallim's chest.

Rothe stretched out his uninjured arm toward Anyara.

"Your staff," he said.

She passed it to him in silence. The Inkallim made to raise his own weapon, but all his strength and grace were gone. He was rocking on his feet. He watched limply as Rothe came up and struck him a great blow on the side of the head. The Inkallim fell. His legs kicked feebly as he lay face-down in the snow.

"Leave him, leave him!" Yvane was shouting. Already, she was heading off, straight down the slope. "He wasn't alone."

Varryn slung his sister's bow across his shoulders with his own and lifted Ess'yr. Her arms and legs dangled limply. Carrying both her and his spear, Varryn began to run after Yvane.

Rothe was scrabbling clumsily in the snow. Blood falling from his wounds left pinpricks of red in the whiteness.

"Where's my sword?" he cried, sounding grief-struck.

"Leave it," shouted Orisian, hauling at his shieldman's arm. Rothe resisted for a moment.

"Rothe! Do as I say. Leave it." Even to his own ears, Orisian's voice had an arresting edge of command to it.

Yvane cried, "We must go!" back over her shoulder.

They took great leaping strides through the snow. Rothe held himself at the back, even though he had nothing now save a knife with which to defend Orisian and Anyara.

Their flight was wild, uncontrolled, but the attack they feared never came. When they broke free of the cloud's embrace they found themselves rushing down toward a distant dark line of trees. The snow was thinning, the ground more even.

Though he could hardly raise his eyes from the point of his next footfall, Orisian was aware of a great vista spread out before them. They had come out onto the northern flank of the Car Criagar and the Dihrve valley lay ahead and below. Beyond that broad plain, like a magnified reflection of the mountains behind them, the immense heights of the Car Dine rose up.

At last, coming to the first scrawny trees, Yvane allowed them to pause. Even Varryn was breathing hard as he knelt and laid

Ess'yr down. A look of concern emerged through the fierce tattoos on his face as he leaned over his sister and listened to her breathing. Delicately, he ran his fingers over her side, feeling for injuries. Then he sat back and gently brushed strands of hair from her forehead.

"How is she?" Orisian panted.

"Broken," Varryn said. He gestured at his own ribcage. "Here."

"*Lamman* root would be best," said Yvane distractedly. She was looking back up the slope, her eyes narrowed. "But we do not have the time to search for it now."

Rothe was at her side, surveying the higher slopes just as she did. The distant banks of cloud that still cloaked the mountains were a blank, impenetrable wall. There was no hint of movement.

"Perhaps they will give up the chase now we have bloodied them," he said.

"Perhaps," murmured Yvane. "Will you allow a *na'kyrim* to bind that wrist for you?"

Rothe nodded in agreement. He turned and watched Varryn as Yvane began rooting somewhere beneath her cloak for bandage materials. "You have a keen aim," he said.

"Kyrinin aim," was Varryn's brusque reply, but after a moment he seemed to think better of his curtness, and he looked up at the shieldman. "Not so keen. I went for the eye."

"A good try, still," replied Rothe. "That arrow saved us a lot of trouble."

Varryn shrugged; it was not as cold a gesture as once might have passed between the two. They rested only for a minute or two, and then resumed a more cautious descent. Ess'yr woke, grimacing in pain, her face whiter than ever it had been before. Varryn supported her as she hobbled down through the woods.

These forests were different to those of the Glas valley. Pines dominated them. Mostly they were small, cold- and wind-bent things, but in places they crowded so close together that they cast a black shade. The earth was carpeted with browned needles and wiry grass. Here and there tree roots had been forced to the surface by hidden rocks or stone faces. The place had a foreign feel, fit for the old tales of savage Kyrinin, watchful Anain or even the wolfish Whreinin.

They had crossed into a land where only masterless humans roamed, where the Bloodoath or the concerns of Lannis and Horin meant nothing. Now more than ever, Orisian thought, they were in the hands of their inhuman companions. This was their land.

In the gathering dusk they made a camp of sorts amidst the trees. Varryn laid a fire against the foot of a sloping rock and then, once Ess'yr was settled by the flames, disappeared into the forest without a word of explanation. Orisian guessed he had gone to search for the root he needed to ease his sister's pain.

There was a great dormant ant hill a few yards from their resting place, a smooth mound of pine needles that bulbed up from the ground. Yvane was crouched beside it, probing it with a thin twig. The image was strangely familiar to Orisian. It was some time before he could recall why: the last time he had been alone with Inurian, the *na'kyrim* had been searching for sea urchins beside Castle Kolglas with a long stick.

"What are you doing?" he asked her, as he had asked Inurian then.

"Distracting myself from our difficulties. Ants make good food if you are hungry enough." She smiled at his involuntary grimace. "Though I suppose we're not that hungry yet." She set aside the twig and rose a little stiffly to her feet.

"I have not stretched my legs so vigorously for a long time," she muttered. There was a touch of irritation in her voice. She disliked her own weakness.

"Mine are getting used to running," he said.

"Well, we may be clear of trouble for now," said Yvane as she led him back toward the fire. "Hopefully we can walk the rest of the way to Koldihrve."

Rothe was sitting on a stone, his unsheathed knife resting on his thigh, gazing into the fire. Orisian felt a twinge of sympathy for his shieldman. It would be a torment to Rothe to be without his sword; unable, as he would see it, to properly protect Orisian. And Orisian had, he glumly reflected, left his own knife — the Inkallim blade — behind, resting in the chest of their pursuer.

Anyara was already dozing, sitting against a tree trunk with her patchy fur jacket draped over her like a blanket. Her head nodded on her chest and every now and again she made a soft murmuring sound.

"We all need some rest," said Yvane softly.

Orisian stretched out close to the fire. He should be afraid, he knew, of what might come in the night. It seemed he was too tired for fear, though, since he soon drifted off toward sleep with the soft crackling of the flames in his ears.

He came briefly to befuddled wakefulness in the depths of the night, roused by some sound. The fire still blazed and he could see nothing beyond its glare. From somewhere in the darkness, muted voices were coming. Drowsy apprehension had just begun to rise in his breast when he recognized them: Rothe and Varryn, deep in conversation. In the few moments before sleep reclaimed him, Orisian recognized that fact for the small wonder it was.

They woke to rain. It was a miserable morning. The fire died quickly. Varryn kicked earth over the embers and then spread them out with his foot. The rain grew heavier as they descended through the forest, but it was at least better than snow and biting wind. They found a rocky stream and drank from it. Ess'yr could not bend to drink, and Varryn raised water to her lips in his cupped palms. Orisian could well imagine the pain each step must bring her. The wound in his own side still made itself known every now and then, not by pain exactly, but a taut tenderness. To see Ess'yr struggling with her own injury brought home how graceful she had been before. He had almost stopped noticing her poise and precision; now that it was stripped from her its absence was glaring, like a bird that could not fly.

The rain eased off toward midday, and the going became easier as the slope flattened out. At last, there came a moment when the gradient disappeared altogether, and for the first time in what seemed an age there was only flat ground beneath their feet and before their eyes. Anyara gave a heartfelt sigh of relief and even Rothe could not keep a slight smile from his lips.

"Welcome to the valley of the Dihrve," said Yvane. "Some call it the Vale of Tears, but we may hope for rather happier times here perhaps."

Varryn exchanged a few words with Ess'yr. They seemed to agree on something.

"There is a *vo'an*," said Ess'yr. "One or two hours. We can rest there."

Nobody disagreed, though Orisian caught a surprised, perhaps even shocked, expression on Anyara's face. It was easy to forget she had not been where he had.

"It'll be fine," he said to her, and tried to put strength into his smile.

Aged willows covered the damp ground. The trees were too uniformly old and thinly spaced to be a *dyn hane,* but still the place had a haunted, wild feel to it, as if it had a life of its own upon which Orisian and the others were intruding. Fallen trunks lay all around, being slowly sucked into the earth by swathes of moss and fungus.

They halted in a clearing and sat on a hummock that was the closest thing to dry ground.

"We are close," Ess'yr said. Her words were breathy, each one costing her some pain. It made Orisian wince in sympathy. "We will go in, ask leave for you to come. Wait here."

"Be certain," said Orisian softly. "No arguments about being sent to the willow this time."

"No," agreed Ess'yr.

"Leave us a spear, at least," said Rothe to Varryn. "We've no weapons save my knife and these walking staffs."

The words seemed to wash straight over the Kyrinin. He and Ess'yr disappeared to the north, leaving the others to sit and watch the clouds scudding overhead. Tiny brown birds were hopping around amongst the undergrowth.

"Are we sure this is safe?" asked Anyara.

"Not entirely," replied Rothe before Orisian could draw breath.

"They wouldn't have brought us here if it wasn't safe," Orisian said.

"That's true enough," said Yvane quietly. "They think we've rid ourselves of hunters, at least for now, or they'd not have left us. Ess'yr certainly would do nothing to put you at risk." She looked from Orisian to Anyara. "Do you understand the *ra'tyn*? The pledge she has made?"

Orisian frowned, not understanding. The word *ra'tyn* was vaguely familiar, but at first he could not say where he had heard it before. Then it came to him that Inurian had spoken it, when he lay by the Falls of Sarn. It had been a part of what he had said to Ess'yr; and Ess'yr had said something, in the moments before Yvane found them in Criagar Vyne, about having sworn an oath of some sort. He had forgotten about it.

"I didn't think so," mused Yvane. "She'll not tell you herself, that's certain. I overheard them talking — arguing would be more precise, I suppose — about it back in the ruins. In any case, you can rest easy that she will not put you in danger."

"But they cannot speak for the wights in this camp," muttered Rothe.

"Things go a little differently in the Dihrve valley," said Yvane. "Huanin and Kyrinin share much of the land here. It's a rough kind of peace but it's peace nevertheless, so I'll give you a word of advice; two, in fact. Do not speak of 'wights' too freely here. It is something you would call an enemy, and as I say, things go a little differently here. Second, no Kyrinin will be willingly parted from spear or bow while they are outside a camp. For a Huanin to be asking for it . . . Varryn bears the full *kin'thyn,* and he didn't get that by being shy about spilling blood. He must like you, or he'd have given you the spear point first."

Rothe lapsed into glum silence after that. Once, Orisian thought, the shieldman might have had something to say about Kyrinin pride.

Time slipped by. They ate and drank. Orisian and Anyara dozed. There was a rustling amongst the trees to the west of them that had Rothe springing upright and clutching his dagger. For a few moments they were all poised, listening intently for any other sound. Then there was a sharp, grunting bark and the sound of some animal bounding off through the woods.

"Marsh deer," said Yvane.

Varryn returned alone. He had been gone no more than a couple of hours.

"Come," was all he said.

This was a very different *vo'an* to the one Orisian had seen before. Emerging from the dense woodland they arrived upon the brink of a lake fringed with vast swathes of reeds and rushes. The winter camp reached out over the marsh and water on stilted platforms and jetties of wood. There were many huts made of animal hides stretched across wooden frames, more permanent structures than the domed tents he had seen in In'hynyr's camp. At the edge of the platforms were tethered rafts of logs which supported more shelters. A powerful scent spilled from sheds where racks of fish hung over smoking fires. The whole place had a settled feel that suggested it had been here for many years; there were probably twice as many Kyrinin here as in the *vo'an* on the southern flanks of the Car Criagar. A few children stopped what they were doing to watch the strange party as Varryn led them up onto one of the platforms, but the adults largely ignored them.

Varryn guided them to a hut out over the water.

"Sleep here," he said. "I speak with the *vo'an'tyr*."

"Where's Ess'yr?" Orisian asked. "Is she all right?"

Varryn nodded. "She will rest. You all rest."

"And tomorrow?"

"Is tomorrow," Varryn said, with the faintest shrug of his shoulders. "No harm comes here."

VII

The Black Road had taken over the old inn at Sirian's Dyke. The inn's staff were dead or had taken flight, like all the inhabitants of the village. Shraeve's Inkallim had put a guard on the stores of ale and wine, but some of the food stocks had been shared out. In the hot, crowded room where weary travelers had rested and slaked their thirst, warriors now jostled for space in a constant hubbub of excited talk and shouts. The mood was good even without the encouragement of drink; almost all of them had been present at the fall of Castle Anduran, and that victory still intoxicated them.

Their advance down the valley had been unopposed, until they came to Sirian's Dyke itself. Just outside the village they had routed a motley force of two hundred Lannis men — warriors and commonfolk mixed together — and they had done it by the strength of their arms alone. The woodwights had melted away, gone to wage their own war against the Fox; almost all of the Tarbains had scattered to plunder hamlets and farmsteads; nobody had seen the *na'kyrim* Aeglyss since Kanin had confronted him in the White Owl camp outside Anduran. It was a purer fight now, Blood against Blood, and tasted the better for it.

Despite the press of bodies in the room, there was space around one table: the best table, close by the blazing fire. Wain, Shraeve and Cannek sat there, eating in silence. In the days since Kanin left for the Car Criagar, Wain and Shraeve had become the center of all attention, the focus of the army's strength, the wellspring of its faith. And so everyone kept a respectful distance from the sister of the new Horin-Gyre Thane and the mistress of the Battle. Cannek of the Hunt passed almost unnoticed, which was as he would wish it.

Shraeve disposed of the bread and meat in front of her methodically, without enthusiasm. One of her Inkallim came and placed a flagon of wine on the table.

"I thought we should allow ourselves some celebration," Shraeve said in response to Wain's questioning look. "They deserve it."

Inkallim were coming out from the kitchens, distributing similar flagons around the room. They were met with roars and cheers that might have shaken loose the roof timbers. Cannek winced at the eruption of joy.

"We agreed to keep it locked away," Wain said.

Shraeve smiled icily. "There's not enough to cause any trouble, and they've fought hard enough to earn it, don't you think?"

Wain glanced around, noting that none of the Inkallim were sharing in the bounty their leader thought they had earned. Shraeve had been more forward since Kanin had left. Before, she had been content to exert absolute power over her own Inkallim; now she was finding small ways to spread her net wider, as if she wanted to test Wain's patience. It might have to come to a head, but tonight was not the time.

Cannek pushed away his plate, leaving half the food uneaten. He drained a cup of wine and rose.

"I will leave you two fell ladies to your pleasantries," he smiled. "I've work to do tonight. We're going to take a look down the road to Glasbridge."

"I've a dozen scouts out that way already," muttered Wain.

Cannek shrugged. "We of the Hunt like to feel useful," he said lightly. "You wouldn't want us loitering around here at a loose end, would you?"

As her fellow Inkallim departed Shraeve laid down a chicken

leg she had been gnawing. She pressed a cloth precisely against her lips, leaving small greasy stains on the material.

"It is best to leave the Hunt to their own devices," she murmured. "However good your scouts are, Cannek's are better. If there was only a single mouse in a field of oats, the Hunt could find it."

"Yet they cannot tell me what has become of Aeglyss, can they? Or is it will not?"

Shraeve gave a disinterested shrug of her shoulders. She was not looking at Wain; her eyes drifted idly over the crowds that filled the inn. Faces were reddening, now that the wine and ale were flowing, and voices grew louder.

"He slipped by all of us," the Inkallim said. "The woodwights are cunning enough to test even the Hunt's skills. Anyway, does it matter? Your brother made it clear he had no further use for him, or for the White Owls."

"It matters little," Wain replied. She was careful to keep her tone flat, unrevealing. In truth, she was uneasy that the *na'kyrim* had disappeared, and with him the alliance — however illusory — he had forged on Horin-Gyre's behalf with the White Owls. Her father had always seen Aeglyss as nothing more than a key to unlock the door to Lannis-Haig, to be discarded once his usefulness was at an end. Now that the breach had come, though, Wain suspected it would have been better had they killed him. As it was, he was wandering around somewhere, out of their sight and out of their reach. However useful he had proved, he had also proven himself unpredictable, perhaps dangerously so.

"I only regret that we don't know where he is," she said, "and what he's doing. I would not want him to turn up again unexpectedly, interfering."

Shraeve gave her a sudden, bleak smile.

"There is no wrong or right on the Black Road, only the unfolding of its inevitable course. You know that as well as I." Then she would say nothing else.

Wain took to her own room not long after. The evening had left a sour, unsettling twist in her thoughts. It did not overly concern her. The Black Road always went its own way; always confounded the expectations of those who walked it. Learning and accepting that was at the root of the creed. Yet . . . given their astonishing success in the last few weeks, it was strange that there was so little room in her mind for joy, for exultation. There were too many things casting small shadows across her to allow for that: Kanin pursuing his own, personal fate in the Car Criagar; Aeglyss and the White Owls off the leash; the Inkallim watching everything with their cold eyes. Wain was no longer sure this was the same war her dead father had set in motion.

* * *

Deep in the heart of the forest that the Huanin called Anlane, but they knew as *Antyryn Hyr* — the Thousand Tree-clad Valleys — the small band of White Owl Kyrinin paused in a glade. They had been walking for two days and two nights, following one of the First Tracks made by the God Who Laughed in the dawn of the five races. Ever since leaving the city in the valley, they had not paused: no sleep, food eaten on the move, no slackening of their steady, remorseless pace southward through the forests that were their home.

Only one of the faithless Huanin had managed to track their departure from the valley. They had killed her, and her hound, on the second day. It would not be fitting for one of the Huanin to follow where they were going. They had stripped her body and left it on open ground where the eaters of the dead would quickly find it.

The *na'kyrim* had remained bound all this time. They kept his arms lashed behind him, and kept him gagged, for they knew that he had a deceitful voice. The lies he told had the power to twist the hearer's mind; the promises he made might put a hunger in the heart, but they had no more substance than the dew glistening on a spider's web. It was in answer to promises broken, to hopes unfulfilled, that they had brought him all this way while their brothers and sisters hunted the enemy in the mountains beyond the valley. Every one of them would prefer to be amongst those making war upon the Fox, for they knew that this would be a war unlike anything that had gone before. The hated Huanin had ruled in the valley for hundreds of years, putting such a barrier between Fox and White Owl that only small raiding parties could make the crossing; now, with the strife between the Huanin tribes, the gate had been thrown open. The Black Road Huanin might have proved no more true to their word, no more trustworthy, than any others of their kind, but they had at least allowed hundreds of White Owls to march across the valley and into the enemy's lands. It would be a bathing of spears to break the hearts of the Fox.

Still, all the promises of friendship, of alliance and benefit, that this *na'kyrim* had brought to the White Owls those many months ago had melted away like snow in the season of breaking buds. These warriors had seen with their own eyes the lord of the Huanin strike down the *na'kyrim,* curse him and cast him out from his councils and confidence. Where were the cattle, the iron that had been promised? Why were there still Huanin villages and huts standing on the naked ground that had been carved out of the *Antyryn Hyr*'s northern flanks? Why had the Huanin lords turned against the White Owls, after so much aid had been given? For all of this, there must be an answering. The *na'kyrim* was the child of a White Owl mother. They had made honest agreements with him, and held fast to them as they would with one of their people. He must answer for the ruin of those agreements.

They were within a day's journey of their destination now. The First Track which they followed would run straight and true — and invisible to all save Kyrinin eyes — down into a great bowl of trees, across the wet, low land beneath that canopy and on to the very heart of their clan, the oldest and greatest *vo'an* of the White

Owls. The camp lay upon the shallow, south-facing slope of a vale of oak and ash trees. Each winter for many lifetimes, hundreds had gathered there to see out the cold months. Their tents would be scattered across the valleyside, half-hidden by the venerable trees that sheltered and guarded them.

The Voice of the White Owl, as always, would have been amongst the first to arrive at those wintering grounds. The great domed tent of many-layered deerskins that was the Voice's winter lodge would have been set up and formed the hub of the sprawling community that grew over the days and weeks. She slept there, and ate there, and gave her judgments. She listened to the songs that were sung on the bare ground before her lodge, and watched the *kakyrin* making their bone poles and weaving the *anhyne* there out of hazel and willow. When she dreamed, her predecessors whispered into her mind, for they knew where to find her. Sometimes, filled with their wisdom, she donned the white-feathered cape and mask and walked amongst her people as something other than herself. At winter's end, when the black ash buds broke, a new Voice for the clan might be chosen, but nothing would change. Next year the Voice, whether old or new, would again be in that valley, in the same tent on the same patch of ground.

And it was to the Voice that they had resolved to take the *na'kyrim.* It was with her he had spoken when he came on behalf of the Black Road Huanin; it was to her he had given false promises. It would be she who passed judgment upon him.

* * *

Wain pushed open the window and leaned out into the dull, cold early morning. The fresh air cut through the stuffy atmosphere of the room and made her shiver. She had slept badly, disturbed as much by her own unsettled spirits as by the noise rising from the inn below.

There were many warriors in the yard, cleaning weapons,

grooming their horses, tending cauldrons of steaming broth, dozing. Some stood around in quiet groups, arms folded and feet shifting against the chill. A few wore capes or coats they had looted from Anduran. It made them look a ragged collection.

Shraeve and a handful of her ravens came striding through the assembly. From her high vantage point Wain could see the uneasy glances, the sharp looks, that followed the Inkallim like a wake. Conversations paused as they drew near, then restarted once they had passed.

Shraeve looked up and nodded at Wain. I'm sister to the Thane, Wain thought, and still the Children of the Hundred think themselves my equal; or my better. She withdrew from the window. A bowl of icy water stood on the table at the foot of the bed. She plunged her face into it. It chased the last remnants of sleep from her.

Shraeve was waiting for her downstairs, feeding logs to the fire that had burned all night. Wain looked about for her own captains, but saw only a couple of them, silently breaking their fasts on bowls of oatmeal.

"Cannek sent word before dawn," Shraeve said. She kicked the fire with a booted foot, sending sparks spinning up the chimney and out across the flagstones.

"He did?" said Wain, casting about irritably for something to eat. Seeing nothing, she snapped at the seated Horin-Gyre warriors. "Find me some bread."

One of the men rose and disappeared in the direction of the kitchens.

"He did," said Shraeve. "There's another company gathered outside Glasbridge. What's left of the Lannis-Haig fighting strength, and half the hale men of the town from the sound of it. Enough to test us, perhaps."

Wain shot an irritated glare at the captain who emerged from the kitchens bearing a platter of bread and cheese for her. She snatched it from his hands.

"Where are my scouts?" she demanded of the startled man. "Why have I had no reports? Go and find someone who can tell me where they are."

The warrior left without hesitation, leaving his companion to hunch a little lower over his bowl of oatmeal and hope to avoid the wrath of the Thane's sister.

"They'll tell you the same as Cannek told me," Shraeve said.

"And why did he not tell me himself?" Wain demanded.

"I have come to tell you. What does it matter who bears the message?"

Wain sat down and began to tear at the bread. She did not like the Glas valley bread; it was not the same as the rich, coarse loaves they made north of the Stone Vale. Shraeve sat down opposite her without waiting for an invitation. The twinned swords strapped across her back loomed on the edge of Wain's vision like upraised fists.

"Very well," Wain said. "How many?"

"We cannot be certain, but Cannek's guess is a thousand Lannis fighting men and at least as many again townsfolk. And a few hundred Kilkry-Haig warriors: the survivors from Grive and a scattering of new arrivals."

Wain began to turn the thick band of gold on the second finger of her left hand. She frowned in concentration, her food forgotten now.

"Fewer than we met at Grive," she mused, "but then, we are far fewer now as well."

She had perhaps a thousand warriors within reach of Sirian's Dyke and fit to take the field. Another three hundred or so were back in Anduran, and must remain there to ensure the town and castle stayed secure. More than a thousand still besieged Tanwrye, along with hundreds from the other Bloods of the Black Road. They could not come to her aid until that obstinate town's garrison was broken. So, to face whatever threat might march up the road from Glasbridge she had at best a thousand swords, and the fifty or so of Shraeve's Battle Inkallim who remained alive and capable of wielding a blade. If Ragnor oc Gyre had answered their calls for aid, if he had sent just a fraction of his strength south . . . but the Black Road did not deal in ifs.

"We can make our stand here as well as anywhere else," she said. "If we take refuge inside Anduran we will only delay matters a little, until they can bring up enough strength to crush us there."

"Indeed," Shraeve agreed. She leaned forward, lowering her voice. "Perhaps we can hope for more than merely making a stand, though. Does your heart not hunger for Glasbridge? It's the last great town of Lannis-Haig. If we break it they'll be cast back all the way to Kolglas; we would hold the entire valley, from the Stone Vale to the sea."

"Of course I hunger for it. It was the home of my forefathers."

Shraeve sank back in her chair. "Your hunger might be sated yet, given the willing sacrifice of a few lives."

Wain sighed. "Whatever you have in mind, Shraeve, just tell me. My belly's too empty for talking in circles."

The Inkallim drove the four great horses past the inn. The beasts were massive, but bedraggled and cowed by the switches the ravens beat them with. Wain watched not the animals, but her own warriors who stood silently watching this strange procession. Wherever the ravens had found these horses — some farm outside Sirian's Dyke, no doubt — they knew how to make them into a spectacle. They herded them right through the village, through the Black Road army, and every curious eye followed their progress. Chains, scavenged from the smithy by the inn, dragged behind the horses, cutting ruts into the mud road.

A crowd followed the Inkallim and their horses to the edge of the village. The Inkallim went on, out onto the marshes that lay along the foot of the Dyke itself. Shraeve stood at Wain's side.

"It will give our people something to remember until their last day dawns," Shraeve murmured.

Wain did not reply. She knew that what Shraeve wanted all

these watching warriors to remember was that it was the Inkallim who had done this. What was about to happen would be a rich and nourishing symbol for the faithful, another story to add to the legends of the Children of the Hundred.

Out on the wettest ground, where sluices and pipes fed water over and through the huge dam and into the reborn Glas below it, some of the Inkallim turned back. Just six of their number remained with the uneasy, disheveled horses. One of them climbed to the top of the dam and stood there for a moment or two, looking north. The breeze stirred his black hair. Wain could imagine the sight that greeted him: the great expanse of listless water and perhaps far out, at the edge of his vision on this cloud-bleared day, the broken remnants of Kan Avor standing proud of the lake. Satisfied, he went back down to the horses, and the great task began.

The Inkallim dug away the earth and turf from the face of the dam; bound chains about the great logs that ran through it; whipped the horses until they put all their huge strength into the effort to pull the structure apart. As time passed, many of the watchers drifted away. The horses labored on, the Inkallim never paused. Timbers and rocks were scattered around the dam's foot. Water trickled through until the ravens were up to their knees. An hour passed, and then a second.

The sound began softly. A seething, hissing, heaving rumble, it built over long seconds. To Wain it was the sound and feel of sun-loosened snow crashing down some far-away mountain slope. Pebbles and clumps of earth were shaken loose from the sloping dam wall. Like blood spurting from myriad tiny wounds, water was flowing through the Dyke. The four great horses began to whinny in fear. They struggled against their chains; one bolted free and went pounding through the marshes in plumes of spray. The six Inkallim stood, gazing up at Sirian's Dyke. One turned toward Wain, Shraeve and the score or so of remaining watchers and raised her arm in silent salute.

And then all thought, all senses, were submerged beneath a great roar as the fabric of Sirian's Dyke began tearing itself apart. The seat of the rupture was deep and low in the dam, and it burst from its base, flicking rocks into the air and releasing jets and cascades of water. Billowing clouds of mist soared up and there was thunder as the center of the Dyke disintegrated and the river, freed of restraint for the first time in more than a century, burst in full, tumultuous flood down toward Glasbridge and the sea, bearing Inkallim and horses away in an instant.

CHAPTER
5
_____

Vale of Tears

Few stories are now told of the time before the Huanin and Kyrinin, the Whreinin and the Saolin walked the world; the time when the One Race was alone upon the face of the earth, before they went to war with the Gods and were unmade. One that is remembered in some places is the tale of how the valley of the Dihrve came to be called the Vale of Tears.

Harigaig kept a herd of great cattle by the mouth of the River Dihrve. One day a daughter of his was keeping watch over the cattle as they grazed at the river's edge. She lay down to rest beneath the Sun's gaze, and the voice of the water sang her to sleep. Then Dunkane, an enemy of Harigaig's from the north, rose up out of the river. He had walked along its bed from its source in the high mountains and come thus secretly to the heart of Harigaig's lands. His had been the soothing voice of the river.

Dunkane stole the cattle and drove them away to the north. When Harigaig discovered the theft, he took up his club and his staff and set out to follow the thief. Dunkane had hidden his tracks, but Harigaig knew many words that were charms, for he had run with the Wildling's Hunt as a child. He spoke to the rocks and the trees and the water, and they told him of his enemy's path. Thus Harigaig found his cattle walled up in a valley in the Tan Dihrin, and Dunkane feasting upon them there. The two faced one another, and grew into giants whose feet broke cliffs and split boulders open. For a *day and a night they fought back and forth across the mountains, until at the dawn of the second day Harigaig crushed Dunkane's head with his club and slew him. He freed his cattle and turned to go south once more, but he had taken grave wounds and as he walked his life began to flow out from his body.*

Now his family — his wife and his three daughters who would one day be the brides of the Gatekeeper — had followed after him, and they took him up and carried him south through the mountains and down the valley, and as they went they wept, for they could see that he would not keep hold of life. When they came to the sea, Harigaig was already dead. They took his body to a headland and cast it into the waves, where it turned to stone and became the island called Il Dromnone, which is, in a tongue long forgotten by all save a few tellers of tales, Isle of Mourning. And the tears shed on the journey of Harigaig's wife and daughters had been so plentiful that the valley down which they had borne him was filled up with them, in great lakes and pools that lie there still. And that is how the valley of the Dihrve found its true name.

from First Tales *transcribed by* Quenquane the Simple

I

In the heart of Kolkyre, atop a mound ringed by a crenellated wall, rose the Tower of Thrones. A bleak grey spike of stone, it dominated the city that lay around it. For two hundred and fifty years this had been the seat of the Kilkry Thanes and from its chambers and council rooms they had, for much of that time, ruled over all the Bloods. The greater power now lay in Vaymouth, but the tower kept its name and the Thanes still dwelled within it.

The Tower of Thrones was already ancient when Grey Kulkain, who was to become the first Thane of Kilkry, made it his home and fortress amidst the chaos of the Storm Years. It came from a time before the Aygll Kingship was born; before even the last of the Whreinin, the wolfenkind, were slain and the Gods departed. Beneath the bustling streets of Kolkyre lay an older place, which here and there reached up through the surface of the city in the form of a derelict wall or a stretch of strangely paved road. The Tower of Thrones alone of all the works of that first city's builders had survived intact. To some, its bleak perfection bore the mark of inhuman makers, and they called it, in hushed tones, the Spire of the First Race. For others, it had been the home of an unnamed human king who came long before the Aygll line, and whose reign and kingdom had passed from memory. Others still whispered of a forgotten *na'kyrim* lord who had raised it up with only the power of the Shared.

From a small, barred window high upon the tower's western flank, Taim Narran could see over the city to the foam-flecked sea beyond. The wind was driving waves up Anaron's Bay, piling them against the docks and quaysides of Kolkyre. Seagulls, grey-white curves against the dark water, were sliding across the wind. They were far away, and far below his lofty vantage point. There was a strange peace to be had from this distancing, Taim reflected, from being so aloof from the flow of events. He had been to Kolkyre many times before in his life, and until now its bustle and vigor — somehow more human and familiar than the chaos of Vaymouth — had been a pleasure. This time, his greatest wish was to be still, and separate, and apart from it all. He breathed deeply, savoring the sea tang borne up on the air.

A thick cough prompted him to turn away from the wide scene. Lheanor, the aging Thane of Kilkry, was sitting and watching him. Long grey hair framed the Thane's face. He was dabbing at his lips with a cloth.

"Forgive me," said Lheanor, "I did not mean to disturb your reverie. It is a long climb to this chamber, and my old carcass protests."

Taim smiled and shook his head. He gestured toward the window. "A beautiful view."

"It is. My father spent many hours here. It made him a touch morose; too much time to reminisce, I think. It reminded him of what we had lost."

"Yes," sighed Taim. "The past must be heavy here."

"Is there anywhere it rests lightly?" Lheanor murmured.

"Not in these days."

"You can tell a good deal about a man from what he feels when he looks out from a great height," the Thane said. "What do you feel?"

"Nothing good. Not today. But it is, nevertheless, a beautiful view."

He settled into a smaller seat beside Lheanor. They did not speak for some time. Taim's eyes closed and he rested. It had been a long time since he rested.

"I am sorry that our re-acquaintance has not been in better times," he heard Lheanor say, and looked round to the old man. "It was a sad enough sight to see you passing through on your way south at Gryvan's bidding. I thought your return, and Roaric's, would be a happier occasion."

"As did I," said Taim. "Roaric cannot be far behind me, though. The times may be dark, but at least he will be home."

"It's a poorer home he'll return to than the one he left. He had a brother then, before he went south." Taim averted his eyes. Lheanor's grief was too painfully apparent. It leaked out in his voice, beneath the words. "And what of your home, Taim? I and my Blood have failed your lord, and you."

"No," protested Taim. "You are the only true friends we have. The failure is not yours. That blame lies elsewhere."

Lheanor's brow was furrowed. "Blame; yes, there should be blame. For this plague of loss. But blame will not breathe life back into the dead. Anduran is gone, half of Kolglas burned, Glasbridge threatened. The enemy must have been at the walls of Tanwrye for weeks now; even if its defenders still hold, they are far beyond our help. As your Thane and all his family must be."

Taim pursed his lips and bowed his head. "I know. I came too late."

"Nonsense," muttered Lheanor. "You have driven yourself and your men to exhaustion getting here now. In any case, if you had come any sooner you would only have added your bodies to those already feeding the crows. Forgive me. I speak poorly. Your family is somewhere in the valley still, I know."

"You need ask no forgiveness of me," replied Taim. "Your son gave his life at Grive. You have already paid a terrible price for your friendship to my Blood. But . . . when I went south Jaen, my wife, went to stay with our daughter's family. In Glasbridge."

The Thane sighed. "I did not know. Ah, I would rather not have lived to see times such as these."

There was such a desolation, Taim thought, behind those weary eyes. Is this what is to become of us all now? Hollowed-out; bereft.

"I try to keep hold of the hope that one of them may still live," Lheanor said. "Naradin, if not Croesan. Even the babe, perhaps. But my heart tells me it is a foolish hope. The hounds of the Black Road have done their work thoroughly. I know you loved Croesan's life as well as you did your own."

"Better. He was a better man than me."

"One of the best. I will miss him. He and I often sat here, talking."

"Of what?"

"What do old men always talk about? Our families. Our harvests, our hunting dogs, the price of furs and wool. He was not quite so old as me, so when I talked about aches and pains he could only listen. He did that well, though." Lheanor smiled a broken smile. "But we did talk of weightier matters, too. We thought our battles were to be fought against the pride of Gryvan and the Shadowhand; that their tithes and ambitions were a more likely threat than war out of the north, for the next few years at least. We hoped to die in our beds."

"The ambitions of the High Thane may be the greater danger, in the end," said Taim. "I heard rumors, on my way."

The Thane of Kilkry gave no sign of being surprised at such a suggestion. He regarded his hands as they lay in his lap. Time had slackened and paled their skin, and patterned them with spots and blemishes. Lheanor ran one over the other thoughtfully.

"Dangerous to place too much faith in whispers," he said without looking up, "but still I'd place more in them than in the Haig Blood. Lagair, Gryvan's Steward here, always seems to be lurking at my shoulder these last few days. His words of condolence and concern are as hollow as a dead oak. Aid has been slow to come from the south; there's no more than a hundred or two here even now. The word is that there are great companies mustering at last, in Vaymouth, but where were they when my son was facing the Black Road? I should have sent every sword I command with Gerain. Perhaps I should march them out now, lead them myself."

Only then did he look up and meet Taim's somber eyes.

"My master in Vaymouth forbids it, though. He forbids me to avenge the death of my own son. I am commanded to await his armies. And I am afraid, Taim. A Thane should not admit to it, but I am. Somehow our enemies have brought the woodwights to their side, and if I march for Anduran, as my heart says I should, what of my villages, my people on my own borders? How has this come to pass, Taim, that Black Road and woodwight stand together against us? I never thought to see such a thing."

"Nor I," said Taim. "But then, I never thought to see any of this come to pass." He gave his head a single, sharp shake as if surprised at what he recalled. "I thought the fighting in Dargannan would be my last. I thought I was going home, and would never leave my wife again."

The narrow door creaked open and Ilessa, Lheanor's wife, entered bearing a tray of tiny cakes. She held it out to Taim. The warrior looked up at her with a weak smile. She wore her years with elegance, possessed of that altogether different kind of beauty that some women found in age.

"I am not accustomed to being waited upon by the wife of a Thane," he said as he took one of the cakes. She smiled. There was compassion in her eyes, a marvelous gentleness in her aged face.

Taim had known Lheanor and Ilessa for much of his adult life, and knew that their feelings for him, and for Croesan and the others, were genuine and deep; strong enough to emerge even out of their own limitless sorrow.

"And I am not accustomed to playing the waiting girl," Ilessa said, "but I thought it better that it should be me who disturbed you. You are much in demand. The High Thane's Steward has been asking for you. He seems to think you and he have much to talk about."

Taim grimaced. "Lagair can wait. I lack the strength to fence with one of Gryvan's mouthpieces at the moment. I might say something better left unsaid."

"I told him I did not know where you were," said Ilessa. She set the tray down and smoothed the front of her dress.

"In truth, I barely know where I am myself," murmured Taim.

"How long will you be staying with us? I visited with your men this morning. They are weary."

Part of Taim would willingly stay here, in this high, cramped chamber with only the sky and wind and gulls for companions, for weeks on end. That part of him had long ago been subjugated, though, by a warrior's sense of duty.

"Only a day or two, my lady," he said with an almost apologetic smile. "You know I must go on, to Glasbridge. Whatever is to become of me and my men, we cannot rest. Not yet."

II

Anyara poked her head out from the hut and found an expectant group waiting. A cluster of Kyrinin children stared at her. They looked soft, pale and harmless. One or two of the younger ones shuffled behind their older comrades as her tousled head appeared. As Anyara hauled herself out onto the wooden boards and stretched the sleep from her limbs, the children backed a few yards further away before re-forming their group. Beyond them, a woman paddled by in a little round boat of taut animal skins. Anyara watched as she coasted effortlessly off along the edge of the reedbeds. A flock of tiny birds burst from the reeds and went churning and chattering away. The lake wore a mirror calm. Scraps of mist hung over the water, obscuring the furthest shores, and the whole scene was eerily beautiful and still.

Anyara had not known what to expect of the *vo'an*. Now, after a night's uneasy sleep, she was still unsure. Like everyone, she had heard tales of how the Kyrinin kept great bonfires burning night and day, or how their children never played but only practiced the killing arts of bow and spear. Or how their old women ate the dead. She was tempted to remain in the hut they had been given and hide away from the unfamiliar sights and sounds and smells that lay outside. These were, after all, Kyrinin, and their kind had killed more than a few of hers over the years. But it was a belief deeply ingrained in her that fear — like grief, or pain — must be mastered, lest it become master in its own right. She did not want Orisian, and certainly not Yvane, to think she was unsettled by this place. So she went walking alone through the *vo'an,* and forced herself to hold her head up and look about her. The gaggle of children followed silently, attentively, in her wake.

She saw a young woman, perhaps her own age though it was hard to tell, dextrously gutting fish with a bone knife. A pair of men, barefoot and leaning on their spears, watched her go by from behind the blue turbulence of their tattoos. She heard lilting voices and from somewhere further away the casual, pitter-patter beat of a small drum being tapped. She smelled the smoke of small fires, meat cooking and the rich scent of the hides stretched over so many of the huts.

Few people paid her much heed, save the group of curious children. It did not feel threatening, but neither did it feel comfortable or entirely safe. She could not read this place as she was able, through birth and belonging, to read Kolglas, Anduran or even

Kolkyre that she had only visited a handful of times. The Kyrinin knew she was out of place just as she did. They did not speak when she was close enough to hear, ignorant though she would have been of what they were saying. Their lack of interest in her was, she felt, as deliberate and conscious as any pointed stares would have been.

It was with some relief that she came to the edge of the settlement, where the platform met the shore. She stepped down onto the ground and walked a little way along the water's edge. The children did not follow her. Tall reeds thronged the shallows and as she tracked a slight curve of the shore they cut off her view of the *vo'an*. Save for the smokesign in the pale sky, she might have been utterly alone in a wilderness. She found a place where the reeds gave way for a stretch and sat on a rock there, gazing out over the lake's flawless surface.

Even as she watched, the morning's thin mist parted and she glimpsed the towering peaks of the Car Dine to the north. She had the sense then of being in a borderland, poised between two worlds. Over the Car Criagar whence she had come lay the real world, of towns and markets and humankind. In the opposite direction, out beyond the Car Dine, lay something else altogether: the fearsome Great Bear Kyrinin; Din Sive, the most ancient forest in all the world, filled with shadows, and then the Tan Dihrin that touched the roof of the sky. Between this quiet lake and the Wrecking Cape which lay uncounted days' journey to the north, there might not be a single human village or farm. She felt herself to be terribly small and fragile, the land and sky to be terribly unlimited.

She had felt something similar five years ago, when she emerged from the grip of the Fever into a world without her mother and her older brother. She felt unutterably vulnerable for months, poised between the tortured sleep of the Fever and a future which she barely recognized. She mastered that feeling in the end, along with the grief that could have crippled her. Now her strength was being tested again. She needed to hold firm, and not just for herself. It had not been just for herself that first time, either. Even then, in the wake of the Fever, part of it had been for Orisian.

She rose briskly to her feet. On impulse, she picked up a small stone and flicked it out over the water. She watched the ripples spreading out from its fall for a few seconds before turning back toward the *vo'an*.

She found Orisian and Rothe sitting on the edge of the platform outside the hut, their naked feet dangling down over the water. The sight was so incongruous — the probable Thane of one of the True Bloods sitting with his shieldman in the midst of a Kyrinin camp as casually as if they were on the harbor's edge in Kolglas — that Anyara almost laughed.

"What's happening?" she asked.

"Nothing," said Orisian. "Varryn came to check on us, but he's gone back to Ess'yr, wherever she is. We're waiting for word."

Anyara lowered herself down to sit beside them.

"Where's Yvane?"

"Gone off," grunted Rothe. "On her own. Didn't say where."

Orisian was picking at a splintered crack in the planking. "She'll be back soon, I'm sure," he said.

"We're trusting her a lot, for someone we hardly know," observed Anyara.

"Indeed," agreed Rothe, "and the Kyrinin, too." To Anyara's keen ear it sounded like a complaint born more out of habit than conviction. And he had not called them woodwights.

Orisian was unperturbed. "Well, Inurian did send us to her. I always trusted what he told me; I won't stop now." He looked at his sister. "In any case, what choice do we have? We do need help, out here. We'd have been dead by now if it had just been the three of us."

They lapsed into silence. Anyara had faith in her brother's judgment; in most things, at least. Growing up amongst men, amidst warriors, could teach a great deal to a girl with the eyes to see, and Anyara had those. She wondered if Orisian was aware of the way he sometimes looked at Ess'yr. Perhaps he did not even know that his eyes followed her with a particular attention that, to Anyara, was instantly recognizable. She had seen men look at her that way in the last two or three years.

It was, though, not a look she had seen from her brother before. His interest in Jienna, the merchant's daughter in Kolglas, had been embarrassingly apparent but it had been an unfocused, overawed kind of fascination. There was little that was childish in the way he watched Ess'yr. It worried her. Any such union would be unthinkable to most of her race, but it was not Ess'yr's inhumanity that bothered Anyara most. Rather, it was fear for Orisian's feelings that stoked her unease. Ess'yr was too hard, too far from what he knew, to be a safe object of her little brother's affection. And she had been Inurian's lover. That was a river with dangerous currents, Anyara thought: one Orisian should have the wit not to swim in.

She could see signs of a change in her brother. He had always been a thinker, always able to see, or imagine, things she could not. But she had been the strong one, on the outside at least, since their mother and brother had died. Before that, it had been Fariel who shone most brightly. Now events were demanding something new of Orisian, and in response to that call he was perhaps beginning to unearth parts of himself that had long been overshadowed. He might be a good Thane, if he lived long enough. Even so, Anyara still saw in him the boy she had chased up and down Kolglas' stairwells, and she was not at all sure that boy could fit Ess'yr into the puzzle his life had become.

Varryn came to fetch them an hour or so later. Wordlessly, he gestured for them to follow him into the heart of the *vo'an*. There, in an open space ringed by skull-adorned poles, Ess'yr was kneeling. A great, bizarre face woven of willow branches stood to one side.

"It's a soulcatcher," Orisian murmured when he saw Anyara

looking at it. "They think it protects them from the dead. It's supposed to be one of the Anain."

It disconcerted Anyara. The fact that the Kyrinin would invoke such sinister creatures as the Anain was too blunt a reminder of the chasm of difference that lay between her and them.

"Stand here," instructed Varryn.

Without further explanation, he went to kneel at his sister's side. He picked up a deerskin bowl that held a dark, viscous liquid. Ess'yr had closed her eyes. Her face was still, almost as if she was asleep. Varryn immersed the point of a long, thin needle in the liquid. He rolled the tool around the bowl, soaking it.

Anyara frowned in confusion.

"The *kin'thyn*," Orisian said. "She's killed her first enemy."

Anyara grimaced as Varryn set down the bowl and moved closer to his sister, the dye-coated needle poised and ready.

"He's going to tattoo her?" she said, almost disbelieving.

There was not so much as a twitch in Ess'yr's face as the skin of her cheek was pierced. Varryn pricked out curling lines, the track of his work marked by beads of blood and dye. Slowly, the pattern took shape. There was something horribly fascinating about the process. This scarring of a woman would never be permitted amongst the Haig Bloods, yet here it was being enacted as a mark of respect. Anyara wondered how Orisian would feel about Ess'yr's perfect skin being thus marred. When she glanced at him, his expression was one of such rapt attention that she was not sure he would think of this as a marring at all.

It lasted almost an hour. Varryn never faltered; Ess'yr never opened her eyes or made a sound. The blood flowed, the *kin'thyn* swooped and swirled its way across the skin. Kyrinin who wandered past sometimes paused to watch for a little while, but seldom tarried long. Though the children were more interested, even their numbers dwindled as the long minutes passed. Eventually Varryn sat back and set needle and bowl aside. He took up a cloth and carefully dabbed at Ess'yr's face.

Ess'yr's eyes flickered open. She gave her brother a simple nod and rose to her feet. She looked over to where Orisian, Anyara and Rothe were standing.

"I thank you," she said.

"What for?" Orisian asked her.

"For leading me to the *kin'thyn*."

Blood was still flowing from the innumerable tiny wounds upon her face. She looked as though she had been mauled in some terrible fight. Anyara almost wanted to look away. Instead, it was Ess'yr who turned and strode off, Varryn following. Orisian gazed after them.

"Lucky you," Yvane said from behind them, a fraction more loudly than was necessary. All three of them started.

"How long have you been there?" Anyara demanded as Yvane smiled with ill-concealed satisfaction.

"Oh, not long. Lucky you, as I said. Most rare nowadays for Huanin to witness the *kin'thyn* being bestowed. An honor, I should say."

Anyara realized that her hand had closed about something in her pocket. She fingered it for a few moments, and then an abrupt pang of guilt shook her as she realized what it was. Carefully she withdrew the short length of knotted cord and held it in her palm.

Orisian did not notice, but Yvane did.

"Now where did you come by that?" the *na'kyrim* asked. Orisian looked down at what Anyara was holding.

"I'd forgotten," she said. "Inurian gave it to me, after we got out of Anduran. He said . . ."

". . . he said it should be buried," Orisian finished for her.

"I'm sorry," said Anyara, and repeated, "I'd forgotten."

Orisian gave the slightest shake of his head, and took the cord between finger and thumb. There was a kind of emptiness in his face as he turned one of the knots in his grip.

"It's what . . ." he said, "it's what the Kyrinin do if they're afraid their body will not be properly buried."

He held it up, and met Anyara's eyes.

"It's his life. Each knot is a piece of his life."

"How do you know that?" Anyara asked quietly.

"Ess'yr and her brother made them before we left their camp."

"Should we bury it, then?"

Orisian did not answer at once. He held the cord as if it was some delicate piece of jewelry. She could not say why, but his expression made Anyara think of their father.

"We should give it to Ess'yr," Orisian said quietly. "It is for her, I think. She will know what to do with it."

"He would have been thinking of you, when he made some of the knots," Yvane said to him. For once her tone was gentle, careful. "The knots may be events, or feelings. Or people. He will have put you into some of them, I am sure."

"Perhaps. I would like to know what they all are; what he was thinking when he made it." He held it by one end so that it hung loosely.

"Even if he had lived, he would not have told you what the knots were," said Yvane. "It is a private thing, a conversation with death."

"I'll take it to Ess'yr," Orisian said.

"No." Yvane's voice was still measured, but firm now. "He gave it to Anyara. That is important, in the way of these things. She is the one who should give it to Ess'yr for burial, if that is what she thinks it best to do."

Orisian held the knotted cord out, and Anyara took it. She coiled it neatly in her hand.

"Will you show me where Ess'yr is?" she asked Yvane, and the *na'kyrim* nodded.

They walked silently through the *vo'an*. It was not far. Varryn was standing outside a low hut. He watched them approach and did not move aside from the entrance.

"Be polite," murmured Yvane, hiding the movement of her lips behind a rub at her nose.

"Varryn, is Ess'yr here?" Anyara asked.

"She rests," the warrior said.

"Can I talk to her? I have something for her."

"Not now. She rests."

"It's important," Anyara said. "I think she would want to see me."

Varryn was unmoved. He reminded Anyara of a Thane's shield-man on some grand ceremonial occasion, rigid with the importance of his role. She did not want to show him the cord — she thought it was something Inurian would have meant for Ess'yr alone — but it seemed the only way to gain admittance. She opened her fingers, exposing the cord in her palm.

"It is Inurian's," she said. "Ess'yr should have it."

And she saw, for the most fleeting of instants, a reaction in Varryn's face. Its presence was too brief, his features too subtly inhuman, for her to be certain of its nature. Perhaps annoyance, perhaps pain. He stared at the cord for a moment or two, then looked away. As she drew breath to ask him again, he moved. A soft prod in her back from Yvane told her not to wait for more of an invitation. She ducked inside the hut.

It was gloomy within. Dark furs and animal skins covered the floor. Grey feathers hung from the hut's wooden skeleton. Ess'yr was lying down. Anyara crouched beside her. Although the poor light hid the worst of what had been done to the Kyrinin's face, the swirling needle tracks were visible, as was her skin's angry reaction. Ess'yr's grey eyes looked out from a wounded visage.

Anyara offered her the cord.

"It is Inurian's," she said. "Orisian thought . . . I thought it should come to you. For you to . . . bury."

Ess'yr sat up carefully, protecting her injured ribs. She took the cord. She hardly looked at it, but closed it in her fist.

"Thank you," she said, so quietly that Anyara almost did not hear.

It felt as though there should be something more to say. Anyara saw no emotion in Ess'yr's face, but those knuckles were white, the pale fingernails digging into the palm of the hand. For the space of a few heartbeats Anyara hesitated and wished that this woman was less of a stranger to her; wished they had something more in common than loss. She rose and turned to go. As she reached for the door flap a thought occurred to her.

"Could Orisian come with you? When you bury it, I mean. Inurian meant a great deal to him, too. It might help him."

Ess'yr looked up. Kyrinin and Huanin eyes met, and there was a flicker of understanding in the gaze. It lasted only a fraction of a moment.

"No," Ess'yr said. "It is not for Huanin to see. It is not . . . allowed."

Anyara nodded, and went out into the daylight.

"I am sorry," she thought she heard Ess'yr say behind her.

"Thank you for asking," was all Orisian said when she told him. He did not seem surprised or hurt at Ess'yr's refusal. Perhaps he knew what to expect, having seen more of the Kyrinin than she had.

Yvane stayed with them. She sat cross-legged outside the hut strengthening the seam on her jacket with a needle and thread she had borrowed from their hosts. She was absorbed in her task, and showed little interest in what Anyara and the others were doing. Orisian was subdued and Anyara thought it best to leave him with his thoughts. She dozed in the hut.

When she woke, feeling better than she had in days, Orisian and Rothe were sparring with sticks on the platform outside. Kyrinin children had assembled once more to observe this strange spectacle. Yvane was also watching, wearing the slightly mocking expression that Anyara thought was on the *na'kyrim*'s face a little too often.

Orisian was working hard. There was sweat on his forehead. Anyara knew what an effort her brother had to make when it came to these things. Now there was a concentration in his work that had never been there before Winterbirth.

The mock fight ended, and Rothe patted his charge on the shoulder.

"Good," the shieldman said. "Better, at least. Your side?"

"I didn't really notice it."

"I did, though. You favor that side a little. It unbalances you. But that will pass."

"And your arm?" Orisian asked, nodding at the bandages around Rothe's wrist.

"Sore. But it does not hamper me."

"Could you teach me?" Anyara asked.

She expected Rothe to dismiss the idea out of hand. The warriors of Lannis-Haig did not teach women how to fight, even — especially — if they were the Thane's sister. Instead the shieldman smiled, almost sadly.

"Perhaps. It's hardly fitting work for a lady, though."

"I've come across one or two people who were keen to kill me, these last few weeks. I wouldn't want it to be easy for them, should I meet them again."

Rothe nodded. "A knife would be better for you than a sword. Or a short Dornach blade, maybe. Perhaps when we are away from here, if you still wish it."

Anyara noted that the shieldman glanced at Orisian with those last words. He wants his approval, she thought. My brother, the Thane. It was an idea it would take her time to get used to.

"Swords are all very well, but they'll not answer every problem," Yvane said. She had begun sewing once more, forcing the bone needle roughly through the hide.

"Not all, but some," replied Rothe.

"Blades were little use against some of the *na'kyrim* who lived long ago."

"A well-aimed bolt always has a use," muttered Rothe.

Yvane snorted. "Dorthyn Wolfsbane had his throat torn out by

451

the last Whreinin of the Redjaw tribe. He laid his hands upon the wound and pressed it closed and made himself whole again. Then he split the wolfenkind open from belly to neck. No mere tale, that. Truth. What use your bolt then?

"And when I was in Highfast, I once read a story of Minon the Torturer. If that tale be true — which I don't claim it is — he was nothing until men broke his bones and took their knives to him. It was his very pain that unlocked the deepest wells of his power. What good a blade if it turns your enemy into something worse?"

Rothe shot the *na'kyrim* a dark look and disappeared into the hut.

"Lacks the stamina for a proper argument," Yvane observed.

"You don't think Aeglyss is like Dorthyn or Minon, do you?" Anyara asked. "I never saw him do anything . . . powerful."

"No," Yvane admitted without looking up from her work. "I shouldn't think he's anything like them. But you would do well not to forget he's not like you, either. Inurian saw enough in him to worry about it. I think you Huanin have forgotten what it was like to have truly great *na'kyrim* amongst you. The only power you recognize now is the kind that lives in swords and Thanes and a rich man's coin chest. Have you really forgotten what the world was like before the War of the Tainted?"

"I know that the *na'kyrim* then were very powerful, if that's what you mean," Anyara replied sharply.

"Half the lords of the Aygll Kingship were *na'kyrim,* once. Oh, it was long ago, when the Kingship was still young and there were hundreds upon hundreds of my kind, but it's true nonetheless. Armies marched behind *na'kyrim* captains. They could bend the Shared to any purpose; shape the world according to their will."

"But not now," said Orisian softly. Yvane glanced up, but Orisian was gazing out over the lake.

"No," the *na'kyrim* acknowledged. "Not now. We are few, and have lost the secrets of those days."

A Kyrinin woman brought them food. She set down bowls of

fish stew and left without a word. The children wandered off, much less interested in the eating habits of their visitors than they had been in the game with the sticks.

As dusk drew in, they retreated inside the hut. Orisian became more and more restless.

"We cannot delay here," he said to Yvane. "We have to move on."

"Tomorrow," agreed Yvane.

"Will Ess'yr come with us?" asked Anyara. She could see from the look on Orisian's face that he had not considered the alternative. It was obvious Yvane had, however.

"I'm not sure. Probably. I think she feels bound to see you safely to Koldihrve, at least. Varryn, I don't know. He would not have come this far if Ess'yr had not made her promise to Inurian."

"The *ra'tyn*?" said Orisian, and Yvane nodded.

"Ess'yr promised Inurian she would get you and your sister to safety. It was a promise asked for, and given, in the knowledge that he was dying; that makes it a serious matter, in the Kyrinin way of thinking. Ess'yr is bound by it, Varryn is not — he's more than a little dismayed that she gave her word, I think. But he will want to stay by his sister, perhaps."

Orisian looked thoughtful. Anyara wondered how he would feel, when they were eventually — inevitably — parted from Ess'yr. Perhaps he was wondering that himself.

"We will have to speak to them tomorrow morning," he said. "Tell them we are moving on. It's up to them what they do."

There was food waiting for them outside the hut the next morning. No one save Ess'yr and Varryn had spoken to them in all the time they had been here, Anyara realized. The hut was provided, food appeared and its remnants were taken away, but not a word — hardly a glance — was given them. The children were the only ones to openly acknowledge their presence in the *vo'an*.

As soon as they had finished eating, Yvane rose to her feet. "I will see if I can find us some food for the journey. And find Ess'yr."

"I'll come," Orisian said. Rothe would not let Orisian go without him, and Anyara had no wish to sit idly by. They all went.

The *vo'an* was quiet. It was a dull morning, with a lethargic feel in the air as if the valley was waiting for some change in the weather before stirring itself into life. They made their way to the center of the camp, and came to the place where poles hung with skulls stood by the soulcatcher. There were few Kyrinin about, and none looked up from their chores as Anyara and the others drew near.

The calm was broken by a flurry of activity. Varryn came out from amongst the huts. Other Kyrinin warriors were striding behind him and Ess'yr was at his side, hobbling uncomfortably. Anyara caught the flash of sympathetic pain that crossed Orisian's features at that sight.

"Oh ho, this doesn't look like a cheerful group," Yvane whispered.

Varryn swept by them.

"We go now," he said.

Ess'yr paused a moment longer, her expression unreadable.

"We are hunted still," she said. "There is another man, with a hound." She gestured back toward the great rise of the Car Criagar.

"Let's hunt him, then," said Rothe fiercely. "There must be a hundred warriors in the camp. We can . . ."

Ess'yr only shook her head and followed after her brother.

Anyara glanced at the knot of Kyrinin who now silently faced them. She felt, for the first time, a sense of threat.

"Come along, then," Yvane said, and set off back the way they had come.

Orisian and Anyara hurried to catch up with her, Rothe lingering for a moment to ensure the Fox did not come after them.

"No point in digging our heels in once they've made up their minds," said Yvane. "They'll not want to get involved in arguments amongst Huanin. Probably blame us for bringing outsiders to their doorstep, as well. All in all, we have outstayed our welcome, I think."

III

Orisian found the Vale of Tears a very different place to his own homeland. The valley was scattered with ramshackle farmsteads. They were smaller and more crudely built than those in the Glas valley, and stood amongst unkempt fields. The soil was heavy and wet; there were many little marshes and beds of rushes. The cattle that grazed the floodplain looked listless and morose.

Time and again, as they made their steady way down toward the sea, they passed by the ruins of abandoned farm buildings. Most were little more than rubble but now and again they would come across the full shell of a house, overgrown by moss and trailing plants. There had been more people here once, Orisian thought, a great many more.

Occasionally they spotted a lone herdsman following along behind his cattle, tapping at their hindquarters with a switch. A hunter crossed their path once, leading a pony that bore the gutted corpse of a deer. He came into sight a hundred or so paces ahead of them, and paused to gaze in their direction for a moment. He was a strange, burly figure almost lost beneath the thick furs he wore. Rothe raised a hand in greeting, but the man did not respond and continued on his way toward a distant shack further out by the river.

They camped by a small grove of trees. Varryn found some kindling, and they soon had a fire alight. Ess'yr lowered herself to the ground with care. For the first few hours after leaving the *vo'an* she had moved well, almost recapturing the lithe grace that had been hers before she was injured. Her stride had shortened and stiffened as the day wore on.

Yvane emerged from amongst the trees, clutching odd, globe-shaped objects in her grubby hands. She smiled at the puzzled expression on Orisian and Anyara's faces.

"Earth mutton," she said. "Never seen it before?"

Anyara and Orisian shook their heads, but Rothe grunted softly.

"Mushroom from underground. Used to be much sought after, that, when I was a child in Targlas," he said. "My father took me searching for it. Don't think anyone goes hunting for it nowadays, though."

"Well, it's still good food in these parts," Yvane said. "The Fox think it something of a delicacy. You should consider yourselves fortunate to be served with such food."

She and Varryn sliced the fungus into thin strips, turning each one briefly over the fire before passing it out. The flavor was good, with a meaty hint beneath the taste of soil.

As they went on down toward Koldihrve, Orisian asked Yvane about the ruined farmhouses that dotted the landscape.

"There were more people here once, and they made a better living from the land," she said.

"That much I'd guessed," said Orisian pointedly.

The *na'kyrim* shot him a wry glance.

"Losing a little of that great gentleness of yours?" she inquired. "Might not be such a bad thing, so long as you don't get carried away. Anyway, this was Aygll land before the War of the Tainted. Went wild in the Storm Years after the Kingship fell, and never got over it."

They passed a dozen Kyrinin who were perhaps making for the *vo'an* on the lakeshore. Varryn exchanged a few soft words with them. From the direction of their glances, it seemed that Ess'yr was the subject of their discussion. One of the travelers produced a small packet from inside his tunic and unwrapped a bound bundle of twigs. Varryn accepted it with a nod of his head and the other Kyrinin went on their way.

When they rested for a time in the early afternoon, Varryn heated some water over a small fire. He dropped the twigs in and let them stew. A sharp, almost acrid, scent rose from the pot. Ess'yr drank the infusion down and afterward a little of the paleness was gone from her cheeks and she walked with an easier stride.

That evening, when they bedded down a short way from the track, Orisian went and sat beside her. No one else seemed to be paying them any attention. He spoke to her quietly.

"How are your ribs?"

She made a dismissive gesture with her hand. "Nothing," she said. "I live still."

Her tattoos were still livid, not yet settled into her skin. They were much less dense than those upon her brother's face. A spiral swung around the swell of her cheek; fronds of dye cupped the corners of her eyes. It was almost beautiful. Only the first *kin'thyn,* Orisian supposed. More would come if she killed again.

"Inurian always seemed to have a cure for any ill," Orisian said. "The same medicines you use, I suppose. He learned them from you? From the Fox, I mean?"

Ess'yr only nodded at that. She was looking at him now, with those still, strong eyes.

"You sent your sister to me," she said. "That was well done."

Orisian knew what she meant: the cord of Inurian's life.

"It was Yvane's idea. It seemed right."

"You feel more clearly than most of your kind," she said and there was the slightest, gentlest of smiles on her delicate lips.

Orisian felt a breath of heat rising in his face. For the first time in many days, he had a glimpse of that Ess'yr he had seen before they reached Anduran: the one who looked at him as if he was Orisian, not just some Huanin. Her hand lay only the shortest of reaches from his own, her fingers pressed softly into the yielding moss.

"You buried it in a *dyn hane?*" Orisian asked.

There was only a fleeting pause. Anyone watching her less carefully than Orisian would have missed the momentary tightening at the corner of her eyes. He wanted to touch her in that instant — to offer comfort — but he did not.

"No," she said. "He was *na'kyrim*. Only half of him was of the true people. But I found a place. I cut a good willow staff. It will leaf when the winter is over."

"Did you . . . How long did you know him for?" Orisian asked her.

She thought for a moment, and he feared she was not going to reply; that, as so often when he asked a question she did not wish to answer, she would not hear it. She did, though.

"Five summers ago. He visited my *a'an*. I saw him, but I did not speak with him until the next summer. He came back."

"And . . ." Orisian had to suppress the urge to cough, "you loved him then?"

"Well enough," was all Ess'yr said, as if he had asked how she liked their campsite. Orisian could not tell whether the question had offended her.

"He was very kind to me," he said. "Always. I would have been very lonely if he had not been there . . . after the Fever. He was always there to talk to, about anything. I will miss him."

And to his surprise she smiled again, the curling lines upon her face flexing themselves gracefully.

"He loved you," she said. Her voice was so gentle, so careful of his feelings, that it gave him the will to take a further step.

"What was it he said to you, by the waterfall? When Varryn was angry. I heard '*ra'tyn,*' and it seemed important. Did it have something to do with me?"

Her gaze flicked down, and he knew that he had reached too far. She gave no sign of anger, and did not shrink away from him, yet he felt the distance between them suddenly yawn. She was no longer Ess'yr, who he knew a little; she became the Kyrinin, who he knew hardly at all.

"That is not spoken of," she said, and turned away from him, a slight rigidity in the movement the only hint of her injury. That, he knew, ended the conversation.

He stayed there for a little while, wrestling with frustration. She made him feel like a child. He knew she did not mean to do it, but still it cut him. His own shortcomings annoyed him more, though. There was some key, he thought, some turn of phrase or way of being, that he lacked. He could not quite close the gap. And yet, if asked, he could not, or would not, have explained precisely why it mattered to him; why he wanted so much to narrow that distance between himself and Ess'yr.

In the morning, they awoke to find Yvane still wrapped in her bedding, her breathing shallow and fluttering. Rothe, who had taken the last watch, said she had been thus for half an hour or more. She would not wake, not even when Orisian gave her shoulder a tentative shake. They spent long minutes in indecision.

"We should get some water from a stream . . ." Rothe was saying when at last Yvane returned to herself, sat up and glared at her audience.

"What are you all looking at?" she demanded, sounding a little groggy.

They busied themselves with the packing away of their simple camp and the sharing out of some food. Only after they were on the move, working their way along a sodden stretch of the track where thick rushes had all but overwhelmed the path, did Orisian ease himself to Yvane's side and ask her what had happened.

"Visited Koldihrve, as I visited Inurian in Anduran," she said. "Best to make sure of some kind of welcome. The place has few comforts to offer, but Hammarn will give us a roof over our heads at least. I think I scared him halfway to death. It's a long time since he saw me like that; I think he'd forgotten. His mind has more holes in it than a mismended net."

She clearly saw or sensed some doubt in Orisian, for she smiled at him.

"Don't worry. Hammarn is just an old, distracted *na'kyrim*. He can be a bit . . . unusual, but his heart is true enough. He's a friend, and will be nothing but delighted to have so many visitors. That's not something you could say for most in Koldihrve."

Orisian did not relish the prospect of arriving in a town of masterless men. He could guess that there would be no warm welcome waiting there. Against that, though, he could set the thought that he was about to see a place where Huanin and Kyrinin lived peacefully alongside one another. He knew of no other place where such a thing would happen in these days. He had not thought of it before, but it was obvious that there would be *na'kyrim* here, and that knowledge quickened his pulse a fraction. Inurian and Yvane were the only *na'kyrim* he had ever known. The only other he had even seen — just for a moment — had been at Kolglas on the night of Winterbirth: Aeglyss.

"Yvane," he asked, "do you know . . . is Koldihrve where Inurian came from? I know his father was from the Fox clan, but I never knew where he grew up."

"No," said Yvane softly. "Inurian was born in a summer *a'an* in the Car Anagais. His mother . . ." She paused and looked at him. "Best to leave that," she said. "It is not the happiest of tales. Don't you think, in any case, that he would have told you himself, if he wanted you to know?"

Orisian gazed at the muddy ground passing beneath his feet.

"Perhaps," he said. "Perhaps he meant to tell me many things one day. He meant to take me with him into the forest, I think. Maybe even next summer."

"Perhaps he did," said Yvane. "I don't think he would have taken any other Huanin, but you . . . yes, perhaps."

She fell silent then, and they trudged along. Flakes of snow began to drift down from the flat, endless clouds. A flight of ducks whirred overhead like fat bolts loosed from some crossbow. Up in the forests on the edge of the Car Criagar a stag bellowed. It was a mournful sound. Some stories said that all the creatures of the world wept when the Gods departed, save the Huanin and the Kyrinin who were the cause of it.

Something else has passed away this time, Orisian thought. Let this night be a warm memory; let it be a seed of life. Those were the words his father had spoken on Winterbirth's eve, as he had done every year for as long as Orisian could remember. But this time the memories of Winterbirth carried nothing of warmth. No seed — at least none with any good in it — had been planted in Castle Kolglas. If spring did come, it would break upon a world changed beyond recognition.

They came to a derelict barn, and rested there for a little while. The snow had turned to desultory sleet. The building's roof was skeletal, its rotting beams exposed like the ribs of some half-decayed carcass deposited by flood waters.

Yvane dozed, huddled in her cloak. Rothe shared some food with Anyara. The two Kyrinin whispered to one another while Varryn applied a balm to the still raw tattoos on his sister's face. Orisian could not settle and wandered listlessly around the barn. There was no sign of fire or storm or other damage. Like all the other abandoned farmsteads they had passed on their journey down the valley, it had been killed by neglect, not some sudden catastrophe.

He clambered into a gap in the wall. The stones were over-grown by a carapace of grey-green lichens. Orisian ran his fingers over them, testing their minutely intricate texture. The wind gusted, throwing a scattering of sharp sleet into his face, and he grimaced, turning his head away.

"Keep under cover," called Rothe. "We don't know who might be watching."

Orisian took a step down from the breach. Something made him look outward once more. He saw a group of figures standing twenty paces or so away: Kyrinin warriors, staring silently at him. Their faces were thick with the tattoos of the *kin'thyn*. For a few seconds he and they were motionless as the sleet swept across them. Then Varryn came soundlessly up to his shoulder, and brushed past him. Orisian watched as Varryn conferred with the newcomers.

"What's happening?" Rothe asked from behind Orisian.

He could only shrug in reply.

After a few minutes, the band of warriors drifted away into the surrounding scrub and Varryn came striding back. His gait was purposeful, almost hasty.

"What news?" Orisian asked, but the Kyrinin ignored him and went to speak with Ess'yr. The language was incomprehensible, but for once the expressions upon their faces were almost eloquent. An intensity entered their eyes as brother and sister talked. There was urgency in their tones. Yvane had stirred herself, and as she listened to the discussion Orisian saw her begin to frown.

Varryn and Ess'yr came to some conclusion, and began rapidly to prepare themselves to move on.

"Will we not wait for the weather to improve?" asked Anyara, contriving a note of innocent inquiry.

"No," Ess'yr said. "We go quickly now."

"What's happened?" said Orisian.

"The enemy are coming."

Yvane was thoughtful as they hastened to keep up with the two Kyrinin, who set a hard pace away from the barn.

"The Inkallim?" Orisian asked, but Yvane shook her head.

"It seems there is war in mountains. Not just a raid: hundreds of White Owls have come north, from the sound of it. I've never heard of so many coming into Fox lands. It's not how the Kyrinin fight their battles, not these Kyrinin at least. They prefer sneaking about in little groups."

"Are they coming this way, then?"

"Probably. The greatest Fox *vo'an* is beside Koldihrve. The White Owls will want that if they've blood on their minds, and they must have a powerful thirst for the stuff for so many of them to come so far. It smells bad to me. Like everything else. If you're not aboard a boat heading south soon you may not be going anywhere."

A strange scene greeted them as they rounded a drift of alder trees and came at last within sight of the sea. Two very different settlements flanked the broad mouth of the River Dihrve. Upon its northern banks lay a chaotic jumble of houses and shacks, sheltering behind a crude ditch and dyke: the masterless town of Koldihrve. To the south of the river was a *vo'an,* a sprawling mass of tents and huts much larger than Orisian had expected. A long wooden trackway raised on poles connected the two settlements across the river. It might have been a vision from the distant past, from the time before the War of the Tainted, when the two races had more in common than distrust and bitterness.

And beyond the ramshackle roofs of Koldihrve was a sight more welcome, and more unexpected, still: the tall masts of a fine sea-going ship at anchor in the estuary.

* * *

Cerys, Elect of Highfast, ran a finger down the hem of her plain brown robe. It was fraying. She must mend it soon, as she had done several times before. Few amongst the *na'kyrim* of Highfast would have begrudged their Elect a new robe but Cerys preferred to set an example. The Thane of Kilkry-Haig still sent an annual boon of coin, and lesser gifts could usually be expected from Kennet nan Lannis-Haig — Inurian's doing, of course — and one or two of the Marchlords on the northern frontier of Taral-Haig. All of that, however, went on food and the materials needed for the great tasks of chronicling and copying. There was little left over for luxuries such as new clothing. When Kilkry had been highest of all the Bloods, things had been easier. Nowadays Lheanor oc Kilkry-Haig must send an ever-growing tithe south to Vaymouth; he had less to spare for the secretive workings of Highfast.

The Elect let the hem fall from between her fingers. She was allowing idle musings to distract her from the demands of the present. Gently, she reached out into the Shared, letting her senses flow with its currents. She felt the presence of those she sought:

the Conclave was gathered in the room that adjoined her own chambers here in the castle's keep.

She did not relish the prospect of this meeting. Disquiet was abroad in Highfast, and it made people irritable and argumentative. There had been too many rumors circulating in recent days; perhaps that at least could be ended by this gathering.

She lowered her chain of office about her neck. It was very simply made — nothing but unadorned links of iron — as befitted what was a symbol of servitude rather than of elevation. To be elected as head of the Conclave lifted the candidate above others only so that the burden of preserving Highfast and its accumulated wisdom should fall more heavily upon their shoulders. The chain's weight tired Cerys, and she never wore it save on official occasions such as this.

Soft conversations died away as she entered the meeting chamber. Every eye was turned upon her. She smiled more resolutely than she felt. There were five other *na'kyrim* present. She would call most of them friends, but that did nothing to dilute the air of tension that filled the chamber. Cerys took her seat at the head of the table and poured herself a beaker of water. A platter of thick-crusted bread was passed to her and she tore off a piece and swallowed it down. A small ritual going back two and a half centuries to the first days of the Conclave in Highfast: that hunger and thirst should be sated, lest their pangs distract from the deliberations to follow. Cerys had little real appetite these days, but the traditions must be respected.

"Has everyone taken food and drink?" she asked, and when all gave their nodded or murmured confirmation, she said, "Let us make a start, then."

She turned to an old, frail-looking man seated beside her. His long hair was cloud-white and his eyes almost entirely misted over. The skin of his face was seamed by a thousand vanishingly fine lines. Olyn was beyond his hundredth year — aged even by the standards of the long-lived *na'kyrim* — and Cerys had hesitated over whether or not to burden him with the delivery of his ill tidings. Even if his body was failing him, however, his mind and his will were as strong as they had ever been. It was his own wish that he should be the one to repeat to the Conclave what he had whispered in the Elect's ear two days ago.

"Olyn has news that I thought all of you should hear," Cerys said. "Olyn, if you please?"

Olyn straightened in his seat and ran a swift tongue over his lips to moisten them.

"The crows have been uneasy this last little while," he said in a wavering voice that ill matched the clarity of the thoughts beneath it. "I have spent much time in the roost, to soothe them. I have slept there on some nights when they have been particularly restless. Four nights ago, I was woken by a great clamor. When I sought its cause, I found that one long gone had returned. Idrin. Inurian's companion."

There was no sound greater than an intake of breath in the room, but Cerys felt the undercurrent of regret. None would fail to understand the meaning of the crow's return. It extinguished, irrevocably, any faint hope that Inurian might still be alive.

"That is a great loss to us," murmured Alian, a beautiful, slight woman. Her head was bowed as she spoke. She would have been too young to have seen much of him when Inurian dwelled here, Cerys thought, yet she feels her life is reduced by his death. Everyone feels that, and rightly.

"We do not know what has happened, but there is no doubting that Inurian is gone," Cerys said. "I have reached out for him — I know others have done the same — and there is no sign. It is, as Alian says, a great loss. He chose to leave this place, but he left his mark upon it just as it did upon him." She glanced at the keeper of crows. "There is more that I wished Olyn to share with you, though."

"It leads us away from the certain," croaked the old, blind man. "I believe that I . . . caught the moment of Inurian's death. There was an instant, a few days ago — I had sunk myself into the Shared — when I think I felt his passing. He ceased to be a presence in the Shared, became a part of its memory."

"That must have been painful," said a tall man whose pale hair was tied back in a braid.

"It was, Mon Dyvain. It was. But there was more to it: another presence, faint and obscure. I do not think Inurian was alone when he died. One of us was there. A *na'kyrim*."

That took a moment or two to sink in. Eshenna broke the contemplative silence. She was the youngest of the Conclave, and had risen to its ranks after being in Highfast for only four years. Her speed of thought and talent in using the Shared had much to do with her rapid elevation, but so did her background: Eshenna had come to Highfast from Dyrkyrnon. That *na'kyrim* sanctuary deep in the marshes of the Heron Kyrinin was a world away from the austere and disciplined atmosphere of Highfast. Only the hidden Inner Court of the Adravane Kingship held a greater concentration of gifted *na'kyrim* than Dyrkyrnon.

It was Eshenna who, of all the members of the council, gave Cerys most cause for concern. The woman had a fire in her that Highfast had not yet turned fully to its own ends. She was as passionate as any in her studies and researches, but the outside world still called to her more strongly than was quite fitting for one of the Conclave.

"Forgive my slowness, Elect," Eshenna said, "but we should be clear about what is being said. Are we to take it that Inurian was killed by one of our own kind?"

Cerys sighed. "As Olyn said, we have left certainty behind. But it seems . . . possible."

"It's hard to believe," Eshenna said. "It must be a long time since *na'kyrim* killed *na'kyrim*."

"It happened in Koldihrve, years ago," said Olyn. "Before that, as far as I know, one would have to go back another two centuries or more, to the early Storm Years. Hyrungyr killed at least two *na'kyrim* on behalf of Amgadan the Wheelwright, who held the castle at Asger Tan. Of course, it was not uncommon before that, during the Three Kingships and the War of the Tainted."

Mon Dyvain was tapping the ancient wood of the table distractedly.

"Ancient history come to life, then," he murmured.

"I think so," agreed Cerys. "Some of you know already, but perhaps others do not: when the Dreamer spoke of Inurian's death, he also referred to someone else. A man, whose presence in the Shared Tyn seems to find . . . unsettling."

"Then it must be true," Eshenna said at once. "Surely it's clear that this man — this *na'kyrim* — the Dreamer spoke of is responsible for Inurian's death."

Cerys regarded the younger woman in silence. There was little more to say.

"What must we do, then?" Eshenna asked.

"There is nothing to do but watch and learn, and seek to understand, as our duties here demand," said Alian.

It was well concealed, and perhaps the others did not notice it, but Cerys caught the slight twitch in Eshenna's face as the young *na'kyrim* suppressed an instinctive, dissenting, response.

"You are most likely right, Alian," Mon Dyvain was saying, "but there are complications here. We know Anduran has fallen to the forces of the Black Road. We know Inurian — peace to him — is dead. The two can hardly be unconnected." He looked around at the other Conclave members. "Well, it must be so, must it not? There is a *na'kyrim,* a murderous one, in the service of the Black Road."

"It must be so," agreed Eshenna. Out of the corner of her eye, Cerys could see Olyn nodding glumly.

"But why would a *na'kyrim* serve the Black Road?" continued Mon Dyvain. "They are not famed for their affection toward us."

"Who is?" Alian asked quietly.

Cerys held up a calming hand.

"Let us not be too hasty with our assumptions," she said. "I share your instincts in this, but true understanding may be hindered by rushing to judgment."

Mon Dyvain inclined his head to acknowledge the soft rebuke.

The Elect's gaze lingered upon one of those who sat around the table: Amonyn. The muscular, elegant man had said nothing so far. That was his way. He listened, and he thought, and he was never anything other than calm. He was also, by the fine margins on which such judgments rested, probably more powerfully imbued with the Shared than anyone else in Highfast. Cerys had seen him quieten a wailing child with a single soothing touch, and bring back from the very edge of death a Kilkry-Haig warrior crushed by falling rocks on one of the mountain trails. She had, for a long time, loved him in the distant, ill-defined way that came easily to the forever childless *na'kyrim,* and they occasionally found solace in one another's arms.

He stirred beneath her questioning look.

"Has the Dreamer spoken again?" he asked.

"He whispers and mumbles. His rest certainly seems disturbed, but the scribes have caught little of it. Nothing of consequence."

Amonyn bestowed a rather sorrowful smile upon her.

"Then I think there is little enough that we can do. It is best to hold fast to our solitude and silence. With the one exception: perhaps Lheanor oc Kilkry-Haig should be told of our suspicions."

Cerys smiled. They thought alike, she and Amonyn.

"With the Conclave's consent, I have a message ready to be carried to the Thane," she said. "It tells him that we believe there to be an unknown *na'kyrim* in the Glas valley and that it is possible — only possible — that he or she is working in the service of the Black Road. We owe the Kilkry Blood that much for maintaining the safety of Highfast for all these many years. What good the warning may do Lheanor, I do not know."

"And that is all we do?" asked Eshenna.

"That is for the Conclave to decide, but I would propose that for now we watch the Dreamer closely and study his words; we remain alert to any further disturbance in the Shared. That, as befits the purposes for which Highfast was first given over to the *na'kyrim* by Kulkain oc Kilkry, we wait and we observe and we learn."

The Elect saw the doubt in Eshenna's eyes. Not outright disagreement, but doubt at the least. She turned to her right. "Alian?" she asked.

"Wait and watch," said Alian without hesitation.

"Wait and watch," agreed Mon Dyvain, and Olyn and Amonyn. And, after only the slightest of pauses, Eshenna.

After the Conclave had dispersed, Cerys retired once more to her austere chambers. She was weary. She carefully lifted the chain from around her neck and returned it to its oak casket. She was the ninth person to hold the office of Elect in Highfast; she often wondered if all those worthy predecessors had felt as unequal to the task as she sometimes did.

The Elect's reverie was disturbed by a gentle rapping at the door. She had half-expected it.

"Come in, Eshenna," she called out.

The youngest member of the Conclave entered with a proper air of humility.

"Forgive me for intruding, Elect," she said.

Cerys dismissed the apology with a wave of her hand and gestured for Eshenna to take a seat.

"It is no intrusion, Eshenna. Being alone with my thoughts is not so restful as once it was. That is true for many of us at the moment, I fear."

Eshenna smoothed her plain dress across her knees. Her troubled mood was as clear as a scar upon the pale skin of her face.

"What was it you wanted to speak with me about?" Cerys asked.

"Nothing, I think, you do not already know, Elect. I have no wish to question the decisions of the Conclave, but . . ."

"But you chafe at the thought of inaction. Of patience," Cerys finished for her.

"As I said, nothing you do not already know."

"I know, too, that you mean well, and that your doubts are honestly held. But what is it that you would have us do, exactly?"

"I am uncertain, Elect. Yet my heart asks for more than simply to wait and watch. I know that Inurian left this place before I arrived, but since I came here I have heard nothing but good of him. Does his death not deserve more of an answer than this? Might not one of us go north, to try to discover what has truly happened?"

"One of us, such as you?" asked Cerys with an arched eyebrow.

Eshenna met her gaze with no outward sign of embarrassment.

"I can conceal myself well enough to pass unnoticed by another *na'kyrim,* if I am not expected or sought. I would not fear to make the attempt, Elect."

"No, I am sure you would not. When Grey Kulkain bade Lorryn come to Highfast and establish a library, and a place of study, he said that he wished him to gather and preserve knowledge, understanding, memory. He had seen how every time tumult swept across the world — the end of the Whreinin, the fall of the Kingships — much of what had gone before was carried off and lost. He and Lorryn hoped that this place would be a storehouse and refuge for knowledge, so that whatever befell the peoples of the world not everything would be forgotten. They were great men, and that was a fine hope. It still sustains me, and all of us here. And you, I believe?"

"Of course, Elect."

"So we hide ourselves behind these thick walls," Cerys said. "We keep ourselves from the gaze of the Huanin in whose lands we dwell. Forgive me if it sounds a foolish question, Eshenna, but why is that?"

There was only the slightest of hesitations before Eshenna's soft-voiced reply.

"Because they fear and mistrust *na'kyrim,* Elect. Because not all share the tolerance that the Thanes of Kilkry have shown us."

"Indeed. Highfast is not only a place of learning. It is haven, too, for our kind. A refuge from the . . . harshness with which both Huanin and Kyrinin are wont to treat us. Just as Dyrkyrnon is. There are few places where such as you and I can live in peace. Would it surprise you if I said I understood the reasons for that? That, sometimes, I can almost sympathize with those who need so little encouragement to turn upon a *na'kyrim* in their midst."

She saw, and felt, the surprise her statement provoked.

"Terrible things were done to many, many *na'kyrim* after the War of the Tainted, in the Storm Years and since. You know that as well as I do, Eshenna. You know, but perhaps do not consider so much, that terrible things were also done by *na'kyrim* themselves before that. Orlane, imprisoning the mind of a king and making him betray his own people. Long before him, there was Minon the Torturer; Dorthyn, who bent all his will and strength to the utter destruction of the wolfenkind, of an entire race. Many of them, Eshenna. Many whose gifts became terrible weapons. The Huanin remember Orlane most clearly, and revile his name most bitterly, but he was not the only one, or even the worst."

"I do not quite understand, Elect," murmured Eshenna.

"It is my responsibility to preserve Highfast and what it contains. The power of the Shared is unwisely used if it is used to interfere in the arguments of the Huanin. We might mean only to do good, but we would nevertheless only remind the humans of what it is they fear.

"If there is truly a *na'kyrim* out there amidst all the slaughter in Lannis-Haig, serving the Black Road, now is not the time to risk Highfast's tradition of discretion. The Kilkry warriors on the battlements above swear their oaths of secrecy, but there's no stilling so many tongues. There are already many more people who know we are here, and what we do, than you might imagine. If it becomes common knowledge that a *na'kyrim* is aiding the Black

Road, who is to say that some of the anger that follows — and it will follow — may not be turned on us? It would be better not to remind the world of our existence."

"Yet," said Eshenna, "if it were true that one of the *na'kyrim* is repeating the errors of the past, does it not fall to us, even more so than to the Bloods, to oppose that error and rectify it?"

Cerys gave a curt laugh. "Nimble, Eshenna. But not nimble enough to sway me. It has taken centuries to gather the wisdom that is recorded here in our books and manuscripts and scrolls. I would not risk that for the sake of correcting another's mistake. Not until we know a good deal more than we do at present."

"You must excuse my obstinacy, Elect. Still, I would have thought that the death of one of our own demanded more of an answer."

"Eshenna," Cerys said levelly, "I grieve for Inurian. But we deal in manuscripts here. In study and memory. Not judgment; not execution. My counsel, and that of the Conclave, is patience. We will wait, and we will watch. If it comes to seem that it is right, and best, for us to do something more, no doubt we will. I cannot keep you here if your heart calls you to leave. Highfast is not a prison. But I must ask you, so long as you wish to remain here, to put your trust in the wisdom of the Conclave, and follow its decisions."

Eshenna bowed her head. "Of course, Elect," she said as she rose to leave.

The door was almost closed behind her when Cerys said, "I would regret it, Eshenna, should you ever choose to leave Highfast. We do need . . . other views to leaven our traditions, sometimes."

"Thank you, Elect," she heard Eshenna say, and then the door clicked shut.

Cerys sighed and ran her fingers through her hair. How sweet a few days of peace, and a few nights of undreaming sleep, would be. She knew she was unlikely to be granted them. Still, there were smaller respites to be found. She opened a cabinet and took out the scented candles that she burned only rarely, and on very particular nights. Amonyn would come to her this evening. They had not spoken of it, but she knew he would come. Tonight they would offer one another what comfort they could against the clamor of the outside world.

IV

Within the walls of Gryvan oc Haig's Moon Palace were stored riches beyond the dreams of all save the most avaricious of souls. There were gemstones from the Karkyre Deeps and the Hills of Far Dyne, bars of solid Kilkry-Haig silver, bale upon bale of the finest furs the northern forests could offer, and vials of Nar Vay dyes worth more than gold. And there were treasures from further afield too: the most delicate, detailed copperwork from Tal Dyre; silks and velvets smuggled out of the far south; pearls the size of bird's eggs from the oyster fields of the Dornach Kingship. It was wealth enough to make a man fall into a stupor of amazement and desire.

As Mordyn Jerain watched his counters at work cataloguing the plunder gathered from Dargannan-Haig towns, it was not precious stones or jewelry or gold coin that he saw. It was power, and influence over the will of men. Mordyn kept his own hoards sealed behind heavy doors and thick walls in his Palace of Red Stone, his personal army sequestered in its barracks. The Chancellor had long ago realized that many of those in Vaymouth had lapsed into a common kind of reasoning: their judgment of what to do in any given situation had become a simple question of what was most profitable for them. He was not one to decry such frailties. Everyone must have some rule to measure their actions against; some had chosen coin, and that gave the Shadowhand the means to influence them.

The Tal Dyreen turned away and left his men to their work. He climbed up through the intricate stairways and passages of the palace. Even as a youth fresh off his father's ship from Tal Dyre it had been obvious to him that the house of Haig stood upon the threshold of enormous power. Now, for all the uncertainties of the situation, he could smell the possibilities afresh. The Dargannan-Haig Blood, an obstreperous child ever since it had been created by Gryvan's grandfather, was broken and would soon be tamed. Lannis, the least of all the Bloods but a long irritation nevertheless, was routed. Even Lheanor oc Kilkry-Haig was weakened and bound now, in time of war, to remember where his proper allegiance lay. All that remained was to drive off the Black Road madmen, and Gryvan could at last turn his full attention upon the prizes to the south: the masterless towns of the Bay of Gold, Tal Dyre and the Dornach Kingship itself. The High Thane might yet, in his lifetime, shape the greatest kingdom the world had ever seen out of these possibilities, and Mordyn would be there at his side as he had always been.

He found Gryvan oc Haig in one of the terrace rooms on the southern side of the palace. The High Thane was reading through papers of some kind, attended by an expectant gaggle of scribes. A songbird chirped in a tall cage wrought from fine threads of precious metal. A flask of wine stood apparently forgotten on a table at the High Thane's side.

Mordyn cleared his throat from a respectful distance. Gryvan looked up, smilingly set the document aside and dismissed his attendants. The Chancellor bowed.

"It is fortunate you came, Mordyn," said the High Thane. "I was minded to send for you."

The Chancellor made to reply, but was distracted by a movement at one of the great open windows that looked out over the terrace. He felt a twinge of irritation as he realized it was Kale, the Thane's shieldman, who had been lurking there unseen. He was like some aging hound unwilling to be parted for even an instant from its master. Mordyn set the distraction aside and smiled at Gryvan.

"I am at your disposal," he said. "The tallying of your recent gains is all but done, and no longer needs my close attention."

"The least of my gains, that loot," said Gryvan. "I find the thought of Igryn safely locked away in my dungeons sweeter than any amount of gemstones. But that is not what I wished of you this afternoon. What word from the north?"

"Nothing new. Most of the valley remains in the hands of the Black Road. Lheanor has, it seems, managed to restrain himself and waits patiently for our armies. If what Lagair tells us is true, the Thane seems to have lost some of his willfulness, since the death of his son."

"You still say it is only the Horin-Gyre Blood that has taken the field?"

"Them and the White Owl Kyrinin. There is no report of any other forces, save a handful of Inkallim. And the ravens are most likely there to keep an eye on Horin-Gyre as much as anything else."

"Very well. Aewult marches for Kolkyre tomorrow, with ten thousand men. So long as he only faces Horin-Gyre, I think we can be certain of a speedy resolution."

"I imagine so," Mordyn murmured. His misgivings about the Bloodheir related not to his prowess on the battlefield but to how he might deal with the aftermath, and with Lheanor oc Kilkry-Haig.

"And Croesan and his spawn, what of them?"

Mordyn studiously placed a troubled expression upon his face.

"No word. All the signs would suggest that not one of Croesan's family has survived. We cannot be certain of it yet, though."

The High Thane, by contrast to his Chancellor, could not keep a smile from his lips. The bird was singing in its cage, the melody spilling out between the golden bars.

"We are fortunate, are we not?" Gryvan said. "Dargannan and

Lannis laid low in a single season. We must give some thought to the future of the Glas valley, once the present situation is resolved. Perhaps we need no more Thanes ruling in Anduran, especially now that it appears there are none to lay claim."

The Chancellor nodded graciously in assent, concealing his disquiet. He could hardly do otherwise, since he had himself long ago planted in Gryvan's mind the idea that a Blood could be unmade just as it could be made. The Aygll Kings, in olden times, had their Wardens who wielded the monarch's authority in the furthest parts of the Kingdom. Why should a High Thane not use his Stewards in the same way? But that had been for later, after the Free Cities on the Bay of Gold, and Tal Dyre, had been added to Gryvan's domains. Taral and Ayth might be subdued and subservient, but until Dargannan, Lannis and Kilkry had been securely and permanently ground down the time would not be right for pulling down the edifice of the Bloods.

"And no Thanes in Dargannan either, perhaps," mused the High Thane.

"We must be careful not to over-reach ourselves," said Mordyn.

"Oh, of course," agreed Gryvan with a nonchalant wave of his hand, as if the Chancellor's caution was some fly to be warded off. "Not yet, I know. Not yet. But we must always be thinking ahead, must we not? You are the one who always tells me that our future glories depend upon our actions today, tomorrow."

"They do."

"It is important that events in Kolkyre and the Glas valley go well. That however things fall out once the Black Road is driven back, they do so in a manner favorable to us."

Mordyn waited patiently for whatever was to follow. It was obvious that the High Thane, in his clumsy way, was preparing the ground for a suggestion — a command, more likely — that his Shadowhand was not going to like.

"My thought is this," Gryvan said, leaning forward with an almost conspiratorial air. "You should go with Aewult to Kolkyre. You will be valuable to him. A guide."

One less disciplined than the Chancellor might have let some hint of his dismay show. The Bloodheir was the last person he desired more time alone with. And scurrying around trying to temper the edge of his ill judgment would be wearying. The Chancellor's mind sifted the options in a moment. There were only two, and his every instinct said the first — trying to change the High Thane's decision — would not work. So, he reasoned with a heavy heart, it must be the second.

"Very well," he said. "I will offer the Bloodheir whatever assistance I can."

"Good." The Thane of Thanes seemed genuinely pleased, perhaps even pleasantly surprised, at Mordyn's acquiescence. "I know, Mordyn, you have your differences with Aewult. I do not blame you. He can be impulsive, careless. A little harsh, perhaps. But he will be Thane after me, as sure as fawns follow the rut. He has much to learn, and I can think of no better teacher than you."

"I will need a little time to put matters in order," the Shadowhand said, with the slightest of bows, "and to placate my wife."

Tara would not be pleased, and her displeasure could be fearsome. She would not accompany him — she was too fond of her comforts to exchange them for wintry Kolkyre — yet his absences pained her more with each passing year. They hurt him as well. When he had been young he might have scoffed at the prospect, for the marriage had been at least partly driven by self-interest on both their parts, but virtually without their noticing it, powerful bonds had grown between the two of them. She had almost died in losing, for the second time, a child of his before its birthing time. The fear he had felt then, as he glimpsed a future without her, had been enough to drive the desire for a son out of his mind. He would never again risk the loss of that which was most precious to him.

The High Thane brushed the bars of the birdcage with a finger. The prisoner hopped a little closer on its perch and leaned forward, half-spreading its wings. When it realized no food was being offered it began to sing again.

"Stupid, these birds," Gryvan murmured, then smiled and shrugged his shoulders. "My wife likes them. What can I do? We are all slaves to those we love."

It was on the eve of his departure that a young manservant came to find Mordyn. He was in his reading chamber, perusing reports from his informants at Ranal oc Ayth-Haig's court in Dun Aygll.

"What is it?" Mordyn demanded irritably.

"There is a messenger here, my lord," the youth said as he bowed. "Not an official one: someone we've never seen before. She insists on speaking only with you, and will not leave. We have her in the guardroom. She is . . . unclean."

"I am not in the mood for messages. Send her away."

"Yes, lord. She did say . . . she did say you would hear her out. She said she brought word for the supplicant."

Mordyn hung his head in thought for a moment.

"You said unclean. How so?"

"The King's Rot, my lord. Foul . . ."

"Very well. Has she been searched?"

"The guards say she is unarmed, lord."

Mordyn went to the guardroom as much out of curiosity as anything. For Torquentine to send his precious doorkeeper in person, the message must be of some import.

When he reached the guardroom, he sent everyone away and sat before Magrayn alone.

"I never thought to welcome you to my home, doorkeeper," he said.

She wore her hood pulled far forward, keeping much of her face in shadow. How the guards must have cursed when they pulled that hood back, Mordyn thought.

"I will not linger," she rasped. "I think your men find my presence unsettling."

"I imagine you're right. Let me hear your master's message, then."

"His exact words: I hear you are bound for Kolkyre, noble Chancellor. There is a man I have heard of, in Lheanor's city. A wretch; worse than that, a leech. Ochan by name, a usurer by nature. And a dealer in stolen goods, a smuggler, a blackguard of the vilest ilk. It would be to the good of the Bloods and all honest traders if he were brought to justice, yet it seems he is under the wing of some protector. There would be no debts between us, should your presence in Kolkyre coincide with this Ochan's fall."

Mordyn laughed. "So I am to be the long arm of Torquentine's revenge upon some minor rival, am I?"

Magrayn remained quite still and quite silent.

"Well, go back and tell your master I will consider it. But make him no promises; be clear on that, Magrayn. No promises. And compliment him on the skills of his eavesdroppers. It's only a day since I decided to go to Kolkyre, after all."

When Torquentine's doorkeeper had departed, Mordyn remained for a minute or two alone in the guardroom, a faint smile playing across his lips. One had to admire Torquentine's presumption. It took a considerable amount of self-confidence to seek to use the Chancellor of the Haig Bloods thus. Still, Mordyn would think on it. There might be some merit in exerting a little of the High Thane's authority in Kolkyre; bringing down someone Lheanor's own people had allowed to prosper would be an elegant demonstration of the Haig Blood's primacy.

V

Koldihrve, Orisian could not help but think, stank. Of fish and freshly butchered meat, of smoke and stagnant pools, of filth: smells he knew well enough from Kolglas, but here they had a different intensity. It was noisy, too. The muddy, puddled streets were filled with shouting and cries. Ear-grating singing assaulted them when they passed by a half-derelict tavern.

There were wild-looking men leading mules laden with furs and carcasses and baskets of turnips; old, crumpled women talking animatedly in doorways or through windows. Scrawny dogs loped up and down, noses to the ground and eyes darting nervously this way and that as if haunted by a lifetime of stonings. The houses were rough and ready, many of them little more than wooden shacks thrown up with whatever timber had come to hand.

Varryn and Ess'yr had parted from them before they entered the town, making for the *vo'an* on the other side of the river. Ess'yr had promised to find them later. Orisian noted the curiosity with which the town's inhabitants watched them pass, even without Kyrinin walking alongside them. There were many frowns, and words muttered behind hands.

"Old Hammarn lives down by the water," said Yvane. She proceeded down Koldihrve's streets utterly oblivious of the unpleasant distractions that assailed them, and the questioning, unfriendly looks cast their way.

They passed by the rotting corpse of a dog half-hidden beneath a wooden boardwalk. A small group of children, their clothes ragged and their faces smudged with dirt, yelled abuse at them, and fled in a squall of laughter when Rothe cast them a black glare.

Even the sea, when they came to it, was a grey and leaden thing compared to the ever-shifting expanse that washed the edge of Orisian's homeland. The water slapped disconsolately upon the muddy shore. There were small boats lying at strange angles here and there, hauled up out of the water and tied down. Koldihrve stood at the highest reach of a long and snaking estuary that protected it from the storms of the open oceans, so there was no need for the protective breakwaters of Kolglas and Glasbridge. There was only a handful of crude wooden jetties. The huts that lined the top of the beach were rickety affairs, half of them made of driftwood.

What caught Orisian's attention more than all this, however, was the ship rocking gently at anchor two or three hundred paces offshore. It was, he was immediately certain, one he had seen before: the Tal Dyreen trading vessel that had been berthed at Glasbridge before Winterbirth. It looked absurdly out of place in this miserable backwater.

Old Hammarn's house was one of the more respectable ones running along the shore. A wattle and daub fence protected it from sea breezes and spray, and the building itself was a solid-looking construction of heavy, if weathered, timbers.

Hammarn himself was a disheveled, almost shriveled, man with straggly hair of the purest white. His face had aged in a way that must surely be his Huanin blood coming to the fore: it was deeply lined and pock-marked. For all his evident years, he bobbed about with the nervous energy of a youth.

He welcomed them in to his little house with cheerful enthusiasm, and almost before they had crammed themselves into its single, chaotically full room he was rooting around in a pile of odd sticks and driftwood. With a flourish he emerged clutching a short, thick piece of wood and thrust it upon Anyara.

"Woodtwine," he exclaimed in a crackling voice. "Finished last week. One of my best, I think, I think."

Anyara, a little taken aback, turned it slowly in her hands. Orisian peered at it, and could see delicate carved figures spiraling around the shaft.

"Saolin, you see," Hammarn said as he jabbed unnervingly at the object with a crooked finger. "The change runs around the wood. Starts with the seal, ends with the horse."

"I . . . I see," said Anyara.

"Old craft, woodtwining. Much practiced by fishermen in these parts in the Kingtimes. Saolin a common theme, but this is a piece twine, not a story twine. Need more wood for a story twine, 'less you have a fine touch. Good one this, though, I think. The best came from Kolkyre, of course. In the old days, that is."

"Hammarn," said Yvane softly. The old man looked from face to face, as if unsure who had spoken. He grinned expectantly at them all, baring uneven teeth blotched with brown. He had the look of a child courting congratulation.

"Be calm for a moment, Hammarn," Yvane said. "Your guests have come a long way."

"Ah," said Hammarn, cowed. "Yes, yes. Not often I have visitors here. Much too exciting." He shuffled his feet and looked more hesitantly at Anyara.

"No harm done," she said. She smiled as she held the wood carving out to him. He took it back with a courteous nod.

Orisian glanced around. The hut's interior was filled with wood and clothing, stones and all manner of odds and ends scavenged from the beach. A lathe rested against one wall, almost hidden beneath a pile of dirty sailcloth. A weary-looking fishing net, apparently unused in years, was draped across another wall. He could hardly imagine that there was room here for all of them to bed down, if that was what Yvane had in mind.

After a deal of searching, Hammarn found them some bread. It was only a little stale. They chewed it in silence for a while. Hammarn ate nothing himself, but watched them, his jaw moving soundlessly in imitation. Orisian cast a more careful eye over his surroundings as he worked at breaking down the bread's stubborn resistance. Hidden here and there amongst the chaos were things that stirred his memory and gave the place an unexpectedly familiar feel. A sack of netting hung in one corner, filled with clay jars and pots, all tightly sealed: the same strange herbs and powders that Inurian had so assiduously collected? Behind the lathe was a pile of thick, leather-bound books so musty and moldy-looking that they could not have been opened in years. The place was almost a decayed, disintegrating version of Inurian's room back in Kolglas. Perhaps Hammarn had once had that same sharp curiosity Inurian possessed. The signs of such a past were here, as if Hammarn had brought with him into the final years of his life all the baggage of another person entirely.

Yvane was watching the track of Orisian's eyes.

"Age brings wisdom to some; for others it bears different fruit," she said. The words were gently spoken, and the older *na'kyrim* only chuckled at them.

"Old Hammarn, yes. Or Hammarn the Quiet." He winked at Orisian. "Quiet, you see, I am. I can smell the Shared, but never touch it, never. Five quiet in the Shared, five waking. In Koldihrve, that is. And old I surely am; really quite old." The last words he spoke faded into silence as he was overtaken by some stray thought.

"I thought there were eleven here?" Yvane said, and her voice brought Hammarn back to himself.

"Ah, indeed," he said sadly. "Brenna fell asleep in the very hour of Winterbirth, two years gone. No waking from such an ill-omened slumber."

Yvane nodded. "It is a long time since I was here. Who is First Watchman, Hammarn? We should speak with him, I suppose. Strangers always cause a stir."

"Oh, still Tomas," said Hammarn, and distaste was apparent in his tone. "Vile Tomas," he whispered conspiratorially, "but tell not I said it."

He looked earnestly at them, and Orisian found himself nodding in assent.

"He'll know you're here well enough," Hammarn mused.

Yvane grunted and glanced at Orisian and Anyara. "Unless Tomas is a changed man, it would probably be better if you kept out of his way. Koldihrve is a rough place, and unlikely to be any gentler if they know they have the ruling line of Lannis-Haig in their midst."

"Not changed a whit," Hammarn was saying. "Always vile. No friend of the Glas valley, that's for certain." He cast a nervous glance at Yvane, and hesitated before continuing. "A fool, but not a great friend of yours either, sweet lady. Not sure he'd be best pleased to see you."

Yvane frowned, but realization quickly followed. "Still angry? It's been, what, four years?"

Hammarn shrugged and grinned.

"I had a disagreement with this Tomas the last time I was here," Yvane explained. "One of the fisherwomen bore a *na'kyrim* baby, and he was making a lot of noise about wanting to know who the father was. He was, and no doubt still is, drunk on his little scent of power, and I told him so. He didn't take it kindly. Well, makes no odds to me if I never see the loathsome man again."

She looked pointedly from Orisian to Anyara with an almost mischievous smile. "And if you should run into him, you can always just pretend to be the children of a woodsman from Anlane or somewhere similar. Shouldn't be a difficult lie: you've collected enough dirt and scratches to pass for beggars."

Anyara and Orisian looked down at their hands and garments. It was true enough, of course. Grime covered their skin; their clothes were filthy and full of rents. Their travels since Winterbirth had left marks outside just as they had within.

When he asked for somewhere to wash, Orisian was directed to a tub of icy water outside, against the seaward wall of the hut. As he made his way to it, he noted a pair of bulky men leaning on quarterstaffs in the road. They watched him quite openly as he disappeared behind the shack.

He pulled off his tunic and dunked his head into the barrel. The water was an invigorating shock and set his face tingling. He shook his head, chill droplets spraying his shoulders and back and making him shiver. He scooped handfuls of water onto his chest and neck and rubbed at the ingrained dirt.

Looking out over the crude fencing, he could see the Tal Dyreen ship rocking gently at its anchor. None of the other vessels along the shore could match it. One or two of them might be fit for the journey around Dol Harigaig to Kolglas or Glasbridge, but at this time of year, when the cold winds came in hard on the coast from the empty reaches of the western oceans, none would be a fast or truly safe choice. The Tal Dyreen vessel was an altogether different proposition. It could carry them south with ease, and it must be bound in that direction anyway. There was nothing to the north save Kyrinin clans. The far distant ports of the Black Road Bloods were guarded by storm, ice and the Wrecking Cape, and even the seamen of Tal Dyre did not dare follow that route.

As he gazed out, a fish-hawk arrowed into the water between land and ship. It vanished for a moment in a plume of spray, then its great wings were levering it skyward again. As it beat away, empty-clawed, it shook itself and shed a shower of seawater.

"No luck," said Hammarn behind him. "Poor bird."

The *na'kyrim* offered Orisian a cloth to dry himself with. "Found it," he said, as if in explanation of something.

"There are men watching your house," Orisian said as he scrubbed at his hair with the cloth.

"Yes, yes. Saw them. Sent by Tomas. Men of his Watch, his clubmen. Told you, didn't I, he'd know you were here." He gave an exaggerated laugh. "They're not here to watch me, that's sure."

Orisian patted his arms and chest dry. Since Hammarn did not seem overly concerned about the clubmen, he saw no point in spending his own worries on them. He nodded in the direction of the ship.

"Do you know where the captain is?"

"Captain? Oh yes, very grand. They're Tal Dyre, you know. Sniffing about after furs, rooting about in our stores." He cast a glance over each shoulder, leaned a fraction closer to Orisian. "Don't much take to them, myself. Not to Tal Dyres, I mean. Always coin, with them, never value. They'll not take my woodtwines. No coin in it."

"Never mind," said Orisian. "You'd not want to sell them to someone who didn't appreciate them anyway, would you?"

Hammarn gave him a broad grin. "Right," the *na'kyrim* said. "Quite right."

"Do you know where the captain is?" Orisian asked again as he handed the damp cloth back. "On his boat or onshore?"

Hammarn shrugged. "Couldn't say. Well, onshore I'd say, since I saw him here yesterday. But now? Who knows? Alehouse, most likely."

"We'll look for him there, then."

"Yes," Hammarn agreed emphatically. "You won't . . . you won't let the sweet lady meet Tomas, will you?"

The look of concern on the old *na'kyrim*'s face was acute.

"Yvane? Well I don't think she wants to, does she? It doesn't sound as if it would be a good idea."

"No, indeed. She's a fine lady, but . . . a fine lady. A good friend, no doubt of that, but not quite gentle. Can be rough. Got stickles on her tongue, if you know what I mean?"

"I do," smiled Orisian.

"Good, good. Wouldn't like trouble. I do like it quiet." He shot a sudden, curious look at Orisian. "Not going to be trouble, is there?"

"I hope not," said Orisian.

"Ah. Good. Only I hear things, you know. There's talk. The Fox aren't happy, not at all."

"We heard there are White Owls in the Car Criagar."

"Oh, yes. Yes, them, but worse too. Mail shirts and crossbows, horses. That must be trouble, mustn't it? When the Road's on the march?"

Orisian felt a twist in his gut, and wanted for a moment to take hold of the *na'kyrim*.

"You mean the Black Road?" he asked. "You mean they're in the mountains too?"

Hammarn nodded glumly. "The Black Road, yes. That must be trouble, mustn't it?"

Yvane, after a display of reluctance, allowed Hammarn to take her off to visit some of the other Koldihrve *na'kyrim*. Orisian went with Rothe and Anyara to find the Tal Dyreen captain. All of them noted, without saying anything to one another, the thickset men armed with staffs who openly followed them as they made their way back into the center of the town.

Warm air carried stale smells out from the gloomy interior of the drinking house. There were places much like this in the poorer quarters of Glasbridge or Anduran, but neither Orisian nor Anyara had ever been inside one. It was not the sort of establishment a Thane's family would frequent. They paused on the boardwalk in front. Rothe stepped forward without hesitation.

"Try not to look anyone in the eye," he muttered over his shoulder. "But don't make it obvious."

Anyara rolled her eyes at Orisian.

There were few customers within, and several of those that were present were slumped in stupor or asleep over tables. A tired-looking serving girl, thin and sallow-skinned, watched them enter but made no move to greet them or offer them anything. The floorboards creaked beneath Orisian's tread.

Edryn Delyne was less opulently dressed than when Orisian had last seen him in the harbormaster's house at Glasbridge. Then, on that pine-scented, wine-warmed night before Winterbirth, the Tal Dyreen had been a picture of elegance; now he wore the clothes of a working sailor. Still, his hair was clean and bright, and his beard was as neatly cropped and pointed as it could be.

He was sitting with two of his crew, nursing a pitcher of frothy ale. For just an instant, there was a flicker of surprise in his face as he recognized Orisian.

"An unexpected meeting," the trader said. The clipped tones of the Tal Dyre cant spilled through into everything he said. "And if my eyes read the resemblance right, this might be the sister that I heard of? The last place to find the Lannis-Haig house, this."

Orisian looked around hurriedly, but no one was paying them any attention. The couple of townsfolk within earshot were in no condition to eavesdrop. Nevertheless, he saw that Rothe was keeping a surreptitious watch on the inn's other patrons.

"I would be grateful if you kept our names to yourself," he

murmured. "We are not known here, and it would seem best if it stayed that way."

One of Delyne's pale eyebrows twitched in wry amusement.

"Ill at ease amongst these masterless folk, are we? Some sense in that. Few friends here for Lannis-Haig strays."

"Perhaps," said Orisian. "But we hope we shall not be here much longer. I was surprised to see your ship here, too. I thought you would be long gone on your way back south by now."

"Ah, would that I was," said Delyne with an elaborate sigh. "The music and warm breezes of Tal Dyre are a sweet thought, but trade's an unforgiving master. No rest, no ease, for me and mine until all that needs to be done is done. Since we last met, I ported in Kolkyre. And what did I find in that noble city? A great desire for fine fox fur; the Furriers in despair at the shortage of material. And there am I knowing there's furs to be had in cold Koldihrve, at a price no man would grudge. So one last run it is, in winter's very teeth, before turning for home."

"You're heading south soon, then," said Orisian, trying to sound casual.

"Back to Kolkyre." The Tal Dyreen nodded. "Not what it once was, some say, but I say a fine city still."

"And might you have room for passengers?" asked Anyara. Orisian sank back in his chair and watched as the Tal Dyreen captain ran frank, appraising eyes over Anyara's face.

"A load of pelts and hides in my hold," he mused. "Little comfort for the likes of you, my lady."

"We've had no comfort since Winterbirth, Captain, and could do without it for a while longer."

Delyne gave her a brief smile. Orisian noticed for the first time how white his teeth were.

"Aye, no doubt. I heard some little whispers before I left Kolkyre: that ungentle times were come to your lands. Sad days. Still, space taken by you is space untaken by money in the making. A pretty mascot for a voyage you are, but there is none matches the beauty of coin."

Orisian almost winced, beset by a premonitory image of Anyara emptying the Tal Dyreen's pitcher over his head, but her warming smile barely flickered.

"We understand, of course," she said. "You must be paid for board and lodging. That is only fair. We will turn our gratitude into hard coin, once we were safely back in harbor."

Delyne looked around, taking in as if for the first time the smoke-blackened walls and the splitting and splintered floorboards. He nodded thoughtfully.

"Yes, a cold harbor this for fine folk. Tight corner, too. The wind tells me swords and spears come this way. A tight corner true enough, when there's no boat here fit for the hard pull around the headland. No boat but one, at least."

Anyara took the sea captain's hand in hers, clutching it tight. "Indeed. We are in your hands, Captain."

Delyne gently eased himself free. "Well. Where is it you're heading for?"

"Kolglas, or Glasbridge," said Orisian. "It matters more that we go quickly than which one we make for."

The Tal Dyreen took a long drink of ale, and licked the froth it left behind from his lips. He put on a gloomy face.

"Off my track, those are. Not my planned course at all."

"Bring that jug with you," Orisian said. "We'll fill it with silver after you put us ashore."

After a moment Delyne gave the slightest of shrugs.

"I'll find a berth, of course, for Lannis-Haig. I cannot be waiting for you, mind. Been here a day longer than wished already, waiting for promised goods. They should be here tomorrow, or perhaps the day after, and we'll be off sharply then."

"We are in some haste," said Orisian. "Gold instead of silver in that jug if we leave tonight."

The Tal Dyreen affected a look of regret. "I've men ashore to be gathered. And the passage out to open water from here's a narrow one, not kind to a vessel the size of mine. By choice I'd not attempt it in the dark. For that gold, though, I'll take her out tomorrow, whether my holds are full or not. The tides will be friendly in the afternoon."

Orisian felt a surge of frustration at the thought of another night's delay. But if a Tal Dyreen said he feared to sail these waters in the dark, it must be right to listen.

"Very well," he said. "Send for us. We'll be at the house of a *na'kyrim* called Hammarn."

"Truly, it is remarkable company Lannis-Haig is keeping in these times," smiled Delyne. "One more matter for agreement: I'll put you ashore wherever you wish, but only if I see safety all about me. A sniff of trouble upon the breeze and I'll not risk one board of my ship or one hair off my men's heads. Not for a hundred jugs filled with coin. You'll ride with us all the way to Kolkyre if I say so."

The deal was struck and Edryn Delyne took his crewmen away.

"I remembered him rather better from Glasbridge," Orisian said.

"He probably didn't have so clear a chance of making a profit then," said Anyara. "You know what they say: a Tal Dyreen scenting gold is like a bear smelling honey. Best not to come between the two of them. In any case, it makes him reliable, doesn't it?"

"I'd sooner trust to something other than greed," sighed Orisian, "but it's a safe enough bargain. Tal Dyreens wouldn't do much trade in Glasbridge, or Kolkyre for that matter, if it was known he'd abandoned us here. He'll be a loyal friend, if for no other reason than that."

"They also say that the only women safe around a Tal Dyreen are the dead and the dying, and the dying only sometimes," Rothe observed.

Anyara shrugged at that. "I can look after myself."

Orisian smiled at the confidence in her voice. Anyara's mood was lighter now that they were drawing closer to safety. The shadow beneath which they had toiled really might be lifting a little, and for the first time in weeks hope did not seem quite such an unreasonable thing.

* * *

No more than half a day's march from Koldihrve, on the northern flank of the Car Criagar, a small hill rose from the thin forest. It was dotted with a few scrawny trees. Kanin had set up his camp on the short turf beneath these ragged sentinels.

The march over the mountains had been hard and fast, though plagued more by cold and snow than by the arrows of wood-wights. There had been no sign of the Fox that Kanin had feared might impede their progress. That, he knew, was because of the hundreds of White Owls surging through the Car Criagar. There were corpses in the forest — tokens of the struggle between the clans — but the cresting wave of savagery was always somewhere ahead of the Horin-Gyre company. Some of the dead Kyrinin they found were mutilated or dismembered. There were men, women and children strung up in trees or impaled upon the ground. A part of Kanin was disgusted at the thought of marching in the tracks of blood-frenzied woodwights. Only the greater need kept his feet on the path: until the children of Kennet nan Lannis-Haig were taken, the task he had promised to undertake was incomplete. The butchery the White Owls spread through the forest served that promise, speeding his descent upon Koldihrve.

On the treeless high ground of the Car Criagar a snowstorm had lashed at them. A slide of rock and snow carried off a few victims. There had been no rest on those hostile slopes, so now, with the peaks behind them, he had ordered a brief pause on this lonely hillock. He did not want to blindly lead weary warriors still further into unknown lands. He sent messengers and scouts racing ahead and waited to see what word they might bring back.

The Thane — he still was not accustomed to thinking of himself as such — was seated on a dusky brown rug, breaking his fast on the same biscuits and gruel that fed his warriors, when a tired-eyed man came scrambling up the hillside and fell to his knees before him. It was one of the sentries posted on the camp's outskirts. Kanin calmly set down his bowl and wiped his lips with his cuff. He waited for the man to speak.

"There is an Inkallim here, lord. One of the Hunt. He would speak with you."

That caught Kanin's attention.

"Bring him to me, then."

The man, when he came striding up out of the forest, was accompanied by a great, thick-jawed hound. The beast loped heavily along at its master's heels. They never leash those creatures, Kanin thought. However ruthlessly trained they were, the Hunt's dogs always had a feral, threatening air. Of course, if they were leashed it might make people less intimidated by them, and that would not accord with the Hunt's desires.

The Inkallim was relaxed and casual, but that could not hide the signs of a hard journey. He was pale and gaunt, befitting a man who had seen little of rest or food in several days. As he halted before Kanin his hound sat at his side and fixed its dark eyes on the Thane. Kanin did not rise from his rug, and after a moment's pause the Inkallim squatted down on his haunches.

"Lord," the man said.

"You are one of Cannek's?"

"Of the Hunt, yes. Two of us came on the trail of the Lannis-Haig girl, up over the tops from the falls where the halfbreed was killed."

"And?"

"There are six of them. Two wights, a *na'kyrim,* a Lannis warrior, the girl and a youth: most likely her brother."

Kanin grimaced and rubbed at his eye in frustration.

"So you've failed to kill them," he muttered.

"My companion made an attempt, as they descended from the mountains. It was unsuccessful. I thought it best to follow at a distance, rather than risk my own death and the loss of their trail."

"Of course. Where are they now?"

"They entered Koldihrve this morning. Had I not seen your approach, I would have pursued them and made another attempt in the town."

"Igris!" Kanin shouted, clambering to his feet. His bowl of gruel toppled as he went, spilling its contents across the rug. The Inkallim's hound sprang to its feet and growled.

Kanin's shieldman trotted up from his post a short distance away.

"Find a rider, with a fast horse," the Thane snapped. "They're to make for Koldihrve. I want a message given to whoever passes for a ruler there: the Black Road is coming, and if the Lannis-Haig children are not delivered up to me I will raze the town to the ground, I will slaughter their stock and drown every child of their own in the river."

Igris nodded and turned away.

"And break camp," Kanin shouted after him. "Everyone is to be mounted and ready by the time that messenger is on his way. I want us within sight of Koldihrve by tomorrow's first light."

VI

The walls of the Lore Inkall's Sanctuary at Kan Dredar enclosed a forest. Hundreds of pine trees stood within their bounds, carpeting the ground with more than a century's needles. They filled the great enclosure with the scent of their sap and the air had a close, embracing feel that only the strongest of winds could disturb. There was seldom any sound beneath their dark green canopy, save the twittering of the small birds that flocked to their shelter in winter or the tolling of a bell to mark some ritual observance. The city in the valley below — the sprawling stronghold of the Gyre Blood — rarely made its presence known. Even the most bullish children of Kan Dredar knew better than to venture over the granite wall of the Sanctuary.

This was Theor's domain, and had been his home for all save the first few years of his life. His parents were a distant memory, almost washed away by time. He had been only five or six — he could not be certain which, since no precise record was kept — when they handed him over to the Inkallim in exchange for a few silver coins. Many others entered the Inkall in the same way. Theor, when he thought of his mother and father at all, was grateful for their decision.

Today, many more people than usual were moving from building to building amongst the Sanctuary's trees. As well as Theor's robed Lore Inkallim, there were warriors of the Battle and grim-faced stalkers and trackers of the Hunt. Such activity was only stirred up by the few formal ceremonies of the year or, as now, by the gathering of the Firsts in the Roundhall. Theor knew that it was a pale echo of what was happening beyond his walls: Kan Dredar was in ferment, the people roused by rumors of great victories won in the south. The talk on the streets and in the markets was of nothing else.

Theor walked alone toward the Roundhall. When these meetings were held, the Firsts came and went without their attendants. The oaken doors of the hall stood open, awaiting him. A single servant was sweeping the tiled floor of the wide, circular chamber. At Theor's arrival, the man quietly left, averting his eyes. The hall was simple, undecorated. A pool of yellowish light fell from candles burning on a central stand. Three chairs were arrayed around its edge. Theor sat and waited.

Nyve of the Battle was the next to enter. Theor's friend walked silently to his chair. They did not look at one another. Avenn came last. The First of the Hunt was a lean, taut woman, several years younger than the two men. Her face, framed by straight black hair, was pock-marked with the scars of a childhood disease. As she took her seat the doors swung shut and the Firsts were alone in candlelight.

"Beneath the unclosing eyes of the Last God all is seen," Theor breathed.

"For his eyes are the sun and the moon," the others said in unison.

"And he sees my heart and my will."

"There is only the Black Road."

"Only the Road."

"Only the Road," Nyve and Avenn repeated.

Tiny echoes from the hall's bare stone walls filled out their voices.

"Ten men were found, crossing the Vale of Stones," Theor said. "They were Horin-Gyre. Old warriors, long settled on farms in the Olon valley; farms they abandoned to go to war."

"There have been others," said Nyve, "even from Ragnor's own garrison here. Three deserters were garroted this week. They claimed they meant to go south. Anduran's fall has set many to dreaming of the homeland, and of the Kall."

"The Kall is for the Lore, not the people, to pronounce. This is not the promised renewal."

"As you say. None would question the Lore's primacy in such a matter."

Theor turned toward Avenn.

"Do you have the answers we sought, First?"

"In part, I think." Her accent was precise, curt: a relic of an impoverished upbringing in the Fane-Gyre mountains. "The message that Vana oc Horin-Gyre's people found on the High Thane's courier is in a cipher we have not seen before. We cannot read it." She saw the disappointment in Theor's eyes, and pressed on quickly before he had a chance to speak it. "But the cipher's form and structure are familiar. No one of Horin-Gyre would have recognized it for what it is; it's fortunate that Vana was willing to pass it to the Hunt. I am told it is most likely a variation on those that Gryvan's Shadowhand introduced in Vaymouth."

"And the messenger himself?" Theor asked darkly. "What did he have to say?"

"He told us as much as he knew before he died. It was not easy to break him, but we found his limits. Although he did not live long enough for us to test him repeatedly, we are confident he told us everything he could. He was bound for Dun Aygll, in the guise of a shepherd. There, he knew only that he was to pass the message to a stallholder in one of the markets."

"It is not much," murmured Nyve.

"It is enough," Theor said.

Avenn nodded. "We deal in likelihoods, in possibilities. But the Hunt's judgment is clear: Ragnor oc Gyre corresponds with the Haig Chancellor. Perhaps with Gryvan oc Haig himself."

"They are one and the same, Gryvan and his Shadowhand," Theor asserted. "The Chancellor holds the reins of the Haig Bloods just as much as the High Thane does."

"In most things, that is true," the First of the Hunt agreed.

"Well, then," sighed Theor, "the time has come for us to make some decisions. The ice is breaking beneath our feet; we must rush onward, or turn back."

"Agreed," Nyve rumbled. "Our High Thane seeks to play the Bloods against one another. The Horin lands have been all but promised to both Gaven and Wyn should Kanin fail to return, so they will not demur if Ragnor withholds his aid. Our Bloods have lost their vigor; forgotten their heritage. Wealth and power in this world please them more than the prospect of the next, and Ragnor fears his wealth and power will be at risk if he tests himself against Gryvan oc Haig. Only Horin out of all of them has kept the creed at its very heart, and now Angain is dead and his son will be abandoned." He shook his head in puzzlement. "It is surprising that the Gyre Thane should so far forget himself."

"It is not so long ago that the Inkall aided a Gyre Thane in humbling Horin-Gyre," Avenn pointed out softly.

"Those were different times," Theor said, "and Ragnor's father a different man. He had no secrets from us. He needed none, since his will ran in the same riverbed as our own. What was done then in the Stone Vale strengthened Gyre, and in those days that meant it strengthened the creed. Our loyalty is first to the creed, second the Gyre Blood and only third the High Thane — the man — himself. If the needs of the first two now dictate it, the last may be set aside."

"We have long known that Ragnor holds us too lightly in his regard," said Nyve. His gaze was wandering over the tiled floor like a man who had dropped some coin and lost it in the pattern. "It has been clear for a long time that there might come a moment such as this, when we must decide whether to put our hand more firmly upon the tiller. I take it we are agreed, that something is wrong . . . rotten . . . when victories such as those Kanin nan Horin-Gyre has won elicit no response from the High Thane?"

Theor and Avenn both nodded.

Nyve rocked his head to one side. Still he did not look up. "Vana oc Horin-Gyre is not Angain's widow for nothing. She is already gathering fresh forces. She may send them to her son's aid even if Ragnor forbids it."

Avenn's voice betrayed an eagerness when she spoke. "Given encouragement, there are many who would march, whether or not Ragnor wishes it."

For the first time, Theor thought he knew what was fated to follow from this meeting, the role they were to play in the unfolding of fate's pattern. He had never doubted the shape of Avenn's instincts: the Hunt always found itself leaders with a taste for the Road's most dramatic twists and turns. Nyve he had not been so certain of. His old friend was harder to read, not given to haste or precipitous action.

"How many more swords can Vana put in the field?" Theor asked.

Nyve glanced at Avenn, silently acknowledging that she might know something he did not. The Hunt had an eye and an ear in every corner of every Blood.

"No more than another thousand," Avenn said. "They are the last, unless she were to leave Hakkan itself defenseless."

"Not many," said Theor. "Whatever happens, we should at least strive to preserve the Horin-Gyre Blood. They must be protected if the creed is to be strengthened rather than weakened by all of this. They are a beacon others can look to, especially now that they have achieved the impossible."

"They are," Nyve agreed. "All would depend upon the commonfolk. Put enough fire in the bellies of his people and even a High Thane cannot disregard it. What does the Hunt say, Avenn?"

"We can stir the villages. Dozens have already gone across the Stone Vale. There is a fervor not seen in many years: feasting and bonfires and telling battle tales. My people could set talk of glory loose in every meeting hall, every farmyard; light a fire the Thanes could not restrain."

"Even with every sword Horin-Gyre can muster and an army of commonfolk alongside them, Kanin could not stand against the full weight of Haig," Nyve observed. He was methodically massaging his crooked fingers. "He will be consumed. As, it seems, Ragnor wishes."

"All might be different, were the Battle to march," Avenn suggested.

Neither Theor nor Nyve replied at once. Nyve's kneading of his fingers did not pause, as if he had not even heard what Avenn said. Theor regarded the First of the Hunt thoughtfully. She was impatient, always eager to be moving on. Perhaps it was for the best. They all knew this was the crux of the decision that must be made.

"That would remove all restraint," Nyve observed quietly.

"Perhaps that is what is required," Theor said. His tone was gentle, conversational. He would not compel his old friend into this. In times such as these, unanimity was important. "If Ragnor oc Gyre has made agreements with the Haig Thane; if he would rather see the Horin-Gyre Blood broken than risk open warfare with Haig; if he prefers playing games of worldly power, and the warm safety of his throne, to seeking the creed's rightful dominion over all people — if all of this is true, then perhaps the time for restraint has passed. War forges a people as the furnace does a sword. It will restore our people's temper. And if the Battle marches, nothing Ragnor can do will stop the fire we set. Thousands — tens of thousands — will follow."

"That's true," Nyve said quietly, "that's true." He lapsed into silence.

Theor thought it best to leave the First of the Battle to his ruminations. He turned to Avenn.

"Tell me, do you remember a conversation we had three years ago? I believe it was at the wedding of the Gaven-Gyre Bloodheir. You made some mention of a woman you had in Kolkyre. A blade, you called her, poised over our enemy's heart."

She smiled. It was a wolfish kind of expression, Theor thought.

"I remember it well. I am surprised you do, Lorekeeper."

"Oh, I find I remember a great many things as I get older. It's perverse, but there you are. If we are to abandon ourselves to fate, shed all restraint, I wonder if the time might not have come to let that blade fall?"

"Gladly, if it is our united will," said Avenn, with a sideways glance at Nyve. "That is one death that would fill our people with belief. Once that head rolled, it is unlikely that anyone could prevent conflagration: not us, not Ragnor, not Gryvan oc Haig."

"We choose how we meet fate, not what that fate is," Theor said. "If it is written that we are to succeed in this, we will do so no matter what dangers or obstacles may seem to bar our way. I do nothing without full consent, but I say the time has come."

Nyve laid his hands like crumpled cloth in his lap. "The Battle will march."

So it is done, Theor thought. For good or ill, we put ourselves in fate's balance; we face a tumultuous future. "We are agreed, then. The Battle will march, a Thane will die and the people will rise. Let it be as it is written."

"As it is written."

"As it is written."

They left as they had come: one by one, alone. Avenn went first, striding out into the day's white light. Theor and Nyve did not speak as they waited for her to disappear from view, but before the First of the Battle followed her out of the Roundhall Theor laid one hand upon his shoulder and let it rest there for a while.

Theor retired early to his private chambers that night. He sent away his servants and dressed himself in his night robes. He opened the carved box at his bedside and removed a scrap of seer-stem. The herb had blackened his lips over the years, and they tingled faintly now, anticipating what was to come. He lay down and slipped the stem into his mouth. He worked carefully at it with his teeth: crushing and squeezing, not breaking it apart. The dark juices oozed out and that familiar, comforting numbness began to spread over his tongue and lips. Slowly, slowly it would spread through his jaw and over his scalp and eventually seep into his mind. Then the visions would come. Sometimes, there was the precious sense of patterns emerging from the chaos of events and lives.

None save the Lore Inkallim were permitted the use of seer-stem. Others, lacking the discipline of a lifetime's schooling in the creed of the Road, could be led astray by the sights the stem offered. The key was to understand that it was not the future that was contained in these fleeting, formless visions, but the past and the present. When Theor dreamed seerstem dreams, he saw all the thousands of paths that had been followed to bring the present into being; he saw, in all their multitudes, the countless tales — finished and unfinished — that the Last God had read from his Book of Lives. But he did not see what was yet to befall those traveling that vast, intricate Black Road.

As he waited for the seerstem to take its effect the First of the Lore watched the flame on the candle by his bed. He was possessed by a vague unease. The weeks and months to come were likely to bring a war greater than any there had been for more than a century. That in itself did not concern him. The Kall would come only when all humankind was bound to the creed of the Black Road; such unity could only be achieved through war and conquest. As the Kall itself was inevitable, so too was eventual victory, whatever the outcome of the present strife.

The roots of Theor's disquiet lay rather in regret. He had thought, when Ragnor first ascended to his throne in Kan Dredar, that he would make a good High Thane. In those early years he had seemed of one mind with his late father: dutiful, secure in his adherence to the creed and to the primacy of its advancement. Somehow, Ragnor had instead become merely a ruler, consumed by the meaningless day-to-day business of power. And they — all of the Inkallim, but most of all Theor himself — had failed in their responsibilities. They had allowed the rot to set in. Once, it might have been cut out with nothing more than a child's woodworking knife; now it would require a sword. Had he allowed the vigilance of the Lore to slip? Was he to blame that they had come to such extremity? In the end, it did not matter. This was the course they were fated to follow. But still, it could not hurt to ensure that no one had any further excuses to forget that the creed was the light that guided all things. When the Battle marched south, it would be fitting for a party of the Lore Inkallim to accompany it.

The seerstem's tingling touch reached behind his ears, worked its way into the bones of his skull. He rested his head on the pillow and closed his eyes. Shapes were beginning to move on the inside of his eyelids. He stilled himself, forcing all thoughts from his mind. He waited to see what would come.

* * *

Taim Narran could not be sure what was being destroyed on the other side of the door. Judging by the sounds that filtered through the heavy oak, it was something substantial. Out of respect for Roaric nan Kilkry-Haig's feelings — and perhaps, if he was honest, out of trepidation — he waited until the noise had subsided before entering.

Lheanor's one surviving son — the Bloodheir, now — stood in the middle of the small room. Fragments of wood were scattered around him on the stone floor. A chair leg still hung, forgotten, from his limp hand. Roaric's head was bowed, his eyes closed, his shoulders slumped. The Thane's son had returned from the south only this morning. He had brought even fewer of his men back alive from Dargannan-Haig lands than Taim had. To be greeted with the news of his brother's death at Grive would have been too much even for one of less tempestuous nature, Taim thought.

Roaric had not registered Taim's presence. He stood quite still, lost in the numb fog of grief. Taim hesitated. He was not sure that he could offer anything to the young man; or that it would be welcomed, even if he could. They had been comrades, though, in Gryvan's war; friends amidst a storm of hostility.

"Roaric," he said softly, then, when there was no response, again more loudly: "Roaric."

The younger man looked up, his eyes wild and bleary. They drifted over Taim, swung around across the window.

"I am sorry," Taim murmured. "You deserved a better homecoming than this. We all did."

Roaric let the chair leg slip from his fingers. It clattered to the floor. He walked to the window, unconsciously kicking aside the detritus of his rage as he went.

"They'll bleed rivers of blood in answer for this, the Black Road," he said thickly. He planted his hands on either side of the window, stared out over his father's city. "I should have been here."

"We both should have been."

"I was proud when my father gave me charge of our armies to march south. Proud! And look at this now. All but a few hundred of the men who marched with me are dead. My brother's dead. We're nothing but shadows of what we once were, Kilkry and

Lannis. We're like sickly children, our strength leaking away from a thousand little sores."

"It's not over yet," said Taim.

"No?" Roaric snapped. He spun away from the window and glared fiercely at Taim. The emotion lasted only for an instant, though. As soon as he saw Taim's face Roaric's own anger sank away. He only shook his head.

"There will be a chance for us to give answer for what has happened," Taim said levelly.

"Perhaps," murmured the Kilkry-Haig Bloodheir. "Perhaps."

"I leave for Glasbridge tomorrow. I wanted to see you, offer my regrets and good wishes, before I left."

"I am sorry to intrude."

The soft voice from the doorway surprised both of them. Ilessa, Roaric's mother, stood there. There was an awful pain in her face, Taim saw, when she looked at her son. She fears for him, he thought.

"There is someone here I think you will wish to see, Taim Narran," Ilessa said. "Will you come with me?"

Taim glanced at Roaric, but the younger man had turned away, almost as if he was ashamed to meet his mother's gaze. With a heavy heart, he followed Ilessa out and down the spiraling stairway that formed the spine of the Tower of Thrones.

"Boats are coming to the harbor," Ilessa said as they went. "They've taken flight from Glasbridge; it's fallen, Taim. Destroyed."

A groan escaped Taim's lips before he could restrain it.

"All is not ill tidings today, though," Ilessa said quickly. "Come, in here."

She ushered him through a doorway, but did not follow. He wondered why for a moment, then his eyes fell upon the room's sole occupant: a slight woman seated at a table. At that sight, Taim's breath caught in his throat and his mind was swept clean of all that had crowded it. Tears sprang to his eyes as she rose from the table and he went to embrace his wife.

"I feared for you," he said as he crushed her to him and felt her arms about his waist. Here was light and hope amidst all the gloom, and he could do nothing more than cling to her.

"And I for you," Jaen replied in an uneven voice. "You have been gone too long this time."

"Yes, far too long." And that was all he could say for a little while.

She told him, later, of Glasbridge's end; of the still, misty morning when a wild flood came out of the north. The Glas became a wall of water roaring down the valley. It swept across the camp of warriors outside the town's northern gate, gathering a cargo of dead men and horses. It piled up against the palisade and the bridges, hammering at them with trees and boulders and corpses carried by the surge. The water swelled and foamed until it tore the great timbers of Glasbridge's stockade out of the earth. The wall of oak that had guarded the town's northern flank was ripped away and carried down to the sea. The flood rushed through the heart of the town. And at last, almost upon the stroke of noon, the stone bridge that had spanned the mouth of the river since the days of the Aygll Kingship broke and crashed with a defeated rumble into the foaming waters.

There were hours of chaos, of noise and fear and anger. At dusk the army of the Black Road came in the wake of the flood, and then there was nothing left but fear.

Taim's wife, his daughter and her husband fought their way to the docks and in the mad tumult of the waterside managed to buy their way onto a little fishing boat. The vessel, laboring beneath a mass of frightened families, struggled out into the estuary. Looking back as they drew close to Kolglas, they had seen the night sky lit by a diffuse orange glow, and they knew that Glasbridge was afire.

Through all this grim tale Taim felt only relief and the lifting of a great burden. His wife and daughter were delivered to him out of the slaughter that had consumed his homeland. Beyond hope, the darkness had seen fit to allow him this one ray of light. When they lay that night in one another's arms for the first time in so long, he found that he still had the capacity, for a time, to believe in — and to accept — sanctuary.

VII

Orisian and Yvane were sitting on the shore behind Hammarn's hut. The *na'kyrim* was scraping dirt from beneath her fingernails with a twig. Orisian was watching Edryn Delyne's ship. Torches had been lit at bow and stern as dusk began to fall. Now and again their light flickered as somebody moved in front of them.

Somewhere out in the gathering gloom a seabird screeched. The cry was not one Orisian recognized from Kolglas. It sounded like the voice of a deserted land. The small boats lying on the mud, and tied to decrepit little jetties, had an abandoned air about them.

"No sign of Ess'yr yet," Orisian said. "Or Varryn. I thought they might have come to find us by now."

"They might have problems of their own, now the White Owls — maybe even the Black Road — are loose in their lands. Anyway, there'll be time enough in the morning, if they've not come to us by then. You said the ship sails in the afternoon?"

Orisian nodded. Yvane was digging at her fingernails with greater vigor. It was obvious she had more to say, and he did not have to wait long to hear it.

"You understand something of the weight the Kyrinin place upon death and the dead?"

"Something."

"They feel the eyes of the dead upon them. They put food out to keep away the restless dead, and have their soulcatchers to snare the ones they can't put off. This *ra'tyn* that Ess'yr has taken on is an oath that may not be broken, because it is given to someone on the brink of death. If she failed that promise, the failure would keep the dead one from his rest and shake him into such anger that no amount of food, or chanting, or drumming would keep him from her. No matter how much he loved her when he lived. It's a serious matter."

"And Varryn doesn't approve," murmured Orisian.

"No. He never liked Inurian in the first place, I would guess. Most Kyrinin think little better of *na'kyrim* than they do of Huanin; I expect Varryn was . . . distressed at his sister's involvement with one of them."

"Still, he's helped her to see her promise through."

"He loves her. And she must have loved Inurian to make it in the first place." She cast aside the stick and scratched at her upper arm. "You understand, then. Ess'yr will die for you if need be, because of that promise. For no other reason. That is the beginning and end of why she has come so far with you, why she has stayed close."

Orisian looked intently at the *na'kyrim*. She pretended not to notice his gaze.

"No other reason," he said, and Yvane gave a quick, emphatic nod.

"None," she said. "It's enough, isn't it?"

"It's enough."

"Good. Tomorrow, then. In the morning, you can say your farewells."

Orisian knew perfectly well that he might never see Ess'yr again once Koldihrve was behind him, and he would be lying to himself if he pretended that thought mattered not at all. Her presence — however distant it might sometimes be — had woken, and now nourished, something deep inside him.

"It won't go well for them, will it? If the White Owls come this far, and the Black Road?" he said.

Yvane folded her hands into her lap.

"It may not. The Fox has never been a large clan. Not many warriors. The townsfolk might help them, but you can never be sure with Koldihrvers. They're not usually the kind of people to put themselves at risk on another's account. But who knows? It's only those Black Road brutes who think the future's carved in stone."

"This is madness," muttered Orisian with sudden bitterness. "None of this would've happened if we hadn't come here."

Yvane's hand twitched, as if she wanted to swat away his thought, but it stayed in her lap.

"Be careful," she said. "Guilt's a dangerous thing. Whoever's fault this is, it's not yours, or your sister's. Fox and White Owl, True Bloods and Black Road: these are old battles. They began long before you were born. Most likely, they'll still be raging long after we're all gone."

A faint shout from the Tal Dyreen vessel drew his eyes up, but there was nothing to see. It was getting darker all the time; the shipboard torches stood out more brightly than ever. One moment he longed to be back at Kolglas or Glasbridge, hungered for the chance to do something more than run from his enemies; the next he was afraid of what he would find there, of what it would mean to be Thane at a time of war. It could have been Fariel; but for the Heart Fever, it could have been Fariel who had to face this. That would have been better for the Blood.

He sighed. He had no wish to dwell on such things.

"You are coming with us, then. On the ship?" he asked.

Yvane wrinkled her nose. It was a sharp, uncharacteristic gesture.

"Seems the wisest course. Much as I like my solitude, I'm no fool. Neither the Vale of Tears nor the Car Criagar seem the most appealing of places at the moment. Can't say I'm overjoyed at the prospect. I've never met a Tal Dyreen, but from what I've heard of them I doubt I'll find them pleasant company."

"What will you do afterward?"

"Thank my good fortune that I've made it out of all this," she said with a shrug. "Curse Inurian for sending you in my direction. Perhaps go to Highfast, which is what he wanted of me all along. Inurian often got his way in the end, I seem to recall."

"Can't you just . . . visit them as you did Hammarn, though?" Orisian asked. "If all Inurian wanted was that they should be told about Aeglyss, about what was happening, can't you do it that way?"

Yvane laughed. She gazed out toward the horizon.

"If I turned up like that in the Elect's chambers, I'd be slapped away and cast out before she even bothered to find out who it was. I've no wish to repeat my experience of trying to eavesdrop on Aeglyss. They're more than a little protective of their privacy in Highfast: uninvited guests, even other *na'kyrim,* don't get a warm welcome. They're frightened, Orisian. All of us are, deep down. You pure-blooded folk have made sure of that, over the centuries.

"Anyway, even if I was given the chance to announce myself, the mere mention of my name . . . well, let's just say I didn't leave there on the best of terms. Oh, they loved Inurian, of course. When he took his leave, it was all kind words, reluctant partings. When I went, it was arguments and ill wishes."

"You didn't like Inurian very much, did you?"

"Ha! There's some precious youthful innocence. To imagine that it's all as simple as like or dislike; love or hate. Inurian and I never did decide which side of the line we fell upon."

Sudden noise from Hammarn's hut had both of them rising sharply and turning. There was shouting, the pounding of a fist on wood. Orisian went first, around to the front of the shack. Three men stood in the roadway: two of them torchbearers, the third a red-faced man with a dented iron helm on his head and a spear in his hand. This third was facing Hammarn, who was struggling to block the doorway with his slight frame. The old *na'kyrim* was agitated, hopping from foot to foot.

"Not a way to treat guests," Hammarn was spluttering, "not at all. Cracking at doors in the dark."

His sideways glance in response to Orisian's appearance made the red-faced man turn around. He had a patchy beard spread sparsely over a scabbed chin. The glare he fixed on Orisian was almost contemptuous.

"This one?" he demanded.

"A guest," Hammarn said irritably before anyone else could reply. "This is Ame," he told Orisian.

The leaden glumness which he put into the phrase, as if he was announcing the arrival of an unpleasant affliction, might have made Orisian smile at another time, but he was tired and had a heavy heart.

"Second Watchman," Ame said gravely. If he had hoped Orisian would be impressed he was disappointed.

"What's happening?" Rothe snapped from over Hammarn's shoulder. The shieldman's abrupt, and bulky, emergence from the shadows within the hut had the two torchbearers taking a nervous step back. Even Ame looked momentarily alarmed before he snapped his attention back to Orisian. He jabbed at him with a stubby finger.

"You're wanted at the Tower," he said.

"Tower?"

"Where Tomas holds court," muttered Yvane.

"He's wanted, you're not," Ame growled at her. "You'll keep out of sight, unless you're a fool."

"My pleasure," Yvane said acidly.

Rothe had pushed past Hammarn and stepped onto the road. He was a good head taller than Ame, and leaned uncomfortably close to the Second Watchman.

"Not clever to throw orders around without knowing who you're talking to," he said.

"It's all right, Rothe," Orisian said quickly. "There's no point in starting arguments. Not now. You and I'll go with them."

He was worried for a moment that they would insist that Anyara came — they must know she was inside, as they'd been watching so closely — but Ame seemed satisfied. He was trying to stretch himself, Orisian noticed, to close the gap a little on Rothe's height.

They went through the dark town in silence. There was nothing left of the day now; the only light was that seeping out between window shutters. Koldihrve was quiet. The air bore the faint smell of meat cooking over a fire.

Ame walked ahead of them, a hint of ungainly swagger in his stride. The First Watchman's abode was the only stone-built structure in the whole town: an old, fragile-looking round tower that stood all of three stories high. A wooden hall and house had been built around it at some time, leaving the tower like a stubby stone finger jabbed up through their midst.

Orisian and Rothe were left to wait in a small, musty room. Voices leaked through from the adjoining hall; Koldihrve's Watch ate and drank well, from the sound of it. Rothe had the look of a man with only a small store of patience left.

"I'll talk to this Tomas and we'll get back to the others," Orisian said. "It won't take long."

His shieldman gave his beard a distracted scratch. "It's not right to have masterless men dragging us this way and that as they like," he muttered.

"We only have to keep them happy until tomorrow. Nothing else matters but getting safely on that ship."

Ame returned. He had shed his helmet and swapped his spear for a hunk of fat-soaked bread. He gestured at Orisian with it. "The First Watchman'll see you."

Rothe rose as well, but Ame waved him back. "The guard dog can stay here, I'd say."

"I don't think so," said Rothe.

"I'll talk to him," Orisian told him. He was surprised at the still calm he felt within. This all felt unimportant, a small detail

510

in the journey to Delyne's ship; just something that had to be shuffled aside to clear their path. "Wait for me here."

Rothe looked doubtful, but settled back onto the bench.

The First Watchman's chamber was simple and sparsely furnished. Tomas himself was a wiry, knotted man who sat low in his chair and regarded Orisian with a sharp eye. There was a wolf's pelt stretched on the wall behind him. Tomas pointed at a stool.

"Way I hear it, there's trouble in the mountains," Tomas said as Orisian was sitting down. His breathing had an uneven edge to it, the air pushed out from his lungs through bubbling phlegm. "White Owl and Fox at each other like stoats. That's no great surprise, but what I hear is it's different this time. Humans up there, too. Now the Fox don't know much about such things, but I'm First Watchman, and I know a thing or two. So when they tell me there's Huanin out there, with women marching alongside men, I think Black Road to myself. Strange times, that the lords of Kan Dredar are wandering in the Car Criagar, seems to me."

"We fled from them," said Orisian, unwilling to say any more than he had to. "It's only luck and chance have brought us here. Some Fox Kyrinin guided us. We would have been finished without them."

He added the last as an afterthought, hoping that it might carry some weight here, where Huanin and Kyrinin lived with only a river between them. The First Watchman ignored it.

"You've the voice of a Lannis boy."

"My name is Orisian. I'm from Kolglas."

Tomas nodded slowly, as if he had already known as much. It was bluff, Orisian decided; a self-important gesture. It seemed very unlikely that Tomas would know the name of Croesan's nephew.

"Not just Kyrinin you travel with," the First Watchman continued. "Yvane, my Watch tells me."

"We met her in the mountains," Orisian said.

"Poor company you keep. But I always say the oathbound're short on judgment."

Orisian started to reply, but Tomas ignored him and continued.

"So who else? Fox, *na'kyrim*; what about the others? A girl, I heard, and a man big enough to be half bear."

"My sister," Orisian said. "And the man's a woodcutter. He was working for my father." With each passing moment he was less inclined to tell Tomas exactly who he was; the worst of the man's hostility was kept just out of sight, but Orisian could see more than enough of it to make him cautious.

"Oh, yes? Well, if you say so. We keep out of other folk's business here. No one'll trouble you if you give us no cause."

He coughed and wiped his mouth with the back of his hand.

"Each of your Thanes, when he's fresh come into his rule, sends messengers trying to persuade us to take his oath. We pay them little heed, and they don't stay long. One sent gifts a while ago; Tavan, if I remember right. I've still got the sword my great-uncle had from his men. Pretty enough on the wall, though I'd have more use for a good bear trap, truth be told. Man who brought it went away with a ringing in his ears. My great-uncle wasn't a man to play pretty with words."

Tomas chuckled, then hawked and spat into a battered tin pot at his feet. The mess accumulated there suggested it had never been cleaned.

"Oaths make men slaves, I reckon," said Tomas. "No place for 'em here."

"You might find a use for that sword, though, if the Black Road comes this way," said Orisian.

Tomas shrugged at that and drummed his fingers on the tabletop.

"We can bend with the wind," he said. "Black Road or your lot makes little odds to us. It's the oath, and what comes with it, that takes a man's freedom. What difference who he's given it to? You're all the same deep down. Oaths like yours only lead to killing and the like, one way or the other."

Orisian bit his lip rather than respond.

"So it's war, is it?" Tomas asked. "On the Glas? Must be, if you've the Black Road up in the hills."

"Fighting, yes. It won't last."

"If you say so," said Tomas with a crooked smile. He was missing at least a couple of teeth. "Bound to run out of people to kill sooner or later, I suppose. I'd not want your troubles in Koldihrve, though."

"There'll be no trouble," Orisian said firmly. "We're taking ship with the Tal Dyreens tomorrow and you'll not see us again."

"Not short of coin, if you've tempted that one into carrying you around. You taking the *na'kyrim* with you?" His voice was thickening all the time, the words rattling in his throat.

"Yvane? Yes, she's coming with us."

"Good enough," Tomas said. "I find you, or her, still here after that boat's gone and I'll want to know why, mind. I look after this town, and I've plenty men'll help me do it. We don't want Lannis folk here any time, but doubly not if the Black Road's rooting around."

"We're gone tomorrow. You won't have to worry about that."

Tomas nodded. He was shaken by a liquid-sounding cough even as he waved Orisian away. Orisian retreated, as if the sound itself might carry disease into his own chest. As soon as he was outside, breathing the cold night air, he set to forgetting the conversation. It did not matter that Tomas seemed a fraction more threatening — perhaps even dangerous — than he had expected. Soon, soon they would be away from this town, and Orisian was confident he would never return.

They slept in Hammarn's hut, all crammed together on the floor with furs and cloth spread over them. The boards were rough on the back, but Orisian slept well. Even when Rothe began to snore — a rumbling, rasping sound vigorous enough to rouse half the town — Orisian woke no more than was needed to prod at his shieldman's shoulder. Rothe shuffled onto his side with an irritated mutter, and the snoring stopped.

Once or twice more, Orisian brushed against the surface of wakefulness. The sighing of tiny waves on the beach infiltrated his sleep, and later the patter of rain on the roof. He heard boat timbers creak, and he heard the breathing of his companions, and pressed in tight in that small hut he was warm. He rested, and though his dreams were troubled they did not disturb him, and in the morning they sank away and he forgot them.

* * *

In that half-hearted dawn, Kanin could see the lights of Koldihrve. They flickered in the grey blur of land, sea and cloud, a feeble and fragile cluster beneath the rain that was starting to fall. The Horin-Gyre Thane glanced upward. An immense host of fat, dark clouds was massing there. A downpour was coming.

He and five of his Shield had outpaced the rest of his company. They waited here, within sight of the town, for the others to catch up. They should be here, Kanin thought angrily. It would still take a good two hours to reach Koldihrve. The going had been slower than he hoped, across this sodden, empty landscape. Every moment of delay cut at him, plunging him deeper and deeper into a black mood.

His mount could sense his temper, and shook its mane uneasily. There was a boggy stream a few paces away; Kanin nudged the horse over to it and loosened the reins to allow it to drink. He patted its neck. It was not the same animal he had picked from his stables all those months ago. But then, none of them could be the same, after such a journey: through Anlane, to Anduran, across the Car Criagar. Its coat had lost its luster, the definition of its muscles had faded. He remembered how it had tossed its head and stamped its feet that morning when he rode out from Hakkan's gate, with Wain at his side. That magnificent arrogance was all but gone now.

"We're not what we were, are we?" he whispered to it.

Igris eased his own mount up alongside the Thane.

"The others are here, lord," the shieldman said.

Kanin glanced around. The remaining forty or so of his warriors were indeed arriving, one by one. They came in an extended line, all looking drained and damp. Their horses were exhausted.

"No sign of that messenger we sent ahead?" Kanin asked.

"Not yet. But he cannot be more than an hour or two ahead of us."

"Very well. We'll pause here, but only long enough to feed and water the horses. We can rest once we've got what we came here for."

Igris nodded curtly.

Kanin dismounted and led his horse gently to a patch of lush grass. They had run out of the oats they had brought as feed the day before, just as they had almost exhausted their own food supplies. Whatever happened in the day now begun, Koldihrve was going to have to provide everything they needed to return over the Car Criagar. And what would they find when they got back to Anduran, Kanin wondered. He spared himself only that one moment to think of Wain. He would see her soon enough.

His horse tore at the grass. The rain was getting heavier; great fat drops pattered down upon them. Kanin shivered. He preferred the clean, dry snow of his homeland to this dank kind of winter.

"Lord," someone shouted. "Wights."

Kanin ducked around behind his horse and followed the pointing arm of the warrior.

There were Kyrinin moving, rushing out from a woodland and onto the flat fields and bogs of the valley. Dozens, then scores. They spilled out in a great wave that flowed over the rushes and through the scrub toward the great River Dihrve. Toward its mouth, and Koldihrve.

"Is it White Owls, or Fox?" Kanin demanded.

No one replied. At this distance, they could not tell.

"Woodwights!" cried Kanin in frustration. Even now, when he had thought himself rid of them, the petty games that Aeglyss and his savages had set in motion were plaguing him.

"It must be the White Owls," suggested Igris, peering through the sheets of rain now crashing down. "They're making for that Fox camp by the river mouth."

Kanin swung up into the saddle. Rain pelted his head and back. Everyone was rushing, filling the air with cries and the clatter of weapons. He did not hear it. He turned his horse in the direction of Koldihrve. The future was there, waiting for him, and he could only advance into it. His sword was naked in his hand.

"The slaughterhouse calls us," he shouted. "We ride!"

VIII

Behind the tent where the Voice of the White Owls dwelled, in a stone-lined pit beneath a roof of oak beams that had been turned hard as rock by time and smoke and heat, the *torkyr* burned. Through day and night, snow and wind, the clan fire would burn all winter long, tended by the chosen guardians who fed it and watched over it. When spring came, and the Voice had chanted over the flames, and the people began to disperse, each *a'an* would take away a single burning brand, so that in all the campfires of their summer wanderings through the furthest reaches of Anlane they carried with them a fraction of the clan's bright soul.

It was to the Voice's tent that the band of warriors brought Aeglyss the *na'kyrim,* bound and gagged by thongs of leather. They tied him to a song staff rising from the ground outside the Voice's tent, and sat cross-legged to wait. They waited for many hours. The sun walked across the sky. Clouds, the scattered raiment of the Walking God, came and went. The *na'kyrim* moaned and bled from his wrists and from the corners of his mouth where the gag had cut his skin. At length a small child, her hair dyed berry-red and holes pierced in her cheeks, came out from the tent and beckoned one of the warriors to come inside. After an hour he re-emerged and gave a slow nod. The *na'kyrim* was untied and ungagged and brought into the presence of the Voice.

She was an aging woman, with skin creased and folded by the years and hair the color of the moon on water. There were others within — the wise, the *a'an* chiefs of last summer, the singers and chanters and buriers of the dead and the *kakyrin* with their necklaces of bone — but it was the Voice alone who spoke with the *na'kyrim*.

They talked for a long time, the old woman and the halfbreed, and of many things. They talked of the clan's history and of its struggles against the Huanin in the War of the Tainted and the centuries since. They talked of the evil done by those who ruled in the city in the valley, their axes and fire that cleared the trees from White Owl lands, and their herds of cattle that reached ever further into Anlane; of the *na'kyrim*'s life, his flight from the White Owl as a child and eventual return, bearing gifts and promises from the cold men of the north. Through it all, the judgment was being formed, built out of the threads of the past that led to the present. Only at the end did they talk of alliances forged in necessity, and of hopes and expectations betrayed.

The Voice asked him, softly, why the lord whose army had passed through the White Owls' forest now turned away his friends and forgot them. Why the promises of friendship the *na'kyrim* had made on that lord's behalf were now so much dust. The *na'kyrim* had no answer to that, but spoke instead in the evil way he had. He spoke, as the White Owls now understood that he had so often before, with a tongue that made truth out of lies, that corrupted the mind's strength and turned judgments inside out. Had there not been so many of them there in the Voice's tent, they might have been deceived, but they had prepared themselves for the dangers of this *na'kyrim*. Some cried out and sang to drown his poisonous words; others belabored him with sticks.

He begged and pleaded but there had, in the end, to be a reckoning. However long his absence, he had been one of the people once, and he was theirs to do with as they would. The Voice gave her judgment and he was dragged out of her presence.

*

The *na'kyrim* struggled and shouted as they bore him away from the *vo'an*, and spoke in a way that threatened to lay wreaths of mist around the thoughts of the warriors. They beat him with the hafts of spears until he was still and silent. Then they carried him up above the valley. Up and up they climbed, until the trees grew wind-bent and the grass beneath their feet became coarse and rough. They climbed into the afternoon, until they pierced the roof of Anlane and came out upon the moors that formed a border-land between forest and sky. And still they went on amongst the rocky ridges and ravines. In time they began to descend again, and at last, upon a promontory of rock that was closely fringed by trees, they came to the Breaking Stone.

The great boulder — the height of two men — stood alone, resting where the Walking God had left it. The Breaking Stone was patterned by lichens older than the clan, older than the Kyrinin. Over and amongst their innumerable pale green and grey shades lay darker stains. Black streaks that would never now be washed away, they scarred the great rock, running down like the tracks of midnight tears from two neat, smooth-sided sockets high upon its face.

The warriors laid the *na'kyrim* on the ground and stripped his clothes from his body. In that muted evening light his skin looked fragile, ashen. He stirred, but they held him firm. They gagged him with a stone wrapped in a strip of cloth. One of them brought out two sharpened, hardened shafts of willow, each the length of an arm and thicker than a man's thumb. The *na'kyrim* writhed. The Kyrinin worked quickly lest he should attempt some trick upon them using his secret skills. They raised his arms and held them tightly as the shafts, twisted and turned to force their way, were driven through his wrists. The *na'kyrim* screamed around his gag and fell into unconsciousness.

Two warriors climbed atop the Breaking Stone and, using ropes of plaited grass tied around his chest, raised him up its face. They held him there while a third reached down and manipulated the willow stakes until they slotted into the sockets in the stone. They slid in, the stone welcoming them as it had dozens of their like before, and the *na'kyrim* hung there, crucified upon the Breaking Stone.

IX

Hunching down against the rain, Orisian and the others crossed the long boardwalk across the mouth of the River Dihrve. Weed and barnacles coated the walkway's supports below the waterline; rot was at work on the parts above. It felt safe enough — the Dihrve was a sluggish, unthreatening thing here at its mouth — but Orisian wondered how much of a life it had left to it.

They had woken to dark skies and miserable rain that gathered strength with every minute. When Orisian said that he was going to find Ess'yr and Varryn, he had half-hoped he could go alone; instead Yvane, Anyara and Rothe all accompanied him. He did not feel he could refuse them.

As they made their way along the shore to the river crossing, he had asked Yvane if an unannounced visit would cause a problem. The *na'kyrim* dismissed the idea.

"They're not so stiff about such things here," she said. "There'd not be so many *na'kyrim* around if they were."

"Ten, Hammarn said," Orisian remembered. "We haven't seen any. Are they hiding?"

"It can't have escaped your notice that everyone keeps themselves to themselves around here. They're all on edge now: everybody's nervous, smells trouble on the wind."

She was right about the ease of entering the *vo'an*. No one tried to stop them as they came off the rickety bridge and walked amongst the tents. It was not, in fact, as disconcerting a place to enter as Koldihrve had been the day before. There was none of the boot-sucking mud that greeted a visitor to the human settlement —

rush matting was spread in broad pathways — and none of the dark glares or muttered asides. It felt safer than the human town, at least to Orisian. The feeling did not last for long.

There was a crowd gathered in the center of the *vo'an,* in a space where the bare earth had been trodden over countless years into the consistency of rock. As they approached the back of the crowd Yvane nudged Orisian with her elbow and pointed discreetly at a pole planted a few paces away. It was bedecked with horns, strings of threaded teeth and animal skulls. The bones looked fresh and unweathered.

"That's bad," Yvane whispered. "A war pole. Means they're expecting deaths."

The Kyrinin crowd stirred gently at their arrival. There was a foul smell, Orisian realized, foul enough to make him almost gag. The crowd thinned a little before them; it let them see what stood at its center.

A wooden frame was there, of the sort used to suspend a carcass while it was butchered. Upon the frame was bound a naked, life-less Kyrinin. His head hung forward and his white hair had fallen across his face like a shroud. From shoulder to hip, long thin strips of skin had been peeled back, wound on sticks. The flaying had left livid, gory bands of raw flesh exposed. He had been disem-boweled, so that his entrails spilled forth to pile upon the ground beneath him. His groin was a bloody mess. An ordurous stench hung suffocatingly in the air and Orisian felt bile in his mouth as his stomach twisted itself. He heard Anyara's faint moan of dis-gust even as he turned away. Three young Fox children were standing close by. They watched him with bland curiosity. One had a bow and quiver — little more than toys — in his tiny, fine hands.

Then Ess'yr was coming around the edge of the crowd. Her brother was a little behind her.

"You should go," said Ess'yr.

"We're leaving," Orisian told her. "On the ship. I wanted to say goodbye."

"We will come to you."

"It'll have to be soon. We'll be gone today." He felt a sharp pang of apprehension. He could not leave her behind without talking to her. To him, if not to her, it was a parting that needed to be marked. He saw that Varryn was regarding him with unreadable eyes.

"Soon," Ess'yr said, and he heard a promise in her gentle voice. "But not now."

"We'd better go," Rothe said quietly. "I don't think this is a good place to be now."

Reluctantly, Orisian agreed. Ess'yr was already turning away, and he was suddenly afraid that he might not see those beautiful features again. He might have tried to call her back, but did not.

Yvane had been talking quietly with a Fox woman, and now rejoined them, her face troubled.

"Let's go," she said.

The four of them walked together out of the camp and over the bridge into Koldihrve. The rain was soaking. It churned up the surface of the river.

"They really are savages," Anyara murmured.

"They are," agreed Rothe, and then to Orisian's faint surprise added softly, "but I've seen worse things done by humans."

"They caught that White Owl not far from here," Yvane said as they stepped back onto the human side of the river. "From the sound of it, there's a lot more where he came from. Very close. There's going to be a good deal of blood spilled."

"Today?" Rothe asked.

"Probably. They say there're scores of White Owls. And your friends from Horin-Gyre too."

"Wait, wait," hissed Orisian, slowing suddenly.

The others looked questioningly at him, and he nodded down the street. Four or five men were standing in the sheeting rain. They were indistinct figures, shapeless cloaks hiding any detail, but nothing about them suggested goodwill. Yvane squinted at them, flicking rainwater from her brow.

"I thought you said you didn't upset Tomas yesterday," she said.

"I didn't," Orisian muttered. "We parted on the best terms I could manage."

He was casting about for another path to take. Every instinct told him this was something more than the simple observation Tomas had kept them under since they arrived in Koldihrve. Already, the men were moving, coming toward them. He could see weapons: staffs and cudgels.

"I'll deal with them," Rothe growled. There was something close to relish in his voice.

"No," Orisian said. "No fighting unless we have no choice. We'll go around them, get out to the ship." Inside, the thought was ringing in his head that he should have called Ess'yr back when she turned away from him. But it was too late for that.

"Down here," he said and led them into a side street. "Yvane, can you find the way to Hammarn's house?"

"I should think so." She brushed past him to take the lead.

The alley narrowed, so that they had to trot along in single file. They passed the backs of small houses and shacks. There were no doors, and the few windows were shuttered. Water was spouting from the roofs, drenching them. The ground was slick mud, constantly treacherous, and littered with broken bits of wood, empty barrels and discarded pots.

"There's a street up ahead," Yvane called. "It's easy from there."

They burst out onto the road, splashing through puddles. The mud was viscous and clinging. Rothe slipped to one knee and Orisian helped him up.

"Oh, dear," Yvane said.

Tomas stood facing them, no more than a dozen paces away. Ame was with him, and three other men of his Watch. The First Watchman wore a thick woolen cloak and held a longsword.

"The very folk we sought," Tomas rasped.

"I see you've taken that sword down from your wall," Orisian said. "Why is that?"

Rothe was stepping forward, but Orisian put a restraining hand on his arm without taking his eyes from Tomas.

"Because it might be I've been played for a fool, that's why," Tomas growled.

"We don't take kindly to being taken for fools by those as think they're our betters," Ame added from behind Tomas. He was eyeing Orisian with a kind of malevolent eagerness. Orisian was acutely, almost agonizingly, aware that he was unarmed. The moment felt pregnant with violence, the hissing rain filled with a pressure that was going to demand release. He and Tomas faced each other.

"Word from the Black Roaders is they're hunting two runaways. Boy and girl," said the First Watchman, his eyes flicking from Orisian to Anyara and back again, "perhaps traveling with Fox Kyrinin, perhaps with a warrior. And not just any ordinary folk these: kin of the Thane himself. Word is there's reward to be had for any who take hold of them, and nothing but strife for those as aids them."

"You told me no one would trouble us, if we gave no cause," Orisian said. He spat rainwater away from his lips. It felt like the air itself was turning to water, like breathing would be impossible soon.

"Cause, is it?" snapped Tomas. "Well, I've cause enough. I've a town to keep safe from harm. We want no part in arguments between Blood lords, but you've put us there. And done it without telling me the truth of who you are."

"Not intentionally," Orisian said as calmly as he could. "Let us be on our way, and the trouble will pass you by."

"You think so?" scoffed Tomas. "I think maybe not."

"Don't imagine you're more important than you are, Tomas," muttered Yvane. The First Watchman shot her such a look of feral contempt it startled even the *na'kyrim*. Orisian groaned inwardly, sensing any chance of a peaceful outcome to this slipping away.

"Don't test me," Tomas snapped at Yvane. "You'll all come to the Tower, and we'll see then what's to be done for the best."

"No," said Orisian heavily. "We can't do that."

He saw Ame's lip begin to twitch into a snarl. He saw Tomas' eyes narrow.

There was a clattering, urgent sound then, from somewhere out in the storm on the town's landward edge. It sounded like pots being hammered together, or a shield being beaten. It sounded like an alarm.

"Tomas! Tomas!" A faint and distant voice, almost lost in the downpour. "They're here! Riders! White Owl!"

Orisian saw the shock that flashed across the First Watchman's face. For an instant he felt sorry for the man. He felt sorry for all of them, as choice and chance collapsed into this one pattern that might kill them all. There were other noises, caught up in the roar of the rainstorm: drums, cries from across the river.

"That's the Fox," said Yvane. "It's starting."

Orisian stared at the *na'kyrim* for a moment.

"Then it is time for us to go," he said.

He flicked a glance at Rothe, striving to ask a question with his eyes. He thought he saw the answer he was looking for. Orisian moved first, his shieldman a moment behind him. Tomas and all his men were staring at Yvane, their aggression momentarily overlaid by confusion and alarm. They were slow.

Orisian hit Tomas around the waist, inside the First Watchman's sword arc before he even realized what was happening. They smacked down together into the mud. Orisian heard the sound of Rothe reaching Ame in almost the same instant, but it barely registered. His whole world had narrowed into a maelstrom of mud and water and the flailing limbs he wrestled with. A detached part of his mind said he was surely going to die here, yet his body had a furious, frenzied hunger for life and he punched and clawed at Tomas like a wild animal.

The First Watchman threatened to lever himself up again, but his hand shot from beneath him. Orisian threw his weight across Tomas' sword arm, pinning it, and raked at his throat with hooked fingers. There was a terrible blow to Orisian's flank, a club landing squarely on his old knife wound. The pain was blinding, but even as he was bludgeoned sideways his fingers clenched reflexively on the First Watchman's throat and he heard a strangulated cry.

Then Orisian rolled free. He got onto one knee, fighting against pain, the mud and the weight of rain. The butt of a staff swept by his face so close he felt it pass. Anyara flung herself at his assailant, shouting furiously. The man slithered sideways, twisting too late to fend her off. Orisian scrambled back to Tomas. The First Watchman was writhing in the mud, pawing vaguely at his throat. Orisian seized his sword and, forgetting everything Rothe had ever taught him, hacked wildly at the man with the staff. The blade found the knee joint and he went down, taking Anyara with him. Orisian staggered to his feet, the sword dragging in the mud, water pouring from him. He gasped for breath, struggled to find Rothe. Ame's dead eye, streaked with dirt, met him. The Second Watchman lay on his side, his neck broken and his battered helm lying in the road collecting rainwater.

Rothe was roaring, howling like some beast in a blood-rage. The two Watchmen he faced were backing away from him, glancing nervously at one another.

"Lannis! Lannis!" Rothe bellowed at them, and at the rain-swept sky, and they ran.

Orisian raised the sword with two hands. The last of Tomas' men had thrown Anyara off him; she sprawled helplessly in the road as he hauled himself upright, leaning heavily on his staff.

"Go," Orisian shouted and thrust the sword forward. Rothe was coming too, reeling as if he was drunk but still roaring. The Watchman hesitated for a moment, saw that he was alone and hobbled away.

Rothe helped Anyara up. He used his right hand only; his left arm hung limply at his side.

"You're hurt?" Orisian called.

"It'll come back," Rothe grunted. "Don't think it's broken. Lucky that Inkallim's hound didn't have longer teeth, or I'd be no use at all." He nodded at the sword Orisian carried and held out his good hand. Without hesitation, Orisian presented the sword to him hilt-first. Even with only one arm, Rothe could put it to better use. The shieldman smiled harshly as he took hold of the weapon.

"Feels better to have my hand on a sword again," he said. He grimaced as he peered at the blade. "Even if it's not been cared for as it should."

The alarm was being rung again, more furiously even than before. It sounded closer too, but in all the tumult of the rain it was hard to be sure. It was, in any case, abruptly cut off. Tomas still lay on the road, struggling to breathe. His teeth were bared. His eyes seemed to be roving about blindly. Orisian, calmer now, felt a moment of horror at what he had done to the man. He saw Rothe eyeing the First Watchman purposefully.

"Leave him," he murmured.

"We should go," Yvane said. "Now."

The rain pounded on the roofs around them, churned the roadway. Other sounds were rising up to compete with the storm. There were cries: panicked voices blurred with the sound of rain. Perhaps even the sound of battle. It was impossible to say where the noise was coming from, but it was not far.

Rothe made them go down the center of the street, fearful that doors or alleyways might hold a surprise. Every muscle in Orisian's body sang with the desire to run, but his wound was acutely painful and Rothe acutely wary. They went cautiously to a corner, and turned into a road that angled toward the sea.

"I hear horses," Yvane said.

Orisian tried, but he could not disentangle the blur of sounds assailing his ears. Perhaps there were hoofs buried in the cacophony.

"Can't tell," shouted Rothe. He was at the rear, constantly turning this way and that, constantly seeking threat. Then, "Here's trouble," he cried.

They all looked, and saw two Koldihrvers staggering out into a junction. The rain put an illusion of distance on the scene, muffled any sound. The men paused, as if unsure of where to go. One of them stared at Orisian and the others. Then three great horses came plunging through the rain and mud, their riders swinging swords. They rode over the Koldihrvers, slamming them down. The horses slithered around. Their hoofs carved troughs into the sodden ground. The riders leaned down and hacked at the fallen men. No cries, no screams, reached Orisian. He saw the riders straighten, though, and master their mounts and come on. The horses stretched their legs and surged through plumes of spray.

"Black Road!" Anyara was shouting.

Rothe had both hands upon the hilt of the old sword now. The riders were bearing down on him; beyond, deeper into the grey rain, Orisian could see more horses appearing.

"Get into a house," Rothe urged through gritted teeth.

Orisian spun, and found two more warriors galloping toward them from the other end of the road. A wild-haired woman was in the lead, leaning forward over her horse's neck, sword held out to the side as if she meant to take a head in the first charge.

"They're behind us," he cried out.

Even as the words left his mouth, a lean, pale-haired figure sprang out from between two houses, lunging to punch a spear into the side of the first horse's neck as it passed. The animal twisted in mid-stride. It crashed down in an eruption of mud and water, flinging its rider loose. The spear splintered and cartwheeled away. Orisian started forward but Ess'yr was ahead of him, whipping out a knife from her belt. She threw herself onto the woman, stabbing precisely for the throat. The fallen horse was thrashing around, unable to rise. The second rider slid to a halt beyond it. Varryn came swiftly and silently from the same alleyway as Ess'yr, and drove his spear up into the man's back. He hooked the Black Roader out of the saddle and cast him down, impaled.

Orisian wheeled about. The three other horsemen were moments from Rothe. The shieldman stood with his feet well spaced, the sword held out before him.

"Come," Ess'yr was shouting at Orisian. She had his arm in a powerful grip and dragged him toward the alley she had emerged from.

"I have to get a sword," Orisian said, casting about for one dropped by the two fallen warriors.

Then Anyara was pushing him from the other side, crying right into his ear, "Move, move!"

Yvane barged into them all and knocked them down. A Black Road horseman surged past, the scything sweep of his blade cutting only the sodden air where Anyara had been standing. They scrambled for the safety of the alley. The road behind them was suddenly full of horses, bursting through the veils of rain.

"Rothe!" Orisian yelled. He could not see his shieldman in the chaos. Varryn ran forward, darting between two rearing horses.

"I will bring him," the Kyrinin snapped over his shoulder as he went.

Orisian thought he heard Rothe shouting, "Make for the ship, Orisian."

Anyara was pulling him down the narrow path. Yvane and Ess'yr were already ahead.

"I'm not leaving anyone," Orisian shouted at his sister.

"They'll find us," she replied without looking round. "You don't want to die here, do you?"

They heard wailing from one of the houses they rushed past. They were moving away from the sea, away from the safety of Delyne's ship, but the alley offered no side turns. It channeled them along its length and spat them out into another street.

There was a woman screaming as she ran down the road. She was hauling a girl after her, dragging her through the mud. The child was crying. Battle spilled into the road beyond them: half a dozen of Koldihrve's Watchmen locked in a doomed struggle with three Horin-Gyre riders. One of the horses reared and twisted away in panic. Its rider was thrown. The other two slashed about them with their swords. Orisian glimpsed a spray of blood; it looked black at this distance, through the rain.

Ess'yr led them away from the fight, pressing close to the houses fronting the street as if they could give some shelter from the horrors consuming Koldihrve.

"Wait," gasped Yvane. She gestured at a shabby house next to them. "There's a path on the other side of these, I think. We can cut back to the sea."

She pushed rather weakly at the door. It opened partway and then stuck. Orisian kicked at it and it smacked open. They tumbled inside. There was only one room: a bed with threadbare blankets, a table, chair and ash-filled fireplace. The occupants had fled, or were fighting or dying somewhere. The rain shook the thin roof. Water ran from their hair, their clothes.

"We can't leave Rothe," Orisian said.

"He knows where we're going," Yvane said. "He'll come to us." She was struggling with the latch on a closed window at the far side of the room. Orisian went to help her.

The shutters came open. Yvane leaned out. Ess'yr was watching the door.

"You left your own people to come to us," Orisian said to the Kyrinin.

Her hair was clinging to the side of her face. Rainwater ran in fine rivulets over her skin. She blinked, and there were droplets upon her eyelashes: silvery beads of rain.

"I must see you safe," she said.

"We have to go," Anyara insisted.

"All right," Yvane said. "I don't see any trouble out on this side. Hammarn's is close. Follow me."

She clambered out of the window onto a wooden walkway that ran along the backs of the houses. Anyara went after her, and then

Ess'yr. Orisian put his hands on the window frame to pull himself out. He swung a leg up and over, and then stopped. A pale glint by the fireplace took his eye: the blade of a thin knife hanging from a hook. He pulled himself back inside. He went across and took the knife in his hand. It was a plain tool, but it was sharp.

"Orisian."

He turned, and thought his heart would stop. A lean, powerful man stood in the doorway. He was half-stooped, for the frame was too low for him. He held a sword; blood and water were dripping together from its blade.

"That is your name, isn't it?" the man said quietly. "Mine is Kanin oc Horin-Gyre."

The crashing of the rain receded; Orisian's vision tightened upon the man standing before him.

Kanin took a single, long step into the room. He straightened up, lifted the point of his sword until it was level with Orisian's chest. Orisian edged toward the window. Kanin surged forward. Orisian hurled himself at the window, launching himself up and out into the rainstorm. He cleared the walkway and sprawled in the road. Mud filled his mouth and nose. He rolled, spitting, in time to see Kanin oc Horin-Gyre putting a foot on the windowsill, pulling himself up into the aperture. Ess'yr was standing to one side, and as the Thane emerged she swung her bow like a club and smashed it into his face. There was a spray of blood and Kanin fell backward into the house with a cry of shock and pain. The impact broke the bow's back, and Ess'yr cast it away as she sprang down into the roadway.

"No sitting around," muttered Yvane as she pulled Orisian to his feet.

They flew down the street and around an acute corner. They cut between houses and came out within sight of the sea. Orisian recognized where they were. Hammarn's hut was there, the door open, Hammarn himself peering out with wide and frightened eyes.

"Is it you? Is it you?" he shouted as they rushed up.

"Yes," Yvane said. "Time to come with us, friend."

The old *na'kyrim* looked startled.

"Can't you hear?" Yvane asked him. "This town's no place to be."

Hammarn cocked his head. Cries and screams were still rising up through the rain.

"Perhaps so," Hammarn grunted. "Maybe so. Better gather myself." He ducked back inside.

"Hammarn . . ." Yvane started to say.

"Let him get what he wants," Orisian said. "We'll wait for Rothe as long as we can. And for Varryn."

Yvane looked back the way they had come.

"That would not be wise," she said.

Orisian faced her without a moment's uncertainty. "Wise or not, I will give them the chance."

He darted around the side of the house, hunching his shoulders fruitlessly against the downpour. The sea was a great shiver of ripples and impacts beneath the rain's assault. Edryn Delyne's ship had its sails set. Figures were moving about on the deck. Orisian waved and shouted, but there was no sign that anyone saw him. He glanced along the storm-swept, muddy shore. There was a long, low rowboat tied up at the nearest of the crude jetties. He returned to the others. They were gathered just inside the doorway. Hammarn was rummaging deep in a pile of driftwood, muttering softly to himself.

"There's a boat we can take," Orisian reported, "but we don't have much time. Delyne's making ready to sail."

He looked at Ess'yr. An unfocused glaze had settled over her eyes. A blurring sheen of rainwater overlay her tattoos, making them seem damaged, impotent.

"What of the *vo'an*?" he asked her.

She gave the slightest shake of her head. "The enemy have come. Many of them."

"I'm sorry."

Orisian felt a hand upon his arm. Anyara was at his side. Her face was mournful. He tried to smile for her.

"I know," he said. "No more time. We can't wait."

Hammarn had collected nothing but woodtwines. He bound a scrap of cloth around the little bundle of carvings and clutched them to his chest like a baby.

"Got it," he said to no one.

Orisian led the way out and made for the shore. He had gone only a few paces when he saw Rothe and Varryn burst out from a side street and come running toward them. The Kyrinin was limping a fraction. Rothe's left arm hung with an ominous looseness. It had taken no mere numbing blow this time: there was blood sluicing away in the rain.

Orisian felt a tremendous surge of relief rush through him.

"Is it bad?" he asked as the shieldman came up to him.

"Not as bad as it could have been," Rothe said with a lopsided smile. "Lucky there's plenty of places too narrow for horses in this dismal town."

When they reached the shore, water running out from the town was cutting channels for itself down the beach. Shells and stones were appearing, eroded out of the mud by the hard rain. They slipped and slithered to the jetty and ran out along its uneven length. The boarding felt treacherous.

Two ropes held the boat. Yvane went to one, Orisian the other. The swollen knot felt huge and solid beneath his numb fingers. He could not get any purchase. He pulled the knife out from where he had tucked it into his belt and began to saw at the sodden fibers. He shot a glance at the ship. Men had gathered at its rail and were gesturing toward them.

"Let me cut it," Rothe said, raising his sword. "Blade's not the sharpest, but it'll do."

Orisian backed away. Rothe's first blow went partway through the rope.

"We go now," Varryn said quietly.

Orisian turned to him. The Kyrinin warrior was impassive, looking not at Orisian but Ess'yr. She did not reply at once. Orisian sought for the words he needed. This once, this one time, he wanted to say the right thing to her.

"Kanin!" Anyara cried. "It's Kanin."

There were riders pounding along the shore, ten or twelve of them. Orisian wiped rain from his eyes. Kanin was to the fore, driving his horse on with wild energy. Orisian heard the chop of another sword blow from behind him.

"It's free," Rothe said. "I'll cut the other."

Yvane gave up her unequal struggle with the second rope. She stood at Orisian's side. The Black Road warriors were close. Fountains of mud and sand erupted at their horses' feet. Orisian could hear the wet thumps of the hoofs.

"Quickly, Rothe," he said.

He watched Kanin coming. He could see the fury in the man's face now, and the great bloody wound Ess'yr had put there with her bow. Orisian was strangely aware of the leaden weight of his soaking clothes. He squeezed the hilt of the knife. Rothe's sword smacked against the rope. The shieldman cursed. Kanin hauled at his reins. His horse came to a ragged halt at the base of the jetty. The other riders gathered around him. They looked as if they had ridden out of the rain-riven sky itself, a wild expression of the storm. Kanin held out his sword, pointing it at Orisian.

"Hold," he cried. "Hold there."

Warriors were dismounting. Orisian could see crossbows being readied.

"Rothe?" asked Orisian without looking round.

"Done!"

A crossbow bolt snapped out, flashing darkly through the rain and past them, out over the sea. An answering arrow sprang from Varryn's bow. It darted past Kanin, thudded into the warrior behind him.

"Get into the boat," said Orisian. "Everyone."

"Oh dear, oh dear," Hammarn was muttering over and over again.

He and Yvane, then Anyara scrambled into the boat. A flurry of bolts hissed down the length of the jetty. Orisian flung himself at the rowboat. Rothe, there beside him, gasped as one quarrel found his shoulder. The boat rocked as the shieldman slumped into it. Orisian struggled to his feet. Yvane was fumbling with an oar; she was staring, as if in surprise, at the crossbow bolt transfixing her upper arm.

Varryn, still standing with Ess'yr on the end of the jetty, loosed another arrow.

"Come on," Orisian shouted at the Kyrinin. "Get in."

"Pull, pull," Anyara was screaming at Hammarn as the two of them hauled at oars. The boat jerked away from the jetty. Orisian reached for Ess'yr.

"Don't be stupid," he shouted. "You can't stay here."

Kanin was rushing down the jetty, his warriors coming behind him like a dark flock of crows stooping out of the rain-lashed sky. Orisian heard Kanin's inarticulate scream of fury. Varryn and Ess'yr looked silently at one another for an instant and then leapt from the jetty. They landed together in the rowboat's stern, so lightly and precisely that it hardly bucked.

Orisian scrambled over Rothe's prostrate form. The warrior was moaning softly. Orisian saw the blood soaking through his shield-man's shirt, but would not allow the sight to touch him. Not yet. There were four oars. Hammarn and Anyara were pulling at two, Yvane struggling with a third.

"No," Kanin was shouting as the boat took another unsteady lunge away from the shore.

More bolts: dark flickers darting out to the boat, slicing through the rain.

"Get down," shouted Orisian, and hunched over his oar. A couple of the quarrels thudded into the hull, the stern; another flew over their heads. He felt his oar shiver and saw a bolt stuck in it, next to his hand. Then nothing. The warriors on the jetty were hurrying to reload. Kanin stood at the furthest point, arms and sword upraised as if to threaten the thick, grey sky itself.

Waves, dragged up by the storm, were slapping at the rowboat's prow. Water sluiced over the sides and around their feet. Spray misted around their heads.

Gasping, spitting salt water from his mouth, Orisian hauled at the oar with all the strength he had left. As they drew clear of Koldihrve he could see, through the teeming rain, the vague shape of Kanin standing impotent and dark over the water, staring out. The Horin-Gyre Thane watched them all the way.

They rode the tide out to the Tal Dyreen ship. The sailors, laughing and shouting excitedly, threw ladders over the side. As they tied ropes about Rothe so that he could be hauled aboard, the huge shieldman fainted away.

Epilogue

I once saw a fragment of a manuscript, found in the ruins of one of Dun Aygll's palaces. It may be truth, it may not, but this is the meat of what it said:

Minon, who was to be the Torturer, and was to cast a dark shadow across his times, gave no sign of what he was to become in his childhood. He had woken only dimly to the Shared, had no talents in its use of any substance, and lived a quiet and gentle life in the woods of the Far Dyne hills.

His father was a man of wicked inclinations, though, and from the cottage where he dwelled with his Kyrinin wife and his na'kyrim son, this man went forth at night to practice murder and thievery. In time his deeds cast a shroud of fear upon those parts and an unnamed lord sent his warriors to rid the country of the bandit. They came one eve upon the cottage of Minon's father. The wife they slew before the hearth, the husband in the stable where he kept his horse. Minon put a knife into the heart of one of the attackers before they bore him to the ground.

Then, such was their anger at his slaying of one of their number, the warriors resolved to put Minon to a cruel death. They bestowed upon that child terrible tortures. But in the extremity of his suffering, there arose in Minon an unsuspected power. Fleeing from the pain and horror of his senses, he found some doorway into the deeper reaches of the Shared that until that moment had been hidden from him, and up out of those deep places there flowed an awful, potent river. All the cruelties his captors had practiced upon him were then revisited tenfold upon them, for Minon broke his bonds and unveiled a terrible visage.

He alone walked away from that cottage and he left nothing but

blood behind him. He went alone into the world and fear and fore-
boding ran before him like fell hounds.

from Secret Tales of the Na'kyrim
collected by A'var of Highfast

I

The harbor of Kolkyre was thronged with boats great and small. The whole city, and the harbor district in particular, was filled with warriors: not just those of Kilkry but also remnants of the army of Lannis-Haig and advance companies of Ayth, Taral and Haig. There were, as well, hundreds of fugitives from the fighting in the Glas valley. Never in living memory had the city been so overflowing with humanity.

Taim Narran pushed his way through the crowds on the waterfront. So great was the press of bodies that he was in danger of losing track of Roaric nan Kilkry-Haig, who was guiding him on his way. Amidst all the grim rumor swirling around Kolkyre, today Roaric was the bearer of only good tidings. The message he brought to Taim in his borrowed chambers in the Tower of Thrones had been so unlooked-for, so joyous, that Taim hardly dared allow his weary heart to believe it.

"Where are they?" Taim shouted above the din.

"At the harbormaster's house," came the reply. "They were on a Tal Dyreen ship that came in an hour ago. They tried for Kolglas, but the captain found out what had happened at Glasbridge from some fishermen and he wouldn't take them up the estuary after that. So he brought them here. They wished to bathe and change their garments before presenting themselves to my father."

When they came to the house Taim could not contain himself, and brushed past the servant who guarded the door. He cast about, his heart thudding, in search of those he had never thought to see again. In the dining hall he found a stranger group than any he might have imagined. Anyara, the niece of his dead Thane, was at a table with two *na'kyrim*: one a small, disheveled old man who looked to be asleep where he sat, the other a woman who turned and fixed him with a penetrating glare. Beyond them, by the fire that roared in the grate, stood two tall Kyrinin — a man and a woman — clad for the forest. They glanced up when he entered and he met their flinty eyes. The woman cast her gaze down again but the man did not, and the ferocious spirals of tattoos upon his face lent his glare a wild edge. Taim found that his voice had fled from his throat.

There were heavy footsteps upon the stairway behind him and Taim turned. Two figures were descending. Rothe Corlyn he knew at once, though his fellow warrior was a changed man: leaner, greyer of face and hair, with one arm bound up in a sling. The shieldman came unsteadily down the stairs, leaning on his companion. It was that companion — a youth, slight of build and tired of countenance — who seized Taim's attention. A youth whose eyes met the old warrior's with a mixture of sadness and resilience, leavened by a spark of recognition. A youth before whom Taim could only fall to one knee and bow his head.

"Orisian," he said. "My Thane. My sword, and my life, are yours."

II

The *na'kyrim* had been upon the Breaking Stone for a full night. Two White Owl warriors sat upon grassy hummocks, watching him. Through their vigil they would neither eat nor sleep nor speak; they would simply wait for the Stone to break the man. They had watched others meet the same end. It seldom took a long time. A mere body could not resist the strength of this boulder, this ancient cage of souls.

Waterskins lay by their sides, along with the fur cloaks they had needed in the coldest depths of the night. Their bows and spears rested against their shoulders. They had barely moved all through the long hours of darkness. The man on the Stone had stirred only briefly in the night, groaning despite the gag that remained in his mouth.

Grey clouds had mustered to stifle the rising sun. The wind fell away. The treetops grew still and a heavy silence descended. The man's blood dried in crusted black rivulets where it had run down from the wounds in his wrists. His head hung forward. He had not moved now for many hours, but still the Kyrinin watched, their eyes caught upon the hook of his naked form. He looked half-dead already.

A buzzard drifted across the sky. It circled, slipping lower and lower by degrees. At length, it glided in toward the Breaking Stone. One of the watchers stretched a leg out and took his bow in his hand. It was not time for the eaters of the dead yet. The bird gave a couple of flaps with its broad wings and lifted itself upward again. It circled a few times more and then headed out over the wide expanse of *Antyryn Hyr,* searching for unguarded prey.

Time passed. The *na'kyrim* moaned but did not wake.

The day moved sluggishly toward night. The grey light faded until the trees and stones lost their shape and detail. Somewhere far away, an owl was calling. It was answered by another, still more distant, and their duet persisted for long minutes. The clouds began to part and through each break in them, starlight shone. The part-moon appeared, spreading a white glow around itself.

The Breaking Stone was bathed in colorless light. The watching Kyrinin saw that the man on the Stone had raised his head. His eyes were unfocused, as if his gaze was fixed upon something far beyond them. A convulsion ran through his chest and upper body, pulling his arms against the stakes that pinned them. His head fell forward again. The watchers unfolded their fur capes, spread them over their shoulders and waited.

In the coldest hour before dawn, the hour when the world was as close to death as it came, the *na'kyrim* began to weep. With their night-tuned sight, the Kyrinin could see the tears coursing down his face, the feverish tremors shivering through his frame. Spittle was foaming around the cloth-wrapped stone that blocked his mouth. The White Owls glanced at one another. It would not be long now.

Yet when the muted, half-hearted daybreak came, the *na'kyrim* still lived. The flow of tears had stopped. He regarded his Kyrinin guards, his eyes bleak and despairing. The White Owls returned his gaze impassively, unflinching.

By the time the day had turned again, falling back toward night, the *na'kyrim* had lived longer than any victim of the Breaking Stone in many years. The clouds scattered in the evening and an orange-yellow light fell upon the great boulder and its burden. Death came stalking across the grass, and breathed upon the *na'kyrim*. Air rattled in his clotted lungs, the muscles in his impaled arms slackened, his head lolled loosely. The two Kyrinin rose and stepped forward to witness the end.

But the end that was coming was not what they thought. The rattle in the *na'kyrim*'s chest stilled. An immense silence fell, and with it the darkness. Tears once more began to fall, but they were of blood, not water. The gaunt head was slowly raised, as if struggling against some awful weight. As the sun slipped away and shadows massed all around, the *na'kyrim* opened his bloody eyes and fixed the Kyrinin with a gaze that spoke no longer of despair, but of a terrible, revelatory horror.

From the balcony on the west face of Highfast, Cerys and Amonyn could see the peaks of the Karkyre Mountains starkly silhouetted by the last vestiges of the fire-red dusk. They stood together, wrapped in a single woolen blanket, snow swirling lightly about them. The heat that Amonyn had woven out of the Shared warded both of them against the elements. It was the faltering of that

heat, the sudden intrusion of the winter's biting chill, that warned
Cerys. In the next moment she had the lurching sense of the world
slipping away from her and but for Amonyn's strong arms holding her up she might have fallen.

"Ah," she breathed as she leaned against him. "What was that?"

"Something . . . someone . . . changed," he whispered, and she
could hear the sudden strain in his voice. Tiny tears were beading
at the corners of his eyes. "Such suffering. Such . . . wonder."

"Elect," someone was calling from the chamber within. "Elect,
the Dreamer . . ." The man's voice was filled with urgency, with
fear. "The Dreamer . . . weeps."

In a bedchamber high in the Tower of Thrones, Yvane the
na'kyrim woke from sleep with a piercing scream. The crisp white
sheets fell from her as she jerked upright, her face slick with
sweat. For long moments she sat thus, her hands clawing at the
bedclothes. Breath would not come to her and she gasped for air.

The door burst open and a guard rushed in: one of Taim's men,
posted outside despite her protestations. He came to the side of
the bed. She turned and stared at him, uncomprehending, still
lost in black nightmare.

"I dreamed of darkness," she said in a cracking, enfeebled voice.
"A man. A terrible, broken man, with nothing but rage in his
heart."

Acknowledgments

I am very grateful for the contribution others have made to the creation and publication of this book. Those I want to thank include:

My agent Sacha Elliot, without whose enthusiasm this might never have happened, and her colleagues Anne Dewe and Tina Betts;

Tim Holman, Darren Nash and Gabriella Nemeth at Orbit, all of whom have made the book better than it would otherwise have been, and Chartwell Illustrators for providing the maps;

Steve Griffin and Criana Connal, for sharing the idea that being a writer is a worthwhile ambition;

My parents, to acknowledge whose contribution in full would need more pages than are available;

And Fleur, who makes no complaint at having to share me with a computer.

LOOK OUT FOR
THE SECOND BOOK
IN THE
GODLESS WORLD TRILOGY:

Bloodheir

extras

orbit

meet the author

BRIAN RUCKLEY was born and brought up in Scotland. After studying at Edinburgh and Stirling Universities, he worked for a series of organizations dealing with environmental, nature conservation, and youth-development issues. Having had short stories published in *Interzone* and *The Third Alternative* in the 1990s, Brian started working as a freelance consultant on environmental projects in 2003 in order to concentrate seriously on his writing, which now takes up almost all his time. He lives in Edinburgh. His Web site and blog can be found at www.brianruckley.com.

interview

Although Winterbirth *is set in a fantasy world, it does feel incredibly realistic. Did the story come first, or the world?*

That's a real chicken-and-egg thing. I don't think one really came before the other. They evolved together, feeding off each other. I had a rough map, and an idea of what life was like for the people who lived in it, at an early stage, but the story was always my main priority — a lot of the details of the world got filled in as the story developed. Making it realistic is just what seemed to come naturally to me.

Do you have a favorite character in Winterbirth*? Why?*

The bad guys tend to be fun to write, although to be honest I don't really think of anyone in the trilogy as "bad guys" — they may behave very unpleasantly at times, but they generally have some sort of reason for doing so. Right now, my favorite's probably one of the "good guys," though: Taim Narran. The more I write him, the more I suspect he might be the closest thing to a hero in the whole trilogy. But it changes all the time: ask me again tomorrow and I'll have a whole different answer.

Similarly, how about a favorite scene?

Tough one. It's hard work, trying to get the written scenes to work half as well as the fantastic, dramatic, gorgeous movie that's playing in your head. There are a couple of scenes with Gryvan, the rather unpleasant High Thane, and Taim Narran in them that come close: they pack quite a bit of character, conflict, and politics into pretty fast-paced scenes, I think. And I do have a soft spot for the Epilogue, which was just a lot of fun to write and hopefully makes the reader curious about what's going to happen next, if nothing else.

Without giving anything away, do you know how the trilogy is going to end?

Yes, the end has always been pretty clear in my mind. From the start, I thought of the story in "beginning, middle, and end" terms. So far, that original ending is still the one I'm aiming for. It still feels to me like the most satisfying conclusion to everything that comes before it (although some of the characters might not be quite so happy about it if they could see what's in store for them).

So, did you always want to be a writer?

It's always been a bit of an ambition. I read lots when I was a kid (still do — if left alone with any form of printed material, I'm pretty much certain to start reading it. Can't help myself). The writing started pretty early too. I wrote a dreadful science fiction epic (with sentient lizards) when I was about eleven.

What or who are the main influences on your writing?

Well, there are too many authors to mention them all by name, really, going all the way to (of course) Tolkien. But I read a lot of history books too, and that affects how I write — makes me quite keen on having a bit of realism to the characters and situations and politics. Plus I've spent most of my life in Scotland, and I think there are quite strong traces of Scottish landscape, climate, and wildlife that show up in *Winterbirth*.

How do you fill your time when you're not writing?

Until recently, I was doing freelance consultancy work for environmental organizations, but that's much reduced now. I'm still a big fan of the natural world, though, and can sometimes be found wandering around in the countryside. Then there's the reading, cinema, computer games to fit in. And I go swimming occasionally, because I'm told it's good for me.

Finally, if you had to pick one historical figure to be stuck on a desert island with, who would you choose?

Alexander Selkirk, the real-life Robinson Crusoe, would be handy to have around. No idea if he'd be good company, but he should have some helpful advice. If that's cheating, how about Homer? I could just laze about, listening to him telling his stories about Troy and Odysseus. Of course, that would only work if he's learned to speak English.

the passage of time

**The Third Age began with the absence
of the Gods, and with chaos. . .**

Year

280   The Adravane and Aygll Kingships arose

451   The Alsire Kingship arose, and the era of the Three Kingships began

775   The Huanin Kingships united against the Kyrinin clans and the War of the Tainted began

788   Tane was destroyed, the Deep Rove was raised by the Anain, and the War of the Tainted ended

793   The last Aygll King was slain, the era of the Three Kingships ended, and the Storm Years began

847   The Bloods — Kilkry, Haig, Gyre, Ayth and Taral — were founded in Aygll lands, and Kulkain oc Kilkry became the first Thane of Thanes; the end of the Storm Years

852   The last Alsire King was slain, and the first King of the Dornach line took his throne

922   The Black Road heresy arose in Kilvale, and was outlawed by the Bloods

942   The Gyre Blood, and all adherents of the Black Road, were exiled beyond the Vale of Stones and founded there the Bloods of the Black Road: Gyre, Horin, Gaven, Wyn and Fane

973 The Lannis Blood was founded, in reward for Sirian's defeat of the invading forces of the Black Road at Kolglas

997 Haig replaced Kilkry as first amongst the True Bloods

1052 The Dargannan Blood was founded

1069 The Lannis-Haig Blood defeated Horin-Gyre in battle at Tanwrye

1097 The Lannis-Haig Blood was afflicted by the Heart Fever

1102 The Dargannan Blood rebelled against the authority of Haig, and Gryvan oc Haig, Thane of Thanes, summoned the armies of the True Bloods to march against them

introducing

If you enjoyed WINTERBIRTH,
keep a look out for

DEVICES AND DESIRES

Book One of the Engineer Trilogy

by K. J. Parker

Devices and Desires is the extraordinary tale of a man who engineers a war to be reunited with his family.

When an engineer is sentenced to death for a petty transgression of guild law, he flees the city, leaving behind his wife and daughter. Forced into exile, he seeks a terrible vengeance — one that will leave a trail of death and destruction in its wake. But he will not be able to achieve this by himself. He must draw up his plans using the blood of others . . .

In a compelling tale of intrigue and injustice, K. J. Parker's embittered hero takes up arms against his enemies, using the only weapons he has left to him: his ingenuity and his passion — his devices and desires.

excerpt from *Devices and Desires*

As soon as Duke Orsea realized he'd lost the battle, the war and his country's only hope of survival, he ordered a general retreat. It was the only sensible thing he'd done all day.

One hour had made all the difference. An hour ago, when he'd led the attack, the world had been a very different place. He'd had an army of twenty-five thousand men, one tenth of the population of the Duchy of Eremia. He had a commanding position, a fully loaded supplies and equipment train, a carefully prepared battle plan, the element of surprise, the love and trust of his people, and hope. Now, as the horns blared and the ragged lines crumpled and dissolved into swarms of running dots, he had the miserable job of getting as many as he could of the fourteen thousand stunned, bewildered and resentful survivors away from the enemy cavalry and back to the relative safety of the mountains. One hour to change the world; not many men could have done such a thorough job. It took a particular genius to destroy one's life so comprehensively in so short a time.

A captain of archers, unrecognizable from a face-wound, ran past him, shouting something he didn't catch. More bad news, or just confirmation of what he already knew; or maybe simple abuse; it didn't greatly matter, because now that he'd given the order, there was precious little he could do about anything. If the soldiers got as far as the thorn-scrub on the edge of the marshes, and if they stopped there and re-formed instead of running blindly into the bog, and if they were still gullible enough to obey his orders after everything he'd let them in for, he might still be relevant. Right now, he was nothing more than a target, and a conspicuous one at that, perched on a stupid white horse and wearing stupid fancy armor.

It hurt him, worse than the blade of the broken-off arrow wedged in his thigh, to turn his back on the dead bodies of his men, scattered on the flat moor like a spoiled child's toys. Once he reined in his horse, turned and rode away, he acknowledged, he'd be breaking a link between himself and his people that he'd never be able to repair. But that was self-indulgence, he knew. He'd forgone the luxury of guilt when he bent his neck to the bait and tripped the snare. The uttermost mortification; his state of mind, his agonized feelings, didn't matter anymore. It was his duty to save himself, and thereby reduce the casualty list by one. He nudged the horse with his heels.

The quickest way to the thorn-hedge was across the place where the center of his line had been. His horse was a dainty stepper, neatly avoiding the tumbled bodies, the carelessly discarded weapons that could cut a delicate hoof to the quick. He saw wounded men, some screaming, some dragging themselves along by their hands, some struggling to draw a few more breaths, as though there was any point. He could get off the stupid white horse, load a wounded man into the saddle and take his chances on foot. Possibly, if there'd only been one, he'd have done it. But there wasn't just one, there were *thousands;* and that made it impossible, for some reason.

Orsea had seen tragedy before, and death. He'd even seen mess, great open slashed wounds, clogged with mud and dust, where a boar had caught a sluggish huntsman, or a careless forester had misjudged the fall of a tree. He'd been there once when a granary had collapsed with fifteen men inside; he'd been one of the first to scrabble through the smashed beams and fallen stone blocks, and he'd pulled two men out of there with his own hands, saved their lives. He'd done it because he couldn't do otherwise; he couldn't turn his back on pain and injury, any more than he could stick his hand in a fire and keep it there. An hour ago, he'd been that kind of man.

A horseman came thundering up behind him. His first thought was that the enemy cavalry was onto him, but the rider slowed and called out his name; his name and his stupid title.

He recognized the voice. "Miel?" he yelled back.

Miel Ducas; he'd never have recognized him. Ten years ago he'd have traded everything he had for Miel Ducas' face, which seemed to have such an irresistible effect on pretty young girls. Now, though, he couldn't see Miel's nose and mouth through a thick splatter of dirt and blood.

"There's another wing," Miel was saying; it took Orsea a heartbeat or so to realize he was talking about the battle. "Another wing of fucking cavalry; reserve, like they need it. They're looping out on the far left, I guess they're planning on cutting us off from the road. I've still got six companies of lancers, but even if we get there in time we won't hold them long, and they'll chew us to buggery."

Orsea sighed. He wanted to shrug his shoulders and ride on — he actually wanted to do that; his own callous indifference shocked him. "Leave it," he heard himself say. "Those lancers are worth more to us than a regiment of infantry. Keep them out of harm's way, and get them off the field as quick as you can."

Miel didn't answer, just pulled his horse's head round and stumbled away. Orsea watched him till he was out of sight over the horizon. It'd be nice to think that over there somewhere, screened by the line of stunted thorns, was that other world of an hour ago, and that Miel would arrive there to find the army, pristine and unbutchered, in time to turn them back.

Orsea still wasn't quite sure what had happened. Last night, camped in the middle of the flat plain, he'd sent out his observers. They started to come back around midnight. The enemy, they said, was more or less where they were supposed to be. At most there were sixteen thousand of them; four thousand cavalry, perched on the wings; between them, ten thousand infantry, and the artillery. The observers knew their trade, what to look for, how to assess numbers by counting campfires, and as each one reported in, Orsea made a note on his map. Gradually he built up the picture. The units he was most worried about, the Ceftuines and the southern heavy infantry (the whole Mezentine army was made up of foreign mercenaries, apart from the artillery), were camped right in the middle, just as he'd hoped. His plan was to leave them till last; break up the negligible Maderi infantry and light cavalry on either side of the center, forcing the Mezentines to commit their heavy cavalry to a long, grueling charge across the flat, right down the throats of his eight thousand archers. That'd be the end of them, the Bareng heavy dragoons and the lancers. If a tenth of them made it through the arrow-storm, they'd be doing outstandingly well; and then Orsea's own lancers would take them in the flank, drive them back on their own lines as the wholesale roll-up started. In would come the horse-archers from the extreme ends of the line, shepherding the Mezentines in on their own center, where the Ceftuines would've been standing helplessly, watching the world collapse all around them. By the time the fighting reached them, they'd be hemmed in on all sides by their own defeated, outflanked, surrounded comrades. The lancers would close the box, and the grand finale would be a long, one-sided massacre.

It had been that, all right.

A deep, low hum far away to his left; Orsea stood up in his stirrups, trying to get a better view, but all he could see was dust. He couldn't even remember which of his units was over that way now. Every part of his meticulously composed line was out of place. When the disaster struck, he'd tried to fight back, pulling men out of what he thought was the killing zone, only to find he'd sent them somewhere even worse. He didn't understand; that was what made him want to sob with anger. He still didn't know how they were doing it, how the bloody things *worked;* all he'd seen was the effects, the clouds and swarms of steel bolts, three feet long and half an inch thick, shot so fast they flew flat, not looped like an ordinary arrow. He'd been there when a volley struck the seventh lancers. First, a low whistling, like a flock of starlings; next, a black cloud resolving itself into a skyful of tiny needles, hanging in the air for a heartbeat before swooping, following a trajectory that made no sense, broke all the known rules of flight; then pitching, growing bigger so horribly fast (like the savage wild animals that chase you in dreams), then dropping like hailstones all around him; and the shambles, the noise, the suddenness of it all. So many extraordinary images, like a vast painting crammed with incredible detail: a man nailed to the ground by a bolt that hit him in the groin, drove straight through his horse and into the ground, fixing them both so firmly they couldn't even squirm; two men riveted together by the same bolt; a man hit by three bolts simultaneously, each one punched clean through his armor, and still incredibly alive; a great swathe of men and horses stamped into the ground, like a careless footstep on a flowerbed full of young seedlings. Just enough time for him to catch fleeting glimpses of these unbelievable sights, and then the next volley fell, two minutes of angle to the left, flattening another section of the line. He couldn't even see where the bolts were coming from, they didn't seem to rise from the surface of the earth, they just materialized or condensed in midair, like snow.

As he watched the bolts fall all around him, he couldn't understand why he was the only one left alive, or how they could aim so precisely to kill everybody else and leave him alone. But of course they could. They could do anything. That was when he'd given his one sensible order, just over an hour ago. A few minutes later, the volleys stopped; there were no coherent bodies of men left to shoot at, and the Mezentine cavalry was surging forward to begin the pursuit and mopping-up. So hard to judge time, when the world has just changed and all the rules are suddenly different, but his best guess was that the disaster had taken ten minutes, twelve at the very most. You couldn't boil a pot of water in that time.

Just a simple steel rod, pointed at one end; he reached out and pulled one out of the ground as he rode. You could use it as a spit; or three of them, tied together at the top, would do to hang a pot from over the fire. They stood up out of the ground, angled, like bristles on an unshaven chin, and there were far too many to count. It'd take weeks just to come round with carts and collect them all up — did the Mezentines do that, or did they leave them, as a monument of victory and a warning to others, till they flaked away into rust? He could imagine them doing that, in this dead, unused plain, which they'd shot full of pins.

I'd have liked just to see one of their machines, he thought, as a sort of consolation prize; but I guess I haven't done anything to deserve that privilege.

He looked back over his shoulder, to see how close the Mezentine cavalry was; but they weren't closing. Instead, they seemed to be pulling back. Well, he could understand that. Why risk the lives of men, even paid servants, when you've got machines to do the work? They'd made their point, and now they were letting him go. So kind of them, so magnanimous. Instead of killing him, they were leaving him to bring the survivors home, to try and find some way of explaining what had become of the dead. (Well, there was this huge cloud of steel pins that came down out of the sky; and the dog ate my homework.) They were too cruel to kill him.

At the thorn hedge, he found what was left of his general staff; twenty out of thirty-six. His first reaction was anger; how could he be expected to organize a coherent retreat without a full staff? (So what are you going to do about it? Write a strongly worded letter?) Then it occurred to him that he wasn't ever going to see those missing faces again, and there was a moment of blind panic when he looked to see who was there and who wasn't. Key personnel — four out of five of the inner circle, but the missing man had to be Faledrin Botaniates; how the *hell* am I going to keep track of duty rosters without Faledrin? The others, the ones who weren't there, were — The shame burned him, he'd just thought *expendable*. He forced himself to go back and repeat the thought. It'd be difficult, a real pain in the bum, to have to cope without them, but a way could be found. Therefore, they were, they'd been, expendable.

There, he'd thought it; the concept he'd promised he'd never let creep into his mind, now that he was the Duke of Eremia. That capped off the day's humiliations, and he was right down there with all the people he despised most. Fine. Now he'd got that over with, it might be an idea to do some work.

They were looking at him; some at his face, some at the blood trickling through the joints of his leg-armor. He'd forgotten all about it.

"What happened to you?" someone said.

The scope of the question appalled him for a moment; then he realized it was just his stupid wound they were talking about. "Friendly fire," he said briskly. "I guess I'm the only man on the field who got hit by one of our arrows." He started to dismount, but something went wrong. His left leg couldn't take any weight, and he ended up in a heap on the ground.

He yelled at them not to fuss as they pulled him to his feet; it was ridiculous, bothering with him when there were thousands of men gradually dying on the other side of the brake. Before he could forbid it, someone sent a runner for the surgeon. Stupid. No time for that.

"We've got to get out of here," someone was saying. "They don't seem to be following up right now, but we've got to assume we'll have their cavalry after us any minute. Does anybody know where anybody is?"

Orsea had views of his own on the subject, but quite suddenly he wasn't feeling too good. Dizziness, like he'd been drinking; and he couldn't think of words. He opened his mouth to say something, but his mind had gone blank. His arms and head seemed to weigh far too much . . .

When he woke up, the sky had turned to canvas. He looked at it for a moment; he could see the weave, and the lines of stitching at the seams. He realized he was lying on his back, on cushions piled on a heap of empty sacks. His throat was ridiculously dry, and he felt so weak . . .

"He's coming round," someone said. (Fine; treat me like I'm not here.) "Go and fetch Ducas, and the doctor."

He knew that voice, but while he'd been asleep, someone had burgled his mind and stolen all the names. He tried to lift his head, but his muscles had wilted.

"Lie still," someone else said. "You've lost a hell of a lot of blood."

No I haven't, he wanted to say. He let his head slip back onto the cushion. There were heavy springs bearing on his eyelids, and the light hurt. "Where is this?" he heard himself say, in a tiny little voice.

"God only knows," someone said, just outside his limited circle of vision. "Just to the right of the middle of nowhere. We've rounded up what we can of the army and the Mezentines seem to have lost interest in us, so we've pitched camp. Miel Ducas is running things; I've sent someone to fetch him."

He definitely knew that voice, but it didn't belong here. It was absurdly out of context; it belonged in a garden, a little square patch of green and brown boxed in by mud-brick walls. His father's house. Now he knew who the speaker was; his second oldest friend, after Miel Ducas. Fancy not recognizing someone you'd grown up with.

"Cordea?" he muttered.

"Right here." There was something slightly brittle about Cordea's voice, but that was only to be expected in the circumstances. "They got the arrow out," he was saying, "they had a hell of a job with it. Apparently it was right up against the artery, nicked it but didn't cut into it. The doctor didn't dare draw it out, for fear of the barbs slicing right through. In the end he had to go in from the side, so you're pretty badly cut up. Infection's the biggest risk, of course —"

"Shut up about my stupid leg," Orsea interrupted. "What about the battle? How many . . . ?"

He couldn't bring himself to finish the question. Simple matter of pronouns; how many of our men did I kill?

"Nine thousand dead." Cordea's voice was completely flat.

"Two thousand badly wounded, another three thousand cut up but on their feet." Cordea paused. "Miel insisted on going back with his lancers and the wagons; he picked up about eight hundred before they started shooting at him. Of course the surgeons can't cope with numbers like that, so we'll lose another two, three hundred just getting home. Actually, it could've been a whole lot worse."

Well, of course it could. But it was plenty bad enough.

"Has anybody got any idea what those things were?" Orsea asked.

Cordea nodded. "Tell you about it later," he said. "Look, it was me said that Miel should take charge; only I couldn't think of anybody else. Are you all right with that?"

Orsea tried to laugh. Talk about your stupid questions.

"Absolutely fine," he said.

"Only, I know you and he don't always get on . . ."

"Cordea, that was when we were *twelve*." He wanted to laugh, but apparently he couldn't. "What about moving on?" he said. "We can't just stay here, wherever the hell we are."

"In the morning. They're shattered, we'd lose people if we tried to move out tonight. We've got sentries, in case they attack."

"How far . . . ?" Dizzy again. He gave in and closed his eyes. If he let himself drift back to sleep, maybe he'd wake up to find it had all been taken care of. He'd never wanted to be a duke anyway. "Ask Miel . . ." he began to say, but the sentence didn't get finished.